# The Ninja

Born and raised in New York City, Eric Lustbader graduated from Columbia University in 1969. Lustbader has had a number of fascinating careers. In addition to having written numerous bestselling novels, including *Black Heart* and *Angel Eyes*, he introduced Elton John to the American music scene. He spent fifteen years in the music industry in various capacities, including working for both Elektra and CBS Records. He is a former writer for *Cash Box* magazine where he wrote lead stories on new rock acts. In that capacity, he was the first person in the United States to predict the success of Jimi Hendrix, David Bowie and Santana, among many others.

Lustbader has taught in the All-Day Neighborhood School Division of the NYC Public School System and has also taught pre-schoolers in special Early Childhood programmes.

Eric Lustbader, who travels worldwide in researching his novels, lives in Southampton, New York, with his wife Victoria Lustbader, who works for the Nature Conservancy.

## BY THE SAME AUTHOR

# ERIC LUSTBADER

# THE NINJA

**HarperCollins**Publishers

HarperCollins*Publishers*
77–85 Fulham Palace Road,
Hammersmith, London W6 8JB

This special edition 1995

Previously published in paperback by HarperCollins 1993
(reprinted once) and by Grafton 1981
(reprinted twenty-two times)

First published in Great Britain by
Granada Publishing 1980

Copyright © Eric Van Lustbader 1980

The Author asserts the moral right to
be identified as the author of this work

ISBN 0 286 13301 6

Set in Granjon

Printed in Great Britain by
HarperCollinsManufacturing Glasgow

# Acknowledgements

Because, in some instances, I met many of the real people in positions which, of necessity, are in this novel, I wish to state that none of the characters drawn here in any way resemble their real-life counterparts who, without exception, were extremely helpful to me.

I would like to thank:

Dr Gita Natarajan, Associate Medical Examiner, City of New York

Lieutenant Jim Doyle, Commander, Village Police, West Hampton Beach

and, especially:

Dr Michael Baden, former Chief Medical Examiner, City of New York

Thanks to the numerous individuals who assisted me with translations, and to my father, who proofed the manuscripts.

Special thanks to Ruth and Arthur for invaluable R&R in Shangri-La.

And to Mom, for her courage.

**FOR SYD**
*with love*

# THE NINJA

---

*Natsu-gusa ya*
  *tsuwamono-domo ga*
    *yume no ato.*
*Summer grass:*
  *of stalwart warriors splendid dreams*
    *the aftermath.*
                              – Matsuo Bashō

*MRS DARLING: Dear night-lights*
*that protected my sleeping babes*
*burn clear and steadfast to-night.*
                    – J. M. Barrie, *Peter Pan*

In darkness there is death.

It was the first thing they had taught him and he never forgot it. He could move unobserved in daylight, too; in other ways. But the night was his special friend.

Now the high piercing sound of the alarm cut through all other nocturnal sounds: the *dree dree dree* of the cicadas, the thunderous crashing of the surf against the grey sand and the black rocks sixty feet below, the wild cry of a disturbed crow far off over the massed treetops.

Abruptly, colour gilded the leaves of the ancient spreading sycamore as lights went on inside the house, but he was already away from the car, deep within the concealing shadows of the carefully sculptured hedge. There was little need of this protection now for he was dressed all in matt black: low boots, cotton trousers, long-sleeved shirt, lacquered reed waistcoat, gloves and a hooded mask that covered all his face save a strip across his eyes that had been smeared with lampblack mixed with a fine charcoal powder to eliminate the possibility of reflection; but his arduous training had been too well ingrained for him to take any target for granted. This precluded the possibility of an error in judgement that could lead to a lapse in security.

The porch light came on, insects fluttering around it. The noise of the car's alarm was too loud for him to be able to hear the door opening but he counted off the seconds in his mind and got it dead on ...

Barry Braughm stepped into the lemon light of the open doorway. He was in jeans and a white T-shirt. His open fly attested to the haste in which he had dressed. He carried a flashlight in his right hand.

From this vantage point on the slight elevation of the doorstep he played the narrow beam around the area of the car. Reflected light from the chrome lanced out into the night and, squinting, he swung the beam away. At this moment he was in no mood to go and fool around with his car – or anything else for that matter.

Not more than half an hour ago he had had a screaming row with Andy, ending up, quite naturally, with him speeding off into the night. Back to the city, Barry supposed. Well, it damn well served him right, cutting off his nose to spite his face. But that was Andy, through and through.

Honest to God, Barry thought angrily, I don't know why I put up with him. And then he shook his head. Yes, you do, he told himself. Well.

He went down the short flight of flagstone steps, careful to give the first one a miss. It was cracked; just one of the things around here Andy had promised to fix this week.

He padded across the wet grass of the lawn to where the car stood, dark and hulking. The wind whistled through the young maple to his left and, farther on, he could just make out the low barrier of the thick hedge. What the hell am I doing with a Mercedes? he asked himself rhetorically. If it had not been for Andy – but Andy loved the creature comforts, wouldn't go anywhere unless it was via first class. That, of course, includes me, Barry thought grumpily. He looked off down the road for a moment as if he might catch a glimpse of Andy's night-black Audi swinging its headlights around the long curve to flood his front lawn. Barry turned abruptly away. Not tonight, he thought. He never recovers this quickly.

He threw the beam of the flash across the top of the hedge as he moved, along the gravel drive to send a quick dazzle of liquid light off the car's bonnet. It grew in intensity as he came up beside the Mercedes.

Goddamned heat, he thought. Always setting off the alarm. And I do not want to sleep alone tonight. Should have thought of that before you called Andy a shit.

He paused for a last look around, then bent and freed the latch, lifting the bonnet. He gazed into the interior, playing the beam over the engine parts, lingering for just a moment on the battery.

Satisfied, he slammed the bonnet and went around the car checking the doors, one by one. The seams of glass and chrome were illuminated as he sought to find any sign of a forced entry. Finding none, he came back to the left side and, bending again, inserted a small metal key into a fixture in the car's side. He turned the key with a quick jerk and silence descended once again. The sound of the cicadas returned and the hiss of the surf gave renewed evidence of its tireless attack upon the slowly eroding shore.

Barry had already turned away on his way back to the house when he thought he heard a brief clatter against the rocks near the edge of the low cliff fronting his property. It sounded to him like the soft noise of running bare feet. He spun around, lifting the flash to scan the area. He saw nothing.

Curious, he went across the lawn and into the high grass which he had never bothered to mow because it was so close to the cliff, emerging seconds later on the slightly elevated portion of land studded with grey slate rocks. He peered along the ridge to both left and right. Directly below him he saw the palely iridescent curl of the tops of the breakers as they rolled noisily in. It's high tide, he thought.

The pain in his chest came totally without warning. He was thrown backwards just as if a hand had come out and pushed him and he stumbled along the dew-slick rocks. His arms flew out to the sides to give him balance and the flash spun end over end like a miniature falling star in the night. He heard quite clearly the sharp *pang* as it bounced off the rocks below and arced into the churning sea like some suicidal firefly. His mouth worked spasmodically. He tried to scream but all he could manage was a kind of gasp, insignificant and irrelevant, and he thought he knew what it must be like for a fish on a line.

His arms and legs felt as if they were full of lead and the air seemed to have run out of oxygen just as if he were lost on an alien planet without the protection of a spacesuit. He was incapable of co-ordinating movement, balanced precariously on the faceted rocks, on the verge of the long drop to the white and black sea. Dimly, he thought he might be having a heart attack and, desperately now, he tried to remember what to do, how to help himself. He died trying to recall ...

With the absence of all movement, a shadow detached itself

from the wall of the hedge, coming swiftly and silently across to the rocks. Even the cicadas, the night birds, were left undisturbed by the passage.

The shadow knelt over the corpse and black fingers worked at something dark and metallic, embedded in the chest just under and to the right of the heart. With a last wrench, the thing was free.

He checked the carotid first, then the eyes, peering intently at the whites for what seemed a long time, then the pads of the fingers.

Softly, to himself, the shadow recited the *Hannya-Shin-Kyō*.

He stood up. The corpse seemed as light as air in his arms. With barely any discernible motion or effort, he launched the corpse out into the night, over the edge, far enough out so that it fell squarely into deep water. Immediately the strong current took it.

Within seconds the shadow had disappeared, having become one with the darkness and having left no trace of its ever having existed.

# First Ring
# THE GROUND BOOK

# I

## West Bay Bridge, Summer Present

When Nicholas Linnear saw them fish the bloated blue-white thing out of the water, he turned right around, walking away, and was far down the beach by the time the real crowd had begun to form.

Flies buzzed furrily along the snaking hillock of sand above the high-tide mark. The spindrift, drying, was like a lock of a child's fine white hair. Beyond, the combers rolled in, purple-blue, then white as their tops turned to foam, spending themselves upon the wet sand at his bare feet.

He dug his toes in, very much as he had done when he was younger, but, of course, it did no good. The sea leached away the footing from under him and he grew shorter by inches as the land was eroded by the tide's inexorable progress.

Until then it had been a quiet afternoon, Dune Road lazy in midweek, even though this was the week after the Fourth of July. He reached unconsciously for the pack of thin black-tobaccoed cigarettes which he no longer carried. He had given up smoking six months ago. He remembered the date well enough because it was the day he had quit his job.

He had arrived at the agency one chill sullen winter's day and had stayed in his office only long enough to place the ostrich-hide briefcase that Vincent had presented him with for no apparent reason – it was some months past his birthday and longer than that since he had been promoted – on his rosewood and smoked-glass desk that was much too modern to hold anything remotely resembling drawers. Then he went out, turning left, past the curious, upturned face of Lil, his secretary, down the beige-carpeted, rose-neon indirectly lit hall. When had he actually made the decision? He had no idea, really. On the way in, in the cab, his mind had been empty, his thoughts like ashes swirled in the dregs of last night's coffee. Nothing else seemed to remain.

He went past the pair of female guardians who, like perfectly carved sphinxes before a great pharaoh's tomb, flanked the enormous carved mahogany door. The thing of it was, they were damned efficient, too. He gave a brief knock and went in.

Goldman was on the phone – the dark blue one, which meant a conversation with a high-level client, rather than the beige one, which would indicate inter-office brainstorming – so Nicholas stared out of the window. They're all high-level these days, he thought. There were days when being on the thirty-sixth floor had its advantages, but this was not one of them. The sky was so dense with leaden clouds that it seemed as if a lid had been clamped down on the city. Perhaps, near night-fall, it would snow again. He couldn't think whether that would be good or bad.

'Nick, my boy!' Goldman cried as he cradled the receiver. 'It must've been ESP, you walking in now! Guess who that was on the phone? No.' He waved one hand. It looked like a duck, eager to take off. 'Better yet, don't guess. I'll tell you. It was Kingsley.' His eyes got big. They always got big when he was excited. 'Know what he said? He was talking my ear off about you and the campaign. The first results are already in. They're "a dramatic improvement", he says. Those are his words, the *schmendrick*. "A dramatic improvement".'

Nearing sixty, Sam Goldman did not look a day over fifty. He was fit and trim and always tanned. This, Nicholas had always supposed, he maintained to set off his shock of brilliant white hair which he wore long and combed straight back. Goldman was enamoured of contrasts. His face was somewhat long, lined, pitted slightly on the crown of each cheek. It was a proud face, dominated by large brown eyes, despite the long nose and generous mouth. He wore a blue pinstripe shirt with solid white collar and a navy and maroon Italian silk tie. He knew how to dress, Goldman did. Despite this, his sleeves were rolled half way up his forearms.

Looking at him now, Nicholas abruptly knew why this was going to be so hard for him to do.

'I'm glad, Sam,' he said.

'Well, sit down, sit down then.' Goldman waved him to a beige suede and chrome chair in front of his enormous desk.

It was not, perhaps, what he would have chosen himself but all his clients were happy with it.

'No, I'm fine where I am, thanks.' Now that he was down to it, he realized that there was just no easy way. 'I'm leaving, Sam.'

'Leaving? What, you want a vacation already? You've only been creative director for six months –'

'Seven.'

'So who's counting? Anyway, you want a vacation? Okay, you got a vacation. Where're you going?'

'I don't think you understand, Sam. I want to leave the company. Resign.'

Goldman swivelled around in his chair, stared out of the window. 'You know, it's going to snow today. On the radio they said no. But I knew better. An old campaigner can always tell. My feet tell me. Every time I play tennis. I said to Edna this morning –'

'Sam, did you hear me?' Nicholas said gently.

'That Kingsley. What a schmuck! He may know publishing but he doesn't know shit from advertising. It took him long enough to come here.' He swivelled back, abruptly. 'You, Nick, you know advertising.'

'Sam –'

'Resign, Nicky? Resign? What's this resign? I don't believe it. You have everything here. Everything. You know how much we're gonna net – not gross, mind you, but net – from this one goddamn campaign of yours?'

'I don't care, Sam.'

'Two hundred fucking thousand, Nick. Now why would you leave?'

'I'm tired, Sam. Honestly. I feel like I've been in advertising so long that lately – lately, I've been waking up feeling like Count Dracula.'

Goldman cocked his head, a non-verbal sign of query.

'You know, like I've been in a coffin.'

'You're going back to Japan.'

'I hadn't really thought about it.' He was far more pleased than surprised; Goldman was unusually perceptive about these things. 'I don't know that it matters.'

'Of course it matters!' Goldman exploded. 'I think about going back to Israel all the time!'

'You didn't grow up in Israel,' Nicholas countered.

'I would have if it'd've been in existence then.' He snorted. 'But that's irrelevant.' He waved a hand again. 'History. History is all that matters.' A call came through for him and he barked at one of the sphinxes outside to jot it down as a call-back. 'Listen, I don't give a good goddamn what we make outa Kingsley, Nicky, you know that. But it's a sign. Can't you see that? You're hot now. I felt it was gonna happen a year ago and now I know I was right. You really want to walk away from that now?'

'I don't think *want* is the right word,' Nicholas said. '*Have* to is more like it.'

Goldman took out a cigar from a thick wooden humidor, contemplated it. 'Nick, I won't bore you by telling you how many bright guys would give their left nut for your job –'

'Thanks,' Nicholas said drily. 'I appreciate that.'

'Everyone's gotta do for himself.' Goldman's eyes regarded the cigar's tip. He took a bite off the end, struck a long wooden match.

'I wish you wouldn't,' Nicholas said. 'I've given up smoking.'

Goldman eyed him, the flame in mid-air. 'Just like you,' he said flatly. 'Everything at once.' He puffed at the flame, flicked the match into a wide glass ashtray. But, unwilling perhaps to admit unconditional defeat, he stuck the cold cigar unhappily in his mouth, chewed on it meditatively. 'You know, Nick, I like to think of myself as more than just your boss. It's been a lotta years since I picked you up right off the boat.'

'Plane.'

Goldman waved his hand. 'Whatever.' He took the cigar out of his mouth. 'As a friend, I think you owe me some kind of an explanation.'

'Look, Sam –'

He put his hand up, palm outwards. 'Hey, I'm not gonna try to stop you from going. You're a big boy now. And I can't say I'm not disappointed, because I am. Why the hell should I lie to you? Only, I'd just like to know.'

Nicholas got up, went over to the window. Goldman swung

his chair around to follow his progress like a radar tracking station.

'It's not even very clear to me yet, Sam.' He rubbed a hand across his forehead. 'I don't know, it's like this place has become a prison. A place to get out of instead of come into.' He turned to face Goldman. 'Oh, it isn't this *place*, itself. There's nothing wrong – I suspect ...' He shrugged. 'Perhaps it's advertising. I feel lost within the medium now, as if the electronicization has no meaning for me. As if I've slipped back, somehow, into another age, another time.' He leaned forwards, a peculiar kind of tension lacing his upper torso. 'And now I'm beginning to feel as if I'm adrift, far out at sea where there's no sign of land in any direction.'

'Then there's nothing I can do to change your mind.'

'Nothing, Sam.'

Goldman sighed. 'Edna will be very upset.'

For several moments their eyes locked in a kind of silent struggle where each, it seemed, was sizing the other up.

Goldman put his thick hands flat on the desk top. 'You know,' he said quietly, 'years ago in the police department of this city it used to be that the only way you got ahead was if you had a rabbi down at headquarters. Someone who looked after you when things got rough or' – he shrugged – 'who knows? Used to be the way of the world – all over.' He put the unlit cigar into the opposite side of his mouth. 'Now, maybe, it's different. Corporations, they don't know from rabbis. You gotta confirm. You gotta suck up to all the vice-presidents, get invited to their weekend parties, be nice to their wives who're so horny and unhappy they'd hump a tree if it could tell them how pretty they look; you gotta live in that certain part of Connecticut where they all live in their two-storey houses with the semi-circular drives. Used to be they had button-down minds; now they got computer minds. That's getting ahead, Nick, business-wise. So they tell me. Me, I wouldn't know. Not first-hand anyway. I'd retire before they'd get me into that kind of trap.' His eyes were clear and they sparkled despite the fact that the light was so dull and leaden. 'Me, I was brought up with rabbis. They're in my system; no way I can get 'em out now, even if I wanted to.' He sat forwards in his high-backed chair, his elbows on the desk top, levelled his gaze at Nicholas. 'You get what I mean?'

Nicholas looked at him. 'Yes, Sam,' he had said, after a time. 'I know exactly what you mean.'

The aching cries of the circling gulls hid the sound of the siren for a time, but, as the ambulance drew nearer, its wailing rise and fall, rise and fall, blotted out all other sound. People were running silently along the expanse of the beach, looking birdlike and rather awkward as they tried to compensate for the too soft footing.

He had come out to West Bay Bridge early in the season. In order to survive now, he had to push it all away from him, into a comforting middle distance, not too close, not too far away. The agency, Columbia, everything. Not even a discovery of some drowned corpse was going to interrupt his solipsistic world; it was too much like the city.

Oddly enough, it put him in mind of the call. It had come only a few days after he had left the agency. He had been in the middle of the *Times*'s Op-Ed page and his second Irish coffee.

'Mr Goldman was good enough to give me your home number, Mr Linnear,' Dean Whoolson said. 'I trust I've not intruded.'

'I still don't understand why you've come to me,' he said.

'It's quite simple, really. There has been, of late, a renaissance of interest in the field of Oriental Studies. The students here are no longer satisfied with the superficiality, shall we say, of many of our oriental courses. I'm afraid they view us as sadly out of date in that area.'

'But I'm hardly qualified as a teacher.'

'Yes, we are well aware of that.' The voice was rather dry, like a pinch of senescent snuff floating through the air. But underneath there was an unmistakable note of sincerity. 'Naturally we are aware that you do not possess a teaching licence, Mr Linnear, but, you see, this course I have in mind would be perfect for you.' He chuckled, an odd, startling sound as if made by a cartoon character. 'For us, too, I might add.'

'But I have absolutely no familiarity with the curriculum,' Nicholas said. 'I wouldn't have any idea where to begin.'

'Oh, my dear fellow, it's a piece of cake,' Dean Whoolson said, his voice now radiating confidence. 'The course is a seminar, you see. Taught by four professors. Well, three now that Dr Kinkaid has fallen ill. It meets twice a week during the spring semester with the four – I'm including yourself, of course – rotating. You see the beauty of it, Mr Linnear? You can leave the curriculum to the others and stick to what you know better than anyone else in the Western Hemisphere.' That strange, oddly likeable chuckle came again, reminding Nicholas of mint chocolates and *crème* sweets. 'I don't imagine you would have to concern yourself with overlapping the others' material, would you? I mean to say,' he rushed on, as if enraptured by the whole-hearted assurance of his own voice, 'the kind of things – uh, insights, as it were – into the Japanese mind are just the kind of things we are looking for. The students would be delighted, no doubt – as would we.'

There was a singing discernible on the line in the ensuing silence between them and, faintly, Nicholas could make out the inconstant sibilances of other voices, like ghosts', raised in argument.

'Perhaps you would care to see the campus,' Dean Whoolson said. 'And, naturally, it is most beautiful in the spring.'

Why not try something different? Nicholas had thought. 'All right,' he had said.

People were still running past him, attracted by the anxiety the wailing siren brought out. A growing knot of curious onlookers hovered, quivering on the borderline between revulsion and fascination, moths circling a flame in an ever-tightening orbit. He concentrated on the sound of the surf, curling and rushing in towards him, calling like a friend, but the human voices, raised in excitement and query, pierced the afternoon like needles. For them it was but a side-show attraction, a chance to turn on the six o'clock news and say to their friends, 'Hey! See that? I was there. I saw it happen,' exactly as if it were Elizabeth Taylor and her touring party who had rolled through that particular stretch of surf, and then, as placidly as if they were contented bovines, return to their icy astringent martinis, the sliced pepperoni that someone had thoughtfully brought out from Balducci's in the city.

His house was of weathered grey shingle and coffee-coloured brick with neither the pop-eyed Plexiglas bubble windows nor the bizarre cantilevered walls that many of the homes had along this stretch. To the right of the house, the dunes abruptly gave way to flat sand, somewhat lower than that of the surrounding area. There had been, until early December, a house worth roughly a quarter of a million dollars on that property, but the winter had been fully as foul as the one in 1977-8 and it had been washed away with much of the land itself. The family was still trying to get the insurance money to rebuild. In the meantime, there was more open space to the side than was usual along this densely populated and highly fashionable beach front.

The breakers seemed to be pounding harder as the tide continued to sweep in and he felt the cold salt water licking up his ankles to his calves. The bottoms of his jeans, though turned up several times, pulled heavy with washed sand. He was reaching down to brush them out when a figure barrelled into him. He fell backwards with a grunt, someone sprawled on top of him.

'Why the hell don't you watch where you're going?' he yelled crossly as he disentangled himself.

'Sorry, but you don't have to scream, do you? It was a simple mistake.'

The first thing he saw was her face, though before that he smelled her perfume, faintly citric and as dry as Dean Whoolson's voice. Her face was extremely close to his. Her eyes he thought at first were hazel but then he saw that they certainly had more green in them than brown. There were one or two red flecks floating in the left iris. Her skin was creamy and lightly freckled. Her nose was rather too wide, which gave her character, and her lips were plump, which gave her an innate sensuality.

He grasped her firmly under the arms and lifted her with him.

She immediately drew away, crossing her arms over her breasts. 'Don't do that.' Still she eyed him, made no move to pass him by. Her fingers curled, rubbing the flesh of her arms as if his grip had bruised her.

23

'Haven't we met before?' he said.

Her lips jerked in a quick quirky smile. 'You can do better than that, can't you?'

'No. I mean it. I've seen you somewhere before.'

Her eyes darted for a moment over his shoulder. When they again alighted on him she said, 'I don't think –'

He snapped his fingers. 'In Sam Goldman's office. The fall or the winter.' He cocked his head. 'I'm not mistaken.'

Her eyes seemed to clear as if, with Sam's name, some almost invisible curtain had been raised within them. 'I know Sam Goldman,' she said slowly. 'I've done some freelance jobs for him.' Now she put one long forefinger up to the centre of her lips, the clear-lacquered nail burnished by the light. The inconstant sound of the voices down the beach seemed to swell like the roar of a crowd at the advent of a grand-slam home run or a bit of defensive heroics in the outfield.

'You're Nicholas Linnear,' she said, and when he nodded she pointed at him. 'He talks about you all the time.'

He smiled. 'But you don't remember our meeting.'

She shrugged. 'I don't know, really. When I'm involved in my work ...' Her shoulders lifted, fell again.

Nicholas laughed. 'I might have been somebody important.'

'Judging by your reputation, you are. But you just walked away from all of it. I think that's odd.'

Squinting up at him, sunglassless, she looked no more than a college girl, as if the sunlight passing through her had somehow illuminated some previously hidden inner innocence. At last her eyes slid away from him. 'What's going on up there, anyway?'

'They found a body in the ocean.'

'Oh? Whose?'

He shrugged. 'I've no idea.'

'Haven't you just come from there?' Her gaze slid back from the distance over his left shoulder, touching his face. It was like a cool summer's breeze after sundown. 'You must've seen them pull it out.' Her eyes were better than arms, keeping him at a carefully measured distance. There was something peculiarly childlike in that, he thought. A hurt child – or scared. It made him want to reach out and touch her reassuringly.

'I left before it happened,' he said.

'Aren't you in the least bit curious?' She seemed unmindful of the wind that flicked at the thick mane of her dark hair. 'It could be someone from around here. You know how incestuous this place is – we're all from the same business.'

'I have no interest in it. No.'

She unfolded her arms, put her hands in the front pockets of her cut-off jeans. She wore a plain, sleeveless top. It was turquoise and set off her eyes. Her firm breasts swelled with her breathing, the nipples visible points. Her waist was narrow, her legs long and elegant. She moved like a dancer.

'But you *do* have interests, I see,' she said flatly. 'How would you feel if I looked at *you* that way?'

'Flattered,' he said. 'I'd certainly feel flattered.'

Justine was an advertising art designer, living four houses down the beach, who found it convenient to work out of the city during the summer.

'I loathe New York in the summer,' she told him the next afternoon over drinks. 'Do you know that I once spent the entire summer in my apartment with the air conditioning on full and never once moving out of the door? I was deathly afraid I'd get overwhelmed by the stench of dogshit. I'd call D'Agostino and have them send up the food and, once or twice a week, the office would send up this big brawny fag – who was doing the director under the desk during coffee breaks – to take my designs and bring me my cheques. But even with that, it wasn't enough and I was forced out. I threw some stuff in a bag and took the first flight out to Paris. I stayed two weeks while the office went batshit looking for me.' She turned her head half away from him, sipping at her manhattan. 'However, when I got back, the only thing that had really changed was that the fag was gone.'

The sun was coming down, the sea devouring its crimson bulk; colour lay shimmering on the water. Then, quite abruptly, it was dark: not even the little lights bobbing far out to sea.

25

It was like that with her, he reflected. Brilliant colour, stories on the surface, but what lay beneath, in the night?

'You're not going back to Columbia,' she said, 'in the fall.'

'No, I'm not.'

She said nothing, sat back on the Haitian cotton couch, her slender arms spread wide along the back; they went out of the pools of lamplight, seemed dark wings, hovering. Then she cocked her head to one side and it seemed to him as if the ice-floe had cracked, coming apart.

'I fell in love with the campus,' he said, deciding to answer her by starting at the beginning. 'Of course, it was the beginning of February, but I could imagine the red brick walkways lined with flowering magnolia and dogwood, quince in among the ancient oaks.

'The course itself – Sources of Oriental Thought – wasn't really too bad at all. The students at least were inquisitive and, when awake, fairly bright – some of them startlingly so. They seemed surprised that I was interested in them.

'I was curious about this, at first, but as the semester wore on, I came to understand what it was all about. The other professors giving the course had appallingly little time to devote to the students; they were extremely busy researching their latest books. And when they were actually teaching, they treated their students with contempt.

'I remember sitting in on a class just after mid-term. Drs Eng and Royston, who taught the meat of the course, announced at the beginning of the session that the mid-term papers had been graded and were ready to be returned. Royston then proceeded to give his lecture. When the bell rang, Eng asked the students to remain seated and, with perfect precision, laid out four piles of papers on the floor at the front of the hall. "Those students with last names beginning with letters $A$ through $F$ will find their papers here," he said, pointing to the pile on his right. And so on. Then they had both turned away and left the hall before the first students even had time to kneel, scrabbling through the piles.

'It was degrading,' Nicholas said. 'That kind of lack of

respect for another human being is something I just cannot tolerate.'

'So you liked teaching.'

He thought that a curious thing to say. 'I didn't mind it.' He made himself another gin and tonic, squeezed a section of lemon before dropping it into the ice-filled glass. 'In the end it was the other professors who made the semester seem long to me. I don't imagine they thought too much of me. After all, the halls of academe are rather closed. Everyone there is bound by the stringency of the situation. "Publish or perish" has become a cliché, I suppose. But for them it's a reality which they must face every day.' He shrugged. 'I imagine they resented my status. I had all the best parts of their life without any of the responsibilities.'

'And Royston and Eng. What were they like?'

'Oh, Royston was okay, I suppose. Rather stuffy in the beginning but he thawed a bit later on. But Eng' – he shook his head – 'Eng was a bastard all right. He had made up his mind about me before we had even been introduced. The three of us happened to be in the lounge one afternoon. "So you were born in Singapore," he said. Just like that. Standing over me, peering down at me through his round wire-rimmed spectacles. That's what they must have been; they were far too old-fashioned to be called glasses. He had a curious manner of speech, his words emerging clipped, almost frozen, so that you could imagine them hanging in mid-air like icicles. "A disgusting city, if you will pardon my saying so. Built by the British, who had no more regard for the Chinese than they did for the Indians."'

'What did you say?'

'Frankly, I was too stunned to say much of anything,' he said gloomily. 'The bastard had hardly said two words to me all semester. He took me quite by surprise.'

'You had no snappy rejoinder.'

'Only that he was wrong. I was conceived there.' He put down his glass. 'I asked Dean Whoolson about it subsequently but he merely brushed it off. "Eng's a genius," was how he put it. "And you know how that sort is sometimes. I must tell you, we are damn lucky to have him here. He almost went to Harvard but we snared him at the last moment. Convinced him of the superiority of our research facilities." He patted me on the back as if I were the department mascot. "Who ever knows with Eng?" he said. "Perhaps he thought you were Malay. We all must make allowances, Mr Linnear." '

'I don't understand that,' Justine said. 'You're not Malay, are you?'

'No, but if Eng thought I was, he might have reason to dislike me. The Chinese and the Malays were constantly at each other's throats in the Singapore area. No love lost there.'

'What are you?' She seemed abruptly quite close to him, her eyes enormous and very luminous. 'There's an Asian hint in your face, I think. In your eyes perhaps, or in the height of your cheekbones.'

'My father was English,' he said. 'A Jew who was forced to change his name so that he could get ahead in business and then, during the war, in the Army. He was a colonel.'

'What was his name? Before he changed it, I mean.'

'I don't know. He wouldn't tell me. "Nicholas," he said to me one day, "what's in a name? The man who tells you that there is some significance in his name is a bare-faced liar." '

'But weren't you ever curious about it?'

'Oh yes. For a time. But after a while I gave up looking.'

'And your mother?'

'Ah. That would depend on whom you spoke to. She always maintained that she was pure-blood Chinese.'

'But,' Justine prompted.

'But in all likelihood she was only half Chinese. The other half was probably Japanese.' He shrugged. 'Not that I was ever certain. It's just that she seemed always to think like a Japanese.' He smiled. 'Anyway, I am a romantic and it's far more exciting to think of her as a mixture. An unusual mixture given the mutual animosity historically between the two peoples. More mysterious.'

'And you like mysteries.'

He watched the sweep of her dark hair, sliding across one cheek, hiding the eye with the crimson motes. 'In a sense. Yes.'

'Your features are all Caucasian,' she said, abruptly switching topics.

'Yes,' Nicholas said. 'Physically I take after my father, the Colonel.' He put his head back on the couch, his hair touching her outstretched fingers for a moment before she moved them back, curling them into a fist. He stared up at the patterned pools of light playing upon the ceiling. 'Inside, though, I am my mother's son.'

Doc Deerforth never looked forward to the summer. This was a curious thing, he thought, because it was invariably his busiest time. The influx from the city never ceased to astound him, the migratory pattern of almost the entire Upper East Side of Manhattan, as fixed and precise as the geese flying their arrowhead formations south in the winter.

Not that Doc Deerforth knew all that much about Manhattan, not these days, at least; he had not set foot in that madhouse in over five years and then it had been only to pay a brief visit to his friend Nate Graumann, New York City's Chief Medical Examiner.

He was quite content to be out here. He had his daughters who, with their own families, visited him regularly – his wife had died of leukaemia over ten years ago, turned to a faded photo – and his work as doctor in West Bay Bridge. Then there was his ancillary M.E. work for Flower at Hauppauge. They liked him there because he was thorough and inventive; Flower kept asking him if he would come to work for the Suffolk County M.E. but he was much too happy where he was. There were friends here, plentiful and warm but, most of all, he had himself. He found that, essentially, he was happy with himself. That did not stop the occasional nightmare, however, from creeping through like a clandestine burglar on the loose. He would still wake up, drenched in sweat, the damp sheets twisted clammily about his legs. Some nights he would dream of white blood but he dreamed of other things as well, dream symbols of his personal fright. At those times he would get up and pad silently into the kitchen, making himself a cup of hot cocoa, and would read, at random, from one of Raymond Chandler's seven novels, finding within that spare inferential prose-style a kind of existential calm amid his private storm, and inside thirty minutes he had returned to sleep.

Doc Deerforth stretched, easing the ache that sat like a stuck pitchfork between his shoulder-blades. That's what comes of working all hours at my age, he thought. Still, he went over his findings once again. It was all there, black and white, the words piling together into sentences and paragraphs, but now he was seeing the meaning for the first time, as if he were an Egyptologist who had at last stumbled upon the Rosetta Stone.

Another routine drowning, he had thought, when they had called him out to Dune Road. Of course he did not mean that. The word *routine* had no place in his vocabulary. Life was the most precious thing in the world to him. But he need not have become a doctor to feel that way. Living through the war in the Pacific Theatre had been enough. Day after day, from his disarrayed jungle camp during the bitter fighting in the Philippines, he had seen the cascades of small one-man planes guided by their kamikaze pilots as they plunged head-long with 2,650 pounds of high explosives in their blunt noses into the American warships. The cultural chasm between East and West could be summed up by those aircraft, Doc Deerforth had always thought. The Japanese name for them was *Ōka* – the cherry blossom. But the Americans called them *baka* – the idiot bomb. Western philosophical thought had no place for the concept of ritual suicide inherent in the Japanese samurai of old. But that was it, really. The samurai survived, despite all obstacles that had been put in his path. Doc Deerforth would never forget the *haiku* which, so the story went, had been written by a twenty-two-year-old kamikaze pilot just before his death; this, too, was tradition: 'If only we might fall / Like cherry blossoms in the spring – / So pure and radiant!' And that, he thought, was how the Japanese felt about death. The samurai was born to die a glorious death in battle.

And all I wanted was for the war to end with my skin intact and my mind unbent.

And it had come to pass, except for the nightmares that haunted him like hungry vampires newly risen from the grave.

Doc Deerforth got up from behind his desk and went to the window. Beyond the fluted layers of the oak leaves that shaded this side of the house from the long afternoon's heat, he saw the expanse of Main Street. Just another weekday in the summer. But that world now seemed a million miles away, as remote as the surface of another planet.

Doc Deerforth turned back into his office and, scooping up the manila folder and its contents, went out of the house, down Main Street towards the one-storey ugly red brick building housing the Fire Department and, beyond a courtyard parking lot, the Village Police.

Half way there, he ran into Nicholas, who was just coming out of the automated doors of the supermarket loaded down with groceries.

'Hello, Nick.'

'Hey, Doc. How are you?'

'Fine. Fine. Just on my way to see Ray Florum.' They had met, as most residents of West Bay Bridge did eventually, along this same Main Street, introduced by mutual acquaintances. It was difficult here, even for the most devoutly reclusive, not to make friends even if they were only of the 'Howdy' variety. 'Just got back from Hauppauge.'

'That body they found yesterday?'

'Yeah.' Doc Deerforth turned his head quickly, spat out a bit of food that had lodged itself between his teeth. He was glad of this diversion. He felt a genuine fear of confronting Florum with what he had. Besides, he liked Nicholas. 'Hey, you might've known him. Didn't live too far from you along Dune Road.'

Nicholas smiled thinly. 'Not very likely –'

'Braughm's his name. Barry Braughm.'

Nicholas felt a queer sense of vertigo for just a moment and he thought of Justine's words on the beach the day she had run into him. *You know how incestuous this place is.* She couldn't know how right she was.

'Yes,' Nicholas said slowly. 'I knew him. When I was in advertising, we worked together at the same agency.'

'Say, I'm sorry, Nick. Did you know him well?'

Nicholas thought about that for a time. Braughm had had

a brilliantly analytical mind. He knew the public perhaps better than anyone at the agency. What a shock to find him suddenly gone. 'Well enough,' he said, thoughtfully.

Swinging her around. Slow-dancing into the night, the screen door bang open, the record-player sending the music rolling in languorous ribbons, drowning the tide. Moving in stereo.

Her arms had trembled when he had first taken them, guiding her out onto the porch. But it was the right thing to do. The perfect thing. She loves to dance, first off. And it was perfectly acceptable for him to hold her this way, even though, quite clearly, rock was sex and dancing was, subliminally, the same thing. What matter? She would dance.

> *She shadows me in the mirror*
> *And never leaves on the light ...*

In giving herself up to the rhythms she was sensual, a kind of glossy exoskeleton dissolving at her feet, unearthing an ardour rich with substantive and elemental fury.

> *Some things that I say to her*
> *They just don't seem to bite ...*

It was as if the music had freed her somehow of her chains, of her wounds – *inhibitions* was a word with far too few ramifications to serve the situation – of her fear, not of him, not of any man, but of herself.

> *She says leave it to me*
> *And everything will be all right.*

With her shoulder touching his and the music filling another room, she said, 'I grew up reading. At first it was anything I could get my hands on. While my sister, always so good with people, was out on dates, I would be gulping down one book or another. Curiously, that didn't last long. I mean, I kept on reading but I quickly became quite discriminating in what I read.' She laughed, a rich happy sound that surprised him in its wholeheartedness. 'Oh, I had my phases, yes indeed! The Tremayne dog books and then Howard Pile – I adored his

*Robin Hood*. One day, when I was about sixteen, I discovered de Sade. It was rather forbidden reading then and therefore exciting. But beyond that, I was struck by much of his writing. And then I had this fantasy that that was the reason my parents had named me Justine. However, when I was older and asked my mother about it, she said, "Well, you know, it was just a name that your father and I liked." It must have appealed to her Continental leanings, I imagine; she was French, you see. But then, oh how I wished that I had never asked her! My fantasy was so much better than the reality of it. Well, what can you expect? They were both banal.'

'Was your father American?'

She turned her face towards him and the warm glow from the living-room lamps burnished one cheek as if by an artist's brush. 'Very American.'

'What did he do?'

'Let's go inside,' she said, turning from him. 'I'm cold.'

First there was the large black and white photograph of a rather heavy-set man with a firm jaw and undaunted eyes. Printed underneath was the legend: *Stanley J. Teller, Chief of Police 1932–1964*. Next to that was a framed copy of Norman Rockwell's *The Runway*.

The office was a spare cubicle with double windows overlooking the courtyard parking lot. There was not much to see out there, this time of the evening.

'Why don't you cut the doubletalk, Doc, and run it by me in plain English,' Lieutenant Ray Florum said. 'Just what's so special about this drowning?'

The subdued crackle of the two-way radio down the hall was a constant background chatter, like being on the telephone with a crossed line.

'That's just what I've been trying to explain to you,' Doc Deerforth said slowly and patiently. 'This man did not die of drowning.'

Ray Florum sat down in his wooden swivel chair. It creaked beneath his weight. Florum was a big man, both in height and girth, which made him the butt of a series of ongoing jokes batted about good-naturedly among his staff. He was commanding officer of the Village Police of West Bay Bridge. He had a beery-cheeked face on which was positioned dead centre, as if it were the bull's-eye of some target, a bulbous red-veined nose. His skin was tanned to the colour of cured leather; his salt-and-pepper hair was cut *en brosse*. He wore a brown Dacron suit not because he liked it but because he had to. He would just as soon have come to work in a flannel shirt and a pair of old slacks. 'What, then,' Florum said equally slowly, '*did* he die from?'

'He was poisoned,' Doc Deerforth said.

'Doc,' Florum said as he wearily rubbed his hand over his face. 'I want this to be real clear, understand? Crystal clear. So perfectly clear that there won't be any possibility of a misunderstanding when I make out my report. Because, beside the State Detectives who, I'm sure you're aware, I'm gonna have to copy on this – and when I do, they're gonna be down here like locusts on a wheat-field asking us to do all their goddamned field work and then sucking us dry – beside those sonsabitches, I've gotta contend with the county bastards who're most probably gonna claim that this thing's in their jurisdiction. And, to top it all off, now that you tell me it's a murder, I'm gonna have Flower rumbling in from Hauppauge on his white horse wondering why our investigation is taking so long and when's he gonna be relieved of the stiff, his staff's so overworked.' Florum slammed the flat of his hand down on the cover of a copy of *Crime in the United States, 1979*. 'Well, this time they're just gonna have to wait long enough so that they're one great step behind me.'

A sergeant came in, handed Florum several typewritten sheets and went out without a word.

'Christ, it makes my blood boil sometimes. I'm no god-damned politician. That's what this job calls for. Who the hell cares whether I know police procedure or not. God!' But he got up, still, and came back with a file which he opened on his desk. He ran a hand through his hair, scratched at his scalp. He began to shift through a number of eight-by-ten black and white prints which, even upside down, Doc Deerforth recognized as shots of the drowned man.

'First of all,' Doc Deerforth said calmly. 'I've taken care of

34

Flower. He won't bother you, at least for the time being.'

Florum looked up briefly, inquisitively, then his gaze returned to the photos. 'Yeah, how'd you work that little miracle?'

'I haven't told him yet.'

'You mean to say,' Florum said, as he reached out an oblong magnifying-glass from a desk drawer, 'that nobody knows about this ... murder but us chickens right here in this room?'

'That's precisely what I mean,' Doc Deerforth said quietly.

After a time, Florum said, 'You know, there's nothing shows up on these photos.' He shuffled the photos like a deck of cards until a close-up of the head and chest of the drowned man was on top. 'Nothing but a routine drowning.'

'You won't find anything there.'

'That's what I said.'

'Doesn't mean, though, that there isn't anything to see.'

Florum sat back in his chair and crossed his hands over his ample belly. 'Okay, Doc. I'm all ears. You tell me about it.'

'What it boils down to is this. The man was dead before he even hit the water.' Doc Deerforth sighed. 'It was something that might have been overlooked by even as good an M.E. as Flower.' Florum grunted but said nothing. 'Look, there is a small traumatic puncture wound in the man's chest, middle-left, and it could easily have been mistaken for a rock scrape – which it is not. The puncture led me to take blood samples, one of which was from the aorta, where this type of poison concentrates; it's flushed from the rest of the bloodstream within perhaps twenty minutes of death, by what means I have no idea. It's a highly unusual cardio-vascular poison.'

Florum snapped his fingers. 'Proof! Heart attack.'

'Yes.'

'You sure about this?'

'About the poison, yes. Otherwise you know I wouldn't have come to you. But I've still got some more tests to run. It appears likely that a sliver of whatever punctured the man's flesh is still lodged in his sternum.'

'There's no exit wound?'

'No.'

'The fall could have dislodged it. Or the sea –'

'Or it was pulled free after the man fell.'

'What you're saying, Doc ...' He paused and, pushing aside the photos, consulted a filled-out preprinted form. 'This guy, Barry Braughm, an account executive at' – here he named Sam Goldman's advertising agency in New York – 'lived at three-oh-one East Sixty-third, was murdered. But in this way? For what reason? He was out here alone. No jealous wife or boy-friend ...' He laughed. 'He's got a sister in Queens whom we've already contacted and interviewed. We checked on his house on Dune Road. Nada. No sign of it being broken into or even that anything was taken. His car was where he had driven it up and parked it in front of the house as secure as Fort Knox. There's nothing to –'

'There's this,' Doc Deerforth said, knowing that, at last, he had come to the moment he had been dreading ever since he had discovered the puncture wound and, subsequently, had pulled the blood from the drowned man's heart. It isn't possible, he kept telling himself, all the time his hands and eyes were running the tests that were confirming it; saying it over and over to himself like a litany against evil. And he felt now rather out of himself, a dreamlike unreality that allowed him to sit in another part of this room and watch himself talking to Ray Florum just as if he were an actor in some film.

From outside there came the sound of a child's laughter, harsh and brittle in the night, transformed by some aural magic into an eerie, other-worldly sound, the mocking shrillness of the macaws' cries in the Philippine jungle.

'It's the poison,' he continued. 'It's a very specific type.' He ran his palms down the sides of his trousers. It had been a long time since he had felt his hands wet with sweat. 'I came across this particular compound when I was stationed overseas.'

'During the war?' Florum said. 'But, good God, man, that's thirty-six years ago. Do you mean to tell me –'

'I could not forget this poison, Ray, no matter how many years have passed. A patrol went out one night. Five men. Only one returned and he just made it to the perimeter. We'd heard no shots; nothing but the birds and the buzz of the insects ... It was odd, that kind of stillness, almost creepy; we'd been fired upon by snipers all through the day and every day for about a week.' Doc Deerforth took a deep breath before plunging onwards. Anyway, they brought me the man who'd come back. He was a boy, really. No more than nineteen. He was still alive and I began to work on him. I did everything I could, everything in and out of the book, but I was helpless. He literally died before my eyes.'

'Dying of this stuff?'

Doc Deerforth nodded bleakly. 'The same.'

'Do you want me to go?' Nicholas asked her.

'Yes,' Justine said. 'No. I don't know.' She stood behind the couch, her fingers pulled distractedly at the tufted Haitian cotton. 'My God, but you confuse me.'

'I don't mean to,' he offered.

'Words don't mean anything.'

He was quite startled to see that her face in profile seemed remarkably different, as if he were seeing her now from the perspective of a different age, some other life. In this respect, she reminded him of Yukio. Of course with Yukio he had always imagined it to be the diverse mixture of her heritage, shrouded in some mysterious world to which he did not belong and to which he had brought but the insight of an alien. That, he knew now, had been a purely Westernized response to what was, quite obviously, inexplicable and it somehow confounded him that here, in the West, it should strike him so differently. Perhaps it was but the passage of time – a certain distancing from the anguish – which enabled him at last to see Yukio for what she really was, to him and to those around her. It was, he thought, the space he had gained from all the ramified, ritualized patterns of his life in Japan, which allowed him to realize the mistakes he had committed, to understand the role of his participation in it all.

Justine stirred on the other side of the couch, as far from him as if she were in another country, and he smelled her fragrance.

'It's late,' she said. But it made no sense, was meant, he supposed, to fill a void that was becoming too threatening for her.

But this kind of inner tension was one of the things that most intrigued him about her. Oh yes, she was extraordinarily beautiful in his eyes; if he had passed her on a busy Manhattan street, he would surely have turned his head, even, perhaps, followed

37

her into Bendel's or Botticelli before he lost her in a swelling crowd; what else does one do with that kind of fantasy? When one followed them up, one was invariably disappointed. Then she would have been on his mind for an hour or so. But so what? Physical beauty, he had learned quite early, was the arbiter of nothing, could even be a dangerous and bloody thing. More than anything else, he needed a challenge, with women as much as with all the interests in his life. For he felt quite deeply that nothing in life was worth possessing without a struggle – even love; especially love. This too he had learned in Japan, where women were like flowers one had to unfold like origami, with infinite care and deliberateness finding that, when fully opened, they were filled with exquisite tenderness and devious violence.

Just the creamy splash of the surf now, the record gathering dust on the immobile turn-table. There came the cry of a gull, lonely and querulous as if it had somehow lost its way.

He wondered what he had to do; whether he really wanted to do anything. After all, there was fear inside him, too.

'Have you been with many women?' she asked abruptly. He saw that her arms, as rigid as pillars, were trembling and that she had brought her head up with an effort. She stared at him, daring him to deride her or, perhaps, revile her, confirming her suspicions of him and, more generally, of men.

'That's an odd question to ask.'

She turned her head slightly and he saw the warm lamplight define the bridge of her nose, slide down into the hollow beneath one eye, at the crest of her neck. The crimson motes were like points of burnished brass; the right side of her face was entirely in shadow. 'Will you answer it?'

He smiled. 'Some that I've not cared about. Few that I have.'

And all the while she watched his eyes for any hint that he might be mocking her. She found none.

'What is it you wish to know, Justine?' he said softly. 'Are you afraid I won't tell you?'

'No.' She shook her head. 'I'm afraid that you will.' Her nails plucked at the nubs of cotton as a musician fingers the strings of a harp. 'I want to and I don't want to,' she said after a while.

He was about to say, with a smile, that it wasn't so serious but he realized that it was; he knew what she was talking about. He came around the end of the sofa, stood by her. 'It's only me, Justine,' he said, 'who's here. There's only the two of us.'

'I know.' But it was not enough because she had said it like a little girl who did not quite believe what she was saying, wanting only some outside reassurance for an important inner act.

She broke away from this tight orbit, perhaps feeling the increasing magnetism beginning to influence the balance, and went across the room to stand in front of the large window. The outside lights were still on, and beyond the porch and the fluttering pitiful moths the sea broke endlessly onto the shore, the sand now as dark as coal.

'You know, for some reason this view reminds me of San Francisco.'

'When were you there?' he asked, coming round and sitting on one arm of the sofa.

'About two years ago, I guess. I was there for eighteen months, almost.'

'Why'd you leave?'

'I – broke up with someone. Came back here. Returned to the East, the prodigal daughter, into the bosom of her family.' For some reason that struck her as funny, but the laugh seemed to strangle and die in her throat.

'You loved the city.'

'Yes,' she said. 'Yes, I did that. Very much.'

'Then why leave it?'

'I – had to.' She lifted her slim hand, then looked at it, surprised that it was in that position. 'I was a different person then. Not at all secure.' She clasped her hands in front of her, arms extended downwards. 'I was so vulnerable. I felt – I guess I felt that I couldn't stay there by myself. There was a kind of wind sailing through me.' As if it were an afterthought, she said, 'It was a stupid situation. *I* was stupid.' She shook her head as if she still could not believe how she had acted.

'I've been there twice,' Nicholas said. 'San Francisco, I mean. I fell in love with it. Its size; its whiteness viewed from Mill Valley.' He was watching the thin line of phosphorescence, almost transparent, that marked the rise of the surf and its subsequent fall to earth, coming in, coming in. 'I used to go down to the shore just to watch the Pacific and think: Here are these waves rolling in, rolling all the way across the world from Japan.'

'Why did you leave?' she asked. 'What made you come here?'

He took a deep breath. 'That's difficult to sum up in words. I suppose it was an aggregate of many things, a slow accretion. My father, you know, he wanted to come to America. He loved Japan. Fought for it, always. He might have come here himself but – it wasn't his karma, I suppose. It was something he regretted.' The spume was like silver lace far away – out there on the bosom of the sea. 'If there is a part of him within me, then he's here now and that makes me feel all right.'

'Do you really believe that? Life after –'

He smiled. 'Oh yes. Oh no. I cannot tell you truthfully. East meets West inside me like swirling currents and there is a kind of tug of war. But about my father, my mother. They are with me, yes.'

'It seems so odd –'

'Only because we are here, standing on a porch in West Bay Bridge. If we were in Asia ...' He shrugged as if this explanation were sufficient. 'And, too, I came here to prove to myself that I could be a Westerner as well as an Easterner. I majored in mass communications at college, launched into the atom age. Advertising seemed a logical choice once I came here and I was lucky enough to find someone who was willing to take a chance on me as a raw trainee.' He laughed. 'It turned out I was a natural.'

She turned her body sideways to the surf, facing him fully. She came and stood next to him. Her long hair swirled, a link; they had not touched. 'Do you want me?' she whispered like the tide. 'Do you want to make love to me?'

'Yes,' he said, watching her eyes, their expanded pupils darkening the green to black. He felt a tightening in his stomach, no longer quite certain of his own ghosts, feeling a filament of fear, a feather brushing the base of his spine. 'Do you want to make love to me?'

She said nothing; he felt the nearness of her hand rather than saw it, mesmerized by her eyes, the glowing motes like magnets. He felt its heat, then the tips of her fingers touched the skin of his biceps, curled around the muscles there, firmly but without squeezing, and it seemed to him that the simple gesture communicated so much that it was as if she had never done it before; that it had never been done to him before in just that way. And that first contact was so electrically tender that he felt the muscles of his thighs trembling, a sighing in his heart begin.

He wrapped her slowly in his arms and he was quite certain she cried out, a tiny burst of erotic emotion, 'Oh!' the abandoned ardour of the music, just before his lips covered hers. Immediately her mouth opened under his and he felt the length of her body pressing against his, building heat at the fulcra of breasts, belly and the juncture of her thighs.

How hot she seemed as his lips caressed her long neck, tracing the rounded edge of her collar-bone. His hands pulled at her shirt. Her lips were at his ear, her tongue circling, circling like that last hungry gull above the night-dark beach, and she whispered, 'Not here. Not here. Please –'

Lifting her arms and the shirt came off; his fingers stroked her spine, the deep long indentation. She shivered and moaned as he licked under her arms, moving slowly to her full breasts, the nipples already hard and puckered.

Her long fingers unfastening the snap of his jeans, her nails clicking together as his open lips covered the upper slopes of her breasts, spiralling inwards. 'Please,' she whispered. 'Please.' And brought him out of the jeans, already half-erect, stroking him softly to full hardness as he sucked her nipples.

He felt the fear give a last flutter, like a tired sigh, before it evaporated utterly. They sank lower and lower, twisting and trembling with anticipation as the remainder of their clothes came off. Her hands moved to push down the pair of thin silk panties but he stopped her, picking her up from the carpet, one hand under her buttocks, the other at the small of her back, lifted her half onto the sofa, moving between her spread thighs, bending, his opened lips finding their soft inner sides, moving slowly upwards, towards the high silk-covered mount. Her fingers were white as they gripped the front edge of the sofa's pillow; his tongue touched the moist silk and she moaned again, her back arching.

He began to lick at her through the thin barrier of the silk and her hands flew to his head, stroking his ears, her wide opened mouth making small involuntary cries as the tension built inside her rapidly. Then he moved aside the sopping silk and buried his face against her. Her nails grazed his back as her long legs jerked convulsively upwards. Her ankles locked against his spine. He moved slightly upwards to her core, sucked it into his mouth. Her loins rolled upwards in powerful thrusts as she cried out, his tongue and lips constantly moving until he felt her shuddering against him, heard her scream, the tenseness dissolving out of her, and wetly, heatedly, she drew him up towards her, her fingers seeking him, her lips wildly on his, wanting him in her now, at this precise moment, more than she wanted anything else, to continue the exquisite heat she felt, to give him pleasure as he had given her.

Her sex felt like a furnace as she guided him into her. She rammed her belly against him as he buried himself to the hilt; they both groaned with the sensation. She surrounded him with her arms, languorously twitching her upper torso so that her lush breasts rubbed back and forth across his chest. She moaned with the intense stimulation to her hard nipples. She licked at his neck as he used his hands on her, all over, increasing her pleasure, riding high within her, and at the end, when she found the tension almost unbearable, when the sweat and the saliva ran down her arms and between her breasts, pooling in her navel, when his frictioning against her was so intense that it took on a kind of third dimension, she used her inner muscles once, twice, heard him gasp, felt herself balancing on the brink, the thudding of their hearts heavy in her inner ear, whispering to him, 'Come, darling, come – ohhh!' gasped out as she felt his probing finger, slick with their mingled juices, at the opening of her anus and lost all control, filled with fire all the way up to her throat.

Dr Vincent Ito stirred the hot chrysanthemum tea steaming in the handleless ceramic cup. Disturbed, several dark bits of crushed leaf swirled upwards from the bottom, circling the surface. They reminded him of floaters. They were coming, he knew, had been for a month or so. Those bodies, once people who had leapt or, unconscious, had, perhaps, been pushed into the East River or the Hudson during the long winter months. Consigned to the deep, they had been preserved by the chill at the bottom, undisturbed by the sluggish currents until the beginning of the summer when the water heated up. At thirty to thirty-five degrees Fahrenheit, bacteria would begin to breed, causing putrefaction and gases that would, eventually, bring the body to the surface, and the floater, months after it had gone in, would be brought to him at the Medical Examiner's building.

That certainly did not bother him. Since he was an associate medical examiner, it was merely part of Vincent's life. An important part, he had admitted to himself long ago. The morgue, in the building's basement, with its steel-jacketed doors stacked one atop the other marked by their neat, typewritten cards, the scrubbed grey tile floor, the great scales upon which the corpses were weighed, was where he lived most of his days. There was nothing ghoulish about it, passing the brown and white bodies laid out on the shining trolleys, bloodless, the great T-shaped incisions across the chest from shoulder to shoulder and down across the abdomen, the epidermis thick like leather, the faces as peaceful as if they slept the sleep of the innocent. It had no effect on him. The interest and, yes, the excitement of forensic medicine was, for him, the intricate puzzle of death. Not so much what it was but rather what had caused it. He was a detective whose work among the dead had, many times, aided the living.

Vincent stared out of the window as he slowly sipped his tea. Darkness still spread itself before the coming dawn: 4:25. He was always up this early.

He stared out at the city, the lighted empty streets of Manhattan. Far away he heard the grinding of a garbage truck making its lentitudinous way along Tenth Street. Then closer by, a police car siren cut abruptly in, shattering the quietude. But it too, after a time, was gone, evaporating into the darkness. Nothing remained in the night but his thoughts, twisting upon themselves.

He felt trapped. *My karma must have been very bad in my*

43

last life, he told himself. Japan seemed as inaccessible as if it were in another time. It no longer seemed possible for him ever to find it again, at least the Japan he had left twelve years ago. For him there was no more Japan; it was but a withered flower – calling him still like a siren of the sea.

Nicholas awoke just before dawn. For just a moment, he was quite convinced that he was in his old house on the outskirts of Tokyo, the Zen garden, the oblique shadows on the wall by his head made by the stand of tall rustling bamboo. He heard a cuckoo's brief call, the rush of the morning's traffic into the city, muffled, funnelled and yet magnified by the distance and the peculiar acoustics of the topography.

He turned his head, still half asleep, saw a female form asleep beside him. Yukio. She had come back after all, he thought. He had known she would. But now to actually have her here beside him –

He sat up abruptly, his heart racing. A runic chanting, as if from far away across the distance of a sea, abruptly metamorphosed into the drifting crash of the surf, coming clear to him through the open window, the cry of the gulls. Still he knew the meaning of that arcane chanting ...

He took several deep breaths. Japan clung to him now like a fine gauzy veil, enmeshing him. What had recalled it to him so intensely?

He looked around, saw the tip of Justine's nose and her soft sensual lips, partly opened as she breathed, the only parts of her not covered by the sheet, blue and white and grey, rippling like the sea. She slept deeply now within its heavy bosom.

What is it about her, he wondered, that pulls me like a current? Oddly, he felt adrift upon the tides. Watching her, the soft rise and fall of her warm body, he knew that he was being drawn back to Japan, into the past where he dared not tread ...

An unutterably delicious sensation woke him. He opened his eyes to find her thighs close to his face. He inhaled her musk, realized her lips were around him. Her tongue licked softly, lasciviously, and he groaned. He reached out to touch her but her thighs moved away. He watched, instead, the movement

44

of her mound, tracing with his eyes the highly arched configuration, deeply bisected at its base, the soft curling hair glistening moistly down the centre, her flesh as tumescent as his, an arrow of delight.

The pleasure ribboned out before him, a highway endlessly extended. Each time he was on the verge of coming, she used her hands on him, lifted her mouth away, encircling the base until the anticipatory spasms subsided. Then she would resume and the crescendo would begin again, over and over until his legs shook and his heart pounded and he felt as if he were burning with a fever, pleasure pooling and radiating at the same time, leaden with the amount of it running through his pelvis and genitals.

He became aware of her breasts swaying against his belly and he reached down, cupping them, rubbing the nipples until, involuntarily, her thighs opened, rushing towards him.

Every touch was now so exquisite that he felt muscles jumping all over his body at each contact. She did something to the head of his penis and he cried out, moving. He clutched at her breasts and she slid up so that his shaft squeezed between them. He buried his face in the crevasse between her thighs, opening his mouth as far as he could as he shot and shot and shot.


Vincent Ito arrived at the Medical Examiner's office on First Avenue at Thirtieth Street at four minutes to eight in the morning. As he pushed through the plate-glass door at the top of the short flight of stairs, he nodded to the uniformed cop on duty and said hello to snowy-haired Tommy, Nate Graumann's chauffeur. As he entered Room 134, he knew he had just enough time to grab a cup of coffee before the morning meeting began.

He turned right through the short hall and into the Chief Medical Examiner's large, crowded office.

Nate Graumann, New York City's Chief Medical Examiner, was a mountain of a man. His eyes were slitted, black and glossy, half hidden within semicircular folds of loose skin, somewhat paler than the colour of that around them. His broad nose had been broken once, perhaps in some night-time street fight in the South Bronx, where he had been born and raised.

His hair was salt and pepper but his moustache was jet black. He looked, in short, like a most formidable opponent – which he was, as the mayor and several members of the city's fiscal control board could easily attest.

'Morning, Vincent,' he called.

'Morning, Nate.' He hurried across the room to the high metal dome of the coffee machine standing like a doge's palace amid the clutter. Hold the sugar, hold the half-and-half, he thought gloomily. I need my caffeine straight this morning.

'Stay a minute, Vincent,' Graumann said, as the assignment meeting broke up.

Vincent sat in a green chair across from the littered desk and handed over the cases he had picked out when Graumann asked to see them.

They were friends, away from their labours here, but those times had seemed to shrink over the years. Graumann had been deputy M.E. when Vincent had first arrived here and, it seemed, there had been more time then. Or perhaps it was just that there had been more money. Their workloads increased as the fiscal crunch fell like the side of a mountain upon them. The city had much larger problems than worrying about the people who were daily bludgeoned, knifed, strangled, drowned, asphyxiated, shot, mangled and blown apart on the city's streets or in the bodies of water throughout its environs. Eighty thousand people die each year in New York City and we get thirty thousand of them, he thought.

'What d'you have on at the moment?' Graumann said.

'Uhm. The Morway thing,' Vincent said, his brow furrowing in thought, 'and the Holloway knifing – I'm due in court on that any moment. The Principal case is about closed – just a few odds and ends left to tie up for the D.A. – the blood analysis should be in this afternoon. And then, oh yeah, Marshall.'

'What's that?'

'Came in late yesterday afternoon. McCabe said it couldn't wait so I began working on it right away. Drowning in the reservoir. McCabe thinks he might have had his head held under. They're holding someone on suspicion, that's why she needs the goods right away.'

Graumann nodded. 'Full load, huh?'

'More than.'

'I want you to go out to the Island for a couple of days.'

'What? In the middle of all this?'

'If it weren't important I wouldn't be asking,' he said patiently, 'would I?'

'But what about –?'

'I'll look after your cases in progress personally. And these' – he picked up the two manila folders, tapping their bottoms on the desk top several times as if straightening them out – 'I'll give to Michaelson.'

'Michaelson is an idiot,' Vincent retorted hotly.

Graumann regarded him placidly. 'He goes by the book, Vincent. He's steady and dependable.'

'But he's so slow,' Vincent moaned.

'Speed is not everything,' Graumann reminded him.

'Tell that to McCabe. She's got the whole office on our case, lately. All those goddamn assistant D.A.s wheedling their way in here mucking things up.'

'It's what they're paid to do, I'm afraid.'

'So what am I doing out on the Island?'

'Paul Deerforth called late yesterday,' Graumann said. 'You remember him?'

'Sure. We met last year when I came out to visit you for a couple of days. West Bay Bridge, right?'

'Uhm, hmm.' Graumann sat forward. 'He's apparently got a problem that's over his head. He has ancillary ties to the Suffolk County M.E.'s office.' He looked down at his steepled nails, back up to Vincent's face. 'He asked for you specifically.'

There was a great fish tank along the left-hand brick wall of the living-room of Nicholas's house. It was, he estimated, big enough to hold fifty gallons of water. But its denizens were no ordinary guppies or gouramis, for the owners had left to him, the summer's tenant, the care of a multitude of salt-water fish whose brilliant colours electrified the surrounding water just as if they were a flock of boldly plumaged birds flitting through some dense tropical world.

He watched Justine's form through this aqueous lens like a

primitive peeping through the foliage at an intruding mem-sahib.

She wore a red bathing suit cut high along the thighs to resemble a dancer's leotard and thus accentuate her long legs. She had a white towel around her neck as if she had just come from a gym. She licked at a running egg yolk between her fingers as she mopped at the plate with a last bite of toast in her other hand. Popping this into her mouth, she turned to look at him.

'Those aren't yours, are they?' she asked.

He had finished feeding them but unaccountably remained in his crouched position, fascinated perhaps by the distortions of the soft currents created by the fish and the bubbling aerator. A certain air of unreality was comforting although he might be more inclined to think of it as an aspect of fantasy.

'Not mine, no,' he said from behind the barrier reef. 'They are the house's true owners.' He laughed and straightened up. 'More so than I, at any rate.'

She stood up, brought the plates to the kitchen. 'Christ, it's raining.' She leaned on the sink with her elbows, stared out of the window. 'I wanted to work outside today.'

The rain pattered lightly against the living-room windows, the flat roof, coming in from the sea. The light was cold and dark, as patchy as marble.

'Do it here,' he said. 'You've got your stuff with you.'

She came out into the living-room, dusted her hands. 'No, I don't think so. If I have to be inside, I might as well use the board.'

She confounded him, and doing nothing was, in its way, just as bad as taking the wrong turn. He despised hesitation.

'Have you brought any sketches with you?'

'Yes, I –' She glanced away towards the large canvas bag by the side of the sofa. 'Of course. Yes.'

'I'd like to see them.'

She nodded, reached out a large blue-paper-covered tablet, handed it to him.

She wandered around the room while he went from page to page. The bubbling of the tank. The muted hiss of the surf.

'What's these?'

He looked up. She was standing in front of a low walnut break-front, hands clasped loosely behind her back. She meant the objects he had hung on the wall one above the other, a pair of scabbarded, gently curving swords. The top one was perhaps thirty inches long, the one beneath perhaps twenty.

He watched the shadowed line of her spine for a moment, compared it with the one in the sketch he held in front of him. 'They are the ancient swords of the Japanese samurai,' he said. 'The longer one is the *katana*, the killing sword; the other, a *wakizashi*.'

'What're they used for?'

'Combat and *seppuku*: ritual suicide. In ancient times, only the samurai were allowed to wear and use the *daisho*, the two blades.'

'Where did you get them?' Still she had not taken her eyes off them.

'They're mine,' he said.

She turned her head and smiled. 'You mean you're a samurai?'

'In a way,' he said seriously and got off the couch. He stood beside her, thinking about the three hours a day he practised.

'Can I see,' she said, 'the long blade?'

Carefully he reached up, took the *katana* off the wall. 'I shouldn't do this.' One hand on the sheath, fingers of his right hand wrapped around the long hilt.

'Why not?'

He pulled slowly, its shining length revealed in a four-inch span. 'The *katana* should be drawn only for combat. It's sacred. Given in the manhood ceremony, christened with its own name, it is the heart and soul of the samurai. This is a *dai-katana*, longer than the standard sword. Don't touch it,' he said sharply and she withdrew the extended finger in alarm. 'It would sever your finger.'

He saw her reflection in the blade, eyes opened wide, lips slightly parted. He could hear her breathing beside him.

'Let me see a little more of it.' She brushed a stray lock of hair out of her eyes. 'It's beautiful. Has it a name?'

'Yes,' he said, thinking of Cheong and Itami. '*Iss-hōgai*. It means "for life." '

49

'Did you name it?'

'No, my father did.'

'I like the name; it fits, somehow.'

'There's magic in a Japanese-forged blade,' he said, replacing the *dai-katana* in its scabbard. 'This particular sword is almost two hundred years old yet its manufacture is so superb that it does not show even a year's wear.' He replaced the weapon. 'The finest blade the world has ever known or ever will know.'

The phone rang and he went to it.

'Nick. It's Vincent.'

'Hey. How are you?'

'Fine. Actually, I'm on my way out to your neck of the woods – or shore, as it were.'

'The Island?'

'Better than that. West Bay Bridge.'

'Hey, that's great. I haven't seen you since –'

'March, if you want to know. Listen, I'm going to be staying at Doc Deerforth's in town.'

'No you're not. You're staying out here by the beach. There's plenty of room; you can't swim in town.'

'Sorry, but this isn't a vacation, and until I find out what's going on I'd better plan to stay with the doc.'

'How's Nate?'

'As usual or thereabouts. There's too much work there for all of us.'

Nicholas glanced at Justine, who was leafing through her sketch-book, one hand run through her thick hair. While he watched, she leaned across the sofa, reached out a pencil from her bag, began to continue the unfinished sketch she had been contemplating.

'Someone there with you?'

'Yes.'

'I see. Well, I'll be out late this afternoon.' He laughed, his voice sounding for the first time thin and strained. 'It must really be something. Graumann's given me the car *and* Tommy. All I have to do is sit in the back seat and take a nap.' He sighed. 'Poor me. A few years ago, before the fiscal crunch, I'd be coming out in a Lincoln. Now I have to be content with a diarrhoea-tan Plymouth.'

Nicholas laughed. 'Give me a ring when you're settled in and you'll come over for a drink.'

'Right. 'Bye.'

He cradled the receiver; sat down next to Justine. His eyes traced the new lines she had made but his mind was far away.


'I think I see now why you asked for me to come out,' Vincent said.

'You know what this stuff is?' Doc Deerforth said.

Vincent rubbed at his eyes with thumb and forefinger. The harsh fluorescent lights hurt his eyes. He reached up, pulled the goose-neck incandescent lamp closer to the sheets of paper he had been reading. 'I don't quite know what to think, to be honest.'

'The man we just saw downstairs did not die of drowning.'

'Of that there is no doubt.' Vincent nodded his agreement. 'Whatever he died of, it wasn't asphyxiation.'

'As you can see,' Doc Deerforth said, indicating the contents of the folder in Vincent's hands, 'he had no previous record of heart failure or any cardiac problem at all; none in his family. He was a perfectly healthy thirty-six-year-old male Caucasian, slightly out of shape but –'

'He died of a massive M.I.' Vincent completed the sentence. 'Heart attack.'

'Induced, I'm convinced,' Doc Deerforth said, bending forward and stabbing at the printed sheet, 'by that substance.'

'Have you fed it through the computer?'

Doc Deerforth shook his head. 'Remember that as far as anyone here is concerned, this is an "accidental death by drowning", at least as of now. Anyway, you must be aware that it would do no good at all.'

'What about the delay in your report to the C.M.E.?' Vincent snapped shut the folder, handed it over to Doc Deerforth.

'Why, didn't I tell you? I'm having a bit of trouble with the man's family.' Doc Deerforth placed the folder under his arm and guided Vincent out of the lab, turning out the lights. The twenty-minute drive back to West Bay Bridge seemed awfully long to him all of a sudden.

*

Justine sat scrunched down in a far corner of the couch, knees drawn up, arms about her legs. Her open sketch-pad lay on the low wooden coffee table in front of them. Across the room, the window-panes were still teary, though most of the rain had dissipated into a low mist.

'Tell me about Japan,' she said abruptly, bringing her face down until it was level with his. Her cool eyes regarded him far from impassively.

'I haven't been back in a very long time,' he said.

'What's it like?'

'Different. Very different.'

'You mean the language.'

'Oh, that's part of it, of course. But it's more basic than that. You can go to France or Spain, have to deal with other languages. But after all, the thought processes are not that much different. Not in Japan. The Japanese confound most Westerners, frighten them, too, oddly enough.'

'Not really,' she observed. 'Everyone's frightened of what they don't understand.'

'And then,' he said, 'there are some who understand right away. My father was one of those. He loved the East.'

'As do you.'

'Yes,' he said. 'As do I.'

'What made you come here?'

He watched her as the darkness came slowly down, as the world outside turned blue, wondering how she could be so insightful in her questions and at the same time so evasive in her answers. Inside the house, where they sat near the bubbling fish tank, the light was like yellow custard.

'I no longer wanted to be in Japan,' he said, recognizing in the simple statement both the truth and the utter insufficiency of the words. But would any words have sufficed? He could not say with any certainty.

'So you came here and went into advertising.'

He nodded. 'In effect, yes.'

'And left your family?'

'I have no family.' The words came out cold and hard, as individually devastating as bullets, and she recoiled.

'You make me feel ashamed that I never talk to my sister,'

she said, turning her face away from him for a moment as if to demonstrate her embarrassment actively.

'You must hate her a great deal.'

She spun her head back. 'That was a cruel thing to say.'

'It was?' He was genuinely surprised. 'I don't think so.' He looked at her. 'Are you indifferent about her? That would be far worse, I think.'

'No,' she said. 'No, I'm not indifferent to her. She's my sister. I – I don't think you could understand,' she finished somewhat lamely and he knew she had meant to say something else, only changing her mind at the last instant.

'Why won't you talk about your father? You spoke about him before in the past tense. Is he dead?'

There was a look in her eyes, a kind of reflective opacity as if she were staring into a fire, as she said, 'Yes. He's as dead as he could possibly be.' She got off the sofa, went over to the fish tank, peering in with a kind of coiled intensity as if she longed to shrink in size and jump into the salt water, becoming one with the crowd idling there. 'What difference could it make to you, anyway? I'm not my father's daughter; I don't believe in all that shit.' But her tone said otherwise and Nicholas found himself wondering just what it was her father had done to her that she should despise him so.

'What about your sister?' he said. 'I'm curious because I was an only child.'

She turned away from the tank, the water's reflection in the overhead light dappling one side of her face as if she were submerged, some exotic sea creature attracted by the motion of his descent. He imagined they were at the bottom of the sea, puckered kelp like stately bamboo waving in the deep current's breeze; he imagined they spoke sonically, bone to bone, vibrations batted back and forth like a tennis-ball.

'Gelda.' Her voice had captured an odd quality that he could not place. 'My older sister.' She sucked in some air. 'You're lucky to be alone; some things shouldn't be shared; some things are better left where they are.'

'Buried in the sand of the sea floor?' he wondered. It seemed irrational to blame her for failing to take him into her confidence yet he found himself annoyed by her obdurate reticence.

Abruptly, he felt a tearing need to share her secrets: her humiliations, her childish maunderings, her hate and love and fear; her shame; the core that made this bolt of silk what it was, as different and fascinatingly imperfect as some strange glowing gem. Her mystery pulled him onwards and, like a marathon swimmer who has reached his limit and, passing it, finds himself about to go under with the realization that he has attempted to discover and defeat something far too powerful for him, he knew that this same realization was the key to his reaching down to find the unplumbed reserves which would carry him onwards to reach the far shore.

But for Nicholas it was somewhat different, for part of him, at least, was well aware of those things which lay hidden there within that interminable beach, and he shuddered to face them again, to gaze upon their hideous countenances. For once before he had come upon them and had almost been destroyed.

They went out of the house into the summer night. The clouds had delivered themselves westward and the sky was at last clear. The stars shone, winking, like ornaments on velvet, making them feel as if the world had wrapped them in a shawl manufactured especially for that occasion.

They strolled along the beach at the waterline, far out, for it was low tide. Their feet picked up the damp sea grapes and their soles felt the brief pain of the fiddler crab shells.

The surf tumbled in low, faintly phosphorescent hillocks that seemed like another world viewed from the wrong end of a telescope. Near to hand, they were alone on the beach; a point of orange, a smokily glowing coal, bespoke a late barbecue in the lee of a dune far down the night.

'Are you afraid of me?' His voice was as light as mist.

'No,' she said. 'I'm not.' She stuffed her hands in the front pockets of her jeans. 'I'm just afraid. It's been with me for more than a year and a half, this fear like a diamond shadow-image I can't manage to shake.'

'We're all afraid – of something or other.'

'Jesus, Nick, don't patronize me. You've never been afraid like this.'

'Because I'm a man?'

'Because you're you.' She stared fixedly away from him, his muscularity. She rubbed her palms along her bare arms; he thought she shivered. 'Oh, Christ.'

He bent down, scooped up a sand-encrusted stone. He wiped it off, feeling its ineffable smoothness against his skin. Time had taken away all the edges; time had dictated its shape. Yet the essence of the stone – its mottled colour, striations, imperfections of structure, density and hardness – remained. Indomitable.

She took the stone from him and hurled it far out into the water. It struck the surface of the sea without a splash and sank from sight as if it had never existed, but Nicholas could still feel the weight of it where it had rested in the palm of his hand.

'It would be so simple,' he said, 'if we could approach people we cared for without any past so we could see them without any colouration.'

She stood silently regarding him and only a slight tremor along her neck told him that she had heard.

'But we can't,' he continued. 'Human memory is long; it's after all what brings us together, what causes that peculiar tingling, sometimes, when we first meet, like a faint but unmistakable brush of recognition – of what? A kindred spirit, perhaps. An aura. It has many names. It exists, invisible but unallayed for all that.' He paused. 'Did you feel it when we met?'

'I felt – something. Yes.' Her thumb stroked the back of his hand, tracing the lines of the bones there. 'A spark from a flame.' She looked down at her feet, at the damp black sand, at the rushing water. 'I'm afraid to trust you.' Her head came up abruptly as if she had made some decision and was now determined to adhere to it. 'My men have been such bastards and – I did the picking, after all ...'

'How can I be any different, is that it?'

'But you are different, Nick. I can feel it.' Yet she took her hand away from his. 'I can't go through it again. I just can't. This isn't a movie. I don't know that everything is going to turn out right.'

'When do you ever know that?'

But she ignored him, continuing, 'We're brought up with a kind of romanticism that's so false it leads us astray. Falling in love and marriage is forever. The movies, then TV told us that, even – especially – the commercials. We're all electronic babies now. So then we pass out of "us" and into "I" – what do you do when the "us" doesn't work and the "I" is far too lonely?'

'You keep searching, I suppose. That's all life is anyway. It's one great search for whatever it is we want: love, money, fame, recognition, security – all of those things. It's the degrees of importance which varies in each individual.'

'Except for me.' Justine's voice was tinged with bitterness now. 'I don't know what I want any more.'

'What was it,' he said, 'that you wanted in San Francisco?' He saw only her outline, an ebon figure in the darkness, blotting out the starlight where she stood.

Her voice, when she answered, was like a wisp out of time, a cold tendril, slightly unearthly, so that he felt a brief shiver run through him.

'I wanted,' she said, 'to be dominated.'

'I still can't believe I said that to you.'

They lay, naked, beneath the sheets in his bed. A beam of moonlight came in through the windows overlooking the sea like an ethereal bridge to another land.

'Why?' Nicholas asked her.

'Because I'm ashamed of it. I'm ashamed I ever felt that way. I don't ever want to be like that again. I reject it.'

'Is it so terrible, then, to want to be dominated?'

'The way I wanted it ... Yes, it was – unnatural.'

'How do you mean that?'

She turned around and he felt the soft press of her breasts against his skin. 'I don't want to talk about it any more. Let's just forget I ever said it.'

He took her bare arms in his hands and looked her full in the face. 'Let's get one thing straight. I am who I am. I'm not – what was that guy's name in San Francisco?'

'Chris.'

'I'm not Chris and I'm not anyone else who's been in your

56

life.' He paused, studying her eyes. 'Do you understand what I'm saying? If you're fearful of the same things happening, then you're bound to see me as Chris or someone else. We all do that at times, unconsciously, because we all have archetypes. But you can't do that now. If you fail, if you don't break through now, you never will. And every man you meet will in some way be Chris and you'll never be free of whatever it is you fear.'

She broke away from him. 'You've got no right to lecture me this way. Who the hell do you think you are? I say one thing to you and right away you think you know me.' She got up off the bed. 'You don't know shit about me. You never will. Who the fuck cares what you have to say anyway?'

He saw her moving away and, a moment later, heard the bathroom door slam.

He sat up, swinging his legs over the side of the bed. The urge to smoke was strong so he turned his mind to other matters. He ran his fingers through his hair, staring sightlessly out at the sea. Even now, Japan lapped at his consciousness. There was a message there, he knew, but because he himself had forced it to be buried so deep, it was slow in working its way upwards to the light.

He stood up. 'Justine,' he called.

The door to the bathroom flew open and she emerged, dressed in a dark tank top and jeans. Her eyes were bright hard points, flashing.

'I'm leaving,' she said tightly.

'So soon?' he was amused by her elaborate melodramatics and, too, he did not quite believe her after all.

'You bastard! You're like all the rest!' She turned towards the hall.

He grabbed her right wrist, whirling her back. 'Where are you going?'

'Away!' she cried. 'Out of here! Away from you, you sono'abitch!'

'Justine, you're acting idiotic.'

Her free hand slashed upwards, struck him across the face. 'Don't you say that to me.' Her tone was low, a growl; her face was an animalistic mask.

Without thinking, he slapped her. The blow was hard

enough so that she reeled backwards against the wall. Immediately, his heart broke and he said her name softly and she came into his arms, her open lips against the tendons of his neck, her hot tears scalding his flesh; she stroked the back of his head.

He picked her up and carried her to the rumpled bed and they made violent love for a very long time.

Afterwards, with her lithe arms about him, her legs twined with his, he said quite seriously, 'That will never happen again. Never.'

'Never,' she breathed, echoing him.

He heard the phone ringing in his sleep and drew himself up through the layers from delta to beta to alpha. Just as he awoke, the muscles in his stomach tightened. He turned over and reached for the receiver; beside him, Justine stirred.

'Hello?' His voice sounded furry.

Justine put her arm across his chest; even her nails were warm.

'Hi! It's Vincent.' There was a pause. 'Say, am I disturbing you?'

'Well, sort of.'

'Sorry, buddy.'

There was only a singing on the line and he woke up. Vincent was too much a Japanese to intrude yet he would not be calling this early unless it was important. It was up to him now, Nicholas knew. If he said 'later', Vincent would hang up and that would be the end of it.

Justine's head moved into the crook of his shoulder and her face went from light to shadow.

'What is it, Vincent? I suspect this isn't a strictly personal call.'

'No. It isn't.'

'What's up?'

'You read about the stiff they took out of the water a couple of days ago?'

'Yeah.' His stomach rolled over. 'What about him?'

'That's why I'm out here.' Vincent cleared his throat, obviously uneasy. 'I'm at the M.E.'s building in Hauppauge. Do you know where it is?'

'I know how to get to Hauppauge, if that's what you're aiming at,' he said shortly.

'I'm afraid I am, Nick.'

He felt as if he were abruptly holding onto three pounds of air. 'What the hell is going on? Why all the goddamn secrecy?'

'I think you ought to see what we've got for yourself.' Vincent's voice seemed strained. 'I don't – I don't want to prejudice you in any way. That's why I'm not giving you anything to think about over the phone.'

'Buddy, you're wrong about that. You're giving me plenty to think about.' He glanced at his watch: 7:15. 'Give me about forty minutes, okay?'

'Sure. I'll meet you outside, guide you in.' There was silence for a moment. 'Sorry, buddy.'

'Yeah.'

When he put down the phone, he found that the palm of his hand was slippery with sweat.

Nicholas looked again at the sliver of metal under the eye of the microscope, a fractional shaving from the small piece Doc Deerforth had recovered from the breastbone of the corpse.

'Here are the spectrometer readouts,' Vincent said, slipping the sheets across the zinc alloy table. Nicholas took his eye from the microscopic fragment. 'We ran it through three times to be certain.'

Nicholas picked up the sheets, running his gaze over the figures. But he already suspected what he would find there. Still, it seemed incredible to him.

'This steel,' he said carefully, 'was manufactured from a particular type of magnetic iron and ferruginous sand. There are perhaps twenty separate layers. The size of the fragment makes it difficult to tell. I'm going by past experience.'

Vincent, whose eyes had never left Nicholas's, took a deep breath, said, 'It wasn't made in this country.'

'No,' Nicholas agreed. 'It was manufactured in Japan.'

'Do you know what this means?' Vincent said. He sat back, including Doc Deerforth in the discussion.

'What can be inferred from that alone?' Nicholas asked.

Vincent took a folder off the tabletop, handed it to Nicholas.

'Take a look at page three.'

Nicholas opened the folder, leafed through the pages. His eyes dropped down the typewritten sheet. He sat perfectly still but, abruptly, he could feel the rushing of his blood through his veins. His heart raced. He was nearing that far shore. He looked up. 'Who did the chemical analysis?'

'I did,' Doc Deerforth said. 'There's no error. I was stationed in the Philippines during the war. I've come across this particular substance once before.'

'Do you know what this is?' Nicholas asked him.

'I can make a pretty good guess. It's a non-synthetic poison that affects the cardiovascular system.'

'It's *doku*,' Nicholas said. 'An enormously powerful poison distilled from the pistils of the chrysanthemum. The technique of its manufacture is virtually unknown outside Japan and even among the Japanese very few know how to make it. Its origins, it is said, lie in China.'

'Then we know how the poison was administered,' Vincent said.

'What do you mean?' Doc Deerforth broke in.

'He means,' Nicholas said heavily, 'that the man was killed by a *shaken* – a Japanese throwing star – part of a *shuriken*, a small-blade arsenal – dipped in *doku*.'

'Which means we also know *who* killed him,' Vincent said.

Nicholas nodded. 'That's right. Only one kind of man could. A ninja.'

For reasons of security, Doc Deerforth hustled them out of the building. They were careful to take with them all the pertinent readouts and evidence.

Since none of them had bothered with breakfast, they stopped on the way back to West Bay Bridge, pulling into a diner right off Montauk Highway that offered authentic Portuguese food.

Over strong black coffee, broiled sardines and clams in a rich steaming winy sauce, they sat and watched the cars silently pass on the highway. No one seemed to want to begin. But someone had to and Vincent said, 'Who's the new lady, Nick?'

'Hmm?' Nicholas turned from the window and smiled. 'Her name's Justine Tobin. She lives right down the beach from me.'

'On Dune Road?' Doc Deerforth said and when Nicholas

nodded, he added, 'I know her. Beautiful girl. Only her name's Tomkin.'

'Sorry, Doc,' Nicholas said. 'You must be mistaken. This Justine's named Tobin.'

'Dark hair, green eyes, one with red motes in it, about five-seven –'

'That's her.'

Doc Deerforth nodded. 'Name's Justine Tomkin, Nick. At least, that's how she was born. You know, Tomkin, as in Tomkin Oil.'

'*That* one?'

'Yep. Her daddy.'

Everyone knew about Raphael Tomkin. Oil was but one of his many multinational moneymakers but by all accounts the most lucrative. He was worth – where had he read it? In *Newsweek*, perhaps – somewhere in the neighbourhood of a hundred million dollars, the last time anybody had bothered to count; at that rarefied level, there did not seem to be much of a reason to do so.

'She doesn't like him much,' Nicholas said.

Doc Deerforth laughed. 'Yah. You could say that. She obviously doesn't want any part of him.'

Nicholas recalled Justine's words, *He's as dead as he could possibly* be. Now he began to understand the irony of that remark. Still, he was annoyed at finding out this way.

'Now, what can you tell me about the ninja?' Doc Deerforth said around a bit of clam flesh.

Outside, a white Ford with black trim pulled up next to the diner. As they watched, a big man with a red face and bulbous nose stepped out and walked towards them.

'Hope neither of you mind,' Doc Deerforth said. 'I phoned Ray Florum when we got here. He's the commander of the West Bay Bridge Village Police. I think he's got a right to hear what's going on. Okay?' Both Nicholas and Vincent nodded their assent. 'Nick?'

'It's okay, Doc,' he said as lightly as he could. 'It just caught me off guard. I didn't expect her to –' He waved a hand in lieu of finishing.

The door opened and Florum pushed into the diner. Doc

Deerforth introduced him around and he sat down. They filled him in.

'Quite literally,' Nicholas said, 'ninja means "in stealth".' Florum poured himself some coffee as Nicholas continued. 'Outside of Japan, there is almost nothing known about ninjutsu, the art of the ninja. Even there, it has been poorly documented primarily because it was knowledge that was both utterly secret and jealously guarded. One was born into a ninja family or one gave up all hope of becoming one.

'As you may know, Japanese society has always been rigorously stratified. There is a highly defined social order and no one would even contemplate deserting his station in life; it's part of one's karma, and this has religious as well as social overtones.

'The samurai, for instance, the warriors of feudal Japan, were gentlemen, of the *bushi* class; no one else was allowed to become a samurai or carry two swords. Well, the ninja evolved from the opposite end of the social spectrum, the *hinin*. This level was so low that the translation of that term means "not human". Naturally, they were a far cry from the aristocratic *bushi*. Yet, as clan warfare increased in Japan, the samurai recognized a growing need for the specific skills of the ninja, for the samurai themselves were bound by an iron-clad code of *bushido* which strictly forbade them many actions. Thus, the samurai clans hired the freelance ninja to perform acts of arson, assassination, infiltration and terrorism which they themselves were duty-bound to shun. History tells us, for instance, that the ninja made their first important appearance in the sixth century A.D. Prince Regent Shotoku employed them as spies.

'So successful were they that their numbers increased dramatically during the Heian and Kamakura periods in Japanese history. They concentrated in the south. Kyoto, for example, was dominated by them at night.

'But the last we hear of them as a major factor in Japan is during the Shimabara war in 1637 when they were used to quell a Christian rebellion on the island of Kyūshū. Yet we know they were active all through the long Tokugawa shōgunate.'

'Just how wide is the scope of their skill?' Doc Deerforth's nostrils were clogged with the rotting stench of the Philippine jungle.

'Very,' Nicholas said. 'From the ninja the samurai learned woodsmanship, disguise, camouflage, codes and silent signalling, the preparation of fire bombs and smoke screens. In short, you would not be wrong to consider the ninja military Houdinis. But each *ryu*, that is, school and, in the ninja's case, clan, specialized in different forms of combat, espionage, lore, and so on, so that one was often able to tell by his methods from which *ryu* a particular assassin came. For instance, the Fodo *ryu* was known for its work with many kinds of small concealed blades, the Gyōkku was expert at using thumb and forefinger on the body's nerve centres in hand-to-hand combat, the Kotto was proficient at breaking bones, others used hypnotism and so on. Ninjas were also quite often skilled *yogen* – that is, chemists.'

There was a heavy silence between them until Vincent cleared his throat and said, 'Nick, I think you ought to tell them the rest of it.'

Nicholas was silent for a time.

'What does he mean?' Florum said.

Nicholas took a deep breath. 'The art of ninjutsu,' he said, 'is very ancient. So old, in fact, that no one is certain of its origin, though speculation is that it was born in a region of China. The Japanese took many things from Chinese culture over the centuries. There is an element of ... superstition involved. One could even say magic.'

'Magic?' echoed Doc Deerforth. 'Are you seriously suggesting ...?'

'In the history of Japan,' Nicholas said, 'it is oftentimes difficult to separate fact from legend. I am not trying to be melodramatic. This is the way it is in Japan. Feats have been ascribed to the ninja that would have been impossible without the aid of some kind of magic.'

'Tall tales,' said Florum. 'Every country's got 'em.'

'Yes. Possibly.'

'And the poison you found?'

'Is a ninja poison. Swallowed, it's quite harmless. A favourite method of administering it was to make a quick-drying syrup

63

of it and coat the *shaken* with it.'

'What's that?' Florum asked.

'These are part of a ninja's arsenal of silent, easily concealed weapons, his short-bladed *shuriken*. The *shaken* is a star-shaped metal object. Flung through the air by the ninja, it becomes a most lethal weapon. And coated with this poison, the weapon need not even puncture a vital spot for the victim to die.'

Florum snorted. 'Are you trying to tell me that that stiff was killed by a ninja? Jesus, Linnear, you said they died out three hundred years ago.'

'No,' Nicholas corrected. 'I merely said that that was the last time they were used in any major way. Many things have changed in Japan since the sixteen-hundreds and the Tokugawa shōgunate, and the country is, in many respects, no longer what it once was. However, there are traditions that are impossible to obliterate by either man or time.'

'There's got to be another explanation,' Florum said, shaking his head. 'What would a ninja be doing in West Bay Bridge?'

'I'm afraid that's something I can't answer,' Nicholas said. 'But I know this. There is a ninja abroad here and in all the world there is no more deadly or clever foe. You must act with extreme caution. Modern weapons – guns, grenades, tear-gas – will give you no security against him, for he knows of all these things and they will not deter him from destroying his intended target and escaping unseen.'

'Well, he's already done that,' Florum said, getting up. 'Thanks for the information.' He stuck out his hand. 'Nice meeting you both.' He nodded. 'Doc.' And with that he left.

The moment Justine heard the knock on her door she felt her heart sink. She put down her pen and, wiping her hands on a chamois cloth, came away from the drawing-board. The light had been just right; she preferred the daylight to the gooseneck lamp clamped to the board, even though its combination of fluorescent and incandescent bulbs gave her a decent approximation of natural illumination.

She let Nicholas in.

'They called you about that body, didn't they?' she said.

He went across the room and sat on the sofa, hands behind

his head. 'What body?'

'You know. The one they took out of the water the day we met.'

'Yes. That's the one.' He looked tired and drawn to her.

'Why did they call you?'

He looked up at her. 'They thought I might be able to help them find out how he died.'

'You mean he didn't drown? But what would you –'

'Justine, why didn't you tell me your father is Raphael Tomkin?'

Her hands, which had been in front of her, fingers interlaced, dropped to her sides. 'What possible reason would I have to tell you?' she said.

'Did you think I'd be after your money?'

'Don't be absurd.' She gave a little laugh but it came out quite strangled. 'I don't have any money.'

'You know what I mean.'

'What difference could it make who my father is?'

'It doesn't, really. I'm more interested in why you chose to change your name.'

'I don't think it's any of your business.'

He got up, went over to look at what she had been working on. 'Nice,' he said. 'I like it.' He went into the kitchen, opened the refrigerator. 'That man was murdered,' he told her over his shoulder. 'By an expert assassin. But nobody knows why.' He took out a bottle of Perrier, opened it and emptied it into a glass. He took a drink. 'Vincent was called in and he in turn asked for my help, because the murderer is in all likelihood a Japanese; a man who kills for money.' He turned round, went back into the living-room where she still stood where he had left her. She stared at him, her eyes very bright. 'Not a hit man – someone you read about in the papers when there's some gangland killing in New Jersey or Brooklyn. No, this is the kind of man you never hear about. He's far too clever to give himself any notoriety except among an *élite* core of potential clients. But I really don't know too much about that end of it.' He looked up at her as he settled himself on the sofa once more. 'Are you getting all this?'

There was silence for a time, just the sound of the surf

seeming far away. She moved, at last, over to the stereo, putting on a record. But almost immediately she took the needle off the groove as if the music were some intruder now to be kept away.

'He called me home during my sophomore year at Smith,' she said with her back to him. Her voice was flat and dry and contained. 'Sent his goddamn private jet for me so I was sure not to miss any of my classes.' She turned round but her head was down, her gaze riveted on a paper-clip she held, working it back and forth until it snapped apart.

'Well, I was, I don't know, I guess "frightened" is the word. I couldn't imagine what emergency he'd called me back home for. I immediately thought of my mother. Funny, not Gelda; she never got sick. Not like Mother.

'Anyway, I was brought into the study and there he was standing before the fire, toasting his hands. I stood watching him with my loden coat brushed with snow, not even bothering to take it off. He offered me a drink.' Her head snapped up and she impaled him with her eyes. 'Can you imagine! He offered me a drink as calmly as if we were business partners about to discuss an important deal.

'It's odd, you know. That's precisely the image I had at the time. It was prophetic. "My dear," he said, "I've got a surprise for you. I've come across a most extraordinary man. He'll be here any moment. I imagine the snow's delayed him a bit. Come. Take off your coat and sit down." But I stayed where I was, dumbfounded. "Is this why you flew me home?" I asked. "Well, yes. I want you to meet him. He's ideal for you. His family's in the right bracket and quite well connected. He's good-looking and a three-letter man to boot." "Father," I said, "you scared me half to death over some mad idea that –" "I scared you?" "Yes, I thought something had happened, to Mother or –" "Don't be so idiotic, Justine! I can't think what I'm going to do with you." I stormed out, furious, and he just couldn't understand what he had done to upset me. It was all done out of love, he told me. "Do you know how much time I spent making this selection?" he said as I went out the door.' She sighed. 'For my father, time was always his most precious commodity.'

'People don't do that any more,' he said. 'Trade off other people as if they were things.'

'Oh no?' She laughed sardonically. 'It happens all the time, all around.' She spread out her arms. 'In marriages, when the woman's expected to perform certain duties; in divorces, when the kids are used as bargaining points; in affairs. All the time, Nick. Grow up, will you?'

He got up off the sofa, annoyed at her height advantage. 'I'll bet your father used to say that to you. "Grow up, Justine."'

'You're a bastard, you know that?'

'C'mon. You're not going to start another fight now, are you? I told you –'

'Bastard!' She leaped across the intervening coffee table, her body crashing against his, her hands flailing against him, but he caught her slender wrists without difficulty, pinioning her.

'Now, listen,' he said. 'I don't mind horsing around with you, but I told you, I'm not Chris and you're not going to provoke a fight with me every time you want some attention. There're other ways to get it. For instance, you could ask.'

'I shouldn't have to ask,' she said.

'Oho! So that's it. I don't have ESP. I'm just a human being. And I don't need psychodramas.'

'But I do.'

'No,' he said, 'you don't.' He let her go.

'Prove it.'

'You're the only one who can do that.'

'Not alone, I can't.' She stared up into his face. Her hand lifted. Her fingertips grazed his cheek. 'Help me,' she whispered. 'Help me.'

His mouth covered her open lips.

It seemed highly improbable that Billy Shawtuck should have got the nickname 'Wild Bill' but nevertheless there it was. He was a ruddy-complexioned man in his early forties, shortish and not even stocky. He always wore long-sleeved shirts, even at the height of summer when, even out here near the shore, there was more sweat than wind around.

Ask his buddies at Grendel's and they would tell you that was because he didn't like to show off his enormous biceps. Of course, if pressed, they would also tell you he came to his nick-name by way of eschewing beers for a double Scotch on the rocks every time. Apparently the heat didn't bother him much.

Billy worked for Lilco, riding power-lines, and, he always said to those he beat at arm wrestling off-hours at Grendel's, he came by his muscles honestly. 'I didn't have to go to no fag gym every day to get these,' he'd say, downing the double Scotch on the rocks in a swallow and raising his arm to order another. 'Shit, my job does all that. Honest work you can sweat at.' Then he would shake his head full of sandy hair. 'I'm not one of those goddamned desk jockeys.'

Grendel's was a local watering hole – almost exclusively blue-collar (the writers had their own favourite) – several miles out-side West Bay Bridge, roadside to Montauk Highway.

Late in the evening, Billy Shawtuck stood in the doorway of Grendel's preparatory to leaving. The sky was turning from indigo to black, the traffic from the highway taking on a spectral quality as headlights and tail-lights flicked by like the inquisitive eyes of nocturnal animals.

On the top of the steps, Billy took a deep breath and cursed the summer influx. We're all gonna die of carbon monoxide poisoning one of these days, he thought.

Not four paces away, his Lilco truck stood waiting for him, but this evening he was reluctant to leave the cheery warmth of the bar. Music blatted at his back from the juke inside. Tony Bennett singing 'I Left My Heart in San Francisco'.

You could take San Francisco, Billy thought, take the whole of the West Coast and shove it up your ass. He'd been out there in the Army and had come to hate it. I didn't leave anything there but a good case of the clap. He laughed. But, damn, I'm sure sorry I took this late job. Time and a half was all well and good but some days – well, some days it just wasn't worth it. He had a feeling that this was one of those days.

Sighing deeply, he went down the stairs but not before giving the finger to Tony Bennett and his shit-ass city.

His mood changed, however, as he banged down one of the dark side roads and he began to whistle tunelessly. He didn't think this job was going to take too long.

And, of course, by that time he was thinking of Hélène and

68

the stuff he had bought her from the Frederick's of Hollywood catalogue. Agh, he thought, maybe it came in the mail today. It was about due.

He was picturing Hélène's long-legged frame in the clothes – he laughed: if you could call them that – as he came around the last bend to the beach-front property and saw the black-clad figure step right into the beam of his left-side headlight.

'What the fuck!' He stepped on the brakes and swerved over to the right shoulder. Leaning out of the window, he called, 'You stupid bastard! I mighta killed you. What's the matter with –'

The door on his side crashed open and it felt as if a tornado hurled him out of the cab. 'Hey!' He rolled across the cool tarmac. 'Hey, buddy!'

He got to his feet in a boxer's semi-crouch, his fists up in front of his chest.

'Not to fool around, you sonovabitch.'

His eyes opened wide as he saw the flash of the long blade in the wash of the headlights. Christ, he thought, a sword. A sword? Jesus, I must be drunk.

A moth batted in the headlight, dazzled, and the cicadas sizzled. Close at hand, the surf hissed and shushed like a nanny calming a crying baby.

He threw a punch. It never connected.

The air in front of him seemed to split apart and vibrated like a bead curtain.

He felt two sensations almost simultaneously. They were the sharpest, most exquisitely painful feelings he had ever experienced.

Once, just outside the base, he had had a scuffle with an M.P. and the bastard had managed to slash him with a knife, wounding him in the side, before he had had a chance to bury his fist in the M.P.'s face. It was the guardhouse for him for that, but he had never felt so satisfied in his life.

But that pain, that burning was nothing to what Billy Shaw-tuck felt now. The blur of the blade pierced the night and then pierced Billy. From the top of his right shoulder down across his abdomen to the left side of his pelvis. His guts began to spill out and his nostrils were suffused with a nauseating stench.

69

'Jesus Chri –'

Then the round wooden pole crashed, whistling like a boy at play, onto his shoulder. He heard the sharp crack as the bones broke but, astoundingly, there was absolutely no pain. Only the feeling that he had been driven straight through the tarmac of the road.

Tears came to Billy's eyes for the first time in years. Momma, he thought, Momma, I'm comin' home.

'I think I know what it is,' she said.

Night had come and a strong wind, springing up from the landward side of the house, rattled the trees outside. Far off a boat hooted once and was still. They lay close together on the bed, enjoying the nearness of their flesh, nothing sexual in it; just two beings, together.

'You won't laugh,' she said, turning her face towards his. 'Promise me you won't laugh.'

'I promise.'

'If I'm hurt – physically – it prepared me, sort of.'

'For what?'

'For the other kind of hurt. The breaking up; the leaving.'

'That seems to me an awfully pessimistic view of life.'

'Yes, it does.'

'He put his arm around her and she put one foot between his, rubbing his shins.

After a time, he said, 'What is it you want?'

'To be happy,' she said. 'That's all.' There is nothing else in the world, she thought, but our linked bodies, our twined souls, and she thought that she had never been as close to anyone as she felt at that moment to Nicholas. Trust had to begin somewhere. Perhaps this was the place for her to start.

She jumped at the sound of an enormous crash that seemed to come from near the front of the house, the kitchen. She cried out as if a cold hand had clutched at her vitals, saw Nicholas sit up, swing his legs over the side of the bed.

He stood up, and as he began to move towards the bedroom door he seemed totally transformed to her. Standing there stark naked, he nevertheless seemed fully clothed, as if his rippling muscles and gleaming sweat-streaked skin were some mysterious raiment cloaking him.

He moved silently towards the lemon light streaming down the hallway. He led with his left foot, his body sideways as if he were a fencer, knees slightly bent, feet not leaving the floor. Down the hallway. He had said not a word to her.

Gathering her wits, she went after him.

His hands were up before him, she saw, their edges reminded her oddly of blades, the fingers as stiff as steel as he moved stealthily into the kitchen.

Past the table, she saw that the window over the sink had been shattered inwards and shards of glass gleamed in the light. She dared not move farther on bare feet. The curtains flapped in the wind rushing in through the rent, whipping against the enamelled walls.

She watched Nicholas move forwards, stop as still as a statue as he peered down at something on the floor on the far side of the table near the window. He stayed in that position for such a long time that she went cautiously across the littered floor to stand behind him. She gasped and turned away. But something drew her eyes inexorably back and she looked again.

On the floor was a black furry mass, large and unmoving. Blood seeped along the floor in several places from under the body, glistening where it shone upon the ruined glass. A strange, astringent smell assaulted her nostrils and she gagged. Her eyes began to blur.

'What –' She gagged again, swallowed hard. 'What is that thing?'

'I'm not sure,' he said slowly. 'It's too big for a bat, at least in this part of the country, and it's not a flying squirrel.'

The phone began to ring and Justine jumped. Her hands gripped her arms. 'I've got goose-flesh,' she said. Nicholas remained where he was, staring down at the black thing that had crashed through the window. 'Blinded by the light,' he said.

Justine went to the far wall and picked up the phone but he seemed oblivious as she spoke for several moments. She had to come back and touch him on the arm. 'Vincent wants to speak to you,' she said.

He looked at her then, tearing his eyes away. 'All right.' His voice seemed thick, his thoughts far away. 'Don't go near it,' he warned as he went to the phone. 'What is it?' he said abruptly.

'I tried you at your place,' Vincent said. 'When there was no answer, I took a chance.' Nicholas said nothing. 'Look, I know what time it is.' His voice rattled against Nicholas's ear, an odd note settled in it. 'It's happened again. Florum just brought in another body. They're photographing it now.' The wind howling in through the broken window seemed chill to Nicholas. He waited, sweat breaking out on his body. He looked at the mess on the floor: the black-furred corpse, the red blood, seeping still as if seeking something or someone. 'Nick, the body has been cut obliquely from shoulder-blade to hip joint as neatly as – It was one cut. Do you understand?'

# II

## Tokyo Suburbs
### Singapore, Summer 1945
### Tokyo Suburbs, Winter 1951

There was a Shinto temple amid the lushest forest Nicholas had ever seen, a mere three hundred metres from the extreme eastern edge of his father's land. Then it was another hundred and fifty or so to the house, a large, delicate, precisely orchestrated structure of traditional Japanese design. The front was L-shaped, preceded, as one came upon it, by an exquisite formal garden which, needless to say, required tireless attention and as much love as a small child.

The irony of the location would come later when, on the far side of the long rolling knoll to the west, they would construct an ultramodern eight-lane superhighway to aid the bustling traffic to and from the heart of Tokyo.

The last traces of Japan's military might had been ground to metal powder, its imperial *daimyo* tried and serving time as war criminals. The Emperor remained but everywhere uniformed Americans basked in what they often laughingly referred to as 'the atomic sunshine'.

Yet Nicholas's history lessons were to begin in another country.

On February 15, 1942, his father told him when he was ten, the British garrison had surrendered Singapore to the attacking Japanese. They held the city for three and a half years until September 1945, when the British reoccupied it. There his father had met his mother, a kind of refugee in the war-torn city. She had been married to a Japanese garrison commander and seeing him blown to bits during the last days of that humid trembling summer perhaps unhinged her for a time.

The first of the British forces were already infiltrating the outskirts of the city and the commander had moved his garrison east to outflank them but, overextending his position, had found himself outflanked. Caught in a murderous crossfire, he had cut down six English soldiers with his *katana* before the

73

rest had sense enough to step back and loft the volley of grenades. There was nothing left of him, not even bones.

Years later, in an old battered shop selling *ukiyo-e* prints in a tiny Tokyo side street, Nicholas had come across a certain print entitled *The End of the Samurai*. It depicted a dismayed warrior's death, his great *katana* flung from his hands by a blast of gunpowder. In that print Nicholas saw, perhaps, the redemption of his mother's first husband, recognizing the historical imperative of that enemy.

His mother had always been a totally apolitical woman. She had married out of love, hardly out of convenience. But with the eventual defeat of the Japanese in Singapore, with the death of her husband, she found that her entire world had exploded into a wilderness that frightened her. This she found utterly consternating. Life, she firmly believed, was for the living. One mourned one's losses and moved onwards. Karma. She believed in that above all else. Not a predestiny – she was no fatalist as many Westerners might mistakenly dub her. She knew, rather, merely how to bow before the inevitabilities of life. As the death of her husband.

But this was a time of momentous changes and, like a beautiful flower caught up in an inexplicable maelstrom, she felt adrift in the riot of chattering gunfire and mortar explosions.

She met Nicholas's father, ironically enough, in the very office where her dead husband had carried on the command of his defeated garrison. She had wandered in there as if it were some Buddhist temple, sacrosanct from the flames of war that rose all about her. Perhaps she had come there because it was one of the only places left in Singapore now that was at all familiar to her. Oddly enough, the thought of fleeing the city never entered her mind. Rather, she wandered the lethal city with little regard to her personal safety.

So much of the city had changed that she was confused, no longer certain where the business district was or where her old apartment had once stood. Piles of rubble were everywhere and the streets were flooded with a tide of children, surging and calling, as if in the aftermath of war's bleak nightmare they had been released from some hideous bondage. It recalled to her the happiness she had felt at New Year's festivals when she had been a girl – liberated for a time from the cares and restrictions of the world. And this, too, confounded her.

Thus for many days she had walked the steaming streets, whirling into dark doorways instinctively as she heard the heavy tramping of the approaching soldiers – she was beyond differentiating one side from another. Miraculously, she avoided serious misadventure.

Karma, she would say later. She survived at the sufferance and the pity of those Chinese folk who spied her and fed her almost as if she were a baby, spooning the thin rice soup between her slack lips, wiping her chin every so often, for she could not perform even this simple act herself. She relieved herself in the gutters and forgot what it was like to take a bath. Those times when she came across running water, as in the fountains still intact which she stumbled across by chance, she thrust her fingers into the spray, staring at it as if it were something she had never seen before. When it rained, she stood still and stared upwards at the billowing clouds, seeking, perhaps, a glimpse of God.

The morning she staggered into the garrison office, Nicholas's father was in the middle of an administrative crisis. Not only were his troops obliged to mop up the last outlying pockets of Japanese opposition but now orders had come down urging him to see to it that his men policed the metropolitan area in an attempt to quell the increasingly violent outbreaks between the Chinese and the Malays who lived constantly in an uneasy half-peace. That left perhaps an hour and a half each day for his men to sleep; it was clearly a situation he could not tolerate and he was in the process of seeking some conciliatory alternative to actively disobeying a direct order. He had, in fact, been sitting in this same wooden slatted chair – the one that had, for the last three years, been the sole property of the dead Japanese garrison commander – since the morning of the previous day.

Except for several hurried trips to the washroom to relieve himself, Colonel Denis Linnear had been right where he was when the dazed woman wandered into his *sanctum sanctorum*. How she had managed to slip past the three sets of guards he was never able to ascertain to his satisfaction. Yet that particular point only manifested itself to him much later. At the time, he was concerned only with her appearance and, as he jumped up from behind his littered desk, his aides seemed more startled by his movements than by the fact that there was an unannounced woman in the room.

'Danvers!' the Colonel called to his adjutant. 'Get a cot in here, on the double!'

The man rushed out and the Colonel was reaching for the woman when she began to fall. Her eyes fluttered closed and she collapsed into his arms.

'Sir?' Lieutenant McGivers said 'About this –'

'Oh, for pity's sake, man, get me a cold cloth,' the Colonel barked irritably. 'And get Grey in here.'

Grey was the garrison surgeon, a tall angular man with a bushy moustache and sun-reddened skin. He arrived just as Danvers was manhandling the cot through the doorway.

'Give him a hand, McGivers, there's a good lad,' the Colonel said to the reappearing Lieutenant. And together they manoeuvred the cot into the room.

The Colonel lifted the woman up, noting her fine Asian features under the layers of dirt and dust, and lowered her gently onto the cot.

He let Grey take over then, going back behind his desk, working on the tail end of his problem with one eye cocked across the room until, at length, the surgeon stood up.

'All right, Lieutenant,' the Colonel said wearily, 'get everyone out of here. We'll reconvene at 0800 hours.' He stood up, passing his long fingers through his hair, and crossed to where Grey stood looking down at his patient.

When they were alone in the room, he said, 'How is she?'

The surgeon shrugged. 'It's hard to say until she comes round and I can run a few more tests. She's obviously suffering from shock and exposure. Several good meals will fix her up, I shouldn't wonder.' He wiped his hands on the cloth he had used to clean her. 'Look here, Denis, I've a lot of young boys to see. If you suspect a problem when she comes round, have Danvers come and fetch me. Otherwise, I think you know what she needs as well as I do.'

The Colonel summoned Danvers and sent him to scrounge up

some hot soup and any pieces of boiled chicken he could find. Then he knelt beside the woman, watching the soft pulse along the long column of her neck.

Thus the first thing Cheong saw when she opened her eyes was the close face of the Colonel. What struck her immediately, she recalled later in recounting the story to Nicholas, were his eyes. 'They were the kindest eyes I had ever seen,' she said in her light singsong voice. 'They were the very deepest blue. I had never before seen blue eyes. I had been outside the city when the British had first come, prior to the outbreak of the war.

'I often think that it was those blue eyes which so startled me, brought me round. Suddenly I remembered the long days after Tsūkō had been killed as if they were part of a film being run off whole for the first time; the pieces at last had knit together. I no longer had gauze in front of my eyes and cotton wool stuffed into my head.

'With that, it all began to pass away from me – as if I were recalling events from some other person's life – the dark terrible last days of the war.

'That is when I knew that your father was part of my karma, in that first moment I saw him, for I have no remembrance of entering the garrison house, of encountering any British soldiers there before him.'

The Colonel took her home at the day's end, in the midst of the long shimmering emerald and lapis lazuli twilight, with the city choked with swirling dust, Jeeps clattering down the streets and soldiers running quick-time along the sidewalks while the Chinese and the Malays paused in their homeward journeys, standing quite still, resolute and quiescent and eternal in their cotton drawstring shorts and sloping reed sedge hats.

As usual it was teeming, and the Colonel had the Jeep brought round, though he was often fond of walking. It took him twenty minutes on average to make the journey from the garrison located near Keppel Harbour almost due north through the city to the house he now occupied. As may be imagined, the command was not over fond of his making this trek on foot and thus he was perforce obliged to be accompanied by two armed men from his garrison as escort from door to door. The

77

Colonel found this a hideous misappropriation of precious man-power but he seemed to have no choice in the matter.

At first he had been assigned an enormous estate near the western tip of the city but he soon found that it was hard by an equally enormous mangrove swamp and being downwind from it was too much even for him. So he had looked around and eventually moved to this current smaller but infinitely more comfortable place.

It was situated on a hill which the Colonel liked quite a bit because when he faced north he could gaze up at Bukit Timah, the island's granitic core and its highest spot. Beyond that dark mass, the hump of some great leviathan, lay the black waters of the Johore Strait and Malaysia, the southernmost tip of the massive block of Asia. On the days when it was particularly hot and humid, when his shirt stuck like hot wax to his skin and the sweat poured from his scalp into his eyes, when the entire city steamed like a tropical rain forest, it seemed to him as if Asia's bulk were sliding slowly downwards onto the top of his head, suffocating him in a blanket of endless marshes, mosquitoes and men; the crick in his neck would return, paining him worse than ever.

But this was all before the appearance of Cheong. To the Colonel it was nothing short of miraculous, as if she had come into his room, not from the streets of Singapore, but from the cloud-filled sky. That first evening, when he had turned her over to tiny Pi to be bathed and clothed, and standing by his polished teak desk, taking his first long drink of the day, he felt the tiredness washing away from him like a residue of salt drowned in a hot shower. He thought only that it was good to be home after so long a time at work. Yet perhaps this had been only the most mundane part of it, for when he recalled that time many years later – as he was often wont to do – he was not at all certain of his motivations or his feelings in the matter. He knew only that when she had been brought back to him in his study, when he saw again her face, for the first time since he had left England in the early part of 1940 to come East, he no longer seemed obsessed with Asia. He stood watching her come towards him, feeling like a house bereft of the ghost that had haunted it for so long, now empty, waiting to be filled by new and more substantial tenants. He recognized then his spirit, unchained at last, dancing inside of him and he felt that here before him was his true reason for seeking out the mysteries of Asia.

He studied her face, using the light of the breaking sky, the day's last light, a spurt before darkness fell completely, with the innate fierceness with which he had applied himself to the destruction of the enemy. This was a most formidable talent in the Colonel, one that was highly respected among the Americans as well as the British military and for which he had been amply rewarded by one battlefield promotion after another.

It was not, he felt, a purely Chinese face. This he derived not from any overt configuration of features but by the overall aspect. There was, for instance, nothing classic about that face. This the Colonel found utterly fascinating, not to mention charming. It was oval, longer than it was full. She had high cheek-bones, very long almond-shaped eyes and a nose less flat than one might normally expect. Her lips were wide and full and, with those eyes, were her most expressive features. Later on, he would be able to tell any nuance of changing mood just by a glance at her lips.

Pi had pulled Cheong's long hair back from her face and, having first endeavoured to do away with the ragged ends, had tied it tightly back with a red satin ribbon so that it hung down across one shoulder in a long ponytail, so thick and gleaming that the Colonel thought of her more at that moment as some mythical creature come to life. She was, he felt, so densely oriental that it was if she were the living embodiment of that vast flat crowded land.

'How are you feeling?' He said this in Cantonese and, when he got no response, repeated the question in Mandarin.

'Fine now. Thank you,' she said, bowing.

It was the first time the Colonel had heard her speak and he was somewhat startled, never having heard such a beautiful and musical voice before. She was tall, almost five-nine, with a figure as slender as a willow but as shapely as any man could wish for.

'It is most fortunate that I met you,' she said, her gaze directed at the floor. She tried in vain to pronounce his last name. 'I am most ashamed,' she said, giving it up at last. 'Pi coached me all through the bath. I am most humbly sorry.'

'Don't be,' the Colonel said. 'Call me Denis.'

This she could manage, pronouncing the *D* sound in a way that had no analogue in the English language. She repeated it twice then said, 'I shall not forget it, Denis.'

By that time, the Colonel knew that he was going to marry her.

When the Colonel received the request by American courier via British liaison to join the American SCAP – the occupation forces – Command in Tokyo as an adviser to General Douglas MacArthur, the first thing he thought of was how he was going to tell Cheong. There was no question of his not taking the assignment. Already he found himself chafing to be in Tokyo.

It was early in 1946 and this part of the world was still reeling from the emotional fall-out caused by the explosions at Hiroshima and Nagasaki; the effect was incalculable, the ramifications endless.

He had been married to Cheong for four months and she was three months pregnant. Still he had no second thoughts about abandoning Singapore, which he thought of as as much his home as England ever was. Beside the fact that he felt it was his duty to take the assignment at SCAP headquarters, he further understood quite keenly the complex problems that had developed within Japan since its unconditional surrender, ending the war, last year and he was eager to immerse himself in what MacArthur had called 'steering a bold new course for Japan'.

The Colonel deliberated only a moment before he called Danvers in and told him that he was leaving for the day; if anything important came up he could be reached at home.

He arrived at the house to find Cheong taking care of him personally, having shooed Pi away from the doorway at the first hint of the jeep turning into the driveway.

'You are home early today, Denis,' she said, smiling.

He climbed out of the Jeep, dismissed the driver. 'I suppose now you'll tell me that I'll be in the way of the servants' cleaning,' he said gruffly to her.

'Oh no,' she cried, linking her arm in his as they went up the stairs and into the house. 'Quite the opposite. I've patted them on the behinds and told them to do the work in the kitchen that they have been putting off for oh-so-long.' They went down the hall and into his study where she poured him a drink.

'Ah,' he said, taking the chill glass from her. 'Have they done anything for which they should be punished?'

'Oh no.' She put her small hand to her mouth as if shocked by the notion.

He nodded, happy inside himself. 'Of course you'd tell me if that were the case, wouldn't you?'

'Not at all.' She indicated that he should sit in his favourite chair and when he was comfortably settled within its soft embrace, his long legs stretched out on the carpet before him, one boot set over the other, she knelt at his side. She wore a deep blue brocaded silk robe with a mandarin collar and wide bell sleeves. Where she had obtained this rather remarkable garment the Colonel could not imagine and he had not the bad taste to ask her. 'That is none of your concern,' she continued. 'I am the mistress of this house. Discipline is here my concern as it is yours downtown.' She meant at the garrison house. 'You must trust me to maintain a perfect aura within our house. Tranquillity is all-important to the health of one's spirit, do you not agree?' And when he nodded, watching her eyes, she continued. 'The tranquillity of one's house is not only confined as to its location and the servants therein but also to its major occupants.' She paused and the Colonel, who had been calmly sipping his drink through all of this discourse, now sat up, placing his glass on the side table by the chair. The Westerner in him longed to take her delicate, capable hands in his, lean towards her and say, 'What is the matter, darling? What's troubling you?' This, he knew, he could not do, for in doing so he would shame her. She had obviously spent much time in the preparation of her presentation. He must honour that by allowing her to come to the point as she might. If there was anything the Colonel had learned by being in the Far East for six years, it was patience, for to fail to learn that lesson swiftly was to court peremptory disaster out here where life was so different, seeming only to float upon the bosom of the eternal Pacific.

'You know, Denis, that tranquillity is only one aspect of the harmony of life. And harmony is what all people strive to achieve. Harmony is the basis of a clear mind, of a good and powerful karma.' She put her fingers along the back of his hand, which lay along the smooth worn wood of one arm-rest. 'You have such a karma. It is very strong, like the thrown net of a master fisherman.' Her eyes looked down at her hands, one atop the other, flashed upwards to his face. 'I am afraid to do anything to destroy that. But now there is more than one to think of. Our karma have meshed and, intertwined, may be all the more powerful for it, yes?' He nodded again and, satisfied that she had both his attention and his agreement, she said, 'Now I must ask something of you.'

'You know that you have only to ask me,' the Colonel said sincerely. 'You, who of all people in this world make me the most happy, can have anything that is mine.'

Yet this heartfelt speech appeared to have little effect on Cheong. 'This thing I must ask you is very large.'

He nodded.

'We must go away from Singapore,' she said boldly. Then, seeing that he did not stop her, she went on in a rush. 'I know that your work means a great deal to you but this is' – she searched for the proper words that would convey her thoughts – 'most imperative for all of us. For you, for me and for the baby.' She placed one palm against her lower belly. 'We must go to Japan. To Tokyo.'

He laughed, struck first by the humour of it and then intrigued by the eeriness.

'This is funny?' she cried, misunderstanding his expression of relief. 'It is bad for us to stay here. Most bad. In Japan our karma will flourish, expand. There lies our – what is the English word? – destiny, is that right? Our destiny.'

'I laughed only at a rather odd coincidence,' the Colonel reassured her. 'It was nothing you said.' He patted her hand. 'Now tell me why we must go to Tokyo.'

'Because Itami is there. She is Tsūkō's sister.'

'I see.' She had told him, quite naturally, of her previous

marriage but, beyond that, they rarely spoke of this portion of her life. 'And what has she to do with our karma?'

'I'm sure that I do not know that,' Cheong said. 'But I had a dream last night.' The Colonel was well aware of how much stock these people put in dream messages. They were not unlike the ancient Romans in this respect. He himself did not, in fact, totally disbelieve in their import. The unconscious, he knew, had more to do with the direction one took in life than most people were willing to admit. And, in any event, dreams were closely linked with the concept of karma and karma was something in which the Colonel had a strong belief. He had spent too many years in the Far East not to have.

'The dream was about Itami,' Cheong said. 'I was in a city. In Tokyo. I was shopping and I turned into a quiet side street. All about me were shops made of wood and paper the way it was in Japan when Tokyo was named Edo and the Tokugawa ruled the shōgunate.

'I passed a shop that had a gaily decorated window and I stopped. In the centre of the window was a doll. It was the most beautiful doll I had ever seen. Its aura was very strong.

'She was of porcelain, this doll, white-faced, dressed elegantly in the *bushi* fashion. Her eyes stared at me and I could not look away. "Buy me," they said.

'The shopkeeper wrapped her up for me in a silken cloth and I took her home. And, as I was unwrapping her, she began to speak. Her voice was imperious and commanding and very, very firm. She was obviously a lady of a high house.

'It was Itami and she said that we must come to her. She said that we must leave Singapore and come to Tokyo.'

'Have you ever met Itami?' the Colonel asked.

'No.'

'Did Tsūkō ever show you a picture of her?'

'No.'

'Yet you are certain that this doll in your dream was Itami.'

'It was Itami, Denis.'

He leaned forward at last and took her hands in his as he had longed to do for some time. Her long nails, he saw today, were lacquered deep scarlet. He traced their satiny smoothness for a moment, savouring the feeling. 'We will go to Japan, Cheong. To Tokyo. We will meet Itami, just as your dream said.'

The smile that spread across her face was like the rising of the sun. 'Oh, yes, Denis? This is really true?'

'It is really true.'

'Then tell me why, for my spirit is happy and cares not but my mind, my mind cries out to know.'

The day before they left, she took him to see So-Peng.

He lived outside the city, to the north-west, in a village of oiled paper and bamboo where no Westerner had ever before set foot. It was not on any map of the region that the Colonel had ever seen. In fact, when Cheong had told him of the location, he had laughed, saying that their destination would be naught but the middle of a mangrove swamp. Nevertheless, she was undeterred and he eventually acquiesced to her wish.

It was Sunday and Cheong insisted that he must not wear his uniform. 'This is most vital,' she had informed him and as he donned his wide-lapelled cream linen suit, white silk shirt and navy regimental tie, he felt somehow spectacularly naked: a daub of crimson in an otherwise emerald jungle, the bull's-eye in an unmissable target. For her part, Cheong wore a white silk dress, embroidered with sky-blue herons, mandarin-collared, floor-length. She looked a dream.

There was brilliant sunlight as they left the city; the heat washed over them in slippery waves. A listless breeze brought with it the foetid stench of the mangrove swamps but always from their left. Twice they were obliged to stop, standing perfectly still as long black and silver vipers writhed obliquely across their path. The first time this happened, the Colonel made a move to kill the serpent but Cheong's firm hand upon his wrist deflected him from his purpose.

Far away, yet seeming as close to them as the flamboyantly painted backdrop to some stage play, the eastern horizon was fairly choked with dark grey clouds piling themselves into the sky like ungovernable children pyramiding themselves dangerously. Above, the sky was a peculiar yellow; no blue was anywhere to be seen; and now and again silent white lightning flickered and forked through the grey, turning its softness for moments to marble. It was difficult to believe that it was so calm and tranquil here where they walked up the winding road, rising along the spine of a sprawling hillock.

Singapore had long since dropped from sight and, like a ship's anchor sent overboard, it seemed to be absolutely gone, part of another world which they had stepped out of and, passing through some invisible barrier, now found themselves in a land quite apart. At least that was how it seemed to the Colonel on that magical afternoon, how it came to him again and again throughout his life in dreams during the mornings' drowsy early hours.

On the far side of the forested hillock, all indications of the road they had been following disappeared and not even the semblance of a path through the foliage presented itself. Yet Cheong seemed to have no difficulty at all in reorienting herself and, taking his hand, guiding them to the village of So-Peng.

It lay in a leafy shallow hollow with the beginnings of a basalt mountain at its back, a natural barrier behind which, perhaps, only the stormy sea lay.

They came upon one house that seemed in all respects similar to those around it and, having climbed its three or four wide wooden steps up from the mud of the streets, now stood upon its front porch, wide as a veranda in the old South of America, covered against the torrential rains and the baking sun of the seasons. Here Cheong bade Denis remove his shoes even as she was doing.

The front door opened and they were ushered into the house by an old woman with steel-grey hair, elegantly coiffed, dressed in a long silk robe the colour of swirled ash. She put her hands together in front of her breasts and bowed to them. They returned the gesture and, as she stood upright and smiled at them, the Colonel saw that she had no teeth. Her face was lined, to be sure, but the flesh still retained a hint of the vitality and beauty that it had obviously radiated in youth. Her black almond eyes were as luminous as lanterns, shining with the inquisitive innocence of the little girl from out of the past.

Cheong introduced the Colonel. 'And this is Chia Sheng,' she said without otherwise identifying her.

Chia Sheng laughed, staring at the Colonel's bulk, and shook her head from side to side as if to say, 'What can one do with young people today?' She shrugged her thin shoulders and clucked her tongue sharply against the roof of her mouth.

Cheong, the Colonel noted, spoke only Mandarin and, without being told in so many words, he was aware that he should do the same.

They were in a room of some considerable size. No other house he had been in in Singapore, not even the main house of the estate bordering the mangrove swamps that had once been his, could boast of such space. The outside façade, he saw, had little relevance once one was inside.

More odd, however, was the fact that this room was covered in tatamis – Japanese reed mats of a specific size by which all rooms in traditional Japanese houses were measured. But more surprises were in store for the Colonel.

Chia Sheng led them wordlessly through this first room, sparsely furnished with low lacquered tables and cushions and little else, down a short dimly lit hallway. Its far wall consisted of an enormous piece of jade so heavily carved that it became a lattice-work. In its centre was a round doorway known, the Colonel had somewhere heard, as a moon gate. These existed on the mainland of China in the houses of the very wealthy during the latter half of the nineteenth century.

Across the moon gate's opening a long bolt of silk hung from a bamboo pole laid crosswise. It was grey. Embroidered upon it was a royal-blue wheel-and-spoke pattern. This seemed oddly familiar to the Colonel, and for long minutes he racked his brain until he recalled that he had seen the self-same bolt of cloth reproduced in a *ukiyo-e* print by Ando Hiroshige. It was one of the *Fifty-three Stations of the Tokaidō* series; he could not remember the title of the print in question. However, it had shown the design to belong to a travelling *daimyo*. Another mystery. The Colonel shrugged inwardly as Chia Sheng led them through the moon gate, white shot with black and green.

They found themselves in a room only a little smaller than the first. On three sides were folding screens of exquisite manufacture, dark colours coming to vibrant life, passing through the years as if they were but veils of smoke.

Scents now invaded his nostrils, the chalkiness of charcoal, the muskiness of incense, and there were others, subtler, delicate cooking-oil, tallow and still others impossible to define.

'Please,' Chia Sheng said, leading them past a low red lacquered table. Freshly cut flowers in a bowl spread themselves at its centre. They disappeared between the ends of two of the screens, which revealed a doorway of blackness, as if it had been cut out of the heart of a piece of onyx.

'The stairs,' Chia Sheng murmured and they ascended. It was a narrow spiral staircase with room enough to climb in single file only.

The stairwell debouched at length upon a kind of tower which struck the Colonel more as a garret. A green-tiled roof was supported at the four corners of the structure by wooden beams. Otherwise there was an unimpeded view on all sides save the one where the basalt mountain, like some awesome leviathan out of mythology, loomed close enough to serve as guardian.

As they came into the garret, the Colonel's eyes fell upon a tall figure gazing out at the riding storm, a long glass held to one eye. This was So-Peng.

'Welcome, Colonel Linnear.' His voice was rich and deep and seemed to set the garret vibrating. His Mandarin was oddly accented; in Western terms one might have said clipped. He did not turn round, did not in any verbal way acknowledge Cheong's presence. Chia Sheng, her mission perhaps at an end, left them, silently descending the winding stair.

'Please come over here and stand by me, Colonel,' So-Peng said. He wore an old-fashioned formal Chinese robe the colour of mother of pearl. It was woven of a material totally unfamiliar to the Colonel, for even the slightest movement of the old man caused its surface to pick up and reflect the fitful light in a most marvellous way.

'Look here,' the old man said, thrusting the glass at the Colonel. 'Look to the storm, Colonel, and tell me what you see.'

The Colonel took the polished brass spyglass, closed one eye and peered through it with the other. Now within the elevation of So-Peng's eyrie, he felt the first tentative touches of the storm they had earlier observed; the wind was rising.

Within the confined circle of his extended vision, he saw the bloom of the clouds, now purple-black like bruises, and, too, the colour of the sky behind the storm had changed. The solid-seeming yellow tinge had been struck through with tendrils of a pale green; such a hue the land-bound world could never produce. Deep-throated rumblings could be heard now and again, rolling over the earth like an invisible *tsunami*, a tidal wave. Dutifully, the Colonel related all he saw.

'And that is all you see,' said So-Peng. There was no hint of an interrogative in his inflection.

Yes, the Colonel was about to say, that is all I can see. But he checked himself at the last moment, certain that there was something out there that the old man wished him to see.

For long moments he moved the eye of the glass over the terrain an inch at a time but he saw nothing new to report. Still, it nagged at him and he moved the glass upwards, scanning. Nothing. Then downwards towards the earth. Below the on-rushing storm, he saw the women in the rice paddies, the flat wet fields without the protection of a single tree or even a make-shift lean-to. Almost in concert, the women bent to their tasks, leaning over, reaching for and pulling at the growing rice. Their skirts were pulled up in the centre, tied in huge knots between their bent legs; woven sacks encircled their backs so that they had the aspect of beasts of burden; water covered their bare feet to the ankle.

'The women are still working,' the Colonel said, 'as if the storm wasn't there.'

'Ah!' So-Peng said, nodding. 'And what does this tell you, Colonel?'

The Colonel took the glass from his eye, lowering it to his side, looking at So-Peng, at his yellow hairless head, the grey wisp of his beard hanging straight down from the ultimate point of his chin, the dark serene eyes regarding him coolly as if from some other age.

'Hmmm,' So-Peng murmured and nothing more. He was fully aware.

'They know something we don't,' the Colonel said.

By that 'we' the Colonel had meant, however implicitly, Westerners. Yet So-Peng now had to make up his mind whether the Colonel was being serious or merely condescending. So-Peng, not unlike every Asian on the continent, had had far more experience with people expressing the latter sentiment. Yet he did not dismiss the Colonel summarily as he very easily might have, so that even at this early stage he must have had an instinctive reaction to this man.

For his part, the Colonel knew only too well that he had come to a crucial nexus in his relationship with Cheong. This man's blessing was imperative for her. Why it had not been necessary at her marriage he could not understand. Yet he knew that for her to depart from Singapore, So-Peng had to become an active agent.

That this house, this town were so isolated, so totally unknown to the Western population, made the Colonel all the more apprehensive. He was painfully aware that many Chinese had no great love for Westerners, those barbarian giants from across the sea. That this dislike – indeed this enmity – was, at its core, mostly justifiable, made no difference to him at this moment.

But the Colonel had a great love for these people, for their life, their history, religion and customs, and it was this knowledge, chiefly, which heartened him now, which prompted him to say, 'There is no doubt, sir, that we have much to learn here but, I feel too, that the most advantageous of situations involves an exchange, initially, of information but, more important, leads from there to an exchange of – confidences.'

So-Peng's hands were inside the wide sleeves of his robe as he crossed his arms over his thin chest. 'Confidences,' he said meditatively as if the word were some new and exotic flavour he was testing on his palate. 'Well, now, Colonel, "confidences" may have many meanings – inflections and contextual placings determine that. Whereby, my boy, I might be led to believe that you had meant by it, secrets.'

'That may not be very far from the mark, sir,' the Colonel replied.

'And what,' said So-Peng, 'makes you think that any such intimacy should be extended to you?'

The Colonel kept his gaze steady, his eyes impaled by those he saw in front of him, and so intense became this look that at length the other's face seemed to disappear, leaving behind that pair of lights swimming alone in the atmosphere, hovering in lambent conversation. 'There is, firstly, respect, sir. Then there is knowledge, knowledge sought and assimilated. There is acceptance, of what is and what was – the understanding of one's role within the matrix. Then there is the curiosity to learn the unknowable. And lastly, there is love.' This being said, the Colonel relaxed somewhat, knowing that he had spoken his heart, expressed himself in a manner both pleasing to himself and honouring his wife. There was naught else to be done now.

Yet when So-Peng next spoke, it was directed not at the Colonel but at his wife. 'Cheong,' he said. 'I believe that Chia Sheng is calling for you. Her voice drifts up to me in this charged air.'

Without a word, Cheong bowed and departed.

The Colonel stayed where he was, silent. Beyond their frail enclosure the storm came on.

'Cheong tells me that you are leaving for Japan shortly.'

The Colonel nodded. 'Yes. Tomorrow. I have been asked to work with General MacArthur in reconstructing a new Japan.'

'Yes. There is much prestige in such work. A place in history, eh, Colonel?'

'I hadn't thought about that, quite frankly.'

'Do you not think,' said So-Peng, 'that this reconstructing, as you put it, is best left for the Japanese people to decide for themselves?'

'That would be the ideal, of course. But unfortunately certain elements within Japanese society have misdirected them throughout the last two decades.' When the other remained silent, the Colonel continued: 'I am certain you are quite aware of their activities in Manchuria.'

'Manchuria!' So-Peng scoffed. 'What have I or my people to do with Manchuria? It is as a slum on the far side of the world to us. I would just as soon allow the Japanese and the Bolsheviks to fight between themselves for it. Manchuria, from my point of view, would be no great loss to China as a whole.'

'But the Japanese sought that land as a foothold into the rest of China. There they would have built their military bases from which they would expand.'

'Yes.' So-Peng sighed. 'Their imperialist nature saddens me deeply – at least it did when I was a youth. Yes, then it was like a thorn in my side, for the Japanese way is the way of militarism. It always has been; it cannot be otherwise. It is the blood flowing out of the centuries and its imperative cannot be denied, neither by politicians' rhetoric nor by any kind of collective amnesia. Do you understand me, Colonel? The Germans deny their racism now. But how foolish, for how can they? Easier to deny that air is the source of one's life.

'China has naught to fear from Japan nowadays. This I tell you as a – confidence, eh? The pressure now comes from the Bolsheviks and they are to be feared more than ever the Japanese were.

'*Bushido*, Colonel. Do you understand this concept?'

The Colonel nodded. 'Yes. I think so.'

'Good. Then you understand what I mean.' He looked out at the sky, entirely grey now and moving, as if some unseen giant were waving a rippling pennant at them. 'That is a measure of friendship, did you know that? Good friendship, I am speaking of now – not a friendship as one might find between business associates or neighbourly acquaintances. In this kind of friendship, which is rarer these days than one might believe, communication no longer becomes a problem or, as it most often is, a barrier. Do you agree with this notion of mine?'

'Yes, sir, most assuredly.'

'Umm. Something told me that you might.' He laughed softly, not unkindly. 'You know, it was a day just like this one when Cheong first came to me. She was a very small child, not even three yet, I believe. Once there had been quite a large family. I don't know whatever happened to them; apparently no one does, for I made many inquiries over a good many years. All fruitless.

'After a while it did not seem to matter at all. This was her family and I could not have loved her more if she were my own daughter. I have many children and now many grandchildren and great-grandchildren. My goodness, so many is their number now that I sometimes confuse a name with the wrong face. But it is excusable. I am an old man and my mind is otherwise occupied with numerous matters.

'But I may tell you with all candour that among all my progeny Cheong has a special place. She is not the fruit of my loins but she most assuredly is the fruit of my mind, do you follow me? This is where she comes from and you must know this, come to understand it for what it is and what it portends before you leave Singapore.'

He was silent for a time now as if he were dreaming of a far-off land or, perhaps, a time long gone. The air seemed to split open and rain slanted down out of the charcoal sky, pattering against the small square roof of the garret, dripping from the diminutive eaves. The green leaves of the trees dipped and shivered under the downpour until, hissing, the world was obliterated as if by a solid wall of water. Leaning slightly over the side, the Colonel could not even make out the lower roof of So-Peng's house. Mist, heavily laden as smoke, drifted up to them. The world was now a grey-green pointillist painting from which only brief shadows emerged as if they were watching the visualization of still-forming thoughts within some godlike brain.

'We seem very alone up here now,' the Colonel said.

So-Peng smiled. 'One is never truly alone in Asia, is that not so?' He stood as still as a statue and it seemed odd to the Colonel that this should be so, primarily because the background was in such violent motion. Spray bouncing up off the sill showered him with a fine mist and he stepped back from the verge a pace, reminded of standing at the bow of a fast cutter on the open seas. 'The world is different here,' So-Peng continued. '*Our* world is different. We are born with, grow up with, indeed live our entire lives with the concept of eternalness always close to us. This – shall we say intimacy – I have often thought is a two-edged sword. It is indubitably our great strength in life but also – this is another confidence – it is our weakness, I fear, our Achilles' heel when it comes to dealing with the West. I am much afraid that too many of my country-men underestimate Westerners precisely because they think of them as barbarians, unable to grasp fully the Eastern concepts of man, honour and the nature of time. This can be lethal. Witness the Japanese. Idiotic, what they attempted! Glorious but idiotic. But the Japanese know well the nobility of failure.

A majority of their national folk heroes would be considered dismal failures by Western standards. It is the nature of their being, the quality of their thoughts that are revered; deeds count for all, in the West. The Protestant ethic, I believe it is called, eh? Well, it is nothing to scoff at, as any Japanese would tell you now. The Protestant ethic is what defeated Japan. It was made to pay dearly for the miscalculation of Pearl Harbor. The United States was truly the sleeping giant; its wrath awesome to behold.' He gazed out upon the frantic rain. The air was heavy with moisture. 'We as yet lack the necessary understanding of the nature of time. We still look to yesterday when its eternalness was all; we have not yet caught up with the present.' He laughed. 'But give us time. We are most ingenious people. Once show us the way and there is our salvation. We are an extremely flexible people. Watch out that we do not catch you and overtake you!'

The faraway, dreaming look left So-Peng's eyes as he turned to the Colonel and said, 'But my personal views of philosophy are no doubt of little interest to you. Words of wisdom – I do not believe in that phrase. One cannot learn wisdom by sitting at another's feet. One must live one's own life, make one's own mistakes, feel one's own ecstasy to learn the true meaning of existence, for it is different in each individual. Fall down, get up, do it all over again in another context. Experience. And learn. That is the only way.

'So. Enough of prattle. I am like an old woman today. Perhaps it is the weather that has made me so. I am loquacious in storms; perhaps it aids my uneasiness. Monsoon season was always a time of terror for me when I was a child.

'A fair enough introduction. You may wonder, Colonel, as to my cultural origins. Well, my father was Chinese. Not a Manchu, thank heaven, but a cultured, quiet mandarin. He was, originally, a merchant, but because of a shrewd mind he soon became an important businessman, emigrating to Singapore when he was thirty-three. Oh, I am from the mainland, certainly; not from here. My mother was a Japanese.' His eyes opened wide. 'Oh, now, Colonel, you needn't look so surprised. Those things happened from time to time. Not, I admit, with any degree of regularity. No, no. And the true nature of my mother's origin was scrupulously concealed for obvious reasons. Her differing features my father explained away by claiming she came from the North of China, near the Russian border where there is much mixed blood, Mongol and Manchu and heaven knows what else.

'However, of Cheong's origins I have no specific information. Perhaps she knows or then again perhaps not. It was never discussed between us. Perhaps, one day, she will tell you. But that, of course, is between the two of you. For myself, I believe it matters little, if at all, for her matrix is here. It is where she grew up; it is what fixed her.

'When one is able to see the matrix from which a precious stone is taken, one is invariably better able to judge the quality of that stone.' He shook his head. 'But this is a somewhat cold example. Let me give you another. One meets an extraordinarily beautiful woman but, in spending time with her, one gradually finds her behaviour somewhat erratic, confusing – in short, incomprehensible. Now, perhaps, one learns, subsequently, that this same woman was the middle daughter of three. It is now possible that one has taken the first step in unravelling the mystery of this beautiful woman's strange behaviour. And, of course, the more one learns, the less odd her behaviour becomes until, at length, it is perfectly understandable.' He sniffed once at the air. 'It will be over soon,' he said. 'Come. Let us descend.'

They sat, the three of them – the Colonel, Cheong and So-Peng – around the red lacquered table in the room of screens while Chia Sheng silently served them course after course of food. The Colonel had not in three years seen so much food at once, nor tasted one dish after another so delicious or so exquisitely presented. There was, firstly, every manner of *dim sum* – tiny delicate rice-dough dumplings, filled with a variety of stuffings. Then there was fish soup, hot and spicy without being in the least heavy. Thirdly, there were six kinds of rice, from the simply boiled white to a kind of double-fried version with minced seafood and cooked egg yolk. The fourth course consisted of a cold salad spiced with white horseradish and cucumber. Then came the main courses: cut fowl, golden brown, crisped, rubbed with coarse salt and herbs; broiled shrimps, hardy langoustes; cracked crabs, their shining cara-paces blue and red, fresh from the boiling water. And lastly, great crescent slices of melon, the juice already running down along the sloping sides, onto the clay plates, like the rivulets of an icy stream.

At last they were through and So-Peng, pushing his rind-garlanded plate from him, heaved a deep sigh and patted his stomach. 'Tell me about your matrix, Colonel,' he said.

And the Colonel told him all about his father, all he had been told about the mother he hardly knew, struck down by diphtheria when he was only two. All about his stepmother, whom he despised for no one particular reason but rather for many diffuse ones. He told So-Peng about his feelings at being an only child, a concept that the other found as fascinating and absorbing as he found it strange. About his boyhood in rural Sussex and the road to school which eventually brought him, as it did to most, to London. Of his burgeoning interest in the Far East, his studies and his eventual enlistment.

'And now,' said So-Peng, 'you are to embark upon a new chapter of your life. You are about to become a politician and more, a maker of history. Very good. Very good. Soon I, too, must leave Singapore for a time. My services are needed else-where. Thus this becomes, truly, a farewell party.' He paused now, as if waiting for something to occur. Long moments passed in silence with just the lentitudinous dripping from the last of the rain leaving the lush loquat trees that surrounded the house.

Presently Chia Sheng appeared, holding a shadowed object close to her. When she reached the table, she lowered the object into So-Peng's hands. This time she did not leave them but stood silently at his side.

So-Peng held the object before him, chest high, and the Colonel saw that it was a copper box perhaps ten inches by eight across, enamelled and elaborately lacquered. On its top was exquisitely painted a fiery, scaled dragon, entwined with an enormous, powerful tiger.

Still holding the box, So-Peng said, 'It is now my duty to apologize to you, dearest Cheong, for being away from Singa-pore on the day of your marriage to Colonel Linnear. I have thought upon this for many months, deciding what would be most appropriate, for, as you know, everything that is mine is yours also. As it is with all my children.' The box was now lowered slowly to the table-top, where it lay like the most exquisite of jewels, newly mined. 'But you mean more to me, Cheong, than all the others, for your love shines all the stronger, all the purer for the hard road you had to endure. No one of all my children, none save you, has ever wanted for anything since the moment of its birth.

'This I have no doubt you already know. But what you are not aware of and what I tell you now is that, of them all, it is your mind alone which has cleaved most closely to my own. This has touched me deeply, for it has happened naturally, with no urging from myself. It is what you yourself wanted and what you now possess.

'Now, on the point of our last farewell – for I fear that we shall never see each other again – this is for you, for your Colonel, for your child about to be born, for your children yet to be conceived. This I give you gladly, with all my love. It comes from me, from Chia Sheng, from the long line of our families. In all the world there is only one. And its contents, too, are the sole sentinels, their like not to be found in any quarter of the globe. This is my legacy. Use it as you may.' His old hands, their long fingers, over which the skin was stretched like patinaed parchment, extended, pushing the box slowly across the table until it passed over the centre meridian. At that point, as if they no longer wielded any power, they relinquished their hold, withdrawing over the empty red expanse of the table to the old man's lap.

The Colonel, holding Cheong's trembling hand in his, stared into So-Peng's eyes. He meant to say something but, whirling upon itself, his mind paralysed his tongue and there he sat, on the near side of the table, as if in a world apart, watching a man who was obviously as important as he was mysterious, not knowing who he was, what he did or why he might be so important, yet, despite that, understanding it all for the first time.

Both the Colonel and Cheong fell in love with the house and its grounds in the suburbs beyond Tokyo. MacArthur had, perhaps quite properly, requested that the Colonel find suitable lodgings within the city proper, to be more accessible to his work. However, he could find no such place, at least none that could satisfy both him and Cheong.

Thus they travelled outside of the city and, almost immediately, came across the house. It was in an area that had, miraculously, escaped the destruction that had devastated fully half of the city and much of the outlying suburbs.

It lay on the eastern verge of an enormous forest of cryptomeria and pine within which the Shinto temple blossomed like some other-worldly flora whose grace of design, quiescence and natural humility instantly bewitched the Colonel's mind, speaking to him more eloquently than even the country's finest speakers the eternalness and dignity of the Japanese spirit. And always when he came in sight of it he thought of So-Peng.

No one knew who had inhabited the house before the Colonel and Cheong moved in, not even Ataki, the wizened old gardener. It had been there, abandoned, for years, he had told the Colonel, though he had come faithfully every day to tend the grounds, and time had dimmed remembrance. Perhaps, the Colonel thought with a certain degree of resignation, he just did not want to say. In any event, it was now the Colonel's.

The formal garden in front of the house was breathtaking, complete with complexly flowering bonsai trees and a shallow stone pool filled with blue-eyed goldfish with fins like fine, gossamer veils (the Colonel quickly bought a tank, setting it up in the kitchen, one of the house's few Westernized rooms, for their warm winter's sojourn).

In the back of the house was another kind of garden altogether, a Zen pebble rectangle with four jutting rocks placed at significant points by the original artist within the uniform expanse, looking, the Colonel thought, like islands jutting from beneath a perfectly calm sea. However, Nicholas pointed out, when he was old enough to speak, they were most surely mountain peaks rising above a cloud-bank: this comment much to the delight of both the Colonel and Cheong. But in any event, the Zen garden was, ironically enough, a place of perfect peace and meditation in a country half-dead, mutilated and charbroiled, struggling now towards a new kind of survival.

Nicholas adored the house and the grounds with an unquench-able passion. He was drawn, over and over, to the Zen garden, where Cheong would often find him sitting thoughtfully, head held in his hands, gazing out over the stark serenity of the rising rocks amid the precisely arranged pebbles. After a time it would be the first place she would look for him.

Nicholas could never decide whether he loved the garden best when he was alone there or when Ataki would come with his water and his rake – to keep the earth beneath from drying out and to make certain that the pebbles were properly aligned – for he adored both the intense solitude of the place ('It's like,' he told the Colonel once, 'you can hear your soul breathing') and watching the old man's preciseness and deft economy of move-ment with the pebbles, which were worn so smooth that Nicholas firmly believed that their origin must have been some point on the island's shoreline, for only the constant action of a motion-filled sea could create such stupendous smoothness.

It appeared to Nicholas that the old man's motions were so utterly effortless that he scarcely seemed to expend any physical energy at all. When he was perhaps six he had asked Ataki how it was he moved the way he did, and when the old man answered with one word, 'bujutsu', Nicholas went to the Colonel straight-way to ask him what it meant. It was no good badgering Ataki, for he would only tell you what he wanted you to know.

'Bujutsu,' the Colonel said, putting down his cup of tea and folding lengthwise the newspaper he had been absorbed in dis-secting, 'means, collectively, all the martial arts of Japan.'

'Then,' Nicholas said clearly, 'I want to learn bujutsu.'

The Colonel regarded his son. He had learned quite quickly that Nicholas never said anything lightly and that now, if he said that he wanted to learn bujutsu, he was quite prepared to take it on; superfluous for the Colonel to tell him how arduous a task it was likely to be.

The Colonel got up from the table and, putting his arm around his son's shoulders, opened the *shōji* – sliding paper and wood walls – so that they could walk outside together.

They stood by the edge of the Zen garden but Nicholas noticed, on looking up at his father, that the Colonel seemed to have fixed his gaze far beyond its border, indeed, beyond even the last boundary of their land, to the rising green swords of the cryptomeria forest.

'Do you know, Nicholas,' the Colonel said in a rather floating voice, 'that within the perimeter of the Shinto temple at the centre of the forest lies a park – a small one, mind you – that is said to contain forty different species of moss?'

'I've never been there,' Nicholas said. 'Will you take me?'

'Perhaps one day,' the Colonel replied, his heart aching, for he knew that there was never enough time and he was here to do a job, a monstrous, bloody, awful job that, nevertheless, needed to be done and, furthermore, needed him to get it done right; these years had been more than enough to grind down a man of lesser courage and perseverance than the Colonel. But each time his tired mind seemed on the verge of faltering, he would recall So-Peng and his son, encompassed in the same thought, and he would go on, through another long night and the subsequent longer day until the weekend came and it would begin all over again. 'But I have never seen that park either, Nicholas. Few save the Shinto priests of that temple have viewed it.' The Colonel took some time now before he continued. 'What I mean to say is that you wish to go where few nowadays would wish to go – and there are many specializations.'

'I wish only to start at the beginning, Father. That is not so much to ask, is it?' Nicholas looked up again.

'No,' the Colonel said, tightening his grip upon his son's shoulders. 'Not too much.' He thought for a moment, his lean face wrinkled along the firm brow. 'I tell you what,' he said at last. 'I'll speak to your aunt about it, all right?'

Nicholas nodded, his gaze lowering from his father's face to the mountains thrusting blindly out of the clouds.

The person to whom the Colonel had referred was, in fact, Itami. Nicholas, knowing her origin, had never really considered her his aunt. Perhaps, after all, this was because he had disliked her for as long as he could remember, and having once formulated this opinion, could never get himself unstuck from it.

It would be no great surprise to learn that his instinctual

dislike of her was only an offshoot of how he reacted to the presence of her husband, Satsugai. In a boy who, from birth, had been taught to attain within himself a calmness of spirit, like a cool guiding stream, it was most disconcerting to come in close contact with Satsugai. He felt, at those times, like an ineffectual moon whirled about by the proximity of a nova. Great turbulent currents, powerful eddies, disturbed his tranquillity, and this inability to return to a semblance of inner balance until Satsugai had left frightened him.

On the other hand, his aunt in no way created the same effect on him. She was an exceedingly small and delicately boned woman, beautiful though, in Nicholas's opinion, the perfect symmetry of her face could not compare to his mother's features.

Itami always wore formal Japanese attire. She was constantly attended by servants. Her diminutive size made all the more fascinating her rather charismatic nature. She was, the Colonel had told him, a member of one of Japan's greatest and oldest houses, of the *bushi* class. She was a samurai lady. She had been married to Satsugai for eleven years and he, as far as Nicholas knew, was a wealthy and influential businessman.

Then there was Itami's son, Saigō. He was a year older than Nicholas, a large burly boy with deep brooding eyes and a cruel and calculating disposition. He spent much time with his father but, on the many occasions when the two families assembled, it was inevitable that Nicholas and Saigō should be thrown together.

It seemed to Nicholas that the other boy hated him almost on sight. Why this should be so he could not imagine. Not until much later. But then he reacted as any boy in any part of the world might to such unadulterated hostility. He returned measure for measure.

It was, of course, Satsugai who had put Saigō up to it. This knowledge, when it came to him, only increased Nicholas's hatred and fear of the man. But then it was also Saigō who introduced Nicholas to Yukio. As it is said, all things in life balance themselves out.

Don't they?

# Second Ring
# THE WIND BOOK

# I

## New York City/West Bay Bridge,
## Summer Present

When the man with the mirrored aviator sun-glasses emerged from the depths of Pennsylvania Station on the Seventh Avenue side he did not look around him; nor did he walk immediately to the kerb, as did most of his fellow passengers, to wave a raised hand to hail a cruising taxi.

Instead, he waited dutifully for the light to change and, when it did, went quickly across the avenue, ignoring the light rain. By the way he walked and, perhaps because of the rather long black duffel bag slung obliquely across his muscular shoulder, one might have thought he was a professional dancer; he moved as effortlessly and as gracefully as the wind.

He wore a short-sleeved navy silk shirt and cotton slacks of the same deep blue, charcoal-grey suede shoes with almost no heel and soles as thin as paper. His face was rather wide; deep lines were scored downwards from each side of his mouth as if he had never learned how to smile. His black hair was cut short and bristly.

On the east side of Seventh Avenue he went by the crowded façade of the Statler Hilton Hotel, crossed Thirty-second Street and, passing up the green and white awning of the Chinatown Express, ducked into the McDonald's next door.

Inside, he went swiftly through the garish yellow and orange interior to a line of telephone booths along one wall. At the side of the extreme left-hand booth was a row of telephone directories encased in steel bindings to discourage theft and vandalism. They hung down in a stand waist-high like quiescent bats in a cave.

The man in the sun-glasses pushed up the Yellow Pages book. Its cover was torn and defaced and the bottom edges of a large hunk of the centre pages were mutilated as if someone had attempted to eat them. He leafed through the book until he came to the section he wanted. He ran one forefinger down the page. Near the bottom, it stopped and the man nodded to himself. He already knew the address but, out of long habit, liked to double-check his information.

Once more outside, he recrossed the avenue, walking west at a brisk pace along the width of the Madison Square Garden complex, and caught an uptown bus on Eighth Avenue. It was crowded. He stood in the hot and airless interior. The bus smelled of stale sweat and mildew.

At the Seventy-fourth Street stop he swung off and walked up one block. There he turned off Central Park West and headed west towards the Hudson River. The rain had ceased for the moment but the sky remained close and dark, as if hung over from a long night of revelry. The air was completely calm. The city steamed.

He found the address approximately midway between Columbus Avenue and Broadway on the north side of the street. His nostrils flared for an instant as he mounted the steps of the brownstone. He opened the glass and wood outer doors and stepped into the tiny vestibule. Before him was a modern steel and wire-glass door securely locked. There was a buzzer on the wall of the vestibule which he pushed firmly. Just above it was a discreet brass plate on which was etched TŌHOKU NO DŌJŌ and, above that, a small oval speaker grille.

'Yes?' came a tinny voice from the grille.

The man with the sun-glasses leaned slightly to the side. 'I wish an appointment,' he said.

He waited, one hand already on the knob of the inner door.

'Please come up. Second floor. Around to the left as far as you can go.'

The door buzzed and he pushed it open.

He could smell the tang of sweat, tinged with the piquant spices of exertion and fear. For the first time since setting foot in the city, he felt at home. Contemptuously, he tossed this feeling aside. He went swiftly and silently up the carpeted stairs.

Terry Tanaka was on the phone to Vincent when Eileen came up to him. Seeing the look in her eyes, he asked Vincent to hold the line and, putting his palm over the phone, said, 'What is it, Ei?'

'There's a man here who wishes to practise today.'

'So? We can handle it. Sign him up.'

'I think you had better take care of this one yourself,' she said.

'Why? What's the matter?'

'Well, for one thing, he's asking to see you. And for another, I've seen the way he walks. He's no student.'

Terry smiled. 'You see how our fame has spread? That piece in *New York* was great.' But when she did not respond, he said, 'That's not all, is it?'

She shook her head. 'The guy gives me the creeps. His eyes ...' She shrugged. 'I don't know. But I wish you'd handle it.'

'Okay. Listen, give him a cup of tea or something. I'll be right there.'

She nodded, giving him a thin smile.

'What was that?' Vincent said in his ear.

Terry uncovered the mouthpiece. 'Oh, nothing probably. Just a client who's spooked Ei.'

'How is she?'

'Fine.'

'And the two of you?'

'Oh, you know. About the same.' Terry gave him a quick laugh. 'I'm still waiting for her to say yés. I've been on one knee so many times, I've worn out four pairs of trousers.'

Vincent laughed. 'We still on for dinner tonight?'

'Sure. As long as it's an early one. I want to see Ei tonight.'

'Sure thing. Just some questions I'd like to ask you. Nick was going to come but –'

'Hey! How is he? He called just before he went out to the Island. Has he been loafing all summer?'

Vincent laughed. 'Yeah. Until I got hold of him. He's got a new woman, too.'

'Good,' Terry said. 'About time.. The ties are still very strong, huh?'

'Yeah.' Vincent knew only too well what Terry meant. 'He sends his love to you and Ei. He'll be in soon, I'm sure, and he'll stop by.'

'Good enough. Hey, my new client will no doubt bite Ei's

head off if I don't run. See you at seven. 'Bye.'

He hung up and went across the room and around the corner to meet Mr Wonderful.

As Terry came up, Eileen Okura felt some of her apprehension dissipate. She had been startled by two separate elements. First, she had not heard the man's approach. Second, his countenance was unusual. He stood now precisely as she had first seen him, duffel bag on his back, sun-glasses swinging from the thumb and forefinger of his right hand. The skin of his face and his hands was far too white for an oriental's. But, she saw, as she glanced at his throat where his shirt was open, this snowy colour predominated only in those areas, for his chest was a darker, more natural hue. It was as if he had been in some kind of hideous accident. An explosion, perhaps, affecting the exposed areas of his flesh. Yet, for all that, it was his eyes which held her. They looked utterly dead, black stones dropped into a stagnant pool of water, they could not conceivably retain any form of emotion. And it was these same eyes which regarded her now as if she were some specimen, stripped and laid out on a sterile surface, ready for dissection. Eileen felt a brief chill wash over her.

'*Watashi ni nanika goyō desu ka*,' Terry said to the man. How may I help you?

'*Anata ga kono dōjō no master desu ka?*' Are you the master of this *dōjō*?

Terry seemed to ignore the abrupt and therefore extremely impolite mode of the other's speech, said, '*Sō dsu.*' Yes.

'*Koko de renshu sasete itadakitai no desu ga.*' I wish to practise.

'I see. Which disciplines are you interested in?'

'Aikido, karate, kenjutsu.'

'For aikido and karate I can surely accommodate you. But as for kenjutsu, I am afraid that it is quite impossible. My instructor is away on vacation.'

'What about yourself?'

'Me? I have given up teaching kenjutsu.'

'I require no instruction. Practise with me for an hour.'

'I –'

'It is better than filling out forms.'

'That it is. My name is Terry Tanaka. And yours?'

'Hideoshi.'

A name from out of the past. Terry nodded. 'All right. Miss Okura will give you the necessary forms. The charge is forty dollars an hour.'

The other nodded curtly. Terry half expected him to produce a plastic wallet filled with travellers' cheques but instead the man peeled off one hundred and twenty dollars in twenties from a roll he kept in his front right-hand trouser pocket.

'Sign there,' Terry said, pointing. He nodded towards a small doorway at the far end of the room. 'You can change in there. Do you have your own robe?'

'Yes.'

'All right. Fine. The *dōjō* proper is one flight up. Which discipline do you prefer to begin with?'

'Surprise me,' Hideoshi said, walking away. He disappeared through the doorway into the darkness of the locker-room beyond.

Terry turned his head away, saw Eileen staring at the empty doorway across the room. There were no shadows. The light filtering in through the half-drawn blinds which covered the high narrow windows, was diffuse enough to put a patina on her glowing skin. She looked slim and tiny, he thought. A pale ballerina about to perform her half of a difficult *pas de deux*.

'Who is he?' Her voice seemed like a whisper in the high-ceilinged room. Above their heads came the thump of the floorboards.

Terry shrugged. He was a big man, perhaps six feet, with wide shoulders and narrow waist and hips. His face was flat, the eyes black above very high cheek-bones. He told Eileen what had transpired.

'You're not going to do it, Terry?'

He shrugged. 'Why not? It's only an hour's practise.' But he knew what she meant and his heart was not nearly so light as his words sounded. He was, along with Nicholas, one of the greatest kenjutsu masters now living outside Japan. At thirty-eight, Terry had already spent three-quarters of his life studying kenjutsu, the ancient Japanese art of swordsmanship. His reason for abruptly abandoning it within the past year might not be altogether easy for a Westerner to understand.

In the first place, no martial art depended solely on physical discipline. In fact, a great percentage was mental. Long ago, he had read Miyamoto Musashi's *Go Rin No Sho*. It was perhaps the greatest treatise on strategy in all the world. Though written in just a few short weeks before the great warrior's death, its knowledge was timeless, Terry thought. Today, he was well aware, many prominent Japanese businessmen mapped out their major corporate advertising and sales campaigns with Miyamoto's principles in mind.

Just about a year ago, he had picked up the *Go Rin No Sho* once again. But, in reading it, he had now found what he believed to be quite different and darker meanings hidden within the logic and vaults of imagination. To devote oneself so religiously to the domination of others was not, he felt, what life was all about. He had been disturbed by dreams, then, black portents without form or face, all the more real and frightening for that. He had felt compelled to rid himself of the volume, throwing it out in the middle of the night, not even waiting until morning.

In daylight, the feeling had remained. He felt as if he had taken a wrong turning in the dead of night and, without warning, had found himself on the lip of a great abyss. There had been a temptation to look over the edge but with it had come the knowledge that if he did he would surely lose his balance and tumble forwards into the darkness. Thus Terry had stepped back and, turning away, had put his *katana* away forever.

And then today, this strange man who called himself Hideoshi appears. Terry shivered inwardly, too much in control to let Eileen see his true emotions. Besides, he did not want to alarm her.

It was surely some kind of omen, for he had no doubt that the man knew well the teachings of Miyamoto. But even beyond this, there was no doubt in his mind that Hideoshi was a *haragei* adept. The concept, stemming from two words, *hara*, meaning centralization and integration, and *ki*, meaning an extended form of energy, was more than intuition or a sixth sense but, as Terry's *sensei* had said, 'a true way of perceiving reality'. It was akin to having eyes in the back of your head, amplifiers in your ears. Yet *haragei* could work both ways: being an ultra-sensitive receiver also made one an excellent transmitter if one came within a certain distance of another *haragei* adept. Terry had picked this up instantly.

'Just another Japanese off the plane from Haneda,' he said nonchalantly to Eileen. He would not, under any circumstances, have told her what he really knew about the man.

'Well, there's something odd about him.' She was still staring at the black doorway, which seemed to gape at her like the mouth of a grinning skull. 'Those eyes –' she shuddered. 'So impersonal, like – like cameras.' She took a step towards Terry. 'What's he doing in there so long, do you think?'

'Meditating, no doubt,' Terry said. He picked up the phone, stabbed the intercom button. He spoke softly and briefly to someone on the third floor, informing him of the new client. He cradled the receiver. 'He'll be another twenty minutes at least,' he said to her. He stared at her long black gleaming hair. Brushed back and unbound, it rushed like a night-dark stream over her shoulders, down her back in a thick cascade, ending at the tops of her buttocks. She started and he said, 'What is it?'

Her head turned. 'Nothing. I just felt you staring at me.'

He smiled. 'But I do that all the time.'

'At night, yes.' Her eyes stayed serious, her pouty lips firm and straight. 'Don't do it here, Terry. Please. You know how I feel about that. We work together and we –' Her eyes met his and for just an instant he felt his heart lurch within him. Was that fear he had glimpsed there lurking like a prowler in the night?

He reached out a hand, pulled her gently towards him. This time she did not resist and, as if seeking warmth, she allowed herself to be cradled, her arms tight around him. She felt safer here, with him so close.

'Are you okay, Ei?'

She nodded wordlessly against his muscles but felt the tears welling up like deep pools within her eyes. Her throat constricted and she could not think why. 'I want to come over tonight,' she heard herself say and she immediately felt better.

'How about every night?' Terry said.

It was not the first time he had said this, though it had been in different ways before. Eileen's response had always been the same, yet now she knew the source of the churning inside her, knew that when he asked her again this evening, as he surely would, her answer would be yes. 'Tonight,' she said softly. 'Ask me tonight.' She dabbed at her eyes. 'When should I come over?'

'I'm having dinner with Vincent. Why don't you join us?'

She smiled thinly. 'Uh-uh. There's too much you guys talk about that I have no interest in.'

'We'll cut that all out tonight. Promise.'

She laughed then. 'No, no. I don't begrudge you that. *Bushido* is important to you.'

'It's part of our heritage. We wouldn't be Japanese without it. I'm not yet that assimilated into Western culture – I'll never be – that I can forget the history of my people –' He paused, seeing her shudder, her eyes flutter closed.

'My people,' her words a ghostly echo. '*Bushido*. I shall die for my Emperor and my beloved homeland.' Tears welled from beneath her lowered lids, turning to minute rainbows. Behind them were galaxies of pain. 'We survived the great firestorm in March' – her whispered words like the shouted cries of the dying – 'when the American armada dropped almost three-quarters of a million bombs filled with napalm; when two hundred thousand Japanese civilians were roasted or boiled alive; when half of Tokyo was cindered; when, the following morning, as you walked down the street, the wild wind took the charcoaled corpses and blew them away like dust.'

'Ei, don't –'

'We moved out, then, away from the war, to Hiroshima in the south but, quite soon, my parents, terrified by all the rumours, packed me off to my grandparents who lived in the mountains.' She looked at his face without really seeing it. 'There was never enough food and slowly we began to die of starvation. Oh, it was nothing very spectacular, merely a kind of all-pervading lassitude. I would sit in the sun for hours unable to think of anything. It took me hours to comb my hair because my arms would hurt, keeping them lifted like that. That was for me. But for my mother and my father there was Hiroshima and the light that fell from the sky.' Her eyes focused and she looked at him steadily. 'What is there for me but shame and hurt? What *we* did and what, in turn, was done to us. My poor country.'

'That's all forgotten now,' he said.

'No, it's not. And you, of all people, should understand that. It's you and Vincent and Nick who talk constantly of the spirit of our country. How can you celebrate the one without feeling shame at the other? Memory is selective, not history. We are what we are. You can't arbitrarily excise the bad, pretend it never existed. Nick doesn't do that, I know. He remembers; he feels the hurt, still. But I don't think you and Vincent do.'

He wanted to tell her of his recent thoughts but he found that he could not. Not now, at least. It was the wrong time, the wrong place, and he had a highly developed sense of these things. Tonight, perhaps. Tonight he would see that it all came down. He watched the diffuse, artist's light on her satin-skinned face, her long slender neck, her slim compact body. It was impossible to think of her as being forty-one; she did not look a day over thirty, even in harsh light.

It was just about two years since they had first met, a year since they had become clandestine lovers – at least as far as those at the *dōjō* were concerned; of course all their friends knew. In that time she had never asked for more, never wanted to know about the future. It was he who, lately, had felt the need for more. And recently he had become aware that, at least partially, the ending of his love affair with kenjutsu had been, simultaneously, the beginning of his love affair with Ei. Now, it seemed to him with pristine logic, that there was nothing more important in life than being with her. The *dōjō*, which he had opened nearly five years ago, was well established and he was more than satisfied that it could run itself for a short while. Time enough for a marriage and a long, leisurely honeymoon somewhere far away. Paris, perhaps. Yes, definitely Paris. It was Ei's favourite city, he knew, and he had never been there. All that remained was for him to ask her. Tonight.

Would she say yes this time? He suspected that she would and his heart fairly danced.

'Tonight,' he said. 'I'll be back by nine, ten if Vincent gets stuck in Island traffic on the way in. But you have a key and some of your clothes are there. Come any time. But bring champagne. Dom Pérignon. I'll bring the caviar.'

It would have been easy for Eileen to ask what all this was for but she felt that it would spoil the moment. There was, after all, plenty of time to find out what she already knew in her heart.

'All right,' she said, her eyes very large now.

He turned, abruptly remembering. 'I'd better get upstairs and prepare the *bokken*. Soon Hideoshi will be through with the others and I want to be ready.'

Justine's eyes were completely dry. This was something new for her but it brought her no solace. Not when the anxiety had come again, a fierce knot in her stomach, a pressure on her chest, constricting her breathing, refusing to go away. There is nothing wrong, she repeated over and over to herself. Nothing. Absolutely nothing. She shivered, feeling cold. Her fingers were like ice.

She stood in the darkened living-room of Nicholas's house, staring out at the mist and rain on this dismal Sunday. Out there, somewhere, was the sea, curling endlessly, but the spiteful rain hid it from her as if it were withholding a bright toy on Christmas morning. She thought about going out there, piercing the mist, finding the ocean for herself, but she lacked, at this moment, the necessary fortitude to brave the weather.

Oh, my God! Oh, my God!

She whirled from the sleeted window-pane, running blindly through the house, groping for the bathroom, and there, at last, she collapsed in front of the toilet, retching.

Her body shook and sweat stood out on her forehead, rolling down into her eyes in tiny stinging rivulets.

After an endless time, when she could no longer stand the stink, she reached out a hand to flush the toilet. It seemed to take all the energy she possessed. But, after that, she somehow found the strength to stand up and bend over the basin.

The cold running water fell on her face like bullets from a gun. She shivered, opened her mouth to get the sour taste out. She could not swallow.

Sitting on the edge of the porcelain bath, feeling the cool bar of it striking across her buttocks, she curled over, putting her head in her arms, her arms on her knees.

She rocked back and forth, thinking, *I can't do it. I can't.*

It was her mind now that did the vomiting. The history of the betrayals unfurling like a hated flag above her head, blotting out all other signs of life. All her men. Timothy, who had been the first, the high-school basketball coach. *I'll be gentle, Justine,* and thrusting savagely into her over and over, enjoying the expression of pain on her face, her crying out into the perfect sterile symmetry of the darkened gym; watching his eyes burn with her instant's fear. Then Jodie, the Harvard man with the laughing eyes and the cruel soul. *I want to be a surgeon, Justine* – and already was. Eddie, who was seeing her and his wife on alternate nights; there was nothing he wanted but them both. And then, in San Francisco, there had been Chris. They had come together, igniting like a bonfire, insatiable, insensate to everything and everyone around them. Or was that only the way it had been with her? She could not bear that truth, even now. Dredging it up was like an act of cruel masochism, like opening the edges of a slowly healing wound and probing for the nerve.

She had used her father's name then – and his money. God only knew how much; certainly she did not. Wasn't it the money that had made her weak and lazy? So easy to pin down the blame, neatly and resolutely; coming back to her father. How she hated him for giving her – those things: his name (she always wrote the word out on the screen of her mind so that she could make the deliberate typo *fame* which was, as far as she was concerned, no error) and his money.

God, this thing makes me nasty and bitter, she thought. As if it's a physical malady that manufactures bile as a by-product. She gagged again but, wrapping her arms around her stomach, she held herself together; there was nothing more to come up; she was empty yet the anxiety made her feel as if she had swallowed a two-by-four whole.

*I can't do it*, she repeated to herself. *I can't.*

She had taken his money – so much of it – not thoughtlessly but wilfully. Because she hated him. But she found that getting it was like having the goblet of wine that was always full no matter how much you drank. What had mattered so much to her was of absolutely no concern to him.

Of course it had mattered very much to Chris, who was the one, after all, who made use of most of the money. At least that was how it had all come down that day when her father had flown in, had come to her house with the battery of local detectives he had hired. It had all been there for her to read in the report. The thing had so shocked her that she had hardly been able to utter a word let alone protest as her father had his men gather up her clothes, all her possessions. He left them to it, hustling her outside and into the waiting limo. She had not said a word all through the flight back east. Her father, sitting across the aisle in the private Lear jet, was too engrossed in reports to notice. She found that she was not hungry, nor was she tired. She was nothing.

It seemed like a long time ago now. Years could be like lifetimes, never like days. This is what came to her on the plane ride back to New York: she saw their old country house, the one in Connecticut that she had loved so much, with the stone walls covered with green creeping ivy, the high leaded-glass windows, the flagstone patio and, across the emerald back lawn, beyond the unpaved avenue, the brick-red of the stables, smelling of hay and manure and horse sweat. How she loved that place; it reminded her of England, somehow. Not like the new place on Gin Lane out on the Island. Her father had sold the old house just after Justine's mother had died, paying two and a half million for the estate on one of the most famous streets in all America.

It was Easter-time in Connecticut. She was eight. Gelda had some friends over, whom she did not like or just did not want to be with. Her mother was gone, having driven into town to do some shopping. She wandered through the enormous old place, the large bright friendly rooms filled, here and there, by the busy servants preparing for a formal party later that evening. Peering out of the window, she discovered that

113

there were a number of cars in the semicircular driveway and, as she went down the long curve of the main stairway to the ground floor, she could just make out voices coming from behind the closed doors of the library. Her hand on the knob, turning, and she pushed.

'Daddy?'

Her father had indeed been inside. He was with a group of men, discussing matters that had no meaning for her.

'Justine,' he said with a frown, 'you must see that I am busy at the moment.' He made no move towards her.

'I just wanted to talk to you.' She felt utterly dwarfed by the circle of men. One of them shifted uncomfortably on the couch, the leather creaking under his weight.

'This is not the time. Shall I fetch Clifford.' The latter had the form but not the inflection of a question.

She looked around mutely.

Her father reached up and pulled a cord. In just a moment, the manservant appeared.

'Yes, sir?'

'Clifford,' her father said. 'See that she is kept occupied until Mrs Tomkin returns, will you? I can't have any more interruptions. Doesn't Gelda have some friends here?'

'Yes, sir.'

'Well, that's the place for her then, eh?'

'Very good, sir.' He turned. 'Come along, Miss Justine –'

But she had already turned, running down the long, high hallway, slamming out through the front door. She could hear Clifford clattering away behind her. She liked Clifford. She spent a lot of her time with him, just talking. But right now she did not feel like being with anyone.

She sped around the side of the house, headed for the stables, and was quite out of breath by the time she got there.

They had six horses. Arabians. Her favourite was King Said. He was her horse, to all intents and purposes. But of course the children, though already good riders, were not allowed on horseback or even in the stables without an adult to supervise.

Justine did not really care about that now. She went down the straw-strewn centre aisle until she came to King Said's stall. She called to him and apparently he heard, for there came to her his slight snorting and stamping; he was eager for a canter. He poked his head out; it bobbed up and down. His powerful neck thrust far above her; his coat shone. She wished that she could reach up and stroke him but she was far too short.

That's when she thought about opening the stall door. She was just lifting the iron latch when Clifford caught up with her.

'Oh, Miss Justine, you must never, never do that –'

But she had already whirled into his arms, clinging to him, crying inconsolably.

The return to New York had presaged a low point in her life. Filled with an anxiety she could not control, she turned in desperation to a psychiatrist. At first it appeared to be no help at all. But that was an unfair assessment. It was, after all, a highly subjective one and she was perhaps so low that she could then perceive no change, however minute. It was like lying sleepless in her bed, staring out of the window at the east, night still clinging tenaciously, looking at her watch, knowing dawn was not far off but seeing no band of light. Not yet.

It was, in retrospect, really a time of retrenchment. She had no job, could not face that, but she began to sketch, returning to the craft she had once loved. Slowly she built up a current portfolio and at length she was ready to go out.

It was not nearly so bad as she had imagined – she had not slept for two nights before the interviews, terrified – and she had got a job at the second agency she went to. But doing a job that she liked, she soon found, was not nearly enough (did she know, then, that she was well again?). Of course she knew why. But the thought of becoming involved again was intolerable to her.

Thus is was that she discovered dance. She went to a class one night with a friend from the office and fell instantly in love. Now she channelled her excess energy into her body, adoring the concept of controlled rhythm, the duality of tension and relaxedness that dance afforded her.

Yet it was not only the dance but also its prelude which fascinated her. Her instructor believed in the discipline of t'ai chi as a warm-up exercise. With this fundamental core assimilated, Justine found to her delight that she could move into virtually any area of dance she chose, from modern to ballet.

She had been at it for just over a year when her instructor said to her, 'You know, Justine, if you had begun the dance when you were a child, you'd be a great dancer today. I say this to you only to give you an accurate idea of where you stand now. You are one of my best pupils because not only is your body responsive but your spirit is within the dance. The greatness is there, Justine, but one unfortunately cannot overcome the advance of time.'

She was filled with pride and happiness. But just as importantly, she knew why. For the first time in her life she felt that she had control of herself as a person; she no longer felt tossed to and fro by the whims of the world. Here, at last, was a control that she could feel directly, that had real meaning for her.

Within the month she had left her full-time job at the agency and had gone into business for herself. The agency still wanted her and she accommodated it. But she was free now to pick and choose the jobs she wanted. She found that within six months of setting up shop she was pulling down three times her old salary in independent billings.

And then she had decided on this house in West Bay Bridge.

And had met Nicholas.

*I can't do it. I can't.*

She stood up and reeled drunkenly out of the bathroom, down the hallway, using her hands, palms outstretched like a blind person, to guide herself through the house. In the living-room she bumped into the bubbling fish tank. All the bright denizens of the deep swam there, tranquil as if anaesthetized – blind, deaf and dumb – as beautiful and as unthinking as the vegetation reaching towards the winking surface. She felt another wave of nausea hit her and she turned away, heading for the front door.

*I can't make the commitment. I can't trust him. Oh, my God! Oh, my God!*

She stumbled out into the rain, tripping down the wooden

116

steps, falling to her knees in the wet sand. It felt like dough, clinging to her jealously.

She crawled a few feet, then, regaining her balance, ran all the way home.

Not long afterwards, Nicholas returned from the beach area where they had found the second body. This time they had waited for him.

*It was one cut. Do you understand?* Vincent had said over the phone. He did indeed understand what that meant. The cut of a *katana*.

The white-skinned corpse was slit from the right shoulder, obliquely down to just above the left hip. One swing, one cut from the finest blade ever known to man. It could easily slash through armour; flesh and bone were as paper to a *katana* wielded by a master swordsman. Ancient blades had been preserved for a thousand years by succeeding generations of warriors, losing not a bit of their original sharpness or effectiveness; and even today no arsenal in the world could claim such a magnificent weapon as the Japanese *katana*.

This was how the second man had died. He lay, as he had been found, cradled by the soft surf and sand. He had not been in the water very long. There was absolutely no question of his being drowned.

But now they had to revise their conclusions radically. Barry Braughm had obviously not been the ninja's only target. But there seemed, on the surface, nothing to connect the two victims. This man was a worker for Lilco – the Long Island power company – blue-collar, lower-middle-class background. Nothing in common, nothing at all.

Yet the ninja was abroad, still killing.

Inside, Nicholas threw off the lightweight khaki slicker. His sneakers and his jeans up to the knees were soaked. But this was of only peripheral interest to him. He was thinking of Justine and the thing that had crashed through her kitchen window in the night. He did not dare to think of what it might be. Besides, it made no sense. Still, he had asked her to stay inside his house and not return home.

She was not there.

He cursed softly and, returning through the living-room,

scooped up his slicker and headed out of the door.

No one answered his knock but, coming down the beach, he had seen the lights burning at the back of the house through the bedroom windows.

He knocked again and, fearful now, tried the door-knob. It gave and he twisted it, went through into the house.

He stopped still as a statue just over the threshold, listening and watching the shadows. Someone was home; there was no intruder. These things he ascertained immediately and simultaneously; his training needed no conscious cueing.

He called her name: 'Justine.'

It was not just the one cut that worried him. Both Doc Deerforth and Vincent had missed the other thing. At least, they had not recognized it for what it was. In leaning over the body, he had chanced to see the top of the left shoulder. The bruise had just begun to darken. He touched it. Below the flesh the clavicle was fractured. Instantly, he was on guard; he had not wanted to alarm the others, even Vincent. If what he believed now was, in fact, the case ...

There had been a man. Miyamoto Musashi. Perhaps Japan's greatest warrior. Among other things, he founded the Niten or Two Heavens school – or *ryu* – of kenjutsu. It taught the art of wielding two swords at once. Another aspect of Musashi, known as Kensei, the Sword Saint, was that he used *bokken* – wooden swords – in actual combat – claiming that he did so because they were invincible.

What all this musing was leading up to was this: the man had been struck *two* blows, not one as Vincent believed. One had been the cut of the steel *katana*, ripping him open, the second had simultaneously crushed his collarbone; this had come from a *bokken*.

'Justine, it's Nick.' There was some movement now from the back of the house.

He was beginning to feel as if, having once been surrounded by confetti floating through the air, he was being confronted by a slowly emerging pattern as the scraps fell to the ground.

And what he saw shook him to his core.

Justine became visible, limned in the light from behind her, sweeping through the half-open bedroom door.

'What are you doing here?'

'Justine?' He knew it was she, just did not believe her tone of voice.

'Why did you come?'

'I told you to stay at my house, away from here.' He tried not to think of the black furry thing full of blood on her kitchen floor. Tried to calm himself, to ignore the fact, as mere coincidence, that it was an animal used by ninja as a ritual warning. It did not work.

'I got claustrophobic, all right? I told you I get that way every once in a while.'

'It's not safe here.'

'What are you talking about? I'm comfortable here. This is my house. *My* house, Nick.' With the light bursting through all around her like an aurora, he could not see her gestures. He did not need to.

'I don't think you understand.'

'No,' she said sadly. 'I'm afraid it's you who don't understand.' She took a step forward. 'Why don't you leave. Please.'

'What's happened?'

'There's – just nothing to say.'

'There has to be.'

'I don't want to talk about it, that's all.'

'You're not the only one who's involved here now.'

'Nick – nobody's involved.'

'You know what I mean.'

'Yes, I do. That's why I'm saying this. I'm – just not ready for anything like this.'

'Like what?'

'Don't force me to spell it out.'

'I just want to know what the hell's got into you.'

'It's just – you don't know me at all. I'm like this. Changeable. Erratic.' She sighed. 'Please go, Nick. Don't make a scene.'

He raised his hands, palms outward. 'No scene.' He walked towards her. 'I just want some answers.'

'You won't find any here. Not today, anyway.' She began to turn away from him, back into the light.

'Justine, wait!' He reached out, touched her arm.

'Get away from me!' she cried, hands pushing at him. And

then calmly whispered, 'Get away from me. I mean it, Nick.'

He turned and left her standing there, a silhouette.

Click. Click-click. Pause. Click-clack-click. *Hail*

As they moved back and forth along the thin line, the diameter of a predetermined circle, Terry felt the fear of an opponent for the first time in his life.

As a master, a *sensei*, fear in kenjutsu was an unknown thing to him. Until now.

It was not so much the fear of defeat – even he had, once or twice, been defeated – though he knew from the opening moments that this man could quite probably take him. No, it was something more subtle than that. It was the manner in which this man – this Hideoshi – fought. Style was imperative in kenjutsu; one could tell much about an opponent by the way he fought. Not only where he had studied and with whom but, on a wider scope, just what kind of man he was. For style was also philosophy and, yes, religion. What one respected and what one held in contempt.

Terry was concerned now because he saw in the other's martial philosophy a lack of regard for human life. Ei had been right on target when she had suggested that the man had the eyes of the dead. They were lustreless and as shallow as glass. Nothing, it appeared, resided behind them. Certainly no feeling. And this worried Terry. He had heard of and had read accounts of samurai in feudal Japan – during the 1600s, just after Ieyasu Tokugawa unified the warring *daimyo* by founding the Tokugawa shōgunate, which would last two hundred years – who cared little or nothing for human life. They were killing-machines, sent out to do their lord's bidding, loyal to him and to *bushido* only. Yet the code of *bushido* had within it the core of compassion, rigid and unassailable though it was. A core these men chose to ignore. He had often wondered what it was that had so corrupted them.

It seemed oddly fitting that, now, he should be confronted by just such a man. It was as if he had stepped out of another age. Karma, Terry thought.

He moved to his left, attacking, but was at once balked. Now their *bokken* whistled through the air, moving so swiftly that, to the untrained eye, it might appear as if the two combatants were wielding enormous fans, so blurred were the weapons' movements.

Terry moved to one knee, sweeping his *bokken* horizontally, but the other used a vertical block. A less experienced swordsman might then have gone for the kill, using the two-handed vertical sky-to-ground sweep. This would have brought instant disaster, for Terry need only have lunged forward several inches, the point of his weapon piercing the attacker's stomach, to vitiate that lethal blow.

Instead, the other stepped back, forcing Terry to regain his feet to continue the match. There had already been two draws and, as the hour was drawing to a close, this would be the last match. Yet, as he blocked several lightning thrusts, Terry had the uncomfortable feeling that he had not seen this man's complete repertory of strategy. Truth to tell, he felt as if the other had been toying with him for all the forty minutes they had been at it.

Annoyed, he struck and struck again. But instead of directly countering, the other's *bokken* cleaved to his as closely as a shadow, moving in concert, always touching. Then they were close together and Terry had his first good look at the other's face. It was just the flicker of an instant, perhaps a tenth of a second when his concentration, his *zanshin* – that is, physical form combined with mental concentration and alertness – wavered. Almost contemptuously, the other flicked at Terry's *bokken* with his own weapon. There was not enough time to react fully and, with the other's *bokken* at his throat, Terry was defeated.

When Justine came out of the bedroom to make herself a drink, it was near sunset. However, looking out of the windows at the front of the house, she saw only thick banks of grey clouds, trailing like streamers left over from a wild party, tattered, shredding in the winds aloft. The wan light bleached out all the colour from the land. The sand looked solid and lumpy like cooling lead.

She stopped, one hand around the neck of the bottle of rum. There seemed to be a shadow on the porch. Letting go of the bottle, she moved slowly to her right to get a better view. She moved past the centre beam between the two picture windows. Curtains fluttered, further obscuring her view. She moved farther to her left and stopped dead still. The shadow had become a silhouette. Someone was out there.

She felt a nameless fear flood her body and, unconsciously, she put a hand up to her throat. Her heart beat like a trip-hammer and Nicholas's words abruptly came to her. *It's not safe here*. Is this what he meant? She wished now that she had paid more attention to what he had been saying, but she had been solely intent on pushing him away, had heard only her own words.

Now she wondered wildly whether she had locked the door after he had left. She thought not but could not be certain. Yet she dared not attract attention by moving to it. She would have to pass directly before the windows. She thought of crawling but was too frightened of making some noise.

Then she thought of the phone. Keeping her eye on the silhouette, she backed up slowly into the hall. She reached down convulsively, almost knocking the receiver to the floor. She went to her knees to retrieve it. She dialled Nicholas's number, closing her eyes, praying he was home. Each solitary ring was like an icicle through her heart. She felt chilled, her flesh raised in goose-bumps as she cradled the phone.

She went silently, on dancer's feet, out to the living-room, sitting on the arm-rest of the sofa, staring at the silhouette. She considered creeping out at the back door. But then what? Pound on a neighbour's door? And say what? That she was afraid of a shadow?

Abruptly, she felt idiotic, like a madwoman trapped within the nightmares of her own mind. And, after all, there had been no movement of the silhouette since she had first glimpsed it. It could be a chair-back or –

She was up and moving without giving herself time to think, to back out. She flung the door open, stepped out on the porch. The air was heavy with the salt of the sea, yet perhaps the humidity was abating somewhat. There was a fresh breeze from the east.

As if she were a mechanical doll, she forced her gaze in the direction of the silhouette.

'Nicholas!' An indrawn breath.

He sat, lotus position, forearms resting easily on the points of his knees, staring seaward.

'What are you doing?' She came around beside him. 'Nick?' She stopped, bending down. 'What the hell are you doing?'

'Thinking.'

'About what?' It was a simple thing to say but perhaps, considering her mood, not a very logical one. She might easily have said, 'Can't you do it somewhere else – away from me?' Yet she had not and this surprised her. She wondered that, in finding him there, a guardian of her house – of her, really – rather than an invader, her anxiety had dissipated as easily as a bad dream. In its place was – what? As she pondered this, she heard him say, 'I'll have to tell you now.'

She reacted better than he might have expected. It was tantamount to saying: You have cancer.

'Are you sure?' she asked.

'I wouldn't tell you if I wasn't. I can't say that I understand it yet but that animal crashing in here was no accident. It was a ninja warning.'

'I may be way off base,' she said levelly, 'but didn't you tell me that one of the ninja's traits was to strike without warning?'

He nodded. 'Yes. That was true, most of the time. But there were occasions – a blood feud, for instance, or where it was specifically ordered or where the ninja wished to boast of invincibility – when a ritual warning was given.'

'But it's crazy,' she protested. 'What would a ninja want with me? I've had no connection ...' She paused but he said nothing, waiting to see if she would figure it out for herself. He did not think he would have to help her.

She got up off the sofa, walked nervously about the living-room, snapping her fingers. She stopped in front of the bar, mixed herself a long white rum on the rocks without offering him one; she was too engrossed. She came back to the sofa, sipped at her drink.

'There's only one thing I can think of,' she said, still somewhat unsure of herself.

'Let's see if we came to the same conclusion.'

'My father.'

'Your father,' Nicholas echoed. 'Raphael Tomkin.' He got up and poured himself a bitter lemon. 'Tell me, what do you know of his business dealings?'

She shrugged. 'Not much more than anyone else, I'm afraid. I never took much interest in it. You know, the basic facts. Oil is the mainstay. The corporation is multinational. That's about it.'

'In other words, not much.'

She winced. 'I told you so.'

'All right. Let's leave that for a while. Now –'

But she had already put a long forefinger against his lips. 'Don't, Nick. Don't ask me. Not now. Not yet. Let's leave things the way they are. Please. Please.'

He watched her eyes, wondered what was missing. Perhaps nothing or then again everything. He did not want that. But now he wanted her more and that called for a compromise. It was an uneasy one, at best, he knew. Talking was always better than not talking; that was a fundamental underpinning to all human relationships. Still, perhaps she was right after all and this was the wrong time. He swallowed half of his bitter lemon.

'What are we to do now?'

A good question, Nicholas thought, looking at her. The ninja meant to kill her, of that there seemed little doubt. This was something he accepted as given, although he could not discount the importance of motivation. But there would be no immediate answer to that, thus he put it out of his mind for the moment. What truly concerned him was the nature of the ninja. It was rare enough to encounter a modern-day villain although, as he had indicated to Vincent and Doc Deerforth, a number did operate clandestinely as independent agents on the highest levels. But to find one adept at the Niten school was quite alarming. It was one of the most difficult of kenjutsu styles to master and it might be indicative of other elements. There was, Nicholas knew well, more than one kind of ninja. Was it a coincidence?

'The only thing to do, for the moment, is to stay with you.'

Justine nodded. Oddly, this did not fill her with fear. Quite the opposite, in fact. She might even begin to relax with it. God knew, she wanted to. Yes, she thought, I *do* want to.

Suddenly she was feeling much better.

Doc Deerforth was dreaming. He lay on the hammock tied to his porch beams, swaying slightly. The delicate, insistent drone of the unceasing rain had lulled him to sleep.

He dreamed of a forest, gleaming like a great emerald, dripping with moisture. But it was not a place of pleasure or beauty. Not for him. He ran through the angled underbrush and, from time to time, as he twisted his head to peer fearfully behind him, he caught a glimpse of the hideous beast that pursued him relentlessly. It was a tiger. Fully ten feet long, the beast seemed to move effortlessly through the thick foliage that otherwise sought to pull him down. Its massive muscles worked with astounding fluidity beneath its glossy striped coat. Now and again, Doc Deerforth's eyes would lock on those of his foe. They glowed green in the night like lambent beacons, lighting the way before it. Yet they were not the shape of cats' eyes but the unmistakable oval – epicanthic fold and all – of a human: a Japanese, to be more specific.

They were the eyes of the ninja Doc Deerforth had encountered just before war's end in the jungles of the Philippines.

Now his way was balked by an enormous stand of bamboo. No matter which way he looked, there was no passage forward. He turned to see the man-beast open its mouth. Hot flame poured out like a river, inundating him in a jelly-like substance that clung to him, stinging like a man-of-war. He writhed, slapping at himself to rid himself of the burning substance. Still it clung to him tenaciously as if it were sentient. He had acquired a second skin: a malignancy which now started to eat into his flesh. His skin curled and cindered, peeling away to tendon and sinew. Only this was left to him, as the substance saturated him, piercing his bones. These were slowly powdered. And all the while the tiger with the ninja's face grinned at him. Then, as he felt all strength running out of him, as if he were urinating his life away, puddling it on the ground before him, the beast lifted its right forepaw. It was a human arm that had been amputated at the elbow. Above, the skin was black, the muscles gone, the arm – what was left of it – virtually fleshless, as if it had been crisped in some terrible swift blast. The tiger with the ninja's face lifted this limb up to him as if to say, 'See this and remember.' On the inside of the arm was tattooed a seven-digit number. Camp, he thought over and over. Camp, camp, camp. He was a jellyfish now, shorn of manhood, even his ape heritage. Beyond that, he now swayed in the jungle; when man was still a part of the gravid seas; before the spark; before the first fish crawled to the edge of its world and became an amphibian; before the land was fit for life. In this jungle sea, he drifted with his implacable foe. 'See, see, see,' said the beast, moving towards him who hung helpless on the tides, the evolutionary avatar. 'No!' cried the jellyfish. 'Don't you see? You'll destroy everyone!' But, unheeding, the man-tiger was upon him. 'This I do for my –'

Doc Deerforth awoke with a start. He was drenched in sweat and his cotton shirt was twisted to one side so that he felt as if he were inside a strait jacket. He gasped, taking several deep breaths. The rain had ceased some time while he was asleep but water still dripped from the eaves, making him think of the sea and the jellyfish and the ninja and annihilation.

Terry was almost killed on his way to meet Vincent. This, in itself, held no import for him; he was far too busy with his thoughts.

He was thinking about Hideoshi as he stepped off the kerb at Sixth Avenue, walking east on Forty-sixth Street. He was meeting Vincent at Michita, a small Japanese restaurant on Forty-sixth between Sixth and Fifth avenues. This place, run in the traditional style – a sushi bar and tatami rooms – was open virtually twenty-four hours a day because it catered, in large part, for the many Japanese businessmen new to the country, still on Tokyo time. It was a favourite haunt of Nicholas's, Vincent's and his because they all felt quite at home there.

He was against the light and, in the gutter, he was almost

run down by an old rattling Checker cab, hurtling up the avenue. The shrill blast of the horn snapped him out of his reverie and he leaped back onto the sidewalk amid the screech of brakes and the heartfelt curses of the obese, shaggy-haired driver. 'Fuckin' asshole gook!' he heard as the taxi swerved past him. He felt the cool breeze of its close passage and then it was accelerating uptown.

This incident, however, did not long deter him from his inner contemplation. Upstairs in the *dōjō*, while he had been preparing his *bokken* for the coming matches, he had observed the man at work on his aikido and, somewhat later, at karate. He had been appalled at the man's strength and agility. Also, it was obvious after a few short moments that he knew far more about strategy than did Terry's instructors. Since opening, the *dōjō* had rapidly built a reputation as being one of the finest facilities of its kind, not only in America, but in all the world. Much of this, of course, came from Terry's astute selection of *sensei*. To a man, his instructors were top-level masters in each of their specialities. To see them thus handled was disquieting indeed. As he went through Michita's thick blond-wood and iron door, he wondered whether he should tell Vincent of Hideoshi's visit.

Eileen went shopping after leaving the *dōjō*. She went cross-town to Bloomingdale's and bought several new pieces of lingerie. On a whim, she picked up a bottle of a cologne she had been meaning to try. On the way back to Terry's she stopped at a liquor store and bought a bottle of 1970 Dom Pérignon.

It was still light when she reached Terry's brownstone. She put the champagne in the refrigerator and threw her Bloomingdale's packages on the wide bed. Returning to the kitchen, she put four eggs in to boil for the caviar, checked to make sure there were enough onions, and bread for toast.

Then she went through into the bedroom and, crossing its ample width, into the bathroom, turning on the shower. She undressed and was about to step into the stall when she remembered something. Without bothering to wrap a towel round her, she returned to the living-room and put a record on the stereo, turning it up so that she could hear it in the shower.

She sang with the water beating down on her, hearing the distant sounds of the music as if from the far side of a waterfall. She imagined herself on a tropical island, bathing in the turquoise water of a deserted lagoon. She washed her hair and soaped her body, revelling in the slipperiness against her skin.

She turned off the water and got out, towelling her hair first. In Terry's full-length mirror, she regarded her naked self critically. She was proud of her body. Her skin was sleek and unblemished, her flesh firm despite her age. Her neck was long and slender, her shoulders as delicate as a china doll's. Her breasts, sloping gently, were still ripe and firm, the nipples dark and long. Her waist was narrow, her hips flaring gently. But it was her legs of which she was most proud. They were long and firm, the muscles taut and supple, the ankles narrow, her feet small. She watched her muscles rippling as she worked the thick blue-green towel over her wet flesh. Her nipples sprang erect at the rough contact and she felt the first beginning warmth as she moved the towel slowly down her belly, between her thighs, back and forth, anticipating Terry's arrival. She loved his hands on her body; they were so soft and gentle and knowing; she abhorred anything rough; he knew she loved that part as much as when he was inside her, both of them coming in concert. She loved to make love to music, the changing melodies, harmonies, tempi somehow enhancing the process. And, of course, the added sounds made vocalizing easier for both of them. She watched the flush of blood throughout her body reflected in the mirror as her thoughts pushed onward, inward. She imagined that Terry was already home, moving around the living-room, preparing the caviar and champagne. She dropped the towel as, with one hand, she rubbed her nipples, with the other she probed gently between her thighs.

After a time, she sighed deeply and stepped out into the bedroom. She crossed to the bed and, bending over, slit open the bag. She took out the bottle of cologne, Chanel No. 19, opened it and dabbed it on her richly glowing skin. Then she stepped into the cream silk teddy she had bought, luxuriating in the feel of the sensuous fabric. This was how Terry would see her when he arrived.

She turned towards the open doorway and a frown creased her brow. Darkness prevailed there and, while it was night now, the sunset having slipped away while she was in the shower, she was certain she had turned on the lights there when she had come in. Or had she? She shrugged and went through the doorway.

Half way to the small porcelain lamp on the table next to the sofa, she paused, turning her head. Had there been some movement in the room to her extreme left? Now she saw only clumps of dense shadows. Outside, a cat yowled twice as if it were being skinned alive, then there was the brief clatter of metal garbage-can lids in the cement alley at the side of the house, coming clear through the wall. The music was still playing. Henry Mancini. A bitter-sweet melody that she knew ended the side of the record. Mancini was so romantic.

She crossed to the table and pressed the switch; the lights in the bedroom went out. She turned round, oblivious for a moment of the fact that the lamp had not lit. The music was over and she was conscious of the minute sounds of the tone arm lifting, setting down on its cradle and the turn-table stopping. There was only one sound now, very close to her, and she realized that it was her harsh breathing.

'Is anyone there?' She felt foolish.

The total absence of sound was infinitely more frightening than if she had heard a voice reply. She looked down at the glowing dial of her watch and all she could think of was: Terry will be home soon.

As if drawn towards the unknown, she went slowly across the living-room until she was standing at the doorway. She peered in, trying to see in the gloom; the curtains were closed and here, at the back of the house, the trees of the back yard intervened behind the closed windows, the working air-conditioner, vitiating the lamps from the neighbouring houses.

She went into the bedroom, her hand feeling along the wall for the light-switch. But before she got to it, she heard the click of the stereo from the other room; heard, after a tiny delay, Mancini's piano and the double bass begin a jazz duet. Soon the drums joined them and then the strings. Last of all was the sax, a crying, almost human voice among the myriad instruments. The music was filled with tension.

She whirled towards the doorway, could not see through it. Something or someone blocked her view. She took a step forward and gasped as something slithered towards her in a blur, wrapped itself around her right wrist.

Crying out inarticulately, she stumbled backwards. She flung up her arm in an attempt to free herself but the thing – whatever it was – followed her silently, relentlessly; the grip on her wrist tightened until she thought her bones might break.

'What do you want?' she said inanely. 'What do you want?' Her mind, numbed by fear, could think of nothing else to say. It was as if the night, through some magical incantation, had become a sentient being.

She felt the edge of the bed against the backs of her knees and, as if this solid barrier brought her back to reality, she launched herself forward. She did not believe in ghosts, not even in the *kami* of her ancestors, as tangible objects able to grasp out at the living. Her mouth opened and she bared her teeth, ready to bite into whatever had hold of her.

She felt the solidness of pressure in front of her and bit down. But at that moment her head was jerked backwards and upwards and her teeth snapped together painfully.

'Oh, my God!' she heard herself say. It seemed to come from another world.

She stared into a face. The head, as, she supposed, was the body, swathed in matt black fabric. A tight hood and a mask that left only the eyes exposed. These were no more than six inches from her own. They were as dead as stones in a pond.

'Oh, my God!' She felt so vulnerable, bent back in a grip she had no hope of breaking, and this, more than anything else, terrified her.

When he moved he was upon her before she could even cry out. She felt his grip shift and it seemed that she was in the grasp of something elemental, like a whirlwind, a force of nature. For surely no man – nothing that was human – could have so much power.

Where his gloved fingers dug into her, they seemed to dissolve her flesh and pulverize the bone beneath. All air was abruptly gone from her lungs; it felt as if she had been thrust to the bottom of the sea. Her insides turned to water. Death rose up on all sides like a spectre on an enormous poster. Her gorge rose and she tried to vomit. She retched pathetically against the restraint to her mouth. She tried to swallow and could not. Her eyes were blurry with tears. She blinked wildly, began to choke on her own vomit.

His face was quite close to hers, but it was as if she had been attacked by an inanimate object suddenly given life. She could smell nothing, see nothing; she had no clue as to what he was feeling, what he might want. She could not even turn her head from side to side, so intense was his grip upon her. Still she struggled merely to swallow and she did, given life once more. But now she saw before her the sloping mountainside in the south of Japan where she had stayed as a child during the last days of the war. She saw as clearly as if she were there again the tall stately pines swaying in the westerly winds, the straggle of *sokaijin* toiling up the long slope, a thin battered line, an exhausted snake that seemed to have no end, no beginning, merely one vast body. She thought of the *zōsui*, the vegetable stew, which had become their staple; the taste of it was strong in her mouth, the smell of the mountain turnips filled her nostrils. She had never thought that she would recall them with such full-bodied accuracy; it was in the nature of human beings to remember pleasure with more clarity than pain.

There was swift movement above her and her silk teddy shredded, parting from her body. She was naked now. Her mind was filled up with Terry now because she was quite certain that this terrifying being would rape her; this secret knowledge of why he had come outraged her and calmed her at the same time. Death seemed to stand away, only a visitor at this feast instead of the guest of honour.

She felt his body over hers, not hot, not cool, but somewhere in between. His was not flesh, but neither was it marble. She felt somehow as if she were being lifted into a cradle, the position familiar. She closed her legs, locking her ankles, resisting him still.

So it was with a great sense of shock that she felt him grasp the pool of her thick hair, pulling it up, winding it with one hand into a long twisted cord.

She stared upwards, above her head. There was sufficient light for her to see it, standing straight as a sword, blacker than the night.

Then, guided by him, it came down, wrapped around her neck. Until, nooselike, it began to tighten about her throat, however, she failed to understand what was about to happen. But as she fought for every breath, her nostrils flaring because his other hand still covered her mouth, she knew that her body was far from his mind. Was he hard? Would he come? Her mind was like a pond filled with squirming eels, monstrously debating these lewd questions while her lungs filled less and less with air.

*No! Please! Take me, don't kill me! Don't! Please!* She tried to scream what her mind formed but the words only came out as animal grunts, further terrifying her. It was as if his inhumanity had somehow managed to strip her of her humanity.

The cord of her hair tightened as he heaved on it, arcing his back precisely as if he were making violent love to her. The muscles of her throat spasmed involuntarily; her lungs burned as if with a corrosive. *This can't be happening*, she thought. *I can't die. I won't! No no no no – !*

And then she was fighting, fighting to perform the most basic of functions which had become as difficult as climbing a mountain. Each breath was the most desperate of struggles.

She fought like a tigress, clawing at him with her nails, punching and slashing, using her knees and thighs in an effort to dislodge him, to deflect him from his monomaniacal purpose, but it was as useless as if she were fighting a brick wall. She was powerless against him. He was beyond the living. He was death.

As she choked on her own vomit, rising again like an inexorable *tsunami*, before her eyes bloomed the final firestorm. As her lungs filled with fluid, as she laboured still for life, Eileen heard clearly the whistling, abrupt and diabolical, directly over her head and, looking skyward, saw the shadow of the lone bomber, coming like an unexpected eclipse, riding before the sun, saw part of it falling away towards the earth, as if it had contemptuously defaecated on the Floating Kingdom, blossoming like a black flower in the bright blue and white sky.

Concussion. The furnace heat of hell. And light like the core of ten thousand exploding suns. Oh, my poor country!

Ashes, floating in the hot wind.

Terry said *sayonara* to Vincent through the taxi's opened window. The day's rain had given the city no relief from the sultry heat and humidity of midsummer. It reminded him of Tokyo.

'I'll call you soon,' he told Vincent.

'Right. Let me know if you have any ideas.' Vincent leaned his elbows on the sill of the window.

Terry laughed. 'I still think you and Nick are making more of this than is there.'

'We aren't making up that poison, Terry,' the other said seriously. 'Or the *katana* wound.'

'I don't know, buddy. There are an awful lot of madmen in this city. What would a ninja be doing here, anyway?'

Vincent shrugged, having no good answer.

'See?'

'Hey, Mac,' the cabdriver growled, turning around. 'Time is money and I ain't got all night. If you're gonna gab why doncha do it on the street, huh?'

'Okay,' Terry said, 'we're off.' He turned his face sideways, smiled and waved to Vincent as the cab pulled away from the kerb.

He gave the driver his address and settled back in the seat. Somehow he regretted not telling his friend about the visitor to his *dōjō* in greater detail. He might have, he supposed, if they had not got so involved in this case that Vincent had been drawn into. Trust him to fabricate something like this. It was the kind of mystery that was just up his alley. Vincent was, Terry suspected, quite bored. Not so much with his job — there were, God knew, enough mysteries there to hold his attention. No, it was more that he was bored with being in

133

America. Perhaps he wanted to go home.

With this, his thoughts turned to Eileen, waiting for him at home. At last all obstacles were washed away. Patience, my *sensei* used to tell me, can often be one's most important weapon. You are too impetuous, my boy. Slow down and enjoy the pace which you yourself set. Abruptly, he remembered the caviar.

He leaned forward, his mouth near the grille bolted to the thick scarred plastic partition separating him from the driver. 'Hey!' he called. 'I forgot. I've got to make a stop at the Russian Tea Room before you take me to the address I gave you.'

The driver cursed and shook his head. 'I'm gettin' 'em tonight all right. Couldn't y've told me soona, fella? Now I gotta go back down Ninth an' cut ova – right into the teeth of th' traffic.' He spun the wheel and, squealing, the cab swerved in mid-flight. There came the answering blare of horns, mingled with shouts and the screech of jammed-on brakes. Terry's driver leaned out of the window and shot his finger into the air. 'Fuck off, y'sonsabitches!' he cried. 'Why doncha learn how tuh drive, yuh assholes yuh!'

Terry took out a pencil and a piece of paper on the way over to the Russian Tea Room, found himself writing down the name, *Hideoshi*. Then, after it, *Yodogimi* and, finally, *Mitsunari*. When he had finished, he stared at what he had written as if they were alien scratchings found on the side of a hill.

The cab jerked to a halt and the driver turned to him. 'Do me a favour, Mac. Don't leave me standin' here holdin' my dick, know what I mean?'

Terry shoved paper and pencil in his pocket and hurriedly left the cab.

It took him only a few minutes to place his order with the *maître d'hôtel* and pay for his two ounces of fresh Beluga. When he returned to the cab, the driver took off as if they were being chased by hijackers. 'Get's so yuh can't tell any more,' he said, eyeing Terry in the rear-view mirror, 'know what I mean? Guys come into the cab lookin' as straight as can be. They ask yuh to stop and right away they take a powder, couldn't find 'em with a battalion, know what I mean? Used tuh be able to tell, years ago; not now. Want me tuh go through the park?'

'Sure,' Terry said. 'Yeah. That'll be fine.'

It did not take long; the park was as still as a tomb, seeming detached from the surrounding sparkle of the high-rise buildings, pristine in the darkness.

He went up the steep stone stairs of the brownstone, whistling softly. He was half way to the third floor landing when he began to discern the Mancini music coming through the door of his apartment. He smiled to himself, feeling warm and confident. Ei loved Mancini.

He turned the key in the lock and went in.

Immediately he knew that he must get into the bedroom. He slammed the door and was in perfect darkness, crouched, then rolling and scrambling across the living-room.

He had smelled/seen/tasted/felt the differences in the apartment and had acted accordingly. He had heard nothing save the music. Mask, he thought. I might otherwise have stopped before I even opened the door. I'm certain I would have. Goddamn that music!

Eileen! his mind cried out just as he was hit.

He was perhaps three-quarters of the way to the half-open doorway to the bedroom. He was struck viciously four times in the first second of the attack. He blocked three blows successfully but that allowed the fourth to get through. It smashed into him just above his right kidney. All the breath went out of him and he keeled over as his leg went numb. He rolled awkwardly across the floor, simultaneously aware of the low light seeping out of the bedroom and a heavy sweetish scent.

A blow whistled through the air near his left ear but he was already rolling away from it. The edge of a table exploded against the side of his face, shards chattering through the air like angry insects. He drew his legs up, kicked out with the soles of both feet in concert. He grunted with the effort, heard an answering sound and then he was up and running as best he could, his right leg dragging a bit behind him.

He went through the doorway at full speed, grabbing its edge as he did so, slamming it to behind him. He turned

135

around thinking: Time. I've got to have time.

The broken figure, one leg still upon the bedspread, drove all rational thought from his mind. His legs turned to water and he felt as if the searing edge of a knife blade were prowling through his guts.

Her face was shadowed and dark, shrouded by wayward tendrils of the night-black hair wound tightly around her neck. Her arms were flung upwards, over her head; her breasts were covered in vomit. His eyes were drawn to the dark patch between her thighs. There were no marks on her body.

He did not have to touch her to know that she was dead but he bent to it anyway because part of his mind said that he must be absolutely certain. He cradled her head in his lap until he heard the sound from beyond the door.

Almost unseeing, he got up, crossed to the opposite wall. His cold fingers closed upon the cool lacquered leather of the slightly curved scabbard that hung on his wall. He brought it to him with great deliberation; the whisper of the naked blade as he unsheathed it was the loudest sound he had ever heard. Louder even than the splintering of the wooden door as it buckled inwards under the enormous force of the karate kick.

The ebon figure stood in the doorway, the *bokken* in his left hand; his right was empty. It was not until this ultimate moment of their confrontation that Terry allowed the thought to surface as a reality. He trembled involuntarily.

'Ninja,' he whispered. He barely recognized his own voice, so clogged was it with emotion. 'You have chosen death in coming here.'

He leaped upon the intervening bed, striking forcefully with his *katana*. It was, he realized instantly, a stupid move, for there was no solid support and therefore not nearly enough power behind the momentum of his strike.

Deftly, with almost no effort, the ninja avoided his strike without even lifting his *bokken*; no need to cross swords, he was saying. You are not even good enough for that.

The ninja whirled away into the darkness of the living-room and Terry had no choice but to follow. Dimly he knew that he was playing into the other's hand; that the background of battle was just as important as the battle itself. He sprinted over Eileen's corpse, his heart constricting, his blood turned to ice. To hell with it! he thought rashly. I can defeat him on any ground. Thus, in his sorrow and his rage, he turned away from all he had been so painstakingly taught.

In the living-room, where Mancini played on obliviously, he saw limned the outline of the *bokken* and immediately went after it.

But the ninja was already in motion, on the attack, and Terry lifted his *katana* into the darkness, bracing for the expected force of the blocked blow against his blade. Thus he was totally unprepared for the violently percussive shock against his exposed chest. He was flung back more than five feet as if by an explosion. He staggered, his ribs and sternum on fire. He ached all the way up to his jaw. 'What – ?' he coughed, confused.

The ninja was again a blur, driving in again. Terry instinctively raised his *katana*, though he was unsure of the point of attack; his vision seemed blurred.

A second blow came against his chest and he flew backwards, going down on one knee. The *katana* in his right hand seemed to weigh as much as a human body. His lungs laboured and he was disoriented.

The third blow hit him just as he had staggered to his feet. This time he perceived what was occurring even as he was slammed back into the wall. He heard rather than felt a crack as if a roof beam had given out and he felt a curious wetness on his left side. Ribs, he thought dully, his seething mind still filled with what was happening to him. It was like a dream; no possible reality could be so fantastic.

Another blow bounced him off the wall and the *katana* pinwheeled from his grasp, a dead star whirling through space. He glanced down at himself, saw the fractured ribs protruding through his rent flesh. The blood was black as ink, running out of him like tap-water down a drain.

It was straight out of the *Go Rin No Sho*. It was the classic Body Strike of which Musashi wrote. Strike with the left shoulder, he wrote, with the spirit resolved, until the enemy is dead. Learn this well. The ninja had, Terry reflected almost disinterestedly. He cared little for his own life now, not with

Eileen lying dead in the next room. But to kill this monster, yes, this still had substance for him.

He began to move forward, up the wall, then off it. But his body refused to respond quickly. He reeled, his eyes on the moving ninja, crossing his arms in front of him to ward off the blow.

It had no effect. He crashed backwards with a grunt of pain, his sternum splintered from the enormous force of the repeated blows. The bone shot through his body as effectively as shrapnel. He looked up once from where he was huddled against the moulding, into the eyes like stones, thinking, Musashi was right after all. The softly swaying Mancini music rang in his ears, recalling Eileen to him. Her warmth suffused him like a lighted fuse, burning its way through him until it reached his brain.

Blood came out of his mouth as he called to her in a voice as fragile as rice paper. 'Eileen,' he called. 'I love you.' His head lolled and his eyes slid shut.

The ninja stood dominant in that black void, seeming scarcely to breathe. He stared at the body before him without emotion. For long moments his senses quested for any sound out of the ordinary. At length, satisfied, he turned away, moving silently across the room. From beneath the sofa he drew out his duffel bag and, drawing open the zipper, carefully placed his *bokken* next to its brother on the top of the contents. In one motion he had closed the bag and hefted it, quitting the apartment without a backward glance.

Behind him, Mancini played on, the slow bitter-sweet melody hinting at lost love, cascading through the room. A deep groan escaped from Terry's cracked lips as he coughed more blood. He lifted his head and, blindly, began to crawl towards the bedroom, not even understanding why, knowing only that he must.

Inch by agonizing inch he moved, crossing the threshold at last, stopping only when he lay panting, drooling blood, beside Eileen's corpse.

Before his face was a cord and, reaching up, he yanked on it. The phone crashed down onto his left shoulder but he was beyond feeling this minute drop within the vast pool of pain that encompassed him. His finger trembling, he dialled seven slow digits. The ringing of the receiver was like the tolling of a far-off temple bell.

But Eileen seemed suddenly so far away from him and he knew she needed him. The receiver slipped through his wet fingers. He crawled across the last miles.

'Hello?' It was Vincent's voice that came dimly through the abandoned instrument. 'Hello? Hello!'

But there was no one now to hear him. Terry lay face down on the black fan of Eileen's hair, his eyes open, unseeing and already glazing over, the blood like a second tongue moving from his lips to hers.

In the living-room, the music was finished.

# II

## *Tokyo Suburbs, Spring 1959-Spring 1960*

'Look here, Nicholas,' the Colonel said one dark and dismal afternoon. Storm clouds hid the crown of Mount Fuji and, occasionally, forked lightning lit the sky; afterwards, the distant roll of thunder.

The Colonel, in his study, had in his hands a lacquered box. On its top was painted a dragon and a tiger, entwined. Nicholas recognized it as the parting gift to his mother and father from So-Peng.

'It is time, I think, for you to see this,' the Colonel said. He picked up his pipe and a zippered pouch of moist tobacco, digging both pipe and forefinger into its depths, filling it. Striking a kitchen match on the edge of his desk, he drew strongly on the pipe, getting it going to his satisfaction before continuing. His long forefinger tapped the top of the box, the tip tracing the lines of the two creatures emblazoned there.

'Nicholas, do you know the symbolic meanings of the dragon and the tiger in Japanese mythology?'

Nicholas shook his head.

The Colonel blew out a cloud of blue aromatic smoke, gripped the pipe-stem with his teeth at one corner of his mouth. 'The tiger is lord of all the land and the dragon, well, he is emperor of the air. Curious, that, I've always thought. The flying serpent, Kukulkān, of Mayan mythology, though he was depicted as being feathered, was also lord of the air. Interesting that two cultures so far from each other should share a major slice of mythology, don't you think?'

'But why did So-Peng give you a Japanese box?' Nicholas asked. 'He was Chinese, wasn't he?'

'Uhm, a good question,' the Colonel said, puffing away. 'One to which, I am afraid, I do not have a satisfactory answer. It is true that So-Peng was Mandarin, but only half so. He made it clear to me that his mother was Japanese.'

'Still, that doesn't explain the box,' Nicholas pointed out. 'It's true enough that you were going to Japan, but this box is ancient, not easily acquirable, especially at that time.'

'Yes,' the Colonel replied, stroking the lid, 'there is little doubt that this had been in his family – quite probably brought by his mother to China – for some time. Now why should So-Peng give this to us? I mean this specific item. Surely it was no whim; he was not that kind of man. Nor do I think it was mere coincidence.' The Colonel rose now and stood by the rain-streaked window. Condensation had made the panes into frosted decorations; winter's chill had not totally been left behind.

'I pondered this for a long time,' the Colonel said, staring out of the windows. He rubbed a small oval, clearing a line of sight as if he were carefully looking out of a besieged fortress's apertures. 'All the way from Singapore to Tokyo, in fact. So-Peng had asked us not to open the present until we had reached Japan and we respected this request.

'At Haneda Airport, we were met by a contingent of SCAP personnel – we had, of course, flown over in a military transport. However, someone else was waiting for us when we landed. Certainly your mother recognized her immediately and so did I, just by the description I had been given by Cheong of her dream. It was Itami and she looked precisely as your mother had dreamed she did.' He shrugged. 'Somehow, I was not amazed. One grows used to such ... phenomena, here; it's a part of life in the Far East, as I've no doubt you will soon learn.

'I was curious, the *rapport* your mother had with Itami. It was as if they had known each other all their lives; as if they were sisters, rather than sisters-in-law. There was absolutely no culture shock as there might have been when a young girl brought up in a tiny Chinese village meets for the first time a grand lady of urban Japanese society. Now this was so even though your mother and Itami are totally different kinds of people.' The Colonel turned around to face his son. 'All the differences you see in them – the warmth in your mother, the steel-like aloofness of Itami; the happiness of your mother, the sadness of your aunt – none of these differences mattered to either of them.

'This, too, I thought about for some time and what I decided was this: although So-Peng told me in so many words that he possessed no knowledge of Cheong's true heritage, yet his present was an oblique way of telling me otherwise.'

'You mean Mother is Japanese.'

'Perhaps part Japanese.' He came and sat down next to his son, putting one hand on his shoulder lovingly. 'But, Nicholas, this is something you must promise never to discuss with anyone, even your mother. I tell you now because – well, because it was information passed on to me. So-Peng believed it was important, therefore it must be, though I myself put little stock in that sort of thing. I am English and a Jew, yet my heart is with these people. My blood sings with their history, my soul resonates with theirs. What use is my lineage to me? I want to make this quite clear to you, Nicholas. I did not renounce my Jewish name; I merely dropped it away. Now I suppose it can be argued that this is the same thing. Not so! I did this not by choice but by necessity. England, as a rule, does not like Jews; never has done so. I found, when I changed my name, many doors opened to me that had hitherto been quite shut. There's a moral question to be answered here, I know. Should one attempt to go through? Yes, say I, and devil take the hindmost. But that's my view. And while my soul is with the Japanese, I am neither Buddhist nor Shinto. These religions hold no particular meaning for me, save for scholarly study. In my heart, I have never renounced my Jewishness. Six thousand years of struggle cannot so easily be bought out. The blood of Solomon and David, of Moses, runs in your veins, too. Never forget that. Whether you choose to do anything about it is purely your concern; I would not tamper with so private a matter. Yet it is my duty to tell you, to give you the facts, as it were. I hope you understand this.' He gazed solemnly at his son for a long moment before he opened the tiger and dragon box, the last gift of the enigmatic So-Peng.

Nicholas looked down, stared into the brilliant fire of sixteen half-inch cut emeralds.

*

Nicholas had been studying bujutsu for nearly seven years now and still felt as if he knew almost nothing. He was strong and his reflexes superb; he went through the drills and exercises with a great deal of concentration and assiduousness but without any special love or feeling. This surprised and concerned him. He had been fully prepared for the hard work, the difficulty, for it was exactly this kind of effort which interested and absorbed him the most. What he had not reckoned on was any indifference on his part. It was not, he reflected one day during floor exercises at the *dōjō*, that he had in any way changed his mind about wanting to learn bujutsu. In fact, if anything, this desire had increased. It was – well, very difficult to put. Perhaps there was no spark there.

Perhaps it was his instructor. Tanka was a stolid, solidly built man who believed a great deal in repeated movements and, it seemed, nothing else. Over and over, Nicholas was obliged to perform the same manoeuvre. Again and again until he felt that the sequence had been engraved upon his brain and nerves and muscles. It was boring work and he hated it. Hated, too, the fact that Tanka treated them as if they were children not yet ready for the adult world.

Ever and again, he would find himself looking over to the far side of the *dōjō* where Kansatsu, the *ryu*'s master, taught individual classes with a select few of the older students. He longed to be there instead of *here* on the dung-heap of unspecialized exercises.

He had come to join the same *ryu* as Saigō – as had been said, through Itami's intervention – and it galled him further that his cousin, being older and having joined the *ryu* earlier than Nicholas, was thus far ahead. This point Saigō brought up to him at every opportunity. At the *dōjō* he was openly contemptuous of Nicholas – as were many of the other students, because of his occidental aspect, feeling that bujutsu, being one of the most traditional and sacred of Japanese institutions, should not be open to a *gaijin*, a foreigner – and never referred to Nicholas as his cousin. However, at home it was quite another matter. He was scrupulously careful to be polite to Nicholas. For his part, Nicholas had given up trying to talk the matter out with Saigō after the third unsuccessful attempt.

Truth to tell, Saigō was a thorn in Nicholas's side at the *dōjō*. When he could have been so much help to the other, he invariably went out of his way to make everything more difficult, even going so far as to become the unofficial ringleader of the 'opposition'.

One evening, the work over with and the showers taken, Nicholas was dressing when five or six of the boys came up in ones and twos until they had surrounded him.

'What are you doing here?' said one of the largest boys. 'This is where we sit.'

Nicholas said nothing, continuing to dress. Outwardly he took no notice, but inwardly his heart was beating like a trip-hammer.

'Don't you have anything to say?' said another boy. He was small and younger than the others but was seemingly emboldened by their surrounding presence. He laughed derisively. 'Maybe he doesn't understand Japanese. Do you think we'll have to speak to him in English like they do with the apes in the zoo?' Everyone laughed.

'That's right,' the big boy said, picking up the cue. 'I want an answer, ape. Tell us why you're here in our spot, stinking it up like a spot of venereal disease.'

Nicholas stood up. 'Why don't you go off and play somewhere where your jokes will be appreciated.'

'Look, look!' cried the small boy. 'The ape speaks!'

'Shut up!' said the big boy, and then to Nicholas: 'I don't much care for your tone, ape. I think you've just said something you're going to regret.' His right hand chopped downward towards Nicholas's exposed neck without warning. Nicholas blocked it and then they were all crowding into him.

Through the *mêlée* he caught a glimpse of Saigō on his way out, oblivious to the raucous disturbance. He called out his name.

Saigō checked and came over. 'Hold on!' he yelled, shouldering his way through the crowd. He shoved them back against the wall, giving Nicholas some breathing space. 'What's going on here?'

'It's the *gaijin*,' the big boy said, his fists still clenched. 'Making trouble again.'

'Oho, is that so?' Saigō said. 'One against six? Hard to believe.' He shrugged, slammed the edge of his hand into Nicholas's stomach.

Nicholas pitched forward onto his knees, his forehead touching the floor as if in prayer. He retched, tried to fill his bursting lungs with air. He gasped like a fish out of water.

'Don't bother these people any more, Nicholas,' Saigō said, standing over him. 'Where are your manners? But what can you expect, fellows. His father's a barbarian and his mother's a *Chinese*. C'mon.' He led them away, leaving Nicholas alone on the floor with his pain.

She had come with her attenuated procession quite unexpectedly during the middle of the week, throwing the entire household into a state of unmitigated panic, initiated, of course, by Cheong, who felt that the house was never clean enough, the food never fine enough, her family never well dressed enough to suit Itami.

She looked like a tiny doll, Nicholas thought, a perfect porcelain thing to be put on a pedestal inside a glass case, protected from the elements. In fact, Itami needed no such exterior protection; she had a will of iron and the power to promote it, even with her husband, Satsugai.

Nicholas watched clandestinely from another room as Cheong herself performed the elaborate tea ceremony for Itami, kneeling on the tatamis before a green lacquered table. She wore a traditional Japanese robe and her long gleaming hair had been put up with ivory sticks. He thought that, at that moment, she had never looked so beautiful or so regal. She was a far cry from the icy aristocracy of Itami, yet perhaps even because of that he had far more admiration for his mother. Of Itami's kind of woman there were plenty in books of photographs he had seen of an older, pre-war Japan. But oh, Cheong! There were none to touch her. She carried with her a nobility of soul that Itami could never hope to attain, not in this life, at least. Though Itami was strong, her magnetism was nothing compared to Cheong's power, for she wielded an inner tranquillity that was as profound as the utter stillness of a hot summer's day, a living jewel, unique. She was, as Nicholas thought of it, of a whole cloth and this he respected and admired above all else.

He had no great desire to talk to Itami but it would have been very bad manners for him to leave the house without acknowledging her presence; his mother would be furious and, quite naturally, blame herself. This he did not want and thus, some time later in the afternoon, he pulled open the *shōji* and stepped through.

Itami looked up. 'Ah, Nicholas, I did not know that you were home.'

'Good afternoon, Aunt.'

'Excuse me a moment,' Cheong said, getting effortlessly to her feet. 'The tea is cold.' For some reason she would not overtly use the servants when Itami was around. She left them alone and Nicholas began to feel uncomfortable under the mute scrutiny of Itami's gaze.

He went over to the window, gazed out at the forest of cryptomeria and pine.

'Do you know,' said Itami, 'that hidden within that forest is an ancient Shinto shrine?'

'Yes,' Nicholas said, turning round. 'My father told me.'

'Have you seen it?'

'Not yet.'

'And did you know, Nicholas, that within that shrine is a park filled with mosses?'

'Forty different varieties, I think, Aunt. Yes, I know of it but I am told that only the priests of the shrine may look upon it.'

'Perhaps it is not so difficult as that, Nicholas. I cannot imagine you wanting to become a priest. It does not suit you.' She rose, said unexpectedly, 'How would you like to take me there? To the shrine and to the park?'

'When? Now?'

'Certainly.'

'But I thought –'

'All things may be possible, one way or another, Nicholas.' She smiled and called: 'Cheong, Nicholas and I are going for a walk. We won't be long.' She turned back to him and reached out her hand. 'Come,' she said gently.

They walked silently until they came to the verge of the forest. There they turned right along the grass for perhaps two hundred metres, when she abruptly guided him inward. He found that they were on a narrow but well-worn track through the trees and underbrush.

'Well, Nicholas, you must tell me how you like your training at the *dōjō*,' Itami said. She walked carefully in her wooden *geta*, using the point of her lacquered paper parasol as a walking-stick to help balance her on the uneven ground.

'It is very hard work, Aunt.'

'Yes.' She waved a hand as if dismissing this statement. 'But this is not something that you had not anticipated.'

'No.'

'Do you enjoy all the hard work?'

He glanced up at her, wondering what she was getting at. He had absolutely no intention of telling her of the growing animosity between himself and Saigō. That would not do at all. He had not even told his parents. 'At times,' he said. 'I would wish to move on.' He shrugged. 'I am impatient, I suppose.'

'There are times when only the impatient are rewarded, Nicholas,' she said, stepping over a tangled root. 'Here, help me the last few feet, won't you?' She gave him her arm. 'Ah, there we are!'

They were in a clearing, and as they moved out from the shade of the pines, Itami lifted her parasol over her head and opened it. Her skin was as white as snow, her lips deep red, her eyes as dark as nuggets of coal.

The deep lacquered wall of the temple was awash in shimmering sunlight so that he was obliged to squint until his eyes accustomed themselves to the brightness. It was as if he were gazing at a sea of gold.

They began to walk along the crushed limestone gravel, a blue-white stippled path that completely encircled the temple; one could tread it forever, never getting closer to or farther away from one's goal.

'But you have survived,' she said softly. 'That is gratifying.' They had reached the verge of the steep wooden steps up to the bronze and lacquered-wood doors which stood open, shadowed, silent, hunkered down comfortably as if waiting for something or someone to arrive. They paused there. She put a hand on his shoulder, so lightly that if he had not seen it, he might not even have felt its weight there. 'I had grave doubts when your father came to me, requesting that I help gain entrance for you in a suitable *ryu*.' She shook her head. 'I had no choice but to acquiesce and honour dictated that I made no comment of my own, but I was concerned.' She sighed. 'In a way I pity you. How strange your life will be. Westerners will never fully accept you because of your oriental blood and the Japanese will despise you because of your occidental features.' Her hand lifted into the air like a butterfly and her forefinger gave him a fragile and fleeting touch on the point of one cheek. She stared at him. 'Even your eyes are your father's. Her hand dropped to her side; it was as if she had never made the gesture. 'But I am not so easily fooled.' She turned her implacable gaze away from him and said, 'Let us go inside and pray.'

'Beautiful, isn't it?' Itami said.

And he had to agree. They stood beside a slow meandering brook which tumbled down across moss-covered rocks from a height of perhaps two metres, certainly not more. Everywhere was green, even the water, even the pebbles. To Nicholas it looked as though there were four thousand species of moss here instead of the forty.

'And peaceful,' she continued. 'It's so peaceful here. The outside world does not exist. Gone.' She folded her parasol in the shade of the overhanging cryptomeria. She inhaled deeply, her small head thrown back. 'It is as if time itself had dissolved, Nicholas. As if there had been no twentieth century, no expansion, no imperialism – no war.' She closed her eyes. 'No war.' He watched her closely until her eyes flew open, staring. 'But there was a war.' She turned. 'Shall we sit on this stone bench? Good. Perhaps the shōgun – one of the Tokugawas, even – sat just here where we are. There. It gives one a sense of history, does it not? A continuity? A feeling of belonging?' She turned to him. 'But not you, I suspect. Not yet, anyway. We are alike in that respect. Oh, yes we are.' She laughed. 'I see by your expression that you are surprised. You shouldn't be. We are both outsiders, you see, forever cut off from that which we desire the most.'

'But how can that be?' Nicholas protested. 'You are a Nobunaga, a member of one of Japan's oldest and most noble houses.'

Itami smiled at him just the way a predator might and he saw her white even teeth, glistening with saliva. 'Oh yes,' she breathed, 'a Nobunaga, indeed. But that, like a great deal else in Japan, is merely the exterior: the gorgeous lacquered coat which hides the rotting hulk underneath.' Her face was no longer beautiful, squeezed as it was by the anguish she felt. 'Listen well to me, Nicholas. Honour has fled us here; we have allowed ourselves to be corrupted by the Western barbarians. We are a despicable race now; we have done such hideous deeds. How our ancestors must shudder in their graves, how their *kami* must yearn for the final resting rather than the return to this – modern society.'

Her voice had risen somewhat and now Nicholas sat quite still beside her, allowing the air to cool. But she would not or perhaps could not rest now. It had been difficult, he suspected, for her to begin this. But, once she had overcome the initial inertia, nothing could stop her.

'Do you know what the *zaibatsu* are, Nicholas?'

'By name only,' he said, once more uncertain of the ground she had put them on.

'Ask your father to explain the *zaibatsu* to you one day, will you? The Colonel knows a great deal about them and you should know, too.' Then, as if it explained it all, she said, 'Satsugai works for one of the *zaibatsu*.'

'Which one?'

'I hate my husband, Nicholas. And, do you know' – she laughed shortly – 'only your father knows why. It is so ironic. But life is ironic. It's a devil withholding from you what you desire the most.' Her tiny hands were clenched like baby fists in her lap. 'What good being a noble Nobunaga when I must forever carry with me the shame of my great-grandfather? My shame is as inescapable to me as your mixed blood is to you.

'My great-grandfather left the service of the shōgun when he was twenty-eight to become a *ronin* – do you know what that is?'

'A masterless samurai.'

'A warrior without honour, yes. A brigand, a thief. He turned mercenary, selling his strong capable arm to the highest bidder. Enraged by this unseemly and dishonourable behaviour, the shōgun sent men out into the countryside to track him down, and when they finally did, they adhered to the order given by the shōgun. No *seppuku* for my great-grandfather; the shōgun would not grant him an honourable way to die. He was carrion now; no longer a *bushi*. They crucified him as they did the scum of the land.

'In most of those cases, the offender's entire family is destroyed – the women and all the children so that his family line, his most prized possession, would be stripped from him. Not this time, however.'

'Why?' Nicholas asked. 'What happened?'

Itami shrugged and smiled wanly. 'Karma. My karma which forms the backbone of my life. I rebel against it; it makes me ache, and at night I cry. I am ashamed to say that. I am a *bushi*, a samurai woman, even in this day and age. Some things time cannot alter. My blood seethes with ten thousand battles; my soul resonates to the sweep of the *katana*, its blade, its fearful shades of steel.'

She stood up, the parasol blossomed like an enormous flower. 'One day you will understand this. And remember. It is difficult now at the *ryu*. Do not interrupt me. I know. But you must never give it up. Do you hear me? Never.' She turned away from him, the soft pastels of the parasol blotting out the smouldering passion in her black eyes. 'Come,' he heard her say. 'It is time we returned to the world.'

'This is *Ai Uchi*,' said Muromachi. He was holding a *bokken* in his hands. Seven students, Nicholas's group, stood in a precise semicircle around him. 'Here at the Itto *ryu*, it is the first teaching; the first of hundreds. *Ai Uchi* means cut the opponent just as he cuts you. It is the timing you will learn here, the one that is basic to kenjutsu. One which you will never forget. *Ai Uchi* is lack of anger. It means to treat an opponent as if he were an honoured guest. It means to abandon your life or to throw away fear. *Ai Uchi* is the first technique and it is the last. Remember that. It is the Zen circle.'

This was the lesson Nicholas had first been taught upon arriving at the *ryu* seven years ago. He did not fully understand it yet he never forgot it. And in the time that followed, as he practised with a cold fury the thousand cuts of the *katana* under Muromachi's tutelage; as he learned the moral teaching of kenjutsu; as the knowledge piled itself upon him with dizzying rapidity, he was ever to think of that first lesson and, in pondering it, feel a calmness, stepping into the eye of the storm each time that storm threatened to overwhelm him.

And he repeated the thousand cuts over and over, feeling as if his arms and his legs were wearing grooves into the air until, at last, his reward manifested itself, when his sword became no sword, his intention became no intention and he knew that that first lesson given to him by Muromachi so long ago was, in fact, the highest knowledge.


Still, he was not satisfied. He was thinking of this late one afternoon when he felt a presence in the room. He looked up but saw no one. The room was deserted and yet he could not get it out of his mind that someone was there. He stood up and was about to call out when he thought it might again be several of the boys lying in wait for him and he kept quiet, not wanting to give them any degree of satisfaction.

He began to move around the room in the dusk. The far side of the empty *dōjō* was streaked with dusty sunlight as red as blood, washed in the industrial haze lying low, its tendrils creeping up Fuji's majestic slopes. Rapidly, his assessment changed. While he was quite certain now that someone was there with him, it also came to him that this person meant him no harm. How he had come to this conclusion he could not have said; it was, rather, a purely automatic response.

Light spilled into the corner of the *dōjō*, touching the edge of the clear-lacquered wooden railing, a fat slice of the raised platform behind it, leaving in dense shadow the corner beam. He was watching this pattern of light and shade when a voice said, 'Good evening, Nicholas.'

The corner shadow had come to life, a figure stepping out

of its concealing pocket, into the light. It was Kansatsu.

He was a thin, slight man, his stiff bristly hair already white. He had eyes that never appeared to move yet took in everything at once.

He made absolutely no sound as he came down off the platform to stand in front of Nicholas who, bare to the waist, felt totally tongue-tied. Kansatsu had barely said three words to him since he had come to the *ryu*. Now they were here together, and Nicholas understood enough to know that the meeting was not accidental.

He saw Kansatsu eyeing him, then the man stepped forward, his outstretched forefinger touching the purple and blue bruise just beneath Nicholas's sternum on the left side.

'These are very bad times for Japan,' Kansatsu said. 'Very sad times.' He looked up. 'The war was joined because of economics and our imperialism dictated that we expand beyond our islands.' He sighed. 'But the war was ill-advised for all that, for it stemmed from greed, not honour. The new Japanese *adds* the gloss of *bushido* to his actions, I am afraid, rather than allowing his actions to evolve from it.' His eyes were sad. 'And now we pay the price. We are overrun by Americans, our new Constitution is American and the entire thrust of the new Japan is to serve the American interests. So strange, so strange for Japan to serve such a master.' He shrugged. 'But, you see, no matter what happens to Japan, *bushido* will never completely perish. We begin to wear Western business suits, our women wear their hair in the American manner; we adopt the Western ways. These things do not matter. The Japanese is like the willow, bending in the wind so that it should not break. These are merely outward manifestations of our desire now for parity in the world. So, too, do the Americans unwittingly serve our purpose, for, with their money, we shall rise more powerful than ever. Yet we must ever look to our tradition, for only *bushido* makes us strong.

'You wish to become one of us,' he said abruptly. 'But this' – he pointed to the bruise that had been inflicted by Saigō – 'tells me that you have not been entirely successful.'

'Success will come in time,' Nicholas said. 'I am learning not to be impatient.'

Kansatsu nodded. 'Good. Very good. Yet one must take the necessary steps.' He put his fingertips together in front of him, began to walk slowly across the *dōjō* with Nicholas beside him. 'I think it is time that you began to work with other *sensei*. I do not want you to give up your very valuable work with Muromachi; rather I want to add to your current schedule.

'Tomorrow you will begin to work with me,' he said, leading Nicholas across the darkened room, 'in *haragei*.'

Nicholas would always separate his relationship with Satsugai into two distinct sections. The specific point of demarcation was the *zaibatsu* party he attended with his parents. It was, of course, quite possible that this changing perception was strictly a function of his own growing up. On the other hand, he had tended to believe that it was just as much a matter of what transpired there that night.

Satsugai was not a large man, either in terms of height or of bulk. Yet for all that he was nevertheless quite remarkable. He was massive through chest and belly, with squat legs and arms that appeared to be far too short for his body. His head seemed to be cemented onto his shoulders without the benefit of an intervening neck. His head was a perfect oval covered on top by jet black hair cut *en brosse* which, to Nicholas at least, added to his military bearing. His face was flat but not in a typically Japanese manner. His eyes, for instance, were distinctly almond-shaped and as glossily black as hard chips of obsidian but they slanted upwards at their outer corners and this oddity, combined with his flat, high cheek-bones and the deep yellow colours of his skin, bespoke his Mongol heritage. Nicholas could think of him, without much difficulty at all, as some reincarnation of Genghis Khan. This was not so outlandish as it at first might seem for, recalling his history, Nicholas brought to mind the Mongol invasions of Japan in 1274 and 1281. Fukuoka, in the south, was their chief target because of its nearness to the Asian shore. Satsugai, Nicholas knew, had been born in the Fukuoka district and though he was, in all ways, purely Japanese – tradition-minded, wholly reactionary – who could say that his ancestors had not been among those most feared mounted nomads?

One might think that, in giving all these particulars of his physical appearance, one should thus be able to define the man. Not so, however. Satsugai was, quite clearly, an individual who was born to lead. Being a native of a land dedicated to the ideal of duty to the group – family elders, the *daimyo* and, ultimately, the shōgun who represented the concept of Japan more forcefully and in a much more real sense than did the Emperor for a span of some two hundred and fifty years – he was nevertheless forever a man apart. Outwardly, quite naturally, this was not so, for he was totally dedicated to Japan, *his* Japan, and to this end he belonged to many groups, not merely one of the *zaibatsu* conglomerates. Yet it became manifestly clear to Nicholas on the night of the party that, inwardly, Satsugai believed himself superior to others. This, curiously enough, was at least part of the basis for his ability in leadership. The Japanese were born followers; they had been bred to follow with blind obedience the dictates of the shōgun even unto death. Was it so surprising then that Satsugai should find a wide following of fanatic supporters? It was a subtle pillow upon which he slept – had Caesar done otherwise? – but none the less it was a prime motivational factor in his life.

Always Itami was by his side. Near him, too, was Saigō as if he were bathing in the energy of a companion sun. However, that night there was a fourth person with them and, from the first moment he saw her, she captivated Nicholas. He leaned over, asked his mother who the girl might be.

'That is Satsugai's niece. From the south,' Cheong said. 'She has come for a brief visit.' By her tone of voice Nicholas could tell that, as far as Cheong was concerned, the visit could not be brief enough. He meant to ask her why it was she disliked the girl but already Satsugai had her in tow and was introducing her to Cheong and the Colonel.

She was slim and tall – willowy, a Westerner might call her. Her dark hair was very long; her eyes seemed enormous, liquid and feral. Her skin was like porcelain, possessing an inner glow quite impossible to duplicate via cosmetics. Nicholas thought she was quite stunning. Her name, so Satsugai informed him when he introduced her separately to Nicholas, was Yukio Jokoin.

She had come with Saigō. He made this plain by keeping within her shadow for most of the evening. Though Nicholas tried, he could not tell whether she wanted this attention or not.

For most of the evening he stewed inside himself, debating whether to ask her to dance. He knew that he wanted to do it; he just did not know what waves his action might cause. Not that he was intimidated by Saigō's close princely protection of her, rather he was burdened by the secrecy of the father, whose relationship with the Colonel was stormy at best.

There was no one's counsel he could seek but his own and, in the end, he decided that he was worrying about something that had significance only for him.

Accordingly, he approached them. It was Yukio herself who provided the opening, for she immediately began to ask him questions about Tokyo, which she had not visited for some time; his immediate impression was that she was fairly well confined to Kyoto and its environs.

Saigō, as might be anticipated, took a rather dim view of his interference and was about to voice his displeasure when his father called for him and, reluctantly, he excused himself.

As he led her onto the dance floor, Nicholas had time to admire her kimono. It was dove-grey with platinum-coloured threads running through it. It was embroidered with the design of a midnight-blue wheel-and spoke pattern typical of the standard of a *daimyo* in feudal times.

She seemed weightless as they danced to the slow music and, holding her close, he felt the heat from her body, the subtle shifting of her flesh beneath the thin kimono.

'We two are both too young to remember the war,' she said, her voice husky. 'Yet we are so much affected by it. Doesn't that seem odd to you?'

'Not really.' He was breathing in the musk of her skin and it seemed to him as if her very sweat were perfumed. 'Isn't history continuous? Incidents don't happen in a vacuum but cause ripples spreading outward, interacting with other ripples, changing their courses and, in turn, being themselves changed.'

'My, what philosophy.' And he thought that she might be mocking him until she laughed and said, 'But I like that theory. Do you know why? No? Because it means that what we do here will affect our histories.'

'What, you mean us?'

'Yes. The two of us. A duo. White and black. Yin and Yang.'

Now while she spoke she had contrived, without Nicholas's being in the least aware, to slide closer to him. Abruptly, as they swayed to the music he found her left leg between his. She pushed discreetly forward and he felt the hot contact with her thigh and then, incredibly, her pubic mound. She continued talking, staring up into his eyes, while she rubbed herself lightly back and forth against him. It was as if they were joined by a hardening fulcrum. Nicholas scarcely dared to breathe lest some precipitous move of his dislodge them from this position. It was an astoundingly intimate gesture, coming as it did in the midst of six hundred or so people, lavishly dressed, still disdainful of new ways or liberal viewpoints. Its highly clandestine nature thrilled him especially when, turning her around, his gaze fell upon Saigō staring at them from the edge of the dance-floor, still engaged in a discussion from which his father would not release him. It was the only time Nicholas would think kindly of the man.

They danced for what seemed like endless moments but when, at length, they parted – with not one word exchanged about the intimacy – he was unaware that he would not see her again for nearly four years.

On Sundays the Colonel slept late. This luxury he permitted himself perhaps because, on a day when he did not work, he was delighted to smash routine to smithereens; though he awoke six mornings a week at precisely six o'clock, he rolled out of bed whenever he wished on that first day of the week.

No one disturbed him then save Cheong, who seemed invulnerable to his infrequent wrath. At times she would stay on the *futon* with him until he was awake but at other times she was up early, working in the kitchen, having shooed the servants away.

Cheong prepared the meals at the week-end. She would have cooked every day, Nicholas knew, because she loved to do it, but the Colonel forbade it. 'Let Tai do the cooking,' he told her somewhat crossly one day. 'That is what she is paid for, after all. Your time should be your own, to do with what you want.' 'Do what?' she had said. 'You know very well what I'm getting at.' 'Who, me?' She pointed to herself. 'Me only ignorant Chinee, Colonel-san.' She said this in pidgin English, though she had superb grasp of that language. She bowed to him over and over. The Colonel was exasperated by her parodies – she was a brilliant mimic, picking up individual accents and idiosyncrasies with astounding rapidity – because they struck so close to reality. He did not like to recall those aspects of the hazed Asian shore so close to them across the *genkainada*: the utter disdain with which the English and the Americans alike treated the Chinese and the Malay; as if they were some subhuman species, suitable only for menial and sexual labours. The Colonel had taken Cheong in his strong sun-browned arms and kissed her hard on the lips, holding her tight around, knowing from experience that this was the only way to silence her, that the expression of his anger would only egg her on.

That particular Sunday morning, Cheong was already up and slicing fresh vegetables when Nicholas came into the kitchen.

Oblique bars of sunlight jazzed the windows, turning them sparkly. The drone of a distant plane could be heard, preparing to land at Haneda. Low on the horizon he could see the flying V of the geese, moving away from the ellipse of the rising sun.

He kissed her and her arms went around him.

'Will you go to the *dōjō* today?' she asked quietly.

'Not if Father will be home.'

She split green beans. 'I think he has a surprise for you today. I was hoping you would decide to stay.'

'I felt I should be here,' he said. 'I wanted to be.'

'There may come a time,' Cheong said without looking up from her cooking, 'when that will not be possible.'

'You mean with Father?'

'No, this applies to you.'

'I don't think I understand.'

'When your father and I left Singapore, So-Peng was al-

157

ready dying. It was to be a relatively slow death and he had much to accomplish before the end. But as he said to me, it would be the last time we would see each other; and he was right.' Her hands moved in a blur along the wooden counter, blithely dissociated from her words. 'I knew that I must take your father and leave Singapore behind forever; our life lay elsewhere; it lay here. But my heart broke at leaving So-Peng. He was my father; so much more than a father and I so much more than a daughter. Perhaps that was so because we had chosen each other; it was our minds rather than our blood that were the same.

'That day, as we left, I paused on the porch of his house as I had done so many times when, as a child, I was about to go out, when So-Peng put a hand on my arm. It was the first and last time he touched me as an adult. Your father was already somewhat ahead on the street. "Now you are me, Cheong," he said to me in the peculiar Mandarin dialect we used only among ourselves in the household.'

'What did he mean?'

'I don't know – I only suspect.' She wiped her hands, dipped them in a bowl of cold lemon water, began to slice again, swiftly and deftly; this time it was cucumbers. 'I cried all the way through the forest until we reached the clearing where the Jeep was parked. Your father, of course, said nothing, though I've no doubt he wanted to; he would not shame me that way.'

'Did you have to leave?' Nicholas asked.

'I did, yes,' she said, for the first time looking up from her work. 'I had my duty to your father. That is my life. I knew it that day and so did So-Peng. It would have been inconceivable to him that I should stay with him, that I should abandon my duty. It could not happen. To abandon duty is to destroy that which makes any individual unique and capable of prodigious feats.

'Duty is the essence of life, Nicholas. It is the only thing over which death has no dominion. It is true immortality.'

As it turned out, the Colonel had the entire day free and, it being spring, he took Nicholas to the Jindaiji Botanical Park in the city for the traditional cherry-blossom viewing.

On the way they dropped Cheong at Itami's; she had promised her she would go with her to see her uncle who was ill.

The morning's haze had lifted and a strong easterly wind had already banished the low-lying mist; wispy cirrus arced like a series of Impressionist paintings newly hung in a museum's vast gallery.

So, too, the park seemed to have been dropped wholesale from out of the heavens. The heavily flowering trees, their long branches bent low under the weight of the palest pink blossoms, took on an ethereal other-worldliness. At other times of the year the park perhaps showed its rather austere beauty. But this was April and the splendour displayed here was breathtaking.

Kimonos and brightly coloured oiled paper parasols were much in evidence as they made their leisurely way along the winding paths beneath the two skies, one low and fragrant, the other far out of reach. They stopped by a vendor selling sweet tofu. The Colonel bought them each a portion and they ate the confection slowly as they moved on. Laughing children passed them, indulged by their parents, and young couples, arm in arm. There were many Americans.

'Father, will you tell me something about the *zaibatsu*?' Nicholas asked.

The Colonel spooned a bit of tofu into his mouth, chewed reflectively. 'Well, I'm sure you know quite a bit already.'

'I know what the *zaibatsu* are,' Nicholas said. 'Four of the largest industrial complexes in Japan. And I know that for a brief time just after the war many of the *zaibatsu*'s top executives were tried for war crimes. I don't really understand that.'

The Colonel was obliged to stoop slightly as they passed beneath low-hanging branches. They might have been flying, passing through rose-coloured banks of clouds. Modern Tokyo seemed never to have existed, to be, rather, a manifestation of some science fiction tale. An Easterner walking here at this time would have no difficulty in understanding this. Symbols abounded in Japan, acquiring their own potency. For the Japanese there was perhaps no more powerful symbol than the cherry blossom. It stood variously for renewal, purification, love and ineffable, timeless beauty: basic concepts to the Japanese spirit. All this passed through the Colonel's mind as he decided where to start.

'As in all things Japanese,' he said, 'the answer is not a simple one. In fact, its origins lie elsewhere: in Japan's long militaristic history. With the beginning of the Meiji Restoration in 1868, Japan made a strong and concerted effort to turn away from both the isolation and the feudalism that marked the two hundred-plus years of the powerful Tokugawa shōgunate. This also meant turning away from the traditionalism which, many felt, was the backbone of Japan's strength.'

They turned off to the right, heading down a shallow incline towards a small lake. The sound of children's voices drifted up to them through the foliage.

'But with this new policy,' the Colonel continued, 'this Westernization, if you will, came, quite naturally, the eroding of the samurai's great power. After all, they had always been Japan's most stalwart traditionalists. Now they were branded reactionaries, for they vigorously opposed all that the Meiji Restoration sought to create. I know that you are well aware that since 1582, when Toyotomi Hideoshi became shōgun, only samurai were allowed to wear two swords – the *katana* was the samurai's province alone. Now this was all changed. The Military Conscription Act forbade the wearing of the *katana* and, by creating a national army composed of 'commoners', effectively did away with the class barrier that had exalted the samurai since its inception in A.D. 792.'

For a time they strolled by the side of the lake, its pure chill blue contrasting with the pink-white of the blossoms. Toy sailboats drifted across the water, their white sails billowing, their tiny captains running gleefully at the verge of the land to keep up with their progress.

'However, the samurai were not so easily beaten,' the Colonel said. The miniature sails, moving so steadfastly over the water, recalled to him perfect prints out of Japan's internecine past. 'A great majority of them fought back directly and, when they were defeated, they formed societies. The main one was called the Genyōsha – the Dark Ocean Society – but there were others such as the Kokuryūkai – the Black Dragon

Society. These societies, which are quite active today, are reactionary organizations that believe strongly in imperialism and a manifest destiny for Japan upon the Asian shore.

'Now the Genyōsha was born in Fukuoka and is based there still. But since that part of Kyūshū is this country's closest approach to the continent, it's not very surprising that the Genyōsha should be most virulent there.'

Nicholas thought of the Mongol invasions, of the violently nationalistic feelings that must have been nurtured there by such precipitous incursions. And this led him back to thoughts of Satsugai.

They found a bench beside the water, sat down. On the far side of the lake a child held a bunch of colourful balloons and, farther away, over the massive treetops, he could see plastered against the sky the quivering fragile presence of a box kite; it was painted in the image of a fire-breathing dragon.

'Having failed in their bid to overthrow the Meiji regime overtly, the members of the Genyōsha next set about subverting the Restoration covertly, from within. They were clever men. They knew that the Meiji oligarchy, which propounded industrialization, would need economic expansion in order to fuel this. To them, this must involve the exploitation and eventual subjugation of China.

'Working within the prescribed political framework of the new Japanese society, the men of the Genyōsha sought to make allies in the highest levels of government. They made their intensive target the members of the General Staff, where a reactionary philosophy was the norm rather than the exception.

'They were aided in this by the upcoming general election of 1882. The Genyōsha made deals with the incumbents. In return for their seeing that these politicians were returned to office, the society was assured that this regime would follow a vigorously imperialistic foreign policy. Accordingly, the Genyōsha hired toughs, importing them into each district of the country. Beatings were not uncommon. It was an election of fear.'

Two American Army officers passed by with their families in tow; they wore their uniforms like a badge of honour, treading the ground like the conquering heroes they were. Perhaps they saw where they were, what went on around them, but surely they understood none of it.

'With the implementation of this policy and the success of Japanese expansion into Manchuria and Shanghai came the vested interests of the Japanese businessman abroad. A growing economy was now crucial to Japan and its rate of growth was prodigious. Out of this cauldron rose the four enormous industrial combines comprising the *zaibatsu*.'

'Then Kansatsu was right when he said that economics must take as much responsibility as militarism for Japan's road to the war,' Nicholas observed thoughtfully.

The Colonel nodded. 'In many ways, Japan was a primitive nation by world standards; the Tokugawas had seen to that. But, on the other hand, they understood perhaps better than any others the purity of their country. But I'm very much afraid it's one of the things that MacArthur missed. Oh, he knew enough about the culture to leave the Emperor just where he had always been despite the hue and cry that he be tried and executed as a war criminal. You see, quite apart from the fact that, from the first, the Emperor had done all in his power to aid the Americans after the war, MacArthur was well aware that any attempt to dethrone him would throw Japan into utter chaos; it was a tradition that even the mighty shōguns dared not tamper with.

'Yet also from the first the Americans propounded the myth that the 'guiding force behind the Japanese war effort came entirely from the military.' He licked at his sticky fingers, took out his pipe. 'Nothing could have been further from the truth. It was the members of the *zaibatsu* who backed the country into a corner from which war became the only viable economic alternative.'

'But what about the Japanese people as a whole?' Nicholas asked. 'Surely they did not want war.'

The Colonel placed his pipe, unlit, between his teeth. He looked up, watching the gentle bobbing of the laden boughs in the wind. 'Unfortunately there is a long history here of the people being led. It comes from being so long in a feudal society, of giving blind obedience to the Emperor, the shōgun, the *daimyo*. It's inbred.' He sat upright, half facing his son on the bench, one hand holding the bowl of his pipe. 'It's not surprising, then, to learn that there was little concerted anti-war sentiment just before the war. In fact, the Social Democrat Party, who had been openly antimilitaristic in their stand when Japan invaded Manchuria, lost much of their constituency in the 1932 general election. It was the tiny but ineradicable Communist Party that became the lone Japanese voice raised against imperialism during that time. It was little more than a reed in a hurricane; the *zaibatsu* and the Genyōsha had efficiently manipulated key individuals in both the government and the media; war became inevitable.'

They both looked up at the sound of running feet. To their left a pair of uniformed policemen rushed down stone steps three at a time, their arms spread wide on either side for balance. People looked up. There was a harsh cry. Children turned; the toy sailboats rocked unattended and unwatched. Several of the American officers hesitated for an instant before taking off after the police. Nicholas and the Colonel stood up and began to drift with the crowd around the left side of the lake.

There was a tour of intervening cherry trees and the foliage was so lush that they could not make out what was happening behind it.

A crowd had formed by the time they arrived, having cut through the grass so as to bypass the crowded steps. Taking Nicholas by the arm, the Colonel shouldered his way through the throng. Already, at the edges, there was some pushing and shoving. The scuffling was brief, however, as more of the metropolitan police arrived on the scene.

The front line of people parted and they saw an expanse of grass like a glade in a forest. There were cherry blossoms scattered upon the grass as if in a hero's welcome home. Nicholas caught a glimpse of a patterned kimono. At first it appeared grey but then, as he was shoved forward by the thrust of the uneasy crowd, he saw that it was composed of thin waved lines of black and white which, at a distance, blended together. It was trimmed in white.

As more policemen pushed themselves through the onlookers, those already in the glade shifted position. As they did so,

Nicholas saw a man kneeling on the grass. His forehead touched the ground littered with blossoms. His right arm was close to his body, the hand invisible within the kimono's folds across his belly. In front of him was a small lacquered rosewood and brass box and a long white strip of silk, partly in shadow.

Behind him, the Colonel gripped Nicholas's shoulders as he said, 'That's Hanshichiro!' He was referring to the great Japanese poet.

Nicholas squirmed to get a better look. He now saw the kneeling man's face between the forest of shifting legs. His hair was iron-grey, his face wide and flat, the features thick. Lines pulled down the corners of his mouth. His eyes were closed. Then Nicholas saw that the silk strip before him was not shadowed but stained. Being porous, it let all the blood through so that it seeped into the earth at Hanshichiro's feet.

'*Seppuku*,' the Colonel said, 'is how it ends for the honourable.'

Nicholas was still thinking of how incredibly ordered it was. He was used to stories of the war; there, death was messy. But here, how serene, how precise, how much like the tide of time it was, while all around its calmness stirred the agitated waters.

'Are you all right, Nicholas?' The Colonel put his hand lightly on his shoulders, looked down at him concernedly.

Nicholas nodded. 'I think so.' He looked up. 'Yes. I guess I am. I feel – a little strange, as if there's been too much to take in suddenly. I – Why did he do it in the park? He wanted everyone to see.'

'To see and take note,' the Colonel said. They had quit the lake, climbing into the heights of the park where the trees blotted out even the surrounding paths. Above, Nicholas could still see the wavering dragon, spitting his fire into the air, as if in defiance of the currents that blew him hither and thither.

'He was a bitter man, firmly embedded in the past. He could never reconcile himself to Japan's new path.' A dark blue baby-carriage filled with pink twins and pushed by a matronly Japanese woman went past them. Hanshichiro was a brilliant artist, obsessed. A man of great honour. This was his way of protesting against Japan's march towards the future, a future which, he felt, would ultimately destroy it.' A young American sailor and his Japanese girl friend approached them from the heights, laughing and clutching each other's hands. The sailor put his arm around the girl, gave her a kiss on the cheek. She giggled and turned her head away. Her hair tossed in the wind, rippling like the dragon's body if he were but articulated.

'There are many others like Hanshichiro,' Nicholas said. 'Wasn't Satsugai born in Fukuoka?'

The Colonel looked reflectively at his son. He stopped and dug in his jacket pocket. He withdrew his tobacco pouch, went about filling his pipe, his thumb tamping at the bowl.

Nicholas, watching the dragon float high above him, over the treetops, said, 'I've read the Constitution, Father. I know that you had a hand in it. It's not Japanese but it's very democratic. Much more so than the policies of the government today. Politically, Japan's gone far to the right, the *zaibatsu* were never dismantled. Most of the pre-war personnel is intact. I don't understand that.'

The Colonel drew out a gunmetal-grey Ronson lighter and, turning his back to the wind, thumbed the long flame to life. He sucked three or four times, deeply, almost with a sigh of contentment, before he flipped the top of the lighter closed. 'I want to know how you feel before I answer that. Do you care that Hanshichiro is dead? Or that you've seen a man take his own life?'

'I don't know. I really don't.' Nicholas put his hand along the black iron railing bordering the path, feeling the cool metal against his skin. 'I don't know whether it has taken effect yet. It's like a movie, not real life. I didn't know him or his work. I guess I'm sad but I don't know why. He did what he wanted to do.'

The Colonel drew on his pipe, thinking of what his son had just said. What had he expected? Tears? Hysterics? He dreaded returning home and having to tell Cheong. She loved the old man's poetry. It was terribly unfair for him to think Hanshichiro's death could touch Nicholas in the same deep way it did him. Their experiences were not the same and neither were the generations; anyway, Nicholas did not yet possess the sense of history that the Colonel and Cheong did.

And, of course, he had quite a different perspective on it. For a moment he thought of Satsugai. There wasn't much Nicholas missed. He would have to watch that from now on.

'Although the American party line was to make the military totally culpable for the war,' the Colonel said, 'it's only fair to say that there was a purge of the *zaibatsu* directly after the war. However, there was so much burning of original documents and deliberate falsification of others that a great many upper-echelon executives slipped through. Others, of course, did not and were tried and convicted of war crimes.' They began to walk towards the eastern gate beyond which their car was parked.

'Now the Americans came in here with the best of intentions.' The Colonel drew on his pipe, exhaled the blue smoke. 'I remember the day we finished drafting the new Constitution and dropped it on the Premier and the Foreign Minister like another A-bomb. They were flabbergasted. It wasn't a Japanese Constitution; its spirit was totally Western, that's certainly true. But it was MacArthur's firm intention to keep the country weaned from its feudal past, which he saw as highly dangerous. Its essence was that all power should be stripped from the Emperor and given into the hands of the Japanese people while maintaining him as the symbol of state.'

'Then what happened?' Nicholas asked.

'In 1947, Washington, through MacArthur, did a complete about-face. Rights were withdrawn, certain war-crime convictions were overturned and the leaders of the *zaibatsu* were restored to their pre-war eminence.'

'It all sounds so contradictory.'

'Only if you look at it from a purely Japanese point of view,' the Colonel said. 'You see, America is deathly afraid of global communism; the Americans will go to any lengths to prevent its spread. Just look at how they've aided Franco in Spain and Chiang Kai-shek out here. Fascism, the Americans feel, is their best weapon against communism.'

'Then the Americans deliberately disregarded their own Constitution for Japan, restoring the reactionary *zaibatsu*, guiding us in a right-wing direction.'

The Colonel nodded but said nothing. He felt now as if he

might never make it to the park gate, as if it were the end of a treacherous overland journey that he no longer had sufficient strength to make. 'Let's sit here a minute,' he said softly. They went carefully over the low railing, sat on a patch of grass filled with sunlight. Still, it seemed chill to the Colonel and he hunched his shoulders against the wind. Sheets of thinly layered cloud passed, now and again, across the face of the sun, causing brief shadows to dance like ghosts across the wide lawn. The cherry blossoms rustled; the cicadas wailed like brass being beaten; a brown and white butterfly darted erratically along the top of the grass, a blithe dancer without a partner. The day seemed like a *haiku* to the Colonel, perfect and sad, bringing tears to the eyes. Why were so many *haiku* sorrowful? he wondered.

The Colonel had witnessed many deaths in his day: the deaths of men he knew and those he did not. One develops over time a kind of shell against which these personal disasters must bounce away; either that or one goes mad. Until death takes on the unreality of a mime show and one no longer contemplates it.

This death in the park, on this sunny spring day, among the children, the inheritors of Japan, was different. The Colonel felt deflated, like Caesar returning home to Rome from the arms of Cleopatra, from eternal summer to the chill of March. He thought of the eagle circling Caesar's statue in the square; the augury. And it seemed to him that this important death, which he had witnessed, was also an augury of sorts. But what it portended he could not say.

'Are you all right?' Nicholas asked. He put a hand on his father's arm.

'What?' For a moment, the Colonel's eyes were far away. 'Oh, yes. Quite all right, Nicholas. Not to worry. I was just thinking of how to break the news of Hanshichiro's death to your mother. She will be most upset.'

He was silent for a time, contemplating the pink-white blossoms all around. After a time he felt calmer.

'Father, I want to ask you something.'

It might have been a moment that the Colonel had dreaded, but Nicholas's tone of voice was such that his father knew

167

that he had spent much time thinking about the question. 'What is it?'

'Does Satsugai belong to the Genyōsha?'

'Why do you ask?'

'It seems a logical question. Satsugai is the head of one of the *zaibatsu*, he is virulently reactionary in his philosophy and he was born in Fukuoka.' Nicholas turned to his father. 'Frankly, I'd be surprised if he wasn't a member. Wasn't it that which allowed him to be restored to power after the 1947 purge?'

'Ah,' the Colonel said judiciously. 'Ah. Very logical assumption, Nicholas. You're quite observant.' The Colonel thought for a moment. To their left several grey plovers broke from the treetops in a flurry and, circling once, headed west into the sun. Farther away, the dragon box kite was being slowly lowered by invisible hands; the day was almost done. 'The Genyōsha,' the Colonel said carefully, 'was founded by Hiraoka Kotarō. His most trusted lieutenant was Munisai Shokan. Satsugai is his son.'

Nicholas waited for a time before saying, 'Is that a yes?'

The Colonel nodded, thinking of something else. 'Do you know why Satsugai named his only son Saigō?'

'No.'

'Remember I told you that, in the beginning, the Genyōsha decided to work within the political framework of the country?'

'Yes.'

'Well, they came to that conclusion the hard way. The Military Conscription Act split the Meiji oligarchy into three factions. One of these was led by a man named Saigō. He was the leader of the ultra-conservative samurai. In 1877 Saigō led thirty thousand of his samurai into the field of battle against a modern conscription army put together by the Meiji government. Armed with rifles and guns, they easily defeated the samurai.'

'Of course!' Nicholas exclaimed. 'The Satsuma Rebellion. I never connected the names before.' He broke off a blade of grass. 'That was the last samurai uprising, wasn't it?'

'The last, yes.' The Colonel got up, feeling at last as if he were ready to face the outside world, Cheong's saddened face.

He could not bear it when she was sad.

They crossed the remainder of the park, passed beneath the high gate. Behind them the sky was clear of dragons, the sun lost within the thickening haze that reddened the sky like a drop of blood on a blotter.

That night they both dreamed of the death of Hanshichiro, each in his own separate way.

# Third Ring
# THE WATER BOOK

# I

## New York City/West Bay Bridge, Summer Present

The grey concrete blocks of Manhattan shimmered under the late July sun. It was sticky. Nicholas could feel the heat penetrating the thin soles of his summer loafers, making even walking uncomfortable.

He stood near the kerb at Seventh Avenue just outside the modernistic marquee of the new Madison Square Garden and Penn Station complex. He glanced up at it, thinking how quickly it had gone out of style. Across from him was the Statler Hilton Hotel and, a block up, the hideous plastic and glass frontage of a McDonald's.

Distractedly, he watched the traffic shooting the lights, weaving lanes; waves of steel. He was thinking of the call that had come in late last night. Vincent's voice had been a terrific blow. Terry and Eileen, murdered. It seemed impossible to imagine. No prowler could possibly have gained entrance to Terry's apartment without his knowing it; he could not have been surprised in that way. How then? Vincent had been peculiarly unforthcoming; his voice had sounded lifeless and, when Nicholas began to press him, he had merely repeated the instructions to be at the Seventh Avenue entrance to Penn Station after taking the first morning train into the city.

The sun burned the streets out of a cloudless sky. Nicholas's shirt stuck to his skin. He ran his fingers through his hair, wishing now that he had had it cut shorter in deference to the heat. The lights were red along the avenue and the heavy air hung like brocaded curtains, stagnant, feeling almost solid with the heat.

It was not Vincent who would be meeting him but, he had been told, a Detective Lieutenant Croaker. Lew Croaker. Nicholas thought he remembered the name. Free time had made *The New York Times* that much more important. A case earlier in the year. Didion. The papers, even the normally staid *Times*, had turned it into a spectacular event, perhaps because it had occurred in the Actium House, the most exclusive new residence building on Fifth Avenue. Croaker had been brought in. He was someone's blue-eyed boy; he got a ton of press, especially on the six o'clock news on TV.

The lights on Seventh changed to green and the traffic resumed its herky-jerky flow, dominated by yellow taxis. Out of this mass of dodging confusion a sleek black limo abruptly appeared. Its tinted glass made it difficult to see inside. It slid to a quiet stop in front of him. The back door on the kerb side opened and Nicholas saw movement on the far side of the seat. A figure leaned forward, beckoned to him. 'Please get in, Mr Linnear,' a vibrant voice said from out of the depths.

As he hesitated, the front door swung silently open and a brawny man in a dark blue business suit with short-cropped brown hair moved forward and guided him into the limo. Both doors swung to with a comfortable *thunk* that bespoke monied engineering and the limo accelerated into the traffic flow.

There was a spaciousness inside not usually an attribute of automobiles and a silence that was truly remarkable. Outside, the city glided by as if pulled on velvet runners. They might have been stationary, a back-drop being rolled by them, save for the slight discomfitures of acceleration and deceleration.

The interior was done all in dove-grey velvet and it was, quite obviously, a custom job; nothing was as one might see it on the showroom floor. It was cool and dim, like the interior of an expensive bar. Even the vibration from the massive V-8 engine was kept to a minimum.

There were three men in the car: a driver, the man in the dark blue business suit who sat on the passenger's side in front and the figure in the back, on the opposite side of the velvet bench seat. This last regarded him now. He was tall and somewhat stocky. He wore a conservative yet impeccable lightweight linen suit. Beneath this, Nicholas could see that there was no fat on him; his bulk was muscle and bone. He had a large head with a somewhat thrusting jaw which, overall, gave him a rather aggressive appearance. This was enhanced by his slanting forehead and short gunmetal-grey hair. His lean cheeks were pockmarked and his deep-set blue eyes, like marble chips, were guarded by black bushy eyebrows. Altogether, Nicholas decided, it was a face that had borne the brunt of many a tough decision and won them all. Nicholas would have cast him as a general and no lower than a five-star.

'Would you care for a drink?' The man beside him had spoken in his commanding voice but it was blue-business-suit who moved, turning his body part-way around on the front seat so that his left arm lay along the velvet top like an implied threat. Nicholas found himself wondering what had happened to delay Lieutenant Croaker.

'Bacardi and bitter lemon, if you have it.' Immediately the blue business suit opened a small door in the centre of the front seat. Nicholas heard the clink of ice against glass. He remained calm, though he still had no idea who these people were. He wanted to keep the man talking. The longer he did that, the sooner he would know who he was.

'You don't look much like your photographs,' the man said almost disgustedly.

As blue-suit stretched to pour the rum, Nicholas caught a glimpse of the butt of a revolver slung with a chamois holster under the man's right armpit. He turned his gaze away, to the city outside. It seemed a thousand miles away. 'That's perfectly understandable,' he said. 'I've never taken a good picture; not to my knowledge, anyway.'

'Your drink,' the man in the dark blue suit said.

Nicholas reached forward through the open partition and, as he did so, he saw from certain minute changes in the other precisely what was coming. Curious, he allowed it to happen. As soon as his hand was through the partition, the man lifted the drink away and grabbed at Nicholas's wrist with his other hand. It was a very swift motion yet, from Nicholas's point of view, slow and clumsy. He could have counteracted it in any number of different ways. Instead, he watched passively as the other gripped his wrist, exerting pressure to turn the hand over. The man peered closely at the edge of Nicholas's hand, which was as hard and calloused as horn. The man lifted his gaze, nodded to the man beside Nicholas, then handed Nicholas his drink.

Nicholas sipped at the Bacardi and bitter lemon, found it

174

quite good. Swallowing, he said, 'Are you satisfied?'

'As to your identity,' said the man beside him, 'yes.'

'You know more about me than I do about you,' Nicholas observed.

The man shrugged. 'That is as it should be.'

'By your standards perhaps.' No one wore sun-glasses or any kind of glasses, for that matter; no one smoked.

'Those are the only standards that count, Mr Linnear.'

'Mind if I light up?' Nicholas's right hand moved towards his trouser pocket and, at the same time, blue-suit's left arm stiffened, moving. He shook his head from side to side.

'You don't want to do that, Mr Linnear,' said the man beside him. 'You gave up smoking more than six months ago.' He grunted. 'Just as well. Those black-tobaccoed cigarettes are certain killers.'

Nicholas was impressed by the depth of their information on him. Whoever this man was, he was not an amateur.

'Did you know, Mr Linnear, that an accumulation of high-nicotine smoke can destroy the taste buds?' He nodded as if this statement needed physical confirmation. 'It's quite true. A group at the University of North Carolina completed the study.' He smiled. 'Ironic, isn't it? The campus is virtually surrounded by tobacco fields.'

'I've never heard of that study,' Nicholas said.

'Well, of course you haven't. The results are quite secret at the moment. They're being timed for release during the annual tobacco growers' convention in Dallas next October.'

'You seem to know a great deal about this study.'

'I should,' the man said, laughing. 'It was funded with my money.' He turned his head away, letting that sink in for several moments.

'How much do you really know about me?' Nicholas prompted. He was almost certain now; the face remained vaguely familiar, at least parts of it.

The man swung around, impaling him on an icy stare. 'Enough to want to talk to you face to face.'

It was the piece he needed. 'I didn't recognize you at first,' Nicholas said. 'I'd never seen you without the beard.'

The man smiled, rubbed at his clean-shaven chin. 'It does

make quite a difference, I'll admit.' Then his face lost all its warmth and it seemed as if the flesh were carved out of granite; the difference was appalling. 'What do you want with my daughter, Mr Linnear?' His voice was like the crack of a whip. Nicholas wondered what it would be like growing up under that fierce domination; he did not envy Justine.

'What does any man want with a woman?' he said. 'Only that, Mr Tomkin. Nothing more.'

Out of the corner of his eye he felt the movement of blue-suit even before it came into his line of vision. He relaxed; now was not the time. The big beefy hands were at his shirt-front. Some of the drink slopped over the side of the glass, ran down his trouser leg, Nicholas supposed that this man would have little trouble in picking up his side of a grand piano. While the man held him from in front, Tomkin leaned over. 'That's not very smart,' he said. His tone had changed again, as quickly and completely as a chameleon switches colour. It was now steel covered thinly by velvet. 'In any event, Justine is no ordinary woman. She's my daughter.'

'Is this how you handled Chris in San Francisco?' Nicholas said.

Tomkin was quite still for a moment; it was a breathless time. Then, without turning his head from Nicholas, he made a small gesture and blue-suit let go his grip. Without a backward glance he pulled himself into the front of the limo and closed the partition. He turned to look through the windshield.

'So that's how it is,' Tomkin said when they were alone. 'Interesting.' He eyed Nicholas. 'My daughter must like you.' Then his tone turned acid. 'Either that or you're a hell of a good lay. She hasn't been with any man for more than two hours since I brought her back. That's a long time for a girl of her age.' Then, as an afterthought, he said, 'She's got problems.'

'Everyone's got problems, Mr Tomkin,' Nicholas said drily. 'Even you.' As soon as he had said it, he regretted opening his mouth. His anger had caused that: not a good sign.

Tomkin sat back, sinking into the cushions. He squinted at Nicholas. 'You're an odd one. I do a hell of a lot of business with the Japs; even go over there three, four times a year.

Never met anyone there like you.'

'I imagine that's a compliment.'

Tomkin shrugged. 'Take it any way you like.' He leaned forward, depressed a hidden stud, and a small desk swivelled out on his side, complete with a miniature gooseneck lamp. Behind the desk was an accordion compartment built into the seat. Tomkin dipped a hand into this, extracted a sheet of paper. It was folded once across its width. He handed it to Nicholas. 'Here,' he said, 'what do you make of this?'

It was a sheet of Japanese rice paper, very fine. Nicholas unfolded it carefully. On it was a symbol, brushed on the centre with black ink. There were nine small diamonds surrounding a large circle like satellites about a sun. Inside the centre circle was the Japanese ideogram for *komuso*, the beggar-ascetic.

'Well?' Tomkin demanded. 'Do you know what it is?'

'Tell me how you got this.' Nicholas lifted his gaze from the crest, saw that those cold blue eyes were clouded with a kind of held-in anxiety.

'It came in the pouch.' And when he saw Nicholas looking at him uncomprehendingly, he added, somewhat irritably, 'The pouch from Japan. Each of our foreign offices has a daily pouch for important messages, when phones are inconvenient or insufficient for relaying data. At first I thought it was some kind of a joke but now ...' He shrugged. 'Tell me what it is.'

'It's a crest,' Nicholas said simply. He handed the sheet back to Tomkin, but he would not take it so Nicholas slid it onto the desk. 'A crest for a ninja *ryu* – a school.' He took a deep breath, weighing his next words carefully, but before he could open his mouth Tomkin was hammering at the smoked-glass partition. Blue-suit turned his head and a part of the glass opened. 'Frank, I want to go to the tower.'

'But, Mr Tomkin –'

'Now, Frank.'

Frank nodded, closed the partition. Nicholas could see him talking to the driver. The limo turned at the next corner, heading east. When they came to Park Avenue South, they made a left, headed north.

Next to Nicholas, Tomkin eyed the folded rice paper as if

something inside it had come to startling life.

Detective Lieutenant Croaker was not happy as he left Captain Finnigan's office early that morning. In point of fact he was on the verge of boiling over. He strode down the fluorescent-lighted corridor, crowded with officers and clerks, in long athletic strides.

'Hey, Lew, wait till I –' But Croaker had already brushed past the sergeant without noticing him and the man shrugged, turned away. Croaker could be like that sometimes and it was best then to stay out of his way.

Reaching his frosted-glass-fronted office, Croaker swung in and pounded his fists against the laminated Formica desk-top. Many was the time he had tried to burn holes in the thing with the end of his cigarette. To no avail. That was modern science for you.

He crashed down into the dark green swivel chair. He stared fixedly at the frosted-glass partition but what he was really seeing was Finnigan's fat mick face, those soft dewy blue eyes staring up at him blankly.

'I want to make this very plain to you, Croaker,' the Captain had said. 'The Didion case is a closed book.' He raised his pudgy hands in front of his face, warding off Croaker's expected protests. 'I know, I know, I put you on it myself. But that was when I thought we could see some quick results. Everyone from the mayor down was howling for a quick arrest. Then the media jumped all over it; you know what they can do.' His hands came down, lying flat on his desk-top. Croaker thought they looked like hams ripe for roasting. 'You know as well as I do the kind of people who live at the Actium House. People like Cardin and Calvin Klein don't like that kind of thing happening where they live. There was an awful lot of pressure.'

Croaker closed his eyes for a moment, counting slowly, one-Mississippi, two-Mississippi, just as he had done when playing football on the streets of Manhattan's Hell's Kitchen when he was a kid. It was either that or belt Finnigan on his fat red nose. His eyes snapped open; they saw the Captain leaning back in his high-backed chair, his hands, fingers interlaced, sitting atop his ample stomach. Croaker wondered how many whiskies the old man had already downed. Inadvertently, he glanced at the spot where the lower right-hand drawer was, where the bottle always lay within easy reach. His gaze swung back to Finnigan's red-veined face. His eyes seemed even more faded in the soft early morning light filtering through the closed shades. Outside, the towers of lower Manhattan rose like blocky giants.

'I know all about that pressure, Captain.' His tone revealed none of his hidden emotion. 'I've lived with that ever since I joined the force ten years ago. What I don't understand is this sudden switch, this about-face.'

'You weren't getting anywhere,' Finnigan said equably. 'I pulled the plug, that's all.'

'Bull! That's a load of –'

'Don't start this with me, Lieutenant.' Finnigan's eyes blazed and a thin line of spittle glistened on his protruding lower lip. 'I'm in no mood for any of your grandstanding.' He sat up, leaning forward, and now his small eyes seemed mean and bitter and altogether merciless. 'You may enjoy a great reputation with the press. I allow that because it's good for the department as a whole; the public responds well to one name, one face. But don't you ever think that that gives you any special privileges in here or out there.' His enormous thumb hooked back over his shoulder, indicating the streets of the city. 'I'm onto your little game and it gets no points with me. You love that attention, the media play. You eat it up like a glutton. But that's okay; that I can handle. What I won't tolerate is you treating me as if I'm some kind of idiot, some kind of moral defective.' He saw the look on the other's face, jumped on it. 'Yeah, that's right: moral defective. You been on the force more than long enough to know the reason why some investigation or other gets snuffed. Someone high up "requested" it. Okay? So now I've spelled it out for you.' His face was red now and the wattles beside his mouth were quivering. 'Believe me, I have thought of getting rid of you so very often, transferring you to some other district. But you're too valuable to me. You're good for at least a couple of mayor's citations for me each year. I don't mind telling you I like that;

it's good for my record.' He stood up now, his thick arms straight columns ending in bunched fists pressed so hard against the desk-top that they had gone white. 'But I'll be goddamned if I'll ever let you pull a stunt like you did with the Lyman thing. That was officially chocked and you went after it anyway. You made me look like a fool to these people here and I'm just lucky that the Commissioner didn't hear about it.' He lifted a finger as big around as a sausage, shaking it in Croaker's direction. 'You'll take this Tanaka-Okura double murder and I don't want to ever hear that you threw a case back at the precinct boys the way you did last night.' He coughed thickly, wiped at his lips with a grey handkerchief. 'What's the matter? You got something against slants? No. So take it and be happy. Be happy that you've got a case to run with.'

Croaker turned to leave but, as his fingers grasped the knob, Finnigan said, 'Oh and, Lieutenant, you know how things function around here. Next time don't make me explain S.O.P. to you as if you were some rookie just off the streets, okay?'

It was at that point that Croaker had decided to continue with the Didion thing on his own. Now he knew that he had to do it all on his own. He could confide in no one at the office and, if he used their resources, which he surely would, he would have to camouflage his intent. He looked at his watch, then at the dregs of old coffee in the stained plastic cup on his desk. He was late for the Linnear pick-up but right now he did not much care; his mind was still on the Didion thing. Finnigan was right in one respect – he had nothing. But only up to a point. The girl had friends somewhere, it had just proved to be a bastard unearthing them. Now he was close to at least one of them. Matty the Mouth had come up with a lead. But he needed a name, an address, or it was useless to him. This was what he was waiting for now; this was why he was so sensitive to being pulled off the case. It was no good telling Finnigan what he had now; no good at all. It would be like talking to the wall. Which was why Croaker always kept his cases to himself; it was part of the reason why he got Finnigan his mayor's citations each year. So it was the one thing Finnigan did not question. In any case, Finnigan could care less about M.O., it was results he craved. Talk about your gluttons! Croaker grunted as he swivelled round in his chair. Those results gave the whisky a fine race for the captain's undivided attention.

Croaker cursed and got up. Time to pick up Linnear.

At approximately the same time, Vincent had been at work in the autopsy room. He had not, of course, been on duty when they had brought Terry's and Eileen's corpses in late last night but he had been called right away – Tallas had thought he should know; she had the soundest judgement of all the associates, he thought. Consequently he had arrived in time to hear the tail end of the argument between the two precinct patrolmen who had responded to the call, and the detective. He was a big burly sonofabitch and he was giving them a tongue-lashing. Vincent had not concerned himself with the noise or the rising tempers. He had wanted to make certain. Perhaps it had all been a ghastly mistake – one of the *dōjō*'s instructors at Terry's apartment – or ... but it had been Terry and it had been Eileen. Dead. It was then that he had remembered the frozen-line call. No one there. Could it have been Terry phoning him? He turned sadly away. It did not matter now.

He put them away for the morning, made sure all their clothes and personal effects were properly tagged and bagged for the detectives who would take the case. Then he had gone home to spend an uneasy night.

It had got to the point where he was content only down in the morgue. There he could work, logically problem-solving, sleuthing his way through the silent mayhem. Sometimes it worked and his report led directly to the arrest of the murderer; at other times he was the only one who could be of solace to the families of the dead who rolled past him each day.

They were like massive hieroglyphs, mute monoliths, waiting to have their arcane messages unearthed. And he the archaeologist of their past.

It was immensely satisfying to him to work here in the dead-house, as many physicians called it. But it was such a misnomer, for here, every day, he and his colleagues were hard at work wresting secrets from death's cold grip. They hacked at it, bringing it down to size, demystifying it, bit by bit, until much of its horror was dissipated. What job could claim more importance for the living?

This morning Vincent now stood in the central room, his back to the tiers of stainless-steel doors. A black man, naked and cool, his head at an angle, lay on a trolley to one side. He stood staring at the swing doors leading into the autopsy room. Behind that barrier, he knew, lay his friend, Terry Tanaka; next would be Eileen. For the first time since coming here, he wondered whether he really wanted to push through those doors. It seemed, all at once, one death too many and he did not feel the same inside any more. He knew that he wanted to return to Japan. But he felt that to be impossible now, as if he had contracted some dread disease in the West, in the city, in New York, and now, transformed inwardly as well as outwardly, he felt as if the culture shock would be the death of him.

Yet, deep inside, he perhaps understood that his only salvation now was to go on. Death had returned to him as it had as a child, a solid wall too high for him to climb over. He knew that he must tear that wall down or go mad and his only path lay within the bright, tidy room inside. There death could be quietly dissected, the wall pulled down one brick at a time until, at last, he would understand what had done this to his friends. For, he found, he wanted desperately to know.

Vincent shook himself and, pushing aside the swing doors, went in to work on the body. Japan, once a dream, had now departed.


The limo pulled out of the traffic flow in the low Fifties, slid quietly to a stop at the kerbside. Frank got out first and opened the rear door for them.

They were on a block dominated by the steel exoskeleton of a building that seemed perhaps three-quarters complete. It was set far back from the street and the pavement had been torn up in order to install brick-red tile. A wooden companion-way had been erected so that pedestrians would not be inconvenienced by the construction. On the south end of the block an enormous cement mixer was drawn up. Multicoloured polka dots had been painted on its revolving barrel. Beside it, an angular crane was in the process of elevating a number of girders.

Part of the building's fashionable black stonework façade was up; chalk marks still criss-crossed some of the blocks, the white and yellow glyphs of the modern world. Still, fully one side was skeletonized like a transparent cocoon beneath which the chrysalis could be seen forming.

They walked along wooden planks laid out while, in the rubble beneath, men with bulging muscles and oil-streaked faces drilled with jackhammers like sullen dentists.

They came into the shade of the roofed walkway. The air was filmed with dust which hung chokingly, settling on their hair and their shoulders like dandruff.

A man with a lean dented face approached them. He wore a bright yellow hard hat. 'Lubin Bros' was stencilled across the front in blue. He smiled broadly when he recognized Tomkin, extended his hand. He led them off to the right into a mobile home which served as construction headquarters. Tomkin introduced him laconically as Abe Russo, the building foreman. Russo shook Nicholas's hand with a firm cool grip. He handed out hard hats for all of them and they left.

Frank led them into the innards of the structure, through the enormous atrium lobby, then along a corridor where bare light-bulbs hung on flex threads and the damp smell of raw concrete filled their nostrils.

Olive-green mats still hung on the walls of the elevator. They took it to the top. In the hall a man as big across as Frank but slightly shorter met them. They went silently down the corridor.

The ceiling was finished, as was the interior wall, in a deep blue fabric, slightly nubby, giving the effect of raw silk. To their right, the outer wall was glass down to the level of their shins, or at least it would be when all the plates were in. Mostly it was a lattice-work of thin-seeming metal, stained orange by the rustproofing. Beyond was the breathtaking panorama of Manhattan, west and north. First the thick buildings on the opposite side of the avenue, then onward, marching in square-cut rows towards the Hudson River. Looking north, he could make out the depression in the elevated surface of Manhattan that was the south end of Central Park.

The corridor gave onto metal-façaded double doors with ostentatious brass door-knobs in the centre of each. To the left, bare wooden doors opened on small offices, floored at this stage only with rough concrete. In several Nicholas could see the huge rolls of carpet, ready to be stapled down.

A warm wind whipped at them, intermittently. It was still hot up here; one could not so easily escape the heat of a summer's day in Manhattan. Soot and grime raced along the bare floor like spindrift, borne on the breeze. The corridor seemed very exposed at this point.

Tomkin paused before the metal doors and looked outward. His arm lifted as if he were about to begin an aria. 'Do you see what I see, Nicholas?' He turned for a moment. 'I *may* call you Nicholas.' But it was a rhetorical question and he continued apace. 'That used to be a big world out there. Used to be something for everyone – at least for anyone with guts enough to go out and get it.' His arm came down, the fingers curled at his side. 'Now it's nothing but a goddamned industrial farmyard. There's no space any more and no time. Do you know what that means, hmm? I'll tell you. There's not enough out there any more. We're all strangling each other in an effort to survive. Oho, yes, you heard me right. It's survival now, not just a matter of making a profit. And the world's homogenized.' He squinted sideways at Nicholas. 'You know what I mean? No? How'd you have liked to've been Marco Polo, eh? Travelling for two and a half years across the endless deadly expanse of Asia; to come at last upon Cathay, a land where no Western man had ever dreamed of, let alone set foot in? Could there be anything in this world to equal such an extraordinary experience? No, I'll tell you a thousand times. No.'

He moved forward as if in a trance, put his hands on the spider-web tracery of the steel superstructure. 'Do you know,' he whispered, 'that I don't know how much money I have. Oh, I could hire a staff to figure it out, except by the time they did the figure'd be totally out of date. Anyway, the sum's far too big to think about comfortably.' His face glistened now with a thin film of sweat. 'There is virtually nothing in this world I can't have if I wish it. Do you believe that?' He turned on Nicholas. His tone of voice had turned savage and the veins stood out on the sides of his temples, pulsing. 'I could have you heaved over the side of this building. Now. Just like that. I could do it with complete immunity. Oh, I might have to suffer through a cursory investigation but that's all.' He waved a hand. 'But I wouldn't.'

'I'm relieved,' Nicholas said, but Tomkin went on as though he hadn't heard him.

'That would be a rather despotic way to act. A flaunting of my power. It doesn't interest me.'

'You sound disappointed.'

'What?' He came back from his reverie slowly. 'Oh, of course not. But let me tell you, like all great men before me I am concerned by mortality – my mortality.' He hesitated. 'I want the best for Justine – for both my daughters.'

For some reason, Nicholas had the distinct impression that Tomkin had been about to say something else entirely. 'Then I'm sure they'll get it,' he said.

'Don't patronize me,' Tomkin said harshly. 'I am well aware of my failings as a father. Justine has problems relating to men and Gelda just divorced her fourth husband and I can't hire enough men to keep her away from the liquor. I keep jumping into their lives. In and out. That's the way it is. If it's hard for either of them to bear, too bad.'

'Justine, at least, doesn't seem to want you jumping at all,' Nicholas pointed out.

'She's got no choice,' Tomkin snarled. 'I'm still her father whatever she cares to say to others. I still love her. I love them both. We're all fucked up, one way or another; their problems are just more visible than most, that's all.'

'Look, Mr Tomkin –'

'Don't screw up now, Nicholas. Not when we're getting along so well.' He spat the words out now as if they were burning the lining of his mouth. 'Sure she hated it when I jumped in two years ago. But what did she know? Christ, she was up to her armpits in shit.' He made a quick violent motion with his head. 'She was following that bastard around like he was God himself.'

'She told me –' Nicholas began.

'Did she tell you that he ran a male stud service? That he was a speed freak? That he liked men more than women? Did she tell you that he tied her up and beat her before laying her? Did she tell you any of that?' His face was mottled with anger and shame and spittle flew uncontrollably from his lips.

'No,' Nicholas said softly. 'She didn't.'

Tomkin laughed harshly, humourlessly, an animal-like sound. 'I'll just bet she didn't.' His head was thrust forward and in that position he looked remarkably like a hunting dog on point. Nicholas found himself wondering if he were the prey. If so, Tomkin had bitten off more than he could chew this time.

'You had no business telling me all this,' he said. His voice rose dangerously.

'What's the matter? Is your stomach turning at the thought?' He smirked. 'Does she disgust you now that you know what kind of woman she really is? Do you hate yourself for ever getting involved with her?'

'It doesn't matter what she did in the past,' Nicholas said slowly. 'And unless she's living in the past, it has no bearing on either of us.' He stared at Tomkin, at the sweating face hovering close in front of him. 'I know what kind of person Justine is, Tomkin. I just wonder whether *you* do.'

For just a moment, Tomkin's eyes seemed to bulge. Then, abruptly, he seemed in total control of himself once again and all signs of anger slipped away from him. He smiled, clapped Nicholas on the back. 'I don't suppose I can be condemned for making certain, can I?'

Nicholas realized just how weak Tomkin was. That was why he made such an overt show of disfranchising his daughters, because they were so important to him – his immortality. Nicholas wondered whether he was reconciled to not having a son to carry on the line.

Oddly, it was this weakness which prevented Nicholas from disliking the man. He had been taught, at the Itto *ryu*, to seize upon an opponent's weakness and thereby bring him crashing down. But outside the *dōjō*, Nicholas had learned that people often lived their lives, or at least a good part of them, out of weakness. It was what made them human, what made them vulnerable; what made them interesting. Take Musashi, for example. If one believed entirely the *Go Rin No Sho*, one saw not a man but a steel monument, invincible and emotionless. However, there were many stories concerning Musashi. The one Nicholas never forgot was the one where Musashi was defeated by a ninja using a paper fan. Ninja were notorious for their harnessing of odylic forces and this, it was commonly believed, was what made Musashi's defeat so effortless. Nicholas, of course, knew that there was more to it than that. Still, it warmed him to know that the great Musashi, the Sword Saint, had after all tasted defeat.

It would be all too easy, Nicholas knew, to dismiss Tomkin as villainous and have nothing more to do with him. But people's façades were all too often just that. He had touched a nerve and had glimpsed for an instant something else in the man, a spark that humbled him, made him human. Moreover, Tomkin was intelligent enough to realize that he had given away this advantage to Nicholas and now Nicholas was intrigued enough to try to find out why. He did not have long to wait.

'I want you to work for me,' Tomkin said easily. 'I want you to find out what's going on. I know all about the Yakuza! I've even had a brush with Shōtō. You've heard of him, no doubt?' Nicholas nodded and he went on. 'Tough cookie, that one. But I managed.' He put his finger and thumb up, pinched his lower lip thoughtfully. 'Don't know anything about ninja, though, and what I don't know about myself I give over to experts.' He stabbed a forefinger. 'You're an expert on these bastards, isn't that right?'

'You could say that.'

'Well, I want to hire you, then. Find out what this is all about.' He produced the folded sheet of rice paper with the ninja crest painted on it, waved it. 'Take the goddamned thing. I don't want it.'

Nicholas did not move. 'When did you get it?' he said.

'Like I said, came in the Japan pouch, let me see, oh, about a week ago.'

A week, Nicholas thought. It could not be a coincidence. Barry's body had been found about that time. Then he had been right. Tomkin was the target. 'I think you've been marked for assassination,' he said.

Tomkin did not even blink. 'All right. It's happened before.'

'Not with a ninja.'

'No,' Tomkin admitted. 'But I told you I've had a spot of Yakuza trouble. Nothing I couldn't handle.'

'This is different.'

'How so? He'll never get to me.'

'There are a thousand ways he could do it but don't waste your time trying to figure out how. You'll never do it.'

'Is this a sales pitch?' Tomkin's eyes had gone hard. 'A little something you just dreamed up to give yourself a raise before you've even started work?'

'I never said I'd take the job.'

Tomkin shrugged. 'Suit yourself. I've got Frank and Whistle there. I'm not worried.'

Nicholas did not even look at them. 'Tomkin, if indeed a ninja has been contracted to assassinate you, he'll go right through those two as if they were stalks of wheat.'

'Like I said, that's some sweet sales pitch you've got.'

'It's no pitch at all. You've made me late for an important appointment. I'm not inter –'

He missed the signal but they were on him, one on each side. Frank's hands hung loosely at his sides, the fingers slightly curled. Whistle's gun was already out. It was a snub-nosed .38 not so good at long range but brutal within fifteen yards. They were way inside that now.

Nicholas was in the classic first position of *yoroi kumi-uchi*, originally grappling in armour but today used quite effectively when one was dressed in Western street clothes.

Whistle's revolver was at the horizontal, his forefinger beginning to squeeze inwards on the trigger. Nicholas stepped forward, jammed his right foot into the man's left instep while at the same time slamming the muzzle of the gun away with the edge of his left hand. There was an explosion and the bullet whined off the inner wall, leaving a grey scar against the blue.

Whistle dropped the useless gun, bringing his right hand upward towards Nicholas's abdomen. He watched it, wide-eyed, as it was halted in mid-flight as if it had come up against a concrete barrier. He winced in pain as it was twisted hard round, felt a hot tearing and then a whiplike snap. At the same instant, Nicholas's left hand smashed into his collarbone and he went down, unconscious.

Frank moved in. He made no move towards the gun under his armpit. His fingers were as straight as boards as he whipped forward.

Nicholas stood motionless, watching the unfolding of the assault. There was plenty of time. He is left-handed, Nicholas thought, and he's expecting karate.

At the point of Frank's attack, Nicholas moved almost languidly, separating the deadly hands. To Tomkin, watching interestedly from the sidelines, it appeared as if he had not moved at all, merely pushed his elbows into Frank's rib cage almost gently. Frank collapsed onto the concrete floor.

'I knew you were good,' Tomkin said excitedly. 'I knew it. The reports said so, but you often can't trust them. Take other people's work for granted and you find yourself in a hole. Happens all the goddamned time.' He stared down at his two incapacitated bodyguards. 'Fucking great, that's all.' He looked up, extended a hand. 'Glad to have you aboard, Nick.'

Nicholas stared at Tomkin's face as he moved away down the corridor towards the elevator. 'I told you, I'm not interested in working for you.' He pressed the button and it glowed. The elevator began its ascent. 'You have no respect for people.' Tomkin came towards him, stepping over the fallen bodies.

'It's not like that.'

'Sure it is. I don't like being manipulated. Any more than I imagine Justine does. I don't owe you a thing, Tomkin. You have no claim over me.'

Behind him the elevator doors opened. He stepped inside.

'Wait a minute, Nick.' Tomkin reached out a hand.

'Don't call me. I'll call you.'

The doors began to close as Nicholas pressed the ground button but Tomkin lunged forward, holding back the doors with his hands. His face was as hard as granite and there was a peculiar feral light in his eyes. 'Aren't you forgetting something?' he spat. 'It's not only my life that's at stake but my daughters', too. You wouldn't want this sonovabitch to get his hands on Justine. Would you? Think about that,' he said savagely and let the doors sigh shut.

On the way down, Nicholas recalled the night he and Justine were together, when that thing came through the kitchen window. Red blood and black fur. The *Kuji-kiri* ninja calling-card, meant to create terror, one of the ninja's most useful weapons. The *Kuji-kiri*, most feared of all the ninja *ryu*. Whose crest was the *komuso* ideogram, circled, surrounded by nine diamonds.

Justine! his mind cried out. He looked up, watching in impatience as the floor numbers flickered by. He wanted to get to a phone immediately.

Outside on the street he saw a dark-haired man with wide shoulders and a pushed-in face. It had character, like a cowboy's. He stood beside a plain white Ford sedan. Even without the removable flashing red light on top, he knew it for a police car. But he had recognized the face. Detective Lieutenant Lew Croaker. He walked out of the shadow of the building's make-shift entrance and, tossing his hard hat to one of the workmen, went down the wooden plank to the kerb.

He had used the phone in Abe Russo's portable headquarters. He had thought about calling Ray Florum, the police lieutenant out at West Bay Bridge, but he knew Justine would never stand for it. Accordingly, he got Doc Deerforth's number from Information and spoke to him for several minutes. He had agreed to look in on Justine every so often.

'Linnear,' Croaker said as he came up to him in the sunshine, 'what the hell were you doing with Raphael Tomkin?' He worked a wooden toothpick between his teeth with two long slender fingers.

'Hello to you, too, Lieutenant.' Nicholas nodded.

'Cut the wise dialogue and get in,' Croaker said, ducking

his head as he sat behind the wheel. 'We've got business to attend to.'

Nicholas opened the door on the passenger's side and got in. As soon as his foot was off the asphalt, the car roared off. He pulled at the door, slamming it shut.

'Didn't your buddy Ito give you specific instructions?' Croaker said. He began to weave through the uptown traffic, heading for the left side of Park Avenue and the street divider.

'Tomkin picked me up while I was waiting for you.'

Croaker snorted. 'Didn't your mother tell you never to get into a car filled with strangers? Jesus! What'd that fucker want with you?'

'I don't have to answer that.'

Croaker swung his head round, unmindful of the tenacious traffic. He glared at Nicholas. 'Listen, buddy, don't give me a hard time. I'm telling you that if it has to do with Raphael Tomkin it fucking *is* my business, get me? Now give!' He braked savagely, in line to make a left onto the downtown side of the avenue.

'What makes you so interested in Tomkin?' Nicholas was tired of being questioned without having any of the answers.

'Now, look, Linnear,' Croaker said, carefully enunciating each word. It was obvious he was holding himself in with an effort. 'I'm doing my best to be civil, to treat you with respect. I've got no beef with you. Yet. But today's just not my day; I'm on a short fuse. That means, you being here beside me, it's not your day either. Now be nice and tell me what I want to know. I promise, it won't hurt.' He leant on the horn, turned down Park.

'I'm seeing his daughter,' Nicholas said. 'He wanted to check me out.'

Croaker hit the steering-wheel with the heel of his hand, bounced up and down. 'Goddamn!' he exclaimed. 'Goddamn! Ho!' He shook his head. 'What do you know!' Then he swore as he was forced to swerve round a slowly cruising cab. He gunned the Ford and they leapt forward into the semicircle of the overpass at Forty-sixth Street. When they emerged, below Forty-second, he said, 'Jesus, I thought I'd pass up the fucking traffic on Second by going down Park but will you look at this.' He gestured at the sea of cars gleaming in the sun ahead of them. They were baking in the interior and the air stank of exhaust and overheated oil. 'To hell with this!' He reached out his left hand, started the siren. On top the red light began to flash. 'Christ,' he said as the cars began reluctantly to part, 'summer in New York!'

They turned east on Thirtieth Street and Croaker cut the siren. 'Which one is it?'

'Which what?'

'Daughter, Linnear. Which daughter? Gelda, the one who like Chivas, or is it the crazy younger one – what's her name?'

'Justine.'

'Yeah. I can never remember it.' He shrugged. 'Too pretty for a Tomkin.' He turned his head, spat the toothpick out of the open window. 'Spoke to her once, couple of months ago. She's kinda hard to forget.'

'Yes,' Nicholas said. 'She's beautiful all right.' He wished he was with her now instead of being in this melting heat on his way to the morgue. Goddamn Tomkin! he thought savagely. Then he smiled inwardly. You could say this for the bastard, he sure knew his people. Which led him to another point. 'You certainly know the family well.'

They had pulled up half way down the block between Third and Second Avenues as traffic piled up at the red light. A refrigerated meat provisions truck was in the process of pulling out into the traffic, its nose canted into the flow.

Croaker turned to look at him, one elbow on the sill of the open window. He had grey eyes and thick hair cut rather long, combed straight back. He looked as if he had been through the wars; like a character out of *From Here to Eternity*. 'You sure are nosy for a civilian.' The line of cars started up, rolling slowly forward after the truck had nosed its way in; it was no faster than a funeral procession. His voice changed gears, softening remarkably. 'Guess the old bastard didn't take it too well, you seeing his baby.'

'You could put it that way.' They had stopped again; the heat was oppressive. 'How'd you find me anyway?'

Croaker shrugged. 'I got to Penn Station in time to see you gettin' into the limo. Frank's a wiseacre.'

'Yeah. I know.' Nicholas grinned. 'He and Whistle tried their best to evict me from the premises.'

Croaker eyed him. 'Don't look like it bothered you none.'

'I wanted to leave anyway.'

Croaker threw his head back and laughed. 'Linnear,' he said, 'you just made my day.'

They soon came to the source of the slow-up. The gutter gurgled and the street swished with running water. Farther down the block four or five shirtless kids, their pants rolled up to their knees, danced about an open fire hydrant. Croaker rolled up his window and they splashed through as if they were in a car wash.

'Do you miss it?' Nicholas asked.

'What? Miss what?' Croaker took them through the intersection on the amber, accelerated.

'Smoking.' He had noticed that the ends of the other's fingers on his right hand were yellowed.

'Goddamn right I miss it,' Croaker growled. 'Why'n hell d'you think I chew these goddamned MintyPicks? Huh! You think I've got time to eat with all the shit coming down in this city? I ain't been in a proper bed in three days.' He hung a left onto First Avenue and, with a squeal of brakes that must have left several inches of rubber on the city's asphalt, he pulled up in front of the turquoise-glazed brick façade of the Chief Medical Examiner's office. He double-parked and they went up the steps.

Croaker led them over to a desk, flipped open a brown plastic case to display his badge and I.D. to the receptionist. The man nodded when Croaker said, 'Dr Ito,' and dialled a three-digit number on the telephone on the small desk.

He looked up as he cradled the phone. 'Dr Ito will be right up, Lieutenant. He's in the morgue.'

Croaker looked around, watched the policeman on duty for several minutes. He did not know the man.

Vincent came out. He was wearing a green lab smock that tied at the back. 'Hello, Nick,' he said gravely. He shook Croaker's hand. He led them back the way he had come, past the identifying room with its hydraulic lift to the morgue and down a set of stairs to the basement.

There was no smell at all down here; Nicholas had always imagined it would stink of disinfectant and formaldehyde. It was silent save for the monotone drone coming from behind a set of swing-doors; an autopsy was in progress. Vincent went to the bank of stainless-steel doors, opened two. Then he described in detail what he had found.

'It was no ordinary intruder who found them,' he concluded. 'You see how the sternum and rib cage are fractured?'

'Christ,' Croaker said. 'I've never seen anything like that. He looks like he's been battered with a baseball bat.'

Vincent shook his head. 'Nothing so crude, Lieutenant. It was a human body.'

Croaker snorted. 'Idiotic! A human body by itself couldn't cause such extensive damage in such a short amount of time. The man must've had fists like hammers.'

'No fists,' Vincent said.

Croaker stared at him. 'I'm sure this is leading somewhere, Doctor.'

'Lieutenant,' Nicholas said. 'Terry was a *sensei*, a master of kenjutsu, karate, aikido. No man alive could get close enough to him to kill him, unless ...'

'Unless what? I want to hear this.' Croaker crossed his legs, leaning nonchalantly against the bank of doors.

'There is a kenjutsu technique, perfected and written about by Miyamoto Musashi, Japan's greatest swordsman. It's called the Body Strike, for obvious reasons. Using one's shoulder –'

'This guy must have been built like a tank,' Croaker said.

'On the contrary,' Nicholas said, 'his stature could have been quite a bit smaller than Vincent's. We are speaking not so much of pure physical strength now, Lieutenant, but of an inner strength.'

'Look, Linnear, the only inner strength I've ever seen is from David Carradine in "Kung Fu" and I didn't believe a bit of it.'

Nicholas smiled. 'Then we must begin to educate you, Lieutenant.'

Croaker stood up, said, 'Then you agree with Ito here. You think these two were killed by a Japanese.'

'Well, I can think of a small number of occidentals who are

kenjutsu *sensei*. But none of them could kill this way. This is a spiritual killing that would be far beyond them.'

Croaker stared down at Terry's smashed chest. 'Ain't nothing spiritual about this, my man. This is the work of a pile driver.'

'Was there any kind of a murder weapon found in Terry's house?' Nicholas asked.

'Just a sword –'

'Terry's *katana*,' Vincent interrupted, his gaze shooting the message, 'lying by his side.'

'Yeah,' Croaker said. 'But no blood on it; nothing like that. No other possible weapon that could've done *that*. But that don't mean shit. The guy could've taken off with it.'

'He didn't,' Nicholas said. 'Lieutenant, killing has been a high art in Japan for almost two centuries. In another time, it was a way of life for the Japanese. And today, though there is the modern Japan which stands in its place, still the old ways remain. Still there is *bushido*, the Way of the Warrior.'

'Yeah? What the hell is it, then?'

Nicholas laughed. 'I don't think I could explain it in a few minutes.'

'That's okay, I've got bags of time.' Croaker extracted a MintyPick from his breast pocket, rolled it between his teeth. 'I ain't eaten in much too long. What say you and I talk this out over a meal?'

Nicholas nodded and Croaker turned to Vincent. 'Say, Doc, I'll sign for the bags while I'm here.'

'Right.' Vincent went round the corner to the small alcove where a number of polythene bundles waited for collection by the police: homicide victims' effects and clothes. Vincent brought two bundles back to Croaker, gave him a form to sign.

Croaker looked up, giving Vincent back his pen. 'I'll be in touch,' he said.

Nicholas's call made Doc Deerforth uneasy, and while Nicholas had been brief, he'd given more than enough for Doc Deerforth to chew on.

He had appointments until twelve-thirty but, directly his last patient said good-bye, he left the office and drove out to Dune Road. He had been in constant touch with Ray Florum, of course, but there had been no progress on the two murder cases and, reluctantly, he had had to let the county detectives in. Not that it would do any good, Doc Deerforth thought sourly as he drove across the steel drawbridge onto Dune Road: the county people were like the Keystone Kops, all gung-ho and no expertise.

He turned right and settled back. Gulls rose, wheeling over the water on his left, circling about the two stories of The Crosstree, Dune Road's newest condominium. It was tan and dark brown with a maze of outside staircases on this, the landward side. Soon the condominiums gave grudging way to private houses.

The thought of the ninja haunted him all the way out to Justine's house. Ever since he had become aware of the evidence, he hadn't had a decent night's sleep. In dreams he would return to the steaming jungles, to the mortar fire by day, the snipers' fire by night. But it was one specific night he dreaded most of all and even in his dreams he fought against remembering. Soon, he knew, he would have to resort to chloral hydrate to knock himself into a dreamless abyss.

He parked the car on the side of the house, took the elevated slatted-wood pathway over the dunes and scrub grass to the beach. He went up the stairs, knocked on the screen door. Behind him the water surged and, down the beach, he could hear the cries of children as they ran into the surf. A shaggy dog barked, leaping along the sand in pursuit of a wobbling Frisbee. The sand was a patchwork of oiled bodies, brightly coloured blankets and striped sun umbrellas. A cool breeze blew in off the water and, for a moment at least, there came the drone of an airplane.

Justine came to the door, opened it. She smiled. 'Hi. What brings you out here?'

'Nothing special,' Doc Deerforth lied. 'I was out this way and thought I'd say hello. Haven't seen you since the beginning of the summer.'

Justine laughed as she stepped back to let him in, 'Thank God that allergy doesn't last for long. I couldn't endure it all summer.' She went into the kitchen. 'Would you like a drink?' And when he nodded, she added, 'Gin and tonic?'

'Fine.'

She went about fixing it.

'Seems quiet around here,' he said. 'Had any visitors?'

'What?' she said over the sound of cracking ice. 'I can't hear you?'

He went into the kitchen. 'Any visitors lately?'

She handed him his drink, began to make hers. 'Only Nicholas.' She tasted it. 'Umm. But that's the way I like it. I've never been comfortable with a lot of people, not at home at least.' They went into the living-room, sat on the sofa. 'In business, it's different. I don't like to mix the two.'

Doc Deerforth nodded. 'I know what you mean. I don't like to either.'

She regarded him over the rim of her tall glass. She pressed the condensation against her lip, rolling the glass. 'Tell me, Doc,' she said. 'You didn't come all the way out here to exchange pleasantries, did you?'

'I came to see how you were.'

'I'm not ill,' she pointed out.

Doc Deerforth smiled. 'I didn't say anything about that. This isn't a business call.'

'I see.' Her eyes wouldn't let him get away. 'Did Nicholas call you?'

He laughed, relieved. 'You know, you remind me of Kathy, my youngest. Nothing gets past her, either.' He shook his head. 'Nicholas called this morning.'

'I wish he'd called me instead,' Justine said. 'I wish he hadn't gone into the city.'

'He had to, from what I gathered.' Doc Deerforth put his drink down. 'Anyway, you could've gone in with him.'

She shook her head. 'Too much work and, besides, they were his friends. I'd just be out of place. I've got no desire to tag along after him.' She took a sip. 'We each have our own lives. Where they touch, well – that's where we love. The involvement – we're like two fiercely spinning wheels, each with its own orbit. We lean towards each other, we touch hesitantly, we calculate how far each of us can go without disturbing the orbits.'

'What happens if you go too far,' Doc Deerforth said, 'and your – orbits, as you put it – are disturbed?'

Justine unfolded herself, went across the room to stare out at the hot beach and the cool curling surf. 'In that event,' she said, her voice as thin as a ghost's, 'I'm afraid it would be disastrous.'

'The girls will take care of you, m'sieur.' The *maître d'hôtel* moved a little to his right, lifting an arm towards the steep, dark staircase. He touched his thin moustache with a forefinger, stroked it.

'You know, I thought you'd take me to that place on Park,' Nicholas said. 'You know, downtown.' They were in the low Fifties on the East Side.

'You mean the Belmore Cafeteria?' Croaker said. 'Jesus, I leave that to the undercover bastards. Christ, I wouldn't go there for a proper meal.'

It was quiet on the second floor; only a table near the door was occupied. The far end of the room was on an elevated platform beside a row of windows.

The two waitresses were pretty. They wore dark tops and short skirts. They spoke with accents.

Croaker requested a window table and one waitress led them up the steps. She left them with menus after taking their drink order.

'How long did you know Tanaka?' Croaker asked. His eyes scanned the opened menu.

'About six years,' Nicholas said. 'We met in kenjutsu class.'

'Here?'

'Yeah. I still go there. I'll take you after lunch.'

'Part of my education, huh? Humm, I think I'll take the bacon and eggs.' The girl came up, placed their drinks on the table; a Kir for Nicholas, a dark Myer's rum on the rocks for Croaker. Croaker gave her his order, Nicholas ordered the same. When she had left, he continued. 'This *dōjō*. Where'd Tanaka get the bread for it?'

'Worked mostly, I expect.' Nicholas took a long swallow of the Perrier. 'And I think he had a bit of money when he came over here. His mother had left him some before she died.'

'How much?'

Nicholas shrugged. 'I have no idea. His family was wealthy but there are nine children.'

'Where are they?'

'As far as I know, they're all in Japan. Terry was the only one who left.'

'And the father?'

'Killed during the war.'

'Um hum.' Croaker shook his head. 'Still, it takes an awful lot of cash or collateral to open up a business here.'

'What are you getting at?'

Croaker shrugged, took a pull of his drink. 'You know about bread. You need, you get. Sometimes it ain't so easy to pay it back. People get antsy; they don't want to wait.'

Nicholas shook his head. 'The only business partner Terry had in the *dōjō* was Chase Manhattan and he paid them off nine months ago. The *dōjō* was thriving.'

'Someone wanted in.'

'Uh uh. Lieutenant –'

Croaker lifted a hand, palm outward. 'Just going over all the possibilities. You so sure he was straight? I mean, you weren't with him twenty-four hours a day.'

'I didn't have to be. I knew him. Believe me, there's no illegal involvement. At least, not in the way you think.'

'Which leads us back to *bushido*, right?' He was interrupted by the food. He waited until the waitress had gone before he said, 'You know, Linnear, for those two stiffs being your friends you certainly aren't broken up about it.'

Nicholas sat perfectly still. A pulse beat strongly in the side of his neck; a cool wind seemed to blow through his brain. There were haunting echoes, as if he were hearing the words of his ancestors carried to him through the corridors of time. Beneath the table, his fingers were as stiff as knives, his thigh muscles like steel. He required no blade, no concealed weapon. There was only himself, as deadly a killing machine as ever was created in any country at any time.

Croaker was staring into his eyes. 'It's all right,' he said softly. He gestured with the tines of his fork, laced with running yolk. 'Your food's getting cold.' He went to work on his own and never knew just how close he had come to being killed.

There was anger and then there was anger. Just as there were insults and there were insults. Lew Croaker was just another dumb Westerner, Nicholas told himself as he ate. He had no idea what he was doing or what effect his words would have. He had said what he had in order to find out, to read their effect in Nicholas's face. There should have been no reaction at all. Bujutsu had taught him that. But it had been a long time and he had been off his guard because he had been with a Westerner.

Which just goes to show you, Nicholas thought. Danger comes cloaked in many forms. Not that he thought of Lew Croaker as any kind of danger, far from it. But, he realized, ignorance brings its own kind of danger and Croaker had unwittingly put his head on the block.

Croaker glanced up at him from time to time as they ate, as Nicholas tried to define the complex concept of *bushido* to him. Obedience might be the basis but, to Western minds at least, that word had such a pejorative nature that it seemed like the wrong beginning. Because *bushido* was defined not only by sociology and religion but by history, too. To Americans, who thought in terms of two hundred years when it came to their own country, the concept of centuries seemed like deep water indeed.

Still, Croaker seemed to absorb it all quite seriously, his interest deepening as Nicholas progressed. At the end, over coffee, Croaker sat back, took out a MintyPick. His eyes wandered for a time, then he said, oddly, 'I got an old lady, who drives me bats. She's never around when I get home.'

'According to you,' Nicholas said, 'you rarely get home.'

Croaker took a swig of the coffee, winced, poured in cream. He broke open a packet of granulated sugar, stirred it in. 'I don't know what it is but I just can't seem to get used to it straight.' He took a swallow, nodded approvingly, looked up. 'All right, I *did* say that, yeah. What I mean is, the odd times I *do* come home, it makes it all the worse, y'know?'

'You need a new job,' Nicholas said pointedly.

'Nah. I think I need a new lady, is all. See, Alison's an endocrinologist. She's been working on a project for three and a half years. It must be a bastard 'cause I don't think they're any closer now than they were when they started.' He rolled the toothpick around his mouth, from one side to the other. 'Recombinant DNA.'

'Clones, huh?'

Croaker liked that; his face brightened. 'Yeah.' He laughed. 'She's building an army of super-fuckin-humans. Gonna make you an' me obsolete, Jack.' He laughed again. 'Nah, nothing so dramatic. They're trying to find a way to alter the DNA in a mother's womb so people with hereditary diseases can have children.' He brooded over his coffee for a while. 'Things haven't been too good for a while. I think it's time to get out.'

'So get out,' Nicholas said.

Croaker looked up. 'Yeah.' There was an awkward silence. 'Listen, about what I said before –'

'Let's go,' Nicholas said, standing up. 'We've got an appointment and it won't do to be late.'

It was cool and dry inside without the benefit of artificial air-conditioning. It was as if they were far below the surface of the earth where it was naturally cool. The summer sun could not penetrate this far.

The walls were of enormous stone blocks, quite thick, so as to be able to retain the coolness even on the hottest of days; there was a second storey to take the brunt of the sun.

Over the sounds of their movement, Croaker could hear faint echoes, like calm voices heard at the bottom of a pond through the intervening water; he could not understand the words but he knew they were there. As they moved closer, he could begin to discern other sounds as well: wordless noises as precise as close-order army drill, recalling to him the long days of basic training in that remote, dusty town in Georgia.

'Film and television discovered the martial arts some years ago,' Nicholas said as they proceeded, 'and turned them into a circus entertainment. As a result, they're taken about as seriously as professional wrestling over here. At best, they are quite misunderstood by Americans.' Nicholas stopped and turned to Croaker. 'The Way is not mere killing. That is a purely Western notion. You pull out a gun and boom! you destroy life. That is not the Way. The basis of all bujutsu is internal.'

They began to walk again and the sounds came nearer now. Croaker thought he heard the rhythmic slap of bare feet against wood, the crack of wood against wood as if a giant were playing an outsized percussion instrument.

'Bujutsu is not something to be taken lightly, Lieutenant, I assure you,' Nicholas continued. 'It is neither a conjurer's trick nor a parlour game amusement, but deadly serious.' He turned his head. 'I trust I'm not being redundant. I'm merely being careful. You see, the average Westerner will never see nor even hear about the true bujutsu adept. Why should he, since the adept neither wishes for nor gets any kind of publicity.

'Despite its violent nature, bujutsu is more in synch with religion – Zen and Shinto specifically – than it is with, say, sports. It is a way of life, governed by *bushido*. An adept would commit *seppuku* – ritual suicide – rather than break the code. Everything in life, Lieutenant – *every thing* – is subject to *bushido*. I hope you can understand that.'

'I'm not certain that I do,' Croaker said truthfully. Yet something swam at the edge of his consciousness, tantalizing him. He wondered what it was, then shrugged mentally, left it alone. Straining after it, he knew, would only push it further away.

'It's not surprising.' Nicholas gave him a bleak smile that contained no warmth. 'For some Westerners it takes years to understand.' He was a bit ahead of Croaker now. 'For others' – he shrugged – 'It never comes at all.'

There was nothing in the world that could make Gelda Tomkin Odile cry, yet she felt close to tears now. She stood in the coolness of her Sutton Place apartment, looking out at the bright sunshine turning the East River solid. It might have been a river of salt for all the reality it had for her. The familiar view looked as flat as a painting and as unappetizing. Perhaps it was a painting, after all, she thought, but she knew that she was not thinking clearly. That was the one thing she was happy about; what she had been searching for. The Chivas was no longer sufficient; and, she thought wryly, it's bad for business. Grass was no damn good. She had found that out a long time ago. Because she could control it and she needed something that controlled her. Hallucinogens were useless to her and opium merely knocked her out. Then she had found that codeine pills in conjunction with the whisky were just what the doctor ordered. She laughed sardonically at that.

The phone rang in the room behind her, a soft burring that was as much a part of the atmosphere of the place as was the long leather couch whose surface could only be warmed by contact with naked flesh.

Gelda stared out of the window, in no hurry to answer the phone; it would continue to ring until she picked it up; if she were not at home or did not want to be disturbed, the machine would have intercepted the call after the first ring. It was Pear who needed her. She could afford to wait.

She wished now that she could cry, but even through the mist of the spirits and the drug she found herself dry, her interior as sere and forbidding as a desert bleached by the sun.

She turned and walked silently across the deep sapphire wall-to-wall carpet of the bedroom. Through the open door she saw the vast expanse of the umber leather couch and the terra-cotta carpet which dominated the living-room – or her work-room as she preferred to call it: they rarely wanted to use the bed any more.

Her thick hair was like honey and, as she passed through a bar of sunlight, it took on the lustre of rich silk. She wore a forest-green natural satin robe, loosely belted, which clung to her like a second skin, showed off her ample cleavage, her long legs, but which concealed those parts of her body which, in her most private thoughts, she despised. There was not a single mirror in the entire apartment, not even over the basin in the bathroom, yet she had a cupboard full, stashed away; it was a popular item.

She picked up the phone. 'Yes.'

'Darling, what took you so long?' Pear said in her ear. 'Something horribly naughty?'

'Not naughty enough.' Gelda closed her eyes.

Pear chuckled. 'That's my girl.' Her voice changed gear abruptly. 'G, are you all right?'

'Sure, why?'

'You haven't been out much lately. Some of the girls were asking, that's all. They miss you.'

'I miss them, too,' Gelda said, wondering whether she meant it or not. 'I've been thinking a lot, Pear.'

'My dearest darling,' Pear said patiently, 'you know that thinking is no good for the soul. You've got to get out more; go to a couple of parties.'

'You know I don't do that sort of thing,' Gelda snapped.

'Please. I wasn't soliciting.' Pear's voice seemed pained now. 'My darling, I care about you. Genuinely care.'

'I'm worth a lot to you.'

'Now you forget that kind of talk. G.' It was Pear's turn to snap. 'You are just being contrary. I know that and I forgive you that statement. There aren't many people I care about in this world – Lord knows, none of the girls – but you're one of them.'

'I'm one of your girls,' Gelda said stubbornly.

She heard Pear's exasperated sigh on the other end of the line. 'Darling, need I remind you *again* that it was you who sought me out? Yes, I provide your clientele, but they're a very special breed, you don't need me to tell you that. One thousand dollars a night is nothing to look down your nose at. You could perhaps make more by the hour but what's the point, darling? That won't make you happy and this does. But I can hardly say that you are one of my *girls*. My God, what a difference! People *ask* for you, my darling. That's the difference.'

'Do you have something for me?' Gelda asked woodenly.

Pear sighed again, giving up for the moment. 'Yes. Dare. The actress. You remember –'

'I remember.'

'She only wanted you.'

'All right.'

'Do you have everything you need?' Pear inquired.

Gelda thought for a minute. 'The chaps were just cleaned but the silk –'

'I'll have Lawless come by with it this afternoon. Anything else?'

Gelda was thinking about the enormous Remington Navy six-shooter with the long octagonal barrel and the polished hardwood stock under her expert guidance. It wasn't called a six-shooter for nothing. 'Yes,' she said dreamily, 'a half pound of lox and four bagels.' She paused for a moment. 'Pear, be sure you tell him no onions; not when I'm working.'

Pear laughed in her ear. 'That's more like it. You know tonight's going to be more pleasure than business.'

There was that to look forward to at least. She turned to look out of the window at the bright brittle sunshine. The phone slid from her grip. The river of salt winked at her, dazzling.

The room itself was constructed entirely of wood. Only wooden pegs and glue had been used in the laying of the boards, shiny with clear lacquer.

It was a rectangle, wider than it was deep, with a high ceiling. The light was soft and well defined in every corner of the room.

It had the look of a gymnasium save for the raised dais with its low wooden railing that ran across the width at the rear of the room. Otherwise it was devoid of furniture or other accoutrements.

There were a dozen men in white cotton leggings and shirts, lined up six against six opposite each other. Each held a polished wooden stick, round with a shallow hilt guard. Croaker would have thought of them as swords had it not been for a total lack of cutting edge or sharp point. The men were maskless. All were Japanese. Most were in their early or middle twenties though he saw one teenager and two who were obviously nearer forty.

A man dressed in grey stood between these two groups, near the stairs leading up to the low dais. He was small in stature. He was hairless, making a judgement of his age somewhat more difficult. Croaker put it somewhere between forty and fifty. The man gave a piercing cry and the two lines advanced two quick steps, engaging each other in what looked to him like ritualized combat using the wooden sticks.

'This is a kenjutsu class, Lieutenant,' Nicholas said. 'The finest in the Western Hemisphere and parts of the East as well.'

Croaker watched, fascinated, as the men advanced and retreated, attacked and parried, crying out in unison. But it all seemed so slow and methodical that he could not see how any of it could be at all useful in a fight.

In moments there came a soft bell tone and, at a sharp command from the *sensei*, the men stepped back and, lifting their swords in unison, bowed deeply to each other. Then they wheeled and broke up into quiet groups. Some walked to the sides of the *dōjō* and sat on their thighs, others bent and stretched where they were. All seemed totally involved in these minute actions.

Nicholas took Croaker across the polished floor to where the kenjutsu master stood. He bowed and said some things, in Japanese, to the small man, who bowed again and extended his hand towards Croaker.

Uncertain, Croaker took it. It was as hard as a block of concrete. The man smiled.

'This is Fukashigi,' Nicholas told Croaker. 'Consider yourself introduced.'

Croaker let go the man's hand, said, 'What happens now?'

'Watch,' Nicholas said.

Fukashigi looked off to his left, spoke in rapid Japanese. A student uncoiled himself and, first pausing to pick up another wooden sword, came quietly over. He bowed to Nicholas, handed him one of the weapons. Fukashigi spoke to him for a short time and at the end his head bobbed once. *'Hai!'* he said in assent.

The student was tall and lanky, with a hard face and quick, intelligent eyes. Both he and Nicholas adopted an opening attitude, feet as far apart as the width of their shoulders, knees slightly bent, both hands on the hilts of their wooden swords.

'Now,' Nicholas said to Croaker, not taking his eyes from the student, 'there are five attitudes in kendo and only five: upper, middle, lower, right side, left side. The first three are

206

decisive; the last two, fluid, used when you encounter an obstruction overhead or on one side. However, this is not the Way. To master the technique, you must have what is commonly known as the "attitude – no attitude". That is, adapt from one to the other as the situation dictates *without thinking* so that your motion from the beginning of the contest to the end is one uninterrupted fluid motion: like the sea. The five elements, Lieutenant, are crucial to kenjutsu.'

And he attacked the student with such blinding speed and ferocity that Croaker literally jumped.

'Approach from the middle attitude,' Nicholas said and he performed it again, slowed down immensely, the motions now magnified. He lifted his sword so that its 'point' was in the student's face. The man immediately attacked and, as he did, Nicholas, with minimal motion, slashed the other's sword to the right.

Nicholas stood with his sword high above his head, the upper attitude. The student struck forwards and, at the same time, Nicholas cut downwards.

Nicholas lowered his sword. The student attacked once more, moving his sword upwards. This time the student blocked him but in that same instant Nicholas's sword freed itself from the block, cut across the other's upper arms in a soft tap.

The student immediately moved to attack, coming in from the right side. Nicholas moved his sword until it was on his left side, below his waist. As the student attacked him, his sword flashed, upwards, scoring along the length and, crossing over, he cut across the man's shoulders.

Now the student attacked from the cut upwards. Blocked, Nicholas slid gracefully into the upper attitude, delivering what would, in actual combat, have been a killing blow to the top of the student's head.

They both stepped back, bowed to each other.

'You see,' Nicholas said, turning to Croaker, 'the basics of kenjutsu.'

'But you're just using wooden practice swords,' Croaker said. 'You can't hurt anybody –'

'On the contrary, these *bokken* are every bit as deadly as the *katana* is. They –'

But in that instant he had whirled, somehow sensing the dual attack from both the student at his side and the *sensei* directly behind him. The student had already been disarmed with one cut and Nicholas was deep within battle with Fukashigi by the time Croaker had time to react to the situation. That would be about a tenth of a second, he calculated dazedly. My God, I saw the attack coming before he did!

The clash of the *bokken* filled the room but the contestants' movements were so swift that they were a mere blur. Croaker stared carefully but, try as he might, he could not distinguish one movement from the next, so fluid were they. He recalled Nicholas's analogy of this movement to the sea and he understood.

Then there came a momentous crashing as Fukashigi landed a ferocious overhead blow against Nicholas's upraised sword. Nicholas was not moved backwards, however, and as he stood immobile, the *sensei* sprang backwards as lightly as a current of air, preparing himself for a second attack. But as the sword moved backwards to gain momentum for the forward thrust, Nicholas was there, extending himself outwards like a river, his own sword following precisely the path of the other's and, beating down the 'point', stabbing inwards at the *sensei*'s head. It touched the tip of the nose but, at the same instant, Fukashigi's left fist was at Nicholas's face in a blow that might have broken his nose and stunned him.

Both stepped back, bowed to each other. Neither of them seemed to be breathing hard.

Doc Deerforth had left. Justine sat over her drawing-board working on a design that had eluded her for four days. Once or twice she seemed to have it conquered only to see it slip away from her as she sketched it out. It was like trying to catch a minnow with your fingers, she decided. At length she threw down her pen in disgust, ripped the sheet of tracing-paper off its drawing-pin anchors and crumpled it up.

She went into the kitchen, fixed herself a tuna fish sandwich. She had chewed at it without really tasting it, thinking of where she had gone wrong; surely the concept was sound enough. She washed the last of the sandwich down with a half glass of orange-juice.

She was dressed in a Danskin bathing suit. For a moment she stood staring at the drawing-board as if it were her enemy. Dangerous, she thought. She knew the signs.

She grabbed a towel and went out of the door onto the beach. She ran now, dropping the towel onto the sand, high-stepping into the breakers, pushing herself through the heavy drag of the cold water until, seeing a wave looming high over her, ready to crash, she dived into its green side.

In solitude, she dimly heard its thunder over her, felt the slight quake of its violent passage. Then she was borne upwards on the swell. She launched out with cupped hands and kicking legs, stroking powerfully outwards, feeling the stretch in her lower back, her shoulders, her thighs. Bubbles streamed like molten metal from the corner of her mouth and she glided effortlessly upwards, breaking the shivering surface, blinking, gulping air before she went under again.

Nicholas filled her thoughts and, despite what she had told Doc Deerforth, she considered going into the city. She hadn't heard from him. Surely that meant he was busy. God, she didn't want that any more. But she wanted him, couldn't help it. She continued to stroke outwards, coming up just long enough to catch sweet air. When she was far enough out, she turned to her right to parallel the shore.

She found herself thinking of the long black and gold lacquered sheath hung on his wall. In her thoughts, she went across the room and, on tiptoes, reached up slowly, freeing it from its hook. It was heavy, satiny, perfectly balanced. She put her left fist around the end of the sheath, her right around the long hilt of the *katana*. Nicholas's *katana*. Inch by inch, as she exerted slow pressure, she saw the gleaming steel appear before her wide-open eyes extending in a crescent horizon. It was a silver dazzle, blinding her, an enormous erection that continued to grow under her ministrations. Breath caught in her throat. Her heart pounded. The pumping blood sang in her ears. And the cool wash of the sea was like a caress over her swimming body. Her nipples erected and she felt an excitement stir between her legs. Still kicking, she put one hand down, cupped her mound. She moaned. Bubbles flew like birds thrown across the sky.

She felt a wash of cold water spiralling up her legs against her working thighs. It was so much like the stroking hand of a lover that, startled, her eyes flew open. The current encompassed her aching loins, now snaked up her torso. She rolled over. It was then that she felt the pull. At first it was only the tiniest of tugs but abruptly, as the tide and her swimming took her along, it wrenched at her.

Her impulse was to gasp but she clamped her teeth shut in time. The undertow was pulling her inexorably out to sea. She tumbled in its grasp, not end over end but around, as if she was a cylinder. Dizzied, she struck out blindly for the shore. She was an excellent swimmer and her breath capacity was good. Still, her first priority was to gain the surface.

Whirling, she struck out upwards but made little headway. The grip upon her was as real as if a sea serpent had appeared from some unseen abyss and had wrapped its slippery coils about her.

She broke the surface, gasping and coughing. But in doing so she had lost ground to the sea. She tried to lift her head, shake her eyes clear of the stinging salt water so that she could get an accurate fix on the shoreline. She was jerked under.

She began to panic. Her stomach heaved and she shivered, not even swimming now but merely struggling futilely. Why hadn't she screamed when she was in the air? She tried to rise again but the fierce grip would not let her. She sank. And in sinking, found her way home. Near the murky bottom the stillness was absolute. She wondered at this for a moment, her mind still trembling in fear until she realized that the tug of the current was gone. She reached out blindly, encountered rock. She pulled, keeping herself at this level, and began to make her way in to shore.

Her lungs turned to fire and once her left thigh seemed seized in a cramp. She let it fall loose for a moment, relaxing her muscles, and it subsided. She went on scuttling over the bottom like an enormous crab. She desperately wanted to shoot upwards to the surface but her terror of the undertow was absolute. She pushed on. Her eyes felt as if they were popping out of their sockets and an unquiet wind blew in her ears, roaring.

At last she felt the warmth of the shallower water and, simultaneously, the gentle push of the tide onto the rising sand.

She sprang upwards, uncoiling her body fully, breaching the surface, sounding like a whale. She gasped and snorted, her insides turning to jelly. She felt the sand against her soles and, as she came out of the water, she found her legs would not support her. She fell to her knees and a wave inundated her. She fell over.

She heard the sound of raised voices as she vomited seawater into the surf. Then strong hands had her under her armpits. Her head hung down on her chest and she coughed.

'Are you all right?'

She tried to nod, only vomited again, heaving wretchedly. She felt the dry sand against her back. She was aware of her whole body gasping. She felt as if she would never get enough air inside her. Her lungs worked like a bellows and the sound was so harsh and rasping to her ears that she might have been an asthmatic. There was a folded towel behind her head, elevating her face. A pins-and-needles tingling broke out along her cheeks and lips. She tried to raise her arms but they felt as if they belonged to another person. There was no strength left within her.

'Take it easy,' someone said above her. 'Take it easy.'

She closed her eyes, feeling as she did so a kind of kinetic vertigo as one does after stepping off a violent ride at an amusement park. In her mind, she still spun in the grip of the undertow. Gradually this faded and, as it did so, her breathing began to return to normal.

'Okay now?'

She nodded, not daring to speak.

'Live around here?' It was a feminine voice.

She nodded.

'We've called for a doctor.'

'I'm all right,' she said. Her voice sounded strange to her.

'He'll be here in a minute.'

She nodded, closing her eyes again. She thought of Gelda

and the time at the seashore when they were both in the water. Perhaps Gelda was nine; she was six. They were playing and, as a joke, she had poked Gelda in the ribs. Her sister had turned to her, a look of fury on her face, and, reaching up her arms, had clamped her hands onto the top of Justine's head. Down Justine had gone, under the water. At first it was all right. But then she wanted to get up, to breathe. Gelda held her down. She struggled, but still Gelda would not relent. In her mind, she pleaded with her sister, then she reviled her. When at last Gelda had let her up, she was hysterical. She ran from the water, crying, right into her mother's arms. She had never told anyone what Gelda had done to her but for a week she would not look at, let alone talk to, her sister. Gelda's only response had been to gloat silently.

Justine opened her eyes to find Doc Deerforth bending over her, talking to her. She reached up and, shuddering, cried against his chest.


When Lieutenant Croaker left Nicholas outside the *dōjō*, he called in through the car radio to see about messages. McCabe wanted him to call back, that was no doubt about the Tanaka-Okura thing; Vegas had dropped in to talk; and Finnigan wanted a progress report.

He was rolling cross-town and the traffic was fierce. 'If you can still catch Vegas, tell him I'll be back around four-thirty, okay?' He did not want to speak to the D.A. yet and as for Finnigan – fuck him!

No other calls. Croaker tried to clear his mind of the anticipation. But oh, how he wanted that call to come in. 'That's it,' he said. 'Patch me through to Vincent Ito at the M.E.'s, will you?' The heat sat in wavy lines along the street. He wiped at his sweating forehead. When Vincent came on the line, Croaker arranged a dinner. Vincent suggested Michita and gave Croaker the address.

Croaker went through Central Park at the Seventy-second Street Transverse and, moments later, he had pulled up outside the three-storey brownstone that housed Terry Tanaka's *dōjō*. There he interviewed all the instructors. He called for a police artist to draw a composite of the strange Japanese who had visited the *dōjō* on the afternoon of the double murder. None of the people he interviewed had seen the man before or since. None knew where he had come from. The aikido *sensei* recalled his name as Hideoshi, but that meant absolutely nothing to Croaker. Still, it was conceivable that the man was the killer or was, at least, tied up with him in some way.

It was well after four by the time he was finished. There had been no prints at Terry's save for the two victims', but . . . but he called for a print team to dust the *dōjō* anyway. It was not good practice to overlook any possibility, however remote. Who knows, he thought, we may be lucky and pull something. Then he asked for a detective sergeant to canvass the block to see if any neighbour had seen the man.

In the office he checked in with Irene, threw the two polythene bags of clothes and personal effects of Terry and Eileen into a corner.

He checked for calls. Nothing.

He was about to open the bundles for tagging when his doorway was darkened by Vegas. He was an enormous man with a full beard and eyes like points of lightning. His skin was so black it took on blue highlights in the fluorescent lighting of the station house.

'Hey,' Croaker said, turning his head.

'What it is.' Vegas's voice was like the rumble of distant thunder.

'Heard you wanted to see me.'

'Yowsah.'

'Take a seat.'

Vegas sat down with a grunt. He wore faded jeans, Texas cowboy boots and a grey and black cowboy shirt with pearl snaps. 'I gots to get outa there,' he said. He meant Narco. 'I am being driven up the fuckin' wall.'

'Sallyson?' He was the Captain.

'You mean Captain Ahab.' Vegas snorted. 'The fuckin' bastard's ready for the funny farm.' He leaned forward, his elbows on his long thighs. 'Look, Lew, I want in here. Homicide.'

Croaker looked at his friend. He had known Vegas for a long time. They had been hooked up in plenty of wild busts;

did each other favours all the time and never did one lightly. 'Finnigan's not an easy sonovabitch to take, my man,' Croaker said seriously. 'He is one mean motherfucker.'

'Don't make no nevermind to me, Jack,' Vegas said. 'Long as I get away from Narco – those boys ain't funny no more.'

Croaker squinted up at him. 'Let's see. Homicide's not the only answer. Why, you could slip right into Vice, no trouble at all.'

Vegas's face looked pained. 'Sheeit! Sure, I could make a bundle, takin' my part of the grease each month. Only trouble is, you sawed-off sonovabitch, those fuckers don't allow no black man in on the big-time scam, you dig? They don' want me over there.'

'Well, Vegas, I sure as hell don't know whether Finnigan would want you either.'

'You know he's an okay motherfucker when it comes to skin, Jack. Wassamatter, don't you want to work with me?'

Croaker laughed. 'I sure as hell would love it but right now the old man ain't too pleased with me.'

'Shit! That ain't no big thing. You know how he is. Next time you land a big one an' the mayor hands him another bronze pin, he'll be back kissin' yo' white ass.'

Croaker grinned. 'Maybe so. Maybe so.'

'Ain't no two ways about it, Jack.'

Croaker longed to tell Vegas about the Didion case: his suspicions and what he was working on. It was only procedure, after all – you needed a back-up in any operation – but he knew that he could not do it. Not that he did not trust the man – they had saved each other's lives too many times for trust ever to be a factor. It was unfair to the other man. It was one thing for Croaker to put himself in departmental jeopardy, quite another to rope someone else in unwittingly.

Croaker reached out, slapped the other's leg. 'Okay, you got it. I'll ask Finnigan soon's I think the time's right and we got a chance of him not biting my head off.'

Vegas gave him a wide grin. 'I dig. I dig.' He got up, towering over Croaker. 'You lay it on him an' we'll see what pops up. Meanwhile, this is one nigger that's got to hit the streets again. Sallyson's given us all quotas to fill, dig? Sheeit!' He turned and waved. 'Later.'

'Lay one on for me,' Croaker said.

Vegas smiled. 'Only on the prettiest one, Jack.'

'I don't know, Nick, it seems as if I've been here for a hundred years.' Vincent looked down at the peanut he was shelling. 'It's funny but Tokyo seems like a dream to me, nothing more.'

'You ought to go back, then. If only for a vacation.'

'Yeah, I suppose I should.' He popped the peanut into his mouth.

They walked down the tiered stone steps into the Central Park Zoo. They strolled over hexagonal tiles, smelling the mingled musk of the animals in the heat. They walked north, towards the Monkey House.

'But I won't. I know that now.'

'There's nothing stopping you. Nothing at all.'

Vincent shook his head. They went down the stone steps to the plaza. On their left, beyond the great empty cage meant to house the avians, they could see the Seal Pond, where now several new sea lions dived and dashed beside the elderly female, the lone survivor of happier years here. 'It's my family, Nick. My sisters. If I went back, I would have to see them. Duty. I can't face them. Not now. Not after what I've become.'

Near the Monkey House a swarthy man with a thick moustache and a sailor hat stood next to a pair of green metal cylinders. He made helium balloons in front of the wide eyes of a group of children. Each time he did it, it seemed like a giant sucking in his breath.

'What have you become?'

The other turned his head. 'That's just it. I don't know any more. But I'm not what I once was. I've been assimilated; I feel as if I've been corrupted by this place. My values have changed. The traditions are crumbling around me.' There was a crowd in front of the gorilla cage watching delightedly as the family inside was hosed down by a female attendant. The mother reached out and, putting her palm against the nozzle, sprayed the onlookers. There were squeals and the crowd broke apart momentarily. Laughing, they surged back towards the cage. Next door, the haughty orang-utan looked on unperturbed, studying the odd creatures through the bars of his cage as if for research for a book.

'Come on,' Nicholas said lightly. 'I remember when we first met. You, Terry and me. It was at Michita, remember? We were all kind of lost then – all in the same way. Which is why, I suppose, we all coalesced at that spot.' He smiled, or tried to at least. 'A bit of home.' He shook his head. 'But what was it that brought *us* together? Was it merely that we were all slightly homesick? I don't think so.'

'Eileen used to say that it was the martial spirit which linked us. Like a magical umbilicus. I think she must have thought we were like children in that way.'

Nicholas shook his head. 'No. You're wrong there. She respected that in us. She didn't – I suspect *couldn't* – understand it. But she recognized its power and would not interfere. That was why she always declined to come when the three of us got together. She knew she would be out of her element even though we would make every effort to make her feel comfortable. Terry told me once that she said she thought she'd only inhibit us, and she was right.'

'I don't know,' Vincent said. 'It all seems so far away to me now, as if we were talking about the customs of Finland. I'm not sure whether *I* understand it any more.'

'That's just talk – so many meaningless words. The way a Westerner would think. Open your mind and you'll still feel it. Being here can't make it go away.' He seemed to be telling himself as well as Vincent. 'We were born in the land of the martial spirit. It binds us more powerfully – timelessly – to one another than a blood bond. What has been taught us will never leave us, you know that. You're still the same person, at the core, who got off that JAL plane twelve years ago.'

'Oh no, I'm not. Not by a long stretch. I don't talk the same, I don't think the same way. America has changed me and the process seems irreversible. I can never go back. I no longer belong to Japan and I don't feel like I belong here. The West has taken something very valuable from me, snatched it away while I wasn't looking.'

'You can get it back. It's not too late.'

Vincent looked at him, put his hands in his pockets and walked on. They were near the arch on top of which perched the famous clock that chimed in each hour with a parade of animals dancing in a semicircle. Beyond was the Children's Zoo, its bright laughter and clip-clop of hastily running feet.

'I haven't told anyone this, not even the police. I got a deadline call the night Terry and Ei were murdered.' He looked up. 'But the more I think about it, the more certain I am that I did hear something, after all. Some music.'

'Do you remember what it was?'

'Yeah. I'm pretty sure it was Mancini.' He did not have to add that Mancini was Eileen's favourite composer.

Vincent shivered. 'It was like Terry was calling to me from beyond the grave.' He lifted a hand hastily. 'I know. I know. I don't believe in that kind of thing. But, damn it! It was as if he was trying to tell me who did it.'

'You mean he *knew* the murderer?'

Vincent shrugged. 'Maybe I'm making too much out of it. I don't know any more. I just wish – I wish you had been in the city that night, that's all. Christ, they were your friends, too!'

Nicholas said nothing, stared at the smiling children eating ices, sticking out their patinated tongues at the solemn apes. He wished he felt something. Grief was a useful emotion; better that than carrying it around with you like a hump. He felt an abrupt stillness as if he were at the eye of a raging hurricane. Safe and protected, he nevertheless was witness to the devastation going on all around him. Was there a way to stop it? He knew a way, most definitely, but he was reluctant to take it. Vincent was still looking at him, as if by his gaze alone he could wrench some confession from Nicholas's bowels. It had to be done, then. As he knew it from the moment the deal had been proposed. There was obligation; there was duty. Vincent was right. They were his friends.

Vincent touched his arm. 'Sorry, old friend,' he said. 'It's me. I'm on edge. You can see it. Jesus, it's not fair to take it out on you.' He smiled thinly. 'You see how Westernized I've become.'

Nicholas returned the smile with more warmth than he

felt. 'No. You were right. Neither of us has forgotten the importance of obligation and duty.'

'Listen, Croaker's invited me to dinner. Why don't you join us? At the place.'

'All right.' Nicholas nodded. 'I'd like that.'

Vincent glanced at his watch. 'Back to the salt-mines. See you later.'

Nicholas searched through the park for a phone, finally went out on Fifth Avenue. He called Justine. Doc Deerforth answered.

'What's the matter?' Nicholas said. His heart was racing.

'A slight accident. Nothing to worry about. But I think you ought to come out if your work permits.'

'What happened?'

'Justine was caught in the undertow. She's all right.'

'Are you certain that's what it was?'

'Reasonably. What do you mean?'

'Were there other people around? Did anyone see anything suspicious?'

'There were plenty of people. A neighbour helped drag her out of the surf. No one mentioned anything else.'

'Can you stay with her until I get there? I'll take the first train out.' He looked at his watch.

'Sure. There's nothing pressing. My service knows where I am. But if there's an emergency –'

'I understand. Doc – tell her I'll be there.'

'When she wakes up. Don't worry.'

He hung up and hailed a cab, took it to Penn Station. Downstairs at the Long Island Rail Road counter he bought a ticket, found that he had twenty-five minutes to spare. He called Tomkin. There was a considerable delay. He stared out at the passing parade of people, scanning unconsciously. A pair of teenagers struggled with enormous knapsacks and, just behind them, a young woman stood against a pillar waiting impatiently to be met. He wondered whether it was her boss who was late.

'Nicholas?' The voice came crisply into his ear.

'Tomkin.'

'I'm glad you called. Have you thought about my offer?'

Bastard, he thought. Bastard to bring Justine into it. But now he knew that Justine *was* a part of it. He hated to be in this position. Methodically, he calmed himself. 'I've thought about it. I'll start work for you today.'

'Good. Why don't you come up to the tower and –'

'No. I'm at Penn Station. I'm taking the next train out to the Island.'

'I don't understand –'

'There's work to do out there. Justine's out there.'

'I see.'

'I'm sure you do,' Nicholas said savagely. 'I'll be in touch tomorrow.'

'Nick –'

The voice was cut off as he cradled the receiver.

The man was on the job. He had come to work for Lubin Bros over a week ago. He had been assigned to a construction site on Ralph Avenue in Brooklyn until Edwards had turned up sick and he had been transferred to the Park Avenue job. Tomkin was paying extra to make certain construction did not fall behind schedule and the management of Lubin Bros was doing everything in its power to keep things moving along. That included making sure there was always a full complement of workers.

The man worked tirelessly at every assignment he was given. He was a good worker and spoke very little; no one noticed him. When he reported that day, his mind had been filled with his work of the night before: early morning, that is. It was a way of thinking about today's assignment. Some new wrinkles were needed, and while his forebrain was recounting last night's work, the subconscious dissected the present problem.

It had been no trouble at all to gain access to the Actium House sub-basement parking lot; he had come in in the empty back seat of a Lincoln Continental which had disgorged its passengers at the street-level entrance. Then it had simply been a matter of waiting.

Tomkin's limo had come down the ramp at ten minutes past

three in the morning. He was a notorious insomniac and spent the better part of each week-day night in his office at the new building.

The powerful headlights had scored the roof of the lot, then dipped as the limo came down the last part of the ramp. The motor thrummed quietly in the dark as the chauffeur rolled it to the parking space and slid in. The motor died.

The man knew by heart the next movements of the chauffeur, but even so he waited a full hour after the other had left. Time was one element that he had plenty of now. It could be the best of friends or the most implacable of enemies, thus he treated it with respect. It never paid to be hasty.

At last he uncoiled himself and moved towards the limo. It was like a shadow on the prowl. In seconds he had the back door of the car open and closed again. Inside, he used a pencil flash and a surgeon's scalpel. Where the plush carpet met the edge of the rear seat, he scored a line with the scalpel. He made a second cut so that the two were in a T shape. Then he peeled back the small flaps and inserted a round object no more than half an inch in diameter and, using an odourless epoxy resin, he closed the flaps carefully. Next he turned his attention to the phone. He opened the box and, ignoring the receiver, placed a second disk on the inside wall of the box. He sat in the back seat precisely where he knew Tomkin sat and opened the box, looking down at the receiver. He could not see the disk. Satisfied, he closed the box. He turned off the pencil flash and let himself out of the limo. Within twenty seconds he was walking down Fifty-first Street, hunched over in his black nylon windbreaker. In all, he had been in the limo precisely nine minutes.

Now as he worked on the riveting in the atrium lobby of Tomkin Industries, the man worked on the problem of getting upstairs.

At lunchtime he took the outside cage elevator up as far as it would go, one floor below Tomkin's office. Here the hall-ways were still raw plaster. Pencil marks were strewn about like engineering graffiti. The corridors were deserted but he was careful enough and there were numerous doorways to plunge into. Every so often he paused and, completely still, listened to the sounds of the building. He would know instantly if there was the slightest change.

He was not worried about his face. There was flesh-coloured putty on his cheeks and the bridge of his nose had been built up. Treated cotton rolls were placed in his mouth between gums and cheek. Too, his posture had changed from the man who had entered Terry Tanaka's *dōjō*. He had become slightly stoop-shouldered and he walked with a noticeable limp, as if one leg were shorter than the other. This was due to an inch lift in his right shoe. Disguising one's face was all well and good but there were a myriad ways one could be identified by an expert. One had to be as meticulous about all parts of the body as one was about the face – the overall image. A disguise had to be total. One needed only the slightest alterations, however, because the idea was camouflage and it did not do to overdo specific characteristics.

He found the fire stairs, went carefully up to the top floor. Here there was much activity. Both workers and Tomkin's staff were present. All the better, he thought.

Tomkin's office, a full corner of the floor, was nine-tenths complete but it had priority because he was already working out of it. Therefore lunch breaks were not observed up here. The morning shift went down to eat while a swing shift arrived to continue the work. The man was just in time to join them. He walked past the steady gaze of Frank, who stood just inside the thick metal doors to the office. This was hardly the most difficult part. It was doing what he had to do in plain sight of everyone.

The answer, of course, was easy. He merely had to look as if he knew what he was doing and no one paid him the slightest attention. It might even have been amusing, the way in which he performed the most clandestine of movements out in the open like the living embodiment of 'The Purloined Letter', if he had allowed himself the luxury of feeling. That, however, was quite impossible for him in this context, thus it was merely an object of intellectual curiosity like a peculiarly striated rock brought home from a summer field trip.

He had, of course, to work in fits and starts: that is, to work on what was his own in between what he was given.

This presented no problems other than extending his time in the office.

He turned it, however, to his own advantage, as was his wont, by using the time to memorize the contours, the tiny nooks and crannies, the open spaces and the closed. He found where the wall was baffled and where it was bare beneath the paint and plaster; where the wiring went and the placement of all of the electrical outlets; where the circuit breakers were and where the auxiliary lighting. At the moment none of these things fitted in with his plans but one never knew when the knowledge might be crucial. Meticulous planning was essential; however, one always had to build into one's plans a bit of leeway because events had a peculiar way of determining themselves and often, *too* often, a random element – an extra guard, a rainstorm, even an unexpected sound; a minute thing that could not be foreseen – slipped in. One never knew.

By one-thirty he was finished and, still under the jaundiced eye of Frank, he went out with the rest of the swing crew. Outside the metal doors, they turned to their right, heading towards the outside cage elevator one floor below. As he was turning the corner, the elevator at the end of the hallway sighed open and Tomkin, accompanied by Whistle, appeared.

The man paused for a moment, his dead eyes glittery. How easy it would be, he thought languidly, to take him out now. Whistle dead on his knees and the big man tumbling through the hot air to the unfinished pavement below. He liked it; it had a certain irony to it. But he did not admire it and that made all the difference in the world. It was not elegant, for one thing, and, for another, there would be little terror in it for Tomkin: just the brief moments he would be airborne, the hot wind in his face while the rubble of the sidewalk reached up for him. What would Tomkin think of in those instants, the man wondered. God? Oblivion? Hell? The man shrugged inwardly. It made little difference. He could understand none of these Western concepts. There was only karma for him. Karma and the *kami* he would inhabit when he died, waiting the prescribed time until he returned in another body, in another life, carrying his karma.

This concept of life that was so basic, so fundamental, was, he knew, beyond the conception of men like Tomkin. This did not make him any easier to kill; the doing was just that much less absorbing. It was the mechanics of the penetration, the sowing of the terror which occupied part of his mind; the act of killing itself would mean as much to him as stepping on a cockroach. After all, that was what Tomkin was. He could never be called a civilized man.

As to the eventual escape, the man knew that on this assignment there was a possibility that it would not happen. It did not faze him in the least, for it was something towards which he had prepared all his life. To die as a warrior was life's highest aspiration, after all, for history recorded the manner of one's death and it was in this that one was remembered forever, not how one lived one's life.

Not that he might ever be caught eliminating Tomkin. It was the other half of his plan: the part that made it all worth while. He was being paid a small fortune to take out Tomkin, but money meant very little to him. In fact, when he had arrived to take a look around – as he had put it to his then potential employers – he had not been certain he would take the assignment. But he had come upon something so startling, so irresistible that he could not refuse. He had learned early to take what life gave. He was being given something now that was so fantastic that he found himself salivating at the prospect. To turn away from such an opportunity would be a crime. The chance would never come again. The set-up would never be so sweet.

And this had been the second reason for not taking Tomkin out at this moment. Besides, it would, by necessity, have to be sloppy; this kind of total improvization went against his grain. He could do it and do it well but he resisted it. He hated to mop up all the loose ends after the fact. He liked things clean and neat; in another life he might have made a superb diamond cutter.

So it was that he just took a long, hard look at Tomkin as he strode down the hallway, unaware that death was at his left hand.

Then the man had moved on, down the unfinished corridor,

223

ducking a loose loop of wire flex hanging from an open panel in the ceiling. In a moment he was through the door to the fire stairs, off the floor.

Once down in the atrium lobby, half in shadows, he poked a finger in his ear as if scratching an itch. In the canal was now placed a flesh-coloured plastic sphere, flattened on the outside. It was totally undetectable. He touched the top of it with the tip of his index finger and began to listen.

Nicholas felt it as he turned away from the line of shining chromium phones along one wall of the station: that premonitory tickle at the base of his neck. He began to walk calmly towards a bookstore, though he had had no intention of going in there. It was merely the way he was headed and he did not want to make any sudden alteration in his movements. He stood by the window, however, instead of going in at the open door. People passed him, going in and out. There was a short line at the cash register; there was a sale on, 20 per cent off the top ten paperback best sellers.

He stood at a slight angle, not looking inside but using the plate glass as one would a mirror. He watched covertly a good section of the station behind him. Observation was made difficult by the poor refraction, the glare of the lights, the distortion of image caused by the glass itself. He accepted all of these and made allowances.

It was not good to stay here too long. He glanced at his watch. He still had fifteen minutes and he had no reason to sit for that time on the waiting train. Especially not now.

He walked away from the bookstore window, moving diagonally across the station. An old woman, her suitcase on wheels, crossed his path and two sailors in crisp whites passed him, one spinning the tail end of a lewd joke to the other. The young woman at the pillar was no longer there; either she had met her date or had given it up; three dark-haired children squired by a dour-looking woman scampered along, laughing and teasing each other. A man in a dark windbreaker stood by the bank of lockers, a lit cigarette dangling from one corner of his mouth. Opposite, a man in a camel-coloured suit flipped through the pages of the current *Hustler*, putting it down as a man with a tan briefcase came up to him. They shook hands and walked off.

Nicholas entered a Nedicks, wedged himself in next to a fat man devouring a slice of coconut cream pie. A dollar bill and some change were on the counter before him; his lips were dotted with pie crust and flecks of ersatz cream. The man ignored Nicholas as he sat down on a stool. He ordered a frank and an orange drink. The columns of the place were mirrored and Nicholas used these to continue his covert surveillance while he ate. He got his food, paid for it.

The feeling was still there, unmistakable. There was only one explanation. He was being observed by a *haragei* adept. The receiver was also a transmitter; there was no way to damp the two-way effect. This one had just come too close, that was all. Careless. And foolish.

Nicholas wiped his lips with the stiff napkin, took one last look in the mirror and went out. He had just over five minutes before the train left and in that time he would have to flush the adept. He had no thoughts now about missing the train; his overriding concern was for Justine. She was most assuredly in danger and he felt totally impotent being so far from her. It was one thing asking Doc Deerforth to look in on her once a day, quite another for him to be there when an emergency arose. Nicholas, rightly, trusted no one but himself in such a situation.

He had one more thing to do. He went to the phones again, called Lieutenant Croaker.

'Yeah.' The voice was harsh and rushed.

'Nicholas Linnear, Lieutenant.'

'What's up?'

'I'm on my way back out to the Island. Justine's had some kind of accident.'

There was some silence. Nicholas was still checking the vicinity.

'Croaker, there's someone following me.'

'Seeing shadows or just too much TV?'

'I haven't seen anyone – yet.'

The singing along the line seemed like a live thing, the only thing to make a sound.

'How do you know there's anyone there?' Croaker asked finally.

'You might not believe me if I told you.'

'Try me.'

'It's *haragei*. Bujutsu training. It's a kind of ESP. A way of looking at the world, sensing things – you might even call it an enlarged sixth sense.'

Nicholas half expected a joke but none seemed forthcoming from the other end of the line.

'Who do you think it is?'

'The ninja.'

There was an indrawn breath. 'Stay there, Linnear, I'll be right over.'

'No good. He'd never stay put that long. Besides, he'd smell you a block away.'

'We can't just sit tight.'

'Believe me, it's the only way. Leave him to me.'

'To you? Where the hell do you come into it?'

'I think he's after Tomkin; Justine, too. That's why I'm going back out.'

'Since when did you get interested in Tomkin's life?' The voice held a hard edge to it now.

'Since I'm working for him. Today.'

He heard the indrawn breath in his ear. 'Shit! Listen, you motherfucker –'

'No, you listen, Croaker. You have no idea of what you are up against. No idea at all. I tried to give you a taste of it today at the *dōjō* but I guess it's true what they say about Westerners: they're too thick-headed ever to be educated.'

He slammed the phone down and went to join the crowd moving down the stairs to Track 17. His scalp tingled all the while. Just as he left the lower level, he thought he caught a glimpse of a face. It was only a glimpse. A ghostly flash, the pale crescent of a face in semi-profile. Something about it stuck with him. He thought fleetingly of reversing his course but the crush of people was enormous.

Then he was on the train, in a window seat. The feeling was gone. Had it ever been there? He knew better than to ask that question of himself. But why would the ninja be following him?

There had to be an answer but he was unable to come up with a satisfactory one.

There was some jostling in the aisles as last-minute passengers squeezed on board. The air-conditioning cut out for a moment and someone moaned. The lights blinked and then full power came on. Everything appeared as it should be.

The bell rang and the doors slid shut with a sigh, sealing them in. A moment later, the train had started up and the platform began to slide away. He looked out of the window. A black man was sweeping up at the end of the platform. Nothing but patterns of light and shadow dictated by the controlled speed of the train.

Then the city was behind him and he was thinking about Justine. He began to doze, his head against the window-pane.

'Tickets, please.'

He started awake, his mind filled with that pale crescent of face, the features oddly indistinct as if he were staring up at the moon through a summer night's mist.

Gelda was laughing. When she laughed her breasts shook, and when her breasts shook, Dare said, she was at her most sensual.

Dare could always make Gelda laugh, which was one of the reasons Gelda enjoyed her. Her body was the other reason.

Dare's skin was a golden brown all over, deeply tanned with no bikini lines. Perhaps it was the natural colour; Gelda never inquired. She was tall, taller at least than Gelda, who was not a small woman. She was long and lean without being thin or over muscular. She had kinky blonde hair which she wore long. It was quite natural.

Dare's legs were even longer than Gelda's. More slender, to be sure, but exquisite just the same. She had small, perfectly round breasts high on her chest, a narrow waist, slender hips. She was boyish and feminine at the same time; there was no touch of the bull in her or in how she dressed. She loved the Old West: the sun-browned masculinity, the fluid musculature of the galloping horse, but most of all she loved the lawlessness.

As Pear had said, this was more pleasure than business.

'I almost found one this time, G,' she was saying now. She lay back languidly in the tub; the strong scent of violets was

227

in the air. Gelda knelt by the side of the tub, working the crystal faucets. Water crashed onto the white porcelain, between Dare's spread legs, against the thick tangled bush of hair now darkened to the colour of caramel by the moisture. Behind them, on the wall, the stained chaps hung like an effigy waiting for the fire to consume it.

'But, you know,' she continued, 'even when it was about to happen, I didn't really believe it.'

'What happened?' Gelda increased the hot water just a bit.

'What happened?' Dare wailed. 'My wonderful Texan, my great Longhorn, my ride of the range turned out to be a fag.' She put her elbows outside the tub, wiggled her ass against the water as it crept up her body. 'He cried in bed with me; told me women intimidate him.' She put her head back, closed her eyes, luxuriating in the wet warmth. 'Oh, I'll never find one.' Her eyes flew open, as grey as Gelda's were topaz. 'But, you know something, I don't think I care any more.' Her voice had lowered to a husky whisper. 'I've got you and there are things in this world that shouldn't be any realer than that.' Her arms lifted and she held them out. 'Come in here, darling. It's cold outside.'

Gelda stood up, slipped off the peach satin robe which hung from her shoulders. It slid to the tile floor with a sensual whisper and Dare shuddered to see her thus naked before her.

Their hands touched as Gelda stepped into the steaming tub and Dare moved to accommodate her.

'There's no one like you,' Dare whispered. 'Not anywhere.' She stroked Gelda's shoulder, the upper slope of her breast. 'It wouldn't make any difference how much you charged.'

Gelda's fingers stroked the other's thigh through the water, using just the tips of her long nails. 'And what,' she said softly, 'if I didn't charge anything at all?'

Dare's brow wrinkled in a frown and Gelda's forefinger smoothed the skin. 'Don't do that,' she said.

'It might have mattered,' Dare said, 'in the beginning. Now I don't suppose it does.' She shrugged. 'The studio gets the bill anyway but even if they didn't ...' Her wide lips curled up in a smile. 'I come to see you, darling. It just happens that you cost money. Who cares? It comes in, it goes out. You're better than a gram of coke or Russian sable by a long shot.'

Gelda smiled. 'I suppose that's a compliment.'

Dare laughed. 'You know it is.' She looked around. 'Where is it?'

Gelda's fingers continued their stroking, softly but insistently. A muscle high up in Dare's thigh jumped and she gasped. Gelda knew her pulse rate was rising. 'There's plenty of time, darling. Relax. It's in a safe place.' Her fingers stroked the supple flesh. 'It'll come out when you're ready.'

Dare's head turned, her hands cupped Gelda's bountiful breasts, her thumbs moving back and forth against the large nipples, feeling them erect. 'Uhm,' she whispered. 'That's what I love about you: the duality. The fire and ice, the soft and the strong, the bitch and the little girl.'

'I'm only a mirror,' Gelda murmured.

'No, that's not true, not with me you're not. I know you love it as much as I do. You can fool all the men but with women it's different. I can tell. You want me as much as I want you.'

Gelda's nails delicately parted Dare's nether lips, probing slowly inward, carefully keeping away from the clit. 'You're the only woman I've wanted this way,' she said.

Dare's hips were pumping, setting off the waves which lapped at the sides of the tub. They were their own universe. The moon's transit, setting off a series of tidal waves.

Gelda worked her other hand around underneath Dare's buttocks, stroking the cleft.

'Oh, oh, oh!' Dare twisted her upper torso, began to suck on Gelda's nipples. 'Ahhh!' The breasts popped out, coated with saliva. 'When I'm filming, I lie in bed at night and think of you. I masturbate while I think of your big breasts, your long legs, your wide cunt. Oh, my God!' She clutched at Gelda's shoulder as she felt the first friction against her clit. 'Oh, now, now, now!'

Gelda reached her hand over the side of the tub, brought the Remington into full view. Dare's eyes were round and luminous, clouded with lust. 'Let me,' she whispered throatily and Gelda let her lick the opening of the barrel. 'Oh, more!' But Gelda had pulled it away and, holding Dare down as she began to struggle slowly, so slowly, she inserted the end between the lips of her vagina. 'Ahhh!' Dare arched her hips upwards and the barrel slid into her, all the way, until the hard protrusion of the hammer mashed against her clit. Gelda needed only to waggle the Remington back and forth twice before she felt the oncoming spasms of delight in Dare. She waited, holding on, licking at her hard nipples as she soared up the orgasmic curve. Dare's body was superbly responsive and she could accurately gauge when she would hit the peak.

Dare convulsed upwards, breaking at last Gelda's hold on her, and as she did so Gelda pulled the trigger. Once. Twice. Six times. And with each shot, Dare cried out as the air-propelled jets of hot water inundated her.

The bathroom was awash in water. Dare shuddered as if with the ague. She wrapped her arms around Gelda, her lips between her breasts, whispered, 'Leave it in, leave it in.' Her eyelids fluttered. 'Oh, my God.' Her breasts heaved as if she had just run a marathon.

'Do it again,' she said. 'Do it again.'

Vincent met Lieutenant Croaker promptly at six-fifteen under Michita's wooden awning. Because of its location, the restaurant was already crowded with people eating a hasty pre-theatre dinner.

The place was L-shaped, dark with wooden walls separating the tables. There was a sushi bar to their left as they walked in which curved around to the shorter leg of the L. It was perhaps three-quarters full. Vincent saw a lone American.

They were led into the rear of the restaurant. Here there were no Western tables but rather a series of private tatami rooms. These traditional areas were covered by the reed mats and contained no chairs, only one low table around which diners sat cross-legged. The tatami rooms were screened by a series of *shōji*.

Vincent ordered *sake* for both of them as they slid off their shoes and climbed into the room. A waiter left buff-coloured menus on the gleaming wooden tables, went to get their drinks.

Croaker put a manila folder on the table, took out two eight-by-ten sheets and placed them side by side in front of Vincent.

'Ever see this man before?'

They were police artist sketches of a man in his thirties, oriental, wide nose, flat cheeks, anonymous eyes. His hair was long.

Vincent studied the drawings carefully before he shook his head. 'No, but to tell you the truth, I'd be surprised if I had.'

'Why?'

'This is the man who came to Terry's *dōjō* the day he and Eileen were murdered, right?'

'How'd you know that?'

The *sake* came and they were silent while the waiter filled the tiny cups. When he had gone, Croaker looked inquiringly at Vincent.

'I had dinner with Terry that night,' Vincent said slowly. 'I did most of the talking.' His voice had turned rueful. 'Now I'm sorry I did because Terry obviously had something on his mind. He spoke briefly about a Japanese who had come in to practise that day. Karate, aikido and – kendo.' He sipped at his *sake* and one hand waved. 'I'm only putting this together now as I talk to you. You see, Bennoku, the *dōjō*'s regular kenjutsu *sensei*, had been on vacation for about ten days. If that man came to Terry for kenjutsu there was only one way he could possibly be accommodated. By Terry himself.'

Croaker shrugged. 'What's so odd about that? Linnear told me that Tanaka was an expert at kenjutsu, a – *sensei*, did you call it?'

Vincent nodded. 'Yeah, but what Nick obviously *didn't* tell you is that Terry had put his *katana* away. He had what I can only describe as a spiritual change of heart. He no longer found pleasure in kenjutsu; he no longer practised it.'

'When did this happen?'

'I'm not really certain. Perhaps as long as six months ago.'

'Then why didn't Linnear tell me?'

Vincent poured more *sake* for them both. 'To tell you the truth, I'm not sure Nick knows. He's – well, he's also had a kind of spiritual change of heart, only he's still going through his and I don't know what it entails. We're still very close, he and I, and he was close with Terry, too, but he'd withdrawn some-what. I'm sure Terry had the opportunity to tell him but I rather think he chose not to.' He shrugged. 'Anyway, if this is the man' – he tapped the drawings – 'he'd be disguised. I might know him or Nicholas might but we'd never be able to tell you from one of those.'

Croaker nodded. 'Okay.' He began to put the drawings away.

Vincent put a hand out. 'Why don't you wait until Nick comes? It couldn't hurt for him to see them.'

'Linnear called me late this afternoon. He went back to West Bay Bridge. His girl had an accident.' He finished putting the drawings away. 'Nobody saw this bastard going in or out. Not at the *dōjō* or Terry's apartment.'

'I'm not surprised. This man's a professional. A highly dangerous professional. I'm afraid you don't know what you're up against here.'

'That's just what Linnear told me,' Croaker growled. 'I don't like hearing it.'

'It's the truth, Lieutenant. You'd better face facts. This guy can put away just about anyone he chooses.'

'Even Raphael Tomkin?'

Vincent nodded. 'Even him.'

'It's been tried a dozen times,' Croaker pointed out. 'By professionals.'

Vincent sighed. 'This professional is different. We are not talking about a hit man from Detroit or wherever they manufacture them.'

'Jersey City,' Croaker said with a thin smile.

'Yeah, well, this is a ninja, Lieutenant. Compared with a professional hit man he's Houdini, Superman and Spiderman all wrapped up into one.' Vincent tapped the table with the tip of his forefinger. 'The man's a sorcerer.'

Croaker stared into the other's eyes, trying to find some hint of irony. He found none. 'You're serious, aren't you?'

'At the risk of sounding medodramatic, deadly serious.'

The waiter returned and they ordered dinner along with more *sake*. 'Take your time,' Vincent told the waiter, who nodded and went out.

'Linnear took me to a kenjutsu *dōjō* today,' Croaker said.

'Which one?'

'I don't know the name of it. I met the *sensei*. Man named Fukashigi.'

There was an odd look in Vincent's eye. 'You're quite a privileged person. Very few Westerners are allowed entrance. And for Nicholas to take you ...' He whistled silently.

'Yeah,' Croaker joked. 'And that was after I'd insulted him. He certainly doesn't hold any grudges.'

Now Vincent's eyes were sad and he said, 'It was not for him to be angry but for you to know that you have now lost face.'

'Lost face? What do you mean?'

'Simply this. Relationships are based on respect – mutual respect. With that comes trust. And obligation. I will not ask you what you did – no, don't tell me, I have no wish to know – but I will say that if you have offended him then his respect for you has lessened.'

'What the hell do I care what he thinks of me?'

'Ah, well, perhaps you don't.' Vincent smiled. 'If that's the case, no more may be said of the matter.' He took a deliberate sip of his *sake*, refilled the cup.

Croaker cleared his throat and, after a time, said, 'Finish your last thought.'

'I was merely going to say that it is not up to Nick to forgive you – that he has already done, otherwise he would not have taken you to see Fukashigi. It is up to you to seek to restore the former balance.'

'How would I do that?' Croaker asked suspiciously.

'Ah, if I knew the answer to that one, I'd be quite the wise man.' Vincent shook his head. 'And tonight, Lieutenant, I'm not feeling wise at all.'

There was a man at the sushi bar with invisible putty on his face. It built up his flat cheekbones, flattened his wide nose, deepened the sockets of his eyes. Even his mother would not have recognized him, and she had been a most intelligent woman.

He was halfway through a plate of sashimi when Vincent and Lieutenant Croaker entered the restaurant and were shown to a tatami room. He did not turn his head but caught them in

233

the periphery of his vision.

Several moments later, he pushed his plate delicately away from him and walked the length of the room to the rest-room. The place was dark and crowded, buzzing with conversation. He had to pass the tatami rooms to get there. The rest-room was empty. He washed his hands, peering at himself in the mirror. The door opened and two men walked in. The man went out, past the thin *shōji* walls. He paid for his meal and left.

Outside in the heat of the summer night, he hailed a cruising taxi. He had to make four switches before he found one suitable for his purposes.

At precisely 8:18 p.m. officer Pete Travine pulled the patrol car over so that the side wheels scraped the kerb. It was his second cruise down Twenty-eighth Street and he was certain now that what he saw in the alleyway between a brownstone and a tailor's shop had not been there when he had made his first trip twenty minutes ago. He had been thinking of the old days, when all cops rode in tandem. Now, because of the city's serious on-going fiscal crisis, they were still experimenting in certain areas with solo patrols, despite concerted PBA opposition.

The radio squawked intermittently, but there was nothing in his vicinity. He parked the blue-and-white and got out a flashlight, played it over the darkened alley. The beam of light hovered over a line of garbage cans painted silver. It was quiet here: no pedestrians, only the soft susurrus of the light traffic along Lexington.

He opened the kerbside door, slid out. With one hand he unsnapped the top of his stiff leather holster, the guard he wore while driving.

He went cautiously across the sidewalk, his flash flicking the darkness. There was an open grille gate leading to four or five steep concrete steps to the alley proper. The right wall – the brownstone's – was blank for all of its three storeys. The left wall had windows beginning on the second storey of the building. There were apartments over the tailor's shop. Odd lighting, subtly kaleidoscopic, leaked from these. Television sets were on.

Travine went down the steps. He thought briefly of calling

in but decided against it. He wanted to have something concrete for them.

Past the line of garbage cans was deep shadow but something protruded part way out into the semi-light, casting strange shadows upwards along the brick wall. It was these that Travine had seen and questioned.

He stood over the shape now. He took his hand from his gun butt, crouched and reached out one hand. An old burlap sack partly covered the shape but this close Travine could see the face, one cheek to the wall. Two fingers laid at the side of the neck confirmed that the man was dead.

Travine got up and, without disturbing anything, went up the steps to the street. He looked both ways. A couple passed, arm in arm, walking downtown along Lex. There was no other movement. He called in, then phoned the M.E.'s office. 'I don't want this to wait until tomorrow,' he told the associate on call. 'I want something tonight.'

Then he went back to the body to I.D. it but there was nothing. No wallet, no money, no cards, nothing. Yet the man was obviously no derelict. He touched the body again. Not yet cold. He stood up. In the distance the night was split by the sound of sirens, growing louder.

Through fingerprints, they were able to establish the identity of the man. That took a little over three hours and at that moment they began to wonder what had happened to his taxi.


Vincent came out of Michita looking for a cab.

He was not a little drunk and not in the least bit ashamed of himself. He felt as light as a balloon despite the sultry, steaming night. All the cares and worries which had clung to him, weighing him down for months, had sloughed away, dead skin shed.

He walked a little unsteadily, realizing it, curious about it, even happy with it. He'd needed this loosening up.

He breathed in the heavy night air, leaden with exhaust fumes, the odours of fried cooking from the corner coffee shop. He felt as if he were on the Ginza in Tokyo, with its bustle, its crowds, its bright neon jungle advertising nightclubs and Western products.

He watched people streaming by him, feeling a bit giddy. He fought down the impulse to giggle and then thought, why not? He giggled out loud. No one appeared to notice.

He began to walk west. Traffic from Sixth Avenue sounded like surf breaking against a far-off shore. He thought of Uraga where the ships of Admiral Perry had docked in 1853, ending two hundred and fifty years of Japanese isolationism. The mysterious surf rolling in towards the Floating Kingdom. Better if we had not given in to that Pacific Overture. Far better. The ageless barrier holding Japan in magical thrall had been breached. It was a mythic tale, as all of Japanese history tended to be, throwing bigger-than-life shadows on the screen of memory.

Down the block, almost at the corner of Sixth, a cab started up, pulling slowly out from the kerb, coming towards him. Just before it pulled abreast, its hack light went on. It caught his eye, a spinning jewel in the night. He was still in Japan.

He waved at it drunkenly and it pulled over to the kerb. A Checker, big and roomy. And air-conditioned.

It was a custom job, not fleet-owned. Inside, there was no plastic partition and the front seats were beige leather buckets.

Vincent gave the driver his address and settled back. The cab started up.

Even in the crowded modern streets of Tokyo, Vincent was thinking, amid the urban clutter, the European business suits, one would abruptly come up an ancient Shinto shrine tucked away somewhere between two buildings. One could hear the ghostly tinkling of the bronze bells, sewn in a vertical strip, green with the patina of time; one could smell the incense gently swirling the air. For those moments the exhaust fumes, the pollution, were eliminated and the soul of ageless Japan reigned unsullied by Western encroachment, summoning the ancient gods.

It was dark in the cab. He gazed out at the glowing lights of the city, realized that they were moving quite slowly. He leaned forward. 'Hey,' he said, 'I'd like to get home within the hour.'

He saw the back of the driver's head move and, raising his gaze, saw his eyes in the strip of the rear-view mirror. He saw that the man was Japanese, looked for his name on the I.D.

card on the extreme right of the dashboard. The light was out and he could not make it out. He spoke to the driver in Japanese, apologizing for his rudeness.

'That's all right,' the man said. 'It's been a hard night for everyone.'

They had come round onto Forty-fifth, heading west. The taxi swung right at the corner onto Eighth Avenue. Here the street was lined on both sides by a combination of junk food restaurants and sleazy porn theatres. The sidewalks were filled with hookers looking to feed their habits, black con men, low-grade pushers and Puerto Rican strong-arm boys: the vast white underbelly of the city in all its gritty, sorrowful splendour.

The driver went through one intersection on the change, hit a red light on the next.

'It's a night like home,' Vincent said in Japanese.

'No one wanted it,' the man said. 'It should never have come.'

Vincent thought again of Perry's four warships, riding in the harbour at Uraga. Perhaps he's right, he thought. We never should have –

The driver had turned round. His face was blue and green in the dancing garish lights from a movie theatre. His mouth opened in a smile. A black oblong that might have belonged to a Nō mask. The eyes were like stones, radiated no possibility of warmth or friendship. This contrast between smile and animosity made him appear to leer frighteningly. Vincent was reminded of the first Nō play he had seen with its terrifying demon's mask; at least that was how it had seemed to him at the age of six.

There was something odd about this face but in the low light he couldn't tell. He leaned forward. It seemed as if the skin on the man's face was blotchy as if –

He drew back, his mind stunned at what it had perceived. But his reflexes had been dulled by the alcohol and, even as he retreated, he saw the man's face ballooning out towards him like the wedge of a viper. The cheeks billowed and the lips curled into an O. A fine mist shot from the aperture, caught him in mid-gasp. He had already inhaled some of the spray before he stopped breathing.

*

Croaker sat in the tatami room, cross-legged, his head propped on one fist, after Vincent had left. He called for more *sake* and thought savagely about going home. He gulped at the liquor. It was cold and he waited patiently for the fresh bottle. He liked the stuff. It had hardly any taste but generated a hell of a high.

He didn't want to go home. No, no, he thought. That's not it. I don't want to go home to Alison. This both surprised and annoyed him. Surprised because even though he had known this might be coming for a while, it had now surfaced so strongly, so blatantly. Annoyed with himself because he had allowed things to slip this far. It wasn't even that he was angry with Alison, he thought. He just didn't want to have anything to do with her any more. He wondered for a time that two people could feel so much together for a time and then, later, not feel anything at all. Part of the human condition, he concluded philosophically, but a hell of a part.

The *sake* came and he allowed the waiter to pour the first cup. He downed it, immediately poured himself another. He itched to call Matty the Mouth but he suspected that if he did he might break this Didion thing to smithereens. It seemed to him now that the entire case was balanced on one shining point: getting the name and address of this broad.

He didn't have to close his eyes to be able to picture again Angela Didion's apartment, but he did so anyway. He went over it all again.

The first thing he noticed when he walked in was the smell. Sickly-sweet, it was ether combined with what? The darkened living-room had given up nothing but in the bedroom he saw the American Indian bone pipe and, sniffing it, smelled the opium. Tasted it on the tip of his tongue. Very high grade indeed. Hardly street stuff. But then this was Angela Didion's bedroom and a woman who was purportedly the world's highest-paid model could hardly be expected to have anything but the best – of everything. He didn't touch the pipe; he didn't touch anything.

Slipping on his surgeon's gloves, he crossed to the closet opposite the enormous bed. The bedroom was all done in midnight blue, from the silk walls to the satin lampshades. There was only one lamp on when he came in, next to the bed. He left the room that way.

Carefully he opened up the sliding door. Inside he found silk dresses, six fur coats, ranging from a full-length dyed Russian sable to a spectacular three-quarter silver lynx. Below, shoes from Botticelli and Charles Jourdan.

On the deep-pile rug between the bed and the closet was a black silk négligé. He skirted that on the way to the bed. It was a custom-made affair, moon-shaped. The sheets were midnight-blue percale but the rumpled quilt was covered in silk. It lay around Angela Didion's ankles like dark surf, ready to claim her.

She lay half on the bed, half off. Her head hung over the edge, the long honey-blonde hair falling on to the floor. She was made up. Her eyes were mascaraed, her cheeks blushed, her lips painted. She was naked save for a thin gold chain which she wore around her waist. There was no other jewellery. She lay on the left side of the bed. The right side was empty but the pillow on that side was indented as if someone had lain there. There were stains on the sheets, still damp. There was no blood. A pillow was wedged beneath the small of Angela Didion's back.

Someone had done quite a job on her. Bruises, just beginning to darken, lay like boils along the sides of her neck, her chest and rib cage, her stomach. Her back was arched as if in ecstasy. There was no expression on her face whatsoever. No sign of pain or fear – or of passion.

It should have been grotesque, would have been with any other victim – Croaker had seen too many like it. But this wasn't anyone, it was Angela Didion. She must have been an extraordinary woman, Croaker thought as he stood staring down at the corpse, because her beauty transcended even this degradation; even death. Croaker knew that he was looking at a magnificent piece of humanity and it saddened him that it should have been destroyed so recklessly. He felt that about most of the bodies he found, if they weren't the punks who got blown away by their own cupidity; the city breathed easier without them.

He tore his gaze away from the bed and, going around it,

knelt beside the black silk garment on the carpet. In this twilight of the room, it was almost invisible: black against the deep blue that was almost black itself.

Dipping one forefinger down, he lifted it up slightly. Bending, he touched his nose to it, breathed in, caught the faint whiff of a perfume. He got up, crossed to Angela Didion's dressing-table. He passed over the ivory brush and comb set, the oval tortoise-shell hand mirror, the odds and ends of mascara, eye-liner, blush, powder, creams, taking them all in as he did so. There were two perfume bottles on a silver tray against the wall. Joy and Bal à Versailles. He sniffed at both of them, one at a time, slowly. Then, to make certain, he returned to the silk négligé, confirming for himself that it exuded another perfume; that it bore the imprint of another woman.

It had taken time and a lot of hard work but, in the end, Matty the Mouth had come through. Now it was this woman's name and address Croaker was anxiously waiting for. Angela Didion's lover. Or, more accurately, one of them. She could not, of course, have been the murderer. Judging from the size of the négligé, she was far too small to have inflicted such terrible wounds on another human adult. *There were no instruments used*, the M.E. had said, *other than the fists*. That meant some-one strong and with a massive build: some of the bruises were quite large.

No, this woman was no murderer but, Croaker was con-vinced, she had been a witness to the murder. She knows, he thought now. She knows. And she's scared shitless of what she's seen. No one had got to her. No one would but Croaker. He must see to that.

Come on, Matty, deliver the goods. He found his hand trembling against the table, stared down at it as if it belonged to someone else. He knew he wanted this conviction badly. More than he had wanted any other in his career. And the hell of it was, he knew who had killed Angela Didion. Knew it as surely as he knew his own name. But without this witness, there was nothing: nothing but conjecture and theory and circumstantial evidence that McCabe wouldn't even touch, let alone ask for an arrest on it. Jesus, he hated counting this heavily on someone else but he had spent seven years cultivating Matty the Mouth and now it looked as if it would finally pay off. If he came through. *When* he comes through, Croaker corrected himself. Think positively.

Which all led him back to this ninja. The case was getting nowhere, spinning on its own momentum. That, Croaker knew from long, hard experience, was extremely dangerous. It meant he had no handle and *that* meant he had no control. People tended to get severely hurt when that happened.

And then there was the problem of Nicholas Linnear. Vincent had been right, he felt instinctively. Linnear had been highly offended by what he'd said. It had been a stupid thing to say. He had known it as soon as he had said it. Now he realized that Linnear might be the key to the case. *He knows more about the ninja than anyone in or out of Japan*, Vincent had said towards the end of the evening. *Trust him. He knows what he's talking about.* Now he's working for that bastard Tomkin, Croaker thought. He had a strong urge to back off then, to let events happen without him. Perhaps Tomkin would fall. But that, he knew, he could never do. It was not the way he wanted it to happen. And then there was the consideration of the four other deaths. If the ninja was after Tomkin, why had he killed four people who did not know the man, let alone have any kind of association with him? No one seemed to know the answer and there was certainly no one on the force he could talk this over with. It came back to Linnear again. If anyone might have a clue, he would.

Croaker looked at his watch, thought about calling Linnear, then quickly changed his mind. The telephone wasn't the right medium and, anyway, he was too high to be able to think things out with enough clarity to satisfy himself. He sighed, finished off the bottle of *sake*. He'd had enough.

Still he could not face the thought of going home. Yet he wanted a woman. Into his mind swam an image and abruptly he was as hard as a bar of iron. Her face seemed familiar but where had he seen her before? Perhaps nowhere. Perhaps on some billboard. The image had surfaced from deep inside of him. Perhaps she was long gone. Or, again, had never even existed.

*

Vincent exhaled in a rush, attempting to free his lungs of the mist. It was a useless gesture, his mind knew, yet his body would not be denied its chance.

His eyes began to burn and tear. He reached blindly for the door-handle. The cab started up as the light changed. He leaned on the handle, got it open on the second try. The city rushed in on him as he half tumbled out. His foot caught for a moment and then he was free, rolling along the street for a moment while horns blared. He could hear the harsh squeal of brakes and muted shouts. Then he was up and running clumsily, slipping on dogshit as if it were a banana peel. He balanced himself with his arms outspread and hit the kerb, sprinted up onto the sidewalk.

Behind him he could feel the looming presence of the Checker cab as the driver pulled hard over and jumped out.

'Hey!' he called. 'Come back! I want my fare!'

Vincent stumbled along the crowded street, bumping into people. Black faces turned, wide-eyed, to stare.

He's a cool bastard, he thought as he was spun around by an enormous black man with an open shirt and tight maroon pants. 'Hey, man! Be cool. Watch yo'self.'

He wove in and out of the crowd, wondering how long he had. He had no illusions about what he had inhaled. Even without the characteristic odour, he would have known it was a neural toxin.

He turned his head but could not see his pursuer. He took a chance, darted off the kerb, trying to hail a passing cab – it was no good expecting a cop to pop up here. But immediately he saw the man stalking him along the periphery of the crowd as, spying Vincent, he leapt forward.

Vincent whirled, darting back into the thick of the throng on the sidewalk. He began to run again but this, he knew, would only spread the toxin more quickly. Already his heart was pounding furiously and the tips of his fingers felt numb: a bad sign. Yet since the man was pursuing him still, perhaps there was a chance that he had not inhaled a sufficient amount of the poison.

Death was very close now, Vincent knew. It rode his shoulder like an expectant predator. He realized now just how much he wanted to live; how strong the drive still was inside him. This knowledge came as a revelation and it buoyed him for a time. He would need all his wits to overcome this demon, he knew. He was overmatched, but he put this thought out of his mind as he ran on and on into the spangled night.

He cut to his right, stumbling off the kerb, but again he was balked by the man. No good. A cab was definitely out.

He coughed as he ran now, trying to retch. He felt as if he could not get enough oxygen into his system. His arms felt weak and he had to force his legs to work. He heard a harsh shout from behind him and the sound of running feet. He pushed his way frantically through the crowd, his mind whirling, trying to alight on some ... The mist! What a fool he'd been! It was being absorbed through the pores of his skin – the burning should have told him. Inhaling was only peripheral.

Have to find ... He was aware of how terribly exposed he was here on this mean street where no help would be forthcoming. A restaurant was no good: too well lighted. He needed some dark place.

It was right in front of him. He put on a last burst of speed, feeling his heart pounding painfully as if it were being overworked.

He skidded to a stop in front of a movie theatre. In front was a billboard dominated by a cut-out of a blonde with large breasts. Beneath it, a blown-up newspaper review of the film. 'An erection!' proclaimed a banner. 'Highest rated!' Vincent shoved a man away from the ticket booth, threw a bill at the man inside the booth. He pushed through the turnstile, ignoring the shouts. 'Hey, mister! Wait! Your change!'

Into the darkness, smelling of mildew, stale sweat and dried sperm. Hazy images moved on the screen and there was the sound of heavy breathing, magnified by the speakers, amplified throughout the theatre. There was a liquid sound and a moaning.

Vincent blinked several times, adjusting to the low light. He looked for the men's room, found that it was two flights up, past the balcony. He didn't think he could make it.

He moved cautiously along the rear aisle, past two people standing watching the screen. He came upon a bank of machines. Popcorn. Candy. Soda.

He dug in his trouser pocket, fumbled out two quarters. He rolled them into the slot, stabbed a button at random. He waited impatiently while the waxed-paper cup clattered down, followed by the soda and the syrup. He stuck his hand in, caught the shaved ice as it came down the vertical chute. He rubbed the ice over his face. He blinked and blinked, feeling the cold water running into his eyes, over his face. Perhaps he had got to it in time. The ice was like a soothing balm, diminishing the pain. There *was* a chance. The cab had been air-conditioned, the windows closed, but he had got out very quickly. He tried to judge the overall time, gave it up as hopeless.

He turned his head to look at the doorway. Someone came in, someone went out. They were shadows to him. Was his pursuer here already? There was no way of knowing and here, in the rear, he was a perfect target.

He turned into the theatre proper, went quickly down the aisle. His vision had seemed to clear and he could see men sitting as still as statues, staring at the screen filled with writhing bodies.

He slipped into a row midway down, moving to his right all the way over until he was wedged against one wall. In the darkest part of the theatre he sat down. The floor was sticky; the place smelled of accelerated age. His head swivelled around. People were coming and going. Flickering light played over their faces. He turned back.

His hands had begun to shake but this might be because of the increased adrenalin. His mouth was dry and his breathing raspy. Otherwise, he felt better than he had before. Obviously the dose had been less than lethal. He tried to relax, breathing deeply, but his side hurt intermittently, perhaps from the frantic running. Meanwhile, his mind was going over the alternatives. There didn't seem to be many. Having come in here, he was now quite effectively trapped. The ninja, too, was here somewhere. If he made a move to leave, he would be dead before he got half way to the door.

He would have to fight. It was the only alternative. He was not a *sensei* or a *haragei* adept as Nicholas was – or Terry had been. He turned his mind away from Terry: that way led to despair; if Terry had been defeated . . .

But Terry had been surprised and then there had been Ei to think of. Vincent was forewarned. He needed time and he was getting it; he was feeling better every moment. Think! he screamed at himself. You've got to get out of this somehow.

There were people in back of him, to his left. Shadows moving in the aisle, up and down, bobbing; rustling as people sat down or got up. Someone slid into his row, one seat away from him, and he stiffened, his eyes sliding that way so that he could see . . . a youngish businessman, clean-cut, Brooks Brothers suit, thin leather attaché case on his knees. A model businessman.

Vincent removed his attention, went back to thinking. Something touched his arm and he jumped, turned his head. It was the businessman, clean-shaven, reddened cheeks, lived just over the river along the Jersey Palisades perhaps with the wife and two kids, the dog and the two cars. The man was tapping him gently on the arm. He leaned forward, his eyes searching Vincent's. He whispered something but Vincent could not hear him over the amplified moaning. He leaned over, across the vacant seat between them. 'Want to move over here next to me?' the man said hopefully.

Vincent stared at him dumbfounded for a full minute until he shook his head violently from side to side, withdrew.

He wiped at his forehead and his fingers came away wet. But he knew what he had to do now and all he could do was wait.

There was a movement along the aisle; a shadow had stopped at the end of his row. Vincent turned his head slightly but all he saw was a black blotch. The businessman who had propositioned him was moving slightly in his seat, his hands invisible under the shield of his attaché case; it was too warm to carry a raincoat.

Someone was coming into Vincent's row now and he held his breath, his heart pumping furiously. Was it the ninja? The figure moved slowly, approaching Vincent. He looked up. The man was just on the other side of the engrossed businessman. He saw a glint of reflected light from the screen dance off the man's eyes. It was the ninja. He bent, said something to the businessman, who moved his legs, not taking his eyes off the screen.

He was coming. Vincent prepared himself for what he had to do. It would take speed and strength and – Now the man was at the seat next to Vincent's. He did not sit down.

Now was the time. Now!

Vincent moved. Nothing happened. His eyes bulged in disbelief. He was paralysed.

He struggled to lift his hands but his arms were immobile, as if they had been encased in lead while his attention had been elsewhere. He tried to stand up but there was no feeling in his legs. No feet, no ankles, nothing. Then he knew with a swift unalterable certainty that the spray had never been meant to kill him but merely to render him motionless.

The shadow loomed over him, blotting out all light. He heard animal cries, lustful sobs; he felt the movement over him with exaggerated slowness, watching calmly and detachedly as the ninja leaned over him and gently put one forearm against his left clavicle. He felt the pressure and his eyes blinked. Perhaps the tip of one finger twitched where it lay on the wooden arm of the seat. There was no fear in him, no sorrow, only an image of Japan, of a rocky seashore outside Uraga with its ramshackle houses, the pure white sails of the fishing boats as they set sail against the red and yellow sunrise. He saw the lone pine standing on the bluff, limned by the light, a dark sentinel standing watch over its homeland

The other forearm broke against the left side of his face, pressing at his ear. The force was enormous. The first arm held the rest of his body immobile. Homeland expanding outward, outward into – *snap!*

# II

## Tokyo Suburbs, Autumn 1963

'This is the perfect place to watch the sun set,' Cheong said. She turned to Tai, handed her the lacquer tray. Tai, bowing, took it and silently left them alone in the kitchen.

'You see, I had your father take the *shōji* out and put the glass in.' She gave a little laugh. 'It scandalized Itami, of course. She would never do a thing like that in *her* house.' She sighed, perfectly serious now. 'Sometimes your aunt can be extremely trying, I am most ashamed to admit.'

'Itami is not blood, Mother.'

She put a slender hand over his and smiled. 'Sometimes, Nicholas, the spirit is more binding than the blood. You may find such a thing out for yourself as you grow older.' She took her hand away. 'Are you hungry?'

'Yes.'

'Good. Tai has made your favourite.' She showed him.

'My favourite is *dim sum*,' he said. 'Tai does not make them as well as you do, though you tell her what to do.'

Cheong laughed and leaning over, kissed his cheek. 'All right,' she said lightly. 'This weekend I'll make you *dim sum*.'

'How many kinds?'

'Enough,' she said. 'Enough.'

She stared out of the window. The sky near the horizon was as lemony as custard but, high aloft, the blue was as deep as midnight. 'You do not get to see this sight often enough, do you?'

'Bujutsu takes a great deal of time, Mother.'

'I know.' She hesitated fractionally. 'Your school work isn't suffering.' It did not seem to be a question.

'There's no problem.'

'You know, my father' – she called So-Peng her father just as if he had sired her – 'used to say, it makes a great deal of difference where you have been. Your ancestors live on in your blood.'

247

'I don't know,' Nicholas said. 'I have a number of American friends who do all they can to break away from such things. You know, their parents and –'

'Then you tell me, my son, if their ancestors have not set the course of their lives?'

He looked at her, thinking that she must, after all, be quite correct.

'Everything your grandfather was, am I,' Cheong said. 'This he bequeathed me long before I left Singapore with your father. In Asia, this is quite special, quite' – she sought for the proper word – 'unique. Now I am able to do the same thing for you.'

'But I know so little about him.'

'In time you will learn. You are young yet.'

'But you were far younger than I am when you began to –'

'Those were different times. Dangerous times. I am very grateful that you could be spared such misery. No one should have to suffer so.' Her beautiful face broke into a smile. 'But let us speak of more pleasant matters.'

I want to know, he told her in his mind. I very much want to know what happened. But, of course, this was something he could not say to her. Never. If she chose to tell him one day ... But she would not. He doubted whether even his father knew. Only Cheong and So-Peng. And he was long dead now.

'Your aunt asked about you today,' she said, breaking into his train of thought. 'She always does when you are not around.'

'It was kind of her to think of me.'

'Yes.' Cheong smiled and touched him. 'You should tell her that. It will make her most happy.'

'I cannot think – that is to say –'

'Nicholas, Itami thinks of us – all of us – as part of her family. She is very fond of you.'

'Sometimes – it's very difficult to know with her.'

'Yes, well, people are complex. They need getting to know. Seeping in. Patience. This is perhaps difficult for you. Your father makes it so. He is patient and impatient.' She shook her head, as if bewildered. 'Very inconsistent, yes. This is still strange to me.' She stroked the nape of his neck. 'You are so much like him in that way. He does not make friends easily as most foreigners seem to do. But then, he is no foreigner.

248

Asia is his home, as it is mine. We are both children of the East, forging our own pasts.'

'It sounds so difficult, so complex.'

She smiled. 'We could live no other way.'

Increasingly now, Satsugai and Itami came to dinner. His aunt had always been somewhat of a fixture around the house – Cheong saw to that. However, now her husband began to accompany her more frequently.

Listening to Satsugai talk, Nicholas began to understand how Japan had been led blindly into the disastrous war by this man and others like him in the powerful *zaibatsu*. Not that Satsugai ever spoke of events before the war or even of the war itself. As far as he was concerned, the war might as well never have occurred. Ostrich-like, he seemed utterly blind to the still quite visible scars strewn throughout the cities and the countryside.

'The communists have always been a problem in Japan, Colonel,' Nicholas recalled his saying one chill autumn evening. The sky was darkening from russet to plum and there was a bitter edge to the wind as it moaned through the pines and the neighbouring cryptomeria, a harbinger of the coming winter. A fine rain fell obliquely, streaming against the large study windows, rolling like silent tears. One wretched wren puttered nervously in a tightening circle beneath the inadequate awning of a carefully pruned hedge just outside the window where the rain had caught like pearls on the oval overlapping leaves, a liquid spider's web spun in glistening precision across the expanse of the foliage. The wren kept its head cocked, eyeing the sky, impatient to be off.

'The Party is not so large, even now,' the Colonel had replied. He tamped down the tobacco in his pipe and carefully lit up. Sweet blue smoke filled the room.

'My dear Colonel,' Satsugai said, 'one cannot use mere *numbers* to define danger, especially here in Japan.' He spoke as if Nicholas's father were some visitor to the country. 'One must take into account the *virulence* of the enemy. These are more than dedicated people we are discussing. They are fanatics to the cause of world communism. One mustn't make the mistake of underestimating them. That is the way they achieve their first foothold.'

The Colonel said nothing, being busy achieving the proper draw on his pipe. It was an umber, rough-hewn brier with a curved stem and a high bowl. It had been with him all through the war and, as such, had become quite dear to him. It was a private symbol to him and, though he had well over twenty-five pipes in his collection, this was the one he invariably smoked now.

One gets some peculiar notions in war, the Colonel thought. Perfectly understandable really because, in the end, when the days are dark with death and the overcast nights filled with a jungle terror, when commanders are mowed down by machine-gun fire and mates are blown to bits by mines a pace away from you or slit from throat to navel by a silent invader, those peculiar notions are all that stand between you and utter madness.

The Colonel had got it into his head that as long as he had that pipe, as long as he could pull his hand away from the hot grip of his smoking Sten gun, reach inside his uniform pocket and feel the irregularity of the outside of its bowl, everything would turn out all right.

He recalled with vivid clarity the morning in the early summer of 1945 when his unit had begun its assault on the perimeter of Singapore. They had just broken camp and were making their way slowly southward, the units in constant walkie-talkie contact.

In the jungle, the Colonel had reached for the comforting bowl of the pipe, found it gone. He paused, peering at the ground behind him, but could find nothing in the muddy tangle of gnarled roots but centipedes and leeches. A creeping sense of panic had overcome him and, without thinking further, he called for his men to backtrack with him until they had returned to the camp area. He found the pipe half-buried in the silty soil and, brushing it off, was about to order his men out when he heard the first of the rolling reports. The ground shook as if in an earthquake. Southward, they saw the violent geysering of earth and foliage, stained red.

Silently, the Colonel waved them out and they crept forward, zigzagging through the dense jungle only to find the entire company ripped apart; those who had not been caught in the cleverly planted minefield had been taken by sniper fire. The Colonel felt in his pocket for the pipe. The brier was warm under his calloused fingers. He hefted his Sten gun and took his men west, through the stinking mangrove swamp, skirting the bloody deathscape, before turning south again. In the dead of night they came upon the Japanese encampment from the rear. They took the perimeter guards out without a sound, stringing them up in the trees as mute witnesses. The Colonel sent half his men into the south-east. At 0400 hours precisely, the Colonel and his men opened fire from their position just south of the encampment. Lead sizzled the air and the Sten guns smoked merrily. Fully half the encampment went down under that withering fire. The other half were not so fortunate. They retreated directly into the line of fire of the second contingent of the Colonel's unit. Caught in a cross-fire, they danced like psychotic marionettes until their bodies literally disintegrated.

At another time the Colonel might have thought it a terrible waste of precious ammunition, but not that searing blast-furnace night; a *Walpurgisnacht*.

'Satsugai,' the Colonel said calmly, the war still vibrating behind his eyes as he languidly blew out a cloud of aromatic smoke, 'you know the history of your country as well as anyone, I daresay. Communism is not a reality for Japan, you know that. There is far too much tradition against that kind of idealized egalitarianism. The idea of commune-izing Japan is ludicrous; the people would never stand for it.'

Satsugai's face held a hint of a steely smile. 'Whatever I believe is of little importance, *hai*? It is what the Americans believe that matters. They understand the communist menace; they know that we of the *zaibatsu* are this country's greatest bulwark against communism. You can't fight it with liberal reform. Your MacArthur found that out in 1947.'

The Colonel's eyes blazed. 'We all had high hopes for the future of Japan, then –'

'Hopes, Colonel, are for the naïve,' the other said blandly. 'Realities must be faced. The mainland is only just across the *genkainada* from Fukuoka. Their threat is quite real, I assure you; they will never stop trying to infiltrate, to subvert the government of Japan. That's why we require firm measures and the strictest enforcement of regulations. Liberalism cannot be tolerated here. Surely you can recognize that.'

'I see only a country being twisted for the ends of certain interests, just as it was during the war.'

For a moment the eyes of the two men locked and it was as if sparks flew from the dynamic friction of the contact.

'If things had been the way they are now in 1873,' Satsugai said softly, 'the *seikanron* would never have gone down to defeat.' He was speaking of the Genyōsha's advocacy of a military campaign against Korea in that year. Its failure to be passed instigated the first overt act of violence by the Genyōsha against the Meiji government, an attempted assassination of Tomomi Iwakura. 'Do not forget, Colonel, that if the *seikanron* had met with success there would have been no fighting in Korea; the communists, when they came, would have been bottled up in Manchuria. As it is' – he shrugged – 'the Americans hurl themselves from war to war without any wholeheartedness.'

'How do you mean?'

'It's obvious, isn't it? You yourself fought in the jungles of the Asian continent. There American tanks and artillery and even large-scale bombing are not the answer. The communists are far too well organized and, in any event, they have a virtually inexhaustible supply of men.'

'Vietnam is no concern of ours.' The Colonel's pipe had gone out but he appeared not to notice.

'Excuse me, my dear sir' – Satsugai crossed his legs, smoothing down the centre creases of his worsted trousers – 'but in that I must say that you are most certainly wrong. If Vietnam falls, Cambodia must certainly be next and then what happens to Thailand? No, the so-called Domino Theory is all too real a possibility; a chilling one, at that.'

The Colonel appeared to be half asleep. His cold blue eyes were hooded, the irises dark beneath. His cold pipe was still stuck firmly in the corner of his mouth. He listened to the hypnotic rattle of the rain against the window-panes, on the eaves, his thoughts filled with history.

So much idealism. It had started out that way, in any case. But MacArthur was such a paranoid bastard. By 1947, the time of the American 'reverse course' in Japan, the United States was no longer so desirous of strict war reparations as such. After all, Japan was demilitarized; that was enough. What began to concern them more and more was that Japan should become their watchdog against communism in the Far East and to this end they began two separate but contiguous courses of action. First, they restored many of the formerly suspect powerful right-wing politicians and businessmen to power and, second, they poured millions of dollars into the Japanese economy until now over 80 per cent of the old pre-war structure and industry were back in operation. In doing so, they allowed a totally *Japanese*-inspired campaign to scour out suspected communists and leftist radicals, doing what they had done in Spain and Iran and South America. Over and over. Only this time, it had hit home.

Outside, the wind had picked up, throwing the rain in hard brittle bursts against the window panes. There was no colour left in the low sky.

That small but intrepid group of men so full of enthusiasm in 1945, certain that their far-reaching vision for a truly democratized Japan, free from feudal encumbrances, was the correct choice for the country. How naïve we all were! the Colonel thought sadly, echoing Satsugai's words. All of them, all my friends are gone now. He watched the rain streaking the glass like tears, cold and forlorn. A violent eddy of wind caught the wet leaves that had fallen since Ataki had last been at the house, sent them skimming through the air, whirling and spinning like miniature airships of alien design. In his twenty-three years in the Far East, the Colonel had never felt more of an alien than he did now. His isolation seemed to him both complete and irreversible. One by one, the members of that inner circle of minds linked in friendship, that core of policy advisers to MacArthur, were either transferred or dismissed. In truth, they were unaware of the political machinations that went on around them or of the increasing instability of MacArthur himself. Still, they had hung on tenaciously, even after the reversal in 1947, hoping against hope that their combined influence could help stem the tide and return the new Japan to the beginnings of democratization. Now, in retrospect, it was so obvious; easy to see just how impotent they had been all along. Policy had been determined on the other side of the world and they were expected to implement, not comment. No one had told them that in the beginning. Terlaine had spoken out and had been summarily dismissed; McKenzie had been crushed, transferred back to the States; and Robinson had left two years ago, retired, having been ground down into the dirt as long as he could take it. Only the Colonel remained, the iron man, outwardly the same. But inside he was sick at heart and terribly disillusioned. He could not bear to believe that his life's work had been utterly meaningless; that what he had fought for for so long and with such unwavering intensity would never become a reality.

But the Colonel could not give up, even now; it was simply not in his nature to contemplate such a thing. He had thought that he had been cleverer than all the rest; he had an ace to play, after all, that the others knew nothing about.

It seems, he thought, that I've played the game and lost. The fox somehow outsmarted me. But it's not over yet. It can't be. I won't let it.

The germ of the idea had come to him the day after Satsugai had been arrested by the SCAP Military Police late in 1946. Ostensibly, there was nothing the Colonel could do about it. Satsugai was well known in Japan, a powerful reactionary who was head of one of the monstrous *zaibatsu* combines. It was inevitable that he should come under suspicion and, subsequently, be arrested as a war criminal.

Itami withstood the shame stoically, as she withstood everything else in life. But Cheong was hysterical. That night, as they lay in bed, she pleaded with the Colonel to intervene. He was high up in the SCAP hierarchy, an adviser to General MacArthur himself. Surely there was some way he could help Satsugai.

'My darling,' he had said, 'matters are not as simple as that. This is a highly charged time. Besides,' he added reasonably, 'Satsugai may indeed be guilty of all they say he is.'

But this only served to infuriate Cheong further. 'It does

not matter,' she said simply. 'He is family.'

'You mean therefore he is no criminal?'

'Yes.'

'Darling, you're talking foolishness.'

'Maybe so.' Her voice was quite serious, containing the undercurrent of strength the Colonel recognized. 'But I tell you that your duty is to your family and if there is a way to help Satsugai you must do it. *Kakujin wa hombun wo tsukusa neba narimasen.*' Everyone must do his duty.

Cheong is a most intelligent person, the Colonel thought, but she can be inordinately stubborn at times. He had known there was no way to deflect her from her purpose; knew, too, that there would be no peace for him at home until he had proved to her that he had done his best to enforce his influence.

He had fallen asleep with that thought in his mind and had awakened just before dawn with the idea blooming already.

There *was* a way to free Satsugai, he was quite certain of that now, but to implement the plan would involve tremendous risk. He had no doubt that he could talk the SCAP tribunal into going along with him. It was purely a matter of whether he wanted to go ahead with it.

In the end, he knew he had little choice. He already understood the precariousness of the advisory board of which he was a member and now he thought of his plan as a kind of insurance policy against the day his job should go sour.

He knew a good deal about Satsugai's background; in fact a good deal more than Satsugai himself was aware. The Fukuoka connection was too obvious to ignore. The Genyōsha had never been an outlaw organization in Japan; records were not too difficult to unearth. The Colonel had taken a clandestine trip south to Kyūshū and had found out the truth. Satsugai was a Genyōsha leader.

At this particular point in time, that sort of information was incendiary. If it came to the attention of the SCAP tribunal, it would not matter how many incriminating documents Satsugai had destroyed in time, he would be executed.

However, the Colonel had absolutely no intention of divulging that piece of information to anyone. In any event, Satsugai's death would serve no purpose. The society would simply elevate another member and go on with its work. That work was totally counterproductive to what the Colonel perceived as the correct course towards Japan's future. He wanted the Genyōsha destroyed. If Satsugai were exonerated, he would be a dog on a leash – the end of which the Colonel had firm hold of. Sooner or later, Satsugai would lead the Colonel home to the centre of the Genyōsha.

The Colonel turned his gaze from the weeping glass into the warmth of his study. He watched the slanted Mongol eyes of his adversary, so well trained that he could see nothing below the surface, nothing that the man did not want him to see.

It seems a long time ago, the Colonel thought now, that I let him go and he has led me nowhere. He has known from the beginning. He knew what I wanted. I have managed to neutralize him as a force but he has otherwise stymied me. The Colonel felt a deep sadness inside himself. It was always his game to win, he thought. I was a fool to think otherwise.

That Satsugai hated him came as no surprise to the Colonel. After all, they were from opposite sides of the political spectrum. And while the Colonel understood better than any Westerner in Japan the importance of the maintenance of its traditions, its heritage, knowing that without those things the country would disintegrate, yet he also understood that the kind of tradition-alism that Satsugai represented was as evil and self-serving as anything in Japan could be. This was a country of heroes, he knew, not of villains. Those were few and far between. At that moment, as he stared into those baleful eyes across the warm expanse of his study, the Colonel knew that he had missed something elementary in the puzzle. There was a piece missing that was, he was convinced, the key to it all. He had believed that he had pierced Satsugai's secret life many years ago and all his actions since then had stemmed from that assumption. He now suspected that assumption, was angry at himself for having been so easily fooled. He played with me as if I were a child, the Colonel thought furiously.

It gave him little comfort at the moment that, by his inter-

256

vening, he had put Satsugai in an agonizing situation. He was in debt to the Colonel, a man he despised. It was an intolerable situation for a Japanese, yet Satsugai bore it well. I have to give him that, the Colonel thought.

My God, he thought, what is it that he has hidden from me all these years? The old warrior is shrewd yet. And then the Colonel understood what he must do. There had already been too much time wasted in an obviously fruitless plot. He had, as Satsugai himself had just said, to face reality. And the reality of this situation was that he must break the stalemate in whatever way was possible. There was only one way now.

The Colonel knew only too well that, as far as Satsugai was concerned, he was invulnerable. He could, for instance, insult Satsugai and the other would not – could not – take action against him. There was an obligation to be met. Satsugai must grin and bear it. The reverse, however, did not hold true.

For a brief moment, the Colonel was filled with a deep regret. Nicholas was still so young. There had been so little time and there were promises he had made that could not now be kept.

The Colonel stared out at the wide expanse of his property, the trees dripping with moisture, bending in the wind. He looked for the wren but it had long gone, perhaps preferring the storm to idleness. So much beauty out there, but this day he could feel no joy.

'What have you learned from the *Go Rin No Sho*?' Kansatsu said one day at the *dōjō*.

'Some of it is obviously quite useful,' Nicholas said, 'though it's mostly common sense.'

'Many consider it a revelatory work.' Kansatsu's tone was entirely neutral, giving Nicholas no clue as to whether or not *he* thought it was so important. His eyes glittered like glass, quite opaque. Behind him the long afternoon slid into the muffled mauve of twilight. The sun was lost in a steep bank of haze; the resulting light, reflective and diffuse, suffused the sky, laminated the trees until the world seemed monochromatic.

'I almost wish you hadn't given it to me.'

'Could you be more specific?'

'Well, there is something – I don't know – disturbing about it.'

Kansatsu said nothing, merely stood waiting. Behind him, the soft clash of *bokken*, the exhaled breaths in unison, filled the place.

'Some might say its purity is its ultimate virtue,' Nicholas said carefully. 'But, to me, it's more of a monomania. There is something intrinsically dangerous in that.'

'Can you tell me what, precisely?'

'Exclusion.'

As if he had been thinking of this all the time, Kansatsu said, 'Do you know anything of the life of Musashi?'

'Not really, no.'

'Miyamoto Musashi was born in 1584,' Kansatsu said seriously. 'As you no doubt know, this was not the best of times for Japan. There was and had been terrible internal strife brought about by the constant internecine warfare waged by the numerous *daimyo*.

'Musashi was a *ronin*, little more than a brigand, really. His family came from the south, in Kyūshū, but by the age of twenty-one he had travelled north to Kyoto and there fought his first battle, decimating a family which had, years before, been responsible for his father's demise.

'There are many, many tales told concerning Musashi and one must be most careful in reading these accounts. As is the case with most historical figures from this country's feudal past, Musashi's history is awash with myth. This blurring of fact and fancy is all well and good for the reader wishing for simple entertainment. But for the serious student of history – and this should include all who study bujutsu – it can be a dangerous trap.'

'But myth sometimes sustains the samurai,' Nicholas said.

'Not so.' Kansatsu's tone was emphatic. 'It is history which must sustain the warrior. History and duty, Nicholas. Nothing more. Myth cannot enter into it, for myth distorts judgement. Even the senses become infected then.

'In bujutsu we deal with most serious matters. The defence of life, yes, but that is not all. Methods of dealing death occupy us daily and there is, literally, no known number to that catalogue. One cannot be taught these things without the concomitant use of responsibility. And myth is the chief eroder of this responsibility. Without *bushido*, you see, we would be nothing more than ninja, common criminals stalking the streets. And it is so easy to slip into myth. So very easy.'

He put his hand out, indicating that Nicholas should sit. 'You have come a long way,' he continued. 'Your technique is flawless and your capacity for learning seems inexhaustible. However, I believe you have gone as far as you can here. There remains for you but one more hurdle and it is the most difficult. In fact, I must tell you that most students who have come this far never go any further.

'Nicholas, you must now find that hurdle within yourself and make the leap. I can no longer aid or even guide you. Either it will be there or it will not.'

'Does this mean you want me to leave the *ryu*?' Nicholas found that he was having difficulty in swallowing.

Kansatsu shook his head. 'I mean nothing of the sort. You are perfectly free to stay here for as long as you wish to stay.'

Nicholas knew that he was missing something and, furiously, he backtracked over the conversation, trying to think what it was. Kansatsu did not seem disappointed with him. On the contrary, there was a subtle undercurrent of excitement running through him. Think! What had he missed?

Kansatsu stood up. 'In lieu of a lesson today,' he said. 'I'd like you to give a demonstration for the class.' He stared down at Nicholas. 'Come along now.'

He went out into the centre of the floor, clapped his hands together once. All sound, all motion immediately ceased and all heads turned expectantly towards him, student and *sensei* alike.

Kansatsu picked four students at what appeared to be random. They were all last-year students and among the biggest physically in the *ryu*. All were older than Nicholas.

Kansatsu turned and beckoned to Nicholas, who walked out to stand beside him. In his right hand he carried a *bokken*. 'Please form up around Nicholas,' Kansatsu said to the students; they moved around him in a rough circle. Kansatsu beckoned to a *sensei*, who gave over his *bokken* to the master. Kansatsu delivered this up to Nicholas. 'Now,' he whispered so that only Nicholas could hear, 'we shall see how well you have digested the words of the Niten *ryu*, Musashi's school.'

He backed away, leaving Nicholas, a *bokken* in each hand, surrounded by the four students. They were all armed with single *bokken*. All of them had been at the *ryu* longer than he.

Darkness falling like a final curtain and he encircled; the stealthy pad of bare feet against polished wood; a sun orbited by four bright moons.

The dragonfly.

It was but one of the *tai-sabaki*, the circular movements consisting of glides and spins developed by Musashi's two-Heavens *ryu*.

He had seen this and others performed to perfection by Kansatsu countless times. He had read about these in numerous texts which the *sensei* had given him. He had, even, practised some on his own. But never in combat.

He must let the strategy of the others dictate his first movements, for only by the convergence of their attacks could he successfully use the *tai-sabaki* and only the *tai-sabaki* would give him a victory against four opponents.

Two came at him, one on each side, both raising their *bokken* in the traditional two-handed kenjutsu grip. Crying aloud, they slashed at him simultaneously.

It was the reverse butterfly. He whirled in an arc and, as he did so, his right-handed weapon swept down, slamming against one student's thighs. At the same time, the second weapon was rising and he continued the swirling motion of his torso, sweeping the rising *bokken* against the second student's windpipe. Both crashed to the ground, were replaced by the second set of adversaries. He had half a mind to use the waterwheel here but changed his mind as the vectors changed, feinting it only.

He split them, whirling still, and, his back arched, his right *bokken* stabbed end first into the mid-section of the student on his left while his left-hand weapon blurred upwards, slamming into the last student's. His *bokken* clattered to the floor. It was the interlacing cross, one of the most difficult of the *tai-sabaki*.

He returned to stillness, his *bokken* poised, quivering the air as if they had a life of their own and wished now to see more action.

'Saigō,' he heard Kansatsu call. The four students quit the field. Saigō stepped into it. He came to the *ryu* now less and less frequently. Nicholas did not know to which *ryu* he belonged; no one seemed to. But he knew that it was none of the ones in the Tokyo area.

Without warning, Saigō ran at Nicholas. His *katana* was still sheathed but in a blur it was out, extending outwards and down towards Nicholas. Saigō had become adept at, among other things, iaijutsu, the art of the 'fast draw'. The object was to incorporate the unsheathing of one's *katana* into the actual thrust against an opponent. The *iai sensei* could kill his enemy before that person was even aware that he had drawn his weapon.

One moment Saigō was unarmed, the next – perhaps a tenth of a second later – he had struck with lethal force. But even as he had used the *iai* draw Nicholas had been swivelling backwards on his right foot so that he now faced Saigō with his left side only. The blow, which had been meant for Nicholas's heart, now swept down into empty air and with his left-hand *bokken* Nicholas made contact, sweeping the *katana*'s blade up and away from him, swivelled again so that for an instant his back was to his opponent, driving the blade away still, using the other's momentum. Then he had completed the circular sweep and his right-hand *bokken* slashed into Saigō's exposed left side. The waterwheel.

He stood now with the entire class watching him, his feet spread, his *bokken* on either side of him, staring down at Saigō's sprawled form. There would be, he knew, a wicked purple welt raising the flesh where he had hit the other which would stay with him for more than a week.

There was absolute silence in the room; the kind of stillness that weighs on the ears until it becomes in itself painful.

Nicholas saw nothing but the face of his cousin staring up at him. Never in his life had he seen a look which contained so much hate. Nicholas had caused him to lose face in front of the *ryu*; he, a graduate, felled by one of the pupils. The intensity of their silent private war was such that for a moment it appeared as if lightning might light the room.

Then Kansatsu had clapped his hands twice and the on-lookers broke up; class was out for the day.

Nicholas found that he was trembling, the muscles jumping as if out of control under the sheath of his skin. Tension and adrenalin both still coursed through him, having been released in enormous quantities by the stress situation. His mind knew that that was over but his body needed more time to accommodate itself to a return to normalcy.

He breathed deeply, in and out. It was like a shudder.

When he returned home that evening, it was not one of the servants who opened the door at his approach. Nor was it Cheong. It was, rather, Yukio.

He had not seen her in three years and then it was only one brief afternoon at a family funeral. It had been three and a half years since their incendiary meeting and he had never forgotten her.

She bowed. 'Good evening, Nicholas.' She wore a dove-grey kimono with platinum-coloured threads running through it vertically. It had a midnight-blue wheel-and-spoke pattern that recalled the signs of the feudal *daiymyo*.

He bowed in return. 'Good evening, Yukio.'

She stood aside for him to enter, her eyes on the floor in front of her. 'You are surprised to see me.'

He put his bag down, never taking his eyes off her face. 'I haven't seen you in years.'

'Aunt Itami brought me this afternoon while you were at the *dōjō*. I came up to stay with them but the house is being partially remodelled, including the spare bedroom.'

He took her through the house, out of the back *shōji*. They stepped out into the night in the Zen garden.

It was clear, just a few stray clouds rising like wisps of smoke low on the horizon. The full moon was enormous, its reflected light turning the air aqueous; everything was bathed in blue shadows. He watched the soft light outline her profile, throwing her eyes into deep shadow. She might have been a statue at the Shinto shrine hidden within the cryptomeria. They

262

might have been under water.

A nightingale called softly from the treetops high over their heads, and farther away came the long, lonely hoot of a snow owl.

'I've never been to Kyoto,' he said. It was where she lived.

'You must come some time.' Her head turned slightly. She was staring at the mountains of the rocks, raising themselves like living entities above the lawn of round stones. Her voice was like velvet in the night. They stood quite still, not touching. 'It's very beautiful.'

Not as beautiful as you, Nicholas thought. He felt his heart beating hard. 'I still remember what happened.'

She turned to face him and the moonlight glinted off her pupils. 'What do you mean?'

Now he felt a fool. 'At the party.' He paused. 'When we danced ...'

She laughed a bit self-consciously. 'Oh, that. I had forgotten.'

He felt a bit deflated. He had felt before that part of her coming here was because of him. He saw how idiotic that was now. That one incident had happened three and a half years ago. Why should she remember it?

'Was Saigo at the *dōjō* today?'

'Yes. I hadn't seen him for some time. He's joined another *ryu*, I expect.'

'Perhaps that's why he goes to Kyūshū a lot.'

He stared at her. 'Kyūshū?'

She nodded. 'It's my Uncle Satsugai's doing, I'm certain. They're always plotting this or that when they're together. I can't imagine that Saigō would take it into his head on his own to go so far away. Anyway, it's a secret, I know that much.'

'How do you know that?'

'I asked Aunt Itami once and she acted as if she hadn't heard a word I'd said.'

'I'm sure it's nothing, then.'

Yukio merely shrugged, putting her arms across her breasts. 'Can we go in? I'm hungry.'

They went into the house and Nicholas excused himself. He went off to his room and, throwing off his dirty robe, padded into the bathroom. He turned on the shower, stepped inside the stall. Someone as traditional as Itami would, perhaps, prefer the bath but Nicholas had no such predispositions.

It was good to feel the hot water on his body and he began to soap himself, his thoughts on the day at the *dōjō*. He had wanted to talk to Kansatsu after the match with Saigō but that had proved impossible. Why hadn't he mentioned the match to Yukio? There had been ample opportunity when she had brought up Saigō. He shrugged, dismissing the thought.

He turned his head, curious. A shadow had been thrown against the frosted glass of the shower-stall. It condensed in size. The person was coming into the bathroom.

He turned off the water, opened the door.

He stood perfectly still. Water beaded his skin, glistening in the fluorescent light of the bathroom, which had turned her skin opalescent.

'You are quite beautiful,' Yukio said. She was naked. She held a bath towel over one arm. She did not offer it to him.

He watched her face for any sign of what she might be thinking. He thought of her words. He saw hunger in her eyes.

He was seventeen and she two years his senior. In terms of chronology it wasn't much but now it seemed like light-years. Despite all his training, his careful schooling, his cool intellect, he felt lost beside her, as if she were some doorway to a world for which he had been totally unprepared.

She took one step towards him. Her lips opened and she said something. It might have been as mundane as 'Do you want this?' He couldn't tell. One leg was extended in front of the other, as his had been earlier at the *dōjō* as the beginning of the interlacing cross. Her tiny ankle, the flesh of the calf, the extended knee, the long sweep of her thigh.

Something inside him, high up at the top of his brain, seemed to rise up, beginning to float away, as if someone unknown had chopped at the last cables holding him to the earth. It went twisting away, diminishing in size with such rapidity that he forgot that it had ever been a part of him.

'Come here,' he said thickly and his hand reached out,

brushing the towel from her arm. It pooled on the glistening tile floor as her arms lifted to him.

'Yukio.' But a breath.

Her breasts were high and round, the dark nipples long and already very hard. Her narrow waist, her creamy belly. The dark mound of her *mons* was highly arched.

Her arms came around him and he enclosed her open mouth.

She slid her body against his, not using her hand at all, only her lips against his own, down his neck, back upwards again, almost desperate in their urgency. Her breasts rubbed along the wet flesh of his chest, picking up the moisture; her mound was against him, gently massaging.

Her lips were at his ear and he heard her whisper, 'Turn on the water.'

He half turned, reaching behind them both to spin the taps. Hot water gushed down, inundating them, and as he turned back to her, he found that he was already deep inside her. He gasped. By what magic had she accomplished that? Sensations rolled like liquid thunder upward from his groin, engulfing him.

As he began to move against her, he saw her head float back, upturned, the wet hair cascading down like a stream at midnight. Her face was in the rush of water, her eyes rolling backwards, and her mouth wide open in a soundless scream. He could hear panting. Her arms came up, reaching over their bobbing heads to grasp the slippery chrome spout. Her knuckles turned white. Her thighs rose until they were locked around his waist and he was supporting her with his body. Her belly ground in hard circular movements as if she could not get enough of him and he was obliged to put his hands on her waist so that she wouldn't throw herself from their wet connection. The fierce heavings of her body mounted. It was like trying to hang on to a wild animal in the shuddering throes of death.

She began to scream now and abruptly he understood why she had wanted the water on. The pleasure was becoming unbearable and his legs began to tremble with the effort and the straining for release. Dimly he became aware that she was saying something to him.

'Hit me,' she moaned. 'Hit me.'

He thought that in this state he must have misheard her but she repeated it over and over, a litany. Her breasts shook, rivulets of moisture ran down her supple flesh. Her body was arched backward, her hands still gripping the spout, their bodies pistoning frantically.

She was gasping and moaning and he didn't think that he could hold out much longer. Her body seemed bottom-heavy.

'Please!' she cried to him. 'Please, please, please!' But he would not raise a hand to her. 'I know,' she gasped out, her lips against his ear. The hot rain crashing against them, her hard nipples scraping his chest. 'I know what happened today – at the *dōjō*.' Her voice was ragged and there were uneven gaps between the words. Still, he heard her. 'I know – oh! Hit me, darling. Hit me!' And then, savagely, 'I fucked Saigō, just as I'm fucking you now!'

He struck her then, as she wanted him to do, indeed, as she needed him to do.

'Oh!' she cried out, her body arching. 'Oh, oh, oh, darling! I'm going!'

And, in that moment, he felt a ring of muscles deep inside her gripping him, clamping his flesh in exquisite torment, and he too cried out, his legs giving way at last. Her fists slipped from the spout and they collapsed to the bottom of the stall, the water on them, all around them, the steam rising. Her arms came around him, pulling him hard against her, both of them still in orgasm.

The clouds were on fire.

The sun, sliding downwards in its arc, broke across the oblique shoulder of Fuji, turning the sky to crimson. As quickly as it had come, the flare faded as the sun dipped behind the mountain and all that was left was traces of pink, slowly healing wounds on the undersides of the passing clouds. Soon they had turned grey. The lights were lit.

Kansatsu sat cross-legged in the centre of the *dōjō*. Nicholas faced him. Nothing was said. The students, the other *sensei* had departed for the night. These two stayed on, breathing.

'Tell me,' Kansatsu said at last, 'what you have learned from the *Go Rin No Sho.*' His eyes remained closed.

'There is good in it,' said Nicholas. 'And evil.'

'That is rare, Nicholas.'

'On the contrary, *sensei.*'

'So?'

'I don't think anything in life is all good or all bad.'

Kansatsu opened his eyes and nodded. 'You have learned well, Nicholas. You are an astute student. It is a bad idea to rely too heavily on one discipline or one strategy set. This quickly becomes ingrained and one's thinking stagnates. Rely only on the situation that presents itself. If you let notions of strategy dictate to you, you will surely be defeated.' He closed his eyes again. 'You would be surprised, Nicholas, at the number of quite good students who make that mistake. *Sensei,* too.'

For a time there was silence between them. From outside Nicholas heard the muffled cough of a car starting. It drove off, the beams from its headlights swinging briefly across his field of vision. Darkness returned. A plover twittered, took off in a soft clatter.

Nicholas cleared his throat. 'I have read it all.'

'And what do you think?'

'To be truthful, I don't know what to think.'

'Do the ninja interest you, Nicholas?'

'Yes.'

'Then why do you hesitate?'

'I didn't know I had.'

'Then you had better look inside yourself.'

He thought for a moment. 'I guess I feel I should have said no.'

'Ah.'

'Ninjutsu seems a forbidden topic.'

'Arcane, yes. Forbidden, no.' Kansatsu stared at Nicholas across the small space between them. 'Even here in Japan, there is surprisingly little known about the ninja. They are from a segment of society about which no Japanese can be proud. But ninjutsu is an ancient art. It came from China, or so it is commonly said. I do not think that anyone could tell you with absolute certainty.

'The ninja were not bound by the Way of the Warrior. *Bushido* was only a word to them. Their rise was swift. Because they were so successful, the *bushi* used them more and more. As their wealth increased, so did the sophistication and diversity of their techniques. There came a time, then, when the samurai came to the ninja to learn. Thus the Way became perverted.

'There are many *ryu* in Japan. More than in any official governmental count. Among these, the variety of disciplines taught is virtually limitless. Good and evil are sometimes propounded indiscriminately.' He did not have to ask if Nicholas was following his line of thought. Darkness, now; the clouds obscuring the moon. Only man-made lights shone.

'To be a true champion, Nicholas, one must explore the darkness, too.'

That evening, Cheong took Nicholas aside. They went into the Colonel's study. It smelled of tobacco smoke and leather. Along with the kitchen, it was a Western room in an otherwise very traditional Japanese house.

Cheong sat sideways on the high-backed wooden chair in front of the Colonel's roll-top desk. Nicholas sat on the leather couch, near her.

'You are happy that Yukio has come to stay with us.' It was not a question.

'Yes,' he said truthfully. 'Is there anything wrong with that?'

Cheong smiled. 'You are growing up but you are still my child. I think I have a right to ask. You don't have to answer me, you know.'

His eyes dropped to his hands for a moment. 'I know that,' he said softly.

She leaned forward, enclosed his hands in hers. 'My darling, you have nothing to fear from me. Whatever you and Yukio do is between the two of you. Your father may not approve but he sees things differently to what we do. He is still a soldier and, therefore, mistrusts everyone and everything.'

Nicholas looked at her. 'He mistrusts Yukio. But what –'

Cheong shook her head. 'It doesn't matter, don't you see that? It's a blind spot he has. Never mind. I'm quite certain he mistrusted So-Peng in the beginning.'

She turned and, opening a drawer in the desk with a key, she produced the dragon-and-tiger box that was So-Peng's parting gift to her and the Colonel. With deft, economical movements of her fingers she opened the box.

'You see,' she said in a hushed voice, 'there are fifteen.' She meant the emeralds. 'There were sixteen, originally. One bought this house.' She looked up at him. 'I'm sure your father told you the story of this present.' Nicholas nodded and she continued. 'What he didn't tell you was its meaning. I'm not certain whether even he knows it fully.' She shrugged. 'And if he did, he would most likely dismiss the idea. He is a most pragmatic man, your father.' She smiled. 'One of his few faults, I'm afraid.'

She put the opened box with its glittering contents in Nicholas's lap.

'You are free to use six of these. To convert into money if your need is sufficient. No, hear me out. I want you to understand this fully; I think you can accept what I'm going to tell you.' She took a deep breath. 'There must never be less than nine emeralds in here. Ever. No matter what the reason, you must not use more than six.

'This is a mystical box, Nicholas. It has certain powers.' She paused, as if waiting. 'I see you're not smiling. Good. I believe it, as did my father, So-Peng. He was a great and wise man in all matters, Nicholas. He was no fool. He knew well that there exist on the Asian continent many things which defy analysis; which, perhaps, have no place in the modern world. They relate to another set of Laws; they are timeless.' She shrugged again. 'So I believe.' She took her hands away from the box, watched his face. 'You are old enough now to form your own opinions about the world and its mysteries. If you believe, then the power will be there for you when some day you need it.'

Night. Nicholas in the living-room, cross-legged in front of the window.

High in the sky, clear now of clouds, the full moon sent reflected light scattering down across the treetops and, closer to him, the formal garden. Intense black shadows streaked the window as the tall pine near the front of the house was illuminated as if by some celestial spotlight. Now and again, as the wind disturbed the branches, the shadows moved up and down, up and down, the motion of a fairyland boat from tales his mother used to tell him as he was falling asleep years ago. That time seemed long gone and Nicholas wondered now whether this was something all people felt: that childhood belonged to another, simpler time when all decisions were minor and seemed of little consequence.

In times gone by, on sleepless nights, that lone pine had been his protector. He knew every configuration, every angle of its branches, every knot along its thick trunk. Now it seemed to him to have been transmogrified. He saw it as an old soldier, a guardian in the night, a friend and an ally. *To be a true champion* ...

His world was changing so swiftly now.

*Haragei* allowed him to become aware of her presence as she stepped into the room. He did not move. He heard her coming towards him. Softly. Softly. Appalled, he found himself getting hard. He willed his erection down but his body would not listen.

She sat down gracefully, facing him, away from the moonlight. Her face black in the dense shadows, her long blue-black hair haloed faintly in platinum light. He thought he could see her entire body beat with the rhythm of her pulse.

He was so acutely aware of her, it was almost painful. The musk of her body, mingled with a perfume he could not identify; a certain heat that transmitted itself physically. But there was more, an almost tangible force. He felt enveloped by her aura.

The house was so still that he could hear the white noise soughing in his inner ear like an internal storm.

He stood up so abruptly that he felt rather than saw her start. Reaching down for her hand, he pulled her up and, opening a *shōji*, took her outside.

Unmindful of the cold, he took her to the periphery of their property, along the verge of the cryptomeria wood, searching for the half-hidden path Itami had shown to him years ago.

At length he found it and plunged with her headlong into

the forest. There was no light to speak of, just dim, luminous patches like odd floating flora where the moonlight penetrated the green canopy high above their heads. Cicadas called shrilly and to one side came a soft scuffling of leaves, a pair of bright red eyes.

They flew along the jungle trail, Nicholas guiding them unerringly as if he were a bat with sonar. They leaped over roots, ducked under black swinging branches and, at last, broke through into the moon-drenched clearing. Before them was the circular path and the closed double doors of the rearing shrine.

She dragged him back to the grass verge, pulling him down beside her. 'Now,' she whispered fiercely. 'I can't wait any more.'

Her robe parted slightly. She was incredible. Her flesh glowed as if with an inner light. He couldn't keep his hands off her. He leaned forward, parting the robe farther. He stroked her thighs until she moaned and, reached out with both arms, drew him over her. Her panting was hot in his ear as his mouth opened, enveloping one nipple, as much of the surrounding breast as he could take. He sucked hard, felt her indrawn breath, the hot scoring of her nails on a line down his ribs. Her thighs surrounded him, her flesh scorching, drawing him inward to her moist centre. She sounded as if she were choking. He could smell her strongly on the night air. Moving snakelike down her writhing body, using his tongue and his lips until he reached her high mound. He rose up, then descended to the soft flesh of her inner thighs. He moved so slowly that, at length, he heard her cry out in longing, felt her fingers in his hair, pulling him up her.

Her buttocks were off the soft damp ground in an attempt to get him to suck her there, where she desired it the most. But he held on, circling, circling, so hard he thought he might never be soft again, until finally he moved, stabbing through the wet dark hair, spreading the flesh beneath. Her hands turned to fists and the cords of her neck tautened. She screamed again and again. There was no stopping the convulsing of her sweat-flecked body.

*

271

'I was born to be something,' she said much later, 'more than what I am now.'

The cryptomeria rustled contentedly above their heads. The earth was soft beneath their spent bodies.

'I'm nothing now.' Her voice was so soft it could have been the night wind. 'Nothing but a reflection.' He did not understand that. 'All my life no one has said one word to me that's meant anything.' She turned her head in the crook of his arm. 'It's all been lies.'

'Even your parents?'

'I have no parents.' She turned over, her buttocks against his thighs.

'Are they dead or ...'

'Did they leave me, do you mean? My father died in the war. He was Satsugai's brother. My uncle never approved of the marriage in the first place.'

'What happened to your mother?'

'I don't know. No one ever said. Perhaps Satsugai gave her a sum of money to leave.'

A whippoorwill trilled, seeming far away. The air was dense with mist though there seemed few clouds in the sky. The moon was low, bloated, tinctured orange.

'I'm surprised Satsugai didn't take you in,' he said.

'You are?' She gave a tiny bitter laugh. 'I'm not. Itami wanted me, I know that. But Satsugai arranged for a couple to take care of me in Kyoto.' She was silent for a time, thinking. 'I asked Aunt Itami once and she said that Satsugai thought they would have many children of their own and he didn't want anything to interfere with his family. It didn't turn out that way, obviously.'

'Then you do have parents.'

'There's something odd about that household.' She was still talking about her uncle. 'I can't put my finger on it. It involves Satsugai and Saigō. Itami's not part of it, though I'm sure she knows what's going on.' There was a dry fluttering over their heads as a plover took off southward. 'I think it has something to do with where Saigō goes.'

'In Kyūshū.'

'Yes.'

'It's a *ryu*, I'll bet.'

She turned over, her eyes luminous and huge in the dark. The heat of her body, its musk, penetrated him. 'But why travel so far? There are plenty of *ryu* in the Tokyo area.'

*There are many* ryu *in Japan.* Kansatsu's words came to him as clearly as a tolling bell. Did he know? Good and evil. White and black. Yin and yang. *One must explore the darkness, too.*

'It must be a very special *ryu*.'

'What?'

He'd said it so softly, thinking out loud, that even this close she had not heard him. He repeated what he'd said.

'But what kind?' she wanted to know.

Nicholas shrugged. 'I'd need to know the town he is going to.'

'But I can find out!' she said excitedly, rising up on one elbow. 'He leaves tonight for Kyūshū. I'll only need to take a peek at his train ticket.'

'Would you do it?'

She gave him a little conspiratorial smile. Lights danced in her eyes. 'If you wanted me to.'

He watched her for a moment, then lay back, hands underneath his head. 'I want to know something.' His throat felt tight. 'I want to know if what you said ... before is true. Did you sleep with Saigō?'

'Does it matter?'

'Yes, it matters.'

She threw her arms around his neck. 'Oh, Nicholas. Don't be so serious always.'

'Did you?'

'It might have happened – once.'

He sat up, staring at her. 'Might?'

'All right. Yes. But – it just happened.'

'The way it just happened with us,' he said nastily.

'Oh no.' Her eyes looked into his. 'That's not the way it happened at all. He's nothing like you.'

'You mean you planned the whole thing with me?' His voice was demanding.

Her eyes flickered down for a fraction of a second. 'I –

didn't know what to think when Aunt Itami told me she was bringing me here. I remembered I wanted to fuck you that night on the dance floor but that was –'

'You told me you didn't remember that!' His tone of indignation concealed his inner delight.

She smiled. 'I lied about that.' She smiled and stuck out her tongue, a very un-Japanese gesture. 'I didn't want to spoil the surprise. I knew the moment I saw you again what I wanted to do.'

'I had no hint when we went out in the garden.'

She shrugged. 'I'm two different people. You've seen both sides.'

'What was it like for you, growing up?'

'Why do you ask?'

He burst out laughing. 'Because I'm interested in you. Why? Do you think I'm after something?'

'Everyone's always after something.'

'Not everyone,' he said softly, pulling her close. 'I'm not.' He kissed her with closed lips. 'I care about you, Yukio. A great deal.'

She laughed. 'Well, at least you didn't say you loved me.'

'I might,' he said seriously. 'I don't know yet.'

She tossed her head. 'Oh, come off it. You know you don't have to say those things to me. They're meaningless. You'll get what you want, don't you know that?'

'I don't understand you.'

'I told you before,' she said patiently. 'I don't need to hear those things. I don't need that illusion. We give each other pleasure. That's enough for me.'

'Is that how it was with Saigō, too?' he asked harshly. 'I meant what I said. I do care about you. About what happens to you. How you feel. If you're happy or if you're sad.'

She stared at him for a long time as if she could find no words to utter. She was watching him carefully. At length she settled back onto the grass.

'When I was a little girl,' she said in a small voice, 'we'd go into the mountains for the summer, to a small town perched high up on the sloping wooded side. The houses, I remember, were all on stilts. It was the first time I'd seen anything like that. It looked like a town out of a story-book.

'My foster parents never had much time for me though Satsugai gave them enough money each month. They never wanted children. So I had a lot of time to myself. I remember that during the days I'd sit in the tall grass, hearing the cicadas in my ears – the shrill metallic sound of the locusts late in the summer ...' She breathed deeply, staring up at the nodding foliage of the cryptomeria. 'The afternoons seemed endless. I'd sit on the mountainside, overlooking the valley. There were two long furrows etched into the foliage, brown and sere, mysteriously bare, as if some giant had scored the land in anger. I used to spend hours wondering who had made those cruel marks.'

'The war, perhaps,' Nicholas said.

'Yes. I never thought of that.' She turned her head away from him. 'But I'd get beaten for staying away so long even though I knew they didn't want me around. There was never any compassion. Never even any understanding. I was like an alien to them, some freak, a miniature adult. It seemed as if they had never been children themselves, had no conception of what it was like to be a child.'

'Yukio,' he said softly, leaning down to kiss her tenderly.

When they broke apart, she said, 'And then there was the bamboo grove. It was somewhat farther down the mountainside. I discovered it quite by accident, early on, when I was lost one afternoon. I used to creep out of the house at night; the darkness stifled me as I lay in bed, sleepless. It became solid, a crushing weight pressing against my eyelids until I had to get out of there.

'It was quite near a stream which bubbled constantly. When there was a moon it looked like it was made of silver. The water was so frigid, it numbed your mouth.

'It was like being at a shrine, standing in that grove, the tall, straight bamboos rising like columns over your head. Their tops sometimes speared the huge orange harvest moon late in the summer, when the locusts were at their most shrill.' She moved against him as if making herself more comfortable. He felt her bare flesh against his. 'It was the only place I could call my own. My secret place. I had sex there for the first time.' He felt the musculature of her body beginning to tremble as if she were cold. 'I brought a boy there. He lived on a near-by farm. It was his first time, too, I think. He'd only seen the cattle do it and he wasn't very good. He was so nervous, wanting to do it the way he'd seen the horses performing. He was so excited, he went all over my thigh.'

'In the West,' Nicholas said, 'they say, "I'm coming." Here, we say, "I'm going." There's a complete reversal.'

'With death, too,' she whispered, 'I've heard it said. Westerners don't understand *seppuku*, do they? They'll turn outwards, instead of inwards, jump off a building –'

'Or blow some poor bastard's head off before they turn the gun on themselves.'

'Odd, isn't it?' She giggled. 'Perhaps they're barbarians, after all.' But she shivered none the less.

'Don't let's talk of death,' he said, holding her.

'No,' she whispered. 'We won't.' She reached between his thighs, caught gently hold of him, stroking.

'Is that all you can think of?' he said thickly.

'It's all I have,' she said in a moan.

# Fourth Ring
## THE FIRE BOOK

# I

## West Bay Bridge/New York City, Summer Present

'No, no, no, no!' she said, laughing. 'Let's forget all about it.'

She ran at him instead of away from him as she had been doing. She leaped in a shallow dive, skidding across the top of a sand dune, wrapped her arms about his ankles, bringing him down.

Justine laughed again, half atop him. Nicholas spat sand out of his mouth, rolled over on his back.

'Very funny!'

She jumped on him, on all fours, and they spun about on the dark sand. A cool breeze came in off the sea, ruffling their hair. The porch lights from the house were diffused by the ground mist, haloed, comforting.

Her face was very close to his, her eyes wide. He could see the red motes as they caught the light. Her long hair was like a bridge between them. Her long delicate fingers were on his cheeks. They had the firmness, the lightness of touch of a sculptor's hands. 'I don't want to be sad, Nicholas,' she said softly.

He kissed her lightly.

'I'm here.'

'I know you are.'

'It's a big thing for me to say. And mean.' She was totally serious now, the playful mood had slipped away. 'I had a lot of time to think about ... things.'

'You mean in bed.'

She shook her head. 'No. In the water. It wasn't my life that flashed before me.' She laughed but it was a rueful sound. 'There was one time when I didn't think I was going to come back up. I had been fantasizing about you while I was swimming. You know, a harmless kind of thing.' Her eyes were almost out of focus, she was so close to him. 'That's not what I thought about when I was under. I thought about what it would be like never to see you again.' Her voice was so soft now that, despite her nearness, he could barely make out what she was saying. She swallowed hard as if the words were sticking in her throat. 'I'm frightened. Frightened of what I'm telling you. It's one thing to admit to the feeling, quite another to voice it, you know?' She gave him a long, hard stare. 'I love you,' she said. 'I can't think of anything else when I'm near you. I usually like to go certain places, be with specific people, but I don't care about any of that when I'm with you. I know that sounds juvenile and romantic but –'

He laughed. 'Romantic, yes. Juvenile, no. And anyway, what's so terrible about being a romantic? I am. Maybe there aren't many of us left, though.'

Her eyes were clear and searching. 'Do you love me, Nick? I want you to be honest. It's all right if you don't. I just need to know the truth.'

He did not know what to say. His mind was alight with memories both pleasurable and painful and he knew then that Yukio was still not gone from him. He felt like a salmon struggling upstream, fiercely fighting the current. But he was no fish and he wondered why he was doing it. What was he fighting, anyway? And what made it so important?

He felt that he had the answers to those questions inside him if only he could pin them down. He still stung from the jibe Croaker had given him in the restaurant and he was angry at himself that it had affected him so. What if Croaker had been right? How deeply had he been affected by Terry's and Ei's deaths? Surely he felt *something*. He must. He was no machine. But he could summon no tears. Perhaps there were other ways to grieve; he knew he was like his mother in that respect. He was far too controlled to allow certain emotions to surface. But with that he was denying a part of himself and that could prove to be disastrous. Without full understanding of himself, he could control no situation. He could be champion of nothing, not the light, nor the dark that thought made him jump as if someone had pricked him. An idea rippled like a banner at the edge of his consciousness ...

'What are you thinking?'

His eyes focused to see her. There was concern on her face. 'You shouldn't make sacrifices,' he said. 'Not for me, not for anybody. It can be dangerous.'

'Damn it! I'm not making sacrifices. Not any more. I'm through with all that. I won't give anything up for you. Not until I'm quite certain it's what *I* want.' Her eyes glittered, fine pinpoints of energy in the darkness. 'Is it so awful that you satisfy me? That I'm content with that? Does part of you rebel against that notion?'

She had cut him to the quick without realizing it. 'Christ, what made you say that?' He sat up, feeling his heart hammering.

'Because it's true?' She tried to look in his eyes. 'I don't know. But I do know how your body reacts to mine. That's communication on the most basic level, the way it was done a million years ago before there were books to talk about or films or plays, any entertainment. When people just had each other. I want to know why you reject that out of hand. Don't you trust your body to tell you what's right? It knows better than your mind what's good for you.' She laughed. 'I can't believe it. You of all people. You've been working with your body all your life and still you don't trust it.'

'You don't know anything about it,' he said shortly.

'Oh, I don't?' She sat up. 'Then you tell me. Explain it to me simply so my poor female brain can understand.'

'Don't be childish.'

'It isn't me who's being childish, Nick. Just listen to yourself. You're terrified of revealing anything of yourself to someone.'

'Didn't you ever think there's a good reason for that?'

'Oh yes. That's why I'm asking you what it is.'

'Maybe it's none of your business.'

'Right. All right,' she flared. 'I can see how far I'm going to get with you.'

'Nowhere, Justine. You don't own me.'

'This is what I get for being honest with you.'

'You want honesty?' Knew he shouldn't do it and didn't care. 'I met your father in the city today.'

Her head came up. She looked incredulous. 'You met my

father? How?'

'He picked me up in his limo outside the station. I got the first-class treatment.'

She stood up. 'I don't want to hear about this.' Her voice was abruptly harsh. She remembered San Francisco all too clearly. Rage built up inside her. She felt impotent against him. Always had. Always.

'I think you should,' he said cruelly. Some part of him egged him on, revelling in the pained expression on her face.

'No!' she cried, putting her palms against her ears. She wheeled away from him.

He got up and went after her, across the cool sand. 'He wanted to know all about us. He knows all about you. What you've been doing. What you haven't.'

'God damn him!' She slipped at the crest of a dune, pulled herself up, whirled on him. Her eyes were feral sparks, as large as beacons. She was white with rage.

'Christ but you're both bastards! Him for doing it and you for telling me. You're a real sonovabitch, you know that?'

All he could think of was pushing her away now. 'He thought I might be another one like Chris –'

'Shut up! Shut up, you cocksucker!'

But he pursued her relentlessly. 'He offered me a job, and you know, the joke of it is I took it. I'm working for him now.'

'How could you do this to me?' she cried. She wasn't talking about the job. 'My God! My God!' Weeping, she hurled herself from him and, stumbling up the sandy steps to her house, she disappeared from his view.

Nicholas broke down and cried, falling to his knees in the unforgiving sand.


'He will soon be here,' said Ah Ma. 'Is everything in readiness?'

'Yes, Mother,' Penny said from her spot at Ah Ma's feet. 'Flower has just returned with the last of the ... ah, items.' Penny's perfect, white face bent over a leather-bound ledger book in which she was writing Chinese characters in vertical lines. She used a thin brush which she dipped periodically in an open bottle of Higgins ink. Her movements were deft and sure.

She considered her mistress's silence, then made a decision. 'Do you think we should be letting this man in here?' She kept her eyes on her writing and, for just an instant, felt her heart contract coldly in her chest at the thought of Ah Ma's possible outburst.

Ah Ma did nothing more, however, than sigh. Penny was quite correct, of course. In days gone by she would never have allowed this to happen. She shrugged mentally. Ah well, times had changed for them all and one must accommodate oneself as best one could. Her voice, when she spoke, conveyed none of this inner dialogue.

'Penny, my precious one, there is, as you well know, a great deal of money involved. I am not a prejudiced person; neither should you be.' But she knew these words to be false, although Penny never would. Ah Ma, now in her late sixties, was Fukienese, from that district of coastal China midway between the cities of Hong Kong and Shanghai. She was one of fifteen children but she had always felt quite apart from them. Perhaps her name had something to do with that. There was a legend of a poor Fukienese girl by that name who sought passage on a junk. In all the port only one would grant her request. Out of port they were beset by a furious typhoon and it had been Ah Ma who had brought the junk safely through. There was a temple to her, Ah Ma knew, at the base of Barra Hill on the island of Macao.

She shifted in her chair and it creaked. She felt the slide of silk against her arm. Through the open window she could clearly hear the clatter from Doyers Street. There was a fish market on the corner which stayed open late. They sold marvellous squid at this time of year. She heard several voices raised in argument and she winced at the Cantonese. Up here in the large suite of apartments which took up the entire third floor of the building only Mandarin was spoken. That was the way it had been in Ah Ma's house when she was a child; that was how it was now.

Ah Ma got up, padded silently over to the window, peering down at the narrow, crowded street. She could, she knew, have had her pick of virtually any location in Manhattan. Over the years there had been many attractive offers to move elsewhere. She had always refused. It seemed right to her that her business should be square in the heart of Chinatown. The area was dim and slightly seedy but it was atmospheric. In many ways it reminded Ah Ma of home. That was what she wanted. Now a millionairess, she was still no more comfortable among the steel and glass towers of uptown Manhattan than she had been with structures like the Chrysler Building when she had first arrived in New York.

Yes, Ah Ma thought now, looking down at the night-dark street, the bright, bustling clutter of the throng, the intermittent odours of fresh fish in the early morning when the catch was brought in downstairs, the delicacy of the steamed *dim sum* from the dumpling house next door, I am very comfortable here. Very much so.

She sighed again. Of course, the Chinatown Planning Council might not be too pleased with her if they knew her real business. But the police were certainly happy with the thousand dollars they picked up each month. She was careful to perform this duty herself and to serve them tea each time they came; it increased her face.

Her home in Foochow was always with her but, oddly, more so as she grew older. Being in Chinatown gave her some small illusion of being home. Not that she would ever consider going back now. She had no great love for the communist Chinese and even now, when it might be feasible for her to return for a visit, she could not bring herself to contemplate the reality of it.

No, she had all that she wanted of Foochow right here.

Around the corner the red and blue neon lights of the restaurants turned the darkness watery with reflected light. It was the Japanese, of course, whom she had learned to hate long before the communists. They had come down the coast, those wealthy, arrogant businessmen, from their deals in Shanghai, already jaded with that city's night-life or just wanting to see a bit more of China. They are so different from the Chinese, Ah Ma thought wonderingly. But of course they do not have our centuries of history to learn from. The Japanese are a relatively new people. When we had already forged dynasties, were experimenting with gunpowder, their islands were inhabited only by the barbarous Ainu – unintelligent savages. If the modern Japanese are descended directly from those people, it's no wonder they're so warlike.

She turned away from her window on Doyers Street, said, 'I want to see him, now, Penny. There must be no mistake.'

Penny nodded, put aside her ledger and pen, stood up and crossed the room.

'Penn ...'

She stopped short, her hand on the door-knob. 'Yes, Mother?'

'He is not from here?'

'No, Mother. He's from uptown.'

Ah Ma nodded. 'Good. I do not want neighbours ... involved.'

In the short space of time Penny was gone, Ah Ma thought about her. She had made the right decision in elevating the girl. She was clever with her mind as well as with her hands. Ah Ma would never admit it openly but there were times when she relied on Penny's judgement, and it disturbed her that she seemed set against the Japanese.

Penny was the name Ah Ma had given to her when she had first applied for a job; Ah Ma gave names to all her girls and henceforth they were known by that name and that name alone. It was neat and tidy and as anonymous as Ah Ma believed her business should be. Besides, it gave her great pleasure to name her 'children'; it pleased her, too, that they should address her by the honorific 'Mother', a word not lightly used in her land.

There would come a time, Ah Ma thought, when she would have to relinquish her hold here. When that eventuality occurred she wanted to be certain that precisely the right hands took over.

Penny came back, ushering in a boy of about eleven. She stopped just inside the threshold, both hands on his shoulders. He stood perfectly still, his eyes incurious. Through the partially open doorway Ah Ma could hear the quiet bustle of the preparations. As planned, there were only one or two guests expected tonight; this, too, was built into the enormous fee she was charging the Japanese. She did not mind.

She looked the boy over. He had clear, smooth skin, a slight Mongol cast to cheeks and eyes. His irises were like chips of coal. His mouth was wide, the lips slightly sensual.

'This is Philip Chen,' Penny said.

'Close the door, precious,' Ah Ma said softly. Her hands were clasped in front of her, the fingers interlaced. She looked at the boy. 'You will have another name while you are here,' she told him. 'Sparrow. This will be how you are summoned, how you will be addressed. Is this understood?'

The boy nodded, then smiled slowly.

'Call me Mother.'

'Yes, Mother.'

'Have you been properly instructed? I don't want any surprises.'

'Yes,' he said happily. 'Penny has explained everything. No problem.'

'Really?' Ah Ma's eyebrows arched. 'That remains to be seen. All right. Leave us now, Sparrow. Find Willow. She will take you to the proper room. You know what to do.'

'Yes, Mother.' He turned and left.

After Penny had shut the door behind him, Ah Ma said, 'Parents?'

Penny shook her head. 'He lives with an uncle who is too drunk to care if he's out all night.'

'The situation is totally secure?'

Penny nodded her head. Her black hair tossed like an animal's mane, 'Willow saw to it personally.'

Ah Ma allowed herself a small smile. 'You have done well, my child.'

Penny bowed her head to cover the flush in her cheeks. It was rare indeed to be addressed in such a loving manner by Ah Ma. 'Thank you, Mother,' she murmured.

Ah Ma went silently to stand in front of Penny. She lifted a hand, tilted her chin up. 'Now tell me what's bothering you,' she said quietly.

Staring into those all-knowing eyes, it was difficult to find words. Penny felt as if her throat had constricted so much that not even air could pass through.

'Come, come, child. Is it the Japanese? What is it about him that offends you so?'

'I am ashamed that my feelings are so transparent,' Penny said sadly. Her eyes dropped for a moment and she felt as if she might burst into tears at any moment.

'Nonsense!' Ah Ma said irritated. 'What is apparent to me is not to others. You have lost no face with me. Please tell me now what I wish to know.'

'It is the drug which bothers me so,' Penny said. 'This is something I don't think we should become involved in.'

For a moment Ah Ma said nothing. She recalled a trip she had taken as a small girl into Shanghai. She could still smell the overpowering, cloying stench of the burning opium. Her nostrils quivered at the memory; she had never smoked but the odour remained with her like a brand.

It had been in the air the night the communists had come for her husband. There had been no sound, no warning. They had been in hiding but the communists had known precisely where to look. They had been traduced.

Ah Ma's husband had been a political activist. His foresight was long-range. He had seen the impending storm of the Communist Revolution, perhaps had even understood its inevitability. Yet he fought against it with unequalled vehemence. 'For once,' he had said in speeches, had written in pamphlets, 'we are in a position to learn from the Japanese. What good did the closed regime of the shōguns do them? There came a time when it became apparent that the country was stagnating, strangling in its hard-bound traditions of iron. The way of the future for the Japanese became Western capitalism. Now see where they are. Can we here in China ignore such a historical example? A communist take-over will seal us off from the West, from the very capitalism which has made such thriving cities of Hong Kong and Shanghai. Thus will China fall behind the rest of the world, a true sleeping giant.'

They burst in, throwing Ah Ma against a wall so that her head banged into the edge of a cupboard. They dragged him out of bed, stripped him, beat him with their heavy sticks, the butts of their rifles. The red star embroidered on their peaked caps, the epaulettes of their stinking uniforms. They had dragged Ah Ma's husband, unconscious and bleeding, from the house. It was the last time she ever saw him. To this day she could not be certain whether he was alive or dead. But she hoped for his sake that he had died quickly. Perhaps he had found a bit of wire or a length of bed-sheet. She did not want to think of what they might have done to his mind.

That was a long time ago but sometimes, on the dismal grey days, when rain lashed the windows and even the street below was obscured, Ah Ma thought that the wound had never quite healed.

She brought her thoughts back to the present, smiled into Penny's eyes. She was so beautiful. Perfect and beautiful. 'It is good you feel that way, my precious,' she said. 'As a rule you know I don't allow drugs of any nature in here. This man is an exception.' He fights the communists in China, in his own way, Ah Ma thought. He believes that his security is total but I know. Of course I know. I would not be who I am otherwise. I know all about everyone who comes here. Without exception. This one merely took more time, more *baht*. But there are always palms willing to be greased; there is a price on all such matters.

'May I know the reason?' Penny asked softly.

Ah Ma patted her shoulder. 'It does not concern you.' She smiled. 'Now go help Willow. It's almost time.'

Penny bobbed her head, her eyes on the floor in front of her. 'Yes, Mother. Right away.'

Ah Ma watched her silently pad out of the room, wondering what the world was coming to.

As for the Japanese, he was, at this time, leaving the movie theatre via its side entrance. He immediately crossed Forty-ninth Street and ran the last several steps to catch a downtown bus. It was fairly crowded but thinned out not long after they passed Thirty-fourth Street.

He swung off one stop from the terminus, walked the rest of the way into the Village. On Eighth Street he turned east until he came to Cooper Square with its black metal cube sculpture balanced on one point. Along one face someone had spray-painted in white 'Zombie loves Karen R'. It seemed to fit.

He caught the City Hall bus on the corner of Eighth and Third Avenue, traced the Bowery as far as Canal Street. There he found the first phone booth. He stared up at the chunky old-fashioned clock above the jewellery store on the corner.

He dialled a number, got the correct time. He hung up and waited precisely one minute and fifty seconds. Then he dialled a local New York number. He detested this procedure but it was a built-in factor and a logical one; he did not fight logic.

At the other end the receiver was picked up. The Japanese read off the seven digits of the number from which he was making the call, then immediately replaced the receiver. He held down the bar while lifting the receiver, placing it against his ear. A woman who had been looking at him turned around disgustedly, searching for another phone.

Four and a half minutes later the phone rang. The Japanese lifted his finger from the bar. The conversation was in Japanese.

'Yes.' He could hear the hollow sound of the overseas line.

'Status.'

'We're running.'

'Tell me more. What results have you?'

'Results?' He seemed somewhat taken aback. 'I'm in place. The buy is running.' *Buy* was his own word for mission.

'I see.' There was a pause during which it was just possible to hear the sibilants of another call far in the open background. 'The line is secure?'

'From this end, absolutely.'

The voice at the other end appeared to disregard the discourtesy. 'We wish a rapid denouement.'

'That was made clear to me in the beginning.' Every fifteen seconds he checked his immediate area. Not that he expected to find anything; one should never forget security. It was all one ever had.

'Precisely.'

'These things can't be rushed. You know that. I work a

288

certain way. This was agreed upon or I never would have taken on the buy.'

'Oh yes. We are well aware of that. But life is ever changing and recent events – events which have taken place while you were out of the country – necessitate a more precipitate closure.'

'I never do things that way. I –'

'You will now.' The voice was as soft as silk, the tone even. There was no haste to the words, no heavy-handed menace. 'It is imperative you close the buy within the next seventy-two hours.'

'I do not think that –'

'Your fee is doubled.'

The line was dead in his hand.

'Good evening,' Ah Ma said. She stitched a smile on her face, extended an arm. 'You honour this house w –'

'Is it all ready?'

Ah Ma kept her annoyance at this serious breach of ritual courtesy out of her voice. She was an extremely orderly woman; she did not take well to disruptions. Or to rudeness. She thought briefly of throwing the Japanese out. Certainly she did not need his money. But he had killed communists in China. Three high officials that she knew of; that surely meant the true figure was higher. She hated the communists far more than the Japanese. Besides, the arrangements had already been made. It would have been a cruel waste of time for her people had she sent him away now.

Ah Ma gave the Japanese her warmest smile. 'All is in readiness, as we discussed.' Covertly, her wide-apart black eyes, as alert as a bird's, studied him. His mood is different, she thought. He seems less relaxed, almost on edge. Perhaps he goes from here to kill another communist. She shrugged inwardly. It was none of her concern.

'Would you care for some tea first?'

'No.'

'Dumplings are just now being prepared.'

He shook his head.

Ah Ma lifted her shoulders. 'As you wish.' Barbarian! she

thought. The amenities mean nothing to him. Time rushes him as if he were a Westerner. Ah well! The Japanese are much like the Westerners now; they are great mimics. 'Willow,' she called softly.

A woman glided up. She was tall and slender, her face bony. This set off her long eyes and full, wide lips. She was most striking. Yet she possessed a remarkable icy detachment. No one could mistake her for one of Ah Ma's girls; one knew immediately, almost instinctively, that she was far more. One had no idea what that might be.

Willow looked at Ah Ma and at no one else.

'Take the gentleman,' Ah Ma said softly, 'to the Gold Suite.' All the rooms used for professional purposes were designated by colour.

Willow bowed and led the man down a dimly lighted hallway. The walls, save for the decorative moulding at floor and ceiling, were covered in blue-green Shantung silk. The carpet was a deep beige, as were the moulding and the closed doors they passed.

They came to the last door on the left and Willow halted. Her hand reached out for the knob.

'Wait a minute.' The man's fingers encircled her slender wrist. He pulled her round to face him. 'Are you going to –' He was speaking in Cantonese, saw the blank look on her face, switched to Mandarin. It was too much to expect that they'd know Japanese. 'Has the old woman fixed you up with me? I told her I didn't want anyone tall.' Willow stared at him mutely. 'Listen, I don't want you. Understand? There's been some mistake.'

Willow dropped her gaze to his fingers holding her.

'Tell the old lady there's been a mistake. For the money I'm –' He stopped, puzzled. She had made no move to break away from him. He had wanted her to struggle, even to whimper. He increased the pressure of his fingers but there was no response. He let go her wrist.

Willow turned and silently opened the door. She did not step over the threshold.

The Japanese went inside and turned around to look at her but the door was already closing behind him.

The room was large. Green carpet covered the floor. The walls were gold; the ceiling, an eggshell white. The room contained a large double bed, a wide sofa and a trio of matching chairs, all done in gold cotton. An open door in the right wall led to a rather large and, upon closer inspection, ornate bath. A highly polished oak armoire stood along the left wall next to a large window.

He crossed to this, looked out on Pell Street. There was a conventional black iron fire escape running up the side of the building; there was no window in the bathroom. Normal security precautions. He turned round.

He saw a young boy and, behind him, a young woman.

'What is your name?' he asked the boy. He did not ask for the woman's name.

'Sparrow.'

'Do you have it?'

The boy nodded, took a step towards the Japanese.

'Stop,' he commanded. 'Give it to the girl.'

The boy turned and handed her something.

'Bring it to me.'

The girl bowed. On her way to him, she stopped to pour a cup of hot *sake*. She handed it to him.

He stared at her, his eyes boring into hers. His hand flipped out in a blur, knocking the cup from her outstretched hand. She stifled a cry at the blow. Her fingers stung terribly.

'Do nothing,' he said coldly, 'unless I command it. Then be quite certain you do precisely as you are told. Is that clear?' The girl nodded dumbly. These remarks seemed directed solely at her. 'Let me see what you have.'

She opened her hand. In it he saw two brown tablets and, beside them, a chunk of a black substance. He picked this up first, sniffed it. He nodded. He placed it back in her hand, picked up the tablets. These he tasted with the tip of his tongue. Satisfied, he told her to grind them up.

This combination of opium and synthetic DMT was not new to him. He had acquired a taste for it from a fellow student years ago. The pressure at the *ryu* had been enormous. *Sake*, of course, was often used as a source of relaxation. But it was not for him; it was not enough.

He watched glassy-eyed as the girl, on her knees, ground the mixture in a stone mortar she had produced from within the armoire.

When she had finished and had filled a pipe for him, he told her to run the water for his bath.

'I can do that,' Sparrow said.

'Stay where you are,' the Japanese barked. His gaze shifted to the girl. 'Do as you are told.'

She bowed her head, half ran across the room. By the time he had the pipe lit, he heard the muted sound of running water.

The Japanese took three long drags at the pipe before he took it out of his mouth. 'Come here, Sparrow. Now inhale. No, deeply. That's right.' He returned the pipe to his mouth, finished smoking. He could hear nothing but the distant water, tumbling. It sounded like a waterfall.

Every time he breathed in now, the air felt chill; on the exhalations, it seemed to burn the lining of his nostrils. He felt his heart pumping, the blood squirting through his veins and arteries. He felt hot.

Gravity pulled upon him as if he were under water. He felt its drag on his arms and legs, on his head and on his penis. His balls seemed to have grown within their sac.

'Come,' he commanded the boy and together they went into the bathroom. The tub was three-quarters full. The girl was on her knees testing the temperature.

'Undress the boy,' he told her. Every time he spoke, he could feel the rumbling vibrations in his chest. The words, gaining substance, seemed to roll around within the cavity, like ripples set in motion, eddying outwards. Some words were as small as insects, as bright and shining. Others were as large and ungainly as giraffes.

The Japanese watched avidly as the girl went to where Sparrow stood on the threshold. 'Do it on your knees,' he told her. He was gratified to see how well she took instructions. He must remember to compliment the old woman.

The boy stood naked, his thin body just beginning to form the musculature of adolescence. The Japanese stared, his pupils dilated. In and out. His breathing like the bellows in a busy forge. The girl sat with her legs folded beneath her. Her head was bowed. Her long black hair hung, shining, down her back.

He bade her undress him next, his shirt first so that she could perform the rest on her knees in front of him. He did not watch her; he watched the boy.

He was hard by the time she had finished and the boy's penis was no longer soft. Without looking at her, he grabbed the girl by the back of her head, pushed her face against his scrotal sac. Her mouth opened. The boy was hard and quivering.

He pushed the girl away from him, stepped into the hot tub. 'Now,' he said to her, 'wash me.'

When this had been completed, he stepped out and instructed her to scrub the bathtub. Only when it was washed and rinsed did he step back in. She ran the water for him again.

Lying back, soaking contentedly, he stared up at the gleaming white ceiling just as if he were alone. He thought about the call and what it meant. He smiled. He had meant to kill Tomkin within three days anyway. He had not been about to reveal that to his employers. The less they knew the better. Once you gave anyone information of any kind, you risked giving them an advantage. That was something the Japanese had never done. He was successful because it was he who held the advantage always. This he had been taught well.

He had to laugh. His body moved, sending wavelets bouncing off the procelain of the tub. By not revealing his plans, he had just had his fee doubled. It had been high enough to begin with and rightly so. Others had tried to kill Raphael Tomkin; none had succeeded. The Japanese had no doubts about his success; none at all. It was, rather, the method that occupied his mind so fully. Yes, his first assessment had been the correct one. Tomkin was most vulnerable in his new office. It was high up, it was isolated, it was surrounded by a warren of tunnels and half-completed passageways into which he could disappear in an instant.

There were, of course, the long-range methods: the rifle, the bomb, and so forth. These were not in the Japanese's repertoire of murder. They were the coward's way; totally Western form of assassination. He did all his work first hand, with his own weapons. There was no honour in killing otherwise. Thus he had been taught. The ninja, too, had their code of honour. It was far from the laws of weak-minded *bushido*, he thought contemptuously, but it governed him none the less. A buy was simply not worth doing if one could not get within arm's length of the objective. And that was all he needed.

So it would happen on the top floor of the office building, in the plush office – that would be superbly fitting. Not tonight and perhaps not the next; there were too many matters to tie up, too many things yet to be settled. The night after next, then. No need to rush it. He went over every phase of the buy again, feeling a tingling in his groin beginning. The only matter that now concerned him – because it was out of his control at the moment – was whether he had been too obvious. Perhaps he had miscalculated in killing Ito. Then he thought: No, it's what I had planned to do from the start. It's what he needs.

The tip of his erect penis breached the water. He stared at it, fascinated.

'Time,' he said and the girl opened the drain. He stood up. The hot water rolled down his flesh. His torso and limbs were hairless.

He stepped out of the tub, brushed aside the thick towel the girl had opened for him. 'No,' he said. 'Lick the water off me.' He watched the boy, who had not moved all this time, as the girl bent to her task.

Yes, he thought. There is plenty of time. Enough for me to return here tomorrow night. Release was instrumental to his functioning properly. Between his spread legs, the girl continued to lick at him.

In the bedroom, he smoked another pipeful, repeating his offer to Sparrow. The girl was the only one who was still dressed. She came and stood before him when he commanded, her eyes at her feet. With one blurred gesture he ripped the silk rob from her. She had small firm breasts, the nipples long and hard. Narrow waist and hips, thick pubic triangle. Her skin was raised in goosebumps. Still she would not look at him; he liked that.

He reached his left hand up. It was so big that his fingers were able to encircle her slender neck completely. Her skin was so soft there. With his other hand he touched her briefly where her flesh was raised, interested in the oddity.

Holding her thus, he drew his right hand away, slapped her breasts so that they shook. She grimaced but made no sound. The Japanese turned his head slightly so that he could see the boy's reaction; he had not moved. The Japanese swung at the girl's breasts again, this time from the opposite side. She gasped and immediately bit her lower lip. Sweat started out along her hairline; her flesh was damp beneath his fingers.

When he hit her a third time, it was with considerably more force. She gave a short cry and her legs collapsed from under her.

The Japanese took her under the arms, threw her on the bed. There was a piece of silk tied to each of the bedposts. He took these and, one by one, tied them around her wrists and ankles until she was spreadeagled, unable to move. Her chest was heaving and it glistened with sweat. She moaned, half unconscious.

The Japanese crossed the room, took the ceramic bottle of *sake* back to the bed and fed it to her. She coughed twice. Her eyes flew open and she swallowed convulsively. He kept the lip of the bottle to her lips until all the liquor was gone. Then he got onto the bed, straddling her. He faced her crotch and spread legs; her breasts were beneath him.

'Come here,' he said to Sparrow. The boy moved to the side of the bed, climbed up into the position the Japanese indicated. He crouched between the girl's legs. His eyes went to her crotch. He fell over, dazed. The right side of his face was numb. Moments later, it began to sting. It was very red.

'Don't do that,' the Japanese said. 'Look only in the direction of *this*.' He pointed to his rampant penis.

Now the Japanese settled over the girl's face. He felt the heat of her breath, the soft tickle as her lips opened. Her tongue began to probe his anus.

'Now,' he commanded the boy. Sparrow leaned forward, opened his mouth.

Soon the Japanese closed his eyes. He began to talk in expletives. Neither Sparrow nor the girl understood his words; they were in Japanese. They could not, however, mistake his tone.

As his excitement mounted, so did the obscenities he uttered. He reached down without knowing it, grabbed painful handfuls of the girl's inner thighs, leaving marks and red welts, and, as he exploded into Sparrow's mouth, he hit her once between her thighs so hard that she fainted with the pain.

Seeing the look in the Japanese's eyes, Sparrow backed away off the bed. It was his turn now.

Doc Deerforth was thinking about the war. He sat in his old wooden chair behind the desk in his office, a cup of steaming coffee half on the pale blue blotter in front of him. His head was turned slightly so that he could gaze out through the screen window, past the ancient oak, out along Main Street. This time of the morning there was little evidence of activity. It was not yet seven o'clock.

Without looking, Doc Deerforth reached for his cup of coffee, took a long sip. He scalded his tongue but he took no notice.

It was quite like malaria, he thought now. Once caught it could never be cured entirely but would return over and over in diminished attacks like an unpleasant reminder of the past. It might even be seasonal, he suspected, coming on most strongly during the hot days of July and August, the dog days when even out here in West Bay Bridge the sun was so withering, the atmosphere so sticky that the leaves on the trees seemed to wilt.

He never seemed to think of the war during the winter.

He picked up the phone, dialled Ray Florum's number at the police station. He let it ring six times before cradling the phone. He had dialled Florum's private line. No one would pick it up but Ray himself.

Where the hell was he? Doc Deerforth thought irritably. Then he glanced at his watch, saw how early it was. Ray didn't come in until around eight. Still, Doc Deerforth wanted to know if there had been any progress towards capturing the ninja. He felt an irrational anger which, he knew, stemmed from fear.

The front-door bell rang and he jumped. For a moment he considered ignoring it, but when it came again, he got up and went through the house.

'Nicholas,' he said, blinking into the light. 'Come in.' He closed the door. 'What brings you here so early? Are you ill?'

'I didn't wake you up, did I?'

Doc Deerforth laughed. 'Hell, no, son. Just sitting here dreaming.' He peered closely at Nicholas. 'You don't look at all well. I think you'd better come along with me.'

'I haven't slept, that's all,' Nicholas said, allowing himself to be led into the house. But instead of taking him into his office, Doc Deerforth led him to the kitchen.

'A good breakfast will do you a world of good,' he said. He opened the refrigerator, took out a carton of orange juice, handed it over. 'Here, help yourself.' He looked up. 'Bacon and eggs all right with you?'

'Hey, you don't have to –'

Doc Deerforth waved away his words. 'Course I don't have to. I *want* to.' He smiled, carrying eggs to the stove. 'Besides, it's been a while since I had a guest for breakfast. Do me good. I've been sitting around too much lately.' He began to prepare the food. He got more coffee going, then put up the bacon. The sizzling of the meat gave him a peculiarly warm feeling. He wondered about that until he recalled he used to cook breakfast for the girls. That seemed so long ago. 'I s'pose you want to know what Florum's been up to,' he said. Nicholas sat down at the table, poured himself some juice. He looked up expectantly. 'Nothing,' Doc Deerforth continued. 'There's not a damn thing for him to go on.'

'I'm not surprised,' Nicholas said. He told the other about what had taken place in the city.

'Friends of yours, huh?' Doc Deerforth said when he had finished. 'That's a bit of bad luck. I'm sorry.' He turned the bacon. 'You think he's really after Raphael Tomkin?'

Nicholas nodded.

'Then why these other killings? None of the victims seem

to have any connection with Tomkin.'

'They don't. At least, not as far as I can tell.'

'Then what's he up to? He could have been in and out half a dozen times by now.'

'I've thought about that.' Nicholas glanced down at his juice as if he might find answers there. 'For one thing, it's not so easy to get to Tomkin. That kind of penetration takes time.'

'All the more reason for him to keep a low profile. They don't like the limelight.' He lifted out the bacon, started on the eggs.

'Normally that's true,' Nicholas agreed. 'But this man's different. He's shrewder than most. Look, he's going up against a man who's been a target three or four times before. There are good reasons why Tomkin is still alive. The ninja figures a simple penetration won't do it. Something a bit more complex is called for. You know how they are. He'll have to go in himself. There'll be no remote-control gadgets; he won't use the long gun.'

'I know.' The kitchen was filled with the smell of the food. Doc Deerforth got out the bread, gave it to Nicholas to toast.

'All right. The idea is to confuse the enemy. It's an ancient form of strategy in kendo and on the battle-field. Use different forms of attacks; attack from different sides. While your enemy is wondering what you're up to, you attack decisively and he's defeated.'

Doc Deerforth eyed Nicholas as he brought the plates over to the table. 'And you think this is what the ninja is doing?'

'It seems logical, yes.'

Doc Deerforth began to eat, frowning in concentration. 'You've thought of other possibilities, naturally,' he said after a while.

Nicholas looked up. 'What other possibilities?'

'I don't know. But they're devious bastards. I could never pretend to know what was in their minds.'

Nicholas looked away for a moment. 'I knew several in Japan.'

Doc Deerforth's eyes blazed briefly. 'Did you?'

'That was years ago.'

'Time doesn't mean anything to them.' Nicholas knew he was talking about his own experience. He put down his fork, said nothing. 'They're not human,' Doc Deerforth said after a time. It was so quiet beween the words that Nicholas could hear the ticking of the clock on the wall. 'At least, there's something quite inhuman about them – as if they were vampires or something. Something supernatural.' His eyes had turned inwards as he strung out the banner of his memory.

'Our war,' he continued, 'was quite different from any other, from what it was elsewhere. Where we were, it was never a matter of companies taking a ridge and holding it in the face of an enemy counter-offensive. There were no front lines, separate territories, retreats or attacks. There was only a kind of holding on. A desperate stubbornness against this terrible fluidity which brought you to the front in the morning and behind the enemy at sunset without having moved at all during the day.

'We were never quite sure just where the enemy was. Specific orders were sporadic at best and, when they came, it seemed clear to us that the generals had no idea of the actual situation. We lived in a kind of loosely controlled state of anarchy. It was our only protection from the panic which continually besieged us.

'The time I'm telling you about was late in the war. Almost all of us had been in the Pacific Theatre from the beginning. Many of us were in no condition to fight. Malaria, amoebic dysentery, those and other diseases I had never encountered before were what we lived with. But, after a while, we began to fear even the cholera less than the nights.

'The nights brought the infiltrations, silent and lethal. We seemed incapable of stemming them. We doubled the perimeter guard, began patrols of the compound itself. Nothing helped. The commander, in desperation, mounted a series of night patrols. They shot at shadows or the calls of night birds. They hit nothing and were, in turn, silently killed.

'These incidents built themselves eerily. Then some idiot mentioned *Dracula*. He had a dog-eared copy of the Bram Stoker novel and it quickly made the rounds. The fear magnified itself. What else could you expect under such circumstanees? Man is notorious for inventing creatures to explain away the otherwise inexplicable. It was something out of a Gothic horror novel. Even now, with so much time in between, it doesn't seem like a joke. We were used to fighting soldiers of flesh and blood, not shadows which melted away in the light. If we could have caught just one, even – caught a glimpse – we'd have had some idea of what we were up against.

'Fear has an uncanny way of escalating. We were none of us cowards. We had all done our share of killing. Even I – even I had been called upon several times ... We were in danger of being overrun. But now we were experiencing something else – something quite beyond our ken. It sounds foolish, I know, but believe me, Nicholas, when I tell you what happened ...

'We were struggling across Leyte. The enormous naval battle of Leyte Gulf was behind us. On the sea the Japanese were destroyed, but on land it was another matter entirely. We did not yet own this small island and Luzon, the main island, was still in Japanese hands. They were undermanned and frightfully undersupplied. We thought we had them beaten at Leyte Gulf; that it was the end.

'It wasn't.

'A new Japanese commander had arrived from Tokyo just before the battle began. Vice-Admiral Ōnishi of the First Naval Air Fleet in Manila. Two days after he arrived, he travelled to Mabalacat, a small town fifty miles to the north-west. It was the site of the Two Hundred and First Air Group. There he chaired a meeting that was, although none of us knew it then, one of the war's most fateful conferences.

'Not long after, we heard the first reports. Many of us, knowing the wildness of rumour, did not believe it. But then, no more than a week later, we saw it for ourselves. At first we thought the Zeros were after us but they screamed by overhead as if we had not existed. Then we saw our ships out to sea, an aircraft carrier and two destroyers. They did not strafe our ships, these Zeros, nor did they dive-bomb them. They merely careened into them. We were certain that the first one had been hit and crashed. But as they one after another followed the same suicidal course, we began to understand. Yet we understood not at all. How could rational men do this? It seemed inconceivable. We thought perhaps they had been brainwashed; the Japanese were notorious for their methods. Anyway, that was the prevailing opinion.

'Yet something about this theory stuck in my mind. I could not believe it. Psychological reorientation takes time, I knew that. Certainly it could not have been accomplished overnight. It took time and that was the one thing the Japanese did not have. No, I was convinced it had to be something else. But what?

'It was the season of rain; there seemed no dry ground on the whole of Leyte. We made progress but not without casualties, of course. One night the unit was forced to move on. There were a number of wounded who needed taking care of. I volunteered to stay behind for a short time so that I could bandage them properly. There was a relief column due in the morning. But the situation was far too volatile and my C.O. insisted I move out with the rest of the unit.

'We made camp just before dawn. Many of us were too tired to fall asleep. We sat around and talked about Dracula. Three men had been killed the night before; the vampire theories were at their height.

'At last I left them, pitched my tent and crawled inside. For a time I could hear their voices as they continued to talk, then the sounds stopped. I wasn't sure whether I had fallen asleep or they had just broken up for the night.

'I was in that odd state between sleeping and wakefulness. I thought I dreamed someone was there, watching me. I tried to wake myself but couldn't. My head felt like it was too heavy to lift up. I strained but nothing happened. It was as if my consciousness had somehow been severed from the nerve impulses which mechanized the muscles. I wanted to look behind me, you know, over my head, certain that was where the danger was coming from. I could make no move.

'Above me a face hovered in the air, disembodied. I don't know when my eyes had actually opened or whether they had ever really been closed. My chest felt heavy and I seemed to have trouble breathing. I felt cold. Not as if the night was chill but from inside. I shivered.

'It was a Japanese face, coal-black as if it had been coated with charcoal or lampblack. It was dull so that no light would reflect off it. His eyes seemed very large. They had an odd light to them as if, while they stared right at me, they were focused on another universe. It was eerie. I had seen something like it once in a hospital when I was in my last year of medical school. We went into the psycho wing and I saw several patients. One was a young man, not far past twenty. His hair was cropped close. He had high cheek-bones and a long thin nose. He could have been a scholar. He was in a strait jacket. I watched his eyes for a long time, while beside me the resident droned his spiel like a carnival barker. This man, this ... creature was far beyond the supposedly modern and humane treatment the resident was describing in such loving detail. This man had reverted. He was certainly no longer human but had returned to the animal state of his ancestors. There was no hint of what we might term "intelligence" in his eyes; at least not as modern man defines intelligence. But I saw cunning there, of a kind and in a strength which terrified me. For a moment I fantasized what it would be like having this man loose in the world. Richard Speck? Gary Gilmore? Jack the Ripper? It was beyond imagining. For this was a man who was clearly beyond morality.

'Now you know some of what I saw in the eyes hovering above me that night on Leyte. But not all. To call this "madness" would be to seriously underestimate it, for it was far more. Ours is a world of order, ruled by laws. From science to morality there are parameters within which we all live. This man did not. He lived outside time as if residing within him, lending him all its ferocious energy, was the essence of chaos. I don't know how to describe it better, but seeing him thus in the flesh only underscored the fact rather than the fiction of his supernatural origins. Perhaps, after all, our vampire stories had not been so far off the mark. I know, I know, this all sounds rather fanciful - pulled out to give a good Gothic kick to this story. I assure you that nothing could be further from the truth.

'While I thought of all this, I felt his movement. He produced a matt black length of cloth and, folding it upon itself, wrapped it painfully tight across my mouth. He was quite close to me now and I saw that he was dressed all in black.

'He hauled me out of the tent and, stooping, slung me over his shoulder.

'He ran.

'He ran without sound. No shadow trailed behind us; we were never in the light. He took a route out of the encampment that was neither direct nor circuitous. It was merely undetectable, as if he were following a path no one else suspected of being there, a path made just for him.

'I didn't struggle. I found myself wondering why I hadn't been killed as the other victims of these silent infiltrations had been. I was amazed. Even upside down I could see well enough to know that he was a magician. No one I knew could possibly have got in and out of our encampment totally undetected as this man had. He moved without seeming motion. That must sound like a contradiction but it's not. He ran with such fluidity that there was no up-and-down motion, merely the sensation of forward movement.

'We were in the jungle now, travelling extremely quickly. In fact, even though the way was now more choked with foliage and underbrush, our speed actually increased. His strength and endurance were exceptional. We were totally alone in the world, or so it seemed to me. It was that time of the night when the nocturnal creatures have crawled back into their holes to sleep and the diurnal animals have not yet awakened. The jungle was quite still, just a sleepy bird calling here and there, the sounds quite isolated and seeming part of another world.

'We travelled thus for perhaps thirty minutes. Then the man stopped abruptly and, spinning me off his shoulder, widened the cloth around my mouth so that I was now blindfold also. He led me, stumbling, through the jungle. His fingers were at the back of my jacket so that, each time I fell, he suspended me as if I was hanging from a coat-hook. It was a terribly dehumanizing thing to do and I tried to shut my mind to it.

'After a time I began to hear voices. I did not speak Japanese but I understood enough to get by; it was something

I did not want him to know. At length the blindfold was removed. We were in the midst of a Japanese camp. It wasn't anything like what I had pictured. In fact, I was aghast; I thought for an instant that he had taken me to a hospital; it hardly seemed like a military camp at all. For one thing, most of the soldiers were either lying down or sitting. I saw no troops as such; no guards.

'We were near the water, though on which side of the island I could not tell. I saw the water clearly through a gap in the vegetation. I watched for a time, totally unmolested, while the man who had brought me spoke with several of his fellows who were identically dressed. These seemed to be the only operational men in the camp. At first I tried to pay attention to what they were talking about, but they were either speaking too fast or in some dialect I had never heard because I couldn't understand them.

'Dawn had broken and there was a white line just above the horizon. I knew I must be looking east. I saw a smudge coming into view and then another Simultaneously, I heard a heavy drone from the north-west, in the direction of Luzon. It was the Two Hundred and First. I looked up. The Zeros were black and bloated against the pale sky. The night's clouds had melted away.

'The Zeros passed low over us, headed out to sea, towards the dark smudges containing the horizon, coming closer.

' "You know they go to attack your ships."

'I started. A thin Japanese stood beside me. He was on crutches. His left trouser-leg was pinned back at the knee but he'd surely die of malnutrition before his stump would begin to bother him.

' "You speak English very well," I said.

' "Yes." He was still staring out at the moving targets as they closed with one another. "They will not come back. None of them. Ōnishi has seen to that." I understand that he meant the new Vice-Admiral. He shook his head sadly. "They say, you know, that he helped Yamamoto plan the Pearl Harbor attack." He clucked his tongue against the roof of his mouth. "It's hard to believe. It seems so long ago." His head turned. "Do you speak Japanese? No? Pity." He turned back. The

Zeros were nearing our ships. You could see the batteries begin to fire. Black clouds with orange bits in their centres exploded, eerily silent until, moments later, the reports found us, shook the air. "No, they won't come back, those boys. They're on a one-way mission."

'Abruptly, his words penetrated the fog which had surrounded me since I had come into the camp. "Do you mean to tell me," I exclaimed, "that they're on suicide missions? The plane and the pilot ...?"

' "One big manoeuvrable bomb, yes." The Japanese stood quite still. Tears seemed to be standing in the corners of his eyes but there was no change in his voice. "Vice-Admiral Ōnishi's idea. It's a desperation move. He had a time convincing the others but he managed it." He said something in Japanese which I took to be a curse. "Not enough of us have died for this 'noble cause'. The Emperor still sends his sons into a war which we have already lost." Far away, on the white and black horizon, the Zeros were leaving the sky.

'There came a sharp call from behind me. I did not need to understand the language to know that my captor wanted me. I walked away from the crippled soldier, saying, "You ought to get something to eat."

'He laughed shortly. "If I could, do you think I'd be here now?"

' "What about a hospital?"

' "Won't take you in unless you bring your own food," he said. His eyes were clear. I could see his ribs underneath his uniform blouse. I thought: What am I doing? He is the enemy. "We're all dying of malnutrition. We can't get into the hospital and our unit's booted us out because we can't fight any more. It's not a soldier's end. There's no honour in any of this." He stared at me and, for a moment, there seemed to be no difference between us.

'Then my captor had hold of me and, barking harshly, he pushed me towards another part of the camp. Here, too, soldiers littered the ground. It seemed pathetic.

'He carried with him a small black satchel which I hadn't noticed before. It was over this that they seemed to be arguing. There were perhaps four of them. They might have been brothers. Now I regretted not asking my unexpected friend who these men were. It was clear that they weren't regular army. To one side, I saw what was obviously a cooking fire. There was a black iron pot. By its side was a small pile of what the Japanese called *kamote*, the diminutive Philippine potatoes that taste rather like a conventional sweet potato. There were also some withered tubers. These were obviously their rations: all the food they possessed.

'The man who had brought me produced a series of cans he had obviously stolen from our camp. How he had spirited this food away I could not imagine, but there it was.

'They began to argue all over again – I suppose about who would get how much. My captor hustled me away, shoved me down towards a group of supine men. It was clear that he wanted me to work on them. Now I understood why I had been spared. He knew very well what I was. I began to wonder what else he knew about me.

'I turned to the soldiers. In truth there wasn't much I could do for them. I was without my instruments and my medicines. But they would not have been much help. My friend had been quite correct in his analysis of the situation. The Japanese were dying of malnutrition.

'At length I got up, went over to the man who had brought me.

' "I'm sorry," I said, "but there's nothing I can do."

'He hit me without warning. I didn't even see where the blow came from. One moment I was standing and talking to him, the next I was on my ass in the mud.

' "They need food," I said inanely.

'He reached down and hauled me up. There seemed to be no expression in his eyes. He hit me again, this time harder, with the edge of his hand. It felt like I had been struck by a cement mixer. I went down and stayed down.

'It was dark when I awoke. I had a splitting headache and my right shoulder didn't seem to work. It was odd. I could wiggle my fingers, even make a loose fist, but I couldn't raise my arm even an inch.

'I was in a tent, lying on something hard. Now I could tell

it wasn't the ground. I had my jacket and fatigue shirt on but no pants. I was naked from the waist down. I tried to move but couldn't. My entire body seemed to pulse with pain. There were flashes behind my eyes and I wondered what he had done to my nerves.

'Shortly after, he came in. I didn't hear him but felt some stirring of the humid air. His face loomed over me. He had removed the lampblack from his face but not the black clothing. This, apparently was his uniform.

' "What is your troop strength?" he asked.

'I understood. Having proved useless in my healing capacity, I was now a fully-fledged prisoner of war. I knew what that meant.

'I told him my name.

' "How much firepower have you?"

'I told him my name.

' "With which units will you rendezvous?"

'I told him my name.

' "What is the American time-table for link-up?"

'This time I varied it. I gave him my rank and serial number.

' "When do the Americans plan to launch their invasion of Luzon?"

' "Luzon has already been invaded," I said. "By the Japanese."

'Then he began to work on me. He used nothing but the ends of four fingers: his two thumbs and forefingers. No blades, no heat, no drugs, no wire, no water. None of the traditional interrogator's tools. He had no need for anything so crude.

'He worked on me for the whole of the night – more than ten hours. Oh, not constantly, of course; I never could have taken that. And at the end of that time there was not a mark on my body.

'He was, truly, a magician. He worked on the nerves. Not just the major nerve centres as might be expected, but the nerve chains themselves. Just his fingers squeezing.

'Everything else ceased to exist. He saw to that. It became, after a while, a kind of sensory deprivation situation: I felt nothing but pain. Even the two or three times I urinated, I couldn't feel it, only smelled it for a time. Then that, too, was obliterated.

'He used pain the way a clever woman can use pleasure. You know the way a woman leads you up the pleasure curve, slowly, lovingly, gently, until you're throbbing for release. She'll bring you to the brink, hold you there for exquisite moments, then stop until the excitement subsides and she starts all over again. Finally, when you come, the sensation is better than it's ever been before. This man used the same principle. You know terrible pain can become its own anaesthetic – just like when you fuck too much, you go numb for a while. So, too, with pain. Even your nerves have a limit, and after a while they just shut down and you feel nothing. That can be your only advantage in intensive interrogation.

'By his very technique, this man avoided that. Again and again, he would bring me slowly up the pain curve, keep me hovering on the brink for long moments – but he never let me topple over into the numbness of the other side. He knew precisely how long I could take it and brought me down each time.

'All the while the questions were repeated over and over. Not shouted, the tone calm and even friendly, he spoke in an intimate voice as if we were close friends meeting in a bar, talking about old times.

'It was odd, this combination. We became, after a while, as intimate as lovers. I wanted to trust him, to tell him all my secrets, to break down the last barriers between us. The pain, too, changed over time. It became – how shall I put it? – less painful? Yes, that's it. Less painful. I still can't understand how it was done. Of course, I knew even then that he was working on my mind as well as on my body. But somehow that didn't help any. I seemed powerless to stop what was happening. I felt things slipping away from me, as if I were losing my balance on slippery ice. Then even the ice was gone and I felt myself settling down into a kind of muddy slime, sinking lower and lower. There seemed to be no bottom.

'All this time the pain was ebbing and, as it did, I felt myself wanting to trust him more. He was my friend and I became guilty at holding out my secrets. How selfish I was! How unworthy of his friendship.

'It was not numbness which overtook me now – I told you he would not allow that. It was another sensation. Pleasure. It crept up on me while I was concentrating on not answering his repeated questions. This was taking more and more energy and once or twice I had to bite my tongue in order to stop myself from telling him everything he wanted to know.

'I felt, at that moment, my self slipping away from me, revealing, underneath, another person I knew not at all. It seemed to me, then, that this man knew more about me than I did and this terrified me.

'Now I found myself wanting to tell him more than ever. Once I did, I was convinced he would hold and comfort me. The pleasure grew. I began to rejoice in the pain, to want it, for it was my link with him and I began to feel that I would be lost without it, that once it ceased I would have nothing and, therefore, be reduced to nothing. Time ceased to have any meaning. There was no past, no future, just an endless now with its bright connection. My mouth was hot with my own blood as I fought to hold back telling him everything.

'Abruptly, it was gone. The pleasure-pain. Everything. I was lost. Alone in the tent, I began to cry, great dry racking sobs – my body had been so depleted of moisture during the night that even tears would not come. I was terrified of being alone, like a child cruelly left by its mother. I had been reduced to a kind of psychological infancy in which I now depended on my inquisitor as a baby does on its mother. I had been left alone so that it would be hammered home. I knew then that the moment he returned and started on me again, I would talk and talk and talk. Nothing would stop me.

'I became abruptly aware of a sound in the tent. It came from behind my head. I thought he had returned and I wept for joy. There came some scraping sounds. I tried to twist my head but I could see nothing except the heavily fluttering tent top.

' "Get up!" It was a harsh whisper in my ear.

' "What?" It sounded moronic. A combination of the de-hydration and my swollen tongue made me sound like a cross between a heavy drunk and a lobotomy case.

'"Get up! Get up! Get up!" the voice hissed.

'I felt hands under my back, forcing me to sit up. It seemed a novel experience. For a moment I stared stupidly down at my body, perhaps expecting to find the flesh shredded into ribbons or blackened bamboo shoots under my nails. There was no mark on me. I shuddered as I forced myself to remember the pain.

'"This way!" the voice said, urgently. "Come on! Move yourself! There's no time to sit around!"

'Gingerly, I swung off the wooden trestle table and turned. It was my friend, the crippled Japanese. His face was drawn with worry. His extended arm held open a flap of the tent on the far side. Through it I could see the bright green of the jungle. The daylight hurt my eyes and for a moment I felt a sense of intense vertigo.

'I stumbled across the room and he had to reach out to stop me from falling over. "I'll never make it," I said.

'"Yes," he whispered, "you will. They won't follow you in the daytime." He gave me some water then looked away from me as I gulped it greedily down. "We've all had enough of this," he said softly. "It's so useless, so pitiable." He moved on his crutches. "Come on. There's no time to lose. We can't let them find you like this, can we?"

'I went to the open tent flap. My chest seemed to be pounding so hard that I thought I might drop dead of a heart attack before I had taken ten paces.

'"I don't know how to thank you," I said as I passed him.

'"Don't," he said. "We're from totally different worlds. We could never understand each other."

'"Oh no?" I stuck out my hand. He touched it for a moment, then released it quickly as if he was embarrassed again. "One last thing," I said. "Who are they?" He knew who I meant.

'"You don't want to know." He began to turn away. The tent flap was coming down like the curtain between our two worlds.

'"Yes I do. Very much."

'His back was already to me. "Ninja" I heard his voice

float back to me as if from a great distance.

'I wished him luck,' Doc Deerforth concluded, 'but I don't think he heard. I turned and ran into the jungle, away from the camp, away from the ninja.'

He sat staring down into the remains of his eggs as if they were a doorway into the past. The skin of his high forehead, where the white hair had receded over the years, was shiny with sweat. For the first time in which seemed like hours, Nicholas heard the stertorous ticking of the clock on the wall.

After a while, Doc Deerforth lifted his head. His eyes seemed weary as they looked into Nicholas's. 'I've never told anyone what happened,' he said softly. 'Not the men in my unit; not my C.O.; not even my wife. I told you, Nicholas, because I was certain you'd understand.' His gaze was steady now, the eyes seeming to bore holes right through Nicholas's skull, X-raying his brain.

'You know, then.'

Doc Deerforth didn't need to nod; his eyes told Nicholas what he wanted to know.

'What are you going to do?'

'Do?' Doc Deerforth seemed genuinely surprised. 'Why, nothing. What *should* I do?'

'I know how you feel,' Nicholas said, 'about them.'

'About that one,' Doc Deerforth corrected him.

'They're like that, most of them.'

'Are they?'

'It's the way they're trained. Their training is even more rigorous than a samurai's because its tradition is bound in such secrecy.'

'Tradition. Odd, isn't it, that such stringent traditionalists should be the perpetrators of such violent anarchy.'

'I never thought of it that way but, yes, you're quite right.'

'I want you to get this one, Nicholas.' Doc Deerforth pushed his cold plate away from him. 'I know you're the only one who can. The police don't know –'

'No, they don't.'

'– anything at all about this. It's very fortunate that you've become involved. Have you thought about that?'

*

The day was bright, not a cloud in the sky. The dazzle of the car's chrome was so intense that he put on his sun-glasses.

Nicholas left the town behind as he drove back out to Dune Road. He slid into the driveway at the side of his house, picked up the *Times* lying outside his door. He glanced uninterestedly at the headlines, went down the steps onto the beach.

He came up on Justine's house from the right, so he could not tell if her car was there. Both the screen door and the outer door were closed but the *Times* had been taken in. He went up the sandy steps.

'She's not in.'

Nicholas turned. Croaker was just coming round from the left side of the house. He was dressed in a rumpled brown suit. His tie was pulled half off. He looked as if he hadn't slept for two or three nights.

'Car's gone.'

'What are you doing here, Croaker?'

'Let's take a walk.'

He led Nicholas down to the beach.

'You're not exactly dressed for it,' Nicholas observed.

'That's all right. I like sand in my shoes. Reminds me of when I was a kid. We used to stay in the city during the summer. Never had any money to go anywhere. We used the hydrants. Turned them on and cooled off.' The water crashed and creamed past them on the right. Far down the beach, blankets were being set up. A portable radio blatted out disco, all booming bass and tattoo percussion. 'There were seven of us. I don't know how my old man made ends meet. But you know, once a month during the summer, as regular as clock-work, he'd call me over just before he went to work. "Lewis," he'd say, "c'mere. I have something for you." He'd give me enough money for a car fare out to Coney Island and an ice-cream. He knew I loved the beach. "Promise me one thing," he'd say every time. "Take a towel. I don't want your mother to worry. Okay"?'

Someone went running out into the surf, laughing. One could see heads bobbing in the water past the surf line. A woman in a one-piece swimsuit walked towards them, a bright beach towel slung nonchalantly over one shoulder. Nicholas thought of Justine, wondered where she'd gone.

'Yeah, we're old friends, the sand and I.'

The woman was close enough for them to see how beautiful she was. Her long hair had been streaked by the sun. She ran past them to meet her lover.

Croaker squinted up at the sun for a moment. 'I threw Alison out of the house last night.'

Nicholas looked at him silently.

Croaker gave him a quick smile that didn't quite reach his eyes. 'Well, it wasn't really like that. I think she wanted to go, too. Getting restless. Yeah. We both were.' He stuffed his big hands in his trouser pockets. 'It was bloodless. Relatively. She'll get over it. These things' – his shoulders lifted and fell – 'you know, they pass and –'

They both stopped at once as if on cue. The sea rolled up near them. Over the slight hump of sand lay a dark straggle of sea grape.

Croaker looked down at his shoes, half sunk in the sand. When he looked up, he said, 'Nick, Vincent's dead. They found him last night.' He didn't say where. 'His neck had been broken.'

Nicholas took a deep breath and sat down in the sand. He wrapped his arms round his legs, stared out to sea.

'Nick ...'

He felt numb, as if his brain had been anaesthetized. He recalled Doc Deerforth talking about pain. This seemed more than enough. This was the day of Terry's and Ei's funeral.

'Jesus,' he said. 'Jesus.'

Croaker crouched down next to him. 'Nick,' he said gently, 'there was no other way to tell you. There was the phone but I couldn't do that.'

Nicholas nodded. Through the numbness, he understood. Croaker had recognized the debt he owed him. He appreciated the fact that the Lieutenant had come all the way out here when he only had to have someone pick up a phone and dial. He remembered that the two had had dinner last night and wondered if this was, in part, Vincent's legacy. If so, it was a fitting one.

'Nick,' Croaker said. He hesitated.

Nicholas's gaze swung round.

'What's going on? You have to tell me.'

'I don't know. What do you mean? I – look, Tomkin's involved. Up to his armpits. He received a ninja warning about a week ago. It fits in. I've seen it. It's authentic. He has a lot of business deals with a number of high-powered Japanese firms. No one's very buddy-buddy in business, least of all them. He crossed them in some way. Anyhow, it's a mortal offence he's committed. There's no doubt they've sent one over to kill him.'

'It's been tried before. Tomkin's a grown-up bastard now. He doesn't need your help.'

Nicholas shook his head. 'That's where you're wrong. Without me, he's a dead man.'

'But it makes no sense, don't you see? The two deaths out here, the three in the city. None have any link with Tomkin.'

'They must have,' Nicholas said, stubbornly. 'Look, he's even made an attempt to frighten Justine.' He told Croaker about the furred thing thrown through the kitchen window.

Croaker looked at him for a moment. Beyond, he could hear the surf hissing as it sucked at the beach front. The sounds of laughter were bright and brittle as if they were made to be broken.

'What if,' Croaker said slowly, 'that message wasn't meant for Justine.'

Nicholas stared at Croaker.

'What do you mean?'

'I think it's time we faced the facts. I think that warning was meant for you.'

Nicholas gave a short, sharp laugh. 'For me? Oh, don't be idiotic. There's no reason –'

'There must be,' Croaker said earnestly. 'Look at the pattern. The two deaths out here. Terry and Eileen. Now Vincent in the city. You're the central point to all the deaths.'

'I didn't know the second man out here.'

'No, but the murder happened close to you.'

'Lew, they happened close to a lot of people.'

'But only to one who's had three friends murdered subsequently.'

It was logical of course, but, Nicholas knew, logic was often not the answer.

He shook his head. 'I don't think I can buy it. As I said, there's no reason. 'It's a smoke-screen.'

'A hell of a smoke-screen!' Croaker snorted.

'It wouldn't matter to him, don't you see? He must know that I'm involved through Justine. *I'm* the danger to him, not you, or Tomkin's muscle. He knows that. No, he's after Tomkin, plain and simple. He's just trying to muddy the water.'

Croaker held up a hand. 'Okay, okay. It was just a theory. But I gotta tell you, I hope you're right because I cared a hell of a lot more about Vincent Ito than I do about Raphael Tomkin.'

Nicholas looked at him. It was as close as they both could come to the outward recognition of their friendship. He smiled. 'Thanks. That means a lot – to me. I know it would to Vincent, too.'

They stood up. Croaker had kept his suit jacket on despite the heat of the day. Now he was sweating profusely and he shrugged out of it. His thin white shirt was stained with sweat.

'You ready to go back?'

Nicholas nodded. 'One thing, Lew.' He hesitated.

'Shoot.'

'You may not want to tell me.'

'Then I won't. Okay?'

Nicholas smiled. 'Okay.' They began to walk up the beach towards Croaker's car. 'What is it between you and Tomkin?'

Croaker opened the door, slung his jacket onto the back seat. He got in behind the wheel. He had parked in the shade but the interior was still hot. Nicholas got in on the passenger's side and Croaker started the engine.

'You're right,' he said. 'I might not want to tell you. And a few days ago, I wouldn't have.' He made a broken U-turn, began to drive up Dune Road towards the bridge across the canal. 'But everything's different now and I guess I figure if I can't trust you, there ain't nobody *to* trust, and I can't live my life like that.'

They rumbled across the bridge, heading past the houses and the small bobbing boats with their stowed outboard motors, towards the highway.

'You know about the Didion thing.'

Nicholas was surprised. 'You mean the murder of that model? Sure, but only what was spread across the papers. I used to see her in practically every magazine I picked up.'

'Yeah,' Croaker said meditatively. 'Beautiful lady. Just beautiful. Like they invented the word for her.'

'It sounds like –'

'Nah. Not what you think.' They swung onto the highway and Croaker picked up speed. The wind was still hot enough to keep them from cooling off. 'But it struck me, you know, that this girl's a person just like everyone else. All anyone thinks of is the image, you know? Her face, her body like that; the façade. No one would stop to think that she might be just as fucked up as all the rest of us, huh? That she belched after a good meal; that she might fart once in a while. Human things.'

He switched lanes, avoiding a blue and white bus, its diesel exhaust asphyxiating. He jammed his horn as they came abreast, then they were shooting away westward.

'Then she was dead and everybody was making a stink. She was a celebrity and responsible for a helluva lot of bread, not to mention the hold she had on a multiple million fantasies. But nobody, I guarantee you, said: There's another life stupidly wasted. Well, buddy, that's what I thought about when I stood there in the middle of her bedroom and looked at her cool body. I thought: She's a human being and I want to know who did this to her.' He shrugged. 'But, hell, I'd do the same for any two-bit whore who got knocked over. Done it mucho times. Doesn't go down well with my captain. But, shit, I never cared a rat's ass about that fucker. "A waste of the taxpayer's money, Croaker," he'd say to me. "Find something more valuable to do with your time." Jesus!' He hit the steering-wheel with his fist. 'Can you beat that? Christ, that bastard's always got one finger in his nose and the other up his ass!

'Anyway, this case turns out to be the ballbuster of all time. I mean, there isn't one goddamned break. All I get is mystery and for that I can go to the movies.

'From what I get from her bedroom, there was someone else there that night. A woman. A woman who had, it appeared, been intimate with Angela Didion and who might conceivably have seen the murder being committed. Only problem is, she's disappeared as if she'd never existed.

'So I'm left with *nada* and the papers are screaming for a solution, which puts the commissioner to screaming at Captain Finnigan, who – but why belabour the point, right? You get the picture.'

They turned off before the multiple exits leading to Manhattan and, in a slow curving glide, moved onto Queens Boulevard. The westbound traffic was only moderate and they made good time.

'Two or three uniforms went through the building doing preliminary checks – seeing who saw what. But it being the Actium House, they were told to step softly and whisper at all times. The result they come back with is nobody knows nothing.

'Okay. Fair enough. But a week later, with everyone screaming for blood – my blood – I decide to take a peek myself. To give you the *Reader's Digest* version so you won't fall asleep from boredom on me, it turns out that the uniform assigned to canvass Angela Didion's floor missed one tenant. Turns out she was away when he came round and had just come back. A little careful digging turns up the interesting fact that she left the morning after the murder – early – for Palm Springs. She stayed for seven days and then returned. She was an older woman. In her late fifties but looking a good ten years older. An alcoholic. I interviewed her at ten in the morning and her breath stank of gin. Her hands shook and she couldn't stop herself from going to the bottle while I was there.'

He turned off Queens Boulevard at Yellowstone Boulevard, went south. They were in Forest Hills.

'But even more interesting was that she swore she saw a man visit Angela Didion – the same man – over the past six months. It might have been going on longer. Six months is when she became aware of him. Apparently there was a fight there one night and from then on she kept a sharp lookout through her door peephole. Nothing better to do with her time.'

He pulled up in front of a medium-sized one-storey building

with a white brick façade. It had dark green, rather ginger-bready trim. A swinging sign on the lawn at the front, black on white, read: PARKSIDE FUNERAL HOME. A large shade elm stood on the other side of the lawn. The wooden doors stood open. As they sat there, several people walked inside. Nicholas recognized one of the *dōjō*'s instructors.

'She gave me a detailed description of the man, Nick. There's no doubt he's Raphael Tomkin.'

'So Tomkin was having an affair with Angela Didion. It's not that surprising, two high-powered people living in the same apartment building. Could she place him there the night of the murder?'

Croaker looked towards the elm. It rustled slightly in a warm desultory breeze. 'She's afraid of flying,' he said finally. 'She took a chloral hydrate with a large slug of gin and passed out at 6 p.m. She didn't get up until about five the next morning.'

'When she left for Key West.'

'Yeah, right.' Croaker turned to him. 'But I know what I know. I've checked and rechecked the movements of all her known intimates. It was Tomkin, all right.'

'You've got no proof, Lew,' Nicholas said. 'You've got nothing.'

'Less than nothing, buddy,' Croaker said morosely. He got out of the car and Nicholas followed him up the flagstone path to the funeral home.

Another of the *dōjō*'s instructors stopped Nicholas on the steps, said several words to him. Nicholas nodded.

'Listen,' Croaker said, pulling Nicholas close to him and lowering his voice, 'the Didion case is officially closed. Finis. Kaput. I got the word the other day from jellybelly Finnigan. This came right from the top; no one would be stupid enough to grease *his* mick palm.'

'Are you saying the police were bought off?'

'What I'm telling you is that if I had any lingering doubts as to Tomkin's complicity in this, they went bye-bye with that order to shut down. Very few people can command that kind of strict hush. He's one of 'em.' His voice was a harsh whisper now, sibilant, lethal. 'But now I got a lead. One of my contacts came through with a make on the other woman in Angela

Didion's apartment the night of the murder. I'm waiting for her name and address. When they come through, I'm gonna nail that sonovabitch's hide to the goddamned wall.'

The service was brief but expressive, half in English, half in Japanese. But it was, basically, an American ceremony, which they had both wanted. Nicholas had been asked to eulogize both Terry and Eileen and he did so. He spoke in Japanese. There was music. A couple, friends of Eileen's. They were professionals and it showed. They played traditional Japanese music on *koto* and *shakuhachi*. And there were the traditional flowers.

Croaker waited until they had walked away from the grave-yard. Behind them, the workmen were beginning to fill in the graves. There seemed to be no sound as the brown earth filled the spaces.

'Nick,' he said, 'what do the names Hideoshi, Yodogimi and Mitsunari mean to you?'

Nicholas stopped and turned away from the sun. He did not want to put on his sun-glasses. 'They're famous names out of Japanese history. Why?'

Croaker seemed to ignore the question. 'Could they be people who are alive today?'

Nicholas shrugged. 'It's possible, I suppose. Sure. They're family names. But those three are linked together by history. The chances –'

'I see what you mean.'

Past them, along the black macadam road, a car door slammed and a motor coughed into life, the sound seeming to float on the hot air. Plane and maple trees rustled their leaves by the side of the path they were on. The heat was mounting.

'You'd better tell me what this is all about.'

Croaker reached inside his coat pocket. He handed over a thin folded slip of what looked like scratch paper. As Nicholas opened it, he said, 'I found this when I was going through Terry's effects the M.E. gave me. It was in his pocket. It might have been made the night he was killed.'

'So?'

'So there was a man – a *Japanese* – at the *dōjō* the afternoon

319

Terry and Ei were murdered. Two of the instructors – Karate and aikido *senseis* –'

'*Sensei.*'

'All right, whatever. They said this man was the best they had ever seen. Afterwards, he had a kendo match with Terry. Vincent told me Terry had been troubled by it when they had dinner together. That was the night of the double murder.'

Nicholas looked at him, ignoring the paper in his hand. It was thin and limp, seeming to be stained with sweat. 'What's the punch-line?'

'This Japanese gave his name as Hideoshi.'

Nicholas looked away for a moment, out over the cemetery. The white marble headstones were brilliant in the burning sun and even the dark grey or striated stones seemed as light as feathers, threatening at any moment to shake free of their moorings and float away into the sky as serenely as clouds. It was the middle of the week; there was little movement along the neat, narrow paths, the close-cropped lawns. Bright blobs of colour, flowers placed precisely at the doorways to heaven, gave the panorama a rather false festiveness as if they stood in the middle of a newly abandoned state fair. At the periphery of his vision, a yellow bulldozer moved fallow earth. Beyond, the highway arched in a steel and stressed-concrete rainbow, its traffic so muted its hiss seemed like the sigh of endless surf.

'In 1598,' Nicholas said, 'Hideoshi, the Kwambaku, he who controlled all the warring *daimyo* of Japan, died. It is commonly believed that he, being a far-sighted man, bequeathed his power to Ieyasu Tokugawa, the strongest member of the governing council. This is not so. Hideoshi's mistress was Yodogimi and she had given him a son. He loved them both and wished, above all else, to have his heir one day rule Japan. Just before his death he asked to see a close friend, Mitsunari the policeman. He told him in strict secrecy to guard Yodogimi and his son. In effect, he set Mitsunari against Ieyasu. "Mitsunari, my friend," he said, "Ieyasu exults in my death though you will see him act otherwise. Do not be deceived. Ieyasu is as clever as he is dangerous. He will, within a short time of my death, seek to become Shōgun. Mitsunari, my friend, you must oppose this with all your might for, to do this, Ieyasu must destroy Yodogimi and the true heir."

'Then, just moments afterwards, Hideoshi received Ieyasu. "You are the strongest of the council," he told him. "Thus you must take over the reins of power after I am gone." "Do not speak of such sad matters, Kwambaku," Ieyasu said, but Hideoshi waved him to silence. "Listen to what I have to say. There is little time. When I am gone, there will be anarchy among the council members. Undoubtedly they will split into factions and the country will be plunged back into civil war. This must be avoided at all costs. You must seize power, Ieyasu. Those other three *daimyo* are as nothing to you. Sweep them aside; rule to forestall a civil war which would rip Japan asunder." And Ieyasu Tokugawa bowed his head in acquiescence.

'Thus did Hideoshi set in motion at the very moment of his death a complex plan for the eventual succession of his heir; thus he hoped to manipulate the destiny of Japan even from beyond the grave. He knew that the moment of his death was most inopportune. His son was still far too young to be able to defend himself or to hold for long the loyalty of all but a tiny fraction of those who were loyal to him. He knew of Ieyasu's ambition to become Shōgun and this he would not permit. That honour must go to his own heir.'

Off to their left, a small funeral procession made its lentitudinous way from the black macadam road from which heat waves rose, along one of the narrow paths towards an open grave. The gleaming casket was already in place, surrounded by garlands of flowers. The mourners were forming up and a slight commotion began as one of the family members collapsed. Distance and the heaviness of the air dampened the sound so that it appeared as if they were viewing a mime show.

'Was Hideoshi successful?' Croaker asked after a time.

'No,' Nicholas said, 'he wasn't.' He was still watching the crowd of people. The person – a woman, it appeared – had recovered and the service commenced. 'For one thing, Ieyasu Tokugawa was far too clever and powerful. For another, Mitsunari gathered a coalition of *daimyo* around him who were just not up to the task of defeating Ieyasu. In 1615 Ieyasu led his forces against those who sought to protect Yodogimi and the heir. They had retreated into the nearly invulnerable castle at Osaka. On June fourth of that year, Ieyasu's forces breached the castle's defences but by that time both Yodogimi and the young heir were already dead; she had killed her son and then committed *seppuku*.'

'Is there a villain in this story?'

There came a flash in the sky and a drone, heavy with vibration, as a 747 headed in to Kennedy.

'I suppose it depends on your point of view,' Nicholas said. 'But I can tell you that Ieyasu was one of the greatest leaders in the history of Japan. Whether Hideoshi understood those qualities in Ieyasu is open to debate. In any case, they were two different kinds of men, and it is impossible, I think, to make an overwhelming case for one against the other. They were both crucial to the development of their country.'

'Yet, in the end, Hideoshi is the loser,' Croaker pointed out. 'His line died with him.' Nicholas said nothing. There was a kind of stillness over the cemetery. People looked like statues, caught within a moment as if part of an old photograph. The hazy spires of Manhattan, sitting astride the horizon in the West, seemed out of place, dropped there by mistake by some drunken stage hand. Croaker's voice had lowered in volume when next he spoke. 'Why would this man take Hideoshi's name – we can be certain it's not his own – when that man failed?'

Nicholas smiled thinly, turned to look at Croaker's face. Odd, he thought. Depending on the intensity of the light and which way it struck, one could see his face as either rugged or battered. But perhaps they were the same, after all. 'That's a totally Western way of viewing history,' he said softly. 'In Japan there is what we call the nobility of failure. Many of our greatest heroes failed in their ultimate objectives. But their *vision* was heroic, as were their subsequent actions. In the West, you revere only the victorious. That's a pity, don't you think?'

Croaker squinted against the glare of the sun. 'You mean this Hideoshi was a hero.'

322

Nicholas nodded. 'Yes.'

'What about the other names on the list? How would they fit in here?'

'Frankly, I don't know, but Terry wasn't just doodling.' He handed the paper back to Croaker.

'Well, I don't get it.'

'Neither do I,' Nicholas said.

There was a kind of stillness in the air that had nothing to do with sadness and death and defeat. Nicholas thought, wonderingly, that it had been some time indeed since he had felt as close to another man as he did now to Lew Croaker.

'You know,' he said, 'when I came to this country years ago, I deliberately put aside a certain part of my life. That is not an easy thing to do – for anyone – but especially for someone brought up in Japan. There was a debt I felt I owed to my father – to the West, really – where it resided inside myself.' Croaker's eyes seemed silvery with the sunlight as he regarded Nicholas silently. He had come to understand the immense importance of this gesture.

'But, abruptly, I stopped. Just like that. It was as if I had suddenly awakened from a long dream-filled sleep. What had I been doing all these years here? What had I accomplished? I would not have myself, feel, as my father had at his death, as if I had squandered the time allotted to me. It was enough that I had been encompassed by *his* sorrow, *his* bitterness. I could not countenance the same thing happening to me.'

They were silent for a time, listening perhaps to the unsteady wind reaching the elms. The sun was very hot.

'And now?' Croaker said with a hint of hesitation; he was still in unfamiliar territory. 'Has anything changed?'

Nicholas laughed, not unkindly but with a sword-sharp edge. 'My whole world has turned upside down. It's as if the intervening years since I came here had never occurred.'

'I'm trying to imagine something like that happening to me.' Nicholas looked at him for a moment in pleasure.

As if by mutual consent, they began to walk slowly down the path towards Croaker's waiting car. Both seemed somehow reluctant to be on their way, as if dreading the frenzy of the city. Just before they reached the car, Croaker said, 'What's your opinion of Justine's old man?'

Nicholas looked at him. 'That's an odd way to put it.'

Croaker shrugged. 'A figure of speech.'

But Nicholas suspected his friend of having inserted a subtle warning. 'I started out by hating his guts,' he said slowly as if formulating his thoughts as he spoke. 'But that's hardly surprising, given Justine's point of view and the way he and I first met. He's deliberate and heavy-handed and used to getting everything he wants. I don't like any of that.'

'I hear a "but" hanging around there some place.'

Nicholas stopped and faced Croaker. 'Look, it would be very easy – and expedient for us all – to write him off as a rich villain out of some dime-store novel but it's not as simple as all that.'

'He's a murderer, Nick.'

'He's vulnerable –'

'Oh, Jesus –'

'He loves his girls, no matter what they think of him. He'd do anything to protect them. And he's not as sure of himself as he ought to be. There's something –'

'It's the grand act he's putting on for you. He needs your help and he knows you're no dummy.'

'I really think you're wrong. He's not as two-dimensional as you make him out to be.'

'All right. Your ninja goes out and kills people,' Croaker said. 'But there must be someone somewhere who he comes home to and loves. He is still what he is.'

'You're ignoring the complexities –'

'He's a fucking shark, man. You'd better face up to it.'

'You're looking at it from only one point of view.'

Croaker shook his head. 'No, Nick. I've just known him longer, that's all.'

On the way into the city, Croaker told Nicholas all he knew about the circumstances of Vincent's death. It wasn't much.

He dropped Nicholas at Tomkin's building on Park and continued downtown. At the office the M.E.'s report on Vincent was waiting for him. He slung his sopping jacket over the back of the grey and dull green chair, took a MintyPick out of his breast pocket, flipped it into his mouth and opened the folder.

What he saw brought the sweat out on his forehead and along the line of his upper lip. He ran a hand through his thick hair and swore under his breath. Then he reached for the phone. There was the minimum of delay.

'Nate?' he said when he got the M.E. on the line. 'Croaker. Thanks for the report on Vincent Ito. Someone must have broken his back to get it here so soon.'

'I did it myself.' Graumann's voice sounded tired. 'We're all still a bit stunned here and –'

'Hey, Nate, I'm working on it.'

'What's up? And don't give me any *schmeer*.'

'Not much,' Croaker admitted. 'Only that it seems related to the deaths of Terry Tanaka and Eileen Okura. They were friends of Vincent's.'

'Yeah, I remember the files. Vincent did the autopsies himself. But how? There's certainly no similarity in M.O.'

Croaker rubbed at his eyes. 'Right now, all I can say is that M.O. doesn't seem very relevant.'

'I see. I phoned Doc Deerforth out on the Island. I wanted it to come from me.'

'How'd he take it?'

'Not well. Look, Lew, we'd – *I'd* appreciate anything you can do – you know . . .' His voice trailed off.

'I know you two were close. Believe me, the minute I have something, I'll be in touch.' He looked up. Vegas was in the open doorway, grinning like a Cheshire cat. He put one finger in the air, put his hand over the speaker, said, 'Hold on, I'll be off in a minute.'

'. . . the funeral arrangements,' Graumann was saying.

'Do that,' Croaker said, 'I want to be there.' He looked down at the report. 'About this chemical substance you found – are you certain –'

'Like I said, I did the autopsy myself. There's no doubt about the finding.'

'Good. That narrows things down considerably.'

'There's absolutely no way the substance could have been

introduced accidentally. It happened shortly before his death.'

'So I see,' Croaker said, reading the typescript. 'A modified nerve toxin; slowed down his muscular responses enough so that –'

'I'd say he was pretty near helpless by the time – by the time it happened.'

'It wasn't injected.'

'No. It would have no effect that way. This is an organic compound we're talking about, not a laboratory synthetic. It must have been sprayed and from close range. He might have known his murderer.'

'Or just not suspected. Anyone – even someone coming quickly out of a crowd – could have sprayed him. Listen, I'll get back to you.'

'Yeah. I just hope it won't be long.'

Croaker cradled the receiver thoughtfully. Still no word from his contact. What was taking so fucking long? 'Come on in,' he said to Vegas. He shifted the MintyPick from one side of his mouth to another. 'Where you been all duded up?' Vegas was wearing a plum-coloured suit with wide lapels and modified flare trousers. Underneath, he wore a pink shirt with a high collar.

'Been out pickin' up the shit,' Vegas said, the wide smile still stitched to his mouth. 'Yeah, real bad shit this time, my man. Took us three months settin' it up.'

Croaker grunted. 'Business as usual.' His mind was on the M.E.'s report.

'No way, man. No way a-tall.' Vegas lounged his huge frame against the open doorway, disdaining the chair inside the office. 'This time I got me a fox among all this shit I just hauled in.'

Croaker clucked his tongue. 'Don't tell me you're planning to mix business with pleasure.'

Vegas shook his head and his grin seemed to expand. 'Uh-uh, not *this* fox. This fox is special.'

'Yeah? They're all the fucking same, man, those cunts you come across.'

Vegas was waiting for this. He poked his forefinger towards Croaker and said, delightedly, 'Not this one. This one's *your* fox, man. I just been her guardian angel till I got her here.'

Croaker looked up, puzzled. 'What the hell are you talking about?'

Vegas laughed good-naturedly. 'What I gots downstairs in the wagon is one piece of high-priced property, man. C'mon, follow me.' Croaker swung his jacket off the chair-back, followed Vegas down the hall.

'This better be worth it,' he said shortly. 'I ain't got time for any of your jive.'

'Oh, no jive, man. No jive.' Vegas laughed again, stabbed the elevator button. 'What I got on ice down in the alley is goin' make your day. Trust me.' He gave a hearty laugh and slapped Croaker on the back as the elevator doors opened and they rode down. They shared the car with a uniform bringing a scruffy-looking Puerto Rican collar down for prints and pics and nothing more was said until they went out through the side entrance.

They came abreast of the police van in the cool dimness of the concrete alley. In this tightly enclosed space, Vegas's body-size was magnified; he was as big as Paul Bunyan amid the White Mountains.

He put an enormous hand on Croaker's shoulder and Croaker was automatically reminded of one of the cases on which they had been teamed. The Atherton thing. Christ, he thought, but that was a bitch! Thought sure we were gonna float away on a sea of blood and never see this goddamned world again. Jesus! He could see it as clearly as if it had just happened: he down with his shoulder shattered by a .45 slug and Vegas rising from the shadows of the burned-out car like an avenging angel. Croaker had fired on his assailant, spinning him around, his second and third shots a useless reflex aimed at the stars. But there was this mountain of a black man with the tyre chain and the snub-nosed pistol the bastard had modified so that it could blast a hole in a brick wall at ten feet; and Vegas took him on with just his bare hands and I never saw anyone go down so hard or so fast from one blow as that motherfucking hood. There were three other corpses that night; Jesus, what fucking mess! Croaker felt the pressure of the other's grip.

'Don't you worry none,' the big man said softly. 'We look out for each other, don't we? I don't give a rat's ass for anyone around here, you know that? They're all a bunch of goddamned hypocrites. I got my job to do, I do it. The rest of them, well, they all got an axe to grind, one way or another. There's always an angle to play out here, ain't that right. War's a perfect place for angles, you know that. The smart make out in wars. They ain't got no conscience, they ain't got no emotion. All they got to worry about is keeping their tails on straight; after that, they got all the time in the world to look for the gravy rollin' in under the dirt and the scum and the –' Vegas stopped abruptly, aware that his grip had tightened painfully on his friend's flesh. He shook his head like a wounded animal. 'Sorry, Soldier, it's been a heavy day.' He smiled ruefully. 'Real heavy duty.'

'It's okay, Spook.' They had given each other nicknames long ago when they had first met; it gave them both a comforting feeling of privacy amid the openness of their days and nights on the force. At times, Croaker thought that this was the falsest feeling in the world, on those days when he felt completely invaded by his job. 'We're two fucking heroes who think that shovellin' shit is heroic.' He laughed. 'But cheer up. What the hell, it could be worse. We could be the ones *makin'* the shit.'

Vegas threw back his head and laughed, the rich sound rolling off the high walls. 'Now, look, here's the dope,' he said. 'We been working, like I said, on this Scarsdale bust for three months, no less. We get a tip to move. We move. Lots of stuff there – enough pills to keep the goddamned Chinese Army awake for a year, a whole lotta horse, carload o' coke an' about a half a ton of reefer madness. Okay, not so bad. That's going on in the back of the place. In the front they got a party going on and everyone gets busted, you know? That's when I saw her. Thought I'd bring her in myself, just in case. I think she's clean but' – he shrugged – 'you know how that is sometimes. Anyway, she's yours if you want her – I can straighten them out upstairs.'

'How can I know if I want her,' Croaker said, 'if I don't know who she is?'

Vegas transferred his hand from Croaker's shoulder to the lever of the back door to the van. 'Sittin' in the dark right in here, man, is Raphael's elder daughter, Gelda Tomkin.'

Croaker felt a jolt race through him just as if he had been doused with ice water.

Vegas leaned on the lever, grinning; the reinforced-steel door swung outward and Croaker stepped in. The door slammed shut behind him.

He stood for a moment in the dimness unmoving, letting his eyes adjust to the low light seeping in through the windshield, washed to a pale grey by the mesh screen dividing the blessed from the damned.

She sat on one of the plain metal benches riveted along either side of the van. Her head was tilted back, resting against the wall. This put her profile into prominence so that he could see the arch of her long forehead, the straight patrician nose, the flair of the highly sensual lips, the long cool sweep of her curving throat. He knew without having to see them now the dark sparks of her eyes, the rather heavy torso with its thrusting breasts and ample hips. Knew, too, the long sweep of the perfect legs from thigh to calf to slim exquisite ankle palely outlined as they stretched out before her; those magnificent legs which, quite inexplicably, made her heaviness an overwhelming asset.

'Well ...' He felt a great weight about his body and an inarticulateness that obliged him to clear his throat and begin again. 'Well, Gelda, what have you been up to now?'

The sharply delineated profile dissolved into sweeping shadow as she turned her head to look in his direction.

'Who the hell are you?' Even in anger there was a rich lustre, a silkiness to her voice that made it seem as if he had spoken to her yesterday instead of several months ago. Even alarm could not diminish its effectiveness.

'Croaker,' he said, moving towards her. 'Lieutenant. Remember me?'

'Should I?' The tone had turned aqueous, soft and languid. The air between them seemed to tremble.

'Maybe. I met you once before.' He stood over her now, not seeing anything in the twilight except the pale sheen from the whites of her large eyes. But he felt her presence acutely and it gave him pleasure to stand thus. 'I interviewed you at the beginning of the summer regarding the Angela Didion murder; we talked about your father.'

'That shit!' Even though she spat it out, there remained an

329

elegance to it. He heard her take a breath. 'Yeah. I remember you. Big dude with a face like Robert Mitchum's.'

His laugh was a brief bark. 'How flattering! Thanks.'

'Don't get cocky. His face looks like it's waged World War Three. So does yours.'

He waited for a moment, then said, 'Mind if I sit down?'

'You mean I've got a choice?' When he didn't answer, he felt her shrug. 'Suit yourself. This isn't my house.'

'That'd be on Sutton Place, right?' he said, sitting down next to her.

Abruptly her head came away from the wall. 'What the hell's going on, anyway?' she snapped. 'Am I going to be booked?'

'That depends.'

'On what?'

But his hand, having dipped into his suit jacket pocket, was a blur and he was already moving. His left hand reached across the space between them. He grasped her wrists together, pulled. At the same time, he flicked on the pocket flash, searching the pale flesh on the inside of her elbows. He tried not to think of the softness of the skin here.

He let her go, sat back. 'I could check the insides of your thighs, too,' he said softly. 'Or you could tell me.' He had used a fair amount of pressure and her wrists must hurt but she made no move to rub them; he liked that. She had a great deal of pride.

'I shoot up through the eyeballs,' she said acidly. 'You've heard of that, I'm sure. Leaves no tracks.' Her head turned then and her cheek lit up as a grillwork of grey and black fell obliquely across her face. She looked like a heroine out of a fifties' *film noir*. Some of the air seemed to go out of her all at once. 'I don't do anything any of you guys don't do. Probably a good deal less. I don't blow coke, for instance.'

He said nothing, sat beside her smelling her scent silently until she turned her head and she was in absolute darkness again. He felt like a blind man, wanting badly, irrationally to see her again. 'Do you believe me?' Her voice had turned small and he wondered how much of an act she was promoting.

He decided to be honest with her; anything less would be useless and potentially dangerous. 'Yes,' he said slowly. 'I believe you.'

'Then I'm free to go?'

'In a minute.' He didn't realize how gentle his voice had become. 'Why the hell are you involved in all this?'

'What, you mean break my poor old father's heart?' She laughed sardonically. 'Come on, what do you want me for?'

'I'm just talking to you,' he said reasonably.

'Yeah, sure. In a police van, home from a bust.'

'That was your choice, not mine.'

She was silent for a moment and, though he couldn't see her, he knew that she was studying him. It could all break apart now, he knew, and held his breath.

She laughed again, a bell-like sound, slightly echoey within the confines of the metal van. 'All right,' she said softly, 'I'll tell you why I do it. I like it, it's as simple as that. It's fun to get paid to fuck. I'm an actress, a model, selling things, just like Angela Didion was. It's all come on, there's no involvement.'

'Never?'

Her head tossed like a bridling horse's and he saw a flash of light across her eyes. 'Sometimes,' she said truthfully, 'with a woman.' She was thinking of Dare. 'Does that shock you?'

'Not really,' he said. 'Did you think it would?'

'I don't know what kind of man you are.'

'I'm just your plain ordinary New York slob.'

'Yeah, I can see that.' She had hurt him and she knew it; she felt he had asked for it.

'What about the booze?' Croaker asked her.

'What about it?' He could hear her voice go hard as her defences came up.

'Still hitting the bottle hard?'

Perversely, she felt herself wanting to tell him the truth, stopped herself in time. 'Not so much any more,' she said. 'I've got my work to keep me warm.'

'No men?'

'What is this, twenty questions?'

'If you want to call it that.'

'I don't want to call it anything,' she said shortly. 'I want to get out of here.'

'I can't detain you any longer.'

'You mean I'm free to go?'

'There are no charges.'

'Now I'm supposed to thank you?'

He knew it was over; that he might just as well have not begun this at all. He felt tired and depressed. 'You're not guilty of anything. You're free to go.' He deliberately used her phraseology.

Still she made no move to go.

He sat stiffly with his back against the wall, his buttocks jammed up against the joining of the bench to the wall. His wrists lay loosely on his thighs. He stared at his hands, could barely make out the pale sheen of his nails.

'What do you want from me?'

Her voice was so soft that for a moment he thought it might be a whisper from his own mind.

'Nothing,' he said. His voice sounded dead. 'I don't want anything from you.'

'In a horses's ass.'

'All right.' His head swung round and he saw that she was staring at him. She blinked once and it seemed that she did so in slow motion. 'I can help you, Gelda.'

'What's that supposed to mean?'

He knew then that he meant what he said, that it was not just his desire to probe for information about Raphael Tomkin; he knew that he had been dreaming about her for the past two weeks. A current of electricity went through him and he half turned towards her. Her eyes seemed to be searching for something in his face.

'Just what it says.'

'I wouldn't trust you if I were drowning and you had the only line.'

'But you *are* drowning,' he said softly. And then, after a time, 'It doesn't have to be like that. The booze and the pills and the – work.' He paused. 'You could go away somewhere.'

'Go away!' she exploded. 'Christ, there's no place far enough to get away from myself.' She put her head back against the metal wall and he saw her soft throat again. 'You want to know how I got my name? Gelda.' She said that last word as if it had a bitter taste. 'I got it because my mother hated.' She laughed humourlessly, the first ugly sound he had heard her utter. 'Oh,

332

not me personally. She would never stoop to anything so personal. She was far too busy detesting the life which bound her like a jealous lover. Being so powerfully rich had been her one dream in life, her overriding goal ... Yes, I guess you could call it that: her goal. Anyway, she found it with my father. Found, too, that it was not what she'd expected it to be – not by a long shot. Oh, she had all the power she had dreamed of and all the money, but living with my father was pure hell and with every moment of their marriage he ground her down.' She sighed. 'I think, in the end, it became a game with him, to try and see how much he could take away from her. Not material things, of course. My God, she had more than enough of those. No, it was in the area that matters most to my father that he denied her: in the mind. I suspect that if she had fought back, she would have eventually emerged bloody but victorious, as they say.

'But she would not. She wanted to hold on to her dream so desperately that she forfeited any kind of courage. She was my father's slave, a slave, more accurately, to his wealth. She was a weak-willed bitch who must have loved the pain which my father inflicted on her. I mean she put up with it, didn't she? Even after –' She stopped suddenly, putting the palm of her hand over her mouth for a moment. 'Christ, what am I saying? And to a cop of all people.' She stifled a nervous laugh. 'I must be out of my mind.'

His heart beat faster as he heard himself say, 'What does all this have to do with how you were named?'

'What?' she said almost absently.

'You were going to tell me about your name.'

'Oh. Oh, yes.' She folded her hands one over the other. She rubbed them against her long thighs, back and forth in a hynotic rhythm. 'I really believe that about the last thing my mother wanted was a child. But my father, as always, insisted on what he wanted. And what he wanted was children. Strangely enough – or not so strangely' – here she gave an odd little laugh – 'he didn't care whether they were boys or girls, just as long as he became a sire. He's old-fashioned that way; he feels it's a sign of manhood.

'But my mother misunderstood him. She supposed that he wanted sons to carry on the Tomkin line and that anything else would be considered a failure. I suppose it's a measure of how far she really was from him that she could have been so wrong about him.

'She was naturally ecstatic that she had given birth to a girl. So she named me Gelda. It was a way of getting back at my father without him knowing, you see. Gelda. Gelding. Get it? Sure you do.' She turned away as if from the memory.

'You could change it,' he said reasonably and for the first time she gave a completely natural laugh. It was quite beautiful, he thought. 'I guess I'm just perverse,' she said. 'I carry it now as a reminder.'

'Of what?'

'What's it your business?' she snapped. All the warmth that, so soon, had suffused her voice, was abruptly gone.

'Look,' he said, 'I'll tell you the truth.' It was a desperate gamble, one which he had hoped not to make. He had no choice now. 'I need your help with an investigation.'

'With what?'

This was it. 'I think your father murdered Angela Didion.'

'So?'

It was not what he'd expected and he was momentarily non-plussed.

Gelda seemed pleased. 'I see you're speechless,' she said, laughing. 'Good for you. Did you think I'd say, "I hate his guts, copper, but he's still my father?" Bullshit. It wouldn't surprise me if he did kill her.'

'You mean, in your opinion, he's capable of murder?' His heart hammered in his chest; this seemed like a straight gift from heaven.

'In my opinion?' She laughed. 'Yes. In my opinion my father's quite capable of murder. Laws, I remember, were not things for him to be concerned with.'

She had moved fractionally so that she was facing him in three-quarters profile and he could see her eyes and the hurt within them, deeply buried.

'Did you know about Angela Didion?' he asked quietly.

'You mean that he was balling her? Sure. I was there one day when she walked in. She did it so you knew right away it was like she owned the place, you know?'

334

'Did you talk with her?'

She smiled. 'We didn't exactly get along. There was a kind of instant repulsion, as if we were magnets with the same polarity.'

'I thought you and your old man didn't get along.'

'We don't.' She seemed quite close to him now, though he had not been aware that any shift had taken place. 'But sometimes my father is impossible to ignore. That happens maybe twice a year.' She shrugged. 'Who knows? Maybe he wants to see if I've changed any.'

'Changed in what way?'

'It's none of –' The fire in her eyes died and she said, quite sweetly, 'That I've given up girls. He can't stand that in me. I suppose that's one of the reasons I like them more than men.' She shrugged. 'A shrink said that to me once. I walked out. I didn't need to pay him fifty dollars an hour to tell me what I already knew.'

'How'd Tomkin come to know at all?'

'About me and girls? Oh, he found me at it one day on the summer estate on Gin Lane out near South Hampton. That was after we'd sold the Connecticut estate; after Mother ... died.'

'What did he do?'

'My mother was a suicide. He –'

'No, I meant when he found you and the other girl.'

'You know, even my sister Justine doesn't know this part of it; I'd never tell her and, God knows, my father never would. He treats her like my mother always did. He dotes on her as if she were a cripple. She was the baby, after all. But she was slim and athletic while I was heavy. No matter what kind of diet they put me on and, believe me, they put me on them all, I never could lose weight. My mother never let me forget that; she made me ashamed of it.'

She paused. 'I don't know how I got on to that.' She wasn't really talking to him any more. 'Anyway, my father found me with this girl. It was about a week before my mother died. Deepest summer. I had met Lisa on the beach – her parents had the estate at the other end of the Lane – her father and stepmother whom she hated. Our hate brought us together, I suppose. But we also loved each other's bodies. Truly. There was a purity to our love that I've never been able to find again.

'It was so hot that day, even so near the water. Everything was lying limp and bedraggled. We were lying at the edge of my estate in the lee of a line of high hedges. We were on the border, clad only in our bathing suits. It was like we were naked, only better. We couldn't keep our hands off each other. We took off our suits and made love. It was very beautiful.

'We were still holding each other wetly when I saw my father. I imagine he had been there for a time, perhaps from the very beginning although I have no true way of knowing.

'He saw me looking at him. His face was red and he seemed to be having trouble breathing. He scrambled towards us in a crouch, screaming. His hands flailed the air. Lisa was terrified. She grabbed her suit and ran off down the beach. My father hadn't even looked at her.

'I lay on the ground, paralysed. With fear, I thought. Now I know better. That first moment when I had looked in his eyes, I knew what he had been doing while he was watching us – it was as unmistakable as the mark of Cain; he made it that way. I might have been horrified but I was not. The idea made me excited; he had watched me make love and I had turned him on.

'I watched him come towards me. There was something clouding his eyes which I couldn't place then. I had never seen him this way before; I was seventeen. He seemed a totally different person to the one I had known as my father; he had come out of himself.

'He took me there where I lay, staring up at him, thinking myself helpless under him. He plunged into me with such force that I cried out and, immediately, I felt his wrist between my lips. I bit down on it with my teeth; I sucked up the blood I had caused to come out of him. I felt as if I were being stuffed all the way up to my throat.

'It was over so quickly that for a moment I thought it had never happened. But there was the salty taste in my mouth and the wet soreness between my legs; I couldn't walk without some pain for two days after.'

She stopped and her head turned. She became aware of him again. 'There, I've said it; I've spewed it all out and now that's supposed to make me feel better. But you know, it doesn't. I still feel the same lousy rotten feeling inside. I loathe myself. Not because he did that to me. But because I didn't fight him; because deep down I didn't want him to stop. I revelled in feeling his come jetting deep inside me. Oh, God! Oh, my God!' She was weeping now, her frame shuddering as if it might shake itself apart.

She fell forward and he caught her. His hands slid under her arms and he stood up with her. Her legs had no strength and he had to support her half propped against him. Her shudders transferred themselves to him as if they were seismic quakes, the vibrations entering him. He felt her long silky hair gently brushing back and forth against the side of his face; the strength of her perfume; the heat of her flesh beneath her elegant clothing.

She cried for a long time and even after her sobs had subsided she continued to cling to him, her hands locked behind his neck.

Then he heard her whispering. 'I must be mad. I must be mad.'

'C'mon.' He said softly but with a great deal of force. 'Let's get you the hell out of here.'

Nicholas thought about the three names as he went up in the elevator to the top of the tower and Raphael Tomkin's plush office. Hideoshi. Yodogimi. Mitsunari. What the hell had Terry meant? Nicholas knew him almost as well as Eileen had but he couldn't fathom this cryptogram. All right. Start at the beginning. Hideoshi is the ninja. Assume? No, it's a given. Then who are Yodogimi and Mitsunari? Were there three people involved? It seemed to go against all the laws of ninjutsu but, of course, it couldn't be ruled out. Deduction was so easy in literature. Elementary, my dear – he wished Holmes were here with him now.

Yet he felt a kind of familiarity with the names. Of course he knew all about the historical personages, their personal histories: the sweep of the past come alive. But this was the present, divorced from the past.

He looked up, watching the neon indicator moving relentlessly from left to right as if ticking off the seconds, the minutes, the years. Time, he thought.

My God! What am I thinking? I've been too long in the West; I've become one of them. He felt then a kind of secret 'shame, something that was difficult to admit to, even within himself.

Wasn't I taught that the present is never divorced from the past? Why have I pushed that away continuously? Why have I suddenly, at age thirty-three, dropped out of life? Given up my job, left the city, begun to hibernate – yes, that's the right word – out on the beach like it was Malibu, some far-off lotus land devoid of worries or responsibilities?

Abruptly he felt something rising within him; something dark and ugly and unstoppable. A *tsunami* – the tidal wave. It reared up at his back, rushing recklessly towards him. Had there been no warning?

There had been plenty of warning. He had just been too preoccupied or merely too dense to see it. Or far too close.

He felt as if he were suffocating and he put his hand out, palm against the textured wall. It was slippery with sweat. He imagined that he was Amelia Earhart blithely flying through the cotton-candy skies on her way to – where? He couldn't remember. No matter. Travelling, working the controls. When suddenly.

Nothing.

Not a thing. No sky, no clouds, no land below, no stars above. Had the past overtaken her, too?

The elevator doors sighed open and he stepped out into the corridor, stiff-legged. He went to the outer edge, looked out at the streaming city through a pane of glass so newly installed that it still carried the wide white X through its centre. He seemed oblivious.

It seemed so obvious to him now. Yukio should have given him the clue. His memory of Yukio stood between him and Justine like a guardian ghost baring her teeth. It was this spectre within him that had hurt Justine so. He clenched his fist unconsciously. Still a part of him after all this time. But he knew how hollow a statement that was. The psyche bore no notion of time, that was a rational response to a basically irrational question.

Abruptly, the force of his feelings for Justine broke the surface like a geyser rupturing the glass surface of a still pond. How stupid could he have been!

Having made up his mind, feeling calmer than he had for a while, he quickly went down the corridor and pulled open the metal doors to Raphael Tomkin's office.

Frank stood just inside. His eyes blazed when he saw Nicholas and his right hand twitched. Nicholas went by him without a second look.

'Hey, you can't –'

But Tomkin had looked up from behind his desk and had already waved him to silence. 'It's all right, Frank,' he said amiably. 'Nicholas is now on the payroll, isn't that right?' He redirected his gaze towards Nicholas.

The office was immense, perhaps slightly smaller than a grand ballroom. This seemed, outwardly, impossibly excessive until one saw that the space was divided up not by walls but by furniture groupings, forming out of the whole a kind of mini-apartment.

Here to the left was what amounted to a living-room with a one-step-down sunken parquet floor surrounded by a C-shaped sofa in crushed velvet from Roche Bobois. A low smoked-glass and chrome coffee table sat in the centre, above which swooped a crescent-necked floor lamp.

To the right, nearer the long bank of windows, was what could be classified as a professional engineer's workroom, complete with drafting table, flexible light source and a black plastic tabouret. Near by was a vertical metal file for storing architectural plans. There was even, on its top, a scale model of the tower as it would look when completed, including the central atrium garden, plaza and trees along its eastern and western peripheries.

Far to the left in the dimness of the office's interior, Nicholas could make out a tiny kitchen with half-refrigerator, a stainless-steel sink and, above, an electric oven. Next to it a door stood open revealing a full-size bath. The rear corner on the left had been transformed into a library. Bookshelves climbed two walls. There were two strong, shaded reading lights hovering at the sides of a pair of clubby high-backed leather chairs which, looked well lived in rather than new. All that was missing was a massive glass ashtray holding a meerschaum.

Lastly, there was the office proper, directly ahead of him, where Tomkin sat now. The magnificent hardwood desk had quite obviously been custom-made. It was a beautifully blank piece of furniture from this side but, on walking around to its reverse side, one found it revealed itself as housing a complex data centre. Nicholas thought it more resembled a console of a 747 than it did anything else. There was a bank of four phones, each colour-coded; a telex; a NYSE ticker; the set of TV monitors for the now obligatory interior surveillance system and a number of other gadgets whose functions totally eluded him.

Tomkin was on the phone. He waved Nicholas to a plush chair in front of the desk. Nicholas looked down. The left armrest contained its own phone. He lifted the receiver, pressed an unlit button for a clear line, dialled Justine's number in West Bay Bridge. He let it ring six times before he hung up. She might just be out on the beach. On an impulse, he tried her city number. No answer.

He got another line, asked Frank for Abe Russo's extension, dialled it. When he got the construction foreman on the line, he asked him for a list of all oriental men currently working on the tower project.

'That'll take some time,' Russo said shortly. 'I got a lotta work. I don't know –'

'Let me put it this way,' Nicholas said slowly. 'If we don't get these names, this project may be halted – permanently.'

'Okay. I'll get it right up to you.'

'I appreciate your assistance,' Nicholas said. 'And, Abe. I want you to do this all yourself. Don't involve anyone, is that clear? And, listen, when you've got the list, I'm going to want to see all the men on that list. Think about how you're going to do that without giving them any advance notice. No leaks, all right? Good.' He hung up, suppressed a desire to try Justine once more.

Tomkin was on the phone for another ten minutes. During that time there was no movement in the office. In the brief silences, Nicholas could hear the gentle hiss of the central air-conditioning. Frank was immobile near the closed doors.

Nicholas got up and, skirting the conversation pit, went back to the library. There was an old-fashioned rolltop desk to one side that he hadn't noticed before. On it he saw several pictures in silver frames that looked Mexican. There were a number of colour shots of the same women at ages varying from perhaps sixteen to late twenties. One was Justine; the other, he surmised, must be Gelda. They were both quite beautiful in very different ways, yet they seemed linked by a hidden quality that defined both. He saw only one photo in which the sisters appeared together. It was a black and white shot, torn at one corner. The two girls stood on a lawn. In the background he could just make out the corner of a building, brick-faced, ivy-covered. It appeared to be part of an estate house. They were ten and seven year old. Justine held up a painted egg. At her feet was a tiny wicker basket. She was smiling at the camera. Gelda, a step behind her, taller and a good deal heavier, had been caught looking off to her left. There seemed, even at that young age, a peculiar gulf between the two, as if one had no cognizance of the presence of the other. They might have been pasted together from different pictures for all the relationship they bore to one another.

'Nicholas?'

Nicholas turned and walked back to the side of the desk. Tomkin stood up, came round. He wore a fox-coloured silk suit, deep yellow-and-white-striped shirt with solid yellow collar and cuffs and a brown silk tie. He extended a hand. It was thick, the back dark with curling hair. He wore a ring of white gold or platinum on his right ring finger; his left hand bore no jewellery at all.

'Glad to see you,' he said. His blue eyes seemed to have a touch of grey to them today. 'I was wondering when you'd show up. What did you find out?'

'I beg your pardon?'

'Information, Nicholas.' He formed the words slowly as if trying to capture the attention of a retarded child. 'You went out to West Bay Bridge because you thought the ninja might be there. At least, that's what you told me over the phone.'

'He wasn't there.'

'Is Justine all right?'

'Perfectly.'

'I don't like your tone of voice.'

'You're not paying me to like my tone of voice, merely to protect you.'

'I have been wondering how you were doing that from Long Island. Remote control, I suppose.'

Nicholas laughed shortly. His eyes were steely. 'Let's cut the crap, Tomkin. You don't have to like me, just be cooperative. Otherwise, I can't do my job.'

'But I do like you, Nicholas. Whatever gave you the idea that I didn't?' Affable now, he guided Nicholas down into the living area. They sat on the couch. It was chocolate brown and luxuriously comfortable.

'Surely you're not surprised to find that I'm – curious, shall we say – about your methodology. After all, Frank here never leaves my side. He gives me a great deal of comfort.'

'Frank is useless,' Nicholas said, 'when it comes to the ninja. He'll get through Frank as if he's not there.'

Tomkin smiled thinly. 'He may get through Frank but if he does, he'll do so with a couple of .45 bullets in him.'

Nicholas shrugged. 'If you choose to take this matter lightly –'

'I assure you, I am not taking this lightly. At all. Else I would not have hired you, understand? Now' – he slapped his thick thigh – 'tell me what you're up to.'

'I'm expecting Abe Russo any minute.'

'What the hell we need him up here for? He's got his hands full keeping to our deadline.'

'The ninja's hall-mark is infiltration,' Nicholas said quietly. 'He won't try to kill you by . . . remote control, as you say.' He grinned. 'He's got to come right up to you – do it himself from arm's length. When Abe gets here, we'll find out if he's in the tower building.'

'Here? But how?'

'The most likely probability is as a worker. He'd be anonymous, have the run of the place. It's only logical.'

At that moment there was a knock on the door and Frank

let Abe Russo in. He carried a sheaf of computer printout paper in one hand. His clothing was rumpled and he wiped a stray lock of sandy hair from his forehead.

'Here it is,' he said, dropping the paper on the coffee table in front of them. 'I've circled all the oriental males. There's thirty-one of 'em,' he continued as they both began to look over the list.

'What are you looking for?' Tomkin said. 'You know his name?'

Nicholas shook his head. 'Even if I did, he'd never use it here.' It was a long shot to expect to find the name Hideoshi on this list but it would have been foolish to have ignored the obvious. 'This it?' he said to Russo.

The other nodded. 'Yeah. Every one. Twenty-five are on the day shift, the rest are on at night.'

'All twenty-five here today?' Nicholas asked. 'None called in sick?'

'None sick. They're all here as far as I can tell.'

'And no one knows about this?'

'Not a one,' Russo said. 'I worked on it alone.'

'Okay,' Nicholas said. 'Let's go.' He stood up.

'What's happening?' Tomkin said.

Nicholas rolled up the paper into a tube. 'I'm going to see all of these men face to face. Every one's a candidate for our ninja.'

Russo took him through the labyrinth of the building and, one by one, the men on the list were interviewed and crossed off the list.

The thirteenth name was Richard Yao. Russo didn't know precisely where he was working at this time of day, so they sought out his unit foreman. They found him supervising the welding going on in one section of the bottom of the atrium lobby. He was a heavy-set man with almost no hair and close-set eyes.

'You just missed him, Abe.' He took a thick cigar stub out of his mouth, used it to point over his shoulder. 'He split.'

'What for?' Russo asked.

'Said he was sick.' He put the cold stub back into his mouth. 'Didn't look too good neither.'

'How long ago did this happen,' Nicholas said.

'Oh, I'd say fifteen – maybe twenty minutes ago. Like I said, you just missed him.' He looked at Russo. 'Anything wrong? He's a good worker.'

Russo's eyes flickered briefly in Nicholas's direction before he shook his head negatively. 'Thanks, Mike. You need another man down here?'

'I could use one.'

'Okay. I'll see to it then.'

On the way back up to the top of the tower, he said, 'What do you think, Mr Linnear?'

'I think,' Nicholas said, 'that we have our man.'

'Well, hey, give me this for a sec –' He took the sheaf of paper from Nicholas's grasp, leafed through the accordion sheets. 'Here!' His forefinger stabbed at the sheet. 'Here's his address, 547 – hey, wait a minute! That address is too far west. It's a phony!'

'I'm not surprised.'

The doors opened and Nicholas sprinted down the corridor, leaving the other behind, staring at him. He pushed past Frank. Tomkin was on the phone, behind his desk. He put a palm over the mouthpiece. 'Well,' he said, 'what gives? Did you find –'

But Nicholas was already at the verge of the desk, his fingertips moving quickly but surely around the rim of the top.

'What the hell –'

'Hang up,' Nicholas said. He was circling the desk, probing. His fingertips never left the surface of the oiled wood.

Tomkin stared down at Nicholas's hands as if they were disembodied entities. He lifted the receiver to his ear, mumbled a few words and hung up.

'Good,' Nicholas said, still moving. 'I'd like to talk to you –'

'About what happened downstairs. Yeah. Yeah.' His blue eyes were open wide as he watched. Across the room, Russo had come in. He stood quietly next to Frank, looking on.

'Right. About what happened downstairs.' Nicholas knelt, began to search under the desk. He spoke as he worked. 'I think we found our man.' Wiring and computer modules. 'The thirteenth. A man named Richard Yao. He was transferred here from a Rubin Bros site in Brooklyn.' Ridged templates: the computer grid. More wiring. 'Not too long ago.' As thick as a rat's nest, colour-coded for easy repair. 'Quite a good worker, so his foreman says.'

'Yeah, so what?' Tomkin's deep-set eyes never left Nicholas's hands. 'What's it to me?'

'He's our man. He split just after I made the call to Russo requesting the list of oriental male workers here at the tower.' One ridge higher than the other and he backtracked with the tips of his fingers just to make certain. He gave a little pull. 'Russo didn't speak to anyone about this little job and there was no time for anyone to get a peek.' Fingers still in darkness with their minuscule prize. 'Just Russo and me and' – he lifted it into the light at last, deposited on the gleaming desk top in front of Tomkin, a bright bit of plastic and metal, thin as a wafer, less than an inch in diameter – 'of course, the telephone.'

Tomkin's face had gone red and his head seemed to tremble somewhat. He reached out one forefinger, pushed hesitantly at the thing as if he thought it might bite him. 'Goddamn it!' he cried. 'Goddamn it! Under my own nose!' He pounded the table, looked up. 'Frank, you sonovabitch! How'd you let that cocksucker in here? I'll kill you!'

Frank stood rooted to the spot, bewildered.

'It's not his fault,' Nicholas said quietly. 'He couldn't know what to look for.'

But Tomkin was beyond calming words. He moved out from behind his desk, the forefinger that had touched the electronic bug waving in the air at his bodyguard. 'Is this what I pay you for, you asshole? That – that *shit* was in here, prowling around! Where the fuck were you? Tell me that! Where the *fuck* were you?'

'I was here all the time, Mr Tomkin,' Frank said hastily. 'Even when you were out to lunch, I was here. I never left, you gotta believe me. This guy must have busted in here at night, after you and me were gone. I don't –'

Tomkin soared forward, slammed Frank with the back of his hand. 'Nobody broke in here, you schmuck – not without my knowing about it the next day.' He watched the bright red stain on Frank's cheek; he could almost feel how hot the skin was. 'No, he was here all right, under our noses. You were just too stupid to have seen him.'

'But I didn't even know who to look for,' Frank said.

'Shut up! Just shut up, will you?' Tomkin turned his back on him. 'Christ, you sound like a baby crying.'

Nicholas had been moving in a half-crouch outwards from the epi-centre of the desk in a tight spiral. It took him ten minutes of intensive search but he found a second bug under one section of the chocolate couch. No one said anything until he was finished.

'I think,' Nicholas said, dusting off his hands, 'that under the circumstances we'd better go downstairs.'

'What for?' Tomkin looked puzzled. 'The room's secure now, isn't it?'

Nicholas nodded. He was already moving towards the door to the corridor. 'Tell you on the way down, okay?'

Tomkin's heavy voice broke the whirring silence of their descent. 'I don't mind telling you that was a good piece of work you did up there, Nick. Damned fine. Thanks.' He sighed. 'You know I regularly have my office and homes electronically vacuumed every six months to weed out surveillance but, Christ, I haven't even moved in here officially.' He ran his fingers through his iron-grey brush of hair. 'Sweet Jesus, when I think of what he might have overheard over those lines! I'd like to rip his throat out!'

The doors slid open and they stepped out into the atrium.

'You don't think the bastard's here somewhere, do you?' Tomkin's head moved from side to side.

'No chance,' Nicholas said, guiding the other man along the lobby. 'He knew security had been broken the minute he overheard my conversation with Russo. He's split. For the time being.'

They went out into the hot sunshine on Park Avenue. Like stepping out onto the surface of a bloated, slowly turning planet, the burning atmosphere so thick it felt like gravity; locked in a pressure chamber.

As they approached the car, the thin, bony chauffeur got out, stood waiting on the broken sidewalk, one hand grasping the door handle.

Nicholas stopped them midway along the plank walkway.

346

The jarring sound of the jackhammers filled the air like a battery of dentists' drills. Tomkin had to lean close in order to hear what Nicholas was saying. He nodded and they climbed into the dim, cool interior of the limo.

They started up immediately, nosing out into the traffic flow. Nicholas began to work. He went to the phone first, unscrewing both ends of the receiver, drew a blank. It had to be a place of easy access, he reasoned. The ninja might have been able to take his time in Tomkin's office but certainly not here. He looked into the well where the receiver was placed; very little room. He used one finger all around the sides. And came up with it. He depressed a button and an inch of window slid silently down. He threw the bug out. The window sighed up.

'Clear?' Tomkin asked.

He held up his hand, inspected all the obvious places; nothing.

'All right.' He sat back up in the seat. 'We're secure.'

'Good.' Tomkin's face relaxed visibly. 'All this has given me the creeps because it's come at the worst time imaginable.' He leaned forward, depressed a hidden stud. A smoked-glass panel slid upwards, cutting them off from the front of the car. Nicholas saw the cross-hatching of the wire mesh embedded within the glass. 'I'm in the middle of one of the biggest deals I've ever made. It takes in corporations on three continents. The amount of money involved, well, it's incalculable. Christ, what I need now is not to be disturbed, so I get this – asshole – hanging around my neck.' He chuckled, his mood shifting abruptly. 'Well, I shouldn't complain, really. This idea originated with the Japanese. Only they were far too timid; they refused to go all the way with it even after I outlined the perfect methodology. Scared, is all. So we had a falling out – of sorts.' He laughed. 'I stole the idea. Shit, they were going to just sit on it for a while, "study" the sampling they already had.' He snorted. 'No one'd get rich *that* way. Then they wanted back in after I had it running. Can you imagine? I told them to fuck off. They had lost a lot of face by then -- too much, I guess. So they've sent the ninja.'

Tomkin settled himself more comfortably against the plush velvet seat. 'Might as well go somewhere now that we're out.'

He flicked a switch, gave the chauffeur an address on the West Side. 'I'm hungry. How about you?'

'I could eat something.'

'Okay. Good.' He closed his eyes for a moment. 'I don't want anything to happen to my girls, understand?'

Nicholas said nothing. He was thinking about what Croaker had told him about this man. He was wondering about the truth.

Tomkin turned his head sharply like a dog at the point. 'I'm quite certain you think I don't give a shit about them. I can imagine the kind of fantasies Justine has told you about me.'

'She really doesn't talk about you much. Does that surprise you?'

'Don't be impertinent with me,' Tomkin said coldly. 'It won't get you very far.' His voice softened somewhat. 'But, to be quite frank, I *am* surprised she hasn't told you all about me.' He waved a hand as if in dismissal. 'It doesn't matter, really. I still love them both. I know I'm not the world's best father but then they leave a lot to be desired as daughters. Let's just say we're all at fault.'

'Perhaps if you didn't use your power with them the way –'

'Ah, then she did talk about me.'

'A bit, yes. Once.'

'My dear boy,' Tomkin said, 'I don't mean to be pompous but money *is* power or, more accurately, it's the other way round. It amounts to the same thing. That's my gift, you see. It's what I excel in. Making decisions, building power, watching the money pour in.' He lifted a knowing forefinger to the side of his nose; absurdly, it made him look like an avuncular character out of a Dickens novel. 'It's also what keeps me alive. I'd be dead tomorrow without that excitement; I can't give it up for anyone, not even my girls.'

'Would you even want to?'

'To be honest, I don't know.' He shrugged heavily. 'But what possible difference could that make? It's a moot point. I don't love them any less for it; I'm merely denied certain things.'

'So are they.'

'Life is tough, huh? I'm glad you figured that out.' He turned his head. 'I guess I was right about you. I like the way you work.'

They crossed Fifth Avenue on Fifty-seventh, heading west. Heavy traffic brought them to a standstill midway along the block. Behind them was the white modernistic sweep of Seven West. Fuel exhaust and the heat combined to streak the air as it rose in waves from the asphalt of the street.

'You know,' Tomkin said while they were stalled, 'money's a funny thing. Most people who don't have it want it very badly. But the ones who have it, if they have any sense at all, know what a fantastic burden it is. There are mornings I don't want to get up and go to the office, despite the excitement. I feel as if my body weighs tons, as if every breath I take is made painful by pressure.' Up ahead, at Sixth Avenue, the light turned green. No one moved. After a moment, horns started blaring.

'But there are decisions to be made,' he continued. 'Decisions involving millions of dollars and the lives of thousands of my employees throughout the world. There's nobody but me to make them.' His voice turned reflective. 'That's excitement enough, don't you think? To know you're performing something in a way no one else can. You know about that as well as I do, eh? You do what you do better than anyone else.'

'And what's that?'

Tomkin's eyes narrowed as if he were looking through cigarette smoke. 'You're a very deadly man, Nick. Don't think I can't feel it. Even before I saw what you could do with Frank and Whistle. Oh, it was nice to see a graphic example of what had been in my mind's eye, of course. But I was as certain of you as I have been of anything. To tell you the truth, I'm glad Justine likes you – I think you'll be good for her. She should get to know what a real man's like.'

The light had turned red again but the horns hadn't diminished.

'What's the problem, Tom?' he said into the grille.

'Bus broken down, Mr Tomkin,' came the electronically filtered reply. 'Won't be long now.'

'Buses,' Tomkin said, readjusting his position. 'Christ, I haven't been on a bus in over thirty years.'

'Money'll do that to you,' Nicholas said blandly.

'The only thing that money does,' Tomkin said sharply, 'is

corrupt.'

Nicholas turned his head. 'Does that include you?'

'We're all susceptible; we all succumb. There're no exceptions, none at all. In that respect, money's the great leveller. It makes fools of us all.' He barked a laugh. 'All those assholes who tell you that money hasn't changed 'em are full of shit. Of course it has. They just like to stare at illusions they build for themselves. As for me, I'm a realist. I take the drawbacks and accept them. Everything has its price tag – you just gotta make sure you got enough to pay.

'Now take my late wife, for example. Jesus, there was a woman who knew sure as hell what she wanted only she didn't have the guts to come to grips with what went along with it. People like her, they piss me off no end, 'cause all they want is to stand and squat in a stream all day long while someone comes and wipes their asses for them three times a day. You think they ever heard of the word *responsibility*? Not a chance.'

They began to move now and the limo slid to a stop at the far corner where Wolf's Delicatessen stood.

'Come on,' Tomkin said. 'I don't know about you but I can't wait to taste a Number One Combination.'

Behind them, in the limo, the second bug, perfectly hidden under the carpet, remained undetected and undisturbed.


'You're not impressed?'

'It seems like a lot of space for one person.'

'I'm claustrophobic.'

Croaker laughed. 'Yeah, well. I could see where you wouldn't be in this place.' He came back from the windows overlooking the East River and Queens. His fingers stroked the butter-soft leather of the brown couch.

'Beautiful,' he murmured.

'It gets a lot of attention.' Her topaz eyes regarded him playfully. 'Why, Lieutenant, I believe you're blushing. Don't tell me you've never met anyone of my profession before – that would be too much to swallow.'

He groaned at the deliberate *double entendre*. 'Do you always talk like that?'

'Only when I'm – only occasionally.' He wondered what she

had been going to say. 'Hey, I'm hungry.' Immediately her face fell. 'But, oh, there's nothing here –'

'That's okay, I've got to –'

'Oh, don't go. Please. Not yet, anyway.' She crossed the room to the phone. 'You deserve some time off – at least to eat. And they know where to reach you if something really hot comes up.'

Yeah, he thought. Like the address of the lady who'll nail your old man to the bathroom wall. He felt immediately embarrassed and wondered why. He'd never felt that way before.

Gelda had her ear to the receiver, was saying, 'I'll order us up some food. How about Italian? Do you like Italian food? I love it.'

'Okay. Fine.'

She nodded, dialled a number, waited a moment. 'Philip,' she said. 'It's G. Yeah, fine. What about you? You sure? You sound a little funny. No? Hey, how'd you like to get me some food. Mario's, yeah. For two. You know what. Okay. 'Bye.' She turned round.

'Who's Philip?' he asked. 'Not a runner or something stupid like that? You wouldn't do something like that to me, would you?'

'Don't worry. No. He's just a kid who hangs around. Does stuff for some – of us.' She saw the look on his face. 'Cut it out. He's got no family but us. We all love him and he knows it. Is that monstrous?'

He smiled. 'Sounds all right.' He moved round to the front of the couch, sat down. 'Feels nice.'

She followed him, said when she was very close, standing over him, 'You should feel it without clothes on.'

He gave a slightly uncomfortable laugh.

Gelda walked towards the bedroom doorway. She began to take off her silk blouse. Before she had disappeared through the doorway, he had seen the flawless expanse of her naked back. Despite the fullness of her breasts, she wore no bra.

'What are you doing?' He got up from the couch, stood uneasily with his hands in his pockets.

'Just changing.' He heard her voice drift back to him. 'Don't worry, I won't attack you.'

'I wasn't thinking of that,' he said not quite honestly.

'Good.'

He heard the sensuous rustle of silk against firm flesh.

'Do you want to come in,' she said, 'so I can see you while we talk?'

'I'm all right out here.' He felt like a schoolboy on his first real date.

'Listen,' she said, 'you've seen my mind. I can't imagine what would embarrass you about seeing my body.'

'Nothing,' he said automatically.

'All right, then.'

He stood where he was for a moment, feeling an outsider in this plush yet intimate landscape. In his mind, he tried to summon up clear images of what she did here but he could find nothing. He had an active imagination; at the moment it had shut down entirely.

He walked to the doorway, stood looking in on the threshold, a *voyeur* at his first peep-hole.

She stood with one leg up on the bedspread, putting on a stocking. A stocking, he thought, not panty hose. The perfect foot was dark, the flesh shining through the silk mesh so that the black was made pale, an altogether new colour. The toes indented the spread as if she had stepped along the crest of a sand-dune. Her legs seemed endless.

She wore bikini panties, a girdle, both flesh-coloured, soft and lacy. Otherwise, she was nude. The effect was startling.

She twisted her head over her shoulder to look at him. Her topaz eyes were very light. She smiled ingenuously. 'There.' The voice was but a wisp. 'That wasn't so bad, was it?'

'I wish you'd put on some clothes.'

She walked across the room. He tried not to stare at the movement of her breasts at each step but he had given himself an impossible task. When she reached the wardrobe she raised her arms and his temperature at the same time. She drew out a forest-green satin robe, came towards him. 'Is that better, Lew – I *can* call you Lew? After all, I threw up all over you in the van; I ought to be able to call you by your first name. At the very least.' She brushed by him, went into the living-room with the ghost of a smile.

He detached himself from the doorjamb, wondering what he

352

was doing still here; always on the job, that's me, he thought. But what was really on his mind was his dark apartment crouching as deserted as Wall Street at a week-end waiting for him to return. Going home to that seemed as out of the question as when it had been filled with Alison's scent.

'Should we go to bed now or after the food gets here?' He could not quite keep the anger out of his voice. There was a degree of control he felt had abandoned him some time when his attention had been elsewhere.

Gelda turned in the middle of the room. Her belted robe opened as if on cue and he saw the gleaming length of one leg. 'Is that what you think?' She was still smiling softly, like the gentle glow from a heavily shaded lamp.

'It's obvious, isn't it?'

'Is it?' One eyebrow arched. 'You know my sexual preference.'

Of course, he had forgotten. Deliberately? He felt an idiot. He put his hands in his pockets again, turned away too embarrassed to apologize. Mental sets, he thought savagely. Isn't it odd how the eyes see one thing and the mind – that great complex monstrosity – makes leaps of illogicality to form conclusions. He felt, abruptly, just as he had that scorching summer's day in Hell's Kitchen when not even the turned-on hydrants helped, when the steaming air hung like layers of blankets your well-meaning but misguided mother had wrapped you in when sick, impossible to take off. Tempers were short and incendiary as if everyone had an itch they couldn't scratch.

The cry came through the wide-open window and he was racing down the dark narrow stairs and into the baking sunshine. Just two doors away, he lay in the alley, his uniform dark with sweat and blood. Trash cans lay tumbled around him, having divulged their slimy secrets as if in one last paroxysm. The grey eyes were open and already glazing; eyes that had always reminded him of a storm-tossed sky. Gentle eyes.

So this was how it ended for Martin Croaker. After twenty-nine years on the New York City Police Force, lying sprawled in an alley piled high with garbage, surrounded by summer stink, fearful rats and incurious roaches, the wail of sirens forlorn in the distance, closing, shot four times forty feet from his own home.

He stared down at the corpse of his father and the world had spun around, canted dangerously on its axis. He felt that, at any moment, its momentum and crazy angle would combine to throw him off.

That's what he wanted, of course, to run far, far away from this stinking hole; never to return. Never.

But that was the easy way out; the coward's way. Not Lew Croaker's way. His father had taught him too well.

So he stayed on. To join the police. Old and grey, his mother had come to his Academy graduation and had cried as he was sworn in.

He had never found the man responsible for his father's death but, after a time, that pain, too, had been put to rest.

He felt her touch his arm; he hadn't realized the wound was still sensitive. After all this time.

'I'm sorry,' she said. 'I shouldn't have teased you. I was just ...'

'What? You were just what?'

Her eyes lowered. 'Happy to be with you.' She tried to make a half joke out of it, failed. 'You make me feel ...'

'What?'

She looked up. 'Just feel.'

He felt torn. 'I bet you could do that and not feel a thing.'

She nodded. 'I could. I'm an actress, of course. Do you distrust me? You couldn't. Not after what you said to me in the van. You took an enormous chance, telling me what you suspect about my father. It was an idiotic thing to do.'

'That's me. Always the idiot.'

'Yes.' Her voice was as soft as silk.

'You know, you could sell me anything.' He said it defensively, because she was so close. He wanted her to know he knew. He felt he needed that precaution now.

'No,' she said, 'I couldn't. Not now, anyway.' She put her fingers along his arm; they seemed very warm. 'The challenge, for myself, is to be honest with you. It's what will make me happy.'

There came the sound of muted chimes.

She disengaged herself from him, disappeared into the old-

fashioned foyer. Her voice floating, 'Hi, darling. Come on in.'
Returning with her arm around a rather tall boy, dark-haired,
almond-eyed. Philip. Croaker turned his back on the proceed-
ings, stared out at the dazzle of the water. A long barge laden
with garbage wallowed slowly up-river, a tug at its side. A man
in a red and white track suit was jogging along the promenade.
He passed the barge, going the other way, and disappeared
from view. He and Gelda in bed – flash of flesh against flesh.

'What happened to you, darling? Your face looks awful.'

Her voice was like the background chatter of a TV left on
at low volume. He wanted that call to come in so bad he could
taste it: the satisfaction of putting a bastard like Tomkin away
for twenty years.

'What in God's name happened to you, darling? You look
like you've been in a fight.'

'No fight, G.'

'Well, what then?'

'Nothing. I fell down ...'

There was a sailboat out there – can you imagine? In the
middle of the goddamned week. The sail white against the
patchwork colours of the buildings on the far shore, scudding
along as effortlessly as a cloud. No pressure out there on the
river, just the wind and the salt spray and a long way until you
reach port. Your own master. Her breasts heavy in his hands;
her lips parting.

'... in an alley. The garbage cans –'

'Don't be an idiot, Philip. And don't lie to me. Darling, you
must tell me what happened. Here, let me put some ice on it –
do as I say.' A soft clatter. 'There.'

There would be time, after Tomkin was put away, to take
some time off. Go to the sea as Melville did when he was sick at
heart and he felt like screaming at anyone who came too close.
Yes, the sea. Not to fish; he hated fishing. But to sail, perhaps.
He'd never done that and it might be time now to try it. Try
her.

'At Ah Ma's – I worked there last night.'

'Well, she'd never do that to you.'

'No. A man –'

'A bastard, that's what. Here, keep the ice on for a little

longer. I forbid you to go there again.'

'But the man is coming here again tonight. She wants to be there –'

'I don't care *what* Ah Ma wants, you're not going. She'll have to learn to do without you.'

'It won't be any good without me.'

'What do you mean?'

'The man wants me. That's how he – ejaculates. I said that right, didn't I?'

'My God – who is this man?'

'I don't know. A Japanese. A very strange man. Eyes like dead stones – you know, like he was from another world.'

But Croaker was already turning, his face flushed with the adrenalin building in his body. 'Talk to me, Philip,' he said slowly and carefully, masking his excitement. 'Tell me about the Japanese with eyes like dead stones.'

Croaker was waiting for them at the tower's Park Avenue side. His big figure was leaning negligently against the side of his unmarked sedan. The detachable red light revolved atop the car, piercing the long twilight's sapphire haze like a lighthouse beacon's unerring warning.

Nicholas emerged from the limo as soon as it pulled over to the kerb just to the uptown side of Croaker. As he went quickly towards the detective, he was acutely aware of Tomkin's presence blooming behind him as Tom, the thin chauffeur, held the heavy door open.

He was aware, too, of the city around him, everything shrouded in blue. The sun was just a memory but its heat refused to leave the asphalt under his shoe soles. The atmosphere was thick with exhaust fumes. The strings of dull yellow cabs along both sides of the avenue seemed like streaming caravans entering and leaving the bowels of the gilt-edged Helmsley Building.

'How's your boss?' Croaker's voice was flat and hard and unyielding; he stared past Nicholas's right shoulder.

Nicholas, feeling the live-wire buildup of tension, said, 'Leave it alone, Lew. Forget about –'

'Too late for that, buddy.'

He felt the presence directly behind him even before he heard

Tomkin's voice say, 'Still patrolling the streets, I see, Lieutenant. Keeping New York safe for us citizens?' The note of sarcasm was unmistakable.

'This city's still dangerous for some,' Croaker said pointedly.

'What the hell's that supposed to mean?'

'Figure it out for yourself, Tomkin.'

'I don't like veiled threats, Lieutenant. Not from anyone. Perhaps I should have another talk with the commissioner and –'

'I knew it was you, you dirty –'

'–we'll see how long you remain a lieutenant –'

'–reassigned now to this case Nicholas was hired for, so I guess we'll be seeing a lot of each other.'

'What?'

There was a malicious grin on his face now, his skin alternately lighter and darker yellow, with the wash of passing headlights from the traffic flow.

Brake lights turned Tomkin's face reddish. 'My God, I won't be saddled with you again!'

'Nothing you can do about it now, I'm afraid. The transfer came down directly from the commissioner himself. Even you won't get him to change that order. He'd look far too foolish, scurrying to rescind a reassignment.'

'Christ, haven't I had enough of you already? You've hounded me about –'

'I'm only here to protect you,' Croaker pointed out, 'and to nail the ninja before he gets you.'

Tomkin's eyes narrowed. The peculiar monochromatic light had washed out all colour from his eyes; they looked oddly pale. 'Wouldn't you just love to sit back and let him do your dirty work? Sure, sure. You could say, "Well, I'm sorry, Captain, but I did my best. I got beaten, is all. Can't blame me for that."'

'Listen, you bastard' – Croaker lunged forward, trying to get around Nicholas's body – 'I do my job better than anyone else in this creepy city and if that means making sure you don't buy it, I'll do it. When I nail you, buddy, it's gonna be for the same reasons –'

'What reasons?' Tomkin snarled. 'You got nothing –'

'No, but I will have,' Croaker shouted. 'And when I do, I'll be coming for you with a warrant that'll stand up to any of your high-priced attorneys!'

'You've got nothing,' Tomkin sneered, 'and you'll get nothing. I was nowhere near Angela Didion the night she was murdered. There's nothing linking me to –'

They were pushing and shoving now. Nicholas heard swift reports on the asphalt as sharp as rifle shots as Tom headed their way. He shouldered the two roughly apart, said, 'Knock it off, both of you.'

Then Tom had hold of his boss and was pulling at him. Tomkin allowed himself to be drawn away from the confrontation but lifted a finger, swung it in the air in Croaker's direction. 'I'm warning you,' he cried, 'this is harassment. I don't want you near me!' And then, lowering his voice, he said to Nicholas, 'He's after me. I don't know why. It's a vendetta. I've done nothing, Nick. What's he doing to me?' He turned away abruptly, walked silently back to the limo with Tom at his side casting a worried glance or two over his shoulder. The revolving red lights played on their backs intermittently.

'Well, that was pretty stupid,' Nicholas said, turning round.

'Oh, who gives a fuck? What are you, my nanny? Jesus!' Croaker disappeared into the car.

Nicholas went slowly around to the passenger's side. He took his time climbing in. Croaker stared fixedly out through the windshield.

'Sorry,' he said, after a time. And then, 'That bastard really boils my blood.'

'The antagonism isn't going to make anything easier.'

Croaker turned his head; looked at Nicholas for the first time since he had got in the car. 'You know, I worry about you, Nick, I really do.' Their reflections in the windshield like a neon sign, blinking on and off in the backwash of traffic headlights, a product advertisement. 'You're a man who never loses control. Don't you ever get angry? Or sad?'

Nicholas thought about Justine. He wanted to see her now, to talk to her more than anything.

'Because I feel sorry for you if you don't.'

'No cause to worry,' he said softly. 'I'm as human as the next person. All too human.'

358

'Hey, you know I'd swear you're making that sound like a liability. We're all born into it, buddy.'

'But me,' he said. 'I grew up thinking there was no room to make a mistake; that it was some kind of failure if I did.'

'But you made them –'

'Oh, yeah.' Nicholas laughed softly, without humour. 'I made plenty of them, especially when it came to women. I trusted when I shouldn't have; now I guess I'm afraid to try it again.'

'Justine?'

'Yeah. We had a heavy row. It's mostly my fault, I see now.'

'You know what I think, buddy?' Croaker said, starting the engine.

'What?'

'I think the problem's not with you and Justine but in the past. What's so wrong in trusting someone? Like I said, we all do it. Sometimes it pays off and sometimes ...' He shrugged. 'But what the hell, right? It's worse never to trust anyone.' He put the car in gear and they edged past Tomkin's limo, pulling over to the left to make the U-turn downtown.

The flood was coming, Nicholas knew. His face was awash in yellow and red, blue in the shadows between light sweeps. The *tsunami*, his personal tidal wave, was roaring blackly just behind him, looming over the world. The past will never die, he thought. Pain surged inside him, threatening to engulf him. All the bitter days, hanging like frost on the ledges of his soul, were returning again despite his careful compartmentalizing; the agony returning like a dull river of lead, climbing through him once more. He lacked the strength to push the memories away any more.

Come! he thought savagely. Here I am; let it happen.

But before the *tsunami* hit, he heard Croaker saying triumphantly, 'But cheer up. We got a break. We may not know who this ninja is but I know where he's gonna be at exactly 11 p.m. tonight.

'We're gonna be there, buddy, waiting. You and me and two blue-and-white backup units. We're gonna nail this bastard before he even gets a chance to get to Raphael Tomkin.'

# II

## *Osaka/Shimonoseki/Kumamoto/Tokyo Suburbs, Winter 1963*

At this time of the year the countryside was bleak and pale. The searingly spectacular deep reds and oranges of the autumnal foliage had already faded, dropped away to dull brown mulch under animals' hooves, and the first snow had obstinately yet to fall to leave the sere land hidden beneath its crisp albescence.

Rolling by rail under a low sky full of incipient rain reminding him of a child's face full of an emotion unacknowledged, it seemed sad to see the lines of bare trees like rough wire approximations of next year's model in among the eternal dark green of the sentinel pines. So forlorn, almost as if God had, after much effort, at last given up on this part of the world.

Nicholas allowed his eyes to focus on the far horizon. The speed blur of the landscape passing closer to hand became dizzying, a brown-black sensation of being whirled about on a funfair ride. Yukio, leaning half across him to get a better glimpse, pressed the side of one hard breast against him. Fingers spread on his thigh to brace herself against the rocking. Nails digging in, giving her purchase. Warmth spread upwards into his groin and he wondered, half-afraid, half-expectant, if her hand would move up with it to cup him.

Opposite, on a seat facing them, a Japanese businessman in a dark-coloured pinstripe and a scrubbed face, calfskin attaché case placed carefully on the seat beside him as mute company, surmounted by a charcoal-grey cashmere overcoat folded meticulously and, atop that, like the miniature couple on a white wedding cake, a black bowler hat – in all, an arcane archaeological pyramid offering no ancestral clues – glanced up from reading the paper. His eyes were given an unnatural size and annularity by his thick round glasses. He blinked much as a fish might upon encountering an unexpected foreign object close to hand. Was he staring at the proximity of her fingertips to his crotch before he returned to his reading? The paper rustled slightly. It might have been a brick wall.

Nicholas could see the flash of reflected light from the curving edge of the thick gold ring. He imagined the man to be an important member of the *zaibatsu*. But which one, he wondered? Mitsubishi, perhaps? Or Sumitomo or Mitsui? Not one of the groups, surely, Fuyo, Sanwa, Dai-Ichi Kangyō. Of the seven lesser konzerns, he was obviously not from Nippon Steel, Toyota or Nissan. No, he had the look about him of the burgeoning electronics firms like Tōshiba-IHI, Matsushita, Hitachi – on second thoughts, scratch Hitachi – or Tōkyū. Did Tōkyū manufacture electronics, come to think of it? He wasn't all that certain.

Perhaps this man's family had started Mitsubishi – the families, he knew, were back-running the *zaibatsu* as they had since the beginning. The American laws that had forced a hiatus had been stricken after only a brief term.

Nicholas stared at the paper barrier as if he had X-ray vision. He could see in his mind the round yellow face, slightly burnished with a light film of sweat, and, below it, the perfect collar white as snow, stiff and starched, the thin dark silk tie the colour of the midnight sky. Here was a symbol of the new Japan: the painful climb out of the stone-age isolationism – oddly, still more pressing than the much more recent war – the human memory is so deliberately and depressingly selective. Adopting the Western mode of dress was just one manifestation of the Japanese cultural drive to catch up with the West. As monomaniacal as Tojo still. Or MacArthur. Our saviour.

Parity was already a fact in Japan and the country was gearing itself up for overdrive, for the great push to surpass those countries from which it had learned. And there would come a day now, Nicholas was convinced, when the Japanese, having proved his economic strength, would shed his Western appurtenances, returning in re-won security to the traditional kimono, robes of state.

They were on the fast train – the express – from Tokyo to Osaka. Out of the window on their right was all of the width of Honshu, the main island. On the other side they could see from time to time the glintings of the sea, throwing bright golden reflections in abstract patterns across the car's ceiling. The vibration from the rails was minimal, as was the noise on this sleek blue and silver liner, quiet, spacious and serene.

Yukio sat back in the seat, linked her arm through his. 'Why don't we stay overnight in Osaka?' she suggested and then, as if in explanation, 'I hate trains.'

Nicholas thought about that. Perhaps it wasn't such a bad idea. The night life there was bright and glossy and he needed cheering up right now.

The little bit of clandestine cloak-and-dagger that Yukio and he had concocted regarding Saigō – he had quite conveniently forgotten whose suggestion it had been – had proved unnecessary. Astoundingly, before she had even had a chance to leave for the dinner at Satsugai's house, where she was to take a peek at Saigō's ticket destination, a note had been delivered to Nicholas. It was in Saigō's hand and it invited him to come to a town called Kumamoto in Kyūshū for a visit during the next few weeks. No reason was given for the invitation. Like everything in Saigō's life, this, too, was meant to be secretive.

Nicholas had read the note with a mounting sense of deflation. Irrationally, he felt as if Saigō had somehow read his mind and he could not throw off the anticipatory overtones the words set off in him, like a far-off bell tolling from some fog-shrouded hillside. 'This will all be unexplored territory,' Kansatsu had said to him, 'if you decide it's what you want. It is totally your decision to make, Nicholas. I cannot guide you. Only say that here you can go no further. For that you must look to the darkness – and the light.' Squelched, his plan had been cruelly revealed as just so much juvenile fantasy and, instead of thinking about why he had been asked south, he made himself busy feeling unhappy, defeated. And to make matters worse, Yukio went to dinner at Satsugai's anyway.

Mountains reared silently through the perspex window, blue-grey, ragged with streaks of snow running down from their summits like spilt cream. One of the three ranges of Alps – the most southerly, headed by Mount Shirane – passed like a cincture about Honshu's waist. Where was he headed now, he wondered. Into the light or the darkness? Did it matter?

'Especially this one,' Yukio said as if there had been no space of silence between. 'I hate this one. All the wide seats, the chrome trim, the bigger windows don't mean a thing to me. It's worse on this one. Because of the silence. The silence makes me restless.' She made a face. 'My foot's asleep.' She shifted, stretching out legs on which she had been sitting. The businessman across the way rattled his paper, peals of warning.

'All right,' Nicholas said. 'Yes.' There seemed no good reason to rush headlong into Kumamoto. Anyway, he'd only been to Osaka once when he was much younger and he was curious to see how much it had changed. Would he recognize it? He thought not.

He felt Yukio's presence close and warm beside him and he wondered if it had been intelligent to take her. In truth it had not been his idea. But after making his decision to accept Saigō's summons, it had proved quite impossible to deflect her. 'It was you, after all,' she had said in her most persuasively accusatory tone, 'who got me involved in this in the first place.' He couldn't recall whether or not that was so. 'It's only fair you take me along now.' She had flung her head back defiantly, sensually – but then, even in anger, she was superbly sensual. 'Besides, if you don't, I'll only come with you on my own. Do you think you could hide from me?' He thought not. Decidedly un-Japanese, he had said to himself while acquiescing. Did the Colonel give in to Cheong in this way?

He often trembled when she was so close to him, his muscles jumping and twitching quite beyond his control. He sometimes clandestinely watched this phenomenon as if he were an outsider. This helped stymie the feelings of terror that rose, fluttering like leathery bats, from the pit of his stomach, rising towards his head. This he knew he must not allow to happen, otherwise he felt he might go mad. She passed a hand across his flesh and thus stirred that hidden pool at the core of his being which he had, for a time, thought closed even to himself. It remained inaccessible to him.

Mr Mitsubishi, face glossy as a horse's hide after a canter, had put his paper down, folding it lengthwise. He proceeded to destroy the pyramid beside him, opening his attaché case, closing it again. On its spotless top he unfolded waxed paper in which was a chicken sandwich. Light lanced from his round glasses as he ate, turning him blind for moments at a time. Perhaps somewhere, Nicholas thought, he had a small bag of crisps or a bar of chocolate.

Behind him, a group of Japanese businessmen, in all respects identical to Mr Mitsubishi, rustled inside their dark three-piece suits like chrysaline insects, black bowlers on their laps, chattering animatedly about the two Jacks, Ruby and Kennedy.

One did not travel to Osaka for culture – one went to Kyoto, the country's original capital, for that. It was commonly said – mostly by the inhabitants of Tokyo – that Osakans were money-mad businessmen, greeting each other on crowded street corners with the all-too-familiar phrase *'Mō kari makka?'* Making any money?

Nicholas had little first-hand knowledge of such affairs yet it was true that secreted along the city's riotous streets, like tiny pockets of the past encysted within the neon age, were numerous shrines to Fudō-miyō-ō, the deity overseeing such matters as concerned the dedicated businessman. These shrines never seemed to lack for attention.

He took them to a smallish modern hotel not far from the Dōtombori where they checked into separate but adjoining rooms. It being still too early for dinner, they immediately set out to see the city.

Yukio insisted on seeing Osaka Castle, that last bastion of refuge of the Toyotomi family, besieged by Ieyasu Tokugawa after he had already assumed the mantle of Shōgun in 1603. It had been erected by Hideoshi Toyotomi – as had much of Osaka – and was completed within three years, in 1586.

'There was a time,' Yukio said as they strolled through the park, bordered at their backs by the modern Osakan skyline, 'when the Lady Yodogimi was my ideal.' The castle loomed through the lowering afternoon, seeming larger than life, a squat pagoda, stolid and boxlike. It was not, Nicholas reflected, the kind of structure that Ieyasu would have had built.

The crowds grew in size as they approached the castle's outward fortifications. 'What I thought was so ... special ... was how she carried on the will of Hideoshi, even after his death, just as if she were a samurai herself. She devoted herself totally to the safety of the heir.'

'Oh yes,' Nicholas said. 'Yes.' They had reached the first of the stonework, massive and hulking in the lengthening shadows. 'To the detriment of the rest of the country. She and Mitsunari plotted –'

'They *plotted* – as you choose to put it – to protect the Shōgun's son. They did what honour dictated.'

Nicholas shook his head from side to side. 'Yukio, Yodogimi was the Shōgun's mistress, not his legal wife. Her aspirations were a bit grandiose.' He waved a hand as if in dismissal. 'In any event, Ieyasu proved a far too potent foe for them.' He stopped.

'You talk as if Yodogimi was some kind of villain in some children's story-book.'

'Well, she hardly had the best interests of Japan in mind, you must admit that.'

'Perhaps the child would have grown up to be this country's finest leader.'

Nicholas looked past her. To their left was a small shedlike structure. The arms house. It was here that Yodogimi had brought her son and their retainers when the end had become inevitable; it was here she took her son's life before committing *seppuku*. 'That's all rather irrelevant, don't you think? In the years it would have taken him to come of age, without one *daimyo* strong enough to become Shōgun and lead Japan, the country would have been plunged again into the civil war from which Hideoshi had saved it. Without Ieyasu's strength, Japan would have been doomed.'

'Still, such a brave woman. Loyal and brave.' Yukio's voice might have been the whisper of the wind. 'So selfless.' She watched the parade of tourists before the shed. 'I admire her so much.'

Hidden, the sun slid downwards to the earth as if too heavy to sustain its own weight. The sky was like grey ribbons fluttering across an excited girl's breast, parting at the soft advance of her lover. There was a brief flash of gold, stonework in flickering torchlight, then it was gone.

'Come on,' he said, taking her hand. 'Onwards and upwards.'

Of course, the original Osaka Castle had been razed in 1615, when it had been overrun by the forces of the Tokugawa; a structure previously regarded as impregnable. This one they strode had been constructed of ferro-concrete in 1931.

Nightside. Along the Dōtombori, jammed with restaurants, shops, news-stands, movie theatres, nightclubs, restless crowds and, above all, the vast spotlit signs glittering in the night, pushing the darkness away as if it held no dominion here. Colours spun, neon lights blinking on, off, on in time to the heartbeat of the shifting traffic.

Time seemed suspended here, as if in a dream these dazzling coloured lights, celebrants of power, called here to summit, would brook no outside interference even from such a basic concept.

A great replica of a crab, crimson and white, its spiny carapace gleaming, so many centred spots focused upon it the light seemed to drip from it like honey, hung over them, a temptation to enter and eat the night away.

They dined in a place of glossy emerald-green lacquered wood and thick bars of mirror-bright chrome as incandescent as neon tubing, replicating portions of their faces as they moved. In a private tatami room, shoeless, stuffing themselves with sashimi and *sake* – did they both appear so much older? – she would not let him forget the castle's awesome history or its daunting inhabitants.

'I suppose I adore her because I am so little like her.' She poured more rice wine with a steady hand.

'Meaning?'

She met his gaze for a moment before her eyes slid away. 'I'm not loyal and I'm not in the least brave. I am only Japanese.' She gave a tiny deprecatory shrug. 'I am a Japanese coward. No one is interested in that. A Japanese without any family: therefore without loyalty.'

'You forget your uncle.'

'No.' She shook her head; her black hair gleamed in the low light. 'I don't forget him. Ever.'

'He's family.'

Her eyes flashed. 'Must everything be spelled out for you? I hate Satsugai. How would you feel about an uncle who would not have you with him, who put you into the hands of –' She swallowed *sake* convulsively.

'One day,' he said, eyes on his plate, 'you will find someone. Fall in love.'

'No loyalty, remember?' Her voice held a tinge of bitterness. 'I was born without it just as I was born without the capacity to love. They are alien concepts to me.'

'Because you think that sex is the only thing you have.'

'The only thing that makes me happy,' she corrected.

He looked up. 'Don't you see that's just because you think of yourself as worthless?' He reached out, covered her hand with his. 'What you really can't conceive of is anyone caring about you – I mean you as a person, not wanting to be with you because of what you can do with your body.'

'You're being an idiot.' But she did not take her hand away and this time she did not look away either.

'If that's what you choose to call it.'

'I do. I have no trust. Truly. Can't you just accept me for what I am? You can't make me over.'

'It's not a question of that. I want what I feel is inside you to have a chance to come out –'

'Oh, Nicholas' – she put her fingers against his cheek – 'why torture yourself by thinking about some future that will not come about. Who knows? I may be dead in a year –'

'Shut up,' he said quickly. 'I don't want to hear you talking like that, understand?'

'Yes,' she said, surprisingly meekly. Her head dipped as if in penance and her thick hair slid across one side of her face like a midnight waterfall. She was the model Japanese wife bowing before the inevitable authority of her husband's words.

'And anyway, who says you're not brave?' He wasn't used to this. He wanted desperately to lean over the table and kiss her half-open shadowed lips, but lacked the nerve. 'Just think of what you've been through, growing up with that couple. That took a lot of strength.'

'You think so?' A little girl now.

The waitress rustled in and knelt by the side of the low table, delivering more food and drink. Nicholas watched her leave as she slipped on her *geta* at the threshold.

'I just said so,' he whispered fiercely. 'What's the matter with you?'

'I don't know.' Dark eyes on the tabletop. 'I don't know.'

He filled her porcelain *sake* cup, white and tiny.

They went out walking, she chattering on animatedly as if nothing untoward had happened, clutching his arm, aimlessly drifting from topic to topic.

Stealing the dark, hiding it in their side pockets as they filtered through the honky-tonk night life, through swirling colours and blaring noise. The air smelt of incense and petrol fumes, the walls of the evening brilliant with the unrelenting marquees here in the city of merchants, erected almost overnight, this new class universally despised by the noble samurai and the lowly peasant alike.

An enormous arcade of pinball wizards they passed up after staring for long moments like the most ignorant of country bumpkins and, farther along, the electronicized insistency of American rock 'n' roll, a quicksilver pulse projecting from a music store's loudspeaker. The wail of harmonized black voices drenched by a wave of strings and the backbeat, always the backbeat like a burnished path guiding you through the melodies. They dance before the lighted window on which is taped a black and white publicity photo, streaked by reflected light: John, Paul, George, Ringo. *Close your eyes and I'll kiss you/ Tomorrow I'll miss you/Remember I'll always be true* ... Around and around. *And then while I'm away/I'll write home every day* ... Red and green and yellow neon bars, swinging her from one to the other; a rock 'n' roll fan overnight. *And I'll send all my loving to you* ...

'Who are they?' says Yukio, slightly out of breath.

'The Beatles,' says the shopkeeper. 'A new band from England.'

And Nicholas buys her the record, imported and exorbitant.

But down the next block they heard the stentorian tones and the intermittent music of the *samisan*. Culture shock. And turned in to investigate.

It was the Bunraku, the traditional puppet theatre, indigenous to Osaka, as the Kabuki was to old Edo. Yukio was delighted and, clapping her hands together as if she were a child, implored him to take her inside. He dug into his pocket, bought them two tickets.

The theatre was nearly full and they had some difficulty finding their seats. The play had just begun but Nicholas knew from the billboards outside that it was famed *Chūshingura*, 'The Loyal Forty-Seven *Ronin*'.

The puppets were magnificent, the principal ones dazzlingly dressed, so complex that they required three men to manipulate them successfully. The master puppeteer for the head, body and right arm, a second for the left arm and the third for the legs or, in the case of the females, the kimono skirts.

They were seated near the back and, some time after they arrived, a couple of marines drifted in. Why they had come to the Bunraku on leave Nicholas could not imagine. One was white, the other black. They might have been waiting for their girls or, perhaps, a third buddy. The white man slid into a row but the black marine turned, stood waiting in the centre aisle.

Nicholas saw Yukio's eyes drifting from the colour of the stage. He saw where she was looking. Like a retriever on point, her gaze locked on the large bulge of his crotch. Colours swam in reflected light, reminding Nicholas of an aquarium his parents had taken him to in Tokyo. It all seemed so unreal. Her lips slightly open, he saw the sharp rise and fall of her breasts as she breathed, as she watched.

In the dimness he felt her fingers between his thighs, caressing, the zipper of his fly being drawn down, the heat enveloping him. Hard. And still she stared, never turning her head, her eyes wide and glittery. His loins turned to water. He wanted to shout to her: *Stop!* But he could not. Had she blinked in all this time? He wanted to take her fingers away from him but he did not. Just sat there watching the Bunraku, the black marine's crotch in the periphery of his vision, ballooning ominously. How big was he? How big could a man be? Was that a criterion for sex appeal, the way Americans felt about big breasts? Did it drive women wild?

The *samisan* played on. The *ronin* fought with proper valour. Yeah, yeah. *Yeah!*

*

'You know what it is I hate about being Japanese?' she said. Streetlight, blue-white through the blinds, threw angular bars of light-shadow-light across the top of the far wall and part of the ceiling.

He turned in the bed. 'What?'

'Not having light eyes.' She sighed and he knew her wide, sensual lips were drawn in a pout. 'The French girls I see in Kyoto and the American ones, too, with their short hairdos and their blue eyes. Funny, I've always dreamed of having green eyes like emeralds.'

'Why think about it?'

'It makes me realize, I think, just how much I dislike myself. Here' – she reached out, took his hand in hers, guided it to the heat between her legs – 'this is the only thing that matters. Right here.'

'No,' he said, taking his fingers away, 'that's not important at all.'

She turned on her side; her voice was light now. 'Not even a little bit?'

He laughed. 'All right, yes. Just a bit, then.' He rose up, leaning over her slightly. Her skin was pale in the half-light, her thick hair a black forest. 'Look, Yukio, I was interested in you before we danced that night.'

'Before I –'

'Rubbed yourself all over me.'

She put her hand out, lightly stroking his chest. A muscle fluttered and he felt the familiar tightening of his stomach. It felt as if a hand were pressing against his lungs, pushing powerfully down so that he had difficulty in breathing. He might have been an asthmatic in fog.

'What is it?' she said just before he whirled away to sit on the edge of the bed. 'What are you afraid of?' she sat up and he felt her looking at him. An odd way to put it. 'Is it me, Nicholas? Are you afraid of me?'

'I don't know,' he said miserably.

And that was the trouble.


They left Osaka on an old pre-war train which, despite its perfect cleanliness, was in marked contrast with the superliner that had brought them to the city.

There were rattles, squeaks and a fair amount of jounces. The swaying, too, was more pronounced but, oddly, the added vibration produced in him a calming effect. His mind kept returning to the Bunraku performance; to, more accurately, Yukio's performance. Was she a nymphomaniac, he wondered? But how could he tell? He did not even know the clinical definition. Was someone who was sexually insatiable a nympho? Could it be that easy to define? He couldn't even say that Yukio was insatiable. Her sexual thirst *could* be slaked. It just took an enormous amount of energy. And, anyway, what if she was? Would that make any difference to him?

He turned away from her presence, staring out of the window. Rattle, rattle. Someone came down the aisle, half fell against her as the train lurched around a turning. The land fell away in a sharp gradient here, giving onto flat fields and rice paddies. He thought he saw cattle standing motionless in the distance. In less than an hour the tracks would turn south-east towards the sea.

The day was bright, the sun burning away the white ground fog by late morning.

Kobe, along with Yokohama, the busiest port in Japan, was already far behind them, with its scores of freighters and its international settlement comprising fully a quarter of the city's population.

We're well away from there, Nicholas thought. Such strictly business-oriented places, like parts of downtown Tokyo, made him nervous. Like airports, they all had a frightening similarity that cut across language and even race. He never knew where he was in airports – he could be anywhere at all in the world and never know it. Railway stations, however, were quite different. Oddly enough, there were no two alike that he had seen and this kind of old-world individualism was comforting to him. Of course, on trains, one could look out of the window and see far more than just grey clouds like wisps of an old man's beard, parting like gossamer. What held the goddamned thing up, anyway?

He tore his eyes away from the ribboning land, glanced around the car. The passengers, too, on this train were different.

The last businessman had debarked at Kobe and now, all around him, he watched the people of the land. A man in blue overalls and thick-soled, high-topped shoes sat with his thickly calloused hands crossed over his lean belly, chin on his chest, legs stretched out, ankles crossed. He had very short hair which was white and a stiff-looking moustache which was black. A farm worker, perhaps, on his way home. Across the car, a fat woman in a bright white and crimson kimono slept peacefully with her mouth open and the breath hissing in and out. Beside her, a squat stack of brown-paper-wrapped parcels. Two kids in Western clothes knelt, arms and elbows along the seat top, making faces at anyone who passed.

'. . . in the back.'

'What?'

'Nicholas, have you been listening to me?'

'No. I'm sorry. I was thinking about the Bunraku.'

She laughed. 'You mean the way I jerked you off.'

'I don't understand,' he said, 'why you feel you have to talk like a sailor. Why, for example, must you say "fuck" instead of "make love"?'

'Because,' she answered seriously, ' "fuck" is exactly what I mean. Have you ever *made love*, Nicholas? tell me what it's like.'

'I make love to you.'

'What are you talking about? We *fuck* like bunnies.'

'I don't think that is what even you do.'

'Oh no?' Her tone rose slightly. 'Listen, Nicholas, I fuck you the way I fuck everyone else. You know what I do with you? Well, I do it with other men, too. With Saigō, for instance.' Now why did she bring him up? 'I come on the edge of his hand, against the instep of his foot, his tongue and his nose, his –'

'All right!' he cried. 'Enough! What the hell do you think you're doing?'

She rubbed herself against him, began to purr like a giant cat. 'Me? I'm just trying to get you excited, that's all. You weren't paying attention to me and I –'

'Jesus!' he said, getting up. 'Is that the way?' He went roughly past her, out into the aisle to the end of the car, stood watching through two sets of glass at the jouncing car behind his. Christ, he thought, did she think telling him about her past conquests would turn him on? What a twisted idea. He felt cold and slightly nauseated. He braced himself against the swaying with a stiff arm against the door frame.

On his right a town flashed by, becoming smaller as they pulled away towards the south-east. He glanced at his watch, calculating distances and speed. That should be Kurashiki. Good. They were but moments away from sighting the northern end of Seto Naikia, the Inland Sea, which he had always found so peaceful and calm during the summers his parents had taken him there as a child.

They plummeted through thick stands of tall gaunt pines, the car darkening abruptly and eerily as if they were in the midst of an eclipse. Then, just as swiftly, the sun broke through again and the foliage fell sharply away on the right, revealing the high bluff along which they raced. Below them, Seto Naikai, glittery with sunlight, dancing like ten thousand golden scimitars, a jewel field.

He watched, transfixed at the sight. But still. Part of his mind was in a film. This was the point when Yukio should come silently up behind him, put her arms around him and tell him she was sorry. This was no film and it never seemed to happen to him that way. And why should he expect it? He did, nevertheless. The eternal romantic.

Islands, so far from home, humpbacked and flat-faced, stretched one after another across the waters of the Inland Sea, all the way to the horizon. Was there really, as he had been told as a child, more land than water here? He could not say he had thought then that it did not matter. They looked like pieces of intricate knitting, these islands, terraced to make them productive; usable land was at a premium in Japan.

One day, he thought, I would like to spend my time just travelling from one island to another, talking to the people there, sitting down to eat with them after helping them in the terraced fields, spending a night here and there. I think that if I did that, I'd probably live out my life and die before I got to the last one. What an idea! Never to go back, only forwards. Each day different from the one before and the one after. Never to get tired; never to get bored. As he was now? Awfully young to feel this way, he mused. But he knew that he was not bored or tired but merely feeling the symptoms of each, hiding what he really felt.

Fear.

In Hiroshima it was a completely different story. In the bay, above which they passed like a wisp of smoke, they saw Miyajima, marked by the great orange and black *torii*, the gate of the Itsukushima Shrine. It was one of the most spectacular sights in all the islands, one of which he had seen many pictures but, until now, had never seen in person.

It hung there as if in mid-air, rising out of the tidal waters like a great three-dimensional cuneiform character written upon the world, mark of the old Japan, a warning never to forget the past.

The train seemed to stand, huffing, for a long time in the Hiroshima Station. All about them were the squat, ugly, industrial structures dominated by a kind of incandescent silence hanging in the air, as thin and brittle as the shell of a robin's egg.

The seat facing them, long vacant through the afternoon, was taken by a gaunt, spare man in a grey and brown kimono. His head was hairless save for a few wisps of white beard hanging from the point of his narrow chin. His skin seemed as translucent as parchment, stretched across high cheek-bones, but underneath his eyes and at the sides of his mouth one could see the masses of wrinkles like the vast accumulation of the years, an ancient tree whose age one could count by the number of rings in its flesh.

His eyes were bright chips as he nodded to them. His hands were lost within the folds of his formal robe.

Soon after, the train gave a little lurch and they began to move slowly out of the station. On the way out, the feeling of oppression only magnified as if all the air had been sucked away and what remained to breathe, if only they should open the window and stick their heads out, was the frosty vacuum of space. They might have been on another planet.

Nicholas felt a creeping in his flesh and he looked out of the window, upwards into the bright porcelain sky, certain he had heard the heavy drone of an airplane.

The train moved with unutterable slowness through the city. For a moment they could see, silhouetted against the near horizon, the shell of the old observatory, standing just as it had been left in 1945, its surmounting hemisphere a bird's-nest skeleton, a lonely, forbidding eyrie for the gulls that swooped low near it but would never touch its inimical skin. Perhaps even after all this time they could still feel the incendiary heat, the hissed outpouring of radiation, carrying it in their bones like a race memory, the survival instinct.

'You want to know the real me?' Yukio said into Nicholas's ear as they both stared at the only monument to what had happened here such a short/long time ago. 'There. You see it. That is what I am like inside. What you see on the outside is all that's left standing.'

Now, he thought, she had become maudlin, turning full circle from her usual sardonic tough-as-nails stance. But, he thought, it was this dichotomy that most intrigued him about her. And he did not for a moment think she was as uncomplicated as she made out. He knew that to be a defence -- her ultimate defence perhaps. Still, he could not stop himself from wondering what manner of unfamiliar territory lay beyond the stone wall she had so effectively erected.

Streamers of cloud flew obliquely across the sky as they left Hiroshima behind, seeming to begin from the ground, reaching up into the very heart of heaven.

'Pardon me,' said the old man across from them. 'Please excuse this intrusion but I could not help wondering.'

He paused and Nicholas was obliged to ask him, 'What were you wondering?'

'If you have ever been to Hiroshima.'

'No,' Nicholas said and Yukio shook her head.

'I didn't think so,' the old man said. 'In any case, you would be too young to remember the old city, to have seen it before the annihilation.'

'Did you?' Yukio asked.

'Oh yes.' He smiled, almost wistfully, and when he did, the wrinkles seemed to fade from his face. 'Yes, Hiroshima was my home. Once. That seems very far away now, I think. Almost as if it were part of another life.' He smiled again. 'And in an important way it was.'

'Where were you,' Nicholas said, 'when it happened?'

'Oh, I was away in the hills.' He nodded. 'Yes, safely away from the firefall. Trees shook miles away and the earth convulsed as if in pain. There was never anything like it. A wound in the universe. It went beyond the death of man or animal or even civilization.'

Nicholas wanted to ask the old man what it was that went beyond all those things but he could not bring himself to do it. He stared, dry-mouthed.

'It was lucky you weren't in the city when the bomb fell.'

The old man regarded Yukio. 'Luck?' he said as if tasting the flesh of some unfamiliar fowl. 'I don't know. Perhaps luck might be a modern equivalent, though an inadequate one. If anything, it was karma. You see, I had been out of the country just prior to the war. I was a businessman in those days and went quite often to the continent. Mostly to Shanghai, where a majority of my selling was done.' For the first time his hands came into view and Nicholas saw the unnatural length of his nails. They were perfectly manicured, buffed and gleaming with clear lacquer. The old man saw the look in Nicholas's eyes, said, 'An affectation I picked up there from the Chinese mandarins with whom I did business and who befriended me. I do not even notice them now, I've grown so accustomed to them. But, of course, these are only of quite a moderate length.' He settled back more comfortably in the seat, began to speak as if telling a bedtime story to his grandchildren. He had a remarkable speaking voice, commanding yet gentle, as well modulated as a seasoned lecturer's. 'We took some time off over a long week-end and, all our business completed, we went into the countryside for a bit of relaxation. I had no idea what to expect, really. These were Chinese, after all. The mandarins have, ah, peculiar tastes in many things. But in business one must learn to be cosmopolitan in one's thinking – especially when it comes to the matter of your clients' personal tastes. Yes, I do not believe that it is good policy to be close-minded or, ah, traditional here. The world supports a myriad cultures, is that not so? Who is to say which is the more valid.' He shrugged his thin sharp shoulders. 'Certainly not I.'

Outside, the afternoon was waning, the oblique cloud-banks streaked with gold and pink on their undersides, a charcoal grey above. The sun was already out of sight below the horizon and in the east the sky was clear, a vast cobalt porcelain bowl, seeming translucent. High up, several first-magnitude stars could already be seen flung aloft as if by a giant hand. The world seemed suffused with an absolute stillness as at the midpoint of a long summer's afternoon when time itself ceases to have any meaning. It was a magical time, made up of fantastic elements having all miraculously arrived at the same spot at one instant, the inaudible sigh the inner ear hears in that last moment in a theatre before the curtain rises.

'They took me on a journey, my mandarin friends. To a town within a town, as I said, outside of Shanghai. It was – excuse me, my dear – a bordello. Not merely the building we went to, oh no. The entire town. Yes, that's right, a city of pleasure. You will forgive me, young lady, parts of this tale. A man on business for weeks at a time – one can ill afford to take one's wife along on such trips for many reasons. And these things become, well, almost an expected part of the trip.

'The mandarins regard sex very highly, oh my, yes, they certaily do. And I cannot say that I blame them.' He gave a little chuckle, not at all smutty but rather avuncular. 'It is, after all, both a necessary and an important part of life, so why not honour it.

'Uhm, in any event it was the most sumptuous, the largest such place I had ever been to. The clientele was strictly mandarin and further, I gathered, only certain families. Extremely exclusive, yes.' His eyes were big and dreamy. 'One could live the rest of one's life there quite easily, I daresay. But, of course, that is not possible. Such places are only for a small amount of time. That kind of rarefied atmosphere would, I imagine, pall after a time. Anyway, I wouldn't want to chance it. Life would most certainly be not worth while if all such spectacular dreams were shattered. Everyone needs time in their life when reality can be set aside, hm?'

The train rattled onwards, across a trestle bridge, plunging into a bleak and scraggy forest of deciduous trees, as forlorn as the ragtag remnants of some defeated army. The light was dying, the clouds stark now in their blackness, only losing definition near the horizon where the haze rendered all colour indistinguishable. Night had swept them up as swiftly as a remonstrating parent.

'So. Here we are in this place. But my purpose is not to tell you all the goings-on there.' He smiled winningly. 'You're young enough not to need any help from me on that score. No. Rather, I wish to tell you about a man I met there.' He held up one long, bony but perfectly straight finger. The long nail gleamed in the artificial light of the car, causing it to look like a street marker. 'Curious. About this man, I mean. He was no client, of that I am certain. Yet neither did he appear to be an employee of the establishment. Certainly I never saw him at work.

'Late in the night, or early in the morning, to be completely accurate, he could be found in the great first-floor parlour – the building had two storeys; it may have been British-made, though certainly for quite a different purpose originally – sitting in one of the overstuffed wing chairs playing a game with red and black marked tiles I had never seen before –'

'Mah-jongg?' Nicholas asked.

'No, not mah-jongg. Another game entirely. One I could never fathom. He would sit there silent and motionless while the girls cleaned up and when they had finished and had left he would begin to play. *Click-click. Click-click.*'

The old man lifted out a cigarette and, with some difficulty, owing to the length of his nails, lit it with a thin gunmetal Ronson. He smiled as one eye squinted up with the smoke. He might once have been an oriental Humphrey Bogart, the expression came so naturally to his face. He twisted the lighter's wide face so that the light glanced off it in a flare. 'A memento of those days, so far away. Belonged to a British diplomat whom I helped out of a spot of trouble there. He insisted I take it. I would have lost face had I not.' He pocketed the Ronson, drew briefly on the cigarette, let the smoke out so that his image was as hazed as the countryside rolling by outside.

'It was impossible for me to sleep in that place – even after I had been satiated. I hope I am being delicate enough, young lady.'

'Perfectly,' Yukio said. Nicholas wondered what the old man would think if he heard the way she threw words around.

'It was my habit to read late at night – I am an insatiable reader. Have been all my life. But one night I felt restless enough to put my book down – I was reading *Moby Dick*. In English, mind you – I don't trust translations; you lose too much – and take a stroll through the first floor.

'*Click-click. Click-click.* I heard the tiles as he moved them. I sat next to him and watched. In those days I was certainly a brash young man. Not rude, mind you. I was far too well brought up by my parents. But I had a spot of – what shall I say? – the impetuosity of youth, yes?

'Now this man was older than I am today, a good deal older, I would say, but then I am an abysmal judge of age so you must not go by me. Still, he was old. Anyone who saw him would certainly say that, yes.

'The odd thing about him was that his nails were so long that he was obliged to wear sheaths to protect them from breaking. These sheaths were something I had read about before. The mandarins were fond of wearing them, as an affectation, I had always supposed, during the turn of the century. However this was the late 1930s. Who in China still kept their nails thus? No one, I had thought. Now I knew differently.

'Usually these sheaths were of lacquer but these, if my eyes did not lie, were made of gold. Solid gold. But how could this be? I asked myself. How could the nails support such a weight? Still, I know gold and there was no doubt.

' "Why have you come here?" asked the man without looking up. *Click-click*, went the tiles. *Click-click.*

'I was so startled that for a moment I could not find my voice and he was obliged to prompt me. "Come, come," he said. Just like the *click-click* of his tiles. The same cadence.

' "Can't sleep," I said, still rather tongue-tied.

' "I never sleep," he said. "But that is because of my advanced age." He looked up at me. "When I was your age, I never missed a night. Perhaps that is why I don't miss it now." He spoke in a rather peculiar dialect. It was Mandarin all right, but the inflections were odd, some nouns clipped at their ends, and so on. I could not place where he was from.

'"I don't often have this trouble," I said, still the dazzling conversationalist. "But you're not that old."

'"Old enough to know that I am going to die soon."

'"Oh, I doubt that."

'He eyed me critically. "Well, sentiment is never very accurate." He began to stack up his tiles, nine to a pile. "But there is no need for concern. I have no fear of death. In fact, I will happily leave here now. I do not want to see what is coming."

'"Coming?" I said like a half-wit. "What is coming?"

'"Something terrible," he said. His hands on the small lacquered folding table looked like shining alien artifacts, newly unearthed. "A new type of bomb with a power beyond anything you can imagine. With enough force to destroy an entire city."

'I shall never forget that moment. I sat as still as a statue, barely breathing. I remember hearing the chirruping of a cicada so clear and near that I thought it must have got itself trapped inside the house. Oddly, I found myself wanting to get up and find it, to free it into the vast darkness which surrounded us.

'I could not move. It was as if his words had pierced my heart, riveting me to the chair in which I sat.

'"I don't understand," I said with a kind of opaque astonishment.

'"It is not likely that you would," he said, finishing stacking his tiles. Then he put them away into an inside pocket of his robe.

'He rose and, for an instant, I thought I might have known him or at least seen him at another, previous time. But I think now it was just the light which made it seem so.'

'What happened then?' Yukio asked.

'What happened?' The old man looked momentarily nonplussed. 'Why, nothing. Nothing at all. "Good evening to you, sir," he said in his somewhat formal way. "I wish you pleasant dreams." Though how he could have meant it after what he had just told me I could not imagine.

'The place was very still after he left and, slumped back in my chair, I imagined I could hear the sound of the grass growing outside where the tree frogs slept. A cloud of mosquitoes whined against the netting.

'At some time I must have gone upstairs – though I have no real remembrance of doing so – to Ishmael and Ahab and the *Pequod*, though I could not well concentrate on even so great a world as Melville's that night.

'His words ran around my head as if he had somehow engraved them upon the grooves of my brain with a cunning scalpel.'

'But how could he have known?' Nicholas asked. 'At that time not even the Americans who eventually comprised the Manhattan Project knew.'

The old man nodded. 'Yes,' he said slowly. 'That is often what I ask myself. From that day in August when I stood on that secluded hillside and felt the earth shake and the sky burn with colour and heard the heat wind coming, I have asked myself that same question. How could he know?'

'And what is the answer?'

The old man looked at them and smiled wanly. 'There isn't one, my friend.' The train was slowing as it came out of a downgrade. Cinders flew, whirled up and around by the wind eddies created by their passage. He stood up and bowed to them, long hands clasped against his flat stomach, nails like translucent chopsticks. 'My station,' he murmured. 'Time to get off.'

'Hey!' Nicholas said. 'Wait a minute.' Forgetting, in his anxiety to know more, his modes of speech, lapsing into the common formation; it lacked the necessary respect a younger person must show towards his elders. It did not matter, however, for the old man had gone, swinging lithely down off the car even before the train had come to its full panting stop. Clouds of steam obscured the windows.

Nicholas came back down the aisle, slumped down in the seat next to Yukio. 'Too late,' he said. 'Too late.'

Now the train picked up speed for the last part of the journey towards Shimonoseki. It was quiet in the car. Even Yukio was silent. She stared at her hands while he looked out of the window.

The night was aflame. They were passing fairly close to one or another of the southern cities – he had no idea which one – which had been turned into a supportive structure for a vast oil refinery. Giant flames leaped and spewed into the darkness like the corona of the sun seen close up in a kind of silent hellish dance. It seemed an inhuman place to work or live, a desolate dreamscape from which there was no exit. It went on and on as they travelled, the lines of red and orange lights leading in inevitable precise rows towards the refinery's main building bulking blackly against the skyline, the bloated billowing flames.

'What did you think of the old man's story?' Yukio said.

He turned his head. 'What?'

'The old man. Did you believe him?'

For some reason he thought of So-Peng. 'Yes,' he said. 'I did.'

'I didn't.' She crossed her legs at the knees, very American. 'Something like that couldn't have happened. Life's just not like that.'

They spent the night in Shimonoseki, so near the water that they could hear it though they could not see it for the thick ground fog. Horns hooted mournfully, deepened by the night air, made somehow mysterious.

She lay with her head on his bare chest, her night-dark hair spread in a fan across his pale flesh. He was a long time falling asleep. He felt her breathing gently, rhythmically through his fingertips, the weight of her on his sternum and rib cage. He wondered what it was about her that drew him so powerfully. And could not even decide why it seemed so important for him to know.

Yukio stirred and it seemed a part of him.

'What is it?' he asked her.

'Oh, nothing.' Her voice was very soft. 'I was just thinking of a story. It's the one my mother told me. The only one I remember. Want to hear it?'

'Yes.'

'Well, once upon a time there was a lady. She lived in a castle in Roku-No-Miya. Where that is no one knows to this day – that's just how my mother used to say it. Anyway, after this girl's parents died, she was brought up by a governess – she was an extremely well-protected girl – and, as the years passed, she grew up into a beautiful young woman.

'One evening she was introduced to a man and, every evening after that, he would come to the castle and she would entertain him until gradually the place took on a festive air.

'But during the long afternoons, while she was alone walking in her gardens, the lady thought of the power of fate. She thought about being dependent upon this man for her happiness. Then she would shrug her shoulders and smile wanly into the sun.

'At night she would lie awake beside her lover, neither happy nor unhappy. What satisfaction she could possess was fleeting.

'But then, one day, even this was to end, for her lover informed her solemnly that he must go with his father to another district to assist him in his new political post. "But," he said, "the assignment is but for five years. At the end of that time I shall return for you. Please do me the honour of waiting for me."

'The lady openly wept, perhaps not from love itself but from the idea of separation.

'In six years, nothing was the same at the lady's castle in Roku-No-Miya. The man had not returned and all the servants had gone as both time and money withered away. The lady and her governess were forced into the old, long-abandoned samurai's quarters to live.

'Now there was only rice to eat and great gaps in the wooden frame of the place let in both wind and rain. At length the governess besought her lady, saying, "Forgive me, lady, but your lover has abandoned you. There is a certain man who has been inquiring about you. Since we have so little money ..."

'But the lady would not listen. "I have no use for other adventures now," she said. "I only wish for the solace of death."

'At that moment, in another district, the lady's lover lay with his new wife. Startled, he sat up in the dark, saying, "Did you hear that?"

' "Go back to sleep, my lord," his wife answered him. "It is only a cherry blossom falling."

'Not over a year later, this man returned to Roku-No-Miya with his wife and retinue. He had paused at a roadside inn to wait out inclement weather and there had sent a number of notes to his former mistress. Not one was answered and thus, piqued, he left his wife at the house of her father and set off in search of the castle at Roku-No-Miya.

'When he arrived, he almost passed it by, so changed was it. The great wood and iron gates that had become so familiar to him were but stumps in the loamy earth and, down the road, the high blue lacquered *torii*, around which he and the lady used to stroll in the spring and summer, was gone.

'The castle itself he found uninhabitable. Some immense storm had completely demolished the east wing and the rest was a shambles.

'In the old samurai's quarters he found only an old, time-weary nun. She was, she said, the daughter of one of the lady's servants. When he inquired after the lady's whereabouts, she said, "Alas, my lord, no one knows."

'He went out searching for her but no one in the district claimed to have seen her.

'One dreary, rain-filled night, he stopped at a crossroads beside a monk and, hearing a voice he was certain was familiar, peered through the loose slats of a board house. Instantly he recognized the withered woman on the floor as his mistress. Rushing with the monk to her side he looked upon her face. She was surely dying and he asked the monk to recite a sutra over her. "Invoke the name of the Amida Buddha," the monk implored the lady. To which she replied, "I see a blazing carriage ... No, it is a golden lotus." "Please, my lady," the monk cried, "you must call out to the Amida Buddha. We have no power over transmigration, otherwise. You must call to Him with all your heart."

' "I see nothing," the lady cried. "Nothing but darkness."

' "My lady –"

' "Darkness and a cold wind blowing. A black wind, so cold."

'The monk did his best to assist her while the man prayed to the Amida Buddha. Gradually the lady's cries grew fainter, at last mingling with the sound of the wind whistling through the trees.'

Yukio was quiet for some time.

'Is that the end of the story?'

'Not quite. On the night of the full moon, some days later, the old monk sat by the same crossroads, pulling his ragged cloak about his bony knees in an effort to keep out the cold.

'A samurai came by singing a song and, seeing the monk, paused to hunker down next to him. "Is this the place?" he asked. "It is said in the district of Roku-No-Miya the weeping of a woman can be heard sometimes at night. What do you know of this?"

'"Listen," was all the monk would say. And the samurai listened. He heard nothing at all save the tiny night sounds. Then, of a sudden, he thought he heard a woman's cry of grief. "What is that?" he said.

'"Pray," said the monk. "Pray for a spirit that knows neither heaven nor hell." But the samurai, having no God, merely looked at the monk and walked on.'

They ate breakfast at the hotel and then went outside. It was cold and damp, the fog still swirling with curled tendrils underfoot. They saw the train on which they had arrived still standing at the station – way station was more like it. It was merely a central platform between two sets of tracks with enormous rough-hewn pillars of wood supporting a slanting, pagoda-like roof, lacquered on top against the debilitating effects of the weather and the salt air, but quite naked underneath. The scent of cedar was still powerful.

As they watched, a skeleton crew swung onto the train and, several moments later, it crawled a small distance onto a section of track set into an enormous disk which, as the train stopped, turned one hundred and eighty degrees. The train now pulled slowly into the opposite side of the platform, ready for the return journey north to Osaka.

The show over, they walked slowly away. The sky was perfectly white, the sun diffuse and ragged within the mist.

They were quite near the harbour and Nicholas could already make out two or three high white sails of the fishing boats manoeuvring carefully away from the quay. Past them, he knew, though hidden now, lurked the flatlands of the Asian shore.

As they came up on the headland, he thought he could make out the dark brown hills, due south, of Bunzen Province across the narrow straits on the island of Kyūshū.

'How peaceful here,' Yukio said, stretching like a cat. 'How different from Tokyo or Osaka or even Kyoto, as if the war never touched this place, nor industrialization. We might be in the seventeenth century.'

'Full of samurai and the ladies of samurai, eh?'

She took a deep breath. 'It's like being at the end of the world – or the beginning.' She turned to him, put her slender fingers around his wrist. He was startled at the nonsexual intimacy it conveyed. The sharp smell of drying fish hung heavily in the air, clinging to their nostrils like paint. Great grey and purple gulls wheeled, crying, in the low sky, half seen. 'Why don't we stay here, Nicholas.'

'Here?'

She nodded her head like a child. 'Yes. Right here. Why not? It's idyllic. The rest of the world doesn't exist here. We can forget. Be free. Start all over again. Like being born again without hurt or sin.' He looked at her and her grip on him tightened convulsively. 'Oh, please,' she said, her voice as hushed and echoey as if she were talking in a cathedral. 'Let's not go on. What for? What can there be waiting in Kumamoto to compare to this? You have me; there's the sea. We could go sailing. Out into the ocean. Even to the continent. It's not so very far away. How much time would it take? And then. And then . . .'

'You can't really mean that,' he said. 'You have to be realistic, Yukio.'

'Realistic?' she cried. 'What do you think I *am* being? There's nothing for me back there.' She flung her arm out to the north, from where they had come. 'There's no love, no life. And to the south, in Kumamoto? What's there? Saigō. Saigō and his damnable secrets. I don't want any part of all that. It terrifies me.'

They had passed a street vendor, shrouded in fog, and Nicholas detached himself from her for a moment, went back, bought two small paper cups of tofu in a sticky sweet brown glaze. He gave her one. A wooden spoon was stuck in the centre of the sweet.

She looked at it, then at him. 'What's the matter with you?' she said. A strong gust of wind, humid with the fecundity of the sea, whipped around them and she had to peel her hair away from her face. A few strands clung to the wet corner of her lips. The rest of her hair, unbound, was like a scarf worn in midwinter, flying out behind her. 'You treat me like a child. You buy me a sweet as if I've just awakened from a nightmare.' She batted the paper cup from his outstretched hand. It hit the ground with a fat splat and stayed there, a misshapen lump of white and brown. 'What I'm feeling is not going to go away, despite what you may think. I go to sleep at night and wake up the next morning hoping that it *is* all a dream. But it's not. Don't you see that?' He began to walk, she with him. 'Nicholas, please.' Her body was bent slightly, either against the wind or against her emotions; perhaps both. 'I'm begging you. Let's stay here. I don't want to go across to Kyūshū.'

'But why not? You knew where we were coming when you insisted I bring you along. What did you imagine would happen?'

'I don't know,' she said miserably. 'I didn't think that far ahead. I'm not like you in that respect. I can't plan ahead. I never know what I am going to do, how I am going to feel until I do it. I didn't go with it all the way until the end. I just wanted to be with you –' Her hand flew to her mouth and her eyes opened wide. She whirled away from him, bent over.

'Yukio –'

'Leave me alone. I don't know what I'm saying any more.'

He threw away the cup, held her by her shoulders. 'I don't understand,' he said. 'Please talk to me.'

'You know I can't do that,' she said, 'very well.' Her back was still to him.

'Yukio' – he held her tighter to him – 'you must tell me.'

'I can't do it. I can't.'

He spun her around. 'Yes you can. I know you can.' He stared into her frightened eyes, enlarged now by incipient tears. 'Will it help if I tell you?'

'Yes. No. I don't know.' But at least she knew what he meant.

'I love you,' he said. 'I don't know how long I've known it and not said it. I –' Was this why he was terrified?

'No. No,' she said. 'Don't say it. Please. I can't bear it. I can't bear it.'

387

'But why not?'

'Because,' she said fiercely, her face wrenched in a snarl, 'I believe you.'

He almost laughed with relief. 'And is that so bad?'

'Don't you understand yet?' Her face was so close to his, her eyes seemed crossed. 'I feel like I'm going to die. I'm not equipped –'

'Yes you are!' He shook her so that her hair flew across her face and her lower lip trembled. 'Everyone is. You just don't know it.'

'I can't handle it.' Her voice was almost a sob. A boat hooted over their shoulders, the rhythmic rumble of its diesel reaching them as a vibration up their legs until it had passed, its green and gold stack lost in the mist. He could not even see as far back up the foreshore to where the vendor must still be, hawking his sweet tofu.

'I am committed now,' he said, deliberately changing the subject. 'I've said I'd come.'

'You can always change your mind. No one's locked you into one decision.' Her voice had taken on a pleading edge. But was it for him or for herself?

'My commitment is to myself,' he said softly. 'I must find out what Saigō is doing in Kumamoto.'

'Why? Why is that so important? Who cares what he's doing? Who is it going to affect? Neither of us. Why can't you just let it go? It's such a small thing.'

'It's not,' he said despairingly. 'It's not a small thing at all.' But he wondered if there was any way he could explain it to her. How could he when he was not even sure he could explain it to himself?

'It's come down to that fight you two had in the *dōjō*,' she said cannily. 'It's like you have each other by the throat and neither of you will let go. You'll destroy each other that way, don't you see? One of you has to let go, otherwise ... Why can't it be you?'

'There's a matter of honour.' He only knew it now, a revelation like the sun as it first slips over the horizon, beginning to defeat the long night's chill.

'Oh, don't give me that one,' she said shortly. 'That kind of honour went out of style a long time ago.'

How little she must understand of life, he thought. 'For some of us, it's never gone out of style.'

'For the samurai,' she said tartly. 'The élite of Japan. The warriors who hurl themselves unhesitatingly into battle. Who live to die in combat?' She laughed, a harsh, discomforting sound. 'Now who needs a strong dose of reality? You're the same, the two of you. Two rabid dogs who'll worry a leg off before they'll give up and let go.'

'Not the same,' he said. 'Not the same at all. Saigō hates everything I stand for. My mixed blood; my love of Japan combined with my *abominable* Caucasian features. It rankles him that someone who looks the way I do should be better than him at anything, especially something so important as bujutsu.'

'Important? What's so goddamned important about bujutsu? What has any of that to do with living, with feeling –'

'You're a good one to talk about that.' Knew it was the wrong thing to say as soon as it was out of his mouth. He saw the look on her face, said, reaching out for her, 'I'm sorry. You know I didn't mean –'

'Oh, you meant it, Nicholas. I'm quite certain of that. And you've a right to say it, I guess. I've been frightened these last few days and now you know how I get when I'm frightened. You've made me feel – something – I was sure was impossible for me. I still don't quite – well, part of the time I want to run away from you and hide and never see another human being for the rest of my life. Is it okay to trust you? I keep asking myself. Isn't it just my cunt and my mouth he's after? But then I think, he's already got those so why go into this at all? It must be real even though every instinct that's still functioning tells me it's not. The past dies very slowly. I keep hearing echoes all around me. When you talk to me, say things, I hear what you're saying but, in my mind, other meanings, hidden and secretive like invisible hieroglyphics, burn themselves into my brain and I hear two different things and I begin a debate as to which of those signals is the real one, the one you mean for me to hear.' She looked at him. 'Does any of this make any sense to you?'

'I think so.'

'I see it doesn't.' Her eyes were so bright they seemed to

glitter despite the lack of any direct light. 'I suppose I am trying to tell you I love you.'

Her arms were around his neck, though how they had got there he had no idea. Hadn't they been at her sides just a moment ago? Had there been any movement since then? What was happening?

They kissed in a kind of timeless moment where even their breath hung suspended, condensed clouds on a chill winter's morning.

They took their bags down to the ferry-boat ticket-taker's, a ramshackle wooden building no larger than an outhouse with an arched window in its front, glassless and inadequately hooded against inclement weather. One could easily freeze to death within such a place.

A young boy in his late teens took the two rail ticket passes Nicholas handed him, stamped and punched them in several places, handed them back.

'The next ferry sails in seven minutes,' he told them. Even here, in such an out-of-the-way town, there was the typical Japanese concern with punctuality.

Yukio was unnaturally quiet until they cast off. But once they were moving, her melancholy seemed to slip away. 'Perhaps there will be a new show in town,' she said gaily. 'Or a riding stable. We could picnic and ride all afternoon.' It was as if the episode on the near shore had never occurred. Still, Nicholas was disturbed in its wake.

Behind them, Shimonoseki drifted away like a dream, beyond the churning white wake of the ferry. Gulls swung gracefully across their bow, wheeling obliquely like a fighter squadron, calling plaintively to each other.

They passed, quite close it seemed in the mist, a pair of fishing boats lying low in the swells, their black nets hauled up the masts like a moron's idea of a sail. A young boy on one of the boats waved excitedly as the ferry passed him by but there were none aboard, it seemed, inclined to return the gesture.

Nicholas's gaze shifted subtly to regard Yukio beside him. Her head was thrown back as if to catch the wan sunlight on the wide planes of her cheekbones, her hair flying to one side, a raven's spread wing. The long line of her neck was exposed, shadowed softly because of the thrust of her chin in this position. The hard jut of her breasts. Was it his imagination or could he see the slight protrusions of her nipples as they poked, erect, through the lace of her bra?

'Why is it, do you think, that Satsugai is afraid of the Colonel?'

The wind tore at her words, flinging over the ferry's side, out towards the bobbing fishing boats, mere black points now, misting to dull grey, and for a moment he was not sure he had heard her right.

'I was not aware that he was.'

She turned towards him, studied his face. 'Oh, yes. But of course. You mean you haven't noticed it? Well, I suppose I shouldn't be so surprised, really. I've spent more time with him than you have.'

'They argue a lot.' He put his elbows along the railing, leaned overboard. He felt her hand on his arm.

'Don't do that. Please.' She laughed. 'If you fell in I'd have to go in after you and I hate the water.'

'Water and trains.'

'Water worse than anything. I don't mind being near it. I like that, in fact. I'm just terrified by the tides and undertow and that.'

'About Satsugai,' he said. 'He and my father are from the opposite sides of the tracks, politically speaking. But that's, well, just talk.'

'Do you imagine that they would be together if it were not for Itami and your mother?'

He looked at the water, dark and light. 'No, I don't suppose so.'

'Right. Well, I know Satsugai. That kind of hate only stems from fear and let me tell you he is not a man who is easily frightened. Whatever the Colonel has on him is potent indeed.'

'I think it's just that Satsugai, being in the *zaibutsu*, was under suspicion as a war criminal for a time. You know, during the purges when the Americans disbanded the traditional family structure of the *zaibutsu*. My father intervened on Satsugai's behalf. I don't know the details but that kind of debt would be a heavy burden for Satsugai to bear.'

'Yes. He prides himself on owing no one and he's more powerful now than he was during the war.' She shook her head. 'To think that's due in part to the Colonel.'

'It's family. That's something my mother is adamant about. Politics are relatively unimportant next to that. Next to my father and me, Itami is her sole family. There is nothing they wouldn't do for one another.'

The fog closed in on them and the day turned chill. The ferry's deep horn sounded at regular intervals, hoarse and mournful. The gulls had gone and now it was even impossible to see the water. They might have been skimming through the air. The whiteness seemed stifling. There was no breeze to speak of. They heard voices, muffled and odd-sounding, from the ferry's far side as if coming to them from across a vast and unfathomable gulf.

All at once the land loomed before them out of the intense mist and, with only a slight bump, the ferry docked against the jute-covered slip. Nicholas wondered how the captain had seen his way across. They could hear the creak of the pilings. Then a dog began to bark hysterically.

To Nicholas the train ride to Kumamoto seemed interminable even though it took merely a fraction of the time it had taken for the bulk of the journey. Perhaps the fog had something to do with it, but he felt now a kind of desperate longing to know what it was that had brought Saigō down here. Kansatsu had been concerned about it. He realized that now, so belatedly. The *sensei* would never have come out and said such a thing, merely implied it. But what could it be about Saigō's visits here that would be so disturbing? And why should it concern Kansatsu at all? These questions gnawed at him as they rode across Kyūshū and he wished with all his might that he had the answers but, of course, that was a useless wish. In fact, any wish, Cheong had told him more than once, is useless. 'If you want something badly enough,' she had said, 'then you must do it. Those who sit and wish for things accomplish nothing.'

Abruptly, he felt resentment welling up inside him for that part of him which was Western in nature. But even so, he knew that that was his turbulent side, filled with energy and longing, impatience and changeability. It was, in short, what made him different.

Yukio, as usual, was filled with lust and, in the jouncing, empty car, she sat on his lap, lifting her skirt up and making the hot connection. Neither of them needed to move at all.

Kumamoto was a town that no doubt in feudal times had been dominated by the stone and mortar castle perched high on a dun-brown hill that in the spring would turn lushly verdant. In these modern times, however, the castle, though still quite imposing, seemed overshadowed by the industrial plant flung across the valley to the north-west. Its fifteen or so smokestacks seemed like inelegant fingers stretching themselves irreverently towards the heavens.

This afternoon, as Nicholas and Yukio stepped off the smoking train, one could not see their tops and the mist made them seem as if they had been covered by gloves.

Oddly enough, Kumamoto itself was not as modern as this new appendage might lead one to believe. There was little evidence of Western erosion and they saw more traditional Japanese garb than they had seen anywhere else in their travels. Even through the mist, which now appeared to be at last lifting, they could see how mountainous Kyūshū was. Dark masses loomed on every side, filling the land with a kind of undulating light and shadow pattern of the kind one might see from an airplane riding high above patchy clouds.

They booked into a hotel along the Street of the Wrestlers. 'Here,' the bustling proprietor said, flinging open the doors to their rooms, 'you will have a perfect view of Mount Aso.' He put down their bags, crossed to the window of Nicholas's room. 'Of course, you'll need a clear day but no doubt by tomorrow you will be able to view, well, perhaps not all five summits but most assuredly Nakadake.' He turned around, rubbing his palms together. 'It's actively volcanic, you know, and always smoking.' He waved one pudgy hand towards the mist outside. 'We get this kind of weather when the wind's the wrong way.' He walked to the door and his finger touched the knob. 'We've had ash and pumice, the sky so dark you'd think it was night, when it erupts.' He shook his head. 'Can you imagine? Coming all that way.' He clucked his tongue against the roof of his mouth. 'Still, one shouldn't complain. Mount Aso brings many people here every year and where would I be without tourism?' He shrugged deprecatingly. Nicholas tipped him and he gave them a rather stiff little bow. 'Anything I can do to make your stay here more pleasant,' he said, opening the connecting door between their rooms before leaving.

Nicholas phoned Saigō but he was not there. He left a message including the hotel's number.

They spent some time searching for a stable but there seemed to be no riding, at least within the town's limits. Yukio could not hide her disappointment.

They ate a light lunch at a tiny teahouse in a square surrounded by trees. Birds called as they flitted from branch to branch. The food was impeccable but Nicholas was not able to eat much. His stomach was tense and he needed to move around.

When they left, they proceeded to walk aimlessly around, through the wide main avenues, down small shop-lined streets, filled with mingled scents and clamouring customers.

They returned to the hotel late in the afternoon with the light receding swiftly from the sky. The mist was gone and the hard shell of the cobalt sky seemed distant indeed.

A message from Saigō was waiting for him. Dinner. Saigō would come to the hotel.

'How long will we be here?' Yukio asked as they were dressing. The door between their rooms was open.

'I don't know. I hadn't thought about it. Why?'

'I want to leave. That's all.'

'We've only just got here.'

'I know, but it already feels like we've been here a year. This is an odd city.'

He laughed, pulling on his trousers. 'You just don't want to be here. Listen, we're not so close to the water here.' He smiled. 'No chance I'll fall overboard.'

Her smile was a bit bleaker than his. 'Yes. Yes. I know. But haven't you noticed? The air here smells different, almost as if it were burnt.'

'It's only the refinery,' he said. 'Or maybe Mount Aso. I've never been near a volcano before. Isn't there one on Hokkaido?'

Saigō arrived promptly just after six. Nicholas opened the door to his room.

'Well, Nicholas, I didn't –' His dark eyes slid across Nicholas's face, over his shoulder. The colour seemed to drain from him. 'What's *she* doing here?' It was said in a hiss but, just as important, in a different speech mode; the polite form had been abruptly dropped.

Nicholas turned his head. 'Yukio? She decided to come with me. Didn't you know she was here?' But of course how could he?

Saigō's angry eyes flicked back to regard Nicholas. The stare was hard and cold. 'You set this up deliberately, didn't you?'

'What are you talking about?'

'You know, don't you? Don't lie to me, Nicholas. She told you everything.'

Nicholas felt her presence close and warm behind him.

'I told him nothing.' Yukio's tone was chill enough to freeze the blood. 'But now that you've brought it up like a hysterical child, perhaps you ought to tell him yourself.'

'Tell me what? Hey, wait a minute!' Saigō had begun a lunge around him towards Yukio. Nicholas stepped into his path, using his shoulder and his left arm as a wedge against the door-frame. Yukio stepped lithely away.

'I think you had better tell me what this is all about.'

Saigō heard the warning note in Nicholas's voice and he felt his blood boil. Leaned forward with the left side of his body, half-concealing the horizontal movement of his right hand and wrist.

Nicholas brought his forearm down in a blur, striking the exposed bone in Saigō's wrist. Physical damage was minimal but nerve disruption was considerable. The hand went numb.

They were very close together and Saigō used his foot, aiming for the side of the knee. The door-jamb was his ally; caught in the force of the blow, Nicholas's knee would shatter like crystal. But he stepped back and the side of Saigō's foot slammed into the wood with a crack as loud and as sharp as that of a house collapsing.

Saigō recovered enough to whirl around and head off down the corridor before Nicholas had a chance to react. Without a word, Nicholas went after him.

Yukio ran to the door. 'Nicholas!' she cried after him. Then she, too, followed in Saigō's wake.

The angel-fish, all grey lace, hovered near the bottom. It's tiny mouth opened and closed. It might have been trying to eat the algae off the side of the tank.

A pair of gourami passed by it, disturbing its concentration, and it darted off behind a group of three or four water plants twisting gently in the clouds of rising bubbles from the aerator.

They stood across the street, in the deep shadow of a doorway. The street was quiet, every step of the few passers-by discernible.

'What are you waiting for?'

'Quiet,' Nicholas said, thinking, twelve, thirteen, fourteen.

A young couple turned a corner, came down the street. He gave the man a quick glance, went back to watching the front door of the fish store where Saigō had disappeared moments before. Twenty-one, twenty-two, twenty-three. When he had reached thirty and there was still no sign, he took Yukio by the hand and went across the street.

A tiny bell rang in the back of the shop like a call to the penitent. It was a narrow, bare-floorboarded place, its walls stocked with glass tanks of varying sizes. Only one or two were dry, cloudy with dust.

A man, thin, worn down by the passage of time, his skin as grey as yesterday's mist, sat on a high wooden stool in front of a wall filled with filters, rolls of clear plastic tubing and stacked boxes of dried fish food.

No one was in the shop.

'Is there a back way out of here?' Nicholas asked him.

'Hm?' He looked up belatedly. 'Oh, yes but –'

Nicholas, with Yukio a step behind him, was already loping past him, through the short, dark passageway and out at the unbolted door.

They found themselves in a dim brick alleyway that was more a cul-de-sac. Only one way for Saigō to have gone and they followed.

They spotted him, already a block away, heading west. Twice

he doubled back and once, when he thought he had lost him altogether, Nicholas began to sweat because he didn't think now that he would get a second chance; Yukio had seen to that. But they got lucky. He had been hidden within a small jostling crowd around a news kiosk, in plain sight, really. It might have been accidental or an extremely sophisticated manoeuvre. There was no way of telling. But the question remained. Why was Saigō taking any precautions at all? Why was he concerned about being followed?

Above their heads a full moon rode, blue-white, as large as a hanging paper lantern, harbinger of winter's first snow. Clouds appearing as flat and substantial as curtains turned the illumination inconstant and, with it, perspective kept changing so that Nicholas was obliged to stop them now and again to check their proximity to the dark, hurrying figure in front.

Once Saigō turned around, his face a pale blur struck by the moonlight, and Nicholas forced Yukio into a doorway, hearing only the soft rasp of her violent breathing and the hammering of his own heart.

Saigō's silhouette was fast diminishing down the dark street and he grabbed her hand, pulling her along until, at length, he saw his quarry pause before a narrow doorway in a rather run-down wood-frame building, windowless and hulking. Disappeared like a nocturnal animal.

Nicholas stood perfectly still in deep shadow with Yukio by his side for several moments. 'Now,' he said in a low tone and took her, running across the wide street.

There was no sign on the building's face to indicate what it might contain; no bells to ring. Nothing. The door was metal, painted in deep red enamel. He grasped the brass handle half expecting the door to be locked. Pulled it open.

Inside, they found themselves in a plain hallway without a true ceiling. A wide industrial-type stairway led upwards; it too was metal. There were no doorways on the ground level. Nor were there any on the first floor, they discovered. There seemed to be a lot of empty space, however.

The building seemed silent but for a peculiar kind of intermittent vibration coming through the rough wooden planks of the vast landings.

They found the one door – closed and padlocked – on the third floor. Yukio coughed twice before putting her palm against her mouth; there seemed to be a great deal of sawdust hanging in the unquiet air.

One had an odd feeling here. Not merely the prickly sensation of trespassing but the uncomfortable hollowness in the pit of the stomach that might come from standing in the foyer of a haunted house at midnight.

'I want to get out of here,' Yukio whispered in his ear. She tugged at Nicholas's arm.

'Shhh.'

He went slowly, cautiously across the landing towards the closed door. He had thought – yes. The light was so dim that he had not been certain. But now as he approached, he saw clearly the sign that had been hand-painted in black ink squarely on the centre of the door: a circle within which were nine black diamonds. They in turn surrounded an ideogram, *komuso*.

Nicholas stared at the sign. Where had he seen that before? Surely he had – a *ryu*. It was a *ryu*. But which one? He had seen this sign quite recently. Just before he had left Tokyo, in fact. A regional offshoot, perhaps. Or –

Abruptly, he reached for Yukio's hand, backing away.

'What is it?' she whispered. 'Where are we?'

'Come on,' he said. And then, jerking her along with him, 'Come *on!*'

Outside in the street he found that he still could not breathe. He began to run down the street with her in tow. The night seemed terribly still, Kumamoto deserted, and he had the impression that they were the only people abroad that night, that they fled through a dreamscape from which they might never emerge.

His head pounded as if it might burst and a kind of fever careened through him. His mind whirled uncontrollably and he only vaguely heard Yukio's panting questions.

He had recognized the sign on the door and, with it, both the reason he had come here after Saigō and the nature of his immediate future.

*

Back at the hotel, he left Yukio to go to her room alone.

'Won't you tell me anything?'

'In a while,' he said, still half distracted. 'Take a bath or something. I'll be in in a little while.'

'You're not going out again,' she said worriedly. 'I don't want to be here alone.'

'Don't worry. I'll just be in the next room.'

Once inside, he crossed to the window. The darkness seemed absolute. But still, perhaps only because the proprietor had mentioned it, he thought he could see the white plume of pumice belching from Nakadake, Mount Aso's fifth column.

There was no doubt in his mind now why Saigō had travelled such a distance to become part of this particular *ryu*, for there were none such as this in the Tokyo area. Kansatsu's words haunted him now with an intensity impossible to ignore: *There are many* ryu *in Japan, Nicholas. Among these, the variety of disciples taught is virtually limitless. Good and evil are sometimes produced indiscriminately.*

No wonder Saigō had been so furtive in his movements: so careful to backtrack.

It would be a natural precaution for a ninja.

For that is precisely what he had become. This Kumamoto *ryu* was no regional offshoot but a centre. *The* centre, to be more accurate.

*The Ninja are not bound by the Way,* Kansatsu had said, and that was correct. Yet ninjutsu was more complex than that and, as in bujutsu itself, there were many types propounded and taught. Good and evil. The black and the red. Kansatsu himself had shown it to Nicholas before he had left Tokyo. Of the red, he had said, far and away the most dangerous, the most virulent *ryu* is the *Kuji-kiri*, 'It is the Chinese word for the "nine-hands cutting", the basis for much of the ninja's real or imagined power. It is said by many that these hand signs are the last remaining vestiges of magic in the world. As for me, I cannot say, but as you yourself have come to understand, there are times when the dividing line between imagination and existence can disappear.' That was when Kansatsu had shown him the symbol of the *Kuji-kiri ryu*. It was the one he had seen on the warehouse door just moments ago.

He heard the water running in the bath next door; Yukio disrobing.

A suspicion was forming in his mind now and the more he thought about it the more certain he became. Had Kansatsu known what it was he would find here? Perhaps he had only suspected. But why was Kansatsu involved at all?

Abruptly, Nicholas had the cold sensation of being manipulated by forces he had not even suspected of existing. It was certain that Kansatsu knew quite a bit more about this situation than he had told Nicholas. Why hold back?

Outside, the moon had slipped its cloud mooring and now rode, unbridled, in the sky. The world was tinged with a blue light, cold and harsh and monochromatic. Far on the horizon – he was certain now – he could make out the rising oblique volcanic cone, its pale umbrella billowing like the aftermath of an explosion seen in slow motion. The still air held the pumice dust in languid suspension like a decadent sprawled across his silk-covered settee.

It seemed to him now that the lines of his life had already been drawn by some other hand at a time when he had been looking elsewhere. As he had said to Yukio this afternoon, he was committed. They had been set against one another, he and Saigō, from the moment they had first met. For what reason he could not yet say, yet it was a reality with which he must now deal.

What to do now?

He knew. He knew. And it terrified him.

The bath-water had drained some time ago. He got up from where he had been sitting in the window-bay and opened the connecting door into Yukio's room.

He paused on the threshold. The lights were extinguished and all seemed still.

He called her name softly.

Blue moonlight was awash along part of the floor, interlaced with the oblique bars of shadow from the casement.

'Yukio?'

He went silently into the room.

And immediately stopped. *Haragei*. Someone else was in the room. He turned his head without moving his body. Saw Yukio lying on the bed, a last bit of light outlining the bridge of her nose. She was on top of the covers. The other side of the double bed had blanket and sheets drawn down. An impression had been made there, as if by another body. She was naked. Her breasts and belly rose and fell in even breathing.

'Welcome, Nicholas.' He turned his head. The chair in the far corner, facing into the room. Moonlight fell part way along its back; its face was in shadow. 'So nice of you to join us.'

'Saigō. How did you get in here?'

'How do you think, Nicholas? How do you think?'

'I imagine there are many ways – for a ninja.'

He seemed unperturbed. 'Quite so, oh yes. But, you see, I didn't need any of them.' He waited a beat. 'Yukio let me in herself.'

'Yukio . . .' He took two steps towards her.

'It won't do any good, Nicholas. She can't hear you.'

'She –'

'Oh no no no no, nothing like that. She's merely sleeping. That's a waste of time. You won't be able to wake her. But don't fret, she's perfectly safe.'

'Wake her up,' Nicholas said. He was sitting on the bed. Her flesh felt cold, raised in goosebumps, but she seemed to be breathing normally.

'I don't think so. At least not yet, anyway.' At last Saigō stood up. He was dressed in a black raw silk suit, rather old-fashioned, somewhat like the ones Chinese mandarins used to wear on formal occasions. His hair had been cut so short that he looked almost bald; the black stubble seemed somehow far more ominous. 'The obvious thing to say now is that I'm sorry to be proved right. About you, I mean. But that would be a lie. I'm not in the least sorry. In fact, I'm delighted. I was right about you all the time. So was my father.' He went into the centre of the room and Nicholas followed him with his eyes.

Saigō shook his head. 'How you ever found out I cannot imagine. I have to give you credit for that.'

'What,' said Nicholas, 'are you talking about?'

Saigō's eyes flashed and his lips curled in a snarl just as if Nicholas had struck him. He flew across the room, grabbed Nicholas by the shirt-front. 'All right,' he whispered savagely, 'I'm through being courteous to you. I see there's no point. Did you really think I didn't know that you were following me?

Do you think you could have if I hadn't wanted you to? You really *are* a fool.'

Nicholas reached up, slammed Saigō's fists from him. They stood, a little apart, eyeing each other, controlling their breathing, like two titans about to do battle over dominion of the world.

'What do you think you're doing to yourself?'

'I'm saving myself,' Saigō said. 'I would have thought it was obvious. I have been accepted into the elite. Beyond *bushi*, Nicholas. Way beyond.' He took a step forward. 'And you can join me.'

'What?'

'Why did you think I asked you down here? This is no vacation spot. And then you show up with *her*. Idiot!'

'I love her.'

'Forget about her. She's nothing. Less than nothing. A whore. Fucking –'

'Shut your *bloody* –!'

'Yes, I forget about your English heritage. So chivalrous!' He took another step forward so their chests almost touched. 'So. Whatever she is or isn't. She no longer exists for you or for me. I am offering you the world, Nicholas. You have no idea. None at all. Ninjutsu is –'

'But why the *Kuji-kiri*? Why black?'

'Oh, I see. I see how it is now. That scum Kansatsu has been talking to you. Yes, it's black ninjutsu, but that is as it should be. We are the strongest, the most potent. With *Kuji-kiri* you become invincible. In all the world, there will be no one to stop you. Think of it, man, unlimited power!'

'There is nothing in that that appeals to me,' and he was spinning down obliquely across the bed, away from Yukio, using the wrist blocks against the darting eye-strikes Saigō drove at him with monstrous swiftness. He retaliated with sword-strikes, three in rapid succession. Thwarted, but that was all right because they had served their purpose and the adrenalin was surging through him like a tidal wave.

He rolled over, Saigō atop him and his immediate concern became the elbow-strike feint followed by a sword-strike aimed at his larynx. He worked his way out of that, found his left arm pinioned beneath the full weight of Saigō's right shoulder.

He was in trouble, he knew. Inside, Saigō, with the ninjutsu training, had an enormous advantage. His only hope was to break away, get some reasonable distance between them.

He began a knee-strike, twisting away at the same time, but Saigō was not fooled and a blow caught the ridge of his collarbone; his frame flexed involuntarily. Still, he was fortunate that the strike was a near-miss.

They were locked now on the floor, part of the counterpane drawn under their straining bodies. There was very little real movement for long minutes as they struggled, fingers grasping wrists, elbows against sternums, a kind of perverse engine, stifling on its own energy output.

It became time to try something else and he slashed upwards with his knee-cap, heard Saigō's grunt and, almost simultaneously, a soft metallic click in front of his face. Saw a small blade, glinting in the moonlight, standing out like a deadly toothpick from between Saigō's first and second finger knuckles. A conjurer's trick. But it was no illusion. He turned his head away as the blade moved infinitesimally towards his eye. There was a peculiar odour and his nostrils flared briefly. Then it was gone and he was concentrating on stepping up the pressure of his forearm against the hand with the blade. He pushed upwards, using all the available leverage. Sweat had broken out along the line of his hair and now it drooled with cruel slowness down his forehead threatening to blur his vision.

But the deadlock was breaking as, bit by bit, he brought the hand backwards, away from him. Then he was free and on his feet. His chest heaved with the intense exertion of the past few moments. He staggered a little, waiting for Saigō to stand. When he did, Nicholas attacked, but perhaps the blow to his collarbone affected him more than he had thought because he was just a little off balance and, as Saigō countered his thrust, he seemed to take an inordinately long time to react.

Now Saigō was at him, seeming faster than ever before. Barely he was able to deflect a fork-strike, but he failed to counter a sword-strike to his neck.

He went down then in a heap. Coughing and gasping, he could not seem to fill his lungs with air. On his back, he saw Saigō standing over him, grinning, as if he knew there would be no more resistance.

Tried to stand up but he had no legs. He used his hand, raised them. Or thought he did; no feeling there, either. He blinked several times, unbelieving. Trapped within a useless body. He glanced down. His hands lay like pale flowers, part of another world. He felt the pounding of his heart unnaturally loud in his inner ear. But that was all.

Saigō bent over him, a sardonic smile on his face. 'Did you think I came unprepared this time?' he said, almost amiable, as one friend to another. 'No, it has all been planned from the very beginning. Yes, Nicholas, even down to Yukio's involvement. She knew about it all. In fact, some of this was her idea. Surprised?'

Nicholas could only open and close his mouth soundlessly like a fish dying of the air. His tongue worked like an idiot's. No, he thought wildly. No no no. It's a lie. It *must* be.

'Well, you shouldn't be. Didn't I tell you she was a whore? Surely she told you we were lovers. Yes, I thought so.'

He turned away and in the half-light Nicholas saw him reach over towards the bed. He grasped Yukio's sleeping form, dragged her across the counterpane. A lamp in front of Nicholas went on and he blinked slowly while his eyes adjusted to the glare. Like having the sun in his eyes.

Yukio! he cried out silently. Yukio!

Saigō had her sitting up now. He had a small capsule in his hand. He broke it in half, waved it under her nose. Her head went back and he followed with the capsule. She shook her head from side to side as if wanting to get away from the expelled contents.

Her eyes came open and her features arranged themselves in a slow, sensual, slavish smile. Her arms came up around Saigō's shoulders. He kissed her roughly and her lips opened like a flower.

Yukio!

Careful to continually stay within Nicholas's line of sight, Saigō caressed her. He rubbed her breasts so that her nipples stood out hard and quivering. He spread her legs, rubbed her there. Yukio began to pant. His fingers came away wet.

He turned her over, bending her across the bed. Her buttocks were pale globes in the harsh light. He dropped his black silk pants. They puddled around his ankles. Spreading her thighs, he rummaged again, anointing his phallus. Then he rammed himself into her anus.

Yukio cried out as he moved on her flesh. From his vantage point Nicholas could see the reddened member sliding in and out. He tried to close his eyes but the gruntings and pantings overwhelmed him, pummelling his brain until his eyes flew open in self-preservation.

Yukio's arms were flung out over her head, her fingers clutching convulsively at the counterpane, drawing it up into bunched, sweaty hillocks. Her eyes were squeezed shut. Her thighs writhed against the bed, pressing her mound down in time to Saigō's thrusts.

All at once, she gave a cry. The counterpane shredded between her frenzied fingers and her thighs drew up convulsively and she shuddered powerfully.

At that moment, Saigō withdrew and a tiny moan of disappointment escaped her lips. His reddened member flicked upward at every pulse.

Saigō bent over Nicholas, flipped him over. It was only then that Nicholas understood the true nature of what was happening.

He felt the first burning penetration, heard Saigō's heavy grunt, felt the great weight of him upon his shoulders and buttocks, coming into him again and again like the tide.

The Colonel returned home quite late.

He sat for a long time behind the wheel of his car smoking his pipe, thinking of nothing. It seemed like days since he had smoked it last and he savoured the mellow bite of the dark tobacco on the back of his tongue and against the roof of his mouth. He thought he might want a drink in a little while.

The moon was a dim smudge low on the horizon, ready to rest for the night. Whatever remained of it. The Colonel slowly rolled up his side window, preparatory to getting out, but he was abruptly suffused with a curious kind of lethargy that left him incapable for the moment of taking any action no matter how minuscule.

I suppose that is to be expected, he thought.

He looked towards the darkened house and he thought of Cheong asleep on their *futon*. How he cherished her. How he had failed her. And himself. And especially Nicholas. He had done the only possible thing but he knew that it was far from enough. He had bolloxed it long ago. Tonight just took some of the sting out of it for him.

What he thought of now was lying to Cheong. He had never done that before and he had no strong desire to do it now. Still, there was no help for it; he understood all too well the consequences of the alternative.

At last he climbed out of the car, shut the door behind him with a soft thunk. The night seemed terribly still.

He went silently around to the side of the house, found the small pile of leaves Ataki had left for the morning's burning. Kneeling down, he set it to flame, listening meditatively to the crisp crackle, inhaling the pungent odour.

He stared into the fire. Odd what one remembers, he thought, in times like these. Like a submarine suddenly surfacing, the memory came to him of the bright summer afternoon when he had been locked in the crucial meeting with Prime Minister Yoshida, debating the specific consequences of the Korean War with John Foster Dulles, General Bradley and Defence Secretary Johnson. Dulles was in Tokyo because among the first American troops being sent into Korea were those who had been occupying Japan since 1945. But that left the bases and approximately a quarter of a million U.S. dependants left unprotected in Japan. The Americans were, of course, against this and they proposed the commencement of a Japanese military.

It was a bombshell proposal because such a force would be in direct violation of Article 9 of the Japanese Constitution written in 1947: 'Land, sea, and air forces, as well as other war potential, will never be maintained.'

In the best of American traditions, Johnson assailed Dulles's stance and the P.M. reacted negatively to Dulles's plea for Japanese remilitarization. However, it was clear that something had to be done. The Colonel proposed that the existing Japanese police force be expanded to approximately 75,000 men, calling it a National Police Reserve. 'We will have an effective army without having to call it that,' the Colonel had said.

For Dulles, of course, this was not enough, but Yoshida, seeing that the Colonel had given him a way out without any loss of face, readily agreed. The plan would have to be, by definition,

Top Secret. Even the recruits, Yoshida insisted, must not know the true purpose for which they were being trained.

The P.M. then set up the Annex of Civil Affairs Section within the existing bureaucracy to be responsible for recruitment and training, and an American officer was put in charge.

Afterwards, Yoshida had asked the Colonel to remain. Tension still laced the room like rancid fruit and the P.M. suggested they take a walk in his gardens.

'I owe you a great debt of thanks,' he had said after the usual amount of conversational courtesies which, even in such a signal situation, could not be ignored.

'The problem is, sir, that the Americans still do not understand us.' He saw Yoshida glance sideways at him. 'Perhaps they never will. They have been here a long time.'

The Prime Minister smiled. 'Remember, Colonel, that there was a time when we did not understand the Americans.'

'But there is, I think, in Japan, a greater ability for cultural absorption.'

Yoshida sighed. 'Yes. Perhaps that is so. But, in any event, I am most grateful to you. Mr Dulles was most anxious to back me into a corner. What he was no doubt leading up to was a Japanese involvement in the Korean War. Why else ask for a sudden enormous military build-up here?' He shook his head, his small hands clasped behind his back. 'It is unthinkable, Colonel, for us to send troops into Korea.'

Unthinkable, the Colonel thought now, kneeling in the brittle night. That time we avoided the unthinkable, by the grace of God. Now it had happened.

The fire was going strong. He reached the cord out of the pocket of his dark nylon jacket, dropped it into the centre of the tiny conflagration.

He was not surprised to see that the knot in its centre was the last to blacken and fall into ashes.

Said goodbye to Mount Aso, hello to Mount Fuji.

It rained most of the way back, drops beading the windowpane, streaking in fat rivulets as they combined. The low sky was black, filled with evil, fulminating clouds. A stiff wind out of the north quarter plummeted the temperatures; winter was here at last.

Nicholas shifted uncomfortably from one buttock to another, finding it painful to sit normally. Someone farther along the car kept fiddling with the tuning dial of a transistor radio: brief bursts of rock music interspersed with a dry, cultured voice announcing the news. Saburō, the leader of the Japanese Socialist Party, was under fire again for his 'structural reform' policies which the Party had adopted a little over two years ago. Speculation was that he would be out soon.

Just north of Osaka, the rain turned to hail, pattering against the windows as it tap-danced along the hull of the train.

Nicholas, scrunched down in the seat, shivered slightly despite the adequate heating. Vaguely, as if the feeling belonged to another person and he had, perhaps, got his lines crossed, he felt hungry. But he had not left his seat since he had boarded this train at Osaka, had collapsed into it. Any movement at all seemed a chore to him now. Perhaps, before they pulled into the station at Tokyo, he would be obliged to relieve himself. He preferred not to think about that now. But then any kind of thought was difficult at the moment. His mind was a wind tunnel, leaves whirled by the same currents, creating precisely the same patterns no matter how many times the tune was replayed.

Hear the groaning, feel the heat on his face: the light – shade off the lamp? Shadows moving, rising, falling, larger than life. Saigō, oddly, making the bed. Yukio, dressed in skirt and blouse, packing rather mechanically. He tried to say something but it was as if his mouth had been packed with dry sand. Was his larynx paralysed as well?

Saigō took her by the arm, bag in her other hand. They both had to step over him to reach the door. Lay there like a quadraplegic, eyes blinking salt sweat and tears. He strained to see her face but it was in partial shadow, her long hair swinging across her cheek.

Saigō stopped her with a word in her ear, leaned backwards and down, his face, shiny with sweat, hovering just over Nicholas's.

'You see how it is now, don't you? There's a good boy.' He sneered. 'And don't bother coming after, hm? There's really no point. Because this is good-bye. No *sayonara* this time. Get it?' He reached out, patted Nicholas's cheek almost tenderly.

'If we ever meet this way again, I'll kill you.'

Shadows looming – were they really people? – and then gone, just the after-image, dark on his retinas. He closed his eyes at last and concentrated on breathing.

The paralysis began to fade some time after dawn, he estimated. He could not be certain of the time because he must have fallen asleep at some point. Only knew that when he awoke just before eight, he could move his fingers and toes.

Within the hour he could stand and even walk steadily. He went into his own bathroom and stayed there for a long time.

His first stop was the warehouse. The character of the street was totally different in the daytime. This was near the centre of the business district and during the day the area was jammed with traffic and pedestrians.

He tried the front door but it was locked. After two complete circuits of the place, he was convinced that there was no other way in. Picking the lock was out of the question.

He went into a near-by tea house for breakfast, sitting at a table that gave him an oblique but clear view of the building's front. He drew a blank and after an hour gave up.

While paying the bill, he asked directions to the local police station. It proved to be a short walk away. He was sent up to the second floor of the wood and brick buildings. The place smelled of cement and turpentine.

The sergeant on duty sat behind a desk that was as battered and scarred as a war veteran. He was a small man, rather young, with a very yellow complexion and a wide moustache meant to disguise his splay teeth. His uniform was so neat that Nicholas could see the creases in his blouse.

He seemed sympathetic, even helpful. He took down all the particulars, including the address of the warehouse. But his eyebrows shot up when Nicholas told him what was behind the red lacquered door on the third floor.

'A ninjutsu *ryu*? Young man, are you certain this isn't some sort of prank? – a college hazing, that sort of thing. Because if it is, I under –'

'No,' Nicholas said. 'It's nothing like that.'

'But surely,' the young sergeant said, stroking his moustache lovingly with one forefinger, 'you know that the ninja no longer exist. They died out, oh, almost a century ago.'

'Do you have any proof of that?'

'Now see here –'

'Please, Sergeant. All I am asking is that you send some men round to the warehouse and check.'

The sergeant took his hand reluctantly from his upper lip, held it out palm first. 'All right, Mr Linnear. All right. Just leave it to me. You go back to your hotel and wait for my call.'

It wasn't until after three.

'Yes?'

'Mr Linnear.' The sergeant's voice sounded weary.

'Did you go to the warehouse?'

'Yes. I went myself. With two patrolmen. It is owned by Pacific Imports.'

'Did you see the sign on the door?'

'There was no sign. Just a plain door.'

'But there must be –'

'The warehouse was closed today but we were able to scare up the watchman. He was good enough to take us through. It's a warehouse. Nothing more sinister.'

'I don't understand.'

'Mr Linnear, perhaps I should send a man over to take a look at your girl friend's luggage. Perhaps we might find some clue to her present whereabouts.'

'Luggage?' Nicholas said, somewhat bewildered. 'Her luggage is gone, Sergeant. I told you.'

The voice at the other end of the line seemed to contract, become somewhat colder. 'No,' the sergeant said, 'you didn't. Mr Linnear, did you and your girl friend perhaps have a row last night? Did she walk out on you?'

'Now listen –'

'Young man, perhaps I should call your parents. Where did you say you were from?'

He waited until long after dark before setting out. It was colder, with a dankness that hung in the air like a steel curtain. What people remained on the streets at this late hour hurried past him, eager to reach the warmth of their destinations.

He went round the block once just to make certain. He saw no one more than once. He stood in a doorway, starting at the front door, shivering slightly as the wind picked up. A bit of newspaper fluttered across the gutter, lifted, then fell, like a mammoth moth searching for a flame.

It took him four minutes to get inside. He was extremely careful. For what seemed a long time he stood with his back against the door, listening for sounds. He needed to pick up and memorize the aural pattern of the place so that, when he began to work, his mind would be attuned to any deviation from the pattern. That kind of thing could mean the difference between making it back out and being trapped in here, the subject of a manhunt. He gave himself ten minutes to be certain; the pattern contained outside traffic sounds and these took the most time to assimilate principally because they were intermittent. Then he went silently up the stairs.

The place appeared deserted but he discounted that, assumed that he was on enemy territory. The sergeant, at the very least, would not be pleased if he was caught trespassing, and he had no desire to involve his father's name in these precincts; the less the Colonel knew of his activities in Kumamoto, the better.

Windowless, the warehouse was just as lightless during the day as it was at night. Time had no meaning here. On the third-floor landing, he reached out a pocket torch, played it on the door.

He stood perfectly still for some moments. Wood creaked somewhere downstairs, a settling rather than from a footstep. Outside, in an alley perhaps, judging by the hollowness of the sound, a dog barked twice and was still. The brief rumble of a truck.

The sergeant had not lied. The door was completely free of any sign.

He went across the landing for a closer look. Rubbed his fingertips over the surface in the light of the torch. Nothing. Had it ever been there? He sprung the padlock.

Fifteen minutes later he was away, walking stiff-legged from the pain down the street. A warehouse. Only a warehouse. And not a sign that it had even been a *ryu*. *Don't bother coming after*. Because we won't be there?

In the railroad car, the radio played a pop song he did not know. Its tempo was fast, its tone optimistic. The passing landscape was blurry with mist and, out of it, the hail, rattling and jumping like ping-pong balls.

Nicholas leaned his head against the perspex, glad of the

chill it afforded. He tried to make a sense of it all. What a superb actress Yukio had been. And what a naïve little boy he had proved to be. It was almost amusing. He working so hard to gain her trust when it was she for whom trust was a meaningless word. No, it was far too dispiriting to be in the least amusing.

But ironic, yes. So ironic.

There was a kind of numbness inside him as if Saigō's cruel intrusion had somehow anaesthetized him, shorting out some spark of current. He thought of Yukio's remark at seeing the bombed-out observatory in Hiroshima. *That is what I am like inside.* Another part of her lie, but it was all too true now of him.

It began to snow, the sky turning white. The silence seemed appalling and absolute after the long siege of the hail. The radio had been switched off at last.

It was the reverse of the story she had told him, he thought, his head pounding. Except he was the lady waiting in vain for the broken promises of her lover to come true. Would Yukio, returning to find him gone, become a nun? For the first time, he began to think of America as more than just a country on the other side of the world. Forsake his beloved Japan? Yes, he thought. Yes. But first ...

With a raucous burst, the radio broke into renewed life ... *I'll pretend that I'm kissing the lips I am missing/And hope that my dreams will come true/And then while I'm away/I'll write home every day/And I'll send all my loving to you ...*

It hardly seemed surprising that Nicholas did not go straight home from the station.

He threw his bags in the back of a taxi and, climbing in after them, gave the address of Kansatsu's *ryu*.

Apparently the snow had been falling in Tokyo for some time. There was already more than an inch on the ground and traffic was snarled. This first snow had come so late in the year that everyone had given up on it and so had been taken by surprise.

The heavily laden windshield wipers gave off a hypnotic *hiss-thunk, hiss-thunk* as they crept through the city in maddening herky-jerky fashion. But once on the highway at the outskirts they made better time; the sanding crews had done their job.

He sat slumped in one corner of the back seat and did not open his eyes until they came to a stop outside the *ryu*. The driver called to him and he asked the man to wait until he was certain someone was still there.

The taxi seemed to sit there in the snow, panting, its exhaust expelled in tiny white bursts. He returned in a moment, paid the driver and hauled out his bags.

Kansatsu served him green tea in one of the *ryu*'s back rooms. The *dōjō*, itself, was deserted. There was no one here save the *sensei* and himself.

'You have had a most difficult trip,' Kansatsu said.

Through an open *shōji*, Nicholas could see the snow silently falling, muffling all sound. In the twilight it seemed more blue than white. Fuji was invisible now, in the weather.

'I can see it on your face.'

So Nicholas told him.

There was a great silence after he had finished, or so it seemed to Nicholas.

'Kansatsu –'

But the *sensei* stopped him. 'Drink your tea, Nicholas.'

Nicholas threw the grey porcelain cup away from him; tea spilled across the tatamis. 'I am tired of being treated like a child! I know what I want to do now – what I *must* do.'

'I think,' said Kansatsu, unperturbed by the outburst, 'that you should go home now.'

Nicholas stood up, his face red with rage. 'Don't you understand what has happened? Have you been listening to what I've been telling you?'

'I have heard every word.' Kansatsu's tone was calm, soothing. 'I sympathize with you. You have confirmed what I have suspected for some time. But no decision can be made in haste. You may think that you know what it is you want to do now but I doubt if you do. Please take my advice and return home. Take some time to think –'

'There are some answers I want from you,' Nicholas said harshly. 'You set me up for this. You knew –'

'I knew nothing. As I said. *Now* I know, as do you. That is better, you will admit, than being unsure. No decisions can be accurately made, no course of action taken, in such circumstances. That is basic. You understand that.' There was a slight interrogative at the end.

'Yes.'

'All right.' Kansatsu sighed and stood up. They faced each other across the low, lacquered table. 'Let me tell you that that which I withheld from you was for your own benefit –'

'My own bene –!'

Kansatsu held up one hand. 'Please allow me to finish my thought. I had, at the time, only conjecture to go on as regards Saigō.' His tone of voice changed, softening somewhat. 'As for yourself, I told you what was in my mind. Working here will no longer well serve either of us. That you have survived your journey to Kumamoto is proof enough of that – if you might be inclined to mistrust my word.'

'I would never –'

'No. I know. You would not.' Kansatsu came round the table, touched Nicholas on the biceps. It was the first such gesture he had ever made towards Nicholas. 'You have been my finest pupil. But the time has come for us to part ways. You must grow along your own path, Nicholas. Too long in this *ryu*, any *ryu*, can be detrimental to that growth. But' – he raised a long forefinger – 'before you decide on where to go, your mind must be clear. And you will admit that you cannot claim such clarity now, hm?'

Nicholas was silent, thinking.

'Take several days, as long as you need, in fact. Then, when you feel you are ready, come to me. I will be here. I shall answer all your questions as best I can. And, together, we will decide on your future.'

'There is something,' Nicholas said at last, 'that cannot be ignored.'

'And what is that.'

'I have an enemy now.' *Don't bother coming after.* 'I invaded their territory! Ignored their warning. When they come, I must be prepared.'

Beside him, Kansatsu had never seemed so old and frail as he stared out at the falling snow.

'I am afraid there's been some bad news.'

He stood with his bags in the doorway of his house. Immediately he thought of Cheong. 'Where's Mother?'

'At your aunt's. Come inside, Nicholas.' The Colonel seemed pale and drawn.

The house seemed subtly different. Emptier.

'What's happened?'

'It's Satsugai,' the Colonel said evenly. He had his pipe in one hand, unlit. 'We tried to reach you in Kumamoto. I finally got hold of Saigō this afternoon. Itami was surprised to learn Yukio decided to stay with him.'

Nicholas felt a knife twisting inside him. *All my loving darling, I will send to you.* There was a silence. He could hear the clock on the mantel in the Colonel's study. All the way in here. Nothing moved outside. It was as if the world had frozen over in a new ice age.

The Colonel cleared his throat. 'Satsugai's been killed. I'm sorry, it's a hell of a homecoming. I can see you didn't have the best of trips.'

Was it so indelibly etched across his face; skywriting that he refused to face?

'How did it happen?'

The Colonel put the pipe stem to his lips, blew sharply outwards to unclog it. He looked at the bowl. 'Robbery, the police think. Satsugai must have surprised the thief.'

'No one else heard him?'

The Colonel shrugged. 'No one else was in the house at the time. Itami was at her sister's.'

'Which one? Ikura?'

'No. Teoke.'

Nicholas disliked Teoke.

'Well.' He went to take his bags into his room. The Colonel stooped to help him and together they went through the house.

'It's so quiet,' Nicholas said. 'Nothing seems right.'

'No,' the Colonel agreed, something far off in his eyes. 'It's never the same.' He sat on the *futon*, pressed his thumb and forefinger against his eyelids. 'The servants have gone with your mother and Ataki won't come today.'

Nicholas began to unpack, separating the soiled clothes from the unworn ones. 'Dad,' he said after a time, 'what do you know of the ninja?'

'Oh, not very much. Why?'

He shrugged, looking down at the shirt he was holding.

'Kansatsu's been talking about them. Did you know that when firearms were first introduced here in 1543 by the Portuguese they were immediately incorporated into ninjutsu techniques? No? And because of that, firearms were shunned by the majority of the other classes – most especially the samurai – until the Meiji Restoration.'

The Colonel got up, went across the room to stand beside his son. 'Nicholas,' he said gently, 'what happened between you and Yukio?' When Nicholas said nothing, he put his hand on his son's shoulder, said, 'Are you afraid to tell me?'

Nicholas turned round to face him. 'Afraid? No. I – It's just that I know how you felt about her. You disliked her from the beginning.'

'So now you won't tell me –'

'I love her,' Nicholas said in anguish. 'And she told me she loved me. And then. And then, it all fell apart just as if it had never existed.' The Colonel's heart ached at the look he saw on Nicholas's face. 'How could she go off with Saigō? How could she do it?' Tears stood in the corners of his eyes. 'I don't understand any of it.'

When he had seen Nicholas standing there in the doorway, the Colonel had felt an enormous urge to tell him everything; to confess. Now he knew that he would never do that; it would be far too selfish. It was a burden designed for him alone. How unfair to make Nicholas carry it for the rest of his life. But he wanted desperately to say something comforting to his son. He was dumbfounded now by his inarticulateness. Is this how I have been with him all his life? he wondered. I don't know what to say; what would calm him. He wished that Cheong were here now and was instantly ashamed of the thought. My God, he thought, am I that estranged from my own son? Is this what my work has done to me? It seemed to the Colonel to be the final irony. And now he realized how he had envied Satsugai's close relationship with Saigō. It was something he could never have with Nicholas. The fault, he saw, lay within himself.

He heard the door chimes ringing. 'Come on,' he said, and they both went to answer it.

A detective sergeant of the Tokyo Metropolitan Police stood on the steps. He was a heavy-set youngish man, seeming ill at ease; he knew all too well where he was. He saluted smartly as the Colonel opened the door.

'Colonel Linnear,' he said. He had restless brown eyes. 'Lieutenant Tomomi asked me to inform you of the investigation's progress.' He did not have to say which investigation. 'Our latest findings indicate that your brother-in-law –'

'He's not my brother-in-law.'

'Sir?'

'Never mind,' the Colonel said. 'Carry on.'

'Yes, sir. We have ruled out burglary. At least, it's no longer at the top of our list.'

'Oh?'

'The coroner's report indicates a double fracture of the cricoid cartilage. In the larynx. He was garrotted. And by a professional. Lieutenant Tomomi believes there is now reason to consider a radical left-wing connection.'

'You mean assassination?'

'Yes, sir. We are bringing suspects in now. You know, the usual activists from the JSP, the communists, so forth.'

'Thank you for informing me, Sergeant.'

'No trouble at all, sir. Good day.' He turned away. Gravel crunched under his high black boots.

In the weeks that followed, the family life slowly restored itself to a semblance of order. But, as the Colonel had remarked, it was not the same.

There was Satsugai's funeral, of course, a strictly formal ceremony, delayed for a time until Saigō returned home.

Nicholas found no sadness inside himself at Satsugai's death. This, of course, was not surprising. But he also found himself oddly anticipating the funeral and did not realize what it was he was anticipating until he saw Saigō and Itami arrive. Then his heart sank. Yukio was nowhere to be seen. For his part Saigō neither looked nor talked to anyone save his mother.

With Saigō's return, Nicholas had expected Cheong to return home. Such was not the case. She continued to stay with Itami for more than a week. She might have, perhaps, stayed indefinitely had not Itami insisted she leave.

The tragedy had aged his mother, Nicholas saw, as much as or even more than it had his aunt. She rarely smiled and she seemed distant as if holding herself together by a supreme act of will.

Further, and, to Nicholas, quite inexplicably, something had changed in her relationship with the Colonel. For as long as Nicholas could remember this had been an unwavering bulwark in his life, the backbone he could always count on. True, the shift was subtle and, perhaps, an outsider might not have picked it up, but it was there none the less and it frightened him. It was almost as if she blamed the Colonel for the tragedy. He had saved Satsugai's life once, wasn't that enough? Nicholas asked himself. He felt she was being unreasonable and, for the first time in his life, he felt himself being pulled by the increasing polarization of his parents.

Itami came almost every day for lunch. On several occasions she brought Saigō along when he was in town. Nicholas missed these meetings, being either at the *ryu*, talking with Kansatsu, or at classes at Tōdai, Tokyo University, but Cheong spoke to him about them when he returned home in the evenings.

The Colonel had taken a week off from work, though he had not taken a vacation in almost a year and a half. He said he was ill and, for the first time since Cheong had known him, he went to a physician. He seemed pale and drawn but she was relieved to find that there was nothing physically amiss.

For his part, Nicholas became engulfed in college life. It was a strange business, Tōdai, but he soon got the hang of it. Once he had passed the enormously difficult entrance exams, he found that he had become a member of the famed *Gakubatsu*, the university clique. He found that Tōdai was one of the world's most exclusive clubs, grooming its graduates for top-line executive positions in government. Had not five of the post-war prime ministers come from Tōdai?

This period of intense self-involvement took Nicholas away from his family and it wasn't until weeks later that he recognized something was amiss. The Colonel had extended his leave of absence. He would rise early in the morning, as was his habit, and wander around the house touching objects as if for the first time. Often he got underfoot and the servants, quite good-naturedly, would steer him into another room or, increasingly – as he had a tendency to wander aimlessly back – outdoors. Then he would spend long hours sitting by the side of the Zen garden as if studying the swirling lines of the gravel. For a man who had been both strong and extremely active all his life, this behaviour was most out of character.

Itami, when she visited, seemed totally attached to Cheong. Increasingly now, she spent the week-ends, often taking long walks with Cheong through the cryptomeria and pine wood to the Shinto temple where she had taken Nicholas that afternoon so long ago. Perhaps they even passed through the spot where he and Yukio had rolled over one another as they had made love. Of what things Cheong and Itami spoke at those times Nicholas had no idea.

One day he came home from his studies earlier than usual and found the Colonel still outside. He was huddled inside his old English great coat. It seemed far too big for him now.

Nicholas skirted the house, went to sit beside him. He was appalled to see the sharp bones standing out along the ridges of the Colonel's cheeks.

'How are you?' he said. His breath frosted in a miniature cloud in front of him.

'Fine,' the Colonel said. 'I am just – tired.' He smiled wistfully. 'Just tired, that's all.' His thin hands fluttered like birds. The backs were dark with liver spots. They settled restlessly on his thighs. 'Don't worry about me. You know, I am thinking of taking your mother away somewhere for a rest. She's still not got over this thing. She needs to get away from here for a while. Forget all about grief. Your aunt hangs on to her now as if she were her only lifeline. It isn't fair.'

'It'll be all right, Dad.'

The Colonel sighed. 'I don't know about that. The world is changing. It's become too complex. I'll never understand it. Perhaps you will. I hope so.' He rubbed his palms up and down his thighs as if they ached. 'Nothing's the way it once was.' He looked away, into the sky. The last of the geese were moving south in giant vees; two fingers lifted triumphantly: the victory sign. 'I had such dreams when I came here. There was so much I could have done.'

'And you have. You've accomplished so much.'

'Like ashes,' the Colonel said. 'I feel as if I've done nothing, merely slid with the tide, taken by forces I knew nothing of.' He shook his head. 'I cannot escape the feelings that perhaps I didn't try hard enough.'

'How can you say that? You gave them everything. Everything.'

'I thought it was the right thing to do. Did I do wrong? I can't say now. I'm pulled in two directions. I wish I had given them more, gone to Washington, pleaded our case there. I wish I had given them less, spent more time with you and your mother.'

Nicholas put his arm around the Colonel's shoulders. How thin they had become. Where had all the hard muscle gone? Not even to fat. It had just disappeared.

'It's all right, Dad.' Such an inane phrase, connoting nothing. He seemed tongue-tied. 'It's all right.'

What was it he really wanted to say?

But something irrevocable had taken place in the Colonel's life and it wasn't all right.

Despite repeated trips to the physician, despite a prescription of potent pills, eating and, finally, injections, he continued to lose weight until there was nothing more anyone could do to sustain him. Ten days after his talk with Nicholas in the Zen garden, he died in his sleep.

The funeral was immense. Most of the arrangements were taken care of by the American military in Tokyo. Mourners came from all over the Pacific and President Johnson sent a personal envoy from Washington. Nicholas thought this man's presence highly ironic, given what he knew of his father's failed ambitions. The Americans had been unwilling to listen to him in life but were anxious to extol him in death. He could not help but resent the man, despite his charm and extreme courtesy, seeing in him not a little of Mark Antony.

The Japanese government, as was its wont, was somewhat more honest. The Prime Minister himself attended, as did many members of the Diet. The Japanese would not forget the Colonel's awesome contributions to their country and they paid their debt – some time later, after a decent interval, Nicholas was approached for training for a high-level governmental post. He politely declined, pleased none the less.

As requested in the Colonel's will, the American Army rabbi conducted the ceremony, which no doubt nonplussed many of the attendance, especially those who had believed they knew the Colonel well. The rabbi had known the Colonel for a long time and when he spoke the eulogy it was with enormous conviction. It was, in retrospect, quite a beautiful ceremony.

'The Tenshin Shoden Katori *ryu* is the only answer now.'

'I believe that is so. Yes.'

'I want to leave and I do not want to leave.'

'I understand this fully, Nicholas.'

Kansatsu's cat's eyes were bright and alive.

He and Nicholas knelt facing each other. Around them was the gleaming empty expanse of the *dōjō*, a deserted beach in the sunlight.

'What will happen to me – there?'

'I am afraid that I cannot tell you. I do not know.'

'Will I be safe?'

'Only you can answer that. But the strength to be so is within you.'

'I am glad you came to the funeral.'

'Your father was a fine man, Nicholas. I knew him well.'

'I did not know.'

'No.'

'Well ...'

'I have prepared your letters of introduction. These include your graduation certificates – with highest honours – from this *ryu*.' His eyes, focused on Nicholas's face, were unwavering; bits of flashing jet. He withdrew from his wide sleeve three tightly rolled sheets of mulberry paper tied with a thin black cord. He extended them and, when Nicholas touched them, it was the only physical link between them. 'Remember,' he said, 'there is a chain. Thin. Link by link it goes. Take care you discover the identity of the next link on, lest the chain break in your hands and you are left defenceless.' Then he handed over the sheets. His hand lowered with a kind of grave finality.

'*Sayonara*, Nicholas.'

'*Sayonara, sensei.*' Tears filled his eyes so fully that he could see only a blur rise and leave the room. *I love you*, he thought. It was what he had wanted to say to the Colonel that day in the Zen garden and hadn't.

He heard no door click shut but abruptly he knew that he was alone in the house of cedar.

Oddly, the first thing he noticed was that the woodbine had died. Ataki no longer came, and during the last weeks the Colonel had been too ill to think of hiring a replacement. The hedges, always so carefully pruned even in winter, were spiky with branches left unchecked. The ground was hard with ice and frozen snow.

He felt a rising desire to run inside and tell Cheong that he was leaving but he was so uncertain of her response that he lingered awhile outside.

Above him the sky was a rich cobalt blue with just a few tracings of high cirrus clouds and, farther down, orange along the horizon where the sun slid through the thick haze. Far away, he thought he could hear the rumbling drone of a 707 coming down at Haneda.

Now he might have regretted cancelling his dinner date with a couple of school chums in the city; he had told Cheong this morning he'd be home late. But, the decision being made to leave for Kyoto where the new *ryu* was located, he had felt the need for completion. And that would not come until he had told her.

Inside, the house was quite still as it had been since the moment he had returned home from Kumamoto, as if that had become some inexplicable nexus point in all their lives. Loss had followed gain and he wondered now if it had been worth it. He thought once more of the day of Roku-No-Miya and her certitude of the implacability of fate. Thought, too, of the Colonel's conviction that he had been taken by forces he knew nothing of. Life could not be so cruelly unfathomable.

He went through the darkened hall, wondering that none of the lights had been lit.

The kitchen was deserted. No one answered his call. He shrugged off his coat, threw it over the back of a chair, went towards the back of the house. Stillness nodded deferentially to him, ancient as time.

He came, at length to his parents' room. The thin paper *shōji* was closed but, beyond, a light was on and he caught the edge of a shadow, moving.

He hesitated, reluctant to disturb Cheong if she was about to rest. Tomorrow, he promised himself, he would take her to the grave and together they would kneel before the marker of new cedar, lighting the incense and saying the prayers in English and in Japanese.

The shadow moved again and he called out her name softly into the falling night. No answer came and cautiously he opened the *shōji*.

He stood perfectly still, one foot in, one out, staring. All the breath had gone out of him. His head pounded and he felt a shock at the base of his neck as if from contact with a live wire.

All the tatamis save one had been taken outside. The *futon* was folded in a neat pile in the far corner. One round white paper-shaded lamp was on against the right wall. Beyond, outside the glass panels of the far wall, lay the blue-whiteness of the snow, virgin, without one footprint to mar its granular surface. It seemed unnaturally pale against the black backdrop of the croptomeria and pine forest. There were no lights in the sky.

The one remaining tatami had been placed in the centre of the room; the surrounding wood floor seemed naked, like raw flesh with the skin stripped away. On it Cheong knelt with her back to him. She wore a formal light grey kimono with obi. The one with the pink roses embroidered across it. Her back was bowed, her head down as if in prayer. The light gleamed on her blue-black hair, immaculately coiffed.

At her right side tiny Itami knelt, sitting at right angles so that he could see her profile. She, too, was dressed formally in a midnight-blue kimono, sleeves edged in crimson, milk-white obi.

The absolute stillness of the room was a tangible force, a rigid barrier holding him from further movement, even from speech.

Then one sound came, as sharp and near and startling as the first break of thunder from an unexpected storm.

It was the slither of steel against a sheath.

Cheong's right arm moved with unnatural speed and for the briefest instant. Nicholas's mind was unaccountably filled with the sight of bursting cherry blossoms, impossibly pink against green foliage. Now that it had commenced, the transition from absolute motionlessness to rapid movement was irrevocable.

Saw the blade flashing platinum as its length caught the

lamplight, as blinding as the sun, slashing inward in the blur of conviction that was necessary. Into the left side of the abdomen.

A thin cry like a startled bird's but no fear and the body remained still. A slight trembling, the perfect folds of the silk disturbed, an eyelash's flutter just before the violent jerk with both hands on the hilt, left to right, horizontally across the abdominal cavity. Only now the shoulders shook somewhat and he could hear a gasping as of a bellows desperately working. Droplets of sweat rolling down her forehead, dropping, darkening the tatami.

This must be a dream.

Saw the tension come into her elbows as she brought the blade upward towards her sternum. Such strength and force of will many men did not possess.

With infinite slowness, as if settling by degrees, fists still locked around the hilt, Cheong's body began to crumple forward, still in total control, a living monument. Her forehead touched the floor before the edge of the tatami.

As if that were a signal, Itami now moved. Her right hand fled to her side. With a harsh rasp, the *katana*, previously hidden within the folds of her kimono, was nakedly revealed and, standing now, she raised it high over her head. The blade commenced its downward motion with a hot hissing sound as if those fearful shades of steel were anxious to feel the warm flesh part.

In an instant, Cheong's head was cleanly severed from her neck. Only then did the body lose its control and collapse completely. Blood seeped darkly, neatly, just a little of it, as if sprinkled there by a decorator.

'No!'

At last released, Nicholas sprang across the room. Itami, staring down at the beautiful head, black and white and crimson, did not even look up.

'What! What!' He could not think. His tongue seemed an impossible weight in his mouth and he resisted the desire to rip it out. He looked at nothing but the body of his mother. And her head.

'It is done now, Nicholas.' Itami's voice seemed distant and gentle at the same time. The bloody *katana* was at her side. 'She is a child of honour.'

# Fifth Ring
# THE NINJA

# I

## New York City/West Bay Bridge, Summer Present

Someone began screaming, even before the lock shattered and the heavy door slammed inward in a crack of thunder.

The room was a shambles.

A bulky shape ran past him, across the room to the open window.

He began to struggle with it immediately because it had been his stupidity that had brought this on and if he did not work it out right now he would be no damn good in the next few hours and that would without a doubt prove fatal. He did not want to die.

Noted in passing the woman spread-eagled on the bed. Her flesh appeared to have been oiled, the light lying in long sweeps whitening the skin. Chinese.

He had known just as they had banged open the front door to Ah Ma's, in the wake of the *tsunami*. Took you bloody well long enough, he berated himself.

The woman stared not at him but at the muscled legs criss-crossing hers, wide shoulders at the edge of the stained coverlet, head off the bed at an odd angle. It was she who was screaming. The silken bond held her from moving. Her eyes were wide enough for him to see the whites all round. She might have been a madwoman and he saw why.

Upside down, Philip looked at him reproachfully, tongue half bitten through between his teeth.

The screaming seemed to go on and on in cadence, as effective as a siren.


'There's another way,' Nicholas had said. 'A better way.' He dipped half a dumpling into its dark brown spicy sauce, popped it into his mouth. 'I don't want any of your men getting hurt.'

Croaker looked at him quizzically. 'You're a strange bird, you know that? It's what we get paid for, us cops – taking risks.'

They were in a dumpling house on Elizabeth Street between

Canal and Bayard. The place was crowded, the noise level high.

'Reasonable risks,' Nicholas pointed out. 'The ninja's a sorcerer of death. They're not going to be prepared for him.'

'Aren't you being just a little bit melodramatic?'

'No.'

Croaker put down his chopsticks, pushed his plate away from him. A waiter immediately came to clear it away. 'All right. What's your idea?'

'Let me go in alone.'

'You're nuts.' He levelled a finger. 'Let me tell you something, Nick. This is a police operation. You know what that means? I could be suspended just for taking you along. And you want me to let you go after him on your own? The commissioner would publicly string up any part of me left intact after Finnigan, my captain, had got through. Uh-uh. You'll just have to be content with the way it is now.'

'You and me then.'

'No dice. That would mean I'd have to leave you to cover the rear. Can't do it.'

'There's going to be trouble, then.'

'Not if we contain him in Ah Ma's. That's what we've got to do.'

What worried him most in those last few moments as they had climbed the steps to Ah Ma's was the tactical disadvantage they were under. True, the element of surprise was in their favour, but only the man up in that suite knew the layout of the place, including the number of exits. Nicholas did not like any part of it.

On the first landing, he stopped Croaker, said, 'You know, if we don't get him within the first few seconds, we've had it.'

'Just concentrate on getting the bastard,' Croaker had said and started up to Ah Ma's door.

Crouching in the dim hallway, Croaker had his .38 in one hand, the warrant in the other. That piece of paper had not been easy to obtain; Ah Ma had many influential friends.

Somewhere behind them the intermittent buzz of a defective light-fixture. A car passed in the street outside, honking its horn. The clatter of running feet. A sharp abrasive laugh.

Then the door was opening, Croaker was pushing aside a tall, elegant Chinese woman. The warrant flew through the air like a broken bird.

And Nicholas saw it all before him as if in a film. The killings, one by one, like links in a chain. One chain. Terry's historical clues. Three signposts: *Hideoshi, Yodogimi, Mitsunari,* as obvious now as if they were glowing neon. Satsugai, Yukio, Saigō. The policeman sent to guard the dead Shōgun's mistress, a close enough approximation.

Idiot! he thought savagely as he stumbled into Ah Ma's after Croaker. Why did I withhold it from myself?

An American man, eyes wide in terror, stood up awkwardly, dumping a tiny Chinese woman onto the floor. He ran from them, through one of the living-rooms, into a side suite.

Croaker was already midway down the long corridor leading to the back suites. Flower, who had opened the door to them, had been calling for Ah Ma. She was calm even in this seeming crisis.

Ah Ma appeared just as Nicholas began following Croaker back through the place.

'What is the meaning of this?' She grabbed at Nicholas. 'How dare you break into my apartment? I have many friends who will –'

'The Japanese,' Nicholas said in perfect Mandarin. Ah Ma started. She was borne along as he rushed through the long corridor. 'Where is he?' Nicholas said. 'He is all we want.' He turned his head slightly. Doors passed them up, half-open, empty rooms lurking, mockingly. 'Are you Ah Ma?' Noise up ahead. Croaker kicking at a locked door.

'He will destroy the place!' Ah Ma cried. She thought of the communists coming in the dead of night, destroying the house before dragging out her husband. But this was America.

Nicholas perceived her agitation. 'The Japanese is a very dangerous man, Ah Ma. He could hurt your girls.'

This she understood immediately and she fell silent, looking at him.

'Where is he?'

'There. There. Take him then.'

He broke away from her, calling, 'The left one. The left!'

428

Croaker swivelled, put a shot through the lock on the left-hand door. He went in with his shoulder and that was when the screaming began.

A blur of movement and Nicholas instinctively threw his arm across his eyes.

Flash of light, blue-white. The stink of cordite.

Croaker reeled and, running, Nicholas saw the last of a leg and shoe disappear through the open window.

'Christ Jesus !'

He turned. Croaker had one hand over his eyes.

'What happened?' His voice seemed hoarse.

'Flash bomb,' Nicholas said. 'A miniature.'

Noise from the corridor, quickening.

'He's gone, Croaker. Out of the rear window.'

Patrolman Tony DeLong received his final instructions from Lieutenant Croaker via the two-way radio and drove the blue-and-white slowly along the length of Pell Street.

'There it is,' said Sandy Binghamton, his partner. 'Pull over.'

DeLong doused the lights, parked the car on a diagonal, blocking the street. It served a dual purpose. It would help keep the suspect within their perimeter if he came out at the back of the building and it would discourage civilians from poking their noses into a potential red sector.

Binghamton was out first, swinging his big black bulk around the right side of the slewed patrol car. He paused, one hand on the chrome, and turned his head back towards the beginning of Pell Street. DeLong, still in the blue-and-white, was at this moment in radio contact with the second car but Binghamton wanted a visual fix. Civilian infiltration could be disastrous at this point and curiosity was a powerful motivator. He took his cap off, wiped his forehead on the sleeve of his uniform.

He turned back, studying the configuration of the end of the street, the specifics of the target building.

DeLong shut down the radio and came out into the street and together they melted into the deep shadows thrown by the architecture on either side. The Lieutenant had been quite insistent on this score. No sound and no sight. He watched the line of windows three storeys up and thought about this. It was an unusual procedure where more than one blue-and-white was being used. But DeLong had no worries. He had faith in the Lieutenant. He had worked with him for just under a year and a half and was now virtually assured, the next time the exam was given, of making sergeant. He wanted that very badly. He had had enough of the uniform division and now he longed for a permanent assignment to a detective squad. There, too, the Lieutenant could help him. And the extra money would come in handy now that Denise was due.

He felt Binghamton's bulk reassuringly near him. They were old partners and this was his lone regret in moving up. He did not want to break up a partnership that had been so successful. But Sandy had no desire to become a detective. He was content to be on the street with the people. 'It's where I belong, man,' he had told DeLong often enough. 'I don't want to be no desk jockey.' It was just that they conceived of the same job in different ways. Lieutenant Croaker's life wasn't filled with paper work but he could not convince Sandy of that. Once the big man had made up his mind about something, it took the devil's own –

Binghamton nudged him but he had already seen it. A hot flash of intense light, followed by a surprisingly soft *phutt*.

'Trouble maybe,' DeLong said. They both drew their weapons, crouched in darkness, waiting tensely.

Movement at the windows, flickerings like a children's shadow play.

'Get ready.' Binghamton's voice was a basso rumble. 'I gotta believe he's on his way out.'

DeLong nodded and, together, they began to edge closer to the rear of the building. They moved as quietly as they could, keeping to the shadows. For the first time, DeLong noticed that several of the streetlights were out. Odd, since the New Chinatown Association lost no time in bringing such problems to the city's attention. But that was New York for you.

They both saw the blur of movement at the same time. DeLong gave his partner a pat and ran across the street into the concealing shadows on the far side. The black man kept his eyes riveted to the building at the end of the street. He knew from long years of experience where DeLong was headed.

They began to close in, keeping the old-fashioned iron fire

escape between them. Looking up, they saw the moving shadow racing over the slats and then – nothing. No vertical movement downwards.

The two men glanced at each other, then, cautiously, they moved forward until they were almost directly beneath the vertical ladder of the fire escape. From this perspective, it seemed an angular jungle of stripes and deep shadows. Randomly spaced lit-up windows made detection that much more difficult – insufficient light in many areas, spurious illumination in others, creating three or more shadows of the same object.

'What the hell happened to him?' DeLong asked.

'I dunno.' Binghamton holstered his .38, swung the iron ladder down with a grate. 'But I'm going up to find out. He may have gone over the roof.' He scrambled up onto the first-floor fire escape landing and drew his gun. Moving quickly and quietly, he climbed upwards. He had difficulty maintaining a clear view through the forest of metal striations.

He paused for a moment on the second floor at the sound of a police siren, rising and falling, as a blue-and-white sped along the Bowery. Apparently it was heading uptown because the sound dopplered abruptly away, sounding odd and echoey in the summer night. Nothing to do with him.

'Anything?'

DeLong's voice drifted up to him along with the background wash of Chinatown, the traffic, slowed along the narrow streets, the distant chattering of a foreign language, singsong, rapid-fire. Gave a negative wave of his free hand and heard the buzzing in the same instant. Some kind of insect. But the impacts – one two three – pinpricks puncturing the flesh of his chest and spinning him around were from nothing so innocuous.

He stumbled, reached out with his left hand, saw a movement, fired, grasped the railing. He thought only of getting enough air into his lungs. The .38 clattered against the iron grillework at his feet.

Turned drunkenly and saw the dark figure before him as if it had appeared out of nowhere. Looked spectral in the wreaths of light and dark stripes, broken into oblique shards like a fun-house mirror as he lurched from side to side. He wanted to vomit.

Impression of a pale face dominated by black almond eyes.

In a moment the eyes moved and a thin line of white lights appeared along their curving edges. Pupils dilated, he saw. Drugs, he thought, irrelevantly. His mouth opened and he grunted like a stuck pig. 'DeLong.' Had it been loud enough? His ears rang as if he had just come from a rock concert.

The figure came at him, ballooning dangerously. He reached out, barring the figure's way with a stiff left arm while he brought his right up to the horizontal so that the gun was brought to bear – where was his gun? His thoughts as slow and stupid as a Neanderthal's.

Felt as if he were at the bottom of the sea, gravity dragging as cruelly at him as if he weighed five hundred pounds. Almost all his strength was now being used to maintain his standing position. His chest was on fire – a cool numbing flame that seemed to set him floating inside himself. His consciousness detached itself from the useless husk of his body. Freed at last, it shot upward through the top of his head and into the humid squalor of the night.

Now the entire blaze of the city was spread out below him, a pinky-blue shell of light pulsing above the building like a shroud. Beyond it, infinite space.

Peering down through the haze, he could just make out in dwindling perspective his swaying body as the shadow ran past it, arm outstretched. He could even make out the pale blob of DeLong's anxious upturned face, moving nervously in the shadows of Doyers Street.

When he looked again his body was toppling ever so slowly, losing its balance. It seemed as if he had to strain to see clearly now, so high was he. Everything cloaked in an aurora and he wondered, fleetingly, whether he had exceeded his limitations and had gone too high.

Like Icarus, he thought. And descended into darkness.

DeLong felt it before he even saw it. Like an elevator unexpectedly coming down, the sheer bulk was oppressive.

He sidestepped, though he had no idea what had been thrown down. Then it landed, quite near him, with a heavy sound that had no analogue in life.

'Jesus Christ!' he said under his breath. He began to sweat.

He knelt beside the crumpled body of his partner. 'Jesus, Jesus. Sandy, what happened?'

Shock. He knew he must look for whoever it was that had done this, but for the moment he was incapable of looking away. The shock. And blood seeping silently in a rivulet along the asphalt. The left side of the head had impacted first, then the shoulder and so on.

DeLong got up and backed away two paces.

Heard a sound, soft as only a cat might make, and he tore his eyes away. Doyers Street had become a trap now for him and he scuttled back into the shadows of a doorway, looking up. For the first time he found himself wondering what the Lieutenant had got them into. Where the hell was he, anyway?

He caught the movement now, this time soundless, along the horizontal plane of the fire escape one flight up. In other circumstances he would have passed it up as an animal prowling the night. Not now. He raised his .38, and, leading the target, squeezed off a shot. The report was very loud in the confined space, echoing off the walls, zigzagging from left to right. The *spang* of the ricochet told him he had hit metal.

'Shit!' He aimed, fired again. This time, no ricochet. Had it been a hit?

There was a vertical and the last horizontal row before the suspect could get to street level and he would be most vulnerable, DeLong reasoned, in descent. With difficulty, he held himself in check. Binghamton's broken body was like a heavy weight close by him and he fought the rising desire to empty his pistol at the moving shape. Wait, he cautioned himself. Wait and get this bastard when he's closer and there's no doubt.

Now the shadow was at the end of the first-floor fire escape landing and DeLong sighted carefully, using both hands, one cupped over the other to steady his aim He fixed on the point of the access to the hanging ladder. His forefinger tightened on the trigger. Wait. Tidal breathing. Wait. Now. Here he comes. Shots, three in rapid fire.

Nothing happened.

DeLong raised his gun, puzzled. Where was the bastard?

Then he picked up movement on the street in the periphery of his vision. Impossible, he thought. How the hell had he made the drop without using the ladder? And without a sound?

He swivelled, legs spread, aiming the .38 in the classic pose he had been taught so well at the Academy. Silence. No movement. He tried to recall the path of the motion and extrapolate...

Felt the presence so close that he was startled. He dropped to one knee, fired fast and accurately on reflex. But in the space of that last instant he saw the figure leap at him. The left hand was extended and DeLong could make out a short black-wood stick, blunt-ended, as big around as his own nightstick. He braced for an overhand blow and thus was totally unprepared for the horizontal thrust. He was dumbfounded by the useless gesture.

The rounded end just touched the cloth of his uniform over his heart. It was only then that he jerked to the searing pain lancing through him as the seven-inch stiletto blade, powered by a high-thrust steel spring, shot out from the end of the wooden stick, puncturing from front to back. It speared his heart, went through one lung and DeLong was dead before he hit the ground.

The flying form was by him, veiled by the first gout of blood, heard DeLong's last gasp which, to the policeman's dying brain, sounded like the loudest shout in the world.

Nicholas led Croaker back through the apartment. Women, half-clothed, stood in the doorways, staring curiously at them.

Ah Ma, having received the warrant papers from Willow, stood stone-faced with Penny at her side. Willow was in the back suite the Japanese had used, seeing to the boy and trying to soothe the girl's shattered nerves. Willow is wonderful in a crisis, Ah Ma thought, resignedly. The way I used to be. She sighed silently. I do not want to go in there, she thought. Once it would have been the first place I'd run. To help. But no more. Times have changed and so have I. She put one arm around Penny's shoulders, as much to keep the girl beside her as to reassure her.

'You should have caught him,' Ah Ma said in Mandarin to Nicholas. 'Now he may come back here. He won't be happy. His security was broken.'

'He won't be back,' Nicholas reassured her. 'He has already killed the leak.'

They had to go out by the front, the long way around, surely, because in the dark and without radio linkage they could not chance egress via the back window. Gunfire still came to them, sporadic and muffled by the intervening walls of the building.

In the hallway a dog was barking and someone one flight down had turned up a TV set, perhaps to drown out the noise from outside.

'Christ!' Croaker said, rubbing at his eyes as they pounded down the stairs. 'What a goddamned mess.'

More shots as they emerged into the hot sticky night and they ran down Doyers, heading for Pell Street.

They saw the blue-and-white first, slewed at an angle.

Nicholas saw the two bodies immediately. One was outlined in the foreground, the other cloaked in a spider's web of shadows at the end of the street. He paused, his eyes searching from left to right and back again.

Croaker pushed past him, his gun at the ready, but checked when he saw the first body. Slowly, warily he went towards it in a semi-crouch and, on one knee, turned it carefully over. He recognized DeLong at once, was appalled at the amount of blood. He searched in vain for any sign of life. His hand came away soaked.

He got up and, crabwise, scuttled quickly down the street, checked Binghamton's cooling body. He stood up and holstered his gun. He came back, passed Nicholas without a word and slid in behind the wheel of the patrol car.

He called dispatch, asking for the meat wagon and the associate M.E. on call. Then he sent out an A.P.B. He was still on the phone when Nicholas came up, leaning on the frame of the open door.

'He's long gone, I'm afraid.'

Croaker cradled the receiver, put his head onto the back of the seat, closing his eyes. 'They were my best team.' His eyes snapped open and his big fist pounded the steering-wheel so hard it jumped. 'The best goddamned team!' He sighed. 'I'm sorry now I didn't listen to you. I don't know who that guy out there is but –'

'Lew,' Nicholas said, 'slide over. I want to talk to you before the crowd comes.'

Croaker turned to look at him as he slid over to the passenger's side. Far off, they could hear the wailing rise and fall of a siren. It could have been an ambulance.

'I know who the ninja is.'

Croaker sat perfectly still for a moment.

'How long have you known?'

Nicholas blew out a breath as if that would relieve the heaviness he suddenly felt. The deaths in the present had combined with the deaths in his past, rushing forward to engulf him once again. He felt very tired and very sad.

'Not long, really. In the hallway outside Ah Ma's.'

'I see.'

And then he told Croaker everything, spewing it all out as if that might cleanse his soul, relieve him of a burden which, he felt now, he had been carrying far too long.

'Do you mean to tell me,' Croaker said, when he had finished, 'that Saigō isn't after Tomkin at all? That he's after you?'

'Yes and no,' Nicholas said wearily. 'He is going to kill Tomkin all right, unless we stop him, but I believe he took on the job to get to me also. It's the only way all of the killings make sense.'

'I see that, of course, but this is like a blood vendetta.'

'It's a matter of honour.'

'But you must have known it was coming.' The siren's wail was louder now, a cry in the night, and the sound of excited voices pitched back at them off the brick walls. 'Weren't you afraid of – ?'

Nicholas gave him a wan smile as he shook his head. Time to go, he thought. 'I am prepared for it. I've been prepared for a long time now.' He climbed out of the car. Every muscle seemed to ache and his head throbbed as if it were in a vice. He leaned in so that Croaker could hear him as the blue-and-white drew up, followed by the ambulance. The street lit up red and white, red and white like the entrance to an amusement park.

'You see, Lew,' he said with infinite slowness, 'I am a ninja, too.'

'Nick, wait!'

But he was already walking past the oncoming people, crowding into the street, into the glare of the dense night.

'Sam.'

Daddy. Daddy. Daddy. He had never said that word in his life yet he thought it now.

'Yes?'

'Sam.'

'Who is this?'

'Are you still my rabbi?'

'Oy, Nick. Nick! Is it really you?' Goldman's voice was light.

'It's me.'

'My God, how are you?'

'All right. How's Edna?'

'Edna? Edna's fine. Dying to see you. Where are you?' Silence. 'Nick, are you all right?'

'To be honest, no.'

'Just a minute. What . . . ?' The sound of muffled voices came to him, a conversation from another world. A world where there were homes and families, children. Mortgage payments and, perhaps, a two-week trip to Europe in the spring. What was he doing here, anyway?

'Listen. Are you in the city? Edna says to come right up. It's a Friday night. She's made chicken soup. With *lokshen*. Your favourite, remember?'

'I remember.' He remembered everything now.

'So come over. We'll eat. We'll talk.' Pause. 'You'll make Edna very happy. She's been worried about you.'

He rested his head against the acoustic panel of the booth. Traffic raced by him, just beyond his reach.

'Yes,' he said after a time. 'Okay. I'll be over.'

He hung up and hailed a cab. The Goldmans lived in the Dakota on Seventy-second and Central Park West. They took the Bowery, which turned into Third Avenue, all the way up to Forty-second Street where the taxi turned left, heading crosstown to Eighth Avenue.

Just after Broadway, Nicholas leaned forward, tapped the intervening plastic partition. 'I've changed my mind. I'll get off here.' He paid and got out.

He had been idly staring out of the left-side window as they passed the long line of movie marquees along that tawdry street when he had seen the film titles.

He watched the two-way traffic, crossed to the south side of the street. He walked west, past a couple of the new-era glass and chrome porn shops, proudly announcing 'Couples Welcome'. The doors were thrown open in one and a tall black man in wide hat and tight green trousers lounged in the doorway. 'Hits,' he murmured, 'loose joints, coke, speed. Quality stuff.'

Now the movie marquees came one after another in a seemingly unending line on both sides of the street. Most were porn houses but one, the one Nicholas had seen from the cab window, was not. Here there was a kung fu triple bill. Two of the films starred Bruce Lee.

Nicholas dug out a buck-fifty and went inside. The place smelt old and musty. It was lighter than was normal in most theatres. There was a crowd of black and Puerto Rican kids clamouring around the soda machine at the back.

He took a seat. The place was almost filled. On the screen Bruce Lee was talking earnestly with a couple of evil-looking Japanese in dubbed English. The audience was noisy, restless for the action sequences. Dialogue they did not appreciate.

Nicholas sat back, watching Lee for a time. The years had not diminished his aura. His spirit seemed to leap off the screen, making the most slipshod productions worth watching.

Nicholas recalled the first time they had met. It had been in Hong Kong, ironically, after the period Lee had spent in Hollywood, working as a bit player in films and TV and teaching stars enough of the martial arts to get by in front of a camera.

He was beginning to be somewhat of a star in his own right then. They had taken to each other immediately but time and logistics had worked against them and they had never seen each other again.

Lee's death had come as a shock to Nicholas. Not that someone would try to kill him – he knew enough about Lee by that time to understand that the man's uncompromising nature had become a thorn in some decidedly unsavoury sides – but that an attempt had succeeded. He had always wondered how it had been done; now he thought he knew.

Outside, it was still stifling and, in this place of hot lights, fast food, dirty dope and even dirtier deals, more so than elsewhere.

It took him fifteen minutes to find an empty cab and half that time to reach the Dakota; there was little traffic.

He had stayed at the decaying theatre just long enough to catch one of Lee's gorgeously choreographed action sequences, motivated, as usual, by revenge. Tonight there seemed nothing artificial about that.

Goldman, dapper as ever in a pale blue pinstripe shirt and midnight-blue linen slacks, met him at the door. He smiled warmly when he saw Nicholas, extending a firm hand. 'Nick. We were getting worried about you.' He turned, still in the doorway. 'Edna, it's him.' He pulled Nicholas inside, pushed a rum on the rocks into his hand. 'Here. It looks like you need this.'

Edna, a dark-haired chubby woman, bustled into the living-room from the swing door to the large kitchen. She beamed, raised her hands. *'Tateleh!'* She kissed Nicholas on both cheeks. She had the kind of incandescent inner warmth that made mere physical beauty irrelevant. 'Where have you been so long, you haven't come to see us?' Her voice held just the right balance between love and reproach.

He smiled thinly. 'It's good to see you both.'

'That's it,' she said as if she had discovered a rare artefact. 'You've lost weight. Come.' She took him by the hand. 'We eat first. Whatever it is you want to talk to Sam about can wait for a full stomach.'

They ate in the kitchen with the yellow and beige wallpaper and the old West Side fixtures, the oval table of fine-grained mahogany richly waxed, covered with a beautiful embroidered white-on-white tablecloth. A brass Menorah stood on a wall shelf above the table, at its centre.

Afterwards, as Edna cleared the dishes, Sam nodded silently to Nicholas and they excused themselves. Edna kissed them both before they left. 'Whatever is wrong,' she told him with absolute faith, 'you can fix it. Right, Sam? Am I right?'

'You're always right.' He ushered Nicholas into the living-room.

Beige and pale green predominated. Edna despised brilliant

primaries, perhaps because she saw her childhood on 189th Street in those colours. The effect was a soothing one, like being in a cool forest during the heat of the day.

They sat on the beige velvet couch and Sam put his feet up on a matching ottoman. An antique clock ticked lightly from its owl-like perch on the white marble mantelpiece. A great bunch of dried eucalyptus in a pale pink ceramic vase stood within the grate, wafting its pungent scent into the room. There was a Utrillo on the opposite wall and, on another, a small Dali. In their bedroom, on pale blue walls, were a Picasso and a Calder which, of course, Edna detested. They were all originals but they were displayed with a pleasing lack of ostentation.

'It has come back,' Nicholas said softly. 'All my past, like a great tidal wave.'

Goldman reached for a hardwood box, took out a cigar, lit it slowly.

'I've lost the present somewhere along the line. I no longer know where I am.'

He deliberately blew the blue smoke away from Nicholas. 'Nicholas, as Shakespeare so cleverly put into Ophelia's mouth, "We know what we are, but we know not what we may be." '

'Sam, I didn't come here for homilies!' he exploded.

'Nor did I mean to give you any.' He took the cigar out of his mouth, laid it on a crystal ashtray. 'Look, it is totally unreasonable to expect to know or understand everything about yourself. The human being is such a complex animal that we have to be content to muddle through things as best we can. Some days, it just doesn't seem nearly enough. At other times ...' He shrugged with some equanimity.

'I understand all that. But you're the expert on history. I am only partly a Jew. I haven't had the training. I don't –'

'It has nothing,' Goldman said seriously, 'at all to do with training. One learns the meaning of being a Jew just as one learns the meaning of being a human being – by living life, not by learning the Torah.

'It comes from what you feel inside and the important thing is that you do not deny what is inside you. Doubt and fears; uncertainty of the present and the future all stem from that. Your self must be free to go in whichever direction it must go.

'The spirit flies, Nicholas – it is the only thing we possess which can. It is a sin to tie it down, to deny your spirit its breath. Life is nothing without it. We merely survive, from day to day, in a kind of unthinking limbo.

'Does this answer your question?'

In the night-silence of the tower on Park Avenue, he sat with Raphael Tomkin. At the moment, Tomkin was on the telephone. Somewhere in the world, it was always some time between nine and five and that meant business was rolling. Decisions, vital to one subsidiary or another, and thus vital to the corporation as a whole, required the mind of the mover and the shaker. Three continents awaited the outcome of such trans-Atlantic or trans-Pacific conversations.

While Tomkin talked on in mega-figures, a kind of semi-secret corporate shorthand, Nicholas looked at the tiny bit of metal and plastic he held between his fingers. He turned it like a miniature world, though in truth it was only a disk and thus flat, so that it caught the lamplight, its face turning to a slow dazzle.

Just possibly, he thought, this little piece of the electronicized present could be the key to it all. The past, the present and the future. It could end right here, if he chose. If he chose.

And he desperately wanted it to be his decision.

He felt, quite rightly, that Saigō had taken all initiative from him and he felt stripped bare, naked and defenceless because he had not seen what was happening.

Saigō had been leading him around by the nose until he was dizzy, laughing all the way. It was a technique from the *Go Rin No Sho*. What was its name? To Hold Down a Pillow. Restrict the enemy's useful actions while encouraging his useless ones. Lead him around as if he had a ring through his nose and, when he is in total confusion, strike.

'Where've you been?' Tomkin asked, cradling the phone. He looked slightly rumpled at this time of the night, his cream-coloured linen suit wrinkled at the insides of the elbows, his medium-width grey silk knitted tie slightly askew. The flesh of his face had lost the pink glow it maintained for most of the day, seemed pummelled into a kind of uneasy truce – submission was a flat-out impossibility – by the long hours. Lines at the corners of his eyes had become noticeable but they merely made him seem that much more human. Nicholas still felt himself wondering which was the façade.

'In Chinatown.'

Tomkin grunted, swivelling round in his high-backed leather chair. His hands played idly across his desk's electronic console as a Greek peasant might fondle his worry beads. 'Chinatown, huh? With that bastard, Croaker, I'll bet.' He stared into Nicholas's face and his eyes, like chips of blue quartz, were merciless. They were sailor's eyes, Nicholas thought. The eyes of a man well seasoned to the sardonic tricks of the sea and the open sky. They were the eyes of a survivor; shipwrecked, his crew drowned, this man would make it onto some beachy shore and, like Crusoe, vanquish time though perhaps not solitude. 'You better not get too friendly with that cop. Just a friendly warning, 'cause I'm waiting for that motherfucker to step one inch out of line. Then I'm gonna break him in two.'

Nicholas thought about what Croaker had told him of Gelda and he had to smile to himself. What would Tomkin do when he found out that Croaker and his daughter were seeing each other? Apoplexy might be an accurate term.

'That bastard's got a hard-on for me and I've got no idea why. He's got this crazy notion that just because I was balling Angela Didion, I killed her.'

Nicholas watched him, rubbing the electronic bug back and forth between the calloused pads of his fingers.

Tomkin snorted derisively through his nostrils, giving Nicholas the image of a horse rearing. 'Hell, that broad got around, you know? Doing people she didn't even know. Got a kick out of that, giving rim jobs to guys she pulled off the street. Just like that – Boom! Only it wasn't always guys, see. The broad was nuts. Definitely nuts. If I'd've known about that – you know, a closet lezzie – I wouldn't have – hell, she disguised it well enough.' He waved a hand and gold glinted. 'Anyway, it's all ancient history now – that's how I see it. But that cop won't let it alone, you know? He's like a fucking dog with an old bone nobody wants but him.'

'He's doing his job.'

'He ain't doing his job!' Tomkin cried. 'That's the whole goddamned issue.' He pounded the table. 'The Angela Didion thing is a dead issue for everyone on the entire fucking New York Police Force except Croaker. What's he think he's got? A calling from God? Well, I'm telling you, he's got nothing. I got his number; loves to see his name in the papers.' He swivelled back and forth in his chair, very fast, as if he had a surplus of nervous energy. 'Goddamned glory hound. He's not gonna ride *me* to any headlines. He needs to be taught a lesson, that's all.' He glanced up, no longer half-talking to himself. 'What about this guy – the ninja?'

'Well, that's what I came to talk to you about. So far, he's been setting the pace. What I think we have to do now is reverse the situation. We have a chance if we can control the environment. We have to, in other words, be on the battleground before him.'

'So? Set it up. That's what I'm paying you for, isn't it?'

'It's not that simple, unfortunately.'

'Well, do what you have to do. I don't care what it is. I want him out of the way. Permanently.'

'It involves you directly.'

'Of course it does. He's been sent here to kill me.'

'He's here to kill me, too.'

'What?'

'I know this man. There is an old score to be settled. It's nothing to do with you.'

'I see.'

'Except that it may lead us to his entrapment.'

'How?'

'Through one of his bugs.' Nicholas lifted the tiny disk so that Tomkin could see it clearly. 'You see, this is currently inactive. It's one of the new contact type, which simply means that once it is reapplied to a surface, it becomes active again.'

A gleam came into Tomkin's icy eyes; deceit was a currency he understood. 'You mean –'

'We reactivate it. And use it. Chances are he'll believe there's been a minor dysfunction and –'

'What if he's smarter than that? This guy's an expert. I've heard stories about ninja –'

'I don't,' said Nicholas, 'think it will matter at all. He wants us both and, if he thinks he can get us together, he'll take the chance, even if there's the suspicion of a trap. It's one I've set up, you see. It's a challenge and he cannot back down without losing an awful lot of face. That he will not do.'

'It amounts to inviting him over,' Tomkin said slowly.

'Yes.'

The blue eyes regarded him cannily. Nicholas could almost hear the sound of his mind ticking over, weighing probabilities just as if he were making a computer-assisted business decision. But then, in a curious kind of way, it *was* a business decision.

'Let's do it.' His voice rang unhesitatingly.

Afterwards, as Nicholas detached the bug and dropped it into the thick cotton bed he had fashioned for it in one of the desk drawers, Tomkin said, 'Can everything be arranged by the night after next?'

'There won't be any problem.'

'Good.' He picked up the phone as Nicholas turned to leave. 'Hey,' he said, 'you didn't tell me you were having problems with Justine.'

Nicholas froze, silently cursing Tomkin. Had he been spying on his daughter again? How else would he know?

'Hit a nerve, didn't I?' He laughed. 'You got a damn good poker-face but I don't need to see your expression to know.'

'Just what *do* you know?'

Tomkin shrugged. 'Just that she's in the city; out with another guy. Don't know who he is but I will soon enough.' He dropped his eyes, began to dial. 'It's too bad, really. I would've liked you two to stay together. You're good for her. Now I'm afraid she's gone back to her old ways.'

'Where is she?'

'Hello? Yes –'

'Tomkin –' Nicholas's tone cut through the space between them.

'Hold the line a moment –' Tomkin put his palm over the receiver. 'What did you say?' His voice had turned a touch treacly.

'Where is she?'

'At a discothèque. On West Forty-sixth Street.' He rummaged

with one hand on his desk-top. 'I know I have the name of it somewhere. At least, I *had* it earlier ... Ah, here it is.' He read off a slip of paper, giving Nicholas the name. His eyes lifted. 'Know it?'

'I don't go to discos, normally,' Nicholas said. His voice was as tight as a coiled spring. Across from him, Tomkin looked as if he had devoured a particularly tasty sweet.

'No, I suppose not. Otherwise you might have run into her before this. It's an old hangout of hers. Perhaps you ought to try it some time.' He turned away to the phone in dismissal.

For a time he spoke as part of a conversation that had no meaning, listening with his free ear to the sound of the elevator's doors sighing shut, the quiet hum of the machine as it took Nicholas down to the lobby far below.

When that sound had ceased, he reached out one hand and opened a desk drawer. Without turning his head, he replaced the receiver of the phone.

He stared down at the bit of plastic and metal with a kind of rapt fascination. A light line of sweat broke out on his forehead, the way it did every time he made a major business decision. His heart thudded and his pulse rate increased.

He licked his lips and, carefully, deliberately, he brought the bug out of its bed and attached it to the side of his desk.

He swung round, away from it so that he looked out on the winking late-night face of the city. West. The entire country was before him though, of course, he could not see it. At length he began to speak.

'I suppose,' he said, almost meditatively, 'it depends on how much you want him. But what if – what if I could *guarantee* Nicholas Linnear. I could hand him to you on a platter. As easy as pie, yes?' He swung round and now he addressed directly the bug hanging like a bloated spider. 'I'll bet that's worth a lot to you. As much as a life. What do you say?'

He reached out and detached the bug, returning it to its drawer, precisely as Nicholas had placed it. Tomkin was a meticulous man.

Then he sat back with his hands behind his head, waiting for the phone call he was certain would come. The fully loaded pistol clinging in its holster to his damp shirt beneath his suit jacket felt heavy and warm and infinitely comforting.

In matters like this, he thought, one never knew.

'Someone wants to see you.'

The phone had rung just after Croaker had walked in but, despite that and despite the fact that she had already put the machine on, Gelda had picked it up herself.

She had come into the living-room to answer the door and both of them were still there in the semi-darkness. She watched him now as she listened to the voice in her ear, as he stood in the oblique bars of light and dark so that they climbed his legs to just above his knees. His face was illumined by the fat wedge of lemon light from the bedroom.

'G, are you there?'

'Yes, Pear.'

'I thought you had drifted away for a moment. Have you popped anything?'

'Not tonight, no.'

He seemed afflicted with a weariness that went far beyond a lack of sleep. It was as if all the endless hours in the office and on the streets and in the courtrooms had built up a sly accretion impossible to discard which now lay heavily upon him like a grey and ageless second skin.

'Just a professional question,' Pear said, mistaking Gelda's silence as an expression of annoyance, 'that's all. Seeing as how there's –'

'Not tonight.'

'I know I haven't given you any notice. That's because it's the Senator.'

Gelda knew what that meant. 'Get him someone else.'

'G,' Pear said slowly and patiently, 'he wants you. There *is* no one else. You know how he is.'

He stood there in the half-light like some mythic animal come to life; a creature someone had mistakenly dressed in human clothes. He seemed only partially aware of her.

'The answer's still no.' She could not be more aware of him.

'And what of Dare when she comes to town again?' Pear had obviously caught something in Gelda's tone of voice.

And, abruptly, Gelda knew that she had answered the phone

*because* he was here. 'No. Even for Dare. Those days are gone. I am out.'

'I see.' There was no hurt in Pear's voice, no hint of recrimination.

Gelda felt light-headed, as giddy as if she had just consumed an entire bottle of Dom Pérignon. She also felt happier than she ever had before.

'We'll miss you, G. *I'll* miss you.' It was like Pear, at a moment like this, not to mention the clients.

'I'll never forget you,' Gelda whispered.

A soft laugh. 'I should hope not. Good-bye, G.'

Gelda put down the receiver, went over to Croaker. 'What happened?' She put her arm round him, walking him into the bedroom.

In the warm lamplight, she saw the dried blood on his hands. 'Won't you tell me?' she said in a voice calmer than she felt. 'You look so sad.'

'I've just come from seeing two families. A pregnant wife and a mother of three small kids.' He looked at her despairingly. 'Have you ever had to tell someone that the person she cares most about is dead?' He took a deep breath. 'Well, I have. But never before when I knew those deaths were my fault.' He stared at his brown hands, stained as if they had been dipped in dye, crusty as if covered in sea salt.

'Why don't we start at the beginning,' she said softly, taking his hands in hers, drawing him forward. 'The blood has to come off first.'

*I knew what I was doing / I knew right from the start / I knew where I was going / There's radar in my heart ...*

The place was all mirrored chrome and black smoked glass, multi-levelled like the hanging gardens with floors of translucent glass under which coloured lights flashed in time to the music.

The air vibrated with percussion and electric voices, strung like a Christmas tree with garlands of perfume and perspiration and burning pot.

*I felt your contact coming / Your star was on my chart / I heard your motors humming / Got radar in my heart ...*

Somewhere was the bar, obscured behind a forest of raised arms, swirling hair, shiny, mindlessly concentrating faces. Dance dance dance: the imperative was clear, treading an atavistic path, the primitive's tribal revivals, an ecstatic communal orgy, trivialized to the point where all possible consequences were nullified.

*The posters on your walls mark every fashion's rise and fall | Why try to keep the past alive/And though I know the time is almost 1984 | It feels like 1965 ...*

Like moving through a dream. All senses assailed relentlessly until distortion grew like weeds in the abandoned front yard of reality. Every step forward carried with it the burden of two in retrograde. He thought of Alice down the rabbit's hole and wondered if Carroll could have had this in mind. Only Coleridge might have dreamsmoked this up; it seemed the habitat of a damaged archangel.

*The music in my room is always slightly out of tune | My harmony is up on trial | And though I know the rhythm you'd prefer me dancing to/I'll turn my revolt into style ...*

At the bar there were leather-padded seats on which no one sat, a line of jackdaws ironically eyeing a busy cornfield in summer.

Nicholas sat and ordered a drink for form's sake. He was not thirsty. He watched the lamé glitter in the spiralling lights, the neon shoes with heels impossibly high. Multicoloured eye make-up seemed to cover half the faces of women who turned towards him again and again in the course of the dance. Flesh was entirely incidental, it seemed; arms and breasts and thighs were painted like lizard skin. Their expressions recalled to him vivid scenes from *Metropolis*.

He was searching for Justine, but in this madhouse it seemed useless: like running after Yukio in Kumamoto. Doors closing in his face as fast as they were opened.

Then what Sam had said to him earlier in the evening began to seep through into his consciousness. What difference did it make what he was now as long as he knew that he wanted to be; what he wanted. It was no longer 1963, part of another lifetime. But he knew that he would never truly be free until he understood it all. Without understanding, he knew, assimilation was impossible. The *kijin* – the goblins of his past – would be appeased by nothing less.

'What are you doing? C'mon, c'mon, c'mon and dance.'

She was a sloe-eyed blonde in a lavender *crêpe de chine* dress which showed off her ample breasts to maximum effect.

*I feel like a wog / People give me the eyes / But I was born just like you you you ...*

'Don't you wanna' – her bird's head swayed seductively – 'get in the swing? C'mon, c'mon.'

'No, I don't think –'

*– like a wog / I don't mean you no harm / I just want to shine your shoes ...*

'– apricorn, right? You must be. Dour.' She pronounced it *dower*. 'All Capricorns are dour. But –'

'I'm not here to dance,' he said, feeling foolish. 'I'm here to find someone.'

*Golly gee / Golly gosh / Don't call me your golliwog ...*

'– do it together.'

*Don't call me, don't call me, don't call me / I'll call you if I want you ...*

'You don't understand. There is a woman here. A woman.'

'So?' She took his hand, crimson nails gleaming, changing colours, lines of light flicking. 'Let's dance, dance, dance until we find her.'

He broke away from her grip.

'Don't you want to have fun?' she cried after him.

*– made me feel like, feel like, feel like a wog ...*

Went up to the second level, blues and greens like a grotto of waving kelp. Synchronization had begun to set in and he felt his pulse throbbing to the beat of the music flailing the air with the abandon of a reaper at his wheat-field.

And, at last, he saw her on the highest level, partly obscured by the scaffolding of the circular staircase. He had to wait several minutes, the narrow path clotted and blocked: dancing up, dancing down.

Disappearing in a wave of arms and heads bobbing and he went up the iron stairs two at a time. Black leather walls like a padded cell, smoked glass far too fragile for the height: what if someone should stumble in thrall and fall? What then?

449

Light in reds and yellows, turning white and grey against the black leather, disconcerting, like seeing a colour TV show on an ancient set: everything somehow just slightly out of phase.

There she was. With a tall broad-shouldered man with lank black hair and the sallow skin of a Puerto Rican. He wore a sleeveless shirt with a red, blue and gold Point Beer button, high-waisted deep red trousers.

*Didn't I hear you cry this morning | Didn't I feel you weep | Teardrops flowing down on me | Like rivers in my sleep ...*

'Justine.'

Her head whipped round and light caught at the crimson flecks in her near eye. Watched him silently until her partner whirled her around in a blur.

'Justine.'

'What'a'you want, man? Don't hassle my chick, hey. Keep cool, okay?'

*Didn't I hear your voice this morning | Didn't you call my name | I heard you whisper softly | But the words were never plain ...*

'Justine. Look at me.' He reached out.

'Hey, man. Hey, hey. No way to act. You ain't listenin'. Drift away now. She don't want no part o' you.'

Noted in passing, the dilated pupils, the reddened nostrils.

'Why don't you go to the men's room and do some blow?'

*That's a strange way to tell me you love me | When your sorrow is all I can see | If you just want to cry to somebody | Don't cry to me ...*

'Now, hey man. I'm through talkin' to you.' The *click* unheard in the throbbing of the leather room but the gleam of the switchblade was unmistakable.

'Justine.'

'Don't talk to her, man.' One shoulder lowered. 'Now this's for you.'

He was very fast and he knew how to use it, trained in the street where there are no rules except the need to survive. This kind could be far more dangerous than the professional because of the unpredictability. The eight-inch blade could rip open his abdomen in a fraction of a second.

Blocked the initial thrust with his left forearm and, pivoting, slammed the edge of his right hand into the Puerto Rican's pelvis. There was no sound save for the music; their violent motions, dancers' movements assimilated into the fierce kineticism of the leather room.

The Puerto Rican's mouth opened wide, his head thrown back in precisely the pose of the man in Munch's *The Scream*. He moved to right himself and Nicholas jammed his shoe against the outer edge of the other's right instep. All balance fled him and he pitched sideways, between two startled couples. His outflung arm smashed someone in the face as she whirled by.

It all might have been a scene from a comic opera but Nicholas did not feel like laughing.

*Here are we | One magical moment | Subject the stuff from where dreams are women ...*

Justine looked from him to the fallen man, clutching his hip. The switchblade lay on the mottled floor like a centrepiece at a bizarre wedding which no one seemed to want to pick up and take home.

'Justine –'

'How did you find me? What do you want from me?'

'Justine.'

'I can't take any more. Please, please, please. Can't you see I've been crying –'

*There are you | Drive like a demon | From station to station ...*

'– over you. Over you.'

'Justine. I came here –'

'And I don't care any more if you know it.'

'– to tell you I love you.'

Tears rolled silently from her eyes. The air was as thick as honey with music: aching voices, insinuating rhythms, erotic percussion. 'Please.' Had she heard him?

'I love you.' They touched in a kind of radiation of energy and mis-spent emotion. 'Justine, I –'

*It's not the side effects of the cocaine | I'm thinking that it must be love | It's too late to be grateful | It's too late to be late again | It's too late to be hateful | It's too late ... | It's too late ...*

'... cried in the sand in front of your house with the night and the sea and that's never happened to me before.' And he thought, lying on the long pale sea-foam sofa with Justine's long warm body next to his: You're wrong, Croaker. I can feel. I *do* feel.

'Don't be ashamed of it.'

'I'm not.' The first faint crumbling of his past, sliding downwards to be buried at last beneath the churning waves of the sea. 'I wouldn't have told you otherwise.'

'It makes me happy.' She put her fingers on his hip as if searching for a lock to open. 'To know that you can be grateful to me for something.' Stockinged, her legs whispered one against the other like cicadas' wings. 'The way I am grateful to you.'

'It's a new feeling.' She watched his eyes turning inward, listening to his words. 'What I did to you was so cruel. But I did it – I did it out of self-defence; a kind of survival instinct. I suddenly felt how close you had come to the core of me and it reminded me –'

Her long hair brushed his shoulder. 'Of what?'

'The sea, a long time ago; the mist and a ferry ride through a cyclorama of Japan.' His lips stayed half open even when he was silent, tidal breathing as one does when dreaming. 'It reminded me of a girl I once loved. The trouble was then, I thought I was still in love with her.'

'Where is she now?'

'I don't know. She could be anywhere – anywhere.' She could feel the rise and fall of his chest and abdomen, as regular as the tide. 'She told me she loved me – she convinced me – I didn't know anyone could be that good at deceit ...'

She smiled, half hidden in the dark. 'If you'd been a woman, you'd know all right.'

'Sometimes I think sex is for the animals.'

It was quiet for some time, just the intermittent hiss of late-night traffic passing outside, remote and inconsequential. Justine was surprised more by his tone; she had never before heard such bitterness and she found herself wondering just what had transpired between him and that girl so long ago.

'I'm jealous,' she said. She thought she might be taking an awful chance. 'I'm jealous of how much of yourself you gave to her.' He was quiet, beside her. 'Never again, Nicholas?' Only her side and hair touched him. 'Who is being punished?'

When he spoke, his voice was tight. With what was he struggling? 'She made me ... feel ...'

'What?'

'Feel, just feel.'

'Is that so terrible?'

'And then she left me. She went off with ...' And he told her what he had never told anyone, flooded with shame.

Justine put her warm lips against his ear, whispered, 'Unzip me, Nicholas.'

He reached out. It came as the rasp of a log cracking, burnt through, subsiding into the hot ashes of the grate.

The top of her breasts shone palely in the firelight like the swelling crests of the sea at dawn. Here, too, there were depths to be plumbed. But the tugging he felt now went beyond his loins; a kind of tidal wash, covering his whole body, sweeping into his head. 'I missed you so much.' And not, any more, Yukio.

She could feel how that had been torn out of him. 'Yes,' she whispered. 'I can see that now. I felt old and tired without you there.' She shrugged out of her shoulder straps.

'Let's not make love right away.'

Her eyes were glittery so close to him, the little fire in the far one like a beckoning beacon homeward bound.

'Say it again.'

'Justine, words sometimes have no meaning at all.'

'Then what does?'

His arms encircled her. 'I'll hold you,' he whispered. 'And you hold me.'

Her fingers brushed his skin, moving.

Fukashigi, the kenjutsu master, awoke at first light with the tendrils of something still in his mind.

The world, this early, was fog-shrouded, familiar landmarks rendered as in a pointillist painting.

Not a dream. Fukashigi did not carry such things into the waking world.

Something had dragged him away from sleep. The tendrils swirled.

And immediately he thought of Nicholas.

It must be time then. And despite all his wisdom, Fukashigi felt the slight thrill of fear shiver him.

He had thought about this time often during long nights when sleep eluded him and now he knew that he had been deluding himself, thinking that this day might never dawn.

Here it was, after all this time.

Time, he knew full well, meant absolutely nothing.

Even with the distances involved, he felt the psychic tuggings like a storm pulling at the moorings of a ship.

The long years in China and Japan seemed like a mist-shrouded dream to him, like the world he saw outside his window. The mind, he knew, could do much, play many tricks, and he wondered this morning which world was truly more the dream. In a way, America could never be as real as those days and nights on the Asian shore with their spices and their mysteries.

There had been time then, unlimited time, it had seemed once, to plunge into each more involving puzzle. And the joy he felt at their eventual unravelling was still unequalled in his life.

There had been, of course, several times when he had cause to regret the life he had carved out for himself. It was, after all, a most perilous path, fraught with real and imagined dangers every step of the way.

Jealousy racked them all like a perennial ague that could never be fully assuaged. There was resentment of anyone new. And especially of one who sought to plumb the depths that had frustrated them all.

And conquered.

Fukashigi sat up on his *futon*, hearing his bones creak. Magic, he thought. What a misunderstood word. Typically Western. He had to laugh.

Then he thought about Nicholas. He did not envy him but then there was no envy in Fukashigi's heart. Had there been ... Fukashigi shrugged his thin shoulders.

Who knows? He thought. But there was excitement inside him again.

Now he thought that he could see clear down to the bottom.

The floor was full of silty hills and fish without colour wove the pattern of their changeless lives through the mud and rocks and sand.

This section of the Straits of Shimonoseki had been haunted for seven hundred years or thereabouts. Ever since the infant emperor Antoku Tennō perished here in a spectacular sea battle along with every other man, woman and child of his Taira clan at the hands of the Minamoto.

There were frequent reports of sightings of the strange Heiké – another name for the Taira – crabs which have human faces on their carapaces and are said to house the *kami* of the long-dead defeated warriors.

They cannot, it is said in legends, find peace and thus, on fog-blanketed nights, fishermen swear they can see odd spectral fires upon the unquiet waters and they refuse to launch their boats, even when the fish are running, for during these terrible nights, the Heiké would rise from the deeps, interfering with passing ships, pulling unwary swimmers downward to their deaths.

And it was to help assuage these lost and unhappy *kami* that the Buddhists built the temple of Amidaji there.

But now, Saigō thought, it is more than ever a haunted place, this Dan-no-ura, for an outpouring of my own soul lies dead and defeated in those waters, come to join the joyless Heiké in their endless journey: there would be no burning fire, no golden lotus hearth for either.

He could see the perfect face lying on the bottom undisturbed as if there were no intervening waves; perfect only now as the features composed themselves in death. A traditional heroine: the pious daughter, the loyal wife, heart filled with sacrifice; all her grievous sins expunged.

It was good, he told himself. It was right; it was just. A death decreed by history.

What else could he have done?

He felt the shortness of breath and the burning tears threatening to destroy his dead eyes with their pitiful flow and he automatically began to chant the *Hannya-Shin-Kyō: Form is emptiness; and emptiness is form ... What is emptiness – that is form ... Perception, name, concept and knowledge, are also emptiness*

*... There is no eye, ear, nose, tongue, body, and mind ...*

In darkness there is sin; in darkness there is death. Sin negates spirit; and the killing of beings without spirit can only be looked on as an act of charity.

But, but, but – how could there be love where sin exists? This was a question that had tortured him for years, more than any other one thing, shaping his life. And as he asked himself the impossible question again, he pounded his closed fists against his forehead and cheek-bones, seeking to destroy that within himself which remained perversely recalcitrant. He could no more drive the memory of her from him than he could relinquish his name and it was just this terrifying obstinacy within himself which had driven him to the drugs. Besides, he believed now that they enhanced his powers.

But surely it had been Nicholas Linnear who had brought him to this sorry state. If it had not been for him, he would not ... they would not ... there would not ...

Lights blazed against his closed eyelids as he beat himself but even they would not drown out the visions of the gentle pale fish at play in the straits. And, O Amida! How the wind howled on that night, snow swirling down like lace curtains, disappearing upon the changeless waves with the black sky so low that neither Kyūshū nor Honshu was visible. Alone in the rocking boat. Did the howling increase at the heavy splash? Did the Heiké know they were about to receive another unrepentant sinner? Unrepentant they must be or why else lie upon the darkest nights as unappeased *kami*?

Ghost lights upon the straits, just as the tales told, and he recited many prayers, as many as he knew, repeating them without surcease until the prow of the boat touched the wooden quay at Shimonoseki and he stood on solid land, shaking and wet with sea-water and sweat despite the snow and the chill north wind.

Still today he could hear that eerie howling like demons calling him back, to complete terrors that had somehow been left undone, circling within his head like black kites descending upon a bloody carcass.

At last, his breath heavy with the aftertaste of psychedelics, drenched in so much sweat that he might have just come from the bath, he fell into a sodden sleep filled with dreams and, worse, the trumpeting echoes of dreams.

Nicholas dreamed: of land's end. And out from the near shore, the very end of it at least, arched a bridge of wood and stone very much like the one at Nihonbashi. And as he started across this bridge, he saw that to either side there was nothing but a hanging mist. He turned round, looking back the way he had come, and was astonished and not a little afraid to see that the strange mist had obscured the land from which he had come, so effectively that he forgot which land that was as well as not knowing towards which land he was bound, as if the mist stirred about inside his head as well as without.

When he was approximately half way across, he thought he could discern a sound, dim and muffled by the mist, but as he drew closer he became more and more convinced that it was the sobbing of a woman.

In time, he was able to make out a darker shape within the mist which, as he approached, coalesced into the form of a young woman. She was tall and willowy and she wore a clinging dress of white silk. It was, he saw now, dripping with water, as if she had just climbed out from the sea, which he supposed this bridge spanned.

She stood with her slim back against the bedewed balustrade, weeping into her hands, and such was the power of her lamentations that Nicholas felt compelled to move closer.

When he was only a few steps from her, he heard her speak: 'Oh, you've come. At last! At last! I had given up all hope!'

'Pardon me.' His voice reverberated within his chest as if it were a cathedral-like cavity. 'My lady, I do not think that I know you, yet you seem to have recognized me. Have you, perhaps, made some error?'

As he said this, he moved his head back and forth in an attempt to get a clear view of her face for, as it was now, he could not truly say whether she was known to him or not. But this seemed quite beyond his present capacity. Between her long dark hair, spread like a sea-fan and strewn with small shells, and the long-fingered hands she continued to press to her face, she remained hidden from his gaze.

'No, there is no error. You are he whom I have sought for all these years.'

'Why do you weep so bitterly, my lady? What ill has befallen you?'

'A most dishonourable death, sir, and until it is avenged my spirit must wander – wander here.'

'I do not see how I can be of help to you, my lady. But if you will allow me to see your face ...'

'It will do you no good to look upon me,' she said so sadly that he felt his heart must break.

'Then I was correct. I do not know you.'

She said nothing and thus he did not know what her answer should be.

'Take your hands away from your face,' he said to her. 'Please, my lady. I cannot assist you otherwise.'

Slowly, as if most reluctant, her long fingers drifted down through the mist and he gasped.

Where the features of her face should have been – eyes, nose, lips and the rest – her skin was as flat and smooth as an egg ...

'– God, Nicholas, what is it?'

His chest heaved as if he had just struggled to finish a marathon, and sweat glistened across his face like rime.

Justine's face, lined with worry, hovered above him, her long hair draped on either side, an electric curtain, a tenuous link.

'What happened?'

'I don't know. You cried out in your sleep –'

'What did I say?'

'I don't know, darling. Nothing recognizable, at least not in English. Something like, oh' – her brow wrinkled in thought – 'minamara no tat-something.'

'*Migawari ni tatsu?*'

'Yes, that's it.'

'Are you certain? Really certain?'

'Yes. Absolutely. You said it more than once. What does it mean?'

'Well, literally, it means, "to act as a substitute".'

'I don't understand.'

'In Japanese folklore there is the belief that a person may give his or her life in order to save another's. It needn't even be a person. It could be a tree, just about anything.'

'What were you dreaming about?'

'I am not certain.'

'Nicholas,' she said with her typical objective intuition, 'did someone give their life for you? – In the dream, I mean?'

He looked at her, put his hand up to her cheek, but it was not her soft flesh he seemed to stroke, certainly not her voice he heard in his head then.

In that heated room of perfect death with his toes touching the hem of his mother's exquisite, perfectly folded kimono and, just a little way beyond, the rivulets of blood dropped like rubies along the floor, Itami said, 'We both must leave now, Nicholas. There is nothing left here for outsiders such as ourselves.'

'Where will you go?' His voice was as dull as lead.

'To China.'

His eyes tracked upward to her white face. 'To the communists?'

She shook her head slightly. 'No. There are others there – who were there long before the communists. Your grandfather, So-Peng, was one such.'

'You would leave Saigō?'

Her eyes were as bright as a bird's. 'Nicholas, did you ever wonder why I had but one child? But no, why should you?' Her lips were turned in a grim smile that chilled him. 'I can only say that with me – with *me* – it was totally a matter of choice, though Satsugai believed otherwise. Oh yes, I lied to him. Willingly. Are you surprised? Well.' She stirred slightly like a sapling in a sudden gust of wind, giving way, giving way minutely. 'I would not have another like him.' Her dark eyes were slits now. 'Do you understand me? I trust you do.'

She looked down briefly at her *katana*, standing on its bloody point. 'Do you hate me? I would not be surprised ... But no, I see that you do not. That gladdens my heart, I cannot tell you how much.

'I love you, Nicholas. Were you my own I could not love you more but I think you already knew that deep inside yourself.' Her head jerked as if she had been abruptly reminded of something. 'These days of *kwaidan* pass through my fingers like so much sand. Time is short and I have much to do.'

He stood in front of her, pale and drawn. He shivered once though no breeze stirred in the room.

'Will you tell me,' he said, 'what honour there is in this?'

'What honour there remains in all the world,' Itami said sadly, 'resides in this room. There is little enough, I fear. Little enough.'

'You must tell me. You must.' His voice was almost a cry and he was certain then he saw tears standing out like soft pearls at the inner corners of her eyes.

'Ah, Nicholas. These tales are not so easily told. You ask me to expose the soul of Japan. I could sooner rip a blade into my own belly.' Her eyes squeezed shut as if she were attempting to brush away a vision from her mind. Her voice was a whisper. 'Ask me anything else. Anything.'

'What will become of you – Aunt?'

Her eyes flew open and she smiled kindly. 'In China I shall travel until I reach the place Cheong bade me go to in her last breath. I will not be there long.' Her hand tightened on the hilt of her *katana*; another drop of blood rolled from the blade's smooth steel surface onto the bare wooden floor.

I must see Fukashigi, Nicholas thought now, staring at Justine in the semi-darkness; time to renew the old vows. And she must leave here; she must be out of harm's way. *Aka i ninjutsu* was the only way now the forces of *Kan-aku na ninjutsu* were stirring, readying themselves to come against him: ancient, implacable enemies arrayed on a modern battlefield. He would need, he knew, all the fearful shades of steel to be victorious this one last time.

When Saigō awoke he was, for just an instant, convinced that it was into death's dark realm. Death held no horror for him but this might only be because life held so little for him. It was the meanest of gifts and, therefore, it meant nothing for him to part with it.

Then he remembered that he had not yet killed Nicholas and he knew that this was life only into which sleep had yet again deposited him.

There was much to be said for revenge, yes. It was all that kept his heart pumping now. He thought of all the money in his swollen bank accounts; the vast acres of land; the four small but rapidly growing electronics konzerns. What did it all amount to? Not even a part of the smallest steel filing from a master swordsmith's forge – ah, no!

Money was merely the sere gateway to power, and power, well, all that was good for was manoeuvrability. Once you could manoeuvre in this atom age, you could accomplish anything.

Yet there was but one thing that Saigō now wished to accomplish and that was to seek out and expunge a life.

Tonight, he thought savagely, lying naked on the *futon*. Pale grey light filtered through the blinds, traipsing across the ceiling like an itinerant priest, his *korom* torn and tattered, its ragged ends taken by the wind.

He marvelled at the weakness of Americans. Such cowards, they surely could not have powerful spirits. How they had won the war he still could not imagine. It would give him great pleasure to see the look on Raphael Tomkin's face as he died beneath the blade of steel. To think that he believed a deal could be so easily arranged. No deal was possible; not after the commencement of a buy.

No, death would come to him tonight, just as it would come to Nicholas.

Perhaps, even, there would be a stalemate between them and death would come to both. This did not concern him. On the contrary, he might have even looked forward to it, knowing that the importance of death lay not in the dying itself but in the *manner* of one's death. How one died was recorded by history and one was remembered as much for the manner of one's death as for one's life.

For Saigō, as for all Japanese warriors from time immemorial, there were only two honourable ways to die: in battle or by one's own hand with calmness and ritual. To die otherwise would mean terrible, insupportable shame throughout eternity, an awful karma brought into the next life or, far worse, carried into the infinity of limbo.

This intimate thanatopsis had made him hard and he almost regretted having killed the Chinese boy. He had been so good. But there had been no choice just as, long ago, there had been no choice –

461

Somewhere in the night he had been full of hate; a pernicious boiling that had all but swamped in his long, exquisite training. It is a true measure of how emotions can warp the soul, he told himself now, sitting up on his single black *futon*, and he cursed the day that Yukio had come into his life. O Amida! he cried silently.

But this early hour was like crystal for him. He had thought, in the dark, to blunder into them tonight. To move fast, fast, fast; to catch them both quickly, Nicholas and Tomkin. But while he had slept in the land of death, his mind had been at work and now he knew that there might be more for him than just the death of those two. He thought of the straits and shuddered. Voices seemed to fill his mind, screaming louder as he inhaled, moaning like the autumn wind as he exhaled. He held his breath, squeezed his eyes shut for long moments until the voices faded.

Yes, he thought, rising and beginning to bathe, his training had taught him that there were things far worse for an enemy than merely slitting his belly.

The world, he knew, was one great wheel, an ellipse one was bound to by karma. Wheels within wheels; plans within plans. By day's end, his mind would be tranquil. Then, if death should come, he would fling wide his arms and welcome it.

It was a splendid day, clear and still cool with just a few touches of gauzy cirrus clouds high up in the west. Far too splendid to spend hanging around the house, Justine thought, as she threw her bags on the bed.

The beach on Dune Road looked inviting as she went round the side of the house and took the car out on to the road.

She went east on the highway, having no specific destination in mind, but seeking the exit for Watermill reminded her of a beach in that area she had heard talked about again and again. Flying Point.

It was no surprise to her that she got lost, but this far out on the South Shore it was difficult to get too lost and at length she found herself at Flying Point beach. She got out and, locking up, went out on the sand.

She was still far too full of energy to lie down so she walked.

The beach was wide, surprisingly free of debris, with sand of a very pale colour.

The surf was up, curling high in a translucent green arc crowned by white spume before tumbling forward onto the sand in a dazzle of silver spray.

It was far from crowded this early in the morning, though the beaches this far out were never jammed the way places like Jones Beach always seemed to be.

It was quiet, peaceful with the repetitive sounds of the sea and the gulls calling as they wheeled into the sun.

The character of the beach changed so subtly that for a long time she was not even aware of any difference, but presently it seemed to her as if it had become somewhat more familiar. For instance, she knew that she was coming upon a narrow spit of land before she turned the curve of the beach and saw it lying before her. As this began to happen more frequently she began to wonder where in fact she was.

Then, as she happened to look up from the beach to the houses she was passing on her right, she saw the familiar spires. She felt a brief twist in her stomach as if she was plunging downward in a high-speed elevator, wondering how she could have been so stupid. Flying Point was just east of South Hampton and Gin Lane.

There it stood in all its looming splendour. The family house.

As she stared, she saw the wooden gate swing open and a figure come down the slatted redwood stairs onto the dunes.

My God, she thought. It's Gelda!

Her first instinct was to turn round and simply walk away but she was rooted to the spot, thinking: what the hell is she doing at the house?

On the sand, Gelda had poised and now she took off her sunglasses.

She's seen me, Justine thought, panic-stricken. I can't walk away now.

Gelda came towards Justine. They stood facing each other on the near-deserted beach at a distance at which a pair of duellists might stand preparatory to firing at each other.

'Justine!'

'Well.'

'What a surprise.' Her eyes had gone dull, as if an iron gate had come crashing down behind them. They talked as stiffly as if they were two strangers awkwardly thrown together at a party neither of them had wanted to attend.

'Are you here with ... anyone?'

The wind whipped about them, making streamers of their hair as if they were pennants on a field of battle.

'No, I'm waiting for someone.'

'I am too.'

'Well.'

'Yes.' She did not want to admit to herself how much Gelda had changed. How beautiful she was now. How gracefully she moved. And behind that, a kind of confidence that – well, she had always had enough confidence for them both. It was Gelda who always had the boyfriends, who was always asked to parties and to football games. It was Gelda who could ice-skate so exquisitely – her movements on the ice totally belying her weight – her dates soon clung to the side railings, watching her with unabashed awe.

Justine was always too young for this or for that; too skinny for the boys to notice her; too clumsy for sports. She drew instead and became more isolated, her envy feeding upon itself like a ravenous cannibal.

'Is Father here?'

Gelda shook her head. 'No, he's in the city.' She hesitated a moment, debating with herself. 'He's in some kind of trouble.'

'That's nothing new.'

'No, but I thought you would be concerned – at the very least. You always were with Mother.'

And there it was, staring at them both in the face like an ugly red sore.

'I can't help the way Mother felt,' Justine said defensively. Anger began to fill her up, and if she had ever entertained the thought of telling her sister about Nicholas it fled now.

'And I can't help being the way I am.'

'That was always your excuse for doing just what you wanted.'

They stared at each other silently. Justine was appalled yet unable to initiate any action. My God, she thought despairingly, we're kids again. We can't think like adults when we're around each other, just intent on hurting each other all over again.

Gelda squinted into the sun. 'D'you want to come inside for a while?'

'No, I –'

'Oh, come on, Justine. You can unbend *that* much, I imagine.'

'You have felt it, also.'

'Yes. During the night. This morning. I don't know when.'

'It is important that you are here.'

'There was nowhere else to go,' Nicholas said.

Fukashigi smiled thinly.

There were no classes today and the *dōjō* seemed enormous in its emptiness. Sadly, it reminded Nicholas of the last time he had seen Kansatsu on the *ryu* outside Tokyo. And it occurred to him that much of his life since then had been spent simply floating, the days and nights gently rocking him as they blended together, lulling him to sleep on the tide of their passage.

What had he really accomplished in America? What could he have done with that time had he stayed in Japan? So much time. And if he had never begun his studies in bujutsu? What then? What would he be now? Some high government functionary, no doubt, with a high salary and a perfect garden. Two weeks each year in Kyoto or somewhere on the seashore, even Hong Kong, perhaps, in a season when it was not overrun by Western tourists. A loyal wife and a family. Children to drool on him and laugh with.

The void, he realized, is only noticeable when it is no longer there. Justine. Justine. Justine. His reward for at last swatting down the past. He very much wished to see again the graves of his parents, to kneel before their *sotoba*, to light the incense sticks, to say the litany of prayer over them.

'You have brought it?' Fukashigi said.

'Yes, I knew I must one day, though I don't know why.'

'Come.'

Fukashigi led him through the abandoned *dōjō*, striped with shadow and pale sunlight bleeding through the ragged rents in the flying lengths of oblique cloud that marbled the summer sky.

At the threshold to the back rooms, Nicholas shed his shoes, Fukashigi his *geta*, and the old man took him to the very rear of the building, to a room with a raised floor of tatamis. He pushed aside the *shōji* and they entered.

Sitting cross-legged, Fukashigi waved his hand gracefully. 'Please place it between us.'

Nicholas put the parcel he had been carrying down onto the tatami and unwrapped it. There was the dragon and tiger box that So-Peng had given to his parents.

'Open it.' Fukashigi's voice held a certain reverence.

Nicholas obeyed, lifting the heavy lid to display the nine cut emeralds.

All of Fukashigi's breath seemed to go out of him as he gazed at those nine bits of mineral which seemed to glow and spark in the low light.

'I never thought,' the old man said softly, 'that I would see such a sight.' He sighed. 'And they are all here. All nine of them.'

He looked up. The square room was immaculate, spacious, harmonious, calming.

'Time changes many things. When you came to me so many years ago in Kyoto it was, I think, only the letter from my friend Kansatsu that stopped me from dismissing you out of hand. Oh, so you did not know that. Well, it is true. And, to be completely truthful, even after I had read the letter, I thought that I might be making a grevious mistake. After all, *Aka i ninjutsu*, history informs us, is no acquired trait but a serious calling – quite as serious, quite as mysterious as the calling to serve Amida Buddha – to which one is born and bred.

'I can tell you that I had grave doubts concerning your entrance into *Aka i ninjutsu*, despite what Kansatsu wrote. He is no ninja, I thought, therefore he cannot know. But a breach of our security had already been created and, of course, you came to me appearing a Westerner. I knew only that Kansatsu had not lost his mind.

'Of course, to have sent you away would have been, I know now, a mistake.' His fingertips caressed the box before him. He smiled. 'You see, I am not, as I understand was so often said of me in those days, omniscient.'

'It is still said.'

The old man inclined his head slightly. 'So? It is, as you can see, an untruth. It was through Kansatsu's intuitiveness that you became the first student of mixed blood at the Tenshin Shoden Katori *ryu*. The only one such. A signal honour; an unorthodox decision on my part. Still, I do not regret it. The *ryu* has had no finer student in all the years that it was mine.'

Now it was Nicholas's turn to incline his head.

'But you came to us for a reason, did you not? And now the time has come. It has begun.'

'I regret to say, *sensei*, that it began some time ago.' And he told the old man about the murders.

Fukashigi sat quite still and there was silence for a time after Nicholas had finished. His head swivelled and his cool gaze swept over Nicholas's face. 'When you joined us you took certain vows, just as you did at every step of your training. You must have known what was commencing the moment you discovered the *shaken* fragment. Yet you took no action. Now, perhaps because of that, many people – three of them your friends – are dead.' His cold eyes seemed as luminous as beacons on a foggy day. 'Are you dead, too, Nicholas?'

Nicholas watched the backs of his hands, stung by the old man's words. 'Perhaps I never should have come to the West. I think I was merely trying to outrun my karma.'

'You know better than that. Wherever you go, it will be the same for you.'

'It sounds like a curse.'

'If one chooses to see one's life in those terms, then it is. But I am surprised that you should think in such a curiously Western mode.'

'Perhaps America has changed me as it did Vincent.'

'Of course only you can know the truth of that –'

'I don't know any more.'

'I suspect that is only because you do not fully comprehend it yet.'

'I am bound up inexplicably with Saigō – and with Yukio – yet –'

'Acceptance of karma should not be confused with fatalism. We are all, to a great extent, masters of our own fate. But also we must learn to bow before the inevitable: this is the true meaning of acceptance and it is only this which brings the harmony without which life is not really worth living.'

'I understand all that,' Nicholas said. 'It is the specifics that still elude me.'

Fukashigi nodded his head and, reaching inside his robe, he withdrew a series of rice paper sheets which had been folded very carefully. They had about them the look of age. Fukashigi handed them across to Nicholas.

'This letter is from Kansatsu. I am following his express instructions in giving this to you now.'

It was a plain black Ford sedan.

Doc Deerforth tried to make out who was in it but the late morning sunlight spun like a nova across the windshield, completely obscuring it.

He watched the sedan long enough to make certain that it was following Justine's brick-red roadster and, still mindful of and not a little curious about Nicholas's warning, he spun the wheel of his car and set off after them both.

He had had a call out along the west end of Dune Road earlier that morning and had come east to look in on Justine. He had still been some distance away when he had seen her take the roadster east. That was when he had picked up the black Ford.

He stayed well back and turned in after seeing the brick-red roadster stop at Flying Point. But, curiously, no one emerged from the black Ford. He waited impatiently for what seemed a long time. He got out of his car, on the point of following her down the beach, when the black Ford started up. Slowly it began to pace her along the beach road.

Doc Deerforth went hurriedly back to his car and got in.

He was sweating profusely by the time he came round the last turn and saw the sedan parked some way from the beginning of Gin Lane.

He was grateful he had not lost it. The traffic was light and he had had to hang back farther than he would have wanted.

More than once the Ford had disappeared for long moments around a serpentine turning.

Now he knew where they were both headed. He recognized Raphael Tomkin's house immediately.

The soles of his shoes crunched on gravel as he got out of the car. He snapped down the sun-glass attachment to his glasses against the fierce glare.

Now he could see into the black Ford. It was empty.

It was quite still here. There was a lone cardinal in a tall pine but it would not sing. He could no longer hear the boom and hiss of the surf, and the lack of that sound was like white noise clattering like thrown stones through his brain.

He began to walk towards the Ford. All sound seemed heightened in the hush. Not even a breeze stirred the high tree-tops. It was very hot.

The black Ford was nearer now, hulking like some sinister castle in the desert. Who would follow Justine? And why? *Look after her*, Nicholas had said. Startled, Doc Deerforth realized he thought of the two of them as if they were his own kids. Just an old man's foolishness, he admonished himself. I miss my two girls, is all.

His shirt was soaked, sticking to his skin like loose folds of ancient flesh. Just as it did, he reflected, in the jungle so long ago. And abruptly, he staggered, experiencing a fierce stab of vertigo. It's the malaria, he thought, steadying himself against a resinous tree trunk. My own form of malaria. Because it's the summer. In the fall, it will pass.

He ran one hand along the burning flank of the Ford, and, bending a bit, peering into the interior. There was nothing to see.

He was still stooped over like that, an old, balding man, sweating in the heat of the afternoon, when the shadow stretched itself across the side of the black sedan.

For a long moment, Doc Deerforth stared at it. It recalled to him a moment in a ballet he had seen a long time ago in the city: the entrance of the Dark Angel. On either side of him, his daughters – they were still young then – had cried at the vision. Black wings clouded the sun and he was abruptly cold.

He began to turn, heard the weird whirring sound at that

same instant. A blur on the periphery of his vision and instinctively he raised his arm in front of his face.

Then something had wrapped itself about his ankles and he was dragged off his feet. Metal links scraped and dug painfully into his flesh. He gasped and twisted, feeling like a fish on a line.

He looked down. A long chain with a weight on its end was strung taut, pulling him into a stand of dense poplars beyond which stretched long fields of corn.

He rolled, puffing; tried to sit up. There was a blade at his throat.

He looked up. Before the sky, as rich a cerulean as he had ever seen it, he saw a face – at least part of one – that made him shudder. All the breath went out of him.

He stared into eyes as dead as stones, madman's eyes. So different from those others long ago; yet the same. The ninja, Doc Deerforth thought. His mind seemed to freeze with the thought, as if there could be no room in the world now for anything else. His life seemed to shrivel down to the size of a pea and, disappearing altogether, become totally insignificant.

Cicadas chimed; flies buzzed. He was back in the Philippines, back in the tent, tied to the table.

And the soft, knowing voice said to him, 'Why have you followed me?'

'Why have you followed the girl?'

There was absolutely no change of expression in those staring eyes, of that he was quite certain. But, without warning, the ninja jerked on the chain and the saw-toothed steel links bit through skin, sawing into tissue, ground against bone.

Doc Deerforth's head flew back and breath whistled through his half-open lips. Blood drained from his face.

'Why have you followed me?'

The words came again and again like a litany, a friar's prayer at day's end – what did they call that? Vespers?

'Why have you followed me?'

Time ceased to exist as the pain rose and fell like the tide – now faster, now slower, so that he had no clear idea of when it would make his jaws clamp together in a rictus, make the sweat fly off him as he jerked this way and that, make his thighs tremble and the muscles in his legs turn to water.

At some point, it was impossible for him to say when, Doc Deerforth knew that there was something different about this one. He was at once more cruel and less removed. And there was an elemental power to him that frightened him to the very core. It was as if the devil himself had come to strip him of life.

That it was his time to die, Doc Deerforth had no doubt. There would be no last-minute rescue this time and he was far too weak and old for muscular heroics. But a human being, until the very moment of death, has certain powers that can only be relinquished voluntarily. Neither time nor terror had dominion over these few last possessions.

The ninja now had one knee across Doc Deerforth's heaving chest. Gently, almost reverently, he took up Doc Deerforth's right hand and, using only the tips of his fingers, broke the thumb. He waited just the right amount of time – the shock had worn off and the pain was a sharp throbbing. He broke the index finger. And so it went, one by one, slowly and inexorably.

Doc Deerforth shuddered, heaved and sighed. He whispered the names of his daughters, of his long-dead wife. He felt, rather than saw, the ninja crouching low to hear his faintly expelled words. A curse and then a sharp crack. Pain flared as his right wrist shattered.

Someone, someone, he thought hazily, will have to call the kids. Then the pain blanketed him and his nerves, vibrating, screaming with agony, pitched him at last into unconsciousness.

A child's high cry perhaps decided Doc Deerforth's fate. It was close at hand and Saigō, abruptly deciding that nothing could be gained from prolonging this game, took up the other end of the saw-toothed *kyotetsu-shoge* and slit Doc Deerforth's throat with the double-edged blade.

'From the beginning,' Nicholas read, 'your father was suspicious of Satsugai. From the first time they met, the Colonel understood that behind the man's vast power in the *zaibatsu* stretched a hidden network of immense size and strength. He suspected, quite rightly, as further investigation bore out, that Satsugai was deeply involved with the Genyōsha. They were, perhaps, most responsible for sowing the seeds that led to the fateful decision to institute the pre-emptive strike at Pearl Harbor.

'Your father wished to crush the forces of Genyōsha and it was to this end that he intervened on Satsugai's behalf when the SCAP tribunal was ready to try him for war crimes. He thought that leaving Satsugai free to pursue his plans would eventually lead to the arrest of the Genyōsha main body itself.

'It was a good plan except that Satsugai discovered it. Now he was eternally in the Colonel's debt – a man who was out to destroy him. This he could not abide. Satsugai was of the old school and most honourable. He knew that he could not touch or interfere with the Colonel in any way.

'Therefore, he sent his son, Saigō, as his emissary of death, sending him into Kumamoto to the most feared of all the *Kan-aku na ninjutsu ryu*, the *Kuji-kiri*.

'Over the years, the Colonel came to understand the nature of his folly. He had gambled heavily and lost. Now Satsugai was forever beyond the law and this had been the Colonel's doing.

'Your father was an Englishman by birth yet he could not have been more Japanese had he been born here and he came to a decision that was uniquely Japanese. He killed Satsugai himself.'

Stunned, Nicholas raised his eyes. And because of that shame to the family, Cheong had committed *seppuku*.

'Continue reading,' Fukashigi said gently. 'There is more.'

'Your father was a fine warrior, Nicholas, and thus none suspected him. Until, that is, Saigō returned home. With the basic elements of *Kan-aku na ninjutsu* already at his disposal, it did not take him long to divine the truth. This knowledge he kept to himself and, while stoking the fires of his hatred in the secret depths of him, he meanwhile presented only the image of a grief-stricken son to the outside world. For already a plan of vengeance had formed in his mind.

'Thus he contrived to be home several times when he knew Itami was coming to your house for the afternoon, when you would not be home. I cannot say whether it happened the first or the second time but it scarcely matters.

'You must know by now what amazing *yogen*' – chemists –

'the *Kuji-kiri* are; how many different and subtle ways they are taught to kill a human being without ever touching him.

'This, I fear, is what happened to your father. Saigō murdered him with slow poison.'

Nicholas felt tears come to his eyes so that he had difficulty focusing on the last several sentences. His fingers gripped the thin rice-paper leaves, shaking.

'Here I must extend to you my most profound apologies. Even though I am not ninja, I feel responsible, at least in part, for your father's death. He was a great friend to me and I feel – even now after the initial sorrow has left me – that I should have known.

'You have become the symbol of my atonement. That you are reading this now with, I trust, my esteemed friend Fukashigi beside you, is proof of that. I am long past knowing.

'I imagine that you were quite surprised on arriving at the Tenshin Shoden Katori *ryu* to find that payment for your long study had already been made in full.

'I trust you understand why I had to do that before I died and pray Amida Buddha that you will forgive an old man's lapse.'

He saw the brush-stroke characters of Kansatsu's name through the well of tears as he cried for the Colonel, who had tried, in his own way, to tell him, and for Cheong. He felt now as if the years had been stripped from him like the red and gold leaves of autumn. And now he wept, too, for his friends, who had loved him and whom he had loved in return. Time enough for them all now.

Beside him, silent as sunlight, Fukashigi sat deep in contemplation, thinking about the cruelties time inflicted upon the young.

'Did you come here to dry out?'

'That's a bit direct, isn't it?'

'Sorry.'

'That's all right. I suppose I deserved it. But, no, I've already done my drying out.'

They sat within the immense oval of the starry living-room. Fully half the walls were glass, open to the sunlight of the beach

and the sea. Above them, the skylight was like a faceted diamond, the largest in the universe, so Justine had always believed
when she was younger. Now, in the morning, the tardy sun had
not yet slipped across its faces and thus they were bathed – as
at evening – in a most flattering indirect light.

The couch upon which they both sat was completely circular
with two breaks, as angular and distinct as the fitted edges of a
Chinese sphere puzzle which someone had once given to Justine
and which she could never quite conquer. They sat on opposite
sides of the morning, their backs as rigid, their eyes as wary
as a pair of cats' on unfamiliar territory.

Tall frosty drinks sat on the tables in front of them, un-
touched, as if for either of them to take the first sip would be to
admit defeat.

'How long will you stay?' That was not what Justine had
meant to say. She had wanted to say, 'I'm glad' because she
found that she was. No one wanted a lush for a sister. It was as
if her tongue cleaved to the roof of her mouth when she wanted
to say something nice to Gelda. I really can't give her anything
at all, she thought in wonder. Not even the tiniest thing. She
felt a wave of shame wash over her like her mother's long
hands, slippery with soap, bathing her.

When she was older, she would wait until everyone had left
the house. She would take a bath and emerge, moist and warm,
one great snowy towel around her thin body and another smaller
one wound about her long hair like a turban. And, as if she
were in some far-off Byzantine city – that must have been from
her constant reading – she would flop down on this very couch,
her back against the foamy cushions, her legs up and dangling
over the back. Thus positioned, she would turn her head, watch
the slow wheel of the day as it streamed in through the skylight
and by its shape and its position in the room could divine the
precise time of day without ever looking upward or out of the
window or at the great clock on the mantelpiece behind her. But
nevertheless its heavy sonorous ticking caused her to dream of
the sunlight as drops of honey, seeping in through the panes of
the skylight, onto her outthrust tongue.

In just this way she amused herself while Gelda was off with
her friends.

With a start, she realized that she had missed Gelda's answer. That was all right; she hadn't meant to ask the question anyway and now had no interest in the response.

'You can stay here as long as you want,' Gelda said.

'Oh, that's all right. I have to be going, anyway.' But she made no move to get up and Gelda chose not to pursue the matter further.

'You'll excuse me, then.' Gelda rose and went through one of the narrow gaps between the couches. 'I'll be around.' She put her hand on the back of the couch. 'You always loved this room best, didn't you?'

'Yes,' Justine said, somewhat surprised.

'I always imagined you would have slept out here if Mother would have allowed it.'

'Yes. That would have been nice.'

'Well.' Gelda's fingers plucked at the fabric. She looked down at her hands, then towards the place where Justine lay half sprawled on the cushions.

'You'll say good-bye before you leave, won't you?'

'Sure.'

Then she was alone in the house – the servants were gone for the week-end – as she had been when she was a child, and her gaze quite naturally fell to the portion of the morning which the skylight let in, reflecting on what it might be like to be a great lady in some time past when there were no cars or phones or even electricity – she always adored candle-light and oil lamps to her meant taking to the sea for years at a time, hunting down the whales, imperilled and exhilarated at the same time. It was something she, as a woman, would never know. Down to the sea in ships and back again with enough oil for all the lamps in Nantucket. I should, she thought, have been born a Starbuck.

And that was how Saigō found her, alone and dazzled, lost within her imagination. She never knew that she had passed into unconsciousness or that anything was done to her while she was out. She might have been sleeping. But she was not.

He worked over her for fifteen minutes, one ear alert for the most minute sound that might herald an interruption. He could not afford that now. He hoped that it would not occur because it would necessitate dragging her away from here and this he did not want to do. She was relaxed here; it was a place she trusted. That made what he had to do that much easier.

During this time, Justine's eyes were open and it could even be said that she saw, in a manner of speaking. But what she saw was only his face, transfigured, like a geological fault line after an earthquake. There was only a little familiarity among the change. It had become a face that was more than human.

It became the ground she walked upon, the food she ate, the water she gulped thirstily down, the air she breathed. It became her world and, finally, her entire universe.

Thus she listened as it spoke to her, this thing – being – which engulfed her, far larger than the diamond that shone above her head. What he did to her was to hypnosis what the atom bomb was to bow and arrow. Here the will of the individual did not loom like an unbreachable wall, stopping them from doing that which they could not do had they been conscious. Now all was possible, for this was different. He was ninja. This was the *Kuji-kiri* and, beyond that, the *Kōbudera*, that which even his *Kan-aku na ninjutsu sensei* feared.

It was magic.

He waited patiently until Nicholas set aside the sheets of rice paper, stained now with tears. It was the end of the long steamy afternoon; the city was slowly cooling as the bloated sun slipped behind the backs of the high steel and glass buildings. But that was outside. In here the West could not intrude. Here the eternalness of the East defied time, shrouding them both. Somewhere, a runic chanting like the call of the cicadas when day is done.

'Kansatsu felt it most prudent to await this time to tell you, Nicholas. Had you been told sooner, you would, no doubt, have sought Saigō out and you were not ready then. He would have destroyed you as easily as he could have done that night in Kumamoto.'

'And now?' His voice was clotted with emotion.

'He may destroy you yet. I am afraid, Nicholas, that he has gone beyond even the Kuji-kiri teachings. He sought out *sensei* who, because of the nature of their teachings, would never be allowed into a ryu, not even the *Kan-aku na ninjutser*. These were mystics steeped in the ancient lore of that portion of China – the central steppes of Mongolia – of which there is little known even today. There is magic in him now, Nicholas, and it has taken him over completely.'

'Well, there is a kind of magic inherent in many of our own ninjutsu teachings.'

'There are imagined magic – that is, illusion – and real magic. The two should not be confused.'

Nicholas knew better than to argue this kind of thing with Fukashigi and he was silent all through the simple meal the *sensei* had prepared. Afterwards, in the darkness of the night, Fukashigi began the ritual that would last until morning.

'Here' – his fingertips touching the opened box lid – 'is the *Kokoro.*' This was a word that, like almost all Japanese words, had many meanings: heart, spirit, courage, resolve, affection, inner meaning, and more. It could, in sum, be said to be the heart of the matter. 'It, too, is real magic. Your mother knew this and, although she suspected your father did not, she knew that you would. It was meant for you.' His young eyes were watchful, full of life and – something more. 'Nine is the key number, Nicholas. There are nine emeralds here. One to break each arm of the *Kuji-kiri* – nine-hands cutting.'

Saigō awoke in the hour before dawn and left his *futon*. There was much to do this last day and the hours seemed to run ahead of him despite his precise organization. He had slept soundly and dreamlessly for the first time in more than a week.

He was on the streets early. He went deep into the East Village, to an enormous army-navy-camping store where he purchased a dark-coloured heavy-weight duffel bag with a triple-weight polythene lining. He tested the duffel bag's sling straps for strength.

Walking crosstown to the IND subway – he was most careful at this stage to take only public transport – he emerged at Forty-seventh Street and walked the block over to Broadway. There he entered a theatrical supply house.

His third stop was at Brooks Brothers, where he purchased a light-weight tan business suit off the rack. The jacket was perfect but he left the trousers with a tailor to be shortened. On his way out, he bought a muted plaid pork-pie hat which looked absurd on him in the light of day but which, he knew, would be perfect at night.

His last stop was in Chinatown, where he picked up a bamboo cane. Then, dropping off his parcels – which included the trousers – he went out again, prowling in search of someone who looked just like him. This was something he had scouted on first arriving in New York. Height, weight, the physical semblance of his physique were all he was concerned with. The face itself would not matter. Not after he got through with it.

Croaker called in twice at half-hour intervals and it was a good thing he did. Either they had misplaced the message the first time or it had not yet come in.

He got it on the second call in.

'Matty called. Didn't leave his –'

'That's okay. I got it.'

In the traffic he began to look for a phone and when he found one, pulled over to the kerb. He dug a dime out of his pocket and dialled. No police lines on *this* call.

'Not here,' Matty the Mouth said in a very bad Italian accent.

'It's Croaker.'

'Oh. Hi.'

'Cut the small talk. You got it?'

'Yeah but it's worth a lotta –'

'Matty, we've already settled on a price.'

'Yeah, well, you see, Lieutenant, what we have here is a fluctuating market.'

'What are you trying to pull?'

'The price is out of date.'

'Look –'

'The situation's changed since we last spoke, is all. Nothing to get your bowels in an uproar about, I still got the goods.'

'I got a notion to haul your ass downtown. How'd you feel about that?'

Matty clucked his tongue against the roof of his mouth. 'Me, Lieutenant? Well, I'd be lying if I said I wouldn't mind, 'cause I would. But I really gotta say that you'd mind even more 'cause then you'd get zip outa me and you know there ain't anywhere else to go on this one.'

Croaker felt a tightening in his stomach. His heart was racing. 'What's happened?' he asked carefully.

'This must be real important to you.'

'Spill.'

'The issue,' he said, 'was cold when we first talked about it.'

'And now –'

'Now it's as hot as Lucifer's hind tit. Lotsa nosing around on the street. Someone else's looking for this dame, too. As a hot item, she's on the top of everyone's list. All of a sudden, like, y'know?'

'But you've got it all. Name, number and address?'

'Lieutenant, when I tell you I got something, it's not on its way in from the Coast. The information's in house.'

'So give it.'

'After we've agreed,' Matty said, 'on the new price.'

'Okay, shoot.'

'Triple.'

'Triple! Are you out of your –'

'Lieutenant,' Matty said reasonably, 'we're talking about my life here. If anyone got wind –'

'Anyone like who? Who's been asking around about this broad?'

'Don't know directly.'

Croaker sighed. 'Maybe you could find out, Matty, there's a good boy.'

'Maybe I could at that. What about the price? Agreed?'

'Agreed.'

'Okay, here's the diamond load.' The name Croaker got was Alix Logan. He also got a phone number and an address in Key West, Florida.

'About the other thing,' Croaker said. 'You better get it to me real soon 'cause I'm likely to head south at any time, get me?'

'That urgent, huh?'

'I can't remember the last time I had a vacation.'

'Will do. You know, Lieutenant, you're really okay. No hard feelings, huh? Business is business, you know?'

'Yeah. Thanks for the vote of confidence. I have a feeling I'm gonna need it.'

'Tell me something.' There was an edge to his voice now as if he had just woken up. 'How big is this thing?'

'What's it to you?'

'Huh! I'm involved, ain't I? Sure. Right up to my armpits. I just wanta know whether I'm standing in a pile of dogshit or –'

'I really can't say yet. The jury's still out. But it just could be.'

'Maybe I oughtta fade, then.'

'Strictly up to you. Might not be such a bad idea.'

' 'Preciate it, Lieutenant.'

'I don't want my wells drying up. Like a Texan that way.'

Matty the Mouth laughed, a dry rasp like a metal file going over an unstripped log. 'Uh yeah! What I am today I owe to you.'

'Just keep it up, Matty. Just keep it up.'

Back in the car, he headed towards the office. Finnigan, the fat mick, would not be at all happy to see him this morning.

Well, to hell with him. Croaker braked savagely, jammed the heel of his hand against the horn rim, stood on the gas. He only hoped that when he returned from Key West with Alix Logan in tow, the bastard would have a stroke.

If he could get her to talk. Fear was a most effective weapon wielded by a knowing hand. Unless he was severely mistaken, his little outburst in Tomkin's face had had its desired effect. A dead issue had become abruptly hot. Now there would be a direct link between Alix Logan and Raphael Tomkin. For a moment he debated bringing Vegas in on this. It would, after all, be helpful to have someone here to round up whoever it was who was nosing around, while he was down in Key West. But he dismissed it almost at once. It wasn't fair to drop such a heavy bag of shit in Vegas's lap. No, he'd just have to look after both ends himself. Timing. He'd need timing.

And a good deal of luck.

'I saw Justine off yesterday,' Nicholas said. 'I asked her to go back out to West Bay Bridge until this is all over.'

Croaker slammed the door to his car, came around to the front where Nicholas was standing. 'Good idea. I asked Gelda to stay with a friend of hers or something. I just wanted her out

480

of the apartment for a while.'

Above them the tower on Park Avenue rose, half-skeletal, half-fleshed, so that it looked like an artist's cross section.

'He up there?' Croaker asked, indicating the building.

'He should be. I cleared all of this with him first.' They began to walk across the wooden planks over the unfinished sidewalk. 'He's got guts, you've got to give him that.'

'Huh. I don't have to give him nothing. If he's agreed to it, five'll getcha ten he's got some angle figured.'

'Sure. Like getting Saigō off his back. Do you think he wants to be hounded?'

Croaker gave him a sideways grin at that. 'Naw. I don't think anyone wants that. Not even him.' They got into the elevator.

'Where are the men?'

'Coming in' – he consulted his watch – 'just about fifty minutes from now. All TPF – Tactical Police Force to you civilians. We've got the works this time: tear-gas, submachine-guns, even a pair of super-snipers with infra-red scopes. Hit a dime at a thousand yards in the dark. And, of course, all the men will be wearing bullet-proof vests – they've all been cleared for hand-to-hand, by the way.' The doors opened on the top floor and they stepped out. 'Tomkin had just better behave himself.'

'Listen, you leave Tomkin to me, okay? Just stay away. He only baits you because he's scared of you.'

'Yeah?' Croaker grinned again. 'Now that's the kind of thing I like to hear.'

Just before they got to the doors of Tomkin's office Nicholas stopped them. 'Remember,' he said, 'I don't want any of your men on this floor. Not for any reason, is that clear? If Saigō gets by them, they are to stay put. I don't want any of them getting in my way. This floor has got to be clear.'

'No sweat. Not that I like it too much but this is his building and you're calling the shots. Seeing as how I didn't do too well two nights ago. I think I can swallow this. Only' – he lifted a forefinger in warning – 'don't expect me to stay down there with them. If he gets away, I'll be up here with you.'

Nicholas nodded. 'As long as you come up via the route we mapped out together. Don't take any unexpected detours.'

'I wish I knew what you had cooked up for this guy.'

'Believe me, it's much better that no one else knows. It's going to come down to him and me, anyway.'

'But all you have is *that*.'

Nicholas hefted his scabbarded *katana*. 'That,' he said, 'is all I am going to need.' He pushed open the door and they went into the great corner office.

Tomkin, seated as usual behind his enormous desk, looked up, frowning. 'Can you believe it?' he growled. 'A goddamned garbage strike. And in the middle of the summer. Christ, those union bastards know how to get blood out of a stone. This place is gonna stink to high heaven before it's even finished.'

The old man stood on the west side of Park Avenue. Although there was little traffic this late at night, he none the less waited for the traffic light on the corner to change in his favour. When at length it did, he started slowly across the wide avenue. He seemed a frail figure from a distance, stooped under the weight of the duffel bag he carried slung over his rounded back. He had splay feet and his bamboo cane aided his slow passage. Because Park Avenue is divided by a rather wide concrete median, he could not make it across on one light.

Standing still on the strip, he looked quizzically about him as a grandfather might, caught dozing in his favourite chair during the day. His head was slow moving and it was some time before his gaze took in the half-finished building on the east side of the avenue. By that time, anyone who might be watching him, even casually, would not have thought it strange that he contemplated the structure for the remaining time until the light returned to green and he made his limping way across the street.

Instead of turning right, he went straight on, due east, towards Lexington Avenue. Once there, he turned south to the end of the block. He had now made a half-circuit along the perimeter of the tower.

There was an old-style phone booth on the corner. One of those with green metal and glass walls all the way down to the pavement. Beside it were black and tan polythene bags of garbage awaiting pickup. He put this makeshift screen between him and the tower as if he were about to head further east.

Now he was in dense shadow and he stood perfectly still, having first altered his image: the duffel bag was at his feet and he stood straight, his shoulders squared. The bamboo cane lay in the gutter, out of sight of even the sparse traffic along Lexington. He was invisible to anyone within the building's periphery.

He waited twenty minutes.

Without bending, he unzipped the duffel bag and worked with deft, economical movements. When he emerged from his cover, he appeared to be a spare, dapper businessman in a conservative suit and a pork-pie hat. As American as apple pie. He remembered to make his strides long and purposeful, knowing that even the most formidable of disguises could be betrayed by the peculiar manner in which an individual walked, the gait as singular as fingerprints.

There had been no movement along the east face but he had seen two blue-and-whites parked along the verge of the north face. They were dark, obviously meant to look empty. He did not think that they were.

Now as he completed his circuit of the tower, his estimation of the New York Police Force rose a couple of notches. In all, he counted half a dozen men either within or around the building. And once he had caught a tiny flash from somewhere above that could only come from the barrel of a rifle.

Not that he particularly cared one way or another how many men they had assigned to protect Tomkin. But one had, of course, to be prepared. However, he detested estimates: on anything. Estimates, he had been taught – and it was most assuredly so – were dangerous. How many men had gone to their deaths by taking an estimated count for real?

He went south on Park, taking it slow and circuitous, arriving back at the phone booth on Lexington a half hour later. Now was not the time to get careless.

The duffel bag was where he had stowed it, between piles of plastic-wrapped garbage. He checked his watch. Thirty seconds. He unzipped the duffel bag for the last time. He took off his light-coloured suit, flipped the hat into the gutter. Then he stooped and threw the contents of the bag over his shoulder in a version of a fireman's lift.

The small but powerful incendiary device he had dropped under a car at the end of the north face of the building in his guise as the old man erupted with a white and green flash into the night. Even a full block away, he could feel the slight concussion as the force of the explosion forced the hot air away from the epicentre. There was a pattering of metal and powdered glass as bright as diamonds in the streetlights. Flame licked skywards.

Crouching, he ran directly towards the building's façade and, within its dense shadows, he went along its south face, through the first-class cover of the dormant machinery – the double shifts had ceased two days ago, after they had discovered he had infiltrated the place as a construction worker. Within four seconds he had disappeared entirely.

Now he went from thick stanchion to thick stanchion, feeling under his fingers the rough texture of the rust-retardant undercoat. Concrete dust still hung in the air and, as he dropped down from the height, free of his heavy burden, he saw that the sharp shadows cast by the huge machines gave the place the rather disconsolate air of a deserted carnival. There had been a carnival once, at Shimonoseki. The thought of it, and the sea slowly closing over, caused him to reach into a side pocket. He put a rough-textured square into his mouth and swallowed.

He squatted, perched like a bird of prey, waiting for the drug to hit. He had been forced to leave the *Kuji-kiri* when he had become careless enough to drop the stuff during practice. Not stupid, he reminded himself. He could not help it; he had been driven to it. By the rocking boat and the howling wind and the heavy splash as the sea closed over –

Hit! In bright light. Form and line became stark, almost two-dimensional, like the backdrop on a theatre stage. It seemed to him that he could see in all directions at once. He became at once more intensely aware of the driving dust in the air. This, too, this little thing could be turned into an advantage. Because of the pollutant, his adversaries' eyes would be forced to blink more rapidly to avoid irritation. That minuscule amount of time would be the difference between life and death for some of them.

He raised his gaze. He hoped that he would not have to use

the thing on the ledge, but if he did . . .

He saw the first one. He was dressed differently from the ones in Doyers Street. Too, he carried himself more confidently.

Saigō spent several minutes studying the policeman. He wanted to know several things before he made a move. Did he have a specific territory assigned to him? And, if so, did it intersect with someone else's?

When he was satisfied, he lifted the double curve from the side and screwed the two pieces together. It became a bow of high-tension plastic with a light aluminium centre and sight.

Interesting, he thought. The explosion had not caused as much havoc as he had thought it might. It had, however, given him enough time to infiltrate the tower's perimeter. But not much more. Now he could hear the piercing wail of the fire-engine as it approached. The policemen here, having at once determined that no person was inside the car or had been hurt while passing by, had left the mop-up to the fire department.

From this vantage point he could see the slight clandestine movement of the sniper. He waited until the policeman on his level was at the extreme edge of his patrol. Fitting a steel-tipped arrow to the bow, he drew back and aimed. These were not normal hunting arrows. Their points were made by the careful layering of steel in precisely the same manner as *katana* were forged. In ancient times, they were known as armour-piercing arrows. They could get through anything short of a two-inch steel block.

He let the arrow fly. There was a quiet humming as of an inquisitive bee and a soft *thunk*. The glint of the rifle's barrel was no longer visible, but the unruffled feathers protruded darkly from the sniper's neck.

The policeman on his level had turned round and was coming back. He stopped directly in front of Saigō and lifted his head. Something dark and wet dripped down onto his shoulder. He shifted his submachine-gun to his left arm, preparatory to phoning in via walkie-talkie.

Saigō leaped at him, an animated shadow. His left arm was lifted high in an arc; it made a hissing sound as it descended. His hand was encased in a thin steel network, running from the wrist out past the fingertips in what amounted to a set of claws, curved and razor-sharp. Articulated steel tendons across the back of the hand, along each finger.

The policeman had time but to open his mouth before the claws ripped viciously through his throat, embedding themselves in his chest, piercing cloth, bullet-proof vest, skin, flesh and internal organs.

There was a great gout of black blood and the body convulsed as if charged with electricity. Strips of flesh as if flayed flew through the air and the stench of death was abruptly as strong as jasmine in some far-off and peaceful clime.

He left the corpse, laughing silently at the ineffectual addition of the vest and retrieved his bow from the dense shadows.

First the vast atrium, he thought. He was in no hurry. Upstairs, they could well wait for him. He visualized Tomkin's broad face slick with sweat in the tense period of not knowing what was happening below.

He moved with no more sound than the passing of the warm night wind through the pillars of the tower. In the next sector he came upon another of the plain-clothesmen. He moved up behind him and, slipping the black nylon cord with its centre knot around his neck, he pulled tight, whipping his wrists powerfully so that the knot bit cruelly into the man's Adam's apple. The back arched as the man fought for breath.

Saigō was momentarily taken by surprise. The man whirled and went for him instead of for the encircling cord. He was monstrously strong and Saigō felt his balance going in these close quarters. He felt the arms, as thick as beams, around his waist squeezing as he squeezed. He stamped with his shoe onto the man's instep and he let go. Saigō hurtled to one side, the momentum too strong to compensate for.

The policeman was on him at once, gasping, his bulk nevertheless stultifying. He used kite- and sword-strikes which were only partially successful but his enormous weight made proper leverage impossible for Saigō.

He fought for the reverse, giving up all but token defence, taking massive punishment, struggling, sweat running down the sides of his neck, staining his black suit.

He cursed himself for the sin of over-confidence and, struggling to free his right hand, he let go a spring blade. It pierced the other's shoulder just centre of the collarbone. The man grunted and, disconcertingly, applied even more force. Saigō heard a sharp crack in his right ear, knew his bow was now useless.

The policeman put all his weight into his knees, which were on Saigō's chest, in an attempt to force all air out. This was a mistake. But how could he know that Saigō could last for at least seven minutes without any air at all?

Saigō now concentrated on the man's upper torso. He lacked the space to use the claws effectively. He stiffened the fingers on his right hand, using them as one would the point of a knife. He rammed them into the man's side just under the rib cage. This time, the protective vest did its work and the killing blow, though painful, was deflected.

In desperation, Saigō used the *tettsui* against the sternum. It cracked and all breath went out of the massive body above him.

Saigō got the reverse at last and now, sitting astride the policeman, rewrapped the cord about his throat, heaving with his arms and shoulders.

He heard it, escalating up the register until the decibels were so high they passed beyond human hearing. He moved at the same time. Felt the white-hot blast along his right temple and, half stunned, began to roll along the atrium floor. Scrambled for the shadows as the deadly sound followed him, whining away in ricochet.

Another sniper! He crouched in the shadow of a thick pillar, hearing the night erupt into sound and motion all around him. Blood seeped from the wound and he automatically put a hand up. Just a crease. Still, he had become careless. *We cannot advocate the use of drugs – any drugs whatsoever –* he heard his *sensei* say. *Drugs tend to narrow consciousness, intensifying the narrow-beam awareness while, at the same time, giving the impression of just the opposite. A false reality set is therefore presented. Narrow-beam consciousness becomes a tendency in any form of combat, especially during the latter stages. Even veterans must guard against it. You must effect the* Rat's Head, Ox's Neck *when this occurs. If preoccupied by minute points, step back and review the combat from a distant stance.*

This is precisely the trap he had set for himself and one into which he had neatly fallen. Otherwise he never would have been grazed by that bullet.

Hearing was still a problem and he scrambled away from the epicentre of the commotion. He needed some time to recover.

Movement to the left and in front of him as he lay at an oblique angle within the building's interior. Above him, the partially completed atrium swept away in a narrowing pattern of dim light and deep shadow, the dark air hovering above him like a column of water, heavy and oppressive.

For the first time he considered the depressing possibility that he had seriously underestimated his foes. He felt helpless and terribly alone as he had that night of the howling winds upon the Straits, carving out a part of him into the deep with dry eyes and trembling hands; as he had the moment he looked down on the face of his dead father. With the only person in the world who understood him now gone, there was room left only for Satsugai's last wishes. Nothing else had seemed to matter. It was as if he had relinquished all control of his life into the grasping hands of some powerful *kami*: a *jikiniki* – the man-eating demon. Perhaps that was all his father had ever been. He had recognized this unassailable monomania even while feeling more respect for him than for anyone else in the world – except perhaps for his namesake. It had occurred to him on first reading that earlier Saigō's history that the *kami* of that great patriot must surely reside within Satsugai. In Buddhist lore this was far from impossible.

Satsugai had taken him over completely from a very early stage. His life had been an extension of his father's and there had been, it seemed, no time at all, to discover what it was about life that Saigō himself could come to enjoy. Now he knew that there was nothing about life he enjoyed: merely the knowledge of unfinished business which drove him onward towards its inevitable conclusion.

He no longer felt alone and afraid. The drug coursed through his system, heightening his senses. His muscles tingled with suppressed energy. It was time to move.

Out from the shadows, he encountered another policeman with a submachine-gun at the ready. They saw each other at the same time. The muzzle of the submachine-gun swung up, centring on Saigō's chest. His finger began to squeeze on the trigger; he stared into Saigō's eyes; his finger froze in place.

Still as a statue, he made no reaction as Saigō raised a blunt, black stick from waist level. The man's eyes seemed blank. Saigō depressed a hidden stud and with a whisper of sound a steel spike four inches long shot into the plain-clothesman's gaping mouth, through the roof, puncturing the brain. He spun around, his finger convulsed on the trigger of his weapon so that it erupted in a short burst, a brief deadly arc.

Saigō was already moving away from the area as the man fell heavily to the patterned tiles of the atrium floor. He could hear the pounding of running feet, the hoarse shouts of the remaining policeman, the static of a walkie-talkie.

He skirted the area overseen by the second long gun, though this was one element which still made him somewhat uneasy. The sniper was potentially as mobile as he was. *Haragei* would protect him from direct assault and, in near-silence, it could negate much of the long gun's threat. But in this commotion he felt cut off from many of his unnatural senses and *haragei* was useless for the kind of distances involved.

He wanted to get upstairs now, but he knew he would not until he had nullified that last threat.

In a leap, he gained the catwalk half way up to the mezzanine. Two shots in rapid succession spun off the metal close by his left side and had he not been moving he would certainly have been hit at least once.

He ran along the catwalk, his forebrain concentrating on what was directly before him as he let his subconscious work out the location of the sniper from the double flashes that had registered on the periphery of his vision.

He ceded conscious control of his body to this part of him, quartering in on the location. All the while, he watched for any movement.

Up ahead were two patches of light with a length of deep shadow in between. To circumvent them would mean to return to ground level. This he did not wish to do, for in doing so he would relinquish his growing advantage over the sniper.

He paused six feet from the first patch of light and, standing perfectly still, surveyed the topography directly in front of him.

He took three deep breaths and sprang forward. One step,

two, and he was in the air, his legs jack-knifed into a diver's tuck so that he passed through the first patch of light as a rotating ball.

He was already arcing downwards when he heard the report of the long gun. In the midst of tumbling, he could not tell how close the sniper had come to him, but he took no chances. Barely had his feet touched the metal catwalk when he had re-launched himself through the air. But now the atmosphere around him seemed thick and humid, as turbulent as cloud turned to smoke.

Automatically he ceased to inhale. Briefly, as he turned over in mid-air, he saw the dull flash of the metal canister rolling along the catwalk in the pool of light. He counted the *spang* and whine of four bullets, a quick heat sear along one calf, and then he was in darkness again, on his feet, hurtling down the catwalk towards the sniper. He ignored the pain in his right leg, compartmentalizing and thus trivializing the nerve shock, the disruption to his thirstily questing senses.

The sniper, seeing at last the full outline of the onrushing figure, did not drop to one knee and aim but turned his rifle crosswise across his body, using it as one might an ancient longstaff. He jammed the heavy stock forward in an attempt to wreck the figure's momentum, felt a jarring crash as it hit a protrusion, the figure's elbow perhaps.

He took one step back and to the side, bringing the muzzle end forward and down in an oblique slash. Saigō struck it away and down with his forearm while extending his leading leg. This brought him within intimate range and he used a kite, the edge on his hand as hard as a block of concrete. The entire right side of the sniper's rib cage collapsed like an eggshell.

The man had time only to grunt once, as if in surprise. As his head and torso came forward, Saigō kicked high, catching him on the bridge of the nose. Skin ripped away and cartilage tore itself from its tendon foundations. Blood gouted and, spinning, the sniper followed his useless weapon, cartwheeling over the side of the catwalk.

Leaping, Saigō was away, racing towards the stairs. At his side, he gripped his scabbarded *katana*.

'They got him. Listen to all that noise.'

He meant the firing.

Tomkin stood behind his desk, torso canted forward at the hips, the way an athlete might hold himself. The columns of his thick arms were rigid, his fists against the desk top.

The sounds of the machine-guns had come like an echoing roll of thunder, amplified and hurled upwards by the vast core of air in the atrium.

Nicholas, at his post near the double metal doors, had not moved at all.

'What do you think, Nick?'

He wondered at Tomkin's sudden nerves. He had been as cool and relaxed as a man about to leave on a long vacation the last time he had seen him. Now he seemed on edge.

Across the room, faced with the reality of the situation, Tomkin was sweating. He was having serious second thoughts about his deal with the ninja. There seemed to be an inordinate amount of activity down there. He knew just how many men Croaker had deployed and with what armaments. Had they got him? It sounded like a world war down there. What if he made it up here? What if I can't trust him? My God, Linnear is my last line of defence and I've sacrificed him.

Tomkin opened his mouth to speak, bit back the words at the last minute. He could not tell Nicholas what he had done, no matter what. He put his shaking hand inside his suit jacket and felt his fingers slip in sweat against the warm edge of his gun. He felt wildly out of place, a piranha stripped of its teeth, watching the shark as it swam ever closer. The feeling did not sit well with him. He enjoyed being in control – at his desk, in the boardroom in the midst of proxy fights, overseas taming recalcitrant buyers – while others hung precariously on to the twists and turns of a destiny he was creating. Now, for this moment, others controlled his life and he felt a brief stab of a fear he had not known since one sun-drenched day sixteen years ago; the house on Gin Lane, the summer's heat, the sound the wind made as it raced through the high beach grass, the dryness of the sand like beads of glass, sounds on the sigh of the wind, a rising and falling tide, moaning, and movement and – Gelda. My God, Gelda. Gelda !

His heart pounded in his chest as upon an anvil and something sat astride his intestines, racing up from his genitals, squeezing, squeezing.

'... better sit down and do as I told you.'

'What? What?'

'Sit down, Tomkin. He'll be coming soon now.'

'Coming? Who?'

'Saigō. The ninja.'

Tomkin's face was shiny in the half-light coming in through the wall of windows to his left. All the lights were off on that floor.

'They didn't get him?'

'I think not.'

'What about all those men – down there?' He was thinking of them as lines of his defence. They could not all be crumbling, so quickly, so easily.

Nicholas misunderstood him. 'I'm surprised you care. This wasn't my idea. It should just have been me and you – and him. They're all innocents down there.'

'Meaning,' Tomkin said, moving a little towards the windows, wondering if Nicholas would follow him as the ninja had suggested he might, 'that we – you and me and the cop – are not.'

Nicholas might have been a statue. 'No. Up here on Olympus morality has little meaning. When you get used to watching people from such a lofty distance their features blur, becoming at last so indistinct that they become as interchangeable as ants – and as insignificant. What does one less ant mean to the course of history? It's too insignificant even to think about.'

'You're crazy,' Tomkin said. 'I don't know what the hell you're talking about.' The trouble is, he thought, I *do* know what he's talking about. He pressed his hands against his temples, squeezing his eyes shut against the sun-dazzle tumble of images limned against his eyelids. Gelda and another girl. How his pulse raced? Now the hatred sluiced like venom through his veins. His head pulsed as if being blown up like a balloon. How could she have ... He'd meted out retribution all right. Deservedly so. His thoughts began to race dangerously.

Where had the days of innocence got to? he asked himself. The Easter egg hunts in Connecticut, the school dances, the easy, laughing summers when the girls would come in from the surf like two brown-skinned mermaids.

Caught in faded photographs, irretrievably caught between Kodak paper and photographic chemicals, as real as Coleridge's dream of Xanadu; gone up in smoke like an addict's hopes.

'You said he's coming.' Tomkin's voice was clotted with emotion and he had to clear his throat before he could continue. 'What are you going to do?'

'Sit down,' Nicholas said. 'I want you away from the windows.'

'I want to know!' Tomkin shouted. 'It's my life!'

'Sit down, Tomkin.' Nicholas's voice was even lower than it had been a moment before. 'Keep yelling and you will guide him right to you.'

Tomkin glared at him for a long moment. His chest heaved beneath his suit jacket. Then, abruptly, he collapsed into his chair.

Nicholas turned his head towards the rear of the office. Next to the open door of the bathroom was a narrow hallway leading first to the electrical and air-conditioning circuits for the floor and then to the offices on the far side of the floor.

He did not believe that Saigō would come through the front doors. For one thing, they were bulky and slow-moving. Too much time and effort was involved in opening them. He could not, of course, discount the ledge outside the windows but, as in the manner of most newer, centrally temperature-controlled buildings, these windows could not be opened. Certainly they were easily breached but that also would take time and, worse, an inordinate amount of sound.

It was logical, then, to expect the attack from the rear of the office. He thought briefly about positioning himself more advantageously, in the air-conditioning alcove, perhaps. But if Saigō chose another way in, he might take too long recovering and he could not chance that.

That Saigō was at this moment on his way up he had no doubt.

It was quiet now, just the gentle white-noise hissing in the inner ear, as of the aftermath of a violent tornado. With the front doors secured, no sound seeped in from the street; all

493

the glass was in place here.

He could hear the sound of Tomkin's heavy breathing, as if he were an asthmatic with his mouth partly open. Where he sat, behind his desk, he was in total shadow.

'Move a bit to your right,' Nicholas said softly. 'No, with the chair. That's right.' He turned his head. 'Now keep still.' A bar of light shone over a portion of the steel-grey hair, quartering the head.

The place was alive with them.

But, of course, that was to be expected.

Two at the entrance to the stairwell, three more guarding the cage elevator. He had not even considered using the main elevator bank.

The easiest thing would have been to use hypnosis. The plan was practical as well as amusing. The idea of having one of those plain-clothesmen shepherding him skyward in the elevator appealed to him. But that would depend on a very specific set of circumstances. Given time, he had no doubt that he could execute them. He did not, at this point, think that he had the time. They would have begun to sort things out down there. They'd turn on the lights, tot up the casualty figures and send for reinforcements. He did not want to risk a get-out through a cordon of a score of men all on the hair-trigger lookout for one thing and one thing alone.

Not that he could not do it but it was foolish to take such risks when there was absolutely no need to.

In the shadows, he reached out four pads from his belt. These he carefully tied, one on each soft-soled shoe and over the palm of each hand. He slung his *katana* obliquely across his back. He could take no step now without attracting attention, for sprouting from the outer side of the pads were two-inch steel spikes set in a complex pattern.

Saigō unwrapped from his waist a long nylon cord, weighted on one end by a small, sharp triangular hook. He looked up, studying the sides of the atrium though he already knew them quite well. He found what he was looking for and began to twirl the weighted cord about his head.

He let it go and it shot high into the atrium, arcing around a

494

transverse iron beam. It was close enough to the wall so that, as he flung himself upwards, he was swung inwards by his momentum. He drew his legs up so that the soles of his shoes faced outwards. He felt the impact as the spiked foot pads dug into the pitted face of the pseudo-marble facing.

This was one of the most ancient of ninjutsu techniques, used for centuries in infiltrating an enemy's castle stronghold. Mere walls, no matter how sheer, could not confound a ninja.

Upwards he went with appalling rapidity. A fly on the wall, he was quite invisible to those below, even had they chanced to look this far up. He had, once again, total security.

To the shocked and bewildered men on the atrium's floor it was as if he had vanished into thin air and this was what they reported to Croaker via walkie-talkie.

The hallucinogen was raging full force within him. His involvement with his immediate environment was total. He could see-smell-taste-hear-feel simultaneously as he crawled up the wall.

Small sounds, brittle and three-dimensional, drifted to him from below, funnelled by the peculiar acoustics. It was curious because he could hear specific sounds with more clarity from this vantage point than he might have if he were still down below: voices talking, shoes pounding against the cool flooring as they called for the ambulances. Do you no good, he thought. Talking, unanswered. The walkie-talkie, he thought. No matter.

The fine dust of his passage took to the slowly swirling air, a minute, ineffectual cyclone passing through the light.

There was silence on the top floor; this was Nicholas's doing; this was why he had insisted that none of Croaker's men be on the floor. Sound was his greatest potential enemy now.

'I want you,' he had said to Tomkin some time before, 'to face away from him when he comes. Do you think you can do that?' Because it was a most difficult thing to turn your back on someone who meant to kill you. But this was essential. Nicholas was afraid of what the *Kuji-kiri* might do to Tomkin. Kick out the glass and take one last step down, that was only one possibility.

'Yes, I can do it.'

He heard the fear shivering Tomkin's voice and wondered again at it.

'Is that where you're going to stand when he comes?'

'Don't worry about that. Just remember what I've told you. If you do anything else, chances are you'll be dead before you know it. This is no time to think about being in control.'

'What can you know about that?' Part of his fear, Tomkin realized belatedly, was that somehow he had recognized a kind of a kindred spirit in Linnear. He had neither the knowledge nor the insight to understand in what way this was so, only knew that it was. This was a deadly man, a sort of a raw animal spirit held in check by a thin veneer of civilization. Tomkin shuddered to think of what might happen if that veneer should crack apart. Perhaps that was why he wanted to trust Linnear with his secrets yet could never bring himself so to unburden himself. Kindred they were and he judged Nicholas in the same light as he judged himself. He would do anything to preserve himself thus –

'I know all about that. I've been too much in control all my life. That's hard to take. Callouses don't grow on hands.'

'What do you mean?' But already he suspected that he knew.

'I feel like my head's been full of novocaine for years.' He paused for a moment, his head cocked at an angle as if listening to a far-off sound, and Tomkin felt his guts turn to water. Was he coming already? Dear God but he wanted to make a break for the bathroom!

'Your daughter's a very special person.'

'Who, Justine?' Tomkin snorted, feeling better now that he was on safe ground again. 'Sure, if you call loony special. I don't.'

'You really are a fool, aren't you?' There was a small silence as they glared across the darkened room at each other. Nicholas wondered if Croaker had overheard all of this and was chuckling to himself.

'It's all a matter of opinion, isn't it?' Tomkin said, backing off somewhat. It would not do to have Linnear angry with him now. 'I mean, I've been through a lot with her. You've only known her a short time. But, listen ' – he tapped a forefinger on the desk top – 'I told you where she was, didn't I? I helped you find her. I want you two to make it. I've told you that and I mean it. You're good for her. Your strength can keep her from going back –'

'You don't know her at all,' Nicholas said. 'She's got more strength than a lot of men I know.' He let that hang in the air. Had it been a glove thrown down at Tomkin's feet? If so, Tomkin chose to ignore it as such.

'Perhaps there has been some change. I haven't seen her for some time, I'll grant you that. I suppose I still think of her as the baby of the family. Gelda, my oldest, always seemed so much more capable of taking care of herself, even when they were both much younger. She was always so much more social than Justine.' Oh yes, social. He had to laugh at that. Women fucking women. My God, where had she picked that up? 'I am afraid we aren't exactly a closely knit family.' How in hell could we be? 'There is little sense of family loyalty among my daughters. I regret that most bitterly but it's to be expected, I suppose. When there is not enough time' – Nicholas could sense the shrug in the dark of the office – 'the children inevitably turn away from their parents, find others who can satisfy their needs.' The finger stopped tapping, hung suspended for a time in the air. 'I imagine you could say that both my daughters are arrested adolescents in a sense. Ah well.'

No one had uttered a word for some time. The silence seemed absolute, totally antithetical to what one comes to expect in any big city. The outside did not exist for any of them. Here they were sealed into a violent world of their own manufacture where the laws of the world did not apply. Now dark and bloody gods stalked these corridors as they did the warren chambers of the Great Pyramid of Cheops. Years falling away like crimson leaves whirled in an autumn storm.

Coming, thought Nicholas. At last he's coming.

He was born into the element earth. *Dai-en-kyō-chi*, as the *Aka i ninjutsu* had taught him: 'Great-round-mirror-wisdom.' This was his strength and he began the *Shū-ji*, the seed-word mantra that would bring him to the final state of preparedness, the death-and-night-and-blood that was ninjutsu combat.

And in the instant following the tiny sound of Saigō's leap onto the top floor, he heard that most unique sound in all the world as he drew his *katana* from its sheath.

*

497

Croaker, you bastard, Nicholas thought, you had better stay out of this. You have been warned. This is between Saigō and me and God help anyone who gets in the way.

Movement on the floor. No one heard but Nicholas. *Haragei*. He could feel the adept's approach. Like an itchy finger in the night, his senses felt the approach. He wore only a light-weight black silk shirt and cotton trousers. He gripped the *katana* with both hands, standing in the attitude of *Happo Biraki*, 'Open on all eight sides', a technique developed by Miyamoto Musashi more than three centuries before. There was no possible ken-jutsu opening for attack. This had been proved long before he had been born.

Energy flowed through him like the current from a generator. The night beat on like a separate heart, with a will of its own, following a destiny no one could yet know.

He saw everything now as segments of a whole, parts fitting into the topography of the floor. The furniture: height, length, depth; fixtures, hangings; the world shrunken into a series of severely confined spaces within which would now take place the dance of death begun so many years ago.

A shadow shifted and Nicholas knew that Saigō was in the narrow hall. He leaped across the room, his *katana* held high above his head, a scream beginning in the recesses of his chest.

His nostrils flared and in mid-air he tumbled head over heels away from the hallway opening. He had caught the smell of it even before he had heard the soft click as it rolled along the floor.

The bathroom door was open and he used that. There was very little light but the percussion, abetted by the confined space, was awesome. He sensed Tomkin leaping to his feet, turning around.

Saigō was already in the room, moving at full velocity, using the noise of the blast for cover. He headed straight for Tomkin.

'Get away from me!' Tomkin cried, raising his hands defensively. He could be dead ten different ways, he realized, before he could draw and fire his gun. 'He's over there!' He pointed frantically to where Nicholas was standing.

Saigō said nothing, but his eyes blazed with a kind of cold fury that sent a tremor of terror through Tomkin's thighs. For the first time in his life he contemplated the coming of death as a real and substantial force. I am already dead, he thought, seeing an element in Saigō's face which, perhaps, had no place in this world. It might have been, had he believed in such a thing, Lucifer himself come to snatch him. He saw the terrible glint of light off the steel claws, extending from the left hand which was raised, beginning its thrust forward towards his chest where a fire burned already.

Then, in less time than, it seemed to him, the blink of an eye, the ninja was knocked sideways, across the floor towards the windows.

Nicholas, his right shoulder lowered, ran lightly after the spinning body, his *katana* held before him in a two-handed grip.

Saigō tumbled head over heels, came up on his feet facing Nicholas. He withdrew his own *katana* with his left hand, made a flicking movement with his right.

Nicholas ducked and leapt at the same time. Something no more than the size of a pea arced high into the air. It bounced once on the floor directly in front of the desk. But Saigō had been slightly off balance when he had tossed it and, on the rebound, the thing hit the overhang of the desk top and, instead of landing behind it, bounced back in front of it.

As it was, the mini-blast blew Nicholas's *katana* from his grasp as it tore away most of the front of the desk, ripping up the carpeting.

Immediately Saigō hurled himself towards Nicholas, who was still scrambling away from the percussion of the explosion.

In the periphery of his vision, Nicholas saw Saigō coming. He was vulnerable and he knew it. No textbook defence was possible from his position, not against someone as skilled as Saigō. His decision was made in a split second. He propelled his body obliquely upwards, using his palms, arms and shoulders for power, and, twisting, his soles caught Saigō's fingers as they curled around the hilt of his *katana*. The angle added to the natural force of the blow and the weapon spun out of his grip and away.

Saigō landed with the claw first and Nicholas countered with sword-strikes to the liver and spleen, missing, but deflecting the attack at the same time.

It was the heart-kite Saigō immediately strove for. Beside the fact that it was lethal, it had the added advantage of forcing a break in a stalemate, a situation that would benefit Nicholas more because of the time factor. Every added second that Saigō took here made the get-out that much more difficult.

Saigō ignored the serpent-strike to his clavicle, biting back on the pain and concentrating on what he had to do. He was on top, part of him stunned by the mode of Nicholas's hand-to-hand defence. It was, in part, ninjutsu but of a kind he had never before encountered. Could it be *Aka i ninjutsu?* he thought wildly. That would be in character. By the Amida! It was ninja against ninja.

He worked out of the four-hands-lock Nicholas had pressed on him and was ready now. For the heart-kite. In less time than it took to think about it, Nicholas would be dead, training or no training.

He jerked away and down as the whine of a bullet passed through the air where his head had been moments ago. Amida! There was another one up here. He cursed himself mightily for becoming so involved with his new knowledge of Nicholas. It was this that had kept him from discerning the third man. Now where was he?

But Nicholas had thrown him the *tettsui-tō* and had already tied him up sufficiently for him to divert his full attention here.

With a frantic effort, he fought Nicholas off and bounded to where he had left his *katana*. Nicholas was after him in a flash, extending his body fully, wrapping his fingers around Saigō's powerful ankles. They crashed together into the drawing-board. Saigō picked up his *katana*. Another bullet richocheted off the corner of the board, spewing splinters into his face, and he rolled away, cursing.

Nicholas went for the sword arm, mindful of all the many *shaken* he knew might pop into his face at any time. He went immediately into the air-sea change to throw Saigō off balance, for he had heard, as he knew his opponent had, the soft hum of the elevator working and when it arrived, he knew, Croaker's men might take no chances this time but flood the floor with tear gas the moment the doors opened.

Saigō knew that he was at the extreme end of his time limit. A new factor had been added that he had not counted on.

Nicholas needed nothing more than a stalemate while he, on the other hand –

He attacked high with a rapid series of strikes aimed for Nicholas's oesophagus, but he was balked and he began to sweat hard. His mind raced but kept coming back to the same point. If both were out of the question, he would have to be content with one and plan for the other later. There was no question of choice.

He let a pair of blows in and doubled over, feigning more pain than he felt. His right hand, in cover, darted within his belt, palming another tiny sphere. This time he must make no error of judgement in his throw.

He turned his head fractionally to get a fix on Tomkin's position and that was when Nicholas knew. He threw himself from his opponent at the same time as Saigō launched the sphere, diving across the desk top, slamming into the immobile Tomkin just as he heard the tiny popping sound behind him. As he pushed Tomkin out of the way, he kicked the massive high-backed chair backwards. At about the same instant, he caught the sound of a shot and what sounded like a high crack of thunder. He hit the floor just as the explosion came.

It was a hot burst of green-white-yellow, behind which came the concussion, the almost physical wave of sound and, just afterwards, the soft pattering of the wrecked furniture like sleet on a frost-filled day.

Nicholas turned over on his back, sat up.

'What – ?'

He put his hand on Tomkin's head, keeping it down. 'Shut up,' he growled thickly.

He saw Croaker's head peering out from behind the top of the long sofa.

'Jesus Christ!' He stood up. 'Is Tomkin okay?'

'Unharmed,' Nicholas said, thinking about how close it had been. Bitterly, he regretted letting Saigō get away. After so many years he wanted only death for death. But the decision had been inconclusive. In one sense, he knew he had been lucky. He had seen the shock in Saigō's eyes as he had learned that Nicholas was ninja. Well, that was some compensation, but it only made the next confrontation that much more dangerous. Tonight he had been unprepared ...

'Christ!' Croaker said again and Nicholas followed his incredulous gaze. 'I wasn't sure that I had seen it just before the blast but now –'

Where the third window panel had been there were now merely shards of glass. Glass littered the carpet, as the night wind had brought some of it back inside.

'Nuts,' Croaker said, slipping his .38 back into its holster. 'The guy must've been nuts – or suicidal.' He turned as the metal door burst open and he waved the men off. 'Downstairs,' he said to a tousle-haired sergeant. 'See what's left of the bastard for the M.E. to scrape off the sidewalk.'

Nicholas had gone to the broken window and was peering out. Croaker came up beside him.

'Can't see anything from this vantage point,' he said, 'but the goddamned red-and-whites from the cars.' He meant the revolving lights.

Tomkin was up behind them, brushing off his suit. It was ruined, whitened from the blasts, as if it had abruptly aged.

Croaker left the room without looking at him.

'Nick.' For the first time in his life he seemed to have trouble talking, and his legs felt rubbery. 'Is he gone?'

Nicholas continued to stare out and down. He could see movement now and lights coming on. They had found the body.

'You saved my life.' Tomkin cleared his throat. 'I want to thank you.' Maybe Nicholas had not heard the exchange he had had with that madman. He had been mad himself to trust him. He knew with a grinding certainty that tore at his guts that, without Nicholas's intervention, he would be dead now. He was in Nicholas's debt and this worried him. He felt anger forcing its way upwards and, for the briefest of instants, he detested himself in precisely the same way he had detested himself as he had arisen, sticky and panting, from the supine body of his daughter so many years ago, in a summer filled with heat and the pounding of the surf. On Gin Lane.

On the street, Nicholas saw that they had already put the corpse into a body bag. He stopped them before they could load it into the ambulance. It was only one of a long line. The associate

M.E., a light-haired woman with a pink complexion, glanced at Croaker, who nodded.

'Not much left after a fall like that,' Croaker said with a curious lack of emotion.

He was right. There was not much left of Saigō's head, his face pulped. One shoulder seemed crushed and the neck at an odd angle.

'Legs're like jelly,' Croaker said as if he relished the thought. 'Not a bone in them now over an inch in length. That right, Doc?'

The associate M.E. nodded wearily. 'Take it away,' she said. 'It's been tagged. I've got more work here.' She turned away and Nicholas could see the parade of stretchers being brought out from the bowels of the building.

Croaker's face was white and drawn as his eyes ticked over the casualties.

'Four dead, Nick.' His voice was a rasp. 'That we know about for sure. There are two others missing and a couple more are down recovering from gas inhalation. Jesus, your friend Saigō kills like other people eat.' He rubbed his fingers over his face. 'I'm glad it's all over. Glad as hell.'

'I'm sorry it had to be this way,' Nicholas said.

'Don't say "I told you so".'

'I wasn't thinking of that at all. I was thinking he's gone now. I can get on with my life. I just want to see Justine.'

'What would make him jump?'

'He was a warrior. To die in battle was what he lived for.'

'I don't understand that kind of philosophy.'

Nicholas shrugged pragmatically. 'It doesn't matter.' He looked around. 'Did you find his *katana*? I'd like to have it.'

'His what?'

'The sword.'

'Oh, that. No. But I don't think they've found all of *him* yet either. It's here, somewhere. We'll find it.'

'I guess it's not very important either.'

Croaker's gaze swept over Nicholas's shoulder. 'Your boss is looking for you, I think.'

Nicholas swivelled and grinned back at his friend. 'Ex-boss, you mean.'

Tomkin, his suit streaked with grey and black, stood at the

open door to his limo. Tom stood at his side, obediently holding the door. The motor seemed to be running. Sirens wailed in ululation for the dead and the night, where they stood at least, seemed very bright.

'Listen,' Croaker said, taking Nicholas's arm and leading him a few paces away along the avenue. 'Before you go. I want to tell you I got that call I've been waiting for. The other woman in Angela Didion's apartment the night she was murdered. I know where she is.'

Nicholas looked at him, then at Tomkin waiting silently beside the limo. 'You're not going to let that go, are you?'

'I can't. I've gotta nail him on this. You should be able to understand. It's a matter of honour. If I don't do it, nobody's gonna be able to.'

'But are you sure of what you've got?'

Croaker stuck a toothpick in the corner of his mouth. His eyes were dark pools. His face seemed more lined tonight than it had two days ago, but perhaps it was only the harsh light. He told Nicholas about his conversation with Matty the Mouth. 'You thought I was just shooting off my big mouth with Tomkin, didn't you? Matty didn't know who else was nosing around about this broad but I'll bet it's Frank who's doing it. You seen him lately? No? Why don't you ask your ex-boss, then, where Frank is, okay?'

'You won't know anything until you talk to the woman, right?'

'Right. That's why I'm taking off for Key West right away. But as far as the department is concerned, it's just a long-overdue vacation.'

'I hope you know what you're letting yourself in for.'

The last ambulance started up, its siren screaming. For an instant they were bathed in the intense crimson glow from its revolving light. Then it had turned a corner and was gone. The night darkened as if from a swiftly advancing storm.

'That's an odd thing to say,' Croaker said, 'coming from you.'

'Nick! Are you coming?' Tomkin's face floated across to them as if from another world.

'In a minute,' Nicholas called without looking over. To Croaker he said, 'You going to see Gelda before you leave?'

'Can't take the time. I'll call her. Anyway, the number she

504

gave me has a 516 area code. She'd never make it in.' He looked down at his feet for a moment. 'I just want to tell her that everything's okay now. And hey,' he said as Nicholas turned to leave, 'you ought to do the same. Justine's probably worried sick.'

When Tomkin saw Nicholas coming, he ducked his head, slid into the limo. Tom held the door until Nicholas got in, then he shut it softly and went around the front.

All the night sounds were gone in the thick, quiet interior. The motor purred richly. The air-conditioning was on.

There was still a lot of police activity going on outside. Nicholas could see Croaker talking to a rather young-looking patrolman. He shook his head once in response to a question and pointed into the bowels of the tower.

'I'm grateful, Nick.' Tomkin put his arm along the top of the back seat, his thick fingers partially curled. 'I mean it. Tomorrow you'll come up to the office for your cheque. Plus a bonus. You deserve it.'

Nicholas sat silently with his scabbarded *katana* across his knees. He put his head back and closed his eyes.

'And we can talk,' Tomkin continued, 'about you staying on in the firm.'

'I'm not interested,' Nicholas said. 'Thanks just the same.'

'Oh now, I wouldn't make a decision like that so hastily.' His voice had lightened somehow. But it was still as deep, ringing with sincerity. 'I could use you. Somewhere high up. You've got remarkable talents.' Tomkin was silent for a time. Even with his eyes closed, Nicholas could tell that he was studying him. 'How'd you like to go back to Japan?'

Nicholas opened his eyes, stared directly ahead at the plastic partition. 'I don't need you for that,' he said slowly.

'No,' Tomkin admitted. 'Decidedly not. You could jump on a plane tonight and be there in ten hours. But if you went with me, it would mean a minimum of, oh, say, a quarter of a million dollars.'

Nicholas turned to look at Tomkin.

'Oh, I am perfectly serious. Just because this ninja has been killed doesn't mean my problems over there are solved. Far from it. I need an expert who –'

Nicholas raised a hand. 'Sorry, Tomkin.'

The other man shrugged. 'Well, you think about it, anyway. There's plenty of time now.'

Behind them, Nicholas could see Croaker climbing into his car.

Tomkin spoke to Tom. 'Let's go over to Third. I want to get a bite to eat before we drop Mr Linnear off.'

The limo started up, heading left on Park, around the median so that they could take the eastbound street fronting the south side of the tower. Nicholas saw Croaker right behind them as he prepared to head back downtown to file his report before driving out to LaGuardia.

'How is Justine?' Tomkin asked.

He really is beneath contempt, Nicholas thought. He wanted to get home so that he could call her. 'Did you have me followed to the disco?'

Tomkin tried to laugh. 'No, no. I knew I could never get away with that. No. Just a father's intuition.'

If it had not been so sad, it might have been funny, Nicholas reflected. He just does not understand. 'She's fine.'

'Good. I'm glad.'

The light changed and they went across the avenue. Tomkin cleared his throat. He almost said something, then seemed to change his mind. They came abreast of the tower. The last few patrolmen were grouped on the broken sidewalk, talking amongst themselves.

'Nick, I know you don't like me much but – still – I'd like to ask you a favour.'

Nicholas said nothing. He watched as through the window the tower began to slide by.

'I want – that is, I *don't* want Justine to be estranged from me. I've done – well, I don't know what to do any more and I thought maybe you could help – bring us together –'

This side of the building was filled with trucks and, midway along the block, a metal and wooden overhang three storeys high that jutted out past the kerb, used to manoeuvre the enormous panes of tinted glass into place.

'I think,' Nicholas said, 'that that has to be between the two of you.'

'But you're already involved,' Tomkin said in his million-dollar-deal voice.

The limo passed beneath the overhang and the night seemed to darken.

Nicholas turned away from the window to look at Tomkin. 'By the way,' he said, 'I haven't seen Frank around for a couple of days. Where is he?'

There came, at that moment, a tremendous crash as the left side of the windshield shattered inwards. Tom seemed to leap from behind the wheel as if he were a speared marlin. He slammed backwards with such force that the plastic partition cracked. His arms fluttered like wings and Nicholas heard a soft moaning sound like a child sick with fever.

Abruptly, Tom's suit jacket ripped and fully three inches of steel rammed itself past his spine. Blood spurted like a geyser and a terrible stench invaded the limo's interior.

'Oh, my God! What – ?' Tomkin's face was pale.

The limo continued to head east along the street, passing the corner and crossing Lexington Avenue.

A great thrashing was coming from the front seat but Tom no longer screamed. Something or someone was squirming its way inside through the great rent in the windshield.

Driverless, the limo wandered to the left, running up on the kerb until its front end smashed into a light stanchion that was part of the new building on the corner.

Blackness in the front of the limo as if the night itself had stolen in.

Nicholas had already taken the *katana* off his lap and was holding it in his left hand. No use drawing it in such a confined space. Beside him, Tomkin was scrabbling at the door handle but it would not open. The automatic door locks were controlled from up front. It had been a security precaution. Now Tomkin cursed it.

Tom's corpse was flung to one side. The smell was so overpowering, it seemed as if there was nothing else in the world.

Something dark pounded at the cracked partition, vibrating it. Nicholas waited until the third blow, timing it in his mind. Then as the fourth blow came he met it with a powerful kick with both feet flat against the plastic. The partition came apart at the force of the blow and Nicholas leaped into the front of the limo.

\*

Saigō had come off the face of the tower, sliding carefully along the narrow ledge from which he had thrown the already dead body.

He had stayed in place long enough to ascertain that the decoy had worked, then slowly made his way within the shadows down the face of the building. Even those few cops still looking up at the shattered window in Tomkin's top-floor office had not seen him. Only Nicholas, had he been down on the street, would have had a chance.

Crouching in the blackness, he had cursed silently for now he felt the sudden touch of fear. Nicholas a ninja! His mind reeled and he popped another rough brown cube into his mouth, chewing on it to make it work all the faster.

Soon the psychedelic was flowing through his system, speeded by the outrush of adrenalin pumping through his veins. Now the sky seemed to explode in a crimson and black mushroom cloud, his muscles bulged; his neck swelled with the power and his vision dazzled as it reached his brain. He was frying in energy.

Then the voices began in his left ear and he lifted one hand, touching a forefinger to the side of his head to settle more comfortably the electronic receiver in his ear canal. He heard Tomkin and Nicholas talking, heard 'Third Avenue' and moved immediately towards the south side of the building where he knew the overhang jutted out into the street. When the limo passed by he swung down so silently and with such remarkable balance that no one inside knew.

He crouched on top and, unsheathing his *katana*, the night wind in his hair, thrust it down and inwards through the windshield, screaming in ecstasy as the car beneath him shuddered like big game being brought down.

Croaker had been about to head south on Park when he thought he saw some movement near Tomkin's limo as it went east. A sound came to him then. He could not identify it but he nevertheless braked hard, swinging the wheel abruptly to the left.

Tyres screeched and his back end skidded outwards. For a long moment he concentrated on holding the turn and not crashing into the median. Horns honked and he cursed softly, fighting the centrifugal force.

Then he was screeching uptown on Park back towards the tower.

In the first moments of shock he was at a distinct disadvantage. Saigō knew this and used it. He ducked under the initial force of Nicholas's lunge and, twisting round, began the *kansetsu-waza* – the dislocation – with the point of his left elbow.

Nicholas, above Saigō, felt rather than saw the lack of resistance and immediately went into the *osae-waza* – the immobilization – defence and got it, deflecting Saigō's elbow while, simultaneously, going on the offensive.

For an instant, Saigō had a short blade free. Then his hand clamped down and they were locked together, joined by the honed steel that was an extension of themselves – the most holy of holies, without which their lives themselves could have no meaning.

Muscles rippled along their hunched backs; sweat streamed from them. Saigō gritted his teeth. Nicholas pressed downwards. It was as if the sun and the moon, offshoots of a single entity, had entered into conflict. Was this the awesome force which bound Cain and Abel, decreeing that their hands be raised against each other?

Now was the time of their desperation. For ninja they were; of *ryu* that were sworn enemies when the silent stars in the sky had different positions, when the summers were perhaps hotter, the winters far colder, the continents even showing the pimply faces of adolescence; such was the nature of endless time into which they had both willingly entered in their youth.

Nicholas went immediately for the air-sea change, to break the deadlock, but this Saigō had apparently been waiting for, for he countered with *shime-waza* – the three-finger strangulation – and caught Nicholas off guard. But the liver-kite, severely foreshortened because of the tight space, broke that. And all the time, Tom flopped intimately against them, his slowly coagulating blood smearing their faces and wrists.

Muscles bulged like puffing engines, veins and rolling sweat ribboning their glossy skin. Their panting breath mingled, magnified in this tiny, overheated space, and their eyes crossed to look at each other. Mere words were, for the moment, beyond them and they hissed their hate at each other in a kind of elemental language that had not been heard since the dawn of man.

The blade of the *tanto* was turned away from him and Nicholas used the angle to force Saigō's wrist backwards. But he was not *Kan-aku na ninja*, not an adept in *koppo*. Saigō, however, was and he knew how to stop this manoeuvre. He drew his right knee up and, simultaneously, began a movement with his right hand. Which was the feint? Or were they both?

In the split second of deciding, Nicholas's grip on Saigō's left wrist loosened and then was dislodged. The point of the *tanto* blurred immediately upwards towards Nicholas's face. He caught the end of the hilt on the outer bone of his wrist, deflecting its flight.

There was only destruction in their hearts; their minds, cleansing themselves of the years of enmity, poured their power into the emotionalism of the moment, stoked by pumping adrenalin and the *hsing-i*, the so-called imaginary mental fist: that is, the enormous force of will their disciplines had imbued them with.

Now Nicholas used the heart-kite to break the deadlock and Saigō, stung and surprised, swung outwards, landing a blow on the side of Nicholas's head.

Immediately he rolled upwards and out through the rent windshield. Nicholas followed, leaping from the bonnet of the stalled limo onto the sidewalk.

He saw Saigō, all in black, standing beyond the bent lightpost. He had thrown aside his *katana*'s scabbard and he held it now in the first position. He did not have to call to Nicholas.

In the periphery of his vision, Nicholas saw a car brake to a halt. Croaker got out. Without turning his head, Nicholas called out, 'Leave us alone! See to Tomkin. He's in the back of the limo.'

Then he advanced on Saigō.

When one is ninja, one sees not only with one's eyes. *Haragei* allows one to see with the entire body. Thus it was that as Nicholas moved towards Saigō, it was his eyes which saw the other's one-handed grip, but his body was already reacting.

Using the *iai* draw, he lifted the blade of his *katana* in time to deflect the pair of *shaken* Saigō had flicked at him almost nonchalantly. They buzzed away like angry bees clattering down the brick steps behind Saigō to the lower plaza of the building. Beside him a modern sculptured waterfall crashed and splattered downwards to rectangular 'rocks' in a pool on the plaza.

Their *katana* clashed together in the Fire and Stones Cut, making them shudder. Only the superbly forged Japanese weapons could survive such power intact.

Saigō seemed frantic. His pupils were so large his eyes seemed all black, so alien that Croaker was transfixed by the *hsing-i*, which he perceived as an almost physical blow.

Saigō attacked strongly and swiftly. His strength was appalling, even to Nicholas. He felt engulfed in a kind of magnetic storm which, swirling him around, threatened to disorient him completely. And he fell back under the onslaught.

He saw Saigō's lips moving slowly and softly and found himself wondering how high he was; how much of the drug was now coursing through him; and how he could use this to his own advantage.

He shook his head as a strike almost slipped through. Abruptly, his arms felt enormously heavy. His eyelids flickered. And there was a wolfish grin on Saigō's face.

Nicholas staggered back, felt running water against the backs of his legs. He was in the waterfall, a steep drop at his back. How had he been turned round?

He felt a sharp pain in his arm, saw Saigō's *katana* streaked with a line of blood like saliva from a mad dog and he knew what was happening to him.

It was the *Kōbudera*. The magic not even the most fanatic of the *Kan-aku na ninja* would touch. Except for Saigō.

Back went Nicholas under the ferocious attack until they were both in the water. Magic was all around him, turning the night crimson. He seemed not to be able to feel his legs; he staggered. His fingers were numb, the grip on his *katana* faltering. His breath came in pants.

And all the while, Saigō came mercilessly on, striking and grinning, his lips invoking the *Kōbudera*.

Nicholas's foot slipped on a piece of sculpture which he could not feel and he almost went down. He was immediately slashed

511

again. Blood sparked the night air. His blood. Agony filled him and it seemed as if he could not breathe. Whatever Fukashigi did during the night, he thought, it is not enough.

The rushing water drenched him and he shuddered. And in that great breath, which reached from his throat all the way down to his toes, came a thin stream of crystal clarity, piercing the fog that had shrouded him.

He thought of Musashi, the Sword Saint, standing in his garden more than three hundred years ago. 'What is the "Body of a rock"?' he was asked. In answer, Musashi summoned a pupil of his and bid him kill himself by slashing his abdomen with a knife. Just as the pupil was about to comply, the Master stayed his hand, saying, 'This is the "Body of a rock".'

This, then, Nicholas did, reaching down inside himself where something he did not even know existed lay in wait. He dragged it up with all his strength and, as Musashi wrote, ten thousand things could not touch him, not Saigō's *katana*, not even the *Kōbudera*.

In a blur, Nicholas cut from left to right with his *katana*. In shock, Saigō lifted up his own blade, his eyes wide and staring.

Blood spurted, brilliantly-red as a cardinal bird's plumage and Saigō's torso arched back, his lips pulled back from his teeth in a rictus.

Water sloshed and sucked as they both struggled to maintain their balance. For Saigō, who had been cut through skin and flesh and even sternum, it was a Herculean task. His *katana* hung from his nerveless left hand, the fingers twitching relentlessly as they sought to do what their torn nerves no longer would allow them to. He weaved from side to side like a lush on one last monumental drunk. He grasped the top of his chest, near his shoulder-blade, but Nicholas, using the point of his *katana*, flicked away the deadly *shuriken* needles he had clutched.

Groaning, Saigō held on to the hilt of his *katana* now, using it like a walking stick to prop himself up. Without its aid, he would have collapsed like an old man.

'Kill me now.' His voice was a harsh gurgle over the restless bubbling of the water rushing over the fall. 'But not until I tell you, cousin, what I have waited long years to tell you.' His shoulder twitched. 'Come closer.' His voice cracked, dropped abruptly in volume. 'Come closer. We cannot have you savour your triumph, ah no!'

Nicholas took a step towards him. His chest and belly were streaked with blood and the iridescent seeping of his organs. For Nicholas, the pain was a dull throbbing all down his arm where Saigō had slashed him.

'You should have cut me when you could,' he said. 'Your spirit was not resolved; the *Kōbudera* consumed you and you slashed me instead. You see what one cut can do.'

Saigō staggered. 'What is that you say, cousin? Come closer still. I cannot hear you.' He grimaced in pain, a fleet passing cloud, and then it was gone, hidden behind all the layers that they had both acquired. This was, perhaps more than any other thing, what set Japan apart from the rest of the world, this bit of hard, unflinching stone beneath all the wrappers – the many, many layers – of distilled duty and filial love. This was why they must go forward always and never take a step back. But, O Amida, their memories were long indeed, stretching, it was said in many tales, beyond the grave itself.

Nicholas wanted to sleep now. His body had dealt with the shock and now, as it damped down on the pain, he was calming. A kind of lassitude was running ...

'You think that you have won but you haven't,' Saigō gasped out. A thin trickle of blood was seeping from one corner of his mouth. His busy tongue flicked at it, as an adder's might, tasting it. 'I see that I had better get on with it ... But won't you come one step closer, cousin, so that I don't have to shout? Good.' His eyes burned coldly. 'You believe that Yukio is alive, somewhere, living the life of a married lady perhaps, and thinking every so often of the old days with you. But, oh no, this is not so!' He began a laugh which ended in a ragged cough. He hawked and spat pinkly between them. He looked into Nicholas's eyes as he said, 'She lies at the bottom of the Straits of Shimonoseki, cousin, precisely where I dumped her.

'She loved you, you know. With every breath she breathed, with every word she spoke. Oh, I could drug her as I did that night with you and, for a time, she would forget you. But each time she would awake and it would be as before.

513

'At last it drove me out of my mind. She was the only woman, the only one ... for me and without her there were only men and more men and still more ...' His eyes blazed like coals, red-rimmed and mad. The trickle of blood had thickened, running like heavy drops from a careless painter's brush, darkening the water.

'You made me kill her, Nicholas,' he said in sudden accusation. 'If she had not loved you –'

'If life was not the way it was –' Nicholas said harshly. His arms were already in motion and the *katana* was a crescent of living light, as if he were the Lord's true messenger, whirring like a living entity through the hot, wet air.

In a bright arc, Saigō's head sailed upwards, tumbling over and over on its final journey like a miniature planet, a crimson streamer like a kite's or a comet's tail laced behind it. Over the edge it went, bouncing downwards across the white steps, a child's lost ball, coming to rest at last at the bottom of the waterfall: on the ninth step from the top.

'– but it is,' Nicholas said, finishing the sentence. At his feet, the water spun, rocking gently as if on a faraway tide, shivering. Caressing Nicholas's spread legs.

Of course, after it was all over Croaker wanted to know just how he had done it, so he made Nicholas come down to the morgue with him to look at the body.

'Can't tell a goddamned thing from this,' he said. 'Christ on a crutch, we'd never have known.'

Nicholas looked down at the battered and broken body. It was Japanese, the same height and weight as Saigō. An exhaustive autopsy would turn up the difference in the musculature, of course; this man could not have been trained as Saigō had been. But that would have happened only if you were *looking* for a difference.

He reached out, turned the head to one side, peered at the neck, touched the side with his fingertips. 'There,' he said.

'What?' Croaker looked at the spot. 'His neck's broken. So what? Happens all the time in a fall.'

'No, Lew. It's the *way* the neck was broken. I've seen that done before, years ago. Bones sheared through as if someone had used a surgical scalpel. No fall can do that. It's *koppo*, Lew. A ninja technique.'

'Christ,' Croaker said. 'He killed a man just to snooker us.'

Nicholas nodded. 'Plans within plans.'

He listened, with nothing but the screen door between him and the coolness of the evening, to the quiet. To the breakers sighing as they rose, curled, and fell again and again like his own tidal breathing.

He was thinking of Japan. Of the Colonel, of Cheong, of Saigō, and especially of Yukio.

All in their rightful places now, the revenge done, all the impossibly tangled cords laid out in their skeins, just as they had once started out; dying as they had been born.

The rage which had filled him up when Saigō had told him seemed like yesterday's ember now. He recalled his dream and the faceless woman was no longer faceless. Only now was he coming truly to understand the enormity of Yukio's sacrifice. She could, at almost any time, have run away from Saigō. And where do you think she would go? Where she wanted to be; at his side. And Fukashigi had said: *You were not ready then. He would have destroyed you* ... Nicholas knew the full measure of the truth of those words. By staying with Saigō, Yukio knew she held in check a measure of his deep anger; at least he had her and Nicholas had not. She gave her life for me. *Migawari ni tatsu.*

*Why do you weep so bitterly my lady? What ill has befallen you? A most dishonourable death, sir, and until it is avenged, my spirit must wander – wander here.*

But no more.

He felt Justine coming quietly up behind him and he felt a vast peacefulness, like coming upon one's own stone cottage at the edge of the sea, guarded by the tall pines one knew so well from infancy. A warm wind blew through his soul and he closed his eyes as he felt her arms steal about him, her lips trace the contours of his cheek.

'Are you all right?'

'Yes. Yes.' They stirred together like two leaves on a branch. 'The sea is so blue now. Bluer than the sky.'

'Because the sky is mirrored in it. See how they're both there?'

'It's the artist in you. You see in colours.'

'But you see it too, don't you?'

'Now you've pointed it out, yes.'

She put her cheek against his shoulder. 'I miss Doc Deerforth.'

'So do I.' He looked out to sea. 'His daughters will be here soon.'

'Saigō must have been at Gin Lane looking for Father, but why Doc?'

'I don't know,' Nicholas said softly. 'Perhaps he saw him and became suspicious.' But his thoughts were far, far away.

After a long time, they made dinner and ate it outside on his porch, and the wind, taking her hair and pulling it to one side as a gentle mother might, whirled their paper napkins out across the dunes to disappear in the surf, platinum and mauve.

A couple walked hand in hand, their bare feet scuffing the sand, leaving a trail of their passage like a pair of crabs. A sleek Irish setter, its glossy coat burnished crimson by the setting sun, ran ahead, barking happily at them, its long tongue lolling as it danced at the edge of the sea.

'Do you want to go back, now?' she asked, her hand in his. 'To Japan.'

He looked at her and smiled. He thought about her father's offer. 'I don't think so.' He sat back in his chair and it creaked a little, a comforting sound like the rattle of lines in the wind aboard ship. 'Oh, one day, perhaps – We'll both go to have a look, as tourists might.'

'You could never be a tourist there.'

'I could try.'

On the near horizon, boats were running back for shore, their sails high and billowing. It might have been a regatta except for the time of day. Music came from somewhere down the beach and was abruptly cut off, as if a door had slammed.

Justine began to giggle.

'What is it?' He was smiling already as one does sometimes, in anticipation of a funny story.

'I was just remembering how you came and took me out of

the disco that night.' Her face abruptly sobered. 'I wish you'd told me,' she whispered, 'all about it.'

'I saw no point in frightening you.'

'I only,' she said, 'would have been frightened for you.'

He stood up, his hands in his pockets, a very Western stance. 'It's all over now, isn't it?' She was looking up at him, her face tilted so that the last of the light reflected off the water, toned her skin, cooling it, making it glow.

'Yes,' he said, rubbing his bandaged arm. 'It's all over now.'

He was on his side, half dreaming, when Justine came out of the bathroom. She turned off the light and, to him, it seemed as if the moon had sunk beneath the rim of the horizon.

He felt her silently get into bed, moving her pillow to a more comfortable position, then the warmth of her body close against him: the line of her spine, the soft curve of her buttocks, her knees against his thighs. Electricity seemed to flow from one to the other.

He thought of Yukio, as the exhaustion rose like fluid, suffusing his limbs and beginning on his torso. He knew now that his fear was the same as his love for her. Her purely elemental sexuality was what drew him to her, what continually aroused him when he was with her. But he had been unwilling, and thus afraid, to acknowledge the balancing half of the equation, that there was, to him also, an elemental sexuality. That Yukio had been able to draw this out of him he had both loved and feared at the same time.

It saddened him greatly that he should have been living a lie for all these years, believing that she had deceived him. But to know now that she had loved him as he had loved her was enough. She was gone from him, had been for a long time, except in his dreams. That memory was his and he would do for her what he did for his parents, light incense and say the prayers for them on the days of their births.

Justine stirred beside him and he turned over on his back. Her right arm was beneath her head, the hand buried to the wrist beneath the crumpled pillow. He heard her soft, even breathing ...

In the high house filled with bars of bright golden sunlight and deep shade falling obliquely across the bare wooden floors Nicholas encountered So-Peng. He seemed not to have aged at all since the time the Colonel and Cheong had come to visit him. Tall and thin with bright black eyes and long hands, longer fingernails which clashed softly like the mandibles of some mythic creature, he stood in the centre of the vaulted room, studying Nicholas.

'You have brought me a fine present. I am most grateful.'

Nicholas looked around, saw nothing. Only he and So-Peng. He did not understand.

'Where am I?'

'Somewhere,' said the old man, 'east of the moon, east of the sun.'

'I don't remember how I got here.' Nicholas felt panic overtake him. 'I'll never find it again.'

So-Peng smiled and his nails clashed together, the brittle sound of cicadas at noon. 'You came here once. You will find your way again.'

And then Nicholas was alone in the high house, staring at himself in a long panel mirror.

Dawnlight, gentle and pale, woke him as it came in through the bedroom window. Justine was still asleep. He lifted the covers lightly, got out of bed.

He washed and dressed silently, went down the hallway into the kitchen to make himself a cup of green tea. He whirled the crushed leaves around and around the cup until they had dissolved. There was a fine froth on top, as pale a green as the mist in the mountains of Japan in autumn.

He sipped once, very slowly, savouring the bitter taste that was like no other in the world. Then he went into the living-room. He turned on the light in the fish tank, fed the inhabitants.

It was a remarkably clear day. Clouds, very high up, stood sharply delineated, their striations as well defined as those in marble. They swayed in the high wind aloft. He opened the door, leaving only the screen door closed against the beach insects. The breeze swept in off the sea, rich and moist.

*

Justine was dreaming of a man whose face seemed to be all mouth. It was a lipless scar, like the horizon on the brink of a savage storm, black and ominous, opening and closing as lurid lightning forked and flickered far out.

It was screaming at her, over and over, the voice just a whisper; each whisper a lash that stung her heart, raising a welt, leaving a scar in its insidious wake.

She tried to get her mind in gear, to think coherently, but the screaming mouth confused her and she lay idling like a car in neutral.

The words the mouth was screaming at her poured down on her like hard rain, making her mind hurt until the only thing she wanted to do was to put her hands over her ears to blot out the terrible noise. But it went on and on and on.

The only way to make the mouth stop was to do what it said.

Now she wanted to wake up. Or she did not. She could not tell which. She began to whimper and cry. In her dream? Or for real? Which did she want to do? Wake up? Or continue to sleep? She was terrified and every moment she remained asleep the fear intensified.

She began to struggle. She felt steel crossing the palms of her hands.

Then her eyes snapped open.

Nicholas was on his knees, sitting straight-backed, facing the windows, the water and the dawn, when Justine came into the room. His eyes were closed, the handle-less cup of green tea steaming in front of him. His spirit expanded, gyring high into the clear sky, reaching towards the high clouds.

Justine, eyes opened wide and burning quiet cold fire, stole silently past the bubbling fish tank. Her pale yellow nightgown swirled about her as if she were immersed in mist, rising up from the floor she walked, enwrapping her torso.

She turned and, reaching upwards with her two hands, unsheathed the *katana* which hung on the wall just below Nicholas's *dai-katana*. She would have taken that but it was just out of her reach.

Now she turns, transfigured. Her eyes are not her own. The colour is all wrong and the crimson motes have been obscured by the new blackness of the irises. Her face, she feels with a mixture of terror and exhilaration, is no longer feminine, though her figure is not altered. Like dark lightning flickering: adder, ant, man-thing. She shakes her head as her vision blurs. Colours seem strange; shapes bulk at her in different proportions. All of it has lost the extra dimensions with which she once saw the world. It is a cold and hateful place; joyless and as sere as the great Gobi.

Air bellows in and out of her lungs as if through some baleful force outside her ken and she curls up inside herself, crying and shivering.

Still her hands are calm and controlled as she places them one over the other around the wound leather handle of the *katana*, feeling its weight and its balance, knowing – and not knowing how she knows – the perfection of it.

Now her bare feet are placed slowly one before the other, at precise angles, as she draws ever closer to the muscular back at the front of the room.

Cool light floods her as she comes out from the shadows and she pauses a moment to allow her eyes to adjust to the glare.

Now she is so close that it seems her harsh breath must brush his skin. Her arms are raised high over her head in preparation for the one lethal blow. One instant and it is all over: the striking of a match in the dark, the flick of one fingernail against another. The difference between life and death.

The tip of the *katana* begins to quiver as the killing energy is built up. One cannot use the *kiai* in this situation – the great scream that releases so much energy. How does she know this? she wonders. One must draw the power upwards from the lower abdomen – more, more, the muscles are so weak.

And it is at this moment, as the *katana* commences its dark downward rush, that her core, at last seeing, begins to uncurl.

*No!* she screamed to herself. *No no no!*

But the blade was already a blur, cleaving the air as it went down and down and, despairing, she knew that it was far too late.

In flight, his spirit seemed to take on the characteristics of an old man. Not any old man but a particular one.

Nicholas, unbound, was old yet seemed not to feel the years. Rather, they hung over one bare, insubstantial arm like a series of silk scarves, each one a different colour, corresponding to its memories.

In the sky of the new day he danced the dance of life, a delighted child who has nevertheless seen many things, experienced many days and nights. He fashioned stalks of wheat from the stuff of the clouds and, grasping one in each fist, swirled them around and around his head like crêpe paper streamers.

Below him the continent of Asia stretched itself like an enormous tiger, yawning in the early morning, just beginning to stir. Yet it was the Asia of another time, before the advent of heavy industrialization, the revolution in China, the devastation of Vietnam and Cambodia. The air was like incense.

Nicholas became aware of Justine and the *katana* at the same instant. Had he not been so far away, the *haragei* would have picked up the intent far sooner. But he was relaxed and, for that moment, went unaware.

But in this last instant he had heard the bolt of black thunder and was already turning as the *katana* rushed down upon him.

There was, of course, no time for cerebration. Had he paused to think, even for the barest of instants, he would have died. As it was, it was closer than he liked to think about.

There are various methods of winning a battle without a sword. The one he knew best was Letting Go the Hilt and he used it now, instinctively reaching up with his arms crossed just past the wrists so that he came in *within* the arc of the blade, slamming Justine's forearms away and up.

He was on his feet and she came at him with a horizontal cut from left to right and he knew then what had happened.

With a shattering cry, he extended his left leg, bending at the knee, and crossed his right arm over his left, applying a blow to her fists with the flat of his hand.

He stamped, startling her, and broke towards the *katana*. Half way there, he realized that the blow he was about to deliver would shatter the bones in her wrists and instead grasped them, wrenching backwards, right over left, until she cried out and the blade clattered to the floor.

Her knee came up and struck him in the pit of his stomach. He bent over and she pounded his back with both her fists.

The breath whooshed out of him but, in falling, he managed to use his forearms to sweep her off her feet. She fell heavily half on top of him and immediately began to strike out.

Nicholas reached up through the rain of blows, touched the side of her neck. Something screamed. It came from her wide-open mouth, it used her vocal cords, but she never could have made that sound on her own. Her strange black eyes flew upwards in their sockets until only the whites showed and then the lids came down and she slumped, unconscious, across him, her long hair half-covering the shining steel blade of the abandoned *katana*.

It had been that second cut. Left to right. Justine was right-handed and would have cut from right to left. It was not Justine who wielded the blade. In any event, she would not have been able to handle the *katana* so well.

Saiminjutsu – the art of ninja hypnotism – was just one of the sub-specialities he had learned years ago. He worked over her for more than four hours – to undo was far more difficult than to do – using everything he had been taught, to exorcize the demon that had been planted in her.

Sweat dripped off them both like rain, mingling on the wooden floor, as he worked on and on until, at last, her body shuddered in his arms and she gave a fierce, startled cry.

Within moments, she was in a sound sleep. But he would not give her up, even then, and held her, cradled protectively in his arms and lap, leaving her only once during the long, heating day to relieve himself and to wet a towel with cool water so that he could place it over her forehead.

For almost all of the time, he stared down into her face, his features somehow different from what they had been earlier. Once, the sound of the quiet bubbling of the fish tank intruded upon his thoughts and he looked briefly over at the denizens of the deep at play among the tall green columns of vegetation and the spiny backs of coloured rocks. They regarded him impassively from beyond the glass, from another world entirely.

By the third day she had recovered fully. Before that, she

slept on and off most of the time as one does when fighting off an evil disease.

During that time, Nicholas fed her and washed her, not minding at all. He would sit on the porch for long hours at a time, staring out at the sea, past the bathers and the sun worshippers as if they did not exist, but he did not go onto the beach nor near the water. He would not go that far away from her.

And when that day dawned when she opened her eyes and they were perfectly clear, the tiny scarlet motes in the left one as brilliant as fires on a plain, he put his arms around her and kissed her.

It was not until he had made them breakfast and she had taken in the paper that he told her what had happened. He told her everything because this was something she must know, to understand that she had had the strength and the courage to pull through. Because he never could have accomplished it on his own. She had fought the *Kōbudera* from the beginning.

'I am strong now.' She laughed. 'As strong as you.'

'In a way,' he said, more seriously than she, 'yes.'

She shuddered. 'Such power needs getting used to.'

She read the paper while he cleaned up and the soft clatter of the dishes in the sink as he washed them made her feel cosy and warm.

'Afterwards,' she said, 'let's go out on the beach.'

'We should. Summer's almost gone. We should make the most of these last days out here. Anyway' – he wiped his hands – 'there are a couple of people in the city I want you to get to know –'

'Nick –' She looked up from the paper.

He came over to where she was sitting. 'Why the look?' He kissed her.

'Look at this.' She pushed the folded paper towards him.

He took it, dropped his gaze from her worried face.

'I ought to call Gelda,' she said as if from a distance.

*Local Policeman Dead in Crash* (he read). The dateline was Key West, Florida. 'Detective Lieutenant Lewis J. Croaker was found dead late yesterday in a rented car, a spokesman for the Monroe County Police Department reported. The car had apparently left the highway at high speed six miles east of Key

West, rolled down an embankment and caught fire. Heavy rains and high winds, which have plagued this area for a day and a half, may have contributed to the accident, the spokesman said.

'Detective Lieutenant Croaker, 43, was apparently in Key West on vacation. Contacted at his office at One Police Plaza, Captain Michael C. Finnigan, Detective Lieutenant Croaker's immediate superior, commented ...'

But Nicholas had already stopped reading. There was a pounding in his chest, a hollow kind of thudding, echoing away as if he stood inside an empty shrine. His vision blurred and he seemed unaware that the paper was shredding through his clenched fingers.

'Nicholas ...' Justine stood beside him, arms crossed, hands clasping her elbows impotently, the physical for the moment put precariously at bay by the emotional. 'I can't believe it.'

But he could, with that typically Asian perspective of the acceptance of events as they evolve. Karma, he thought savagely. But Croaker's death was like a knife thrust into his bowels, a kind of seething pain that would not dissipate.

Then he recalled why Croaker had gone to Key West. He read the article again, this time from first sentence to last. On vacation, indeed. As if Croaker's *kami* hovered in close asylum at his right hand, he heard again, *He's a murderer, Nick. If I had any lingering doubts as to Tomkin's complicity in the Angela Didion case, they went bye-bye with that order to officially shut down. He's a shark, man. You'd better face up to it.* A hot wind from the cemetery, out from the shade elms, assailed him as he began to see past events in a chill new light. The confrontations between Tomkin and Croaker had been deliberate. Croaker had wanted to needle Tomkin, perhaps provoking him into making some precipitous move, like an attempt to silence Croaker. Now it had come, the whisper of the gibbet. And Frank, Tomkin's chief bodyguard, had been gone several days, who knew where?

*I've gotta nail him on this. It's a matter of honour.* Every remembered word a knife twist. *If I don't do it, nobody's gonna be able to.*

He got up and went to the phone, his mind abruptly quite

clear, and dialled a number. His whole body seemed to ac
if he had been recently beaten. He did not think it fair
this should have happened to them; friendship as special as thi
was meant to be savoured, not snatched away by a thief in the
night. He felt strongly as if they had both been cheated. This,
he knew, was Western thinking and he set it aside, compartmentalizing it, as he had been taught, just as someone places a
treasured item on a high shelf, out of harm's way. Still, for the
briefest moment, he could picture the four of them on a long
sleek sloop, wet from the salt spray, laughing and carefree, the
sun in their eyes. Then he banished the vision, letting it part
from him as if it were the last ray of the sun slipping below the
dark horizon. But did that change anything? Not at all, as he
had already seen. Love and friendship were inextricably entwined in Japan and he was, after all the time in the West, the
clothes, the new veneers, an Easterner, now and forever. He
knew this with an abrupt and wrenching conviction that both
thrilled and calmed him. He had a sense of place now, as well
as a sense of time.

And sacrifice, revenge, the cornerstones of Japanese history,
were both a part of him, too. This had been Itami's last message
to him, though, at the time, he had not fully understood.

Croaker's death made it all too plain.

Now a quote attributed to Ieyasu Tokugawa flew through
his head like a bird of prey, circling in the sky of his mind. He
knew what to do.

'What is it?' Justine asked him. Her voice was thick as if she
were still in shock.

He put his finger to his lips, said into the phone, 'Is he in?
It's Nicholas Linnear.' He waited a moment. Justine came up
behind him, entwining her arms around him.

Frank answered. So he had returned. Bastard. But his voice
was controlled as he said, 'Had a good vacation? Yeah. Too bad
you missed all the excitement.' He felt the press of her breasts
against his back. He put one arm around behind him, holding
her. 'Sure. Next time I see you, I'll tell you all about it.' And
thought: It might be a lot sooner than you think. Frank said
to hold on a minute.

He closed his eyes briefly, saw the sea at that time of day

when the sun, having left the sky, turns it into the brightest piece of topography; in twilight, the water shines like a carpet of light.

'Hello,' he said. 'I've thought about your offer. Yes. Yes, I know what I said then.' His eyes snapped open and Justine, so close against him, felt the tension flooding through him and wondered at the disparity between his words and his feelings. 'But things have – changed a bit. I've reconsidered. Yes. I thought you might be.' Oh, Ieyasu! How right I shall prove you! 'Any time you say.' His knuckles went white as they gripped the receiver. 'Yes. I just read about it in the paper. Sure. A friend. I got to know him a bit.' Justine, sensing his mounting anger, pressed herself more tightly to him as if her presence might mollify him in some way. Nicholas, feeling her warmth seep into him, knew that quite soon – certainly before they went down to the beach – he would want to make love to her, need to even as he grieved for his friend. Perhaps because of it. He was returning to life now and so was she.

'In a week?' he said. 'No, I don't think there will be a problem. You'll just need to fill me in on all the details. But even that ... Well, we can go over it on the plane, can't we? Yes. Yes.' He listened for a moment more, his mind far away. 'I'll see you, then. Soon. Very soon.'

He was one now with Ieyasu, with his words: *To come to know your enemy, first you must become his friend.* He drew all the warmth he could from Justine, now. Because he had gone cold with the realization that Tomkin had sent Frank out to find the woman in Key West. And then Croaker had been killed in Key West. *Murder.* The word rang like a heavy bell in his mind. If not for you – he thought into the phone as he cradled it.

*And once you become his friend, all his defences come down. Then can you choose the most fitting method for his demise.*

# Afterword

There are, in Japanese martial philosophy – which incorporates many elements of both the Buddhist and Shinto religions – five cardinal signs: Ground, Water, Wind, Fire and the Void.

Miyamoto Musashi's *Go Rin No Sho* exists * to this day. It is, literally, *A Book of Five Rings*.

*The Ninja,* too, is a book of five rings.

* *A Book of Five Rings* by Miyamoto Musashi, translated by Victor Harris, is published by The Overlook Press, Woodstock, New York.

# Eric Lustbader

All these books are available from your local bookseller or can be ordered direct from the publishers.

To order direct just tick the titles you want and fill in the form below:

Name:_____

Address:_____

_____

Postcode:_____

Send to HarperCollins Paperbacks Mail Order, Dept 8, HarperCollins *Publishers*, Westerhill Road, Bishopbriggs, Glasgow G64 2QT.
Please enclose a cheque or postal order or your authority to debit your Visa/Access account –

Credit card no:_____

Expiry date:_____

Signature:_____

to the value of the cover price plus:
UK & BFPO: Add £1.00 for the first book and 25p for each additional book ordered.
Overseas orders including Eire: Please add £2.95 service charge. Books will be sent by surface mail but quotes for airmail despatches will be given on request.

**24 HOUR TELEPHONE ORDERING SERVICE FOR ACCESS/VISA CARDHOLDERS –**
**TEL: GLASGOW 041 772 2281 or LONDON 081 307 4052**